ANTHONY TROLLOPE

Three Great Novels

ANTHONY TROLLOPE

Three Great Novels

The Warden

Barchester Towers

An Eye for an Eye

MAGPIE
London

This edition first published by Magpie Books Ltd in 1994,
a division of Robinson Publishing

Magpie Books Ltd
7 Kensington Church Court
London W8 4SP

ISBN 1-85487-370-9

A copy of the British Library Cataloguing in Publication
Data for this title is available from the British Library.

Printed and bound by Firmin-Didot (France),
Group Herissey. No d'impression : 27423.

CONTENTS

INTRODUCTION

Anthony Trollope was a Londoner, born in 1815 (Waterloo year), the son of an unsuccessful barrister who became an equally unsuccessful farmer. Anthony's schooldays were by his own admission unhappy, and frequent changes of school as funds straitened cannot have helped. In 1834 his father's bankruptcy and exile to Belgium ended all prospect of a University education. His resourceful mother (with whom his dealings remained relatively cool) supported the younger members of the family by means of her pen, producing a brilliantly splenetic travel-book, *Domestic Manners of the Americans*, and, in quick succession, a series of combative, controversial novels. Anthony was turned loose to earn his living. After a brief spell as a teacher he entered the permanent Civil Service as a Post Office clerk at a salary of one hundred pounds a year. For a man whose later life was marked by conscientiousness and efficiency in everything he did, the beginnings of Trollope's official career were inauspicious. He quarrelled with his superior, Colonel Maberly, and departmental tradition maintains that he was once minuted as a 'very bad clerk'. It was only when he was posted to Ireland (to get him out of the way?) in 1841 that his stock began to rise. He married, started a family, moved to a large house in Essex, rose steadily in the Post Office and became its favourite ambassador on foreign Postal missions. Meanwhile literary ambitions began to surface, and he published two wholly creditable – if not particularly successful – novels with an Irish setting, *The Macdermots of Ballycloran* (1847) and *The Kellys and the O'Kellys* (1848). Only after the failure of an historical novel called *La Vendée* (1850) and a five-act play in blank verse entitled *The Noble Jilt* (no one would stage it!)

did he settle to the manner and material for which he is best known.

The Warden (1855) and *Barchester Towers* (1857), reprinted here, are the first two novels in a series of six set in Trollope's imaginary 'forty-first county' of Barsetshire – the others are *Dr Thorne* (1858), *Framley Parsonage* (1860), *The Small House at Allington* (1864) and *The Last Chronicle of Barset* (1867) (Trollope's own favourite among all his novels). In the early 1850s Trollope had temporarily left Ireland to conduct a professional survey of south-western England (the postal rounds needed rearranging in the wake of the introduction of the Penny Postal service). In the course of this job he visited Salisbury, and (as he tells us in his *Autobiography*) it was 'whilst wandering there on a midsummer evening round the purlieus of the cathedral' that he conceived *The Warden*. Both *The Warden* and its sequel, *Barchester Towers*, show how comfortably upholstered Anglican sinecures – the products of centuries of tasteful inertia – are subject to the burning-glass of 'New Men and New Measures'. In *The Warden* a radical local politician means to do away with the Wardenship of Hiram's Hospital – a nice little moneyspinner for a harmless old clergyman addicted to early Church Music. In *Barchester Towers* a whole tribe of brisk Evangelicals – dapper Bishop Proudie, overweening Mrs Proudie and time-serving Mr Slope – try to force-feed the 'High and Dry' clergy of Barchester with a diet of grandiloquent humility, judgmental sermons and 'Bishop's Barchester Young Men's Sabbath Evening Lectures'. Trollope handles both crises with exemplary (and customary) fairmindedness, neither sentimentalising the conservatives nor unfairly stigmatising the apostles of progress. Though he admits his own High Church sympathies, he assures us that the pushy Low Church chaplain Mr Slope is 'not in all things a bad man', that 'he believed in the religion which he taught.' The Bishop and his wife (perhaps his best-known comic creations) tug even more firmly at his heartstrings: he follows them through three subsequent novels and to the far end of their lives, admitting after he finally killed Mrs Proudie off in *The Last Chronicle*' that he spent much time 'in company with her ghost'.

It was while engaged in the writing of *Barchester Towers* that Trollope evolved the celebrated (and to some tastes distressingly mechanical) methods of composition that were to serve him until the end of his literary career, and which resulted in a 'pile' of sixty-five books (forty-seven of them novels) by the time of his death in 1882. He wrote at a constant rate of two hundred and fifty words every quarter of an hour. He paid a faithful Irish groom to wake him at five-thirty, put in a three-hour stint before going on to his day's labours at the Post Office, and recorded the progress of each book faithfully in a ledger, so that his conscience might be suitably pricked by any daily shortfall. He became adept at writing anywhere: on buses, trains, even in the cabins of ocean liners. He plumed himself on keeping deadlines, and confessed that there was for him 'no human bliss equal to twelve hours of work with only six hours in which to do it.' And after all this grind Trollope left behind him not an array of prolix potboilers, but, in the words of Gordon Ray, 'more novels of lasting value than any other writer in English.' Three of the most representative of these novels are combined in the present volume: to *The Warden* and *Barchester Towers* is added *An Eye for an Eye*, which Trollope wrote in 1870, but kept in a drawer until he cleared a space for it in his busy publishing schedule in 1879. He need not have been so modest. *An Eye for an Eye* is a story of towering maternal passion on the steepling Atlantic cliffs of County Clare: evidence that Trollope was not averse to exploring the byways of Victorian sexual irregularity, nor to a whiff of sensation in the Wilkie Collins style, and that what Henry James famously called his 'complete appreciation of the usual' included an interest in the most extraordinary states of mind.

Julian Thompson
Brackley, 1994

BOOK 1

The Warden

CHAPTER I

Hiram's Hospital

THE Rev. Septimus Harding was, a few years since, a beneficed clergyman residing in the cathedral town of —; let us call it Barchester. Were we to name Wells or Salisbury, Exeter, Hereford, or Gloucester, it might be presumed that something personal was intended; and as this tale will refer mainly to the cathedral dignitaries of the town in question, we are anxious that no personality may be suspected. Let us presume that Barchester is a quiet town in the west of England, more remarkable for the beauty of its cathedral and the antiquity of its monuments, than for any commercial prosperity; that the west end of Barchester is the cathedral close, and that the aristocracy of Barchester are the bishop, dean, and canons,[1] with their respective wives and daughters.

Early in life Mr Harding found himself located at Barchester. A fine voice and a taste for sacred music had decided the position in which he was to exercise his calling, and for many years he performed the easy but not highly paid duties of a minor canon. At the age of forty a small living in the close vicinity of the town increased both his work and his income, and at the age of fifty he became precentor of the cathedral.[2]

Mr Harding had married early in life, and was the father of two daughters. The eldest, Susan, was born soon after his marriage; the other, Eleanor, not till ten years later. At the time at which we introduce him to our readers he was living as precentor at Barchester with his youngest daughter, then twenty-four years of age; having been many years a widower, and having married his eldest daughter to a son of the bishop, a very short time before his installation to the office of precentor.

Scandal at Barchester affirmed that had it not been for the beauty of his daughter, Mr Harding would have remained a minor canon; but here probably Scandal lied, as she so often does: for even as a minor canon no one had been more popular among his reverend brethren in the close than Mr Harding; and Scandal, before she had reprobated Mr Harding for being made precentor by his friend the bishop, had loudly blamed the bishop for having so long omitted to do something for his friend Mr Harding. Be this as it may, Susan Harding, some twelve years since, had married the Rev. Dr Theophilus Grantly, son of the bishop, Archdeacon of Barchester, and rector of Plumstead Episcopi, and her father became, a few months later, precentor of Barchester Cathedral, that office being, as is not usual, in the bishop's gift.[3]

Now there are peculiar circumstances connected with the precentorship which must be explained. In the year 1434 there died at Barchester one John Hiram, who had made money in the town as a wool-stapler, and in his will he left the house in which he died and certain meadows and closes near the town, still called Hiram's Butts, and Hiram's Patch, for the support of twelve superannuated wool-carders,[4] all of whom should have been born and bred and spent their days in Barchester; he also appointed that an almshouse should be built for their abode, with a fitting residence for a warden, which warden was also to receive a certain sum annually out of the rents of the said butts and patches. He, moreover, willed, having had a soul alive to harmony, that the precentor of the cathedral should have the option of being also warden of the almshouses, if the bishop in each case approved.

From that day to this the charity had gone on and prospered – at least, the charity had gone on, and the estates had prospered. Wool-carding in Barchester there was no longer any; so the bishop, dean, and warden, who took it in turn to put in the old men, generally appointed some hangers-on of their own; worn-out gardeners, decrepit grave-diggers, or octogenarian sextons, who thankfully received a comfortable lodging and one shilling and fourpence a day, such being the stipend to which, under the will of John Hiram, they were declared to be entitled. Formerly, indeed – that is, till within some fifty years of the present time – they received but sixpence a day, and their breakfast and dinner was found them at a common table by the warden, such an arrangement being in stricter conformity with the absolute wording of old Hiram's will: but this was thought to be inconvenient, and to suit the tastes of neither warden nor bedesmen,[5] and the daily one shilling and fourpence was substituted with the common consent of all parties, including the Bishop and the Corporation of Barchester.

Such was the condition of Hiram's twelve old men when Mr Harding was appointed warden; but if they may be considered as well-to-do in the world according to their condition, the happy warden was much more so. The patches and butts which, in John Hiram's time, produced hay or fed cows, were now covered with rows of houses; the value of the property had gradually increased from year to year, and century to century, and was now presumed by those who knew anything about it, to bring in a very nice income; and by some who knew nothing about it, to have increased to an almost fabulous extent.

The property was farmed by a gentleman in Barchester, who also acted as the bishop's steward – a man whose father and grandfather had been stewards to the bishops of Barchester, and farmers of John Hiram's estate. The Chadwicks had earned a good name in Barchester; they had lived respected by bishops, deans, canons, and precentors; they had been buried in the precincts of the cathedral; they had never been known as griping, hard men, but had always lived comfortably, maintained a good house, and held a high position in Barchester society. The present Mr Chadwick was a worthy scion of a worthy stock, and the tenants living on the butts and patches, as well as those on the wide episcopal domains of the see,⁶ were well pleased to have to do with so worthy and liberal a steward.

For many, many years – records hardly tell how many, probably from the time when Hiram's wishes had been first fully carried out – the proceeds of the estate had been paid by the steward or farmer to the warden, and by him divided among the bedesmen; after which division he paid himself such sums as became his due. Times had been when the poor warden got nothing but his bare house, for the patches had been subject to floods, and the land of Barchester butts was said to be unproductive; and in these hard times, the warden was hardly able to make out the daily dole for his twelve dependants. But by degrees things mended; the patches were drained, and cottages began to rise upon the butts, and the wardens, with fairness enough, repaid themselves for the evil days gone by. In bad times the poor men had had their due, and therefore in good times they could expect no more. In this manner the income of the warden had increased; the picturesque house attached to the hospital had been enlarged and adorned, and the office had become one of the most coveted of the snug clerical sinecures attached to our church. It was now wholly in the bishop's gift, and though the dean and chapter, in former days, made a stand on the subject, they had thought it more conducive to their honour to have a rich precentor appointed by the bishop, than a poor one appointed by themselves. The stipend of the precentor of Barchester was eighty pounds a year. The income arising from the wardenship of the hospital was eight hundred, besides the value of the house.

Murmurs, very slight murmurs, had been heard in Barchester – few indeed, and far between – that the proceeds of John Hiram's property had not been fairly divided: but they can hardly be said to have been of such a nature as to have caused uneasiness to any-one: still the thing had been whispered, and Mr Harding had heard it. Such was his character in Barchester, so universal was his popularity, that the very fact of his appointment would have quieted louder whispers than those which had been heard; but Mr Harding was an open-handed, just-minded man, and feeling that there might be truth in what had been said, he had, on his instalment, declared his intention of adding twopence a day to each man's pittance, making a sum of sixty-two pounds eleven shillings and fourpence,[7] which he was to pay out of his own pocket. In doing so, however, he distinctly and repeatedly ob-served to the men, that though he promised for himself, he could not promise for his successors, and that the extra twopence could only be looked on as a gift from himself, and not from the trust. The bedesmen, however, were most of them older than Mr Harding, and were quite satisfied with the security on which their extra income was based.

This munificence on the part of Mr Harding had not been unopposed. Mr Chadwick had mildly but seriously dissuaded him from it; and his strong-minded son-in-law, the archdeacon, the man of whom alone Mr Harding stood in awe, had urgently, nay, vehemently, opposed so impolitic a concession: but the warden had made known his intention to the hospital before the archdeacon had been able to interfere, and the deed was done.

Hiram's Hospital, as the retreat is called, is a picturesque build-ing enough, and shows the correct taste with which the ecclesiast-ical architects of those days were imbued. It stands on the banks of the little river which flows nearly round the cathedral close, being on the side furthest from the town. The London road crosses the river by a pretty one-arched bridge, and, looking from this bridge, the stranger will see the windows of the old men's rooms, each pair of windows separated by a small buttress. A broad gravel walk runs between the building and the river, which is always trim and cared for; and at the end of the walk, under the parapet of the approach to the bridge, is a large and well-worn seat, on which, in mild weather, three or four of Hiram's bedesmen are sure to be seen seated. Beyond this row of buttresses, and further from the bridge, and also further from the water which here suddenly bends, are the pretty oriel windows of Mr Harding's house, and his well-mown lawn. The entrance to the hospital is from the London road, and is made through a ponderous gateway under a heavy stone arch, unnecessary, one would suppose, at any time, for the protection of twelve old men, but greatly con-ducive to the good appearance of Hiram's charity. On passing through this portal, never closed to anyone from six a.m. till ten p.m., and never open afterwards, except on application to a huge, intricately hung, medieval bell, the handle of which no uninitiated intruder can possibly find, the six doors of the old men's abodes are seen, and beyond them is a slight iron screen, through which the more happy portion of the Barchester *élite* pass into the Elysium of Mr Harding's dwelling.[8]

Mr Harding is a small man, now verging on sixty years, but bearing few of the signs of age; his hair is rather grizzled, though not grey, his eye is very mild, but clear and bright, though the double glasses which are held swinging from his hand, unless when fixed upon his nose, show that time has told upon his sight: his hands are delicately white, and both hands and feet are small; he always wears a black frock-coat, black knee-breeches, and black gaiters, and somewhat scandalizes some of his more hyper-clerical brethren by a black neck-handkerchief.[9]

Mr Harding's warmest admirers cannot say that he was ever an industrious man; the circumstances of his life have not called on him to be so; and yet he can hardly be called an idler. Since his appointment to his precentorship, he has published, with all possible additions of vellum, typography, and gilding, a collection of our ancient church music, with some correct dissertations on Purcell, Crotch, and Nares.[10] He has greatly improved the choir of Barchester, which, under his dominion, now rivals that of any cathedral in England. He has taken something more than his fair share in the cathedral services, and has played the violoncello daily to such audiences as he could collect, or, *faute de mieux*,[11] to no audience at all.

We must mention one other peculiarity of Mr Harding. As we have before stated, he has an income of eight hundred a year, and has no family but his one daughter; and yet he is never quite at ease in money matters. The vellum and gilding of *Harding's Church Music* cost more than anyone knows, except the author, the publisher, and the Rev. Theophilus Grantly, who allows none of his father-in-law's extravagances to escape him. Then he is generous to his daughter, for whose service he keeps a small carriage and pair of ponies. He is, indeed, generous to all, but especially to the twelve old men who are in a peculiar manner under his care. No doubt with such an income Mr Harding should be above the world, as the saying is; but at any rate, he is not above Archdeacon Theophilus Grantly, for he is always more or less in debt to his son-in-law, who has, to a certain extent, assumed the arrangement of the precentor's pecuniary affairs.

CHAPTER 2

The Barchester Reformer

MR HARDING has been now precentor of Barchester for ten years; and, alas, the murmurs respecting the proceeds of Hiram's estate are again becoming audible. It is not that anyone begrudges to Mr Harding the income which he enjoys, and the comfortable place which so well becomes him; but such matters have begun to be talked of in various parts of England. Eager pushing politicians have asserted in the House of Commons, with very telling indignation, that the grasping priests of the Church of England are gorged with the wealth which the charity of former times has left for the solace of the aged, or the education of the young. The well-known case of the Hospital of St Cross[1] has even come before the law courts of the country, and the struggles of Mr Whiston,[2] at Rochester, have met with sympathy and support. Men are beginning to say that these things must be looked into.

Mr Harding, whose conscience in the matter is clear, and who has never felt that he had received a pound from Hiram's will to which he was not entitled, has naturally taken the part of the Church in talking over these matters with his friend, the bishop, and his son-in-law, the archdeacon. The archdeacon, indeed, Dr Grantly, has been somewhat loud in the matter: he is a personal friend of the dignitaries of the Rochester Chapter, and has written letters in the public press on the subject of that turbulent Dr Whiston, which, his admirers think, must well nigh set the question at rest. It is also known at Oxford that he is the author of the pamphlet signed 'Sacerdos'[3] on the subject of the Earl of Guildford and St Cross, in which it is so clearly argued that the manners of the present times do not admit of a literal adhesion to the very words of the founder's will, but that the interests of the church for which the founder was so deeply concerned are best consulted in enabling its bishops to reward those shining lights whose services have been most signally serviceable to Christianity. In answer to this, it is asserted that Henry de Blois, founder of St Cross, was not greatly interested in the welfare of the reformed church, and that the masters of St Cross, for many years past, cannot be called shining lights in the service of Christianity; it is, however, stoutly maintained, and no doubt felt, by all the archdeacon's friends, that his logic is conclusive and has not, in fact, been answered.

With such a tower of strength to back both his arguments and his conscience, it may be imagined that Mr Harding has never felt any compunction as to receiving his quarterly sum of two hundred pounds. Indeed, the subject has never presented itself to his mind in that shape. He has talked not infrequently, and heard very much about the wills of old founders and the incomes arising from their estates, during the last year or two; he did even, at one moment, feel a doubt (since expelled by his son-in-law's logic) as to whether Lord Guildford was clearly entitled to receive so enormous an income as he does from the revenues of St Cross, but that he himself was overpaid with his modest eight hundred pounds – he who, out of that, voluntarily gave up sixty-two pounds eleven shillings and fourpence a year to his twelve old neighbours; he who, for the money, does his precentor's work as no precentor has done it before, since Barchester Cathedral was built – such an idea has never sullied his quiet, or disturbed his conscience.

Nevertheless, Mr Harding is becoming uneasy at the rumour which he knows to prevail in Barchester on the subject. He is aware that, at any rate, two of his old men have been heard to say that if everyone had his own, they might each have their hundred pounds a year, and live like gentlemen, instead of a beggarly one shilling and sixpence a day; and that they had slender cause to be thankful for a miserable dole of twopence, when Mr Harding and Mr Chadwick, between them, ran away with thousands of pounds which good old John Hiram never intended for the like of them. It is the ingratitude of this which stings Mr Harding. One of this discontented pair, Abel Handy, was put into the hospital by himself; he had been a stonemason in Barchester, and had broken his thigh by a fall from a scaffolding, while employed about the cathedral; and Mr Harding had given him the first vacancy in the hospital after the occurrence, although Dr Grantly had been very anxious to put into it an insufferable clerk of his at Plumstead Episcopi, who had lost all his teeth, and whom the archdeacon hardly knew how to get rid of by other means. Dr Grantly has not forgotten to remind Mr Harding how well satisfied with his one and sixpence a day old Joe Mutters would have been, and how injudicious it was on the part of Mr Harding to allow a radical from the town to get into the concern. Probably Dr Grantly forgot, at the moment, that the charity was intended for broken-down journeymen of Barchester.

There is living at Barchester a young man, a surgeon, named John Bold, and both Mr Harding and Dr Grantly are well aware that to him is owing the pestilent rebellious feeling which has shown itself in the hospital; yes, and the renewal, too, of that disagreeable talk about Hiram's estates which is now again prevalent in Barchester. Nevertheless, Mr Harding and Mr Bold are acquainted with each other; we may say, are friends, considering the great disparity in their years. Dr Grantly, however, has a holy horror of the impious demagogue, as on one occasion he called Bold, when speaking of him to the precentor; and being a more prudent far-seeing man than Mr Harding, and possessed of a stronger head, he already perceives that this John Bold will work great trouble in Barchester. He considers that he is to be regarded as an enemy, and thinks that he should not be admitted into the camp on anything like friendly terms. As John Bold will occupy much of our attention, we must endeavour to explain who he is, and why he takes the part of John Hiram's bedesmen.

John Bold is a young surgeon, who passed many of his boyish years at Barchester. His father was a physician in the city of London, where he made a moderate fortune, which he invested in houses in that city. The Dragon of Wantly inn and posting-house belonged to him, also four shops in the High Street, and a moiety of the new row of genteel villas (so called in the advertisements), built outside the town just beyond Hiram's Hospital. To one of these Dr Bold retired to spend the evening of his life, and to die; and here his son John spent his holidays, and afterwards his Christmas vacation, when he went from school to study surgery in the London hospitals. Just as John Bold was entitled to write himself surgeon and apothecary, old Dr Bold died, leaving his Barchester property to his son, and a certain sum in the three per cents to his daughter Mary, who is some four or five years older than her brother.

John Bold determined to settle himself at Barchester, and look
after his own property, as well as the bones and bodies of such of
his neighbours as would call upon him for assistance in their
troubles. He therefore put up a large brass plate with JOHN BOLD,
SURGEON on it, to the great disgust of the nine practitioners who
were already trying to get a living out of the bishop, dean, and
canons; and began housekeeping with the aid of his sister. At this
time he was not more than twenty-four years old; and though he
has now been three years in Barchester, we have not heard that
he has done much harm to the nine worthy practitioners. Indeed,
their dread of him has died away; for in three years he has not
taken three fees.

Nevertheless, John Bold is a clever man, and would, with
practice, be a clever surgeon; but he has got quite into another line
of life. Having enough to live on, he has not been forced to work
for bread; he has declined to subject himself to what he calls the
drudgery of the profession, by which, I believe, he means the
general work of a practising surgeon, and has found other employment. He frequently binds up the bruises and sets the limbs of such
of the poorer classes as profess his way of thinking – but this he
does for love. Now I will not say that the archdeacon is strictly
correct in stigmatizing John Bold as a demagogue, for I hardly
know how extreme must be a man's opinions before he can be
justly so called; but Bold is a strong reformer. His passion is the
reform of all abuses; state abuses, church abuses, corporation
abuses (he has got himself elected a town councillor of Barchester,
and has so worried three consecutive mayors, that it became
somewhat difficult to find a fourth), abuses in medical practice,
and general abuses in the world at large. Bold is thoroughly
sincere in his patriotic endeavours to mend mankind, and there
is something to be admired in the energy with which he devotes
himself to remedying evil and stopping injustice; but I fear that he
is too much imbued with the idea that he has a special mission
for reforming. It would be well if one so young had a little more
diffidence himself, and more trust in the honest purposes of others
– if he could be brought to believe that old customs need not
necessarily be evil, and that changes may possibly be dangerous;
but no, Bold has all the ardour, and all the self-assurance of a

Danton,⁴ and hurls his anathemas against time-honoured
practices with the violence of a French Jacobin.

No wonder that Dr Grantly should regard Bold as a firebrand,
falling, as he has done, almost in the centre of the quiet ancient
close of Barchester Cathedral. Dr Grantly would have him avoided
as the plague; but the old doctor and Mr Harding were fast friends.
Young Johnny Bold used to play as a boy on Mr Harding's lawn;
he has many a time won the precentor's heart by listening with
wrapt attention to his sacred strains; and since those days, to tell
the truth at once, he has nearly won another heart within the
same walls.

Eleanor Harding has not plighted her troth to John Bold, nor has
she, perhaps, owned to herself how dear to her the young reformer
is; but she cannot endure that anyone should speak harshly of
him. She does not dare to defend him when her brother-in-law is
so loud against him; for she, like her father, is somewhat afraid
of Dr Grantly; but she is beginning greatly to dislike the archdeacon. She persuades her father that it would be both unjust and
injudicious to banish his young friend because of his politics; she
cares little to go to houses where she will not meet him, and, in
fact, she is in love.

Nor is there any good reason why Eleanor Harding should not
love John Bold. He has all those qualities which are likely to touch
a girl's heart. He is brave, eager, and amusing; well-made and
good-looking; young and enterprising; his character is in all
respects good; he has sufficient income to support a wife; he is her
father's friend; and, above all, he is in love with her: then why
should not Eleanor Harding be attached to John Bold?

Dr Grantly, who has as many eyes as Argus,⁵ and has long seen
how the wind blows in that direction, thinks there are various
strong reasons why this should not be so. He has not thought it
wise as yet to speak to his father-in-law on the subject, for he
knows how foolishly indulgent is Mr Harding in everything that
concerns his daughter; but he has discussed the matter with his
all-trusted helpmate, within that sacred recess formed by the
clerical bedcurtains at Plumstead Episcopi.

How much sweet solace, how much valued counsel has our
archdeacon received within that sainted enclosure! 'Tis there

alone that he unbends, and comes down from his high church pedestal to the level of a mortal man. In the world Dr Grantly never lays aside that demeanour which so well becomes him. He has all the dignity of an ancient saint with the sleekness of a modern bishop; he is always the same; he is always the archdeacon; unlike Homer, he never nods. Even with his father-in-law, even with the bishop and dean, he maintains that sonorous tone and lofty deportment which strikes awe into the young hearts of Barchester, and absolutely cows the whole parish of Plumstead Episcopi. 'Tis only when he has exchanged that ever-new shovel hat[6] for a tasselled nightcap, and those shining black habiliments for his accustomed *robe de nuit*,[7] that Dr Grantly talks, and looks, and thinks like an ordinary man.

Many of us have often thought how severe a trial of faith must this be to the wives of our great church dignitaries. To us these men are personifications of St Paul: their very gait is a speaking sermon; their clean and sombre apparel exacts from us faith and submission, and the cardinal virtues seem to hover round their sacred hats. A dean or archbishop, in the garb of his order, is sure of our reverence, and a well-got-up bishop fills our very souls with awe. But how can this feeling be perpetuated in the bosoms of those who see the bishops without their aprons,[8] and the archdeacons even in a lower state of dishabille?[9]

Do we not all know some reverend, all but sacred, personage before whom our tongue ceases to be loud, and our step to be elastic? But were we once to see him stretch himself beneath the bedclothes, yawn widely, and bury his face upon his pillow, we could chatter before him as glibly as before a doctor or a lawyer. From some such cause, doubtless, it arose that our archdeacon listened to the counsels of his wife, though he considered himself entitled to give counsel to every other being whom he met.

'My dear,' he said, as he adjusted the copious folds of his nightcap, 'there was that John Bold at your father's again today. I must say your father is very imprudent.'

'He is imprudent – he always was,' replied Mrs Grantly, speaking from under the comfortable bedclothes. 'There's nothing new in that.'

'No, my dear, there's nothing new – I know that; but, at the present juncture of affairs, such imprudence is – is – I'll tell you what, my dear, if he does not take care what he's about, John Bold will be off with Eleanor.'

'I think he will, whether papa takes care or no; and why not?'

'Why not!' almost screamed the archdeacon, giving so rough a pull at his nightcap as almost to bring it over his nose; 'why not! – that pestilent, interfering upstart, John Bold – the most vulgar young person I ever met! Do you know that he is meddling with your father's affairs in a most uncalled for – most –' And being at a loss for an epithet sufficiently injurious, he finished his expressions of horror by muttering, 'Good heavens!' in a manner that had been found very efficacious in clerical meetings of the diocese. He must for the moment have forgotten where he was.

'As to his vulgarity, archdeacon,' (Mrs Grantly had never assumed a more familiar term than this in addressing her husband) 'I don't agree with you. Not that I like Mr Bold – he is a great deal too conceited for me; but then Eleanor does, and it would be the best thing in the world for papa if they were to marry. Bold would never trouble himself about Hiram's Hospital if he were papa's son-in-law.' And the lady turned herself round under the bedclothes, in a manner to which the doctor was well accustomed, and which told him, as plainly as words, that as far as she was concerned the subject was over for that night.

'Good heavens!' murmured the doctor again – he was evidently much put beside himself.

Dr Grantly is by no means a bad man; he is exactly the man which such an education as his was most likely to form; his intellect being sufficient for such a place in the world, but not sufficient to put him in advance of it. He performs with a rigid constancy such of the duties of a parish clergyman as are, to his thinking, above the sphere of his curate, but it is as an archdeacon that he shines.[10]

We believe, as a general rule, that either a bishop or his archdeacons have sinecures: where a bishop works, archdeacons have but little to do, and vice versa. In the diocese of Barchester the Archdeacon of Barchester does the work. In that capacity he is diligent, authoritative, and, as his friends particularly boast, judicious. His great fault is an overbearing assurance of the virtues

and claims of his order, and his great foible is an equally strong
confidence in the dignity of his own manner and the eloquence
of his own words. He is a moral man, believing the precepts which
he teaches, and believing also that he acts up to them; though we
cannot say that he would give his coat to the man who took his
cloak, or that he is prepared to forgive his brother even seven
times.[11] He is severe enough in exacting his dues, considering that
any laxity in this respect would endanger the security of the
church; and, could he have his way, he would consign to darkness
and perdition not only every individual reformer, but every committee and every commission that would even dare to ask a
question respecting the appropriation of church revenues.

'They are church revenues: the laity admit it. Surely the Church
is able to administer her own revenues.' 'Twas thus he was
accustomed to argue, when the sacrilegious doings of Lord John
Russell[12] and others were discussed either at Barchester or at
Oxford.

It was no wonder that Dr Grantly did not like John Bold, and
that his wife's suggestion that he should become closely connected
with such a man dismayed him. To give him his due, the archdeacon never wanted courage; he was quite willing to meet his
enemy on any field, and with any weapon. He had that belief in
his own arguments that he felt sure of success, could he only be
sure of a fair fight on the part of his adversary. He had no idea that
John Bold could really prove that the income of the hospital was
malappropriated; why, then, should peace be sought for on such
base terms? What! bribe an unbelieving enemy of the Church with
the sister-in-law of one dignitary, and the daughter of another –
with a young lady whose connections with the diocese and
chapter of Barchester were so close as to give her an undeniable
claim to a husband endowed with some of its sacred wealth! When
Dr Grantly talks of unbelieving enemies, he does not mean to
imply want of belief in the doctrines of the Church, but an equally
dangerous scepticism as to its purity in money matters.

Mrs Grantly is not usually deaf to the claims of the high order
to which she belongs. She and her husband rarely disagree as to
the tone with which the church should be defended; how singular,
then, that in such a case as this she should be willing to succumb!

The archdeacon again murmurs 'Good heavens!' as he lays himself beside her, but he does so in a voice audible only to himself, and he repeats it till sleep relieves him from deep thought.

Mr Harding himself has seen no reason why his daughter should not love John Bold. He has not been unobservant of her feelings, and perhaps his deepest regret at the part which he fears Bold is about to take regarding the hospital arises from a dread that he may be separated from his daughter, or that she may be separated from the man she loves. He has never spoken to Eleanor about her lover; he is the last man in the world to allude to such a subject unconsulted, even with his own daughter; and had he considered that he had ground to disapprove of Bold, he would have removed her, or forbidden him his house; but he saw no such ground. He would probably have preferred a second clerical son-in-law, for Mr Harding, also, is attached to his order; and, failing in that, he would at any rate have wished that so near a connection should have thought alike with him on church matters. He would not, however, reject the man his daughter loved because he differed on such subjects with himself.

Hitherto Bold had taken no steps in the matter in any way annoying to Mr Harding personally. Some months since, after a severe battle, which cost him not a little, he gained a victory over a certain old turnpike woman in the neighbourhood, of whose charges another old woman had complained to him. He got the act of Parliament relating to the trust, found that his *protégée*[13] had been wrongly taxed, rode through the gate himself, paying the toll, then brought an action against the gate-keeper, and proved that all people coming up a certain by-lane, and going down a certain other by-lane, were toll-free. The fame of his success spread widely abroad, and he began to be looked on as the upholder of the rights of the poor of Barchester. Not long after this success, he heard from different quarters that Hiram's bedesmen were treated as paupers, whereas the property to which they were, in effect, heirs, was very large; and he was instigated by the lawyer whom he had employed in the case of the turnpike to call upon Mr Chadwick for a statement as to the funds of the estate.

Bold had often expressed his indignation at the malappropriation of church funds in general, in the hearing of his friend the precentor; but the conversation had never referred to anything at Barchester; and when Finney, the attorney, induced him to interfere with the affairs of the hospital, it was against Mr Chadwick that his efforts were to be directed. Bold soon found that if he interfered with Mr Chadwick as steward, he must also interfere with Mr Harding as warden; and though he regretted the situation in which this would place him, he was not the man to flinch from his undertaking from personal motives.

As soon as he had determined to take the matter in hand, he set about his work with his usual energy. He got a copy of John Hiram's will, of the wording of which he made himself perfectly master. He ascertained the extent of the property, and as nearly as he could the value of it; and made out a schedule of what he was informed was the present distribution of its income. Armed with these particulars, he called on Mr Chadwick, having given that gentleman notice of his visit; and asked him for a statement of the income and expenditure of the hospital for the last twenty-five years.

This was of course refused, Mr Chadwick alleging that he had no authority for making public the concerns of a property in managing which he was only a paid servant.

'And who is competent to give you that authority, Mr Chadwick?' asked Bold.

'Only those who employ me, Mr Bold,' said the steward.

'And who are those, Mr Chadwick?' demanded Bold.

Mr Chadwick begged to say that if these inquiries were made merely out of curiosity, he must decline answering them: if Mr Bold had any ulterior proceeding in view, perhaps it would be desirable that any necessary information should be sought for in a professional way by a professional man. Mr Chadwick's attorneys were Messrs Cox and Cummins, of Lincoln's Inn. Mr Bold took down the address of Cox and Cummins, remarked that the weather was cold for the time of the year, and wished Mr Chadwick good morning. Mr Chadwick said it was cold for June, and bowed him out.

He at once went to his lawyer, Finney. Now, Bold was not very fond of his attorney, but, as he said, he merely wanted a man who knew the forms of law, and who would do what he was told for his money. He had no idea of putting himself in the hands of a lawyer. He wanted law from a lawyer as he did a coat from a tailor, because he could not make it so well himself; and he thought Finney the fittest man in Barchester for his purpose. In one respect, at any rate, he was right: Finney was humility itself.

Finney advised an instant letter to Cox and Cummins, mindful of his six and eightpence.[14] 'Slap at them at once, Mr Bold; demand categorically and explicitly a full statement of the affairs of the hospital.'

'Suppose I were to see Mr Harding first,' suggested Bold.

'Yes, yes, by all means,' said the acquiescing Finney; 'though, perhaps, as Mr Harding is no man of business, it may lead – lead to some little difficulties; but perhaps you're right. Mr Bold, I don't think seeing Mr Harding can do any harm.' Finney saw from the expression of his client's face that he intended to have his own way.

CHAPTER 3

The Bishop of Barchester

BOLD at once repaired to the hospital. The day was now far advanced, but he knew that Mr Harding dined in the summer at four, that Eleanor was accustomed to drive in the evening, and that he might therefore probably find Mr Harding alone. It was between seven and eight when he reached the slight iron gate leading into the precentor's garden, and though, as Mr Chadwick observed, the day had been cold for June, the evening was mild, and soft, and sweet. The little gate was open. As he raised the latch he heard the notes of Mr Harding's violoncello from the far end of the garden, and, advancing before the house and across the lawn, he found him playing: and not without an audience. The musician was seated in a garden chair just within the summer-house, so as to allow the violoncello which he held between his knees to rest upon the dry stone flooring; before him stood a rough music desk, on which was open a page of that dear sacred book, that much-laboured and much-loved volume of church music, which had cost so many guineas; and around sat, and lay, and stood, and leaned, ten of the twelve old men who dwelt with him beneath old John Hiram's roof. The two reformers were not there. I will not say that in their hearts they were conscious of any wrong done or to be done to their mild warden, but latterly they had kept aloof from him, and his music was no longer to their taste.

It was amusing to see the positions, and eager listening faces of these well-to-do old men. I will not say that they all appreciated the music which they heard, but they were intent on appearing to do so; pleased at being where they were, they were determined, as far as in them lay, to give pleasure in return; and they were not unsuccessful. It gladdened the precentor's heart to think that the old bedesmen whom he loved so well admired the strains which were to him so full of almost ecstatic joy; and he used to boast that such was the air of the hospital, as to make it a precinct specially fit for the worship of St Cecilia.[1]

Immediately before him, on the extreme corner of the bench which ran round the summer-house, sat one old man, with his handkerchief smoothly lain upon his knees, who did enjoy the moment, or acted enjoyment well. He was one on whose large frame many years, for he was over eighty, had made small havoc – he was still an upright, burly, handsome figure, with an open, ponderous brow, round which clung a few, though very few, thin grey locks. The coarse black gown of the hospital, the breeches, and buckled shoes became him well; and as he sat with his hands folded on his staff, and his chin resting on his hands, he was such a listener as most musicians would be glad to welcome.

This man was certainly the pride of the hospital. It had always been the custom that one should be selected as being to some extent in authority over the others; and though Mr Bunce, for such was his name, and so he was always designated by his inferior brethren, had no greater emoluments than they, he had assumed, and well knew how to maintain, the dignity of his elevation. The precentor delighted to call him his sub-warden, and was not ashamed, occasionally, when no other guest was there, to bid him sit down by the same parlour fire, and drink the full glass of port which was placed near him. Bunce never went without the second glass, but no entreaty ever made him take a third.

'Well, well, Mr Harding; you're too good, much too good,' he'd always say, as the second glass was filled; but when that was drunk, and the half-hour over, Bunce stood erect, and with a benediction which his patron valued, retired to his own abode. He knew the world too well to risk the comfort of such halcyon moments, by prolonging them till they were disagreeable.

Mr Bunce, as may be imagined, was most strongly opposed to innovation. Not even Dr Grantly had a more holy horror of those who would interfere in the affairs of the hospital; he was every inch a churchman, and though he was not very fond of Dr Grantly personally, that arose from there not being room in the hospital for two people so much alike as the doctor and himself, rather than from any dissimilarity in feeling. Mr Bunce was inclined to think that the warden and himself could manage the hospital without further assistance; and that, though the bishop was the constitu-

tional visitor,[2] and as such entitled to special reverence from all
connected with John Hiram's will, John Hiram never intended
that his affairs should be interfered with by an archdeacon.

At the present moment, however, these cares were off his mind,
and he was looking at his warden as though he thought the music
heavenly, and the musician hardly less so.

As Bold walked silently over the lawn, Mr Harding did not at
first perceive him, and continued to draw his bow slowly across
the plaintive wires; but he soon found from his audience that some
stranger was there, and looking up, began to welcome his young
friend with frank hospitality.

'Pray, Mr Harding; pray don't let me disturb you,' said Bold;
'you know how fond I am of sacred music.'

'Oh! it's nothing,' said the precentor, shutting up the book, and
then opening it again as he saw the delightfully imploring look of
his old friend Bunce. Oh, Bunce, Bunce, Bunce, I fear that after all
thou art but a flatterer. 'Well, I'll just finish it then; it's a favourite
little bit of Bishop's;[3] and then, Mr Bold, we'll have a stroll and a
chat till Eleanor comes in and gives us tea.' And so Bold sat down
on the soft turf to listen, or rather to think how, after such sweet
harmony, he might best introduce a theme of so much discord, to
disturb the peace of him who was so ready to welcome him kindly.

Bold thought that the performance was soon over, for he felt
that he had a somewhat difficult task, and he almost regretted the
final leave-taking of the last of the old men, slow as they were in
going through their adieus.

Bold's heart was in his mouth, as the precentor made some
ordinary but kind remark as to the friendliness of the visit.

'One evening call,' said he, 'is worth ten in the morning. It's all
formality in the morning; real social talk never begins till after
dinner. That's why I dine early, so as to get as much as I can of
it.'

'Quite true, Mr Harding,' said the other; 'but I fear I've reversed
the order of things, and I owe you much apology for troubling you
on business at such an hour; but it is on business that I have called
just now.'

Mr Harding looked blank and annoyed; there was something in
the tone of the young man's voice which told him that the inter-

view was intended to be disagreeable, and he shrank back at
finding his kindly greeting so repulsed.

'I wish to speak to you about the hospital,' continued Bold.

'Well, well, anything I can tell you I shall be most happy –'

'It's about the accounts.'

'Then, my dear fellow, I can tell you nothing, for I'm as ignorant
as a child. All I know is that they pay me £800 a year. Go to
Chadwick, he knows all about the accounts; and now tell me, will
poor Mary Jones ever get the use of her limb again?'

'Well, I think she will, if she's careful; but, Mr Harding, I hope
you won't object to discuss with me what I have to say about the
hospital.'

Mr Harding gave a deep, long-drawn sigh. He did object, very
strongly object, to discuss any such subject with John Bold; but
he had not the business tact of Mr Chadwick, and did not know
how to relieve himself from the coming evil; he sighed sadly, but
made no answer.

'I have the greatest regard for you, Mr Harding,' continued
Bold; 'the truest respect, the most sincere –'

'Thank ye, thank ye, Mr Bold,' interjaculated the precentor
somewhat impatiently; 'I'm much obliged, but never mind that;
I'm as likely to be in the wrong as another man – quite as likely.'

'But, Mr Harding, I must express what I feel, lest you should
think there is personal enmity in what I'm going to do.'

'Personal enmity! Going to do! Why you're not going to cut my
throat, nor put me into the Ecclesiastical Court –'

Bold tried to laugh, but he couldn't. He was quite in earnest,
and determined in his course, and couldn't make a joke of it. He
walked on awhile in silence before he recommenced his attack,
during which Mr Harding, who had still the bow in his hand,
played rapidly on an imaginary violoncello. 'I fear there is reason
to think that John Hiram's will is not carried out to the letter, Mr
Harding,' said the young man at last; 'and I have been asked to
see into it.'

'Very well, I've no objection on earth; and now we need not say
another word about it.'

'Only one word more, Mr Harding. Chadwick has referred me
to Cox and Cummins, and I think it my duty to apply to them for

some statement about the hospital. In what I do I may appear to be interfering with you, and I hope you will forgive me for doing so.'

'Mr Bold,' said the other, stopping, and speaking with some solemnity, 'if you act justly, say nothing in this matter but the truth, and use no unfair weapons in carrying out your purposes, I shall have nothing to forgive. I presume you think I am not entitled to the income I receive from the hospital, and that others are entitled to it. Whatever some may do, I shall never attribute to you base motives because you hold an opinion opposed to my own, and adverse to my interests: pray do what you consider to be your duty; I can give you no assistance, neither will I offer you any obstacle. Let me, however, suggest to you, that you can in no wise forward your views nor I mine, by any discussion between us. Here comes Eleanor and the ponies, and we'll go in to tea.'

Bold, however, felt that he could not sit down at ease with Mr Harding and his daughter after what had passed, and therefore excused himself with much awkward apology; and merely raising his hat and bowing as he passed Eleanor and the pony-chair,[4] left her in disappointed amazement at his departure.

Mr Harding's demeanour certainly impressed Bold with a full conviction that the warden felt that he stood on strong grounds, and almost made him think that he was about to interfere without due warrant in the private affairs of a just and honourable man; but Mr Harding himself was anything but satisfied with his own view of the case.

In the first place, he wished for Eleanor's sake to think well of Bold and to like him, and yet he could not but feel disgusted at the arrogance of his conduct. What right had he to say that John Hiram's will was not fairly carried out? But then the question would arise within his heart: Was that will fairly acted on? Did John Hiram mean that the warden of his hospital should receive considerably more out of the legacy than all the twelve old men together for whose behoof the hospital was built? Could it be possible that John Bold was right, and that the reverend warden of the hospital had been for the last ten years and more the unjust recipient of an income legally and equitably belonging to others? What if it should be proved before the light of day that he, whose life had been so happy, so quiet, so respected, had absorbed £8,000, to which he had no title, and which he could never repay? I do not say that he feared that such was really the case; but the first shade of doubt now fell across his mind, and from this evening, for many a long, long day, our good, kind, loving warden was neither happy nor at ease.

Thoughts of this kind, these first moments of much misery, oppressed Mr Harding as he sat sipping his tea, absent and ill at ease. Poor Eleanor felt that all was not right, but her ideas as to the cause of the evening's discomfort did not go beyond her lover, and his sudden and uncivil departure: she thought there must have been some quarrel between Bold and her father, and she was half angry with both, though she did not attempt to explain to herself why she was so.

Mr Harding thought long and deeply over these things, both before he went to bed, and after it, as he lay awake, questioning within himself the validity of his claim to the income which he enjoyed. It seemed clear at any rate that, however unfortunate he might be at having been placed in such a position, no one could say that he ought either to have refused the appointment first, or to have rejected the income afterwards. All the world – meaning the ecclesiastical world as confined to the English Church – knew that the wardenship of the Barchester Hospital was a snug sinecure, but no one had ever been blamed for accepting it. To how much blame, however, would he have been open had he rejected it! How mad would he have been thought had he declared, when the situation was vacant and offered to him, that he had scruples as to receiving £800 a year from John Hiram's property, and that he had rather some stranger should possess it! How would Dr Grantly have shaken his wise head, and have consulted with his friends in the close as to some decent retreat for the coming insanity of the poor minor canon! If he was right in accepting the place, it was clear to him also that he would be wrong in rejecting any part of the income attached to it. The patronage was a valuable appanage⁵ of the bishopric; and surely it would not be his duty to lessen the value of that preferment which had been bestowed on himself; surely he was bound to stand by his order.

But somehow these arguments, though they seemed logical,

were not satisfactory. Was John Hiram's will fairly carried out? that was the true question: and if not, was it not his especial duty to see that this was done – his especial duty, whatever injury it might do to his order – however ill such duty might be received by his patron and his friends? At the idea of his friends, his mind turned unhappily to his son-in-law: he knew well how strongly he would be supported by Dr Grantly, if he could bring himself to put his case into the archdeacon's hands, and to allow him to fight the battle; but he knew also that he would find no sympathy there for his doubts, no friendly feeling, no inward comfort. Dr Grantly would be ready enough to take up his cudgel against all comers on behalf of the church militant, but he would do so on the distasteful ground of the Church's infallibility. Such a contest would give no comfort to Mr Harding's doubts; he was not so anxious to prove himself right, as to be so.

I have said before that Dr Grantly was the working man of the diocese, and that his father the bishop was somewhat inclined to an idle life: so it was; but the bishop, though he had never been an active man, was one whose qualities had rendered him dear to all who knew him. He was the very opposite to his son; he was a bland and a kind old man, opposed by every feeling to authoritative demonstrations and episcopal ostentation. It was perhaps well for him, in his situation, that his son had early in life been able to do that which he could not well do when he was younger, and which he could not have done at all now that he was over seventy. The bishop knew how to entertain the clergy of his diocese, to talk easy smalltalk with the rectors' wives, and put curates at their ease; but it required the strong hand of the archdeacon to deal with such as were refractory either in their doctrines or their lives.

The bishop and Mr Harding loved each other warmly. They had grown old together, and had together spent many, many years in clerical pursuits and clerical conversation. When one of them was a bishop and the other only a minor canon they were even then much together; but since their children had married, and Mr Harding had become warden and precentor, they were all in all to each other. I will not say that they managed the diocese between them, but they spent much time in discussing the man who did, and in forming little plans to mitigate his wrath against church delinquents, and soften his aspirations for church dominion.

Mr Harding determined to open his mind, and confess his doubts to his old friend; and to him he went on the morning after John Bold's uncourteous visit.

Up to this period no rumour of these cruel proceedings against the hospital had reached the bishop's ears. He had doubtless heard that men existed who questioned his right to present to a sinecure of £800 a year, as he had heard from time to time of some special immorality or disgraceful disturbance in the usually decent and quiet city of Barchester: but all he did, and all he was called on to do on such occasions, was to shake his head, and to beg his son, the great dictator, to see that no harm happened to the church.

It was a long story that Mr Harding had to tell before he made the bishop comprehend his own view of the case; but we need not follow him through the tale. At first the bishop counselled but one step, recommended but one remedy, had but one medicine in his whole pharmacopoeia strong enough to touch so grave a disorder – he prescribed the archdeacon. 'Refer him to the archdeacon,' he repeated, as Mr Harding spoke of Bold and his visit. 'The archdeacon will set you quite right about that,' he kindly said, when his friend spoke with hesitation of the justness of his cause. 'No man has got up all that so well as the archdeacon'; but the dose, though large, failed to quiet the patient; indeed it almost produced nausea.

'But, bishop,' said he, 'did you ever read John Hiram's will?'

The bishop thought probably he had, thirty-five years ago, when first instituted to his see, but could not state positively: however, he very well knew that he had the absolute right to present to the wardenship, and that the income of the warden had been regularly settled.

'But, bishop, the question is, who has the power to settle it? If, as this young man says, the will provides that the proceeds of the property are to be divided into shares, who has the power to alter these provisions?' The bishop had an indistinct idea that they altered themselves by the lapse of years; that a kind of ecclesiastical statute of limitation barred the rights of the twelve bedesmen to any increase of income arising from the increased value of property. He said something about tradition; more of the many learned men who by their practice had confirmed the present arrangement; then went at some length into the propriety of maintaining the due difference in rank and income between a beneficed clergyman, and certain poor old men who were dependent on charity; and concluded his argument by another reference to the archdeacon.

The precentor sat thoughtfully gazing at the fire, and listening to the good-natured reasoning of his friend. What the bishop said had a sort of comfort in it, but it was not a sustaining comfort. It made Mr Harding feel that many others – indeed, all others of his own order – would think him right; but it failed to prove to him that he truly was so.

'Bishop,' said he, at last, after both had sat silent for a while, 'I should deceive you and myself too, if I did not tell you that I am very unhappy about this. Suppose that I cannot bring myself to agree with Dr Grantly! – that I find, after inquiry, that the young man is right, and that I am wrong – what then?'

The two men were sitting near each other – so near, that the bishop was able to lay his hand upon the other's knee, and he did so with a gentle pressure. Mr Harding well knew what that pressure meant. The bishop had no further argument to adduce; he could not fight for the cause as his son would do; he could not prove all the precentor's doubts to be groundless; but he could sympathize with his friend, and he did so; and Mr Harding felt that he had received that for which he came. There was another period of silence, after which the bishop asked with a degree of irritable energy, very unusual with him, whether this 'pestilent intruder' (meaning John Bold) had any friends in Barchester.

Mr Harding had fully made up his mind to tell the bishop everything; to speak of his daughter's love, as well as his own troubles; to talk of John Bold in his double capacity of future son-in-law and present enemy; and though he felt it to be sufficiently disagreeable, now was his time to do it.

'He is very intimate at my own house, bishop.' The bishop stared; he was not so far gone in orthodoxy and church-militancy as his son, but still he could not bring himself to understand how so declared an enemy of the establishment could be admitted on terms of intimacy into the house, not only of so firm a pillar as Mr Harding, but one so much injured as the warden of the hospital.

'Indeed, I like Mr Bold much, personally,' continued the disinterested victim; 'and to tell you the "truth" ' – he hesitated as he brought out the dreadful tidings – 'I have sometimes thought it not improbable that he would be my second son-in-law.' The bishop did not whistle; we believe that they lose the power of doing so on being consecrated; and that in these days one might as easily meet a corrupt judge as a whistling bishop; but he looked as though he would have done so, but for his apron.

What a brother-in-law for the archdeacon! what an alliance for Barchester Close! what a connection for even the episcopal palace! The bishop, in his simple mind, felt no doubt that John Bold, had he so much power, would shut up all cathedrals, and probably all parish churches; distribute all tithes among Methodists, Baptists, and other savage tribes; utterly annihilate the sacred bench, and make shovel hats and lawn sleeves as illegal as cowls, sandals, and sackcloth![6] Here was a nice man to be initiated into the comfortable arcana of ecclesiastical snuggeries; one who doubted the integrity of parsons, and probably disbelieved the Trinity!

Mr Harding saw what an effect his communication had made, and almost repented the openness of his disclosure; he, however, did what he could to moderate the grief of his friend and patron. 'I did not say that there is any engagement between them. Had there been, Eleanor would have told me: I know her well enough to be assured that she would have done so; but I see that they are fond of each other; and as a man and a father, I have had no objection to urge against their intimacy.'

'But, Harding,' said the bishop, 'how are you to oppose him, if he is your son-in-law?'

'I don't mean to oppose him; it is he who opposes me: if anything is to be done in defence, I suppose Chadwick will do it. I suppose –'

'Oh, the archdeacon will see to that: were the young man twice his brother-in-law, the archdeacon will never be deterred from doing what he feels to be right.'

Mr Harding reminded the bishop that the archdeacon and the reformer were not yet brothers, and very probably never would be; exacted from him a promise that Eleanor's name should not be mentioned in any discussion between the father bishop and son archdeacon respecting the hospital; and then took his departure, leaving his poor old friend bewildered, amazed, and confounded.

CHAPTER 4

Hiram's Bedesmen

THE parties most interested in the movement which is about to set Barchester by the ears were not the foremost to discuss the merit of the question, as is often the case; but when the bishop, the archdeacon, the warden, the steward, and Messrs Cox and Cummins, were all busy with the matter, each in his own way, it is not to be supposed that Hiram's bedesmen themselves were altogether passive spectators. Finney, the attorney, had been among them, asking sly questions, and raising immoderate hopes, creating a party hostile to the warden, and establishing a corps in the enemy's camp, as he figuratively calls it to himself. Poor old men; whoever may be righted or wronged by this inquiry, they at any rate will assuredly be only injured; to them it can only be an unmixed evil. How can their lot be improved? all their wants are supplied; every comfort is administered; they have warm houses, good clothes, plentiful diet, and rest after a life of labour; and above all, that treasure so inestimable in declining years, a true and kind friend to listen to their sorrows, watch over their sickness, and administer comfort as regards this world, and the world to come!

John Bold sometimes thinks of this, when he is talking loudly of the rights of the bedesmen, whom he has taken under his protection; but he quiets the suggestion within his breast with the high-sounding name of justice – 'fiat justitia ruat cœlum'.[1] These old men should, by rights, have one hundred pounds a year instead of one shilling and sixpence a day, and the warden should have two hundred or three hundred pounds instead of eight hundred pounds. What is unjust must be wrong; what is wrong should be righted; and if he declined the task, who else would do it?

'Each one of you is clearly entitled to one hundred pounds a year by common law': such had been the important whisper made by Finney into the ears of Abel Handy, and by him retailed to his eleven brethren.

Too much must not be expected from the flesh and blood even of John Hiram's bedesmen, and the positive promise of one hundred a year to each of the twelve old men had its way with most of them. The great Bunce was not to be wiled away, and was upheld in his orthodoxy by two adherents. Abel Handy, who was the leader of the aspirants after wealth, had, alas, a stronger following. No less than five of the twelve soon believed that his views were just, making with their leader a moiety of the hospital. The other three, volatile unstable minds, vacillated between the two chieftains, now led away by the hope of gold, now anxious to propitiate the powers that still existed.

It had been proposed to address a petition to the bishop as visitor, praying his lordship to see justice done to the legal recipients of John Hiram's Charity, and to send copies of this petition and of the reply it would elicit to all the leading London papers, and thereby to obtain notoriety for the subject. This it was thought would pave the way for ulterior legal proceedings. It would have been a great thing to have had the signatures and marks of all the twelve injured legatees; but this was impossible: Bunce would have cut his hand off sooner than have signed it. It was then suggested by Finney that if even eleven could be induced to sanction the document, the one obstinate recusant might have been represented as unfit to judge on such a question – in fact, as being *non compos mentis*[2] – and the petition would have been taken as representing the feeling of the men. But this could not be done: Bunce's friends were as firm as himself, and as yet only six crosses adorned the document. It was the more provoking, as Bunce himself could write his name legibly, and one of those three doubting souls had for years boasted of like power, and possessed, indeed, a Bible, in which he was proud to show his name written by himself some thirty years ago – 'Job Skulpit'; but it was thought that Job Skulpit, having forgotten his scholarship, on that account recoiled from the petition, and that the other doubters would follow as he led them. A petition signed by half the hospital would have but a poor effect.

It was in Skulpit's room that the petition was now lying, waiting such additional signatures as Abel Handy, by his eloquence, could obtain for it. The six marks it bore were duly attested, thus:

his   his   his

Abel + Handy, Greg^y + Moody, Mathew + Spriggs,

mark   mark   mark

etc., and places were duly designated in pencil for those brethren who were now expected to join: for Skulpit alone was left a spot on which his genuine signature might be written in fair clerk-like style. Handy had brought in the document, and spread it out on the small deal table, and was now standing by it persuasive and eager. Moody had followed with an inkhorn, carefully left behind by Finney; and Spriggs bore aloft, as though it were a sword, a well-worn ink-black pen, which from time to time he endeavoured to thrust into Skulpit's unwilling hand.

With the learned man were his two abettors in indecision, William Gazy and Jonathan Crumple. If ever the petition were to be forwarded, now was the time, so said Mr Finney; and great was the anxiety on the part of those whose one hundred pounds a year, as they believed, mainly depended on the document in question.

'To be kept out of all that money,' as the avaricious Moody had muttered to his friend Handy, 'by an old fool saying that he can write his own name like his betters.'

'Well Job,' said Handy, trying to impart to his own sour, ill-omened visage a smile of approbation, in which he greatly failed; 'so you're ready now, Mr Finney says; here's the place, d'ye see' – and he put his huge brown finger down on the dirty paper – 'name or mark, it's all one. Come along, old boy; if so be we're to have the spending of this money, why the sooner the better – that's my maxim.'

'To be sure,' said Moody; 'we a'n't none of us so young: we can't stay waiting for old Catgut no longer.'

It was thus these miscreants named our excellent friend: the nickname he could easily have forgiven, but the allusion to the divine source of all his melodious joy would have irritated even him. Let us hope he never knew the insult.

'Only think, old Billy Gazy,' said Spriggs, who rejoiced in greater youth than his brethren, but having fallen into a fire when drunk, had had one eye burnt out, one cheek burnt through, and one arm nearly burnt off, and who, therefore, in regard to personal appearance, was not the most prepossessing of men; 'a hundred a year, and all to spend: only think, old Billy Gazy'; and he gave a hideous grin that showed off his misfortunes to their full extent.

Old Billy Gazy was not alive to much enthusiasm – even these golden prospects did not arouse him to do more than rub his poor old bleared eyes with the cuff of his bedesman's gown, and gently mutter, 'he didn't know, not he; he didn't know.'

'But you'd know, Jonathan,' continued Spriggs, turning to the other friend of Skulpit's, who was sitting on a stool by the table, gazing vacantly at the petition. Jonathan Crumple was a meek, mild man, who had known better days; his means had been wasted by bad children, who had made his life wretched till he had been received into the hospital, of which he had not long been a member. Since that day he had known neither sorrow nor trouble, and this attempt to fill him with new hopes was, indeed, a cruelty.

'A hundred a year's a nice thing, for sartain, neighbour Spriggs,' said he: 'I once had nigh to that myself, but it didn't do me no good.' And he gave a low sigh, as he thought of the children of his own loins who had robbed him.

'And shall have again, Joe,' said Handy; 'and will have someone to keep it right and tight for you this time.'

Crumple sighed again – he had learned the impotency of worldly wealth, and would have been satisfied, if left untempted, to have remained happy with one and sixpence a day.

'Come, Skulpit,' repeated Handy, getting impatient, 'you're not going to go along with old Bunce in helping that parson to rob us all. Take the pen, man, and right yourself. Well,' he added, seeing that Skulpit still doubted, 'to see a man as is afraid to stand by hisself, is, to my thinking, the meanest thing as is.'

'Sink them all for parsons, says I,' growled Moody; 'hungry beggars, as never thinks their bellies full till they have robbed all and every thing.'

'Who's to harm you, man?' argued Spriggs: 'let them look never so black at you, they can't get you put out when you're once in – no, not old Catgut, with Calves to help him!' I am sorry to say the archdeacon himself was designated by this scurrilous allusion to his nether person.

'A hundred a year to win, and nothing to lose,' continued

Handy, 'my eyes! – Well, how a man's to doubt about sich a bit of cheese as that passes me – but some men is timorous – some men is born with no pluck in them – some men is cowed at the very first sight of a gentleman's coat and waistcoat.'

Oh, Mr Harding, if you had but taken the archdeacon's advice in that disputed case, when Joe Mutters was this ungrateful demagogue's rival candidate!

'Afraid of a parson,' growled Moody, with a look of ineffable scorn; 'I tell ye what I'd be afraid of – I'd be afraid of not getting nothing from 'em but just what I could take by might and right – that's the most I'd be afraid on of any parson of 'em all.'

'But,' said Skulpit, apologetically, 'Mr Harding's not so bad – he did give us twopence a day, didn't he now?'

'Twopence a day!' exclaimed Spriggs with scorn, opening awfully the red cavern of his lost eye.

'Twopence a day!' muttered Moody with a curse; 'sink his twopence!'

'Twopence a day!' exclaimed Handy; 'and I'm to go, hat in hand, and thank a chap for twopence a day, when he owes me a hundred pounds a year; no, thank ye; that may do for you, but it won't for me. Come, I say, Skulpit, are you a going to put your mark to this here paper, or are you not?'

Skulpit looked round in wretched indecision to his two friends. 'What d'ye think, Billy Gazy?' said he.

But Billy Gazy couldn't think: he made a noise like the bleating of an old sheep, which was intended to express the agony of his doubt, and again muttered that 'he didn't know'.

'Take hold, you old cripple,' said Handy, thrusting the pen into poor Billy's hand: 'there, so – ugh! you old fool, you've been and smeared it all – there – that'll do for you – that's as good as the best name as ever was written': and a big blotch of ink was presumed to represent Billy Gazy's acquiescence.

'Now Jonathan,' said Handy, turning to Crumple.

'A hundred a year's a nice thing, for sartain,' again argued Crumple. 'Well, neighbour Skulpit, how's it to be?'

'Oh, please yourself,' said Skulpit; 'please yourself, and you'll please me.'

The pen was thrust into Crumple's hand, and a faint, wander-

ing, meaningless sign was made, betokening such sanction and
authority as Jonathan Crumple was able to convey.

'Come, Job,' said Handy, softened by success, 'don't let 'em have
to say that old Bunce has a man like you under his thumb – a man
that always holds his head in the hospital as high as Bunce
himself, though you're never axed to drink wine, and sneak, and
tell lies about your betters, as he does.'

Skulpit held the pen, and made little flourishes with it in the air,
but still hesitated.

'And if you'll be said by me,' continued Handy, 'you'll not write
your name to it at all, but just put your mark like the others' –
the cloud began to clear from Skulpit's brow – 'we all know you
can do it if you like, but maybe you wouldn't like to seem uppish,
you know.'

'Well, the mark would be best,' said Skulpit: 'one name and the
rest marks wouldn't look well, would it?'

'The worst in the world,' said Handy; 'there – there': and
stooping over the petition, the learned clerk made a huge cross on
the place left for his signature.

'That's the game,' said Handy, triumphantly pocketing the
petition; 'we're all in a boat now, that is, the nine of us; and as
for old Bunce, and his cronies, they may –' But as he was hobbling
off to the door, with a crutch on one side and a stick on the other,
he was met by Bunce himself.

'Well, Handy, and what may old Bunce do?' said the grey-
haired, upright senior.

Handy muttered something, and was departing; but he was
stopped in the doorway by the huge frame of the newcomer.

'You've been doing no good here, Abel Handy,' said he, ''tis
plain to see that; and 'tisn't much good, I'm thinking, you ever do.'

'I mind my own business, Master Bunce,' muttered the other,
'and do you do the same. It a'n't nothing to you what I does – and
your spying and poking here won't do no good nor yet no harm.'

'I suppose then, Job,' continued Bunce, not noticing his
opponent, 'if the truth must out, you've stuck your name to that
petition of theirs at last.'

Skulpit looked as though he were about to sink into nothing
with shame.

'What is it to you what he signs?' said Handy. 'I suppose if we all wants to ax for our own, we needn't ax leave of you first, Mr Bunce, big a man as you are: and as to your sneaking in here, into Job's room when he's busy, and where you're not wanted –'

'I've knowed Job Skulpit, man and boy, sixty years,' said Bunce, looking at the man of whom he spoke, 'and that's ever since the day he was born. I knowed the mother that bore him, when she and I were little wee things, picking daisies together in the close yonder; and I've lived under the same roof with him more nor ten years; and after that I may come into his room without axing leave, and yet no sneaking neither.'

'So you can, Mr Bunce,' said Skulpit; 'so you can, any hour, day or night.'

'And I'm free also to tell him my mind,' continued Bunce, looking at the one man and addressing the other; 'and I tell him now that he's done a foolish and a wrong thing: he's turned his back upon one who is his best friend; and is playing the game of others, who care nothing for him, whether he be poor or rich, well or ill, alive or dead. A hundred a year? Are the lot of you soft enough to think that if a hundred a year be to be given, it's the likes of you that will get it?' – and he pointed to Billy Gazy, Spriggs, and Crumple. 'Did any of us ever do anything worth half the money? Was it to make gentlemen of us we were brought in here, when all the world turned against us, and we couldn't longer earn our daily bread? A'n't you all as rich in your ways as he in his?' – and the orator pointed to the side on which the warden lived. 'A'n't you getting all you hoped for, ay, and more than you hoped for? Wouldn't each of you have given the dearest limb of his body to secure that which now makes you so unthankful?'

'We wants what John Hiram left us,' said Handy; 'we wants what's ourn by law; it don't matter what we expected; what's ourn by law should be ourn, and by goles³ we'll have it.'

'Law!' said Bunce, with all the scorn he knew how to command – 'law! Did ye ever know a poor man yet was the better for law, or for a lawyer? Will Mr Finney ever be as good to you, Job, as that man has been? Will he see to you when you're sick, and comfort you when you're wretched? Will he –'

'No, nor give you port wine, old boy, on cold winter nights! he

won't do that, will he?' asked Handy: and laughing at the severity
of his own wit, he and his colleagues retired, carrying with them,
however, the now powerful petition.

There is no help for spilt milk; and Mr Bunce could only retire
to his own room, disgusted at the frailty of human nature – Job
Skulpit scratched his head – Jonathan Crumple again remarked
that 'for sartain, sure a hundred a year was very nice' – and Billy
Gazy again rubbed his eyes, and lowly muttered that 'he didn't
know'.

CHAPTER 5

Dr Grantly Visits the Hospital

THOUGH doubt and hesitation disturbed the rest of our poor warden, no such weakness perplexed the nobler breast of his son-in-law. As the indomitable cock preparing for the combat sharpens his spurs, shakes his feathers, and erects his comb, so did the archdeacon arrange his weapons for the coming war, without misgiving and without fear. That he was fully confident of the justice of his cause let no one doubt. Many a man can fight his battle with good courage, but with a doubting conscience; such was not the case with Dr Grantly. He did not believe in the Gospel with more assurance than he did in the sacred justice of all ecclesiastical revenues. When he put his shoulder to the wheel to defend the income of the present and future precentors of Barchester, he was animated by as strong a sense of a holy cause as that which gives courage to a missionary in Africa, or enables a sister of mercy to give up the pleasures of the world for the wards of a hospital. He was about to defend the holy of holies from the touch of the profane; to guard the citadel of his church from the most rampant of its enemies; to put on his good armour in the best of fights; and secure, if possible, the comforts of his creed for coming generations of ecclesiastical dignitaries. Such a work required no ordinary vigour; and the archdeacon was, therefore, extraordinarily vigorous: it demanded a buoyant courage, and a heart happy in its toil; and the archdeacon's heart was happy, and his courage was buoyant.

He knew that he would not be able to animate his father-in-law with feelings like his own, but this did not much disturb him. He preferred to bear the brunt of the battle alone, and did not doubt that the warden would resign himself into his hands with passive submission.

'Well, Mr Chadwick,' he said, walking into the steward's office a day or two after the signing of the petition as commemorated in the last chapter; 'anything from Cox and Cummins this morning?' Mr Chadwick handed him a letter, which he read, stroking the tight-gaitered calf of his right leg as he did so. Messrs Cox and Cummins merely said that they had as yet received no notice from their adversaries; that they could recommend no preliminary steps; but that should any proceeding really be taken by the bedesmen, it would be expedient to consult that very eminent Queen's Counsel, Sir Abraham Haphazard.

'I quite agree with them,' said Dr Grantly, refolding the letter. 'I perfectly agree with them. Haphazard is no doubt the best man; a thorough churchman, a sound conservative, and in every respect the best man we could get – he's in the house,[1] too, which is a great thing.'

Mr Chadwick quite agreed.

'You remember how completely he put down that scoundrel Horseman about the Bishop of Beverly's income;[2] how completely he set them all adrift in the earl's case.' Since the question of St Cross had been mooted by the public, one noble lord had become 'the earl', par excellence, in the doctor's estimation. 'How he silenced that fellow at Rochester.[3] Of course we must have Haphazard; and I'll tell you what, Mr Chadwick, we must take care to be in time, or the other party will forestall us.'

With all his admiration for Sir Abraham, the doctor seemed to think it not impossible that that great man might be induced to lend his gigantic powers to the side of the Church's enemies.

Having settled this point to his satisfaction, the doctor stepped down to the hospital, to learn how matters were going on there; and as he walked across the hallowed close, and looked up at the ravens who cawed with a peculiar reverence as he wended his way, he thought with increased acerbity of those whose impiety would venture to disturb the goodly grace of cathedral institutions.

And who has not felt the same? We believe that Mr Horseman himself would relent, and the spirit of Sir Benjamin Hall give way,[4] were those great reformers to allow themselves to stroll by moonlight round the towers of some of our ancient churches. Who would not feel charity for a prebendary, when walking the quiet length of that long aisle at Winchester, looking at those decent houses, that trim grassplat, and feeling, as one must, the solemn, orderly comfort of the spot! Who could be hard upon a dean while wandering round the sweet close of Hereford, and owning that in that precinct, tone and colour, design and form, solemn tower and storied window, are all in unison, and all perfect! Who could lie basking in the cloisters of Salisbury, and gaze on Jewel's library,⁵ and that unequalled spire, without feeling that bishops should sometimes be rich.

The tone of our archdeacon's mind must not astonish us; it has been the growth of centuries of Church ascendancy; and though some fungi now disfigure the tree, though there be much dead wood, for how much good fruit have not we to be thankful? Who, without remorse, can batter down the dead branches of an old oak, now useless, but, ah! still so beautiful, or drag out the fragments of the ancient forest, without feeling that they sheltered the younger plants, to which they are now summoned to give way in a tone so peremptory and so harsh?

The archdeacon, with all his virtues, was not a man of delicate feeling; and after having made his morning salutations in the warden's drawing-room, he did not scruple to commence an attack on 'pestilent' John Bold in the presence of Miss Harding, though he rightly guessed that that lady was not indifferent to the name of his enemy.

'Nelly, my dear, fetch me my spectacles from the back room,' said her father, anxious to save both her blushes and her feelings.

Eleanor brought the spectacles, while her father was trying, in ambiguous phrases, to explain to her too-practical brother-in-law that it might be as well not to say anything about Bold before her, and then retreated. Nothing had been explained to her about Bold and the hospital; but, with a woman's instinct, she knew that things were going wrong.

'We must soon be doing something,' commenced the archdeacon, wiping his brows with a large, bright-coloured handkerchief, for he had felt busy, and had walked quick, and it was a broiling summer's day. 'Of course you have heard of the petition?'

Mr Harding owned, somewhat unwillingly, that he had heard of it.

'Well,' – the archdeacon looked for some expression of opinion, but none coming, he continued – 'We must be doing something, you know; we mustn't allow these people to cut the ground from under us while we sit looking on.' The archdeacon, who was a practical man, allowed himself the use of everyday expressive modes of speech when among his closest intimates, though no one could soar into a more intricate labyrinth of refined phraseology when the Church was the subject, and his lower brethren were his auditors.

The warden still looked mutely in his face, making the slightest possible passes with an imaginary fiddle-bow, and stopping, as he did so, sundry imaginary strings with the fingers of his other hand. 'Twas his constant consolation in conversational troubles. While these vexed him sorely, the passes would be short and slow, and the upper hand would not be seen to work; nay the strings on which it operated would sometimes lie concealed in the musician's pocket, and the instrument on which he played would be beneath his chair; but as his spirit warmed to the subject – as his trusting heart, looking to the bottom of that which vexed him, would see its clear way out – he would rise to a higher melody, sweep the unseen strings with a bolder hand, and swiftly fingering the cords from his neck, down along his waistcoat, and up again to his very ear, create an ecstatic strain of perfect music, audible to himself and to St Cecilia, and not without effect.

'I quite agree with Cox and Cummins,' continued the archdeacon: 'they say we must secure Sir Abraham Haphazard. I shall not have the slightest fear in leaving the case in Sir Abraham's hands.'

The warden played the slowest and saddest of tunes: it was but a dirge on one string.

'I think Sir Abraham will not be long in letting Master Bold know what he's about. I fancy I hear Sir Abraham cross-questioning him at the Common Pleas.'

The warden thought of his income being thus discussed, his modest life, his daily habits, and his easy work; and nothing issued from that single cord, but a low wail of sorrow. 'I suppose they've sent this petition up to my father.' The warden didn't know; he imagined they would do so this very day.

'What I can't understand is, how you let them do it, with such a command as you have in the place, or should have with such a man as Bunce; I cannot understand why you let them do it.'

'Do what?' asked the warden.

'Why, listen to this fellow Bold, and that other low pettifogger, Finney – and get up this petition too: why didn't you tell Bunce to destroy the petition?'

'That would have been hardly wise,' said the warden.

'Wise – yes, it would have been very wise if they'd done it among themselves. I must go up to the palace and answer it now, I suppose; it's a very short answer they'll get, I can tell you.'

'But why shouldn't they petition, doctor?'

'Why shouldn't they!' responded the archdeacon, in a loud brazen voice, as though all the men in the hospital were expected to hear him through the walls; 'why shouldn't they? I'll let them know why they shouldn't: by the by, warden, I'd like to say a few words to them all together.'

The warden's mind misgave him, and even for a moment he forgot to play. He by no means wished to delegate to his son-in-law his place and authority of warden; he had expressly determined not to interfere in any step which the men might wish to take in the matter under dispute; he was most anxious neither to accuse them nor to defend himself. All these things he was aware the archdeacon would do in his behalf, and that not in the mildest manner; and yet he knew not how to refuse the permission requested.

'I'd so much sooner remain quiet in the matter,' said he, in an apologetic voice.

'Quiet!' said the archdeacon, still speaking with his brazen trumpet; 'do you wish to be ruined in quiet?'

'Why, if I am to be ruined, certainly.'

'Nonsense, warden; I tell you something must be done – we must act; just let me ring the bell, and send the men word that I'll speak to them in the quad.'

Mr Harding knew not how to resist, and the disagreeable order was given. The quad, as it was familiarly called, was a small quadrangle, open on one side to the river, and surrounded on the others by the high wall of Mr Harding's garden, by one gable end of Mr Harding's house, and by the end of the row of buildings which formed the residences of the bedesmen. It was flagged all round, and the centre was stoned; small stone gutters ran from the four corners of the square to a grating in the centre; and attached to the end of Mr Harding's house was a conduit with four cocks covered over from the weather, at which the old men got their water, and very generally performed their morning toilet. It was a quiet, sombre place, shaded over by the trees of the warden's garden. On the side towards the river, there stood a row of stone seats, on which the old men would sit and gaze at the little fish, as they flitted by in the running stream. On the other side of the river was a rich, green meadow, running up to and joining the deanery, and as little open to the public as the garden of the dean itself. Nothing, therefore, could be more private than the quad of the hospital; and it was there that the archdeacon determined to convey to them his sense of their refractory proceedings.

The servant soon brought in word that the men were assembled in the quad, and the archdeacon, big with his purpose, rose to address them.

'Well, warden, of course you're coming,' said he, seeing that Mr Harding did not prepare to follow him.

'I wish you'd excuse me,' said Mr Harding.

'For heaven's sake, don't let us have division in the camp,' replied the archdeacon: 'let us have a long pull and a strong pull, but above all a pull altogether; come, warden, come; don't be afraid of your duty.'

Mr Harding was afraid; he was afraid that he was being led to do that which was not his duty: he was not, however, strong enough to resist, so he got up and followed his son-in-law.

The old men were assembled in groups in the quadrangle – eleven of them at least, for poor old Johnny Bell was bedridden, and couldn't come; he had, however, put his mark to the petition, as one of Handy's earliest followers. 'Tis true he could not move from the bed where he lay; 'tis true he had no friend on earth, but those whom the hospital contained; and of those the warden and his daughter were the most constant and most appreciated; 'tis true that everything was administered to him which his failing body could require, or which his faint appetite could enjoy; but still his dull eye had glistened for a moment at the idea of possessing a hundred pounds a year 'to his own cheek', as Abel Handy had eloquently expressed it; and poor old Johnny Bell had greedily put his mark to the petition.

When the two clergymen appeared, they all uncovered their heads. Handy was slow to do it, and hesitated; but the black coat and waistcoat, of which he had spoken so irreverently in Skulpit's room, had its effect even on him, and he too doffed his hat. Bunce, advancing before the others, bowed lowly to the archdeacon, and with affectionate reverence expressed his wish, that the warden and Miss Eleanor were quite well; 'and the doctor's lady,' he added, turning to the archdeacon, 'and the children at Plumstead, and my lord'; and having made his speech, he also retired among the others, and took his place with the rest upon the stone benches.

As the archdeacon stood up to make his speech, erect in the middle of that little square, he looked like an ecclesiastical statue placed there, as a fitting impersonation of the church militant here on earth; his shovel hat, large, new, and well pronounced, a churchman's hat in every inch, declared the profession as plainly as does the Quaker's broad brim; his heavy eyebrows, large open eyes, and full mouth and chin expressed the solidity of his order; the broad chest, amply covered with fine cloth, told how well-to-do was its estate; one hand ensconced within his pocket evinced the practical hold which our mother Church keeps on her temporal possessions; and the other, loose for action, was ready to fight if need be in her defence; and below these the decorous breeches, and neat black gaiters showing so admirably that well-turned leg, betokened the decency, the outward beauty and grace of our church establishment.

'Now my men,' he began, when he had settled himself well in his position; 'I want to say a few words to you. Your good friend, the warden here, and myself, and my lord the bishop, on whose behalf I wish to speak to you, would all be very sorry, very sorry indeed, that you should have any just ground of complaint. Any just ground of complaint on your part would be removed at once by the warden, or by his lordship, or by me on his behalf, without the necessity of any petition on your part.' Here the orator stopped for a moment, expecting that some little murmurs of applause would show that the weakest of the men were beginning to give

way; but no such murmurs came. Bunce, himself, even sat with
closed lips, mute and unsatisfactory. 'Without the necessity of any
petition at all,' he repeated. 'I'm told you have addressed a petition
to my lord.' He paused for a reply from the men, and after a while
Handy plucked up courage, and said, 'Yes, we has.'

'You have addressed a petition to my lord, in which, as I am
informed, you express an opinion that you do not receive from
Hiram's estate all that is your due.' Here most of the men expressed
their assent. 'Now what is it you ask for? what is it you want that
you haven't got here? what is it –'

'A hundred a year,' muttered old Moody, with a voice as if it
came out of the ground.

'A hundred a year!' ejaculated the archdeacon militant, defying
the impudence of these claimants with one hand stretched out and
closed, while with the other he tightly grasped, and secured within
his breeches pocket, that symbol of the Church's wealth which his
own loose half-crowns not unaptly represented. 'A hundred a
year! Why, my men, you must be mad; and you talk about John
Hiram's will! When John Hiram built a hospital for worn-out old
men, worn-out old labouring men, infirm old men past their work,
cripples, blind, bedridden, and such like, do you think he meant
to make gentlemen of them? Do you think John Hiram intended
to give a hundred a year to old single men, who earned perhaps
two shillings or half a crown a day for themselves and families in
the best of their time? No, my men, I'll tell you what John Hiram
meant; he meant that twelve poor old worn-out labourers, men
who could no longer support themselves, who had no friends to
support them, who must starve and perish miserably if not protected by the hand of charity; he meant that twelve such men as
these should come in here in their poverty and wretchedness, and
find within these walls shelter and food before their death, and
a little leisure to make their peace with God. That was what John
Hiram meant: you have not read John Hiram's will, and I doubt
whether those wicked men who are advising you have done so.
I have; I know what his will was; and I tell you that that was his
will, and that that was his intention.'

Not a sound came from the eleven bedesmen, as they sat listening to what, according to the archdeacon, was their intended

estate. They grimly stared upon his burly figure, but did not then express, by word or sign, the anger and disgust to which such language was sure to give rise.

'Now let me ask you,' he continued, 'do you think you are worse off than John Hiram intended to make you? Have you not shelter, and food, and leisure? Have you not much more? Have you not every indulgence which you are capable of enjoying? Have you not twice better food, twice a better bed, ten times more money in your pocket than you were ever able to earn for yourselves before you were lucky enough to get into this place? And now you send a petition to the bishop, asking for a hundred pounds a year! I tell you what, my friends; you are deluded, and made fools of by wicked men who are acting for their own ends. You will never get a hundred pence a year more than what you have now: it is very possible that you may get less; it is very possible that my lord the bishop, and your warden may make changes –'

'No, no, no,' interrupted Mr Harding, who had been listening with indescribable misery to the tirade of his son-in-law; 'no, my friends. I want no changes – at least no changes that shall make you worse off than you now are, as long as you and I live together.'

'God bless you, Mr Harding,' said Bunce; and 'God bless you, Mr Harding, God bless you sir, we know you was always our friend' was exclaimed by enough of the men to make it appear that the sentiment was general.

The archdeacon had been interrupted in his speech before he had quite finished it; but he felt that he could not recommence with dignity after this little ebullition, and he led the way back into the garden, followed by his father-in-law.

'Well,' said he, as soon as he found himself within the cool retreat of the warden's garden; 'I think I spoke to them plainly.' And he wiped the perspiration from his brow; for making a speech under a broiling midday sun in summer, in a full suit of thick black cloth, is warm work.

'Yes, you were plain enough,' replied the warden, in a tone which did not express approbation.

'And that's everything,' said the other, who was clearly well satisfied with himself; 'that's everything: with those sort of people one must be plain, or one will not be understood. Now, I think they did understand me – I think they knew what I meant.'

The warden agreed. He certainly thought they had understood to the full what had been said to them.

'They know pretty well what they have to expect from us; they know how we shall meet any refractory spirit on their part; they know that we are not afraid of them. And now I'll just step into Chadwick's, and tell him what I've done; and then I'll go up to the palace, and answer this petition of theirs.'

The warden's mind was very full – full nearly to overcharging itself; and had it done so – had he allowed himself to speak the thoughts which were working within him, he would indeed have astonished the archdeacon by the reprobation he would have expressed as to the proceeding of which he had been so unwilling a witness. But different feelings kept him silent; he was as yet afraid of differing from his son-in-law – he was anxious beyond measure to avoid even a semblance of rupture with any of his order, and was painfully fearful of having to come to an open quarrel with any person on any subject. His life had hitherto been so quiet, so free from strife; his little early troubles had required nothing but passive fortitude; his subsequent prosperity had never forced upon him any active cares – had never brought him into disagreeable contact with anyone. He felt that he would give almost anything – much more than he knew he ought to do – to relieve himself from the storm which he feared was coming. It was so hard that the pleasant waters of his little stream should be disturbed and muddied by rough hands; that his quiet paths should be made a battlefield; that the unobtrusive corner of the world which had been allotted to him, as though by Providence, should be invaded and desecrated, and all within it made miserable and unsound.

Money he had none to give; the knack of putting guineas together had never belonged to him; but how willingly, with what a foolish easiness, with what happy alacrity, would he have abandoned the half of his income for all time to come, could he by so doing have quietly dispelled the clouds that were gathering over him – could he have thus compromised the matter between the reformer and the conservative, between his possible son-in-law, Bold, and his positive son-in-law, the archdeacon.

And this compromise would not have been made from any prudential motive of saving what would yet remain, for Mr Harding still felt little doubt but he should be left for life in quiet possession of the good things he had, if he chose to retain them. No; he would have done so from the sheer love of quiet, and from a horror of being made the subject of public talk. He had very often been moved to pity – to that inward weeping of the heart for others' woes; but none had he ever pitied more than that old lord, whose almost fabulous wealth, drawn from his church preferments, had become the subject of so much opprobrium, of such public scorn; that wretched clerical octogenarian Croesus,[6] whom men would not allow to die in peace – whom all the world united to decry and to abhor.

Was he to suffer such a fate? Was his humble name to be bandied in men's mouths, as the gormandizer of the resources of the poor, as of one who had filched from the charity of other ages wealth which had been intended to relieve the old and the infirm? Was he to be gibbeted in the press, to become a byword for oppression, to be named as an example of the greed of the English church? Should it ever be said that he had robbed those old men, whom he so truly and so tenderly loved in his heart of hearts? As he slowly paced, hour after hour, under those noble lime trees, turning these sad thoughts within him, he became all but fixed in his resolve that some great step must be taken to relieve him from the risk of so terrible a fate.

In the meanwhile, the archdeacon, with contented mind and unruffled spirit, went about his business. He said a word or two to Mr Chadwick, and then finding, as he expected, the petition lying in his father's library, he wrote a short answer to the men, in which he told them that they had no evils to redress, but rather great mercies for which to be thankful; and having seen the bishop sign it, he got into his brougham[7] and returned home to Mrs Grantly, and Plumstead Episcopi.

CHAPTER 6

The Warden's Tea Party

AFTER much painful doubting, on one thing only could Mr Harding resolve. He determined that at any rate he would take no offence, and that he would make this question no cause of quarrel either with Bold or with the bedesmen. In furtherance of this resolution, he himself wrote a note to Mr Bold, the same afternoon, inviting him to meet a few friends and hear some music on an evening named in the next week. Had not this little party been promised to Eleanor, in his present state of mind he would probably have avoided such gaiety; but the promise had been given, the invitations were to be written, and when Eleanor consulted her father on the subject, she was not ill pleased to hear him say, 'Oh, I was thinking of Bold, so I took it into my head to write to him myself, but you must write to his sister.'

Mary Bold was older than her brother, and, at the time of our story, was just over thirty. She was not an unattractive young woman, though by no means beautiful. Her great merit was the kindliness of her disposition. She was not very clever, nor very animated, nor had she apparently the energy of her brother; but she was guided by a high principle of right and wrong; her temper was sweet, and her faults were fewer in number than her virtues. Those who casually met Mary Bold thought little of her; but those who knew her well loved her well, and the longer they knew her the more they loved her. Among those who were fondest of her was Eleanor Harding, and though Eleanor had never openly talked to her of her brother, each understood the other's feelings about him. The brother and sister were sitting together when the two notes were brought in.

'How odd,' said Mary, 'that they should send two notes. Well, if Mr Harding becomes fashionable, the world is going to change.'

Her brother understood immediately the nature and intention of the peace-offering; but it was not so easy for him to behave well in the matter as it was for Mr Harding. It is much less difficult for the sufferer to be generous than for the oppressor. John Bold felt that he could not go to the warden's party: he never loved Eleanor better than he did now; he had never so strongly felt how anxious he was to make her his wife as now, when so many obstacles to his doing so appeared in view. Yet here was her father himself, as it were clearing away those very obstacles, and still he felt that he could not go to the house any more as an open friend.

As he sat thinking of these things with the note in his hand, his sister was waiting for his decision.

'Well,' said she, 'I suppose we must write separate answers, and both say we shall be very happy.'

'You'll go, of course, Mary,' said he; to which she readily assented. 'I cannot,' he continued, looking serious and gloomy; 'I wish I could, with all my heart.'

'And why not, John?' said she. She had as yet heard nothing of the new-found abuse which her brother was about to reform; at least, nothing which connected it with her brother's name.

He sat thinking for a while till he determined that it would be best to tell her at once what it was that he was about: it must be done sooner or later.

'I fear I cannot go to Mr Harding's house any more as a friend, just at present.'

'Oh, John! Why not? Ah, you've quarrelled with Eleanor!'

'No, indeed,' said he; 'I've no quarrel with her as yet.'

'What is it, John?' said she, looking at him with an anxious, loving face, for she knew well how much of his heart was there in that house which he said he could no longer enter.

'Why,' said he at last, 'I've taken up the case of these twelve old men of Hiram's Hospital, and of course that brings me into contact with Mr Harding. I may have to oppose him, interfere with him, perhaps injure him.'

Mary looked at him steadily for some time before she committed herself to reply, and then merely asked him what he meant to do for the old men.

'Why, it's a long story, and I don't know that I can make you understand it. John Hiram made a will, and left his property in charity for certain poor old men, and the proceeds, instead of going to the benefit of these men, goes chiefly into the pocket of the warden, and the bishop's steward.'

'And you mean to take away from Mr Harding his share of it?'

'I don't know what I mean yet. I mean to inquire about it. I mean to see who is entitled to this property. I mean to see, if I can, that justice be done to the poor of the city of Barchester generally, who are, in fact, the legatees under the will. I mean, in short, to put the matter right, if I can.'

'And why are you to do this, John?'

'You might ask the same question of anybody else,' said he; 'and according to that, the duty of righting these poor men would belong to nobody. If we are to act on that principle, the weak are never to be protected, injustice is never to be opposed, and no one is to struggle for the poor!' And Bold began to comfort himself in the warmth of his own virtue.

'But is there no one to do this but you, who have known Mr Harding so long? Surely, John, as a friend, as a young friend, so much younger than Mr Harding –'

'That's woman's logic, all over, Mary. What has age to do with it? Another man might plead that he was too old; and as to his friendship, if the thing itself be right, private motives should never be allowed to interfere. Because I esteem Mr Harding, is that a reason that I should neglect a duty which I owe to these old men? or should I give up a work which my conscience tells me is a good one, because I regret the loss of his society?'

'And Eleanor, John?' said the sister, looking timidly into her brother's face.

'Eleanor, that is, Miss Harding, if she thinks fit – that is, if her father – or rather, if she – or, indeed, he – if they find it necessary – but there is no necessity now to talk about Eleanor Harding; but this I will say, that if she has the kind of spirit for which I give her credit, she will not condemn me for doing what I think to be a duty.' And Bold consoled himself with the consolation of a Roman.[1]

Mary sat silent for a while, till at last her brother reminded her that the notes must be answered, and she got up, and placed her desk before her, took out her pen and her paper, wrote on it slowly –

MY DEAR ELEANOR,

I –

and then stopped, and looked at her brother.

'Well, Mary, why don't you write it?'

'Oh, John,' said she, 'dear John, pray think better of this.'

'Think better of what?' said he.

'Of this about the hospital – of all this about Mr Harding – of what you say about those old men. Nothing can call upon you – no duty can require you to set yourself against your oldest, your best friend. Oh, John, think of Eleanor; you'll break her heart and your own.'

'Nonsense, Mary; Miss Harding's heart is as safe as yours.'

'Pray, pray, for my sake, John, give it up. You know how dearly you love her.' And she came and knelt before him on the rug. 'Pray give it up. You are going to make yourself, and her, and her father miserable: you are going to make us all miserable. And for what? For a dream of justice. You will never make those twelve men happier than they now are.'

'You don't understand it, my dear girl,' said he, smoothing her hair with his hand.

'I do understand it, John. I understand that this is a chimera – a dream that you have got. I know well that no duty can require you to do this mad – this suicidal thing. I know you love Eleanor Harding with all your heart, and I tell you now that she loves you as well. If there was a plain, a positive duty before you, I would be the last to bid you neglect it for any woman's love; but this – oh, think again, before you do anything to make it necessary that you and Mr Harding should be at variance.' He did not answer, as she knelt there, leaning on his knees, but by his face she thought that he was inclined to yield. 'At any rate let me say that you will go to this party. At any rate do not break with them while your mind is in doubt.' And she got up, hoping to conclude her note in the way she desired.

'My mind is not in doubt,' at last he said, rising; 'I could never respect myself again, were I to give way now because Eleanor Harding is beautiful. I do love her: I would give a hand to hear her tell me what you have said, speaking on her behalf; but I cannot for her sake go back from the task which I have commenced. I hope she may hereafter acknowledge and respect my motives, but I cannot now go as a guest to her father's house.' And the Barchester Brutus[2] went out to fortify his own resolution by meditations on his own virtue.

Poor Mary Bold sat down, and sadly finished her note, saying that she would herself attend the party, but that her brother was unavoidably prevented from doing so. I fear that she did not admire as she should have done the self-devotion of his singular virtue.

The party went off as such parties do: there were fat old ladies in fine silk dresses, and slim young ladies in gauzy muslin frocks; old gentlemen stood up with their backs to the empty fireplace, looking by no means so comfortable as they would have done in their own armchairs at home; and young gentlemen, rather stiff about the neck, clustered near the door, not as yet sufficiently in courage to attack the muslin frocks, who awaited the battle, drawn up in a semicircular array. The warden endeavoured to induce a charge, but failed signally, not having the tact of a general: his daughter did what she could to comfort the forces under her command, who took in refreshing rations of cake and tea, and patiently looked for the coming engagement: but she herself, Eleanor, had no spirit for the work; the only enemy whose lance she cared to encounter was not there, and she and others were somewhat dull.

Loud above all voices was heard the clear sonorous tones of the archdeacon as he dilated to brother parsons of the danger of the Church, of the fearful rumours of mad reforms even at Oxford,[3] and of the damnable heresies of Dr Whiston.

Soon, however, sweeter sounds began timidly to make themselves audible. Little movements were made in a quarter, notable for round stools and music stands. Wax candles were arranged in sconces, big books were brought from hidden recesses, and the work of the evening commenced.

How often were those pegs twisted and retwisted before our friend found that he had twisted them enough; how many discordant scrapes gave promise of the coming harmony! How much the muslin fluttered and crumpled before Eleanor and another nymph were duly seated at the piano; how closely did that tall Apollo[4] pack himself against the wall, with his flute, long as himself, extending high over the heads of his pretty neighbours; into how small a corner crept that round and florid little minor canon, and there with skill amazing found room to tune his accustomed fiddle!

And now the crash begins: away they go in full flow of harmony together – up hill and down dale – now louder and louder, then lower and lower: now loud, as though stirring the battle; then low, as though mourning the slain. In all, through all, and above all, is heard the violoncello. Ah, not for nothing were those pegs so twisted and retwisted – listen, listen! Now alone that saddest of instruments tells its touching tale. Silent, and in awe, stand fiddle, flute, and piano, to hear the sorrows of their wailing brother. 'Tis but for a moment: before the melancholy of those low notes has been fully realized, again comes the full force of all the band – down go the pedals, away rush twenty fingers scouring over the bass notes with all the impetus of passion. Apollo blows till his stiff neckcloth is no better than a rope, and the minor canon works both arms till he falls in a syncope of exhaustion against the wall.

How comes it that now, when all should be silent, when courtesy, if not taste, should make men listen – how is it at this moment the black-coated corps leave their retreat and begin skirmishing? One by one they creep forth, and fire off little guns timidly, and without precision. Ah, my men, efforts such as these will take no cities, even though the enemy should be never so open to assault. At length a more deadly artillery is brought to bear; slowly, but with effect, the advance is made; the muslin ranks are broken, and fall into confusion; the formidable array of chairs gives way; the battle is no longer between opposing regiments, but hand to hand, and foot to foot with single combatants, as in the glorious days of old, when fighting was really noble. In corners, and under the shadow of curtains, behind sofas and half hidden by doors, in retiring windows, and sheltered by hanging tapestry, are blows given and returned, fatal, incurable, dealing death.

Apart from this another combat arises, more sober and more serious. The archdeacon is engaged against two prebendaries,[5] a

pursy full-blown rector assisting him, in all the perils and all the
enjoyments of short whist.[6] With solemn energy do they watch the
shuffled pack, and, all-expectant, eye the coming trump. With
what anxious nicety do they arrange their cards, jealous of each
other's eyes! Why is that lean doctor so slow – cadaverous man
with hollow jaw and sunken eye, ill beseeming the richness of his
mother church! Ah, why so slow, thou meagre doctor? See how
the archdeacon, speechless in his agony, deposits on the board his
cards, and looks to heaven or to the ceiling for support. Hark, how
he sighs, as with thumbs in his waistcoat pocket he seems to
signify that the end of such torment is not yet even nigh at hand!
Vain is the hope, if hope there be, to disturb that meagre doctor.
With care precise he places every card, weighs well the value of
each mighty ace, each guarded king, and comfort-giving queen;
speculates on knave and ten, counts all his suits, and sets his price
upon the whole. At length a card is led, and quick three others
fall upon the board. The little doctor leads again, while with
lustrous eye his partner absorbs the trick. Now thrice has this been
done – thrice has constant fortune favoured the brace of prebendaries, ere the archdeacon rouses himself to the battle: but at
the fourth assault he pins to the earth a prostrate king, laying low
his crown and sceptre, bushy beard, and lowering brow, with a
poor deuce.

'As David did Goliath,' says the archdeacon, pushing over the
four cards to his partner. And then a trump is led, then another
trump; then a king – and then an ace – and then a long ten, which
brings down from the meagre doctor his only remaining tower of
strength – his cherished queen of trumps.

'What, no second club?' says the archdeacon to his partner.

'Only one club,' mutters from his inmost stomach the pursy
rector, who sits there red-faced, silent, impervious, careful, a safe
but not a brilliant ally.

But the archdeacon cares not for many clubs, or for none. He
dashes out his remaining cards with a speed most annoying to his
antagonists, pushes over to them some four cards as their allotted
portion, shoves the remainder across the table to the red-faced
rector: calls out 'two by cards and two by honours, and the odd
trick last time', marks a treble under the candlestick,[7] and has dealt

round the second pack before the meagre doctor has calculated his losses.

And so went off the warden's party, and men and women arranging shawls and shoes declared how pleasant it had been; and Mrs Goodenough, the red-faced rector's wife, pressing the warden's hand, declared she had never enjoyed herself better; which showed how little pleasure she allowed herself in this world, as she had sat the whole evening through in the same chair without occupation, not speaking, and unspoken to. And Matilda Johnson, when she allowed young Dickson of the bank to fasten her cloak round her neck, thought that two hundred pounds a year and a little cottage would really do for happiness; besides he was sure to be manager some day. And Apollo, folding his flute into his pocket, felt that he had acquitted himself with honour; and the archdeacon pleasantly jingled his gains; but the meagre doctor went off without much audible speech, muttering ever and anon as he went 'three and thirty points', 'three and thirty points!'*

And so they all were gone, and Mr Harding was left alone with his daughter.

What had passed between Eleanor Harding and Mary Bold need not be told. It is indeed a matter of thankfulness that neither the historian nor the novelist hears all that is said by their heroes or heroines, or how would three volumes or twenty suffice! In the present case so little of this sort have I overheard, that I live in hopes of finishing my work within 300 pages, and of completing that pleasant task – a novel in one volume; but something had passed between them, and as the warden blew out the wax candles, and put his instrument into its case, his daughter stood sad and thoughtful by the empty fireplace, determined to speak to her father, but irresolute as to what she would say.

'Well, Eleanor,' said he, 'are you for bed?'

'Yes,' said she, moving, 'I suppose so; but, papa – Mr Bold was not here tonight: do you know why not?'

'He was asked; I wrote to him myself,' said the warden.

'But do you know why he did not come, papa?'

'Well, Eleanor, I could guess; but it's no use guessing at such things, my dear. What makes you look so earnest about it?'

'Oh papa, do tell me,' she exclaimed, throwing her arms round him, and looking into his face; 'what is it he is going to do? What is it all about? Is there any – any – any –' she didn't well know what word to use – 'any danger?'

'Danger, my dear, what sort of danger?'

'Danger to you, danger of trouble, and of loss, and of – Oh papa, why haven't you told me of all this before?'

Mr Harding was not the man to judge harshly of anyone, much less of the daughter whom he now loved better than any living creature; but still he did judge her wrongly at this moment. He knew that she loved John Bold; he fully sympathized in her affection; day after day he thought more of the matter, and, with the tender care of a loving father, tried to arrange in his own mind how matters might be so managed that his daughter's heart should not be made the sacrifice to the dispute which was likely to exist between him and Bold. Now, when she spoke to him for the first time on the subject, it was natural that he should think more of her than of himself, and that he should imagine that her own cares, and not his, were troubling her.

He stood silent before her awhile, as she gazed up into his face, and then kissing her forehead he placed her on the sofa.

'Tell me, Nelly,' he said (he only called her Nelly in his kindest, softest, sweetest moods, and yet all his moods were kind and sweet), 'tell me, Nelly, do you like Mr Bold – much?'

She was quite taken aback by the question. I will not say that she had forgotten herself and her own love in thinking about John Bold, and while conversing with Mary: she certainly had not done so. She had been sick at heart to think that a man of whom she could not but own to herself that she loved him, of whose regard she had been so proud, that such a man should turn against her father to ruin him. She had felt her vanity hurt, that his affection for her had not kept him from such a course; had he really cared for her, he would not have risked her love by such an outrage; but her main fear had been for her father, and when she spoke of danger, it was of danger to him and not to herself.

She was taken aback by the question altogether: 'Do I like him, papa?'

'Yes, Nelly, do you like him? Why shouldn't you like him; but that's a poor word – do you love him?' She sat still in his arms without answering him. She certainly had not prepared herself for an avowal of affection, intending, as she had done, to abuse John Bold herself, and to hear her father do so also. 'Come, my love,' said he, 'let us make a clean breast of it: do you tell me what concerns yourself, and I will tell you what concerns me and the hospital.'

And then, without waiting for an answer, he described to her, as he best could, the accusation that was made about Hiram's will; the claims which the old men put forward; what he considered the strength and what the weakness of his own position; the course which Bold had taken, and that which he presumed he was about to take; and then by degrees, without further question, he presumed on the fact of Eleanor's love, and spoke of that love as a feeling which he could in no way disapprove: he apologized for Bold, excused what he was doing; nay praised him for his energy and intentions: made much of his good qualities, and harped on none of his foibles; then, reminding his daughter how late it was, and comforting her with much assurance which he hardly felt himself, he sent her to her room, with flowing eyes and a full heart.

When Mr Harding met his daughter at breakfast the next morning, there was no further discussion on the matter, nor was the subject mentioned between them for some days. Soon after the party Mary Bold called at the hospital, but there were various persons in the drawing-room at the time, and she therefore said nothing about her brother. On the day following, John Bold met Miss Harding in one of the quiet sombre shaded walks of the close: he was most anxious to see her, but unwilling to call at the warden's house, and had in truth waylaid her in her private haunts.

'My sister tells me,' said he, abruptly hurrying on with his premeditated speech, 'my sister tells me that you had a delightful party the other evening. I was so sorry I could not be there.'

'We were all sorry,' said Eleanor, with dignified composure.

'I believe, Miss Harding, you understood why, at this moment –' And Bold hesitated, muttered, stopped, commenced his explanation again, and again broke down.

Eleanor would not help him in the least.

'I think my sister explained to you, Miss Harding?'

'Pray don't apologize, Mr Bold; my father will, I am sure, always be glad to see you, if you like to come to the house now as formerly; nothing has occurred to alter his feelings; of your own views you are, of course, the best judge.'

'Your father is all that is kind and generous; he always was so, but you, Miss Harding, yourself – I hope you will not judge me harshly, because –'

'Mr Bold,' said she, 'you may be sure of one thing; I shall always judge my father to be right, and those who oppose him I shall judge to be wrong. If those who do not know him oppose him, I shall have charity enough to believe that they are wrong, through error of judgement; but should I see him attacked by those who ought to know him, and to love him, and revere him, of such I shall be constrained to form a different opinion.' And then curtseying low she sailed on, leaving her lover in anything but a happy state of mind.

CHAPTER 7

The Jupiter

THOUGH Eleanor Harding rode off from John Bold on a high horse, it must not be supposed that her heart was so elate as her demeanour. In the first place, she had a natural repugnance to losing her lover; and in the next, she was not quite so sure that she was in the right as she pretended to be. Her father had told her, and that now repeatedly, that Bold was doing nothing unjust or ungenerous, and why then should she rebuke him, and throw him off, when she felt herself so ill able to bear his loss? – but such is human nature, and young-lady-nature especially. As she walked off from him beneath the shady elms of the close, her look, her tone, every motion and gesture of her body, belied her heart; she would have given the world to have taken him by the hand, to have reasoned with him, persuaded him, cajoled him, coaxed him out of his project; to have overcome him with all her female artillery, and to have redeemed her father at the cost of herself; but pride would not let her do this, and she left him without a look of love or a word of kindness.

Had Bold been judging of another lover and of another lady he might have understood all this as well as we do; but in matters of love men do not see clearly in their own affairs. They say that faint heart never won fair lady; and it is amazing to me how fair ladies are won, so faint are often men's hearts! Were it not for the kindness of their nature, that seeing the weakness of our courage they will occasionally descend from their impregnable fortresses, and themselves aid us in effecting their own defeat, too often would they escape unconquered if not unscathed, and free of body if not of heart.

Poor Bold crept off quite crestfallen; he felt that as regarded Eleanor Harding his fate was sealed, unless he could consent to give up a task to which he had pledged himself, and which indeed it would not be easy for him to give up. Lawyers were engaged, and the question had to a certain extent been taken up by the public; besides, how could a high-spirited girl like Eleanor Harding really learn to love a man for neglecting a duty which he assumed! Could she allow her affection to be purchased at the cost of his own self-respect?

As regarded the issue of his attempt at reformation in the hospital, Bold had no reason hitherto to be discontented with his success. All Barchester was by the ears about it. The bishop, the archdeacon, the warden, the steward, and several other clerical allies, had daily meetings, discussing their tactics, and preparing for the great attack. Sir Abraham Haphazard had been consulted, but his opinion was not yet received: copies of Hiram's will, copies of wardens' journals, copies of leases, copies of accounts, copies of everything that could be copied. and of some that could not, had been sent to him; and the case was assuming most creditable dimensions. But above all, it had been mentioned in the daily *Jupiter*.[1] That all-powerful organ of the press in one of its leading thunderbolts launched at St Cross, had thus re-marked:

Another case, of smaller dimensions indeed, but of similar import, is now likely to come under public notice. We are informed that the warden or master of an old almshouse attached to Barchester Cathedral is in receipt of twenty-five times the annual income appointed for him by the will of the founder, while the sum yearly expended on the absolute purposes of the charity has always remained fixed. In other words, the legatees under the founder's will have received no advantage from the increase in the value of the property during the last four centuries, such increase having been absorbed by the so-called warden. It is impossible to conceive a case of greater injustice. It is no answer to say that some six or nine or twelve old men receive as much of the goods of this world as such old men require. On what foundation, moral or divine, traditional or legal, is grounded the warden's claim to the large income he receives for doing nothing? The contentment of these almsmen, if content they be, can give him no title to this wealth! Does he ever ask himself, when he stretches wide his clerical palm to receive the pay of some dozen of the working clergy, for what service he is so remunerated? Does his conscience ever entertain the question of his right to such subsidies? Or is it possible that the subject never so presents itself to his mind; that he has received for many years, and intends, should God spare him, to receive for years to come, these fruits of the industrious piety of past ages, indifferent as to any right on his own

part, or of any injustice to others! We must express an opinion that
nowhere but in the Church of England, and only there among its priests,
could such a state of moral indifference be found.

I must for the present leave my readers to imagine the state of
Mr Harding's mind after reading the above article. They say that
forty thousand copies of the *Jupiter* are daily sold, and that each
copy is read by five persons at the least. Two hundred thousand
readers then would hear this accusation against him; two
hundred thousand hearts would swell with indignation at the
griping injustice, the barefaced robbery of the warden of Barchester Hospital! And how was he to answer this? How was he to
open his inmost heart to this multitude, to these thousands, the
educated, the polished, the picked men of his own country; how
show them that he was no robber, no avaricious lazy priest
scrambling for gold, but a retiring humble-spirited man who had
innocently taken what had innocently been offered to him?

'Write to the *Jupiter*,' suggested the bishop.

'Yes,' said the archdeacon, more worldly wise than his father,
'yes, and be smothered with ridicule; tossed over and over again
with scorn; shaken this way and that, as a rat in the mouth of a
practised terrier. You will leave out some word or letter in your
answer, and the ignorance of the cathedral clergy will be harped
upon; you will make some small mistake, which will be a falsehood, or some admission, which will be self-condemnation; you
will find yourself to have been vulgar, ill-tempered, irreverend,
and illiterate, and the chances are ten to one but that being a
clergyman you will have been guilty of blasphemy! A man may
have the best of causes, the best of talents, and the best of tempers;
he may write as well as Addison,[2] or as strongly as Junius;[3] but
even with all this he cannot successfully answer, when attacked by
the *Jupiter*. In such matters it is omnipotent. What the Czar is in
Russia, or the mob in America, that the *Jupiter* is in England.
Answer such an article! No, warden; whatever you do, don't do
that. We were to look for this sort of thing you know; but we need
not draw down on our heads more of it than is necessary.'

The article in the *Jupiter*, while it so greatly harassed our poor
warden, was an immense triumph to some of the opposite party.

Sorry as Bold was to see Mr Harding attacked so personally, it still gave him a feeling of elation to find his cause taken up by so powerful an advocate: and as to Finney, the attorney, he was beside himself. What! to be engaged in the same cause and on the same side with the *Jupiter*; to have the views he had recommended seconded, and furthered, and battled for by the *Jupiter*! Perhaps to have his own name mentioned as that of the learned gentleman whose efforts had been so successful on behalf of the poor of Barchester! He might be examined before committees of the House of Commons, with heaven knows how much a day for his personal expenses – he might be engaged for years on such a suit! There was no end to the glorious golden dreams which this leader in the *Jupiter* produced in the soaring mind of Finney.

And the old bedesmen, they also heard of this article, and had a glimmering, indistinct idea of the marvellous advocate which had now taken up their cause. Abel Handy limped hither and thither through the rooms, repeating all that he understood to have been printed, with some additions of his own which he thought should have been added. He told them how the *Jupiter* had declared that their warden was no better than a robber, and that what the *Jupiter* said was acknowledged by the world to be true. How the *Jupiter* had affirmed that each one of them – 'each one of us, Jonathan Crumple, think of that' – had a clear right to a hundred a year; and that if the *Jupiter* had said so, it was better than a decision of the Lord Chancellor; and then he carried about the paper, supplied by Mr Finney, which, though none of them could read it, still afforded in its very touch and aspect positive corroboration of what was told them, and Jonathan Crumple pondered deeply over his returning wealth; and Job Skulpit saw how right he had been in signing the petition, and said so many scores of times; and Spriggs leered fearfully with his one eye; and Moody, as he more nearly approached the coming golden age, hated more deeply than ever those who still kept possession of what he so coveted. Even Billy Gazy and poor bedridden Bell became active and uneasy, and the great Bunce stood apart with lowering brow, with deep grief seated in his heart, for he perceived that evil days were coming.

It had been decided, the archdeacon advising, that no remonstrance, explanation, or defence should be addressed from the Barchester conclave to the editor of the *Jupiter*, but hitherto that was the only decision to which they had come.

Sir Abraham Haphazard was deeply engaged in preparing a bill for the mortification of papists, to be called the 'Convent Custody Bill',[4] the purport of which was to enable any protestant clergyman over fifty years of age to search any nun whom he suspected of being in possession of treasonable papers or jesuitical symbols: and as there were to be a hundred and thirty-seven clauses in the bill, each clause containing a separate thorn for the side of the papist, and as it was known the bill would be fought inch by inch by fifty maddened Irishmen, the due construction and adequate dovetailing of it did consume much of Sir Abraham's time. The bill had all its desired effect. Of course it never passed into law; but it so completely divided the ranks of the Irish members, who had bound themselves together to force on the ministry a bill for compelling all men to drink Irish whiskey, and all women to wear Irish poplins, that for the remainder of the session the Great Poplin and Whiskey League was utterly harmless.

Thus it happened that Sir Abraham's opinion was not at once forthcoming, and the uncertainty, the expectation, and suffering of the folk of Barchester was maintained at a high pitch.

CHAPTER 8

Plumstead Episcopi

THE reader must now be requested to visit the rectory of Plumstead Episcopi; and as it is as yet still early morning, to ascend again with us into the bedroom of the archdeacon. The mistress of the mansion was at her toilet; on which we will not dwell with profane eyes, but proceed into a small inner room, where the doctor dressed and kept his boots and sermons; and here we will take our stand, premising that the door of the room was so open as to admit of a conversation between our reverend Adam and his valued Eve.

'It's all your own fault, archdeacon,' said the latter; 'I told you from the beginning how it would end, and papa has no one to thank but you.'

'Good gracious, my dear,' said the doctor, appearing at the door of his dressing-room, with his face and head enveloped in the rough towel which he was violently using; 'how can you say so? I am doing my very best.'

'I wish you had never done so much,' said the lady, interrupting him; 'if you'd just have let John Bold come and go there, as he and papa liked, he and Eleanor would have been married by this time, and we should not have heard one word about all this affair.'

'But, my dear –'

'Oh, it's all very well, archdeacon, and of course you're right; I don't for a moment think you'll ever admit that you could be wrong; but the fact is, you've brought this young man down upon papa by huffing him as you have done.'

'But, my love –'

'And all because you didn't like John Bold for a brother-in-law. How is she ever to do better? papa hasn't got a shilling; and though Eleanor is well enough, she has not at all a taking style of beauty. I'm sure I don't know how she's to do better than marry John Bold, or as well indeed,' added the anxious sister, giving the last twist to her last shoestring.

Dr Grantly felt keenly the injustice of this attack; but what could he say? He certainly had huffed John Bold; he certainly had objected to him as a brother-in-law, and a very few months ago the very idea had excited his wrath: but now matters were changed; John Bold had shown his power, and, though he was as odious as ever to the archdeacon, power is always respected, and the reverend dignitary began to think that such an alliance might not have been imprudent. Nevertheless, his motto was still 'no surrender'; he would still fight it out; he still believed confidently in Oxford, in the bench of bishops,[1] in Sir Abraham Haphazard, and in himself; and it was only when alone with his wife that doubts of defeat ever beset him. He once more tried to communicate this confidence to Mrs Grantly, and for the twentieth time began to tell her of Sir Abraham.

'Oh, Sir Abraham!' said she, collecting all her house keys into her basket before she descended; 'Sir Abraham won't get Eleanor a husband; Sir Abraham won't get papa another income when he has been worreted[2] out of the hospital. Mark what I tell you, archdeacon: while you and Sir Abraham are fighting, papa will lose his preferment; and what will you do then with him and Eleanor on your hands? besides, who's to pay Sir Abraham? I suppose he won't take the case up for nothing?' And so the lady descended to family worship among her children and servants, the pattern of a good and prudent wife.

Dr Grantly was blessed with a happy, thriving family. There were, first, three boys, now at home from school for the holidays. They were called, respectively, Charles James, Henry, and Samuel. The two younger (there were five in all) were girls; the elder, Florinda, bore the name of the Archbishop of York's wife, whose godchild she was; and the younger had been christened Grizzel, after a sister of the Archbishop of Canterbury. The boys were all clever, and gave good promise of being well able to meet the cares and trials of the world; and yet they were not alike in their dispositions, and each had his individual character, and each his separate admirers among the doctor's friends.

Charles James[3] was an exact and careful boy; he never committed himself; he well knew how much was expected from the eldest son of the Archdeacon of Barchester, and was therefore mindful not to mix too freely with other boys. He had not the great talents of his younger brothers, but he exceeded them in judgement and propriety of demeanour; his fault, if he had one, was an over-attention to words instead of things; there was a thought too much finesse about him, and, as even his father sometimes told him, he was too fond of a compromise.

The second was the archdeacon's favourite son, and Henry[4] was indeed a brilliant boy. The versatility of his genius was surprising, and the visitors at Plumstead Episcopi were often amazed at the marvellous manner in which he would, when called on, adapt his capacity to apparently most uncongenial pursuits. He appeared once before a large circle as Luther the reformer, and delighted them with the perfect manner in which he assumed the character; and within three days he again astonished them by acting the part of a Capuchin friar to the very life.[5] For this last exploit his father gave him a golden guinea, and his brothers said the reward had been promised beforehand in the event of the performance being successful. He was also sent on a tour into Devonshire; a treat which the lad was most anxious of enjoying. His father's friends there, however, did not appreciate his talents, and sad accounts were sent home of the perversity of his nature. He was a most courageous lad, game to the backbone. It was soon known, both at home, where he lived, and within some miles of Barchester Cathedral, and also at Westminster, where he was at school, that young Henry could box well and would never own himself beat; other boys would fight while they had a leg to stand on, but he would fight with no leg at all. Those backing him would sometimes think him crushed by the weight of blows and faint with loss of blood, and his friends would endeavour to withdraw him from the contest; but no, Henry never gave in, was never weary of the battle. The ring was the only element in which he seemed to enjoy himself; and while other boys were happy in the number of their friends, he rejoiced most in the multitude of his foes.

His relations could not but admire his pluck, but they sometimes were forced to regret that he was inclined to be a bully; and those not so partial to him as his father was observed with pain that, though he could fawn to the masters and the archdeacon's friends, he was imperious and masterful to the servants and the poor.

But perhaps Samuel was the general favourite; and dear little Soapy,[6] as he was familiarly called, was as engaging a child as ever fond mother petted. He was soft and gentle in his manners, and attractive in his speech; the tone of his voice was melody, and every action was a grace; unlike his brothers, he was courteous to all, he was affable to the lowly, and meek even to the very scullery maid. He was a boy of great promise, minding his books and delighting the hearts of his masters. His brothers, however, were not particularly fond of him; they would complain to their mother that Soapy's civility all meant something; they thought that his voice was too often listened to at Plumstead Episcopi, and evidently feared that, as he grew up, he would have more weight in the house than either of them; there was, therefore, a sort of agreement among them to put young Soapy down. This, however, was not so easy to be done; Samuel, though young, was sharp; he could not assume the stiff decorum of Charles James, nor could he fight like Henry; but he was a perfect master of his own weapons, and contrived, in the teeth of both of them, to hold the place which he had assumed. Henry declared that he was a false, cunning creature; and Charles James, though he always spoke of him as his dear brother Samuel, was not slow to say a word against him when opportunity offered. To speak the truth, Samuel was a cunning boy, and those even who loved him best could not but own that for one so young he was too adroit in choosing his words, and too skilled in modulating his voice.

The two little girls Florinda and Grizzel were nice little girls enough, but they did not possess the strong sterling qualities of their brothers; their voices were not often heard at Plumstead Episcopi; they were bashful and timid by nature, slow to speak before company even when asked to do so; and though they looked very nice in their clean white muslin frocks and pink sashes, they were but little noticed by the archdeacon's visitors.

Whatever of submissive humility may have appeared in the gait and visage of the archdeacon during his colloquy with his wife in the sanctum of their dressing-rooms was dispelled as he entered his breakfast-parlour with erect head and powerful step. In the presence of a third person he assumed the lord and master; and that wise and talented lady too well knew the man to whom her lot for life was bound, to stretch her authority beyond the point at which it would be borne. Strangers at Plumstead Episcopi, when they saw the imperious brow with which he commanded silence from the large circle of visitors, children, and servants who came together in the morning to hear him read the word of God, and watched how meekly that wife seated herself behind her basket of keys with a little girl on each side, as she caught that commanding glance; strangers, I say, seeing this, could little guess that some fifteen minutes since she had stoutly held her ground against him, hardly allowing him to open his mouth in his own defence. But such is the tact and talent of women!

And now let us observe the well-furnished breakfast-parlour at Plumstead Episcopi, and the comfortable air of all the belongings of the rectory. Comfortable they certainly were, but neither gorgeous nor even grand; indeed, considering the money that had been spent there, the eye and taste might have been better served; there was an air of heaviness about the rooms which might have been avoided without any sacrifice of propriety; colours might have been better chosen and lights more perfectly diffused: but perhaps in doing so the thorough clerical aspect of the whole might have been somewhat marred; at any rate, it was not without ample consideration that those thick, dark, costly carpets were put down; those embossed, but sombre papers hung up; those heavy curtains draped so as to half exclude the light of the sun: nor were these old-fashioned chairs, bought at a price far exceeding that now given for more modern goods, without a purpose. The breakfast-service on the table was equally costly and equally plain; the apparent object had been to spend money without obtaining brilliancy or splendour. The urn was of thick and solid silver, as were also the teapot, coffeepot, cream-ewer, and sugar-bowl; the cups were old, dim dragon china, worth about a pound a piece, but very despicable in the eyes of the uninitiated. The silver forks were so heavy as to be disagreeable to the hand, and the breadbasket was of a weight really formidable to any but robust persons. The tea consumed was the very best, the coffee the very blackest, the cream the very thickest; there was dry toast and buttered toast, muffins and crumpets; hot bread and cold bread, white bread and brown bread, home-made bread and bakers' bread, wheaten bread and oaten bread, and if there be other breads than these, they were there; there were eggs in napkins, and crispy bits of bacon under silver covers; and there were little fishes in a little box, and devilled kidneys frizzling on a hot-water dish; which, by the by, were placed closely contiguous to the plate of the worthy archdeacon himself. Over and above this, on a snow-white napkin, spread upon the sideboard, was a huge ham and a huge sirloin; the latter having laden the dinner-table on the previous evening. Such was the ordinary fare at Plumstead Episcopi.

And yet I have never found the rectory a pleasant house. The fact that man shall not live by bread alone seemed to be somewhat forgotten; and noble as was the appearance of the host, and sweet and good-natured as was the face of the hostess, talented as were the children, and excellent as were the viands and the wines, in spite of these attractions, I generally found the rectory somewhat dull. After breakfast the archdeacon would retire, of course to his clerical pursuits. Mrs Grantly, I presume, inspected her kitchen, though she had a first-rate housekeeper, with sixty pounds a year; and attended to the lessons of Florinda and Grizzel, though she had an excellent governess with thirty pounds a year: but at any rate she disappeared: and I never could make companions of the boys. Charles James, though he always looked as though there was something in him, never seemed to have much to say; and what he did say he would always unsay the next minute. He told me once, that he considered cricket, on the whole, to be a gentleman-like game for boys. provided they would play without running about; and that fives, also, was a seemly game, so that those who played it never heated themselves. Henry once quarrelled with me for taking his sister Grizzel's part, in a contest between them as to the best mode of using a watering-pot for the garden flowers; and from that day to this he has not spoken to me, though he speaks at me often enough. For half an hour or so I certainly did like Sammy's gentle speeches; but one gets tired of honey, and I found that he preferred the more admiring listeners whom he met in the kitchen-garden and back precincts of the establishment; besides, I think I once caught Sammy fibbing.

On the whole, therefore, I found the rectory a dull house, though it must be admitted that everything there was of the very best.

After breakfast, on the morning of which we are writing, the archdeacon, as usual, retired to his study, intimating that he was going to be very busy, but that he would see Mr Chadwick if he called. On entering this sacred room he carefully opened the paper case on which he was wont to compose his favourite sermons, and spread on it a fair sheet of paper, and one partly written on; he then placed his inkstand, looked at his pen, and folded his blotting paper; having done so, he got up again from his seat, stood with his back to the fireplace, and yawned comfortably, stretching out vastly his huge arms, and opening his burly chest. He then walked across the room and locked the door; and having so prepared himself, he threw himself into his easy chair, took from a secret drawer beneath his table a volume of Rabelais, and began to amuse himself with the witty mischief of Panurge;[7] and so passed the archdeacon's morning on that day.

He was left undisturbed at his studies for an hour or two, when a knock came to the door, and Mr Chadwick was announced. Rabelais retired into the secret drawer, the easy chair seemed knowingly to betake itself off, and when the archdeacon quickly undid his bolt, he was discovered by the steward working, as usual, for that church of which he was so useful a pillar. Mr Chadwick had just come from London, and was, therefore, known to be the bearer of important news.

'We've got Sir Abraham's opinion at last,' said Mr Chadwick, as he seated himself.

'Well, well, well!' exclaimed the archdeacon impatiently.

'Oh, it's as long as my arm,' said the other; 'it can't be told in a word, but you can read it'; and he handed him a copy, in heaven knows how many spun-out folios, of the opinion which the attorney-general[8] had managed to cram on the back and sides of the case as originally submitted to him.

'The upshot is,' said Chadwick, 'that there's a screw loose in their case, and we had better do nothing. They are proceeding against Mr Harding and myself, and Sir Abraham holds that, under the wording of the will and subsequent arrangements legally sanctioned, Mr Harding and I are only paid servants. The defendants should have been either the Corporation of Barchester, or possibly the chapter or your father.'

'W–hoo!' said the archdeacon; 'so Master Bold is on a wrong scent, is he?'

'That's Sir Abraham's opinion; but any scent almost would be a wrong scent. Sir Abraham thinks that if they'd taken the corporation, or the chapter, we could have baffled them. The bishop, he thinks, would be the surest shot; but even there we could plead that the bishop is only visitor, and that he has never made himself a consenting party to the performance of other duties.'

'That's quite clear,' said the archdeacon.

'Not quite so clear,' said the other. 'You see the will says, "My lord, the bishop, being graciously pleased to see that due justice be done." Now, it may be a question whether, in accepting and administering the patronage, your father has not accepted also the other duties assigned. It is doubtful, however; but even if they hit that nail – and they are far off from that yet – the point is so nice, as Sir Abraham says, that you would force them into fifteen thousand pounds' cost before they could bring it to an issue! and where's that sum of money to come from?'

The archdeacon rubbed his hands with delight; he had never doubted the justice of his case, but he had begun to have some dread of unjust success on the part of his enemies. It was delightful to him thus to hear that their cause was surrounded with such rocks and shoals; such causes of shipwreck unseen by the landsman's eye, but visible enough to the keen eyes of practical law mariners. How wrong his wife was to wish that Bold should marry Eleanor! Bold! why, if he should be ass enough to persevere, he would be a beggar before he knew whom he was at law with!

'That's excellent, Chadwick – that's excellent! I told you Sir Abraham was the man for us'; and he put down on the table the copy of the opinion, and patted it fondly.

'Don't you let that be seen, though, archdeacon.'

'Who? – I! – not for worlds,' said the doctor.

'People will talk, you know, archdeacon.'

'Of course, of course,' said the doctor.

'Because, if that gets abroad, it would teach them how to fight their own battle.'

'Quite true,' said the doctor.

'No one here in Barchester ought to see that but you and I, archdeacon.'

'No, no, certainly no one else,' said the archdeacon, pleased with the closeness of the confidence; 'no one else shall.'

'Mrs Grantly is very interested in the matter, I know,' said Mr Chadwick.

Did the archdeacon wink, or did he not? I am inclined to think he did not quite wink; but that without such, perhaps, unseemly gesture he communicated to Mr Chadwick, with the corner of his eye, intimation that, deep as was Mrs Grantly's interest in the matter, it should not procure for her a perusal of that document; and at the same time he partly opened the small drawer, above spoken of, deposited the paper on the volume of Rabelais, and showed to Mr Chadwick the nature of the key which guarded these hidden treasures. The careful steward then expressed himself contented. Ah! vain man! he could fasten up his Rabelais, and other things secret, with all the skill of Bramah or of Chubb;⁹ but where could he fasten up the key which solved these mechanical mysteries? It is probable to us that the contents of no drawer in that house were unknown to its mistress, and we think, moreover, that she was entitled to all such knowledge.

'But,' said Mr Chadwick, 'we must, of course, tell your father and Mr Harding so much of Sir Abraham's opinion as will satisfy them that the matter is doing well.'

'Oh, certainly – yes, of course,' said the doctor.

'You had better let them know that Sir Abraham is of opinion that there is no case at any rate against Mr Harding; and that as the action is worded at present, it must fall to the ground; they must be nonsuited if they carry it on; you had better tell Mr Harding that Sir Abraham is clearly of opinion that he is only a servant, and as such, not liable – or if you like it, I'll see Mr Harding myself.'

'Oh, I must see him tomorrow, and my father too, and I'll explain to them exactly so much – you won't go before lunch, Mr Chadwick: well, if you will, you must, for I know your time is precious;' and he shook hands with the diocesan steward, and bowed him out.

And the archdeacon had again recourse to his drawer, and twice read through the essence of Sir Abraham Haphazard's law-enlightened and law-bewildered brains. It was very clear that to Sir Abraham the justice of the old men's claim or the justice of Mr

Harding's defence were ideas that had never presented themselves. A legal victory over an opposing party was the service for
which Sir Abraham was, as he imagined, to be paid; and that he,
according to his lights, had diligently laboured to achieve, and
with probable hope of success. Of the intense desire which Mr
Harding felt to be assured on fit authority that he was wronging
no man, that he was entitled in true equity to his income, that he
might sleep at night without pangs of conscience, that he was no
robber, no spoiler of the poor; that he and all the world might be
openly convinced that he was not the man which the *Jupiter* had
described him to be; of such longings on the part of Mr Harding,
Sir Abraham was entirely ignorant; nor, indeed, could it be looked
on as part of his business to gratify such desires. Such was not the
system on which his battles were fought, and victories gained.
Success was his object, and he was generally successful. He conquered his enemies by their weakness rather than by his own
strength, and it had been found almost impossible to make up a
case in which Sir Abraham, as an antagonist, would not find a
flaw.

The archdeacon was delighted with the closeness of the reasoning. To do him justice, it was not a selfish triumph that he desired;
he would personally lose nothing by defeat, or at least what he
might lose did not actuate him; but neither was it love of justice
which made him so anxious, nor even mainly solicitude for his
father-in-law. He was fighting a part of a never-ending battle
against a never-conquered foe – that of the Church against its
enemies.

He knew Mr Harding could not pay all the expense of these
doings; for these long opinions of Sir Abraham's, these causes to
be pleaded, these speeches to be made, these various courts
through which the case was, he presumed, to be dragged. He knew
that he and his father must at least bear the heavier portion of this
tremendous cost; but to do the archdeacon justice, he did not
recoil from this. He was a man fond of obtaining money, greedy
of a large income, but open-handed enough in expending it, and
it was a triumph to him to foresee the success of this measure,
although he might be called on to pay so dearly for it himself.

CHAPTER 9

The Conference

ON the following morning the archdeacon was with his father betimes, and a note was sent down to the warden begging his attendance at the palace. Dr Grantly, as he cogitated on the matter, leaning back in his brougham as he journeyed into Barchester, felt that it would be difficult to communicate his own satisfaction either to his father or his father-in-law. He wanted success on his own side and discomfiture on that of his enemies. The bishop wanted peace on the subject; a settled peace if possible, but peace at any rate till the short remainder of his own days had spun itself out; but Mr Harding required, not only success and peace, but he also demanded that he might stand justified before the world.

The bishop, however, was comparatively easy to deal with; and before the arrival of the other, the dutiful son had persuaded his father that all was going on well, and then the warden arrived.

It was Mr Harding's wont, whenever he spent a morning at the palace, to seat himself immediately at the bishop's elbow, the bishop occupying a huge armchair fitted up with candlesticks, a reading table, a drawer, and other paraphernalia, the position of which chair was never moved, summer or winter; and when, as was very usual, the archdeacon was there also, he confronted the two elders, who thus were enabled to fight the battle against him together; and together submit to defeat, for such was their constant fate.

Our warden now took his accustomed place, having greeted his son-in-law as he entered, and then affectionately inquired after his friend's health. There was a gentleness about the bishop to which the soft womanly affection of Mr Harding particularly endeared itself, and it was quaint to see how the two mild old priests pressed each other's hands, and smiled and made little signs of love.

'Sir Abraham's opinion has come at last,' began the archdeacon. Mr Harding had heard so much, and was most anxious to know the result.

'It is quite favourable,' said the bishop, pressing his friend's arm. 'I am so glad.'

Mr Harding looked at the mighty bearer of the important news for confirmation of these glad tidings.

'Yes,' said the archdeacon, 'Sir Abraham has given most minute attention to the case; indeed, I knew he would – most minute attention, and his opinion is – and as to his opinion on such a subject being correct, no one who knows Sir Abraham's character can doubt – his opinion is, that they haven't got a leg to stand on.'

'But as how, archdeacon?'

'Why, in the first place – but you're no lawyer, warden, and I doubt you won't understand it; the gist of the matter is this: under Hiram's will two paid guardians have been selected for the hospital; the law will say two paid servants, and you and I won't quarrel with the name.'

'At any rate I will not if I am one of the servants,' said Mr Harding. 'A rose you know –'

'Yes, yes,' said the archdeacon, impatient of poetry at such a time. 'Well, two paid servants, we'll say; one to look after the men, and the other to look after the money. You and Chadwick are these two servants, and whether either of you be paid too much, or too little, more or less in fact than the founder willed, it's as clear as daylight that no one can fall foul of either of you for receiving an allotted stipend.'

'That does seem clear,' said the bishop, who had winced visibly under the words servants and stipend, which, however, appeared to have caused no uneasiness to the archdeacon.

'Quite clear,' said he, 'and very satisfactory. In point of fact, it being necessary to select such servants for the use of the hospital, the pay to be given to them must depend on the rate of pay for such services, according to their market value at the period in question; and those who manage the hospital must be the only judges of this.'

'And who does manage the hospital?' asked the warden.

'Oh, let them find that out; that's another question; the action is brought against you and Chadwick, and that's your defence, and a perfect and full defence it is. Now that I think very satisfactory.'

'Well,' said the bishop, looking inquiringly up into his friend's face, who sat silent awhile, and apparently not so well satisfied.

'And conclusive,' continued the archdeacon; 'if they press it to a jury, which they won't do, no twelve men in England will take five minutes to decide against them.'

'But according to that,' said Mr Harding, 'I might as well have sixteen hundred a year as eight, if the managers choose to allot it to me; and as I am one of the managers, if not the chief manager, myself, that can hardly be a just arrangement.'

'Oh, well, all that's nothing to the question; the question is, whether this intruding fellow, and a lot of cheating attorneys and pestilent dissenters, are to interfere with an arrangement which everyone knows is essentially just and serviceable to the Church. Pray don't let us be splitting hairs, and that amongst ourselves, or there'll never be an end of the cause or the cost.'

Mr Harding again sat silent for a while, during which the bishop once and again pressed his arm, and looked in his face to see if he could catch a gleam of a contented and eased mind; but there was no such gleam, and the poor warden continued playing sad dirges on invisible stringed instruments in all manner of positions: he was ruminating in his mind on this opinion of Sir Abraham, looking to it wearily and earnestly for satisfaction, but finding none. At last he said, 'Did you see the opinion, archdeacon?'

The archdeacon said he had not – that was to say, he had – that was, he had not seen the opinion itself; he had seen what had been called a copy, but he could not say whether of a whole or part; nor could he say that what he had seen were the *ipsissima verba*[1] of the great man himself; but what he had seen contained exactly the decision which he had announced, and which he again declared to be to his mind extremely satisfactory.

'I should like to see the opinion,' said the warden; 'that is, a copy of it.'

'Well, I suppose you can if you make a point of it; but I don't see the use myself; of course it is essential that the purport of it should not be known, and it is therefore unadvisable to multiply copies.'

'Why should it not be known?' asked the warden.

'What a question for a man to ask!' said the archdeacon, throwing up his hands in token of his surprise; 'but it is like you – a child is not more innocent than you are in matters of business. Can't you see that if we tell them that no action will lie against you, but that one may possibly lie against some other person or persons, that we shall be putting weapons into their hands, and be teaching them how to cut our own throats?'

The warden again sat silent, and the bishop again looked at him wistfully: 'The only thing we have now to do,' continued the archdeacon, 'is to remain quiet, hold our peace, and let them play their own game as they please.'

'We are not to make known then,' said the warden, 'that we have consulted the attorney-general, and that we are advised by him that the founder's will is fully and fairly carried out.'

'God bless my soul!' said the archdeacon, 'how odd it is that you will not see that all we are to do is to do nothing: why should we say anything about the founder's will? We are in possession; and we know that they are not in a position to put us out: surely that is enough for the present.'

Mr Harding rose from his seat and paced thoughtfully up and down the library, the bishop the while watching him painfully at every turn, and the archdeacon continuing to pour forth his convictions that the affair was in a state to satisfy any prudent mind.

'And the *Jupiter*?' said the warden, stopping suddenly.

'Oh! the *Jupiter*,' answered the other. 'The *Jupiter* can break no bones. You must bear with that; there is much of course which it is our bounden duty to bear; it cannot be all roses for us here,' and the archdeacon looked exceedingly moral; 'besides the matter is too trivial, of too little general interest to be mentioned again in the *Jupiter*, unless we stir up the subject': and the archdeacon again looked exceedingly knowing and worldly wise.

The warden continued his walk; the hard and stinging words of that newspaper article, each one of which had thrust a thorn as it were into his inmost soul, were fresh in his memory: he had read it more than once, word by word, and what was worse, he fancied it was as well known to everyone as to himself. Was he to be looked on as the unjust griping priest he had been there described? Was he to be pointed at as the consumer of the bread of the poor, and to be allowed no means of refuting such charges, of clearing his begrimed name, of standing innocent in the world, as hitherto he had stood? Was he to bear all this, to receive as usual his now hated income, and be known as one of those greedy priests who by their rapacity have brought disgrace on their church? and why? Why should he bear all this? why should he die, for he felt that he could not live, under such a weight of obloquy? As he paced up and down the room he resolved in his misery and enthusiasm that he could with pleasure, if he were allowed, give up his place, abandon his pleasant home, leave the hospital, and live poorly, happily, and with an unsullied name, on the small remainder of his means.

He was a man somewhat shy of speaking of himself, even before those who knew him best, and whom he loved the most; but at last it burst forth from him, and with a somewhat jerking eloquence he declared that he could not, would not, bear this misery any longer.

'If it can be proved,' said he at last, 'that I have a just and honest right to this, as God well knows I always deemed I had; if this salary or stipend be really my due, I am not less anxious than another to retain it. I have the well-being of my child to look to. I am too old to miss without some pain the comforts to which I have been used; and I am, as others are, anxious to prove to the world that I have been right, and to uphold the place I have held; but I cannot do it at such a cost as this. I cannot bear this. Could you tell me to do so?' And he appealed, almost in tears, to the bishop, who had left his chair, and was now leaning on the warden's arm as he stood on the further side of the table facing the archdeacon. 'Could you tell me to sit there at ease, indifferent, and satisfied, while such things as these are said loudly of me in the world?'

The bishop could feel for him and sympathize with him, but he could not advise him, he could only say, 'No, no, you shall be asked to do nothing that is painful; you shall do just what your heart tells you to be right; you shall do whatever you think best yourself. Theophilus, don't advise him, pray don't advise the warden to do anything which is painful.'

But the archdeacon, though he could not sympathize, could advise; and he saw that the time had come when it behoved him to do so in a somewhat peremptory manner.

'Why, my lord,' he said speaking to his father: and when he called his father 'my lord', the good old bishop shook in his shoes, for he knew that an evil time was coming. 'Why, my lord, there are two ways of giving advice; there is advice that may be good for the present day; and there is advice that may be good for days to come: now I cannot bring myself to give the former, if it be incompatible with the other.'

'No, no, no, I suppose not,' said the bishop, reseating himself, and shading his face with his hands. Mr Harding sat down with his back to the further wall, playing to himself some air fitted for so calamitous an occasion, and the archdeacon said out his say standing, with his back to the empty fireplace.

'It is not to be supposed, but that much pain will spring out of this unnecessarily raised question. We must all have foreseen that, and the matter has in no wise gone on worse than we expected; but it will be weak, yes, and wicked also, to abandon the cause and own ourselves wrong, because the inquiry is painful. It is not only ourselves we have to look to: to a certain extent the interest of the Church is in our keeping. Should it be found that one after another of those who hold preferment abandoned it whenever it might be attacked, is it not plain that such attacks would be renewed till nothing was left us? and that if so deserted, the Church of England must fall to the ground altogether? If this be true of many, it is true of one. Were you, accused as you now are, to throw up the wardenship, and to relinquish the preferment which is your property, with the vain object of proving yourself disinterested, you would fail in that object, you would inflict a desperate blow on your brother clergymen, you would encourage every cantankerous dissenter in England to make a similar charge against some source of clerical revenue, and you would do your best to dishearten those who are most anxious to defend you and uphold your position. I can fancy nothing more weak, or more wrong. It is not that you think that there is any justice in these charges, or that you doubt your own right to the wardenship: you are convinced of your own honesty, and yet would yield to them through cowardice.'

'Cowardice!' said the bishop, expostulating. Mr Harding sat unmoved, gazing on his son-in-law.

'Well, would it not be cowardice? would he not do so because he is afraid to endure the evil things which will be falsely spoken of him? Would that not be cowardice? And now let us see the extent of the evil which you dread. The *Jupiter* publishes an article which a great many, no doubt, will read; but of those who understand the subject how many will believe the *Jupiter?* Everyone knows what its object is; it has taken up the case against Lord Guildford and against the Dean of Rochester, and that against half a dozen bishops;[2] and does not everyone know that it would take up any case of the kind, right or wrong, false or true, with known justice or known injustice, if by doing so it could further its own views? Does not all the world know this of the *Jupiter?* Who that really knows you will think the worse of you for what the *Jupiter* says? And why care for those who do not know you? I will say nothing of your own comfort, but I do say that you could not be justified in throwing up, in a fit of passion, for such it would be, the only maintenance that Eleanor has; and if you did so, if you really did vacate the wardenship, and submit to ruin, what would that profit you? If you have no future right to the income, you have had no past right to it; and the very fact of your abandoning your position, would create a demand for repayment of that which you have already received and spent.'

The poor warden groaned as he sat perfectly still, looking up at the hard-hearted orator who thus tormented him, and the bishop echoed the sound faintly from behind his hands; but the archdeacon cared little for such signs of weakness, and completed his exhortation.

'But let us suppose the office to be left vacant, and that your own troubles concerning it were over; would that satisfy you? Are your only aspirations in the matter confined to yourself and family? I know they are not. I know you are as anxious as any of us for the church to which we belong; and what a grievous blow would such an act of apostasy give her! You owe it to the church of which you are a member and a minister, to bear with this affliction, however severe it may be: you owe it to my father, who instituted you, to support his rights: you owe it to those who preceded you to assert the legality of their position: you owe it to those who are to come after you, to maintain uninjured for them that which you received uninjured from others; and you owe to us all the unflinching assistance of perfect brotherhood in this matter, so that upholding one another we may support our great cause without blushing and without disgrace.'

And so the archdeacon ceased, and stood self-satisfied, watching the effect of his spoken wisdom.

The warden felt himself, to a certain extent, stifled; he would have given the world to get himself out into the open air without speaking to, or noticing those who were in the room with him; but this was impossible. He could not leave without saying something, and he felt himself confounded by the archdeacon's eloquence. There was a heavy, unfeeling, unanswerable truth in what he had said; there was so much practical, but odious common sense in it, that he neither knew how to assent or to differ. If it were necessary for him to suffer, he felt that he could endure without complaint and without cowardice, providing that he was self-satisfied of the justice of his own cause. What he could not endure was that he should be accused by others, and not acquitted by himself. Doubting, as he had begun to doubt, the justice of his own position in the hospital, he knew that his own self-confidence would not be restored because Mr Bold had been in error as to some legal form; nor could he be satisfied to escape, because, through some legal fiction, he who received the greatest benefit from the hospital might be considered only as one of its servants.

The archdeacon's speech had silenced him – stupefied him – annihilated him; anything but satisfied him. With the bishop it fared not much better. He did not discern clearly how things were, but he saw enough to know that a battle was to be prepared for; a battle that would destroy his few remaining comforts, and bring him with sorrow to the grave.

The warden still sat, and still looked at the archdeacon, till his thoughts fixed themselves wholly on the means of escape from his present position, and he felt like a bird fascinated by gazing on a snake.

'I hope you agree with me,' said the archdeacon at last, breaking the dread silence; 'my lord, I hope *you* agree with me.'

Oh what a sigh the bishop gave! 'My lord, I hope you agree with me,' again repeated the merciless tyrant.

'Yes, I suppose so,' groaned the poor old man, slowly.

'And you, warden?'

Mr Harding was now stirred to action – he must speak and move, so he got up and took one turn before he answered.

'Do not press me for an answer just at present; I will do nothing lightly in the matter, and of whatever I do I will give you and the bishop notice.' And so without another word he took his leave, escaping quickly through the palace hall, and down the lofty steps, nor did he breathe freely till he found himself alone under the huge elms of the silent close. Here he walked long and slowly, thinking on his case with a troubled air, and trying in vain to confute the archdeacon's argument. He then went home, resolved to bear it all – ignominy, suspense, disgrace, self-doubt, and heart-burning – and to do as those would have him, who he still believed were most fit and most able to counsel him aright.

CHAPTER 10

Tribulation

Mr Harding was a sadder man than he had ever yet been when he returned to his own house. He had been wretched enough on that well-remembered morning when he was forced to expose before his son-in-law the publisher's account for ushering into the world his dear book of sacred music; when after making such payments as he could do unassisted, he found that he was a debtor of more than three hundred pounds: but his sufferings then were as nothing to his present misery – then he had done wrong, and he knew it, and was able to resolve that he would not sin in like manner again; but now he could make no resolution, and comfort himself by no promises of firmness. He had been forced to think that his lot had placed him in a false position, and he was about to maintain that position against the opinion of the world and against his own convictions.

He had read with pity, amounting almost to horror, the strictures which had appeared from time to time against the Earl of Guildford as master of St Cross, and the invectives that had been heaped on rich diocesan dignitaries and overgrown sinecure pluralists. In judging of them, he judged leniently; the whole bias of his profession had taught him to think that they were more sinned against than sinning, and that the animosity with which they had been pursued was venomous and unjust; but he had not the less regarded their plight as most miserable. His hair had stood on end and his flesh had crept as he read the things which had been written; he had wondered how men could live under such a load of disgrace; how they could face their fellow-creatures while their names were bandied about so injuriously and so publicly – and now this lot was to be his – he, that shy retiring man, who had so comforted himself in the hidden obscurity of his lot, who had so enjoyed the unassuming warmth of his own little corner, he was now to be dragged forth into the glaring day, and gibbeted before ferocious multitudes. He entered his own house a crestfallen, humiliated man, without a hope of overcoming the wretchedness which affected him.

He wandered into the drawing-room where was his daughter; but he could not speak to her now, so he left it, and went into the book-room. He was not quick enough to escape Eleanor's glance, or to prevent her from seeing that he was disturbed; and in a little while she followed him. She found him seated in his accustomed chair, with no book open before him, no pen ready in his hand, no ill-shapen notes of blotted music lying before him as was usual, none of those hospital accounts with which he was so precise and yet so unmethodical: he was doing nothing, thinking of nothing, looking at nothing; he was merely suffering.

'Leave me Eleanor, my dear,' he said, 'leave me my darling for a few minutes, for I am busy.'

Eleanor saw well how it was, but she did leave him, and glided silently back to her drawing-room. When he had sat awhile, thus alone and unoccupied, he got up to walk again – he could make more of his thoughts walking than sitting, and was creeping out into his garden, when he met Bunce on the threshold.

'Well, Bunce,' said he, in a tone that for him was sharp, 'what is it? do you want me?'

'I was only coming to ask after your reverence,' said the old bedesman, touching his hat; 'and to inquire about the news from London,' he added after a pause.

The warden winced, and put his hand to his forehead and felt bewildered.

'Attorney Finney has been there this morning,' continued Bunce, 'and by his looks I guess he is not so well pleased as he once was, and it has got abroad somehow that the archdeacon has had down great news from London, and Handy and Moody are both as black as devils; and I hope,' said the man, trying to assume a cheery tone, 'that things are looking up, and that there'll be an end soon to all this stuff which bothers your reverence so sorely.'

'Well, I wish there may be, Bunce.'

'But about the news, your reverence?' said the old man, almost whispering.

Mr Harding walked on, and shook his head impatiently. Poor Bunce little knew how he was tormenting his patron.

'If there was anything to cheer you, I should be so glad to know it,' said he, with a tone of affection which the warden in all his misery could not resist.

He stopped, and took both the old man's hands in his. 'My friend,' said he, 'my dear old friend, there is nothing: there is no news to cheer me – God's will be done': and two small hot tears broke away from his eyes and stole down his furrowed cheeks.

'Then God's will be done,' said the other solemnly, 'but they told me that there was good news from London, and I came to wish your reverence joy; but God's will be done'; and so the warden again walked on, and the bedesman looking wistfully after him, and receiving no encouragement to follow, returned sadly to his own abode.

For a couple of hours the warden remained thus in the garden, now walking, now standing motionless on the turf, and then, as his legs got weary, sitting unconsciously on the garden seats, and then walking again. And Eleanor, hidden behind the muslin curtains of the window, watched him through the trees as he now came in sight, and then again was concealed by the turnings of the walk; and thus the time passed away till five, when the warden crept back to the house and prepared for dinner.

It was but a sorry meal. The demure parlourmaid, as she handed the dishes and changed the plates, saw that all was not right, and was more demure than ever: neither father nor daughter could eat, and the hateful food was soon cleared away, and the bottle of port placed upon the table.

'Would you like Bunce to come in, papa?' said Eleanor, thinking that the company of the old man might lighten his sorrow.

'No, my dear, thank you, not today; but are not you going out, Eleanor, this lovely afternoon? don't stay in for me, my dear.'

'I thought you seemed so sad, papa.'

'Sad,' said he, irritated; 'well, people must all have their share of sadness here; I am not more exempt than another: but kiss me, dearest, and go now; I will, if possible, be more sociable when you return.'

And Eleanor was again banished from her father's sorrow. Ah! her desire now was not to find him happy, but to be allowed to share his sorrows; not to force him to be sociable, but to persuade him to be trustful.

She put on her bonnet as desired, and went up to Mary Bold; this was now her daily haunt, for John Bold was up in London among lawyers and church reformers, diving deep into other questions than that of the wardenship of Barchester; supplying information to one member of parliament, and dining with another; subscribing to funds for the abolition of clerical incomes, and seconding at that great national meeting at the Crown and Anchor a resolution to the effect that no clergyman of the Church of England, be he who he might, should have more than a thousand a year, and none less than two hundred and fifty. His speech on this occasion was short, for fifteen had to speak, and the room was hired for two hours only, at the expiration of which the Quakers and Mr Cobden were to make use of it for an appeal to the public in aid of the Emperor of Russia;[1] but it was sharp and effective: at least he was told so by a companion with whom he now lived much, and on whom he greatly depended – one Tom Towers,[2] a very leading genius, and supposed to have high employment on the staff of the *Jupiter*.

So Eleanor, as was now her wont, went up to Mary Bold, and Mary listened kindly while the daughter spoke much of her father, and, perhaps kinder still, found a listener in Eleanor while she spoke about her brother. In the meantime the warden sat alone, leaning on the arm of his chair; he had poured out a glass of wine, but had done so merely from habit, for he left it untouched: there he sat gazing at the open window, and thinking, if he can be said to have thought, of the happiness of his past life. All manner of past delights came before his mind, which at the time he had enjoyed without considering them; his easy days, his absence of all kind of hard work, his pleasant shady home, those twelve old neighbours whose welfare till now had been the source of so much pleasant care, the excellence of his children, the friendship of the dear old bishop, the solemn grandeur of those vaulted aisles, through which he loved to hear his own voice pealing; and then that friend of friends, that choice ally that had never deserted him, that eloquent companion that would always, when asked, discourse such pleasant music, that violoncello of his – ah, how happy he had been! but it was over now; his easy days and absence of work had been the crime which brought on him his tribulation; his shady home was pleasant no longer; maybe it was no longer his; the old neighbours, whose welfare had been so desired by him, were his enemies; his daughter was as wretched as himself, and even the bishop was made miserable by his position. He could never again lift up his voice boldly as he had hitherto done among his brethren, for he felt that he was disgraced; and he feared even to touch his bow, for he knew how grievous a sound of wailing, how piteous a lamentation, it would produce.

He was still sitting in the same chair and the same posture, having hardly moved a limb for two hours, when Eleanor came back to tea, and succeeded in bringing him with her into the drawing-room.

The tea seemed as comfortless as the dinner, though the warden, who had hitherto eaten nothing all day, devoured the plateful of bread and butter, unconscious of what he was doing.

Eleanor had made up her mind to force him to talk to her, but she hardly knew how to commence: she must wait till the urn was gone, till the servant would no longer be coming in and out.

At last everything was gone, and the drawing-room door was permanently closed; then Eleanor, getting up and going round to her father, put her arm round his neck, and said, 'Papa, won't you tell me what it is?'

'What what is, my dear?'

'This new sorrow that torments you; I know you are unhappy, papa.'

'New sorrow! it's no new sorrow, my dear, we have all our cares sometimes,' and he tried to smile, but it was a ghastly failure; 'but I shouldn't be so dull a companion; come, we'll have some music.'

'No papa, not tonight – it would only trouble you tonight': and she sat upon his knee, as she sometimes would in their gayest moods, and with her arm round his neck, she said, 'Papa, I will not leave you till you talk to me; oh, if you only knew how much good it would do to you, to tell me of it all.'

The father kissed his daughter, and pressed her to his heart; but still he said nothing: it was so hard to him to speak of his own sorrows; he was so shy a man even with his own child.

'Oh, papa, do tell me what it is; I know it is about the hospital,
and what they are doing up in London, and what that cruel
newspaper has said; but if there be such cause for sorrow, let us
be sorrowful together; we are all in all to each other now: dear,
dear papa, do speak to me.'

Mr Harding could not well speak now, for the warm tears were
running down his cheeks like rain in May, but he held his child
close to his heart, and squeezed her hand as a lover might, and
she kissed his forehead and his wet cheeks, and lay upon his
bosom, and comforted him as a woman only can do.

'My own child,' he said, as soon as his tears would let him speak;
'my own, own child, why should you too be unhappy before it is
necessary: it may come to that, that we must leave this place, but
till that time comes, why should your young days be clouded?'

'And is that all, papa? If that be all, let us leave it, and have light
hearts elsewhere: if that be all, let us go. Oh, papa, you and I could
be happy if we had only bread to eat, so long as our hearts were
light.'

And Eleanor's face was lighted up with enthusiasm as she told
her father how he might banish all his care; and a gleam of joy
shot across his brow as this idea of escape again presented itself,
and he again fancied for a moment that he could spurn away from
him the income which the world envied him; that he could give
the lie to that wielder of the tomahawk who had dared to write
such things of him in the *Jupiter*. That he could leave Sir Abraham,
and the archdeacon, and Bold, and the rest of them with their
lawsuit among them, and wipe his hands altogether of so sorrow-
stirring a concern. Ah, what happiness might there be in the
distance, with Eleanor and him in some small cottage, and
nothing left of their former grandeur but their music! Yes, they
would walk forth with their music books, and their instruments,
and shaking the dust from off their feet as they went, leave the
ungrateful place. Never did a poor clergyman sigh for a warm
benefice more anxiously than our warden did now to be rid of his.

'Give it up, papa,' she said again, jumping from his knees and
standing on her feet before him, looking boldly into his face; 'give
it up, papa.'

Oh, it was sad to see how that momentary gleam of joy passed away; how the look of hope was dispersed from that sorrowful face, as the remembrance of the archdeacon came back upon our poor warden, and he reflected that he could not stir from his now hated post. He was as a man bound with iron, fettered with adamant: he was in no repect a free agent; he had no choice. 'Give it up!' Oh, if he only could: what an easy way that were out of all his troubles!

'Papa, don't doubt about it,' she continued, thinking that his hesitation arose from his unwillingness to abandon so comfortable a home; 'is it on my account that you would stay here? Do you think that I cannot be happy without a pony-carriage and a fine drawing-room? Papa, I never can be happy here, as long as there is a question as to your honour in staying here; but I could be gay as the day is long in the smallest tiny little cottage, if I could see you come in and go out with a light heart. Oh! papa, your face tells so much; though you won't speak to me with your voice, I know how it is with you every time I look at you.'

How he pressed her to his heart again with almost a spasmodic pressure! how he kissed her as the tears fell like rain from his old eyes! how he blessed her, and called her by a hundred soft sweet names which now came new to his lips! how he chid himself for ever having been unhappy with such a treasure in his house, such a jewel on his bosom, with so sweet a flower in the choice garden of his heart! And then the floodgates of his tongue were loosed, and, at length, with unsparing detail of circumstances, he told her all that he wished, and all that he could not do. He repeated those arguments of the archdeacon, not agreeing in their truth, but explaining his inability to escape from them; how it had been declared to him that he was bound to remain where he was by the interests of his order, by gratitude to the bishop, by the wishes of his friends, by a sense of duty, which, though he could not understand it, he was fain to acknowledge. He told her how he had been accused of cowardice, and though he was not a man to make much of such a charge before the world, now in the full candour of his heart he explained to her that such an accusation was grievous to him; that he did think it would be unmanly to desert his post, merely to escape his present sufferings, and that, therefore, he must bear as best he might the misery which was prepared for him.

And did she find these details tedious? Oh, no – she encouraged him to dilate on every feeling he expressed, till he laid bare the inmost corners of his heart to her. They spoke together of the archdeacon, as two children might of a stern, unpopular, but still respected schoolmaster, and of the bishop as a parent kind as kind could be, but powerless against an omnipotent pedagogue.

And then, when they had discussed all this, when the father had told all to the child, she could not be less confiding than he had been; and as John Bold's name was mentioned between them, she owned how well she had learned to love him – 'had loved him once,' she said, 'but she would not, could not do so now – no, even had her troth been plighted to him, she would have taken it back again – had she sworn to love him as his wife, she would have discarded him and not felt herself forsworn, when he proved himself the enemy of her father.'

But the warden declared that Bold was no enemy of his, and encouraged her love; and gently rebuked, as he kissed her, the stern resolve she had made to cast him off; and then he spoke to her of happier days when their trials would all be over; and declared that her young heart should not be torn asunder to please either priest or prelate, dean or archdeacon. No, not if all Oxford were to convocate together,[3] and agree as to the necessity of the sacrifice.

And so they greatly comforted each other – and in what sorrow will not such mutual confidence give consolation! – and with a last expression of tender love they parted, and went comparatively happy to their rooms.

CHAPTER II

Iphigenia

WHEN Eleanor laid her head on her pillow that night, her mind was anxiously intent on some plan by which she might extricate her father from his misery; and, in her warm-hearted enthusiasm, self-sacrifice was decided on as the means to be adopted. Was not so good an Agamemnon worthy of an Iphigenia?[1] She would herself personally implore John Bold to desist from his undertaking; she would explain to him her father's sorrows, the cruel misery of his position; she would tell him how her father would die if he were thus dragged before the public and exposed to such unmerited ignominy; she would appeal to his old friendship, to his generosity, to his manliness, to his mercy; if need were she would kneel to him for the favour she would ask; but before she did this, the idea of love must be banished. There must be no bargain in the matter. To his mercy, to his generosity, she could appeal; but as a pure maiden, hitherto even unsolicited, she could not appeal to his love, nor under such circumstances could she allow him to do so. Of course when so provoked, he would declare his passion; that was to be expected; there had been enough between them to make such a fact sure; but it was equally certain that he must be rejected. She could not be understood as saying, Make my father free and I am the reward. There would be no sacrifice in that – not so had Jephthah's daughter saved her father[2] – not so could she show to that kindest, dearest of parents how much she was able to bear for his good. No; to one resolve must her whole soul be bound; and so resolving, she felt that she could make her great request to Bold with as much self-assured confidence as she could have done to his grandfather.

And now I own I have fears for my heroine: not as to the upshot of her mission – not in the least as to that; as to the full success of her generous scheme, and the ultimate result of such a project, no one conversant with human nature and novels can have a doubt; but as to the amount of sympathy she may receive from those of her own sex. Girls below twenty and old ladies above sixty will do her justice; for in the female heart the soft springs of sweet romance reopen after many years, and again gush out with waters pure as in earlier days, and greatly refresh the path that leads downwards to the grave. But I fear that the majority of those between these two eras will not approve of Eleanor's plan. I fear that unmarried ladies of thirty-five will declare that there can be no probability of so absurd a project being carried through; that young women on their knees before their lovers are sure to get kissed, and that they would not put themselves in such a position did they not expect it; that Eleanor is going to Bold only because circumstances prevent Bold from coming to her; that she is certainly a little fool, or a little schemer, but that in all probability she is thinking a good deal more about herself than her father.

Dear ladies, you are right as to your appreciation of the circumstances, but very wrong as to Miss Harding's character. Miss Harding was much younger than you are, and could not, therefore, know, as you may do, to what dangers such an encounter might expose her. She may get kissed; I think it very probable that she will; but I give my solemn word and positive assurance, that the remotest idea of such a catastrophe never occurred to her, as she made the great resolve now alluded to.

And then she slept; and then she rose refreshed, and met her father with her kindest embrace and most loving smiles; and on the whole their breakfast was by no means so triste[3] as had been their dinner the day before; and then, making some excuse to her father for so soon leaving him, she started on the commencement of her operations.

She knew that John Bold was in London, and that, therefore, the scene itself could not be enacted today; but she also knew that he was soon to be home, probably on the next day, and it was necessary that some little plan for meeting him should be concerted with his sister Mary. When she got up to the house, she went as usual into the morning sitting-room, and was startled by perceiving, by a stick, a greatcoat, and sundry parcels which were lying about, that Bold must already have returned.

'John has come back so suddenly,' said Mary, coming into the room; 'he has been travelling all night.'

'Then I'll come up again some other time,' said Eleanor, about to beat a retreat in her sudden dismay.

'He's out now, and will be for the next two hours,' said the other; 'he's with that horrid Finney; he only came to see him, and he returns by the mail-train tonight.'

Returns by the mail-train tonight, thought Eleanor to herself, as she strove to screw up her courage – away again tonight – then it must be now or never; and she again sat down, having risen to go.

She wished the ordeal could have been postponed: she had fully made up her mind to do the deed, but she had not made up her mind to do it this very day; and now she felt ill at ease, astray, and in difficulty.

'Mary,' she began, 'I must see your brother before he goes back.'

'Oh yes, of course,' said the other; 'I know he'll be delighted to see you'; and she tried to treat it as a matter of course, but she was not the less surprised; for Mary and Eleanor had daily talked over John Bold and his conduct, and his love, and Mary would insist on calling Eleanor her sister, and would scold her for not calling Bold by his christian name; and Eleanor would half confess her love, but like a modest maiden would protest against such familiarities even with the name of her lover: and so they talked hour after hour, and Mary Bold, who was much the elder, looked forward with happy confidence to the day when Eleanor would not be ashamed to call her her sister. She was, however, fully sure that just at present Eleanor would be much more likely to avoid her brother than to seek him.

'Mary, I must see your brother, now, today, and beg from him a great favour,' and she spoke with a solemn air, not at all usual to her; and then she went on, and opened to her friend all her plan, her well-weighed scheme for saving her father from a sorrow which would, she said, if it lasted, bring him to his grave. 'But Mary,' she continued, 'you must now, you know, cease any joking about me and Mr Bold; you must now say no more about that; I am not ashamed to beg this favour from your brother, but when I have done so, there can never be anything further between us'; and this she said with a staid and solemn air, quite worthy of Jephthah's daughter or of Iphigenia either.

It was quite clear that Mary Bold did not follow the argument: that Eleanor Harding should appeal, on behalf of her father, to Bold's better feelings, seemed to Mary quite natural; it seemed quite natural that he should relent, overcome by such filial tears, and by so much beauty; but, to her thinking, it was at any rate equally natural that, having relented, John should put his arm round his mistress's waist, and say, 'Now having settled that, let us be man and wife, and all will end happily!' Why his good nature should not be rewarded, when such reward would operate to the disadvantage of none, Mary, who had more sense than romance, could not understand; and she said as much.

Eleanor, however, was firm, and made quite an eloquent speech to support her own view of the question: she could not condescend, she said, to ask such a favour on any other terms than those proposed. Mary might, perhaps, think her high-flown, but she had her own ideas, and she could not submit to sacrifice her self-respect.

'But I am sure you love him – don't you?' pleaded Mary; 'and I am sure he loves you better than anything in the world.'

Eleanor was going to make another speech, but a tear came to each eye, and she could not; so she pretended to blow her nose, and walked to the window, and made a little inward call on her own courage, and finding herself somewhat sustained, said sententiously, 'Mary, this is nonsense.'

'But you do love him,' said Mary, who had followed her friend to the window, and now spoke with her arms close wound round the other's waist. 'You do love him with all your heart – you know you do; I defy you to deny it.'

'I –' commenced Eleanor, turning sharply round to refute the charge; but the intended falsehood stuck in her throat, and never came to utterance. She could not deny her love, so she took plentifully to tears, and leant upon her friend's bosom and sobbed there, and protested that, love or no love, it would make no difference in her resolve, and called Mary, a thousand times, the most cruel of girls, and swore her to secrecy by a hundred oaths, and ended by declaring that the girl who could betray her friend's love, even to a brother, would be as black a traitor as a soldier in a garrison who should open the city gates to the enemy. While they were yet discussing the matter, Bold returned, and Eleanor was forced into sudden action: she had either to accomplish or abandon her plan; and having slipped into her friend's bedroom, as the gentleman closed the hall door, she washed the marks of tears from her eyes, and resolved within herself to go through with it. 'Tell him I am here,' said she, 'and coming in; and mind, whatever you do, don't leave us.' So Mary informed her brother, with a somewhat sombre air, that Miss Harding was in the next room, and was coming to speak to him.

Eleanor was certainly thinking more of her father than herself, as she arranged her hair before the glass, and removed the traces of sorrow from her face, and yet I should be untrue if I said that she was not anxious to appear well before her lover: why else was she so sedulous with that stubborn curl that would rebel against her hand, and smooth so eagerly her ruffled ribands? why else did she damp her eyes to dispel the redness, and bite her pretty lips to bring back the colour? Of course she was anxious to look her best, for she was but a mortal angel after all. But had she been immortal, had she flitted back to the sitting-room on a cherub's wings, she could not have had a more faithful heart, or a truer wish to save her father at any cost to herself.

John Bold had not met her since the day when she left him in dudgeon in the cathedral close. Since that his whole time had been occupied in promoting the cause against her father, and not unsuccessfully. He had often thought of her, and turned over in his mind a hundred schemes for showing her how disinterested was his love. He would write to her and beseech her not to allow the performance of a public duty to injure him in her estimation; he would write to Mr Harding, explain all his views, and boldly claim the warden's daughter, urging that the untoward circumstances between them need be no bar to their ancient friendship, or to a closer tie; he would throw himself on his knees before his mistress; he would wait and marry the daughter when the father had lost his home and his income; he would give up the lawsuit and go to Australia, with her of course, leaving the *Jupiter* and Mr Finney to complete the case between them. Sometimes as he woke in the morning fevered and impatient, he would blow out his brains and have done with all his cares – but this idea was generally consequent on an imprudent supper enjoyed in company with Tom Towers.

How beautiful Eleanor appeared to him as she slowly walked into the room! Not for nothing had all those little cares been taken. Though her sister, the archdeacon's wife, had spoken slightingly of her charms, Eleanor was very beautiful when seen aright. Hers was not one of those impassive faces which have the beauty of a marble bust; finely chiselled features, perfect in every line, true to the rules of symmetry, as lovely to a stranger as to a friend, unvarying unless in sickness, or as age affects them. She had no startling brilliancy of beauty, no pearly whiteness, no radiant carnation: she had not the majestic contour that rivets attention, demands instant wonder, and then disappoints by the coldness of its charms. You might pass Eleanor Harding in the street without notice, but you could hardly pass an evening with her and not lose your heart.

She had never appeared more lovely to her lover than she now did. Her face was animated though it was serious, and her full, dark, lustrous eyes shone with anxious energy; her hand trembled as she took his, and she could hardly pronounce his name, when she addressed him. Bold wished with all his heart that the Australian scheme was in the act of realization, and that he and Eleanor were away together, never to hear further of the lawsuit.

He began to talk, asked after her health – said something about London being very stupid, and more about Barchester being very pleasant: declared the weather to be very hot, and then inquired after Mr Harding.

'My father is not very well,' said Eleanor.

John Bold was very sorry, so sorry: he hoped it was nothing serious, and put on the unmeaningly solemn face, which people usually use on such occasions.

'I especially want to speak to you about my father, Mr Bold; indeed, I am now here on purpose to do so. Papa is very unhappy, very unhappy indeed, about this affair of the hospital: you would pity him, Mr Bold, if you could see how wretched it has made him.'

'Oh Miss Harding!'

'Indeed you would – anyone would pity him: but a friend, an old friend as you are – indeed you would. He is an altered man;

his cheerfulness has all gone, and his sweet temper, and his kind
happy tone of voice; you would hardly know him if you saw him,
Mr Bold, he is so much altered; and – and – if this goes on, he will
die.' Here Eleanor had recourse to her handkerchief, and so also
had her auditors; but she plucked up her courage and went on
with her tale. 'He will break his heart, and die. I am sure, Mr Bold,
it was not you who wrote those cruel things in the newspaper –'

John Bold eagerly protested that it was not, but his heart smote
him as to his intimate alliance with Tom Towers.

'No, I am sure it was not; and papa has not for a moment
thought so; you would not be so cruel – but it has nearly killed
him. Papa cannot bear to think that people should so speak of him,
and that everybody should hear him so spoken of – they have
called him avaricious, and dishonest, and they say he is robbing
the old men, and taking the money of the hospital for nothing.'

'I have never said so, Miss Harding. I –'

'No,' continued Eleanor, interrupting him, for she was now in
the full floodtide of her eloquence; 'no, I am sure you have not,
but others have said so; and if this goes on, if such things are
written again, it will kill papa. Oh! Mr Bold, if you only knew the
state he is in! Now papa does not care much about money.'

Both her auditors, brother and sister, assented to this, and
declared on their own knowledge that no man lived less addicted
to filthy lucre than the warden.

'Oh! it's so kind of you to say so, Mary, and of you too, Mr Bold.
I couldn't bear that people should think unjustly of papa. Do you
know he would give up the hospital altogether, only he cannot.
The archdeacon says it would be cowardly, and that he would be
deserting his order, and injuring the Church. Whatever may
happen, papa will not do that: he would leave the place tomorrow
willingly, and give up his house, and the income and all, if the
archdeacon –' Eleanor was going to say 'would let him', but she
stopped herself before she had compromised her father's dignity;
and giving a long sigh, she added – 'Oh, I do so wish he would.'

'No one who knows Mr Harding personally accuses him for a
moment,' said Bold.

'It is he that has to bear the punishment; it is he that suffers,'
said Eleanor; 'and what for? what has he done wrong? how has

he deserved this persecution? he that never had an unkind thought in his life, he that never said an unkind word!' and here she broke down, and the violence of her sobs stopped her utterance.

Bold, for the fifth or sixth time, declared that neither he nor any of his friends imputed any blame personally to Mr Harding.

'Then why should he be persecuted?' ejaculated Eleanor through her tears, forgetting in her eagerness that her intention had been to humble herself as a suppliant before John Bold – 'why should he be made so wretched? Oh! Mr Bold' – and she turned towards him as though the kneeling scene were about to be commenced – 'oh! Mr Bold, why did you begin all this? you whom we all so – so – valued!'

To speak the truth, the reformer's punishment was certainly come upon him, for his present plight was not enviable; he had nothing for it but to excuse himself by platitudes about public duty, which it is by no means worthwhile to repeat, and to reiterate his eulogy on Mr Harding's character. His position was certainly a cruel one: had any gentleman called upon him on behalf of Mr Harding he could of course have declined to enter upon the subject; but how could he do so with a beautiful girl, with the daughter of the man whom he had injured, with his own love?

In the meantime Eleanor recollected herself, and again summoned up her energies.

'Mr Bold,' said she, 'I have come here to implore you to abandon this proceeding.'

He stood up from his seat, and looked beyond measure distressed.

'To implore you to abandon it, to implore you to spare my father, to spare either his life or his reason, for one or the other will pay the forfeit if this goes on. I know how much I am asking, and how little right I have to ask anything; but I think you will listen to me as it is for my father. Oh, Mr Bold, pray, pray do this for us – pray do not drive to distraction a man who has loved you so well.'

She did not absolutely kneel to him, but she followed him as he moved from his chair, and laid her soft hands imploringly upon his arm. Ah! at any other time how exquisitely valuable would have been that touch! but now he was distraught, dumbfounded, and unmanned. What could he say to that sweet suppliant; how explain to her that the matter now was probably beyond his control; how tell her that he could not quell the storm which he had raised?

'Surely, surely, John, you cannot refuse her,' said his sister.

'I would give her my soul,' said he, 'if it would serve her.'

'Oh, Mr Bold,' said Eleanor, 'do not speak so; I ask nothing for myself; and what I ask for my father, it cannot harm you to grant.'

'I would give her my soul, if it would serve her,' said Bold, still addressing his sister; 'everything I have is hers, if she will accept it; my house, my heart, my all; every hope of my breast is centred in her: her smiles are sweeter to me than the sun, and when I see her in sorrow as she now is, every nerve in my body suffers. No man can love better than I love her.'

'No, no, no,' ejaculated Eleanor, 'there can be no talk of love between us; will you protect my father from the evil you have brought upon him?'

'Oh, Eleanor, I will do anything; let me tell you how I love you!'

'No, no, no,' she almost screamed; 'this is unmanly of you, Mr Bold. Will you, will you, will you leave my father to die in peace in his quiet home?' and seizing him by his arm and hand, she followed him across the room towards the door. 'I will not leave you till you promise me; I'll cling to you in the street; I'll kneel to you before all the people. You shall promise me this, you shall promise me this, you shall –' And she clung to him with fixed tenacity, and reiterated her resolve with hysterical passion.

'Speak to her, John; answer her,' said Mary, bewildered by the unexpected vehemence of Eleanor's manner; 'you cannot have the cruelty to refuse her.'

'Promise me, promise me,' said Eleanor; 'say that my father is safe – one word will do. I know how true you are; say one word, and I will let you go.'

She still held him, and looked eagerly into his face, with her hair dishevelled, and her eyes all bloodshot. She had no thought now of herself, no care now for her appearance, and yet he thought he had never seen her half so lovely; he was amazed at the intensity of her beauty, and could hardly believe that it was she whom he had dared to love. 'Promise me,' said she; 'I will not leave you till you have promised me.'

'I will,' said he at length, 'I do – all I can do, I will do.'

'Then may God Almighty bless you for ever and ever!' said Eleanor; and falling on her knees with her face on Mary's lap, she wept and sobbed like a child: her strength had carried her through her allotted task, but now it was well nigh exhausted.

In a while she was partly recovered, and got up to go, and would have gone, had not Bold made her understand that it was necessary for him to explain to her how far it was in his power to put an end to the proceedings which had been taken against Mr Harding. Had he spoken on any other subject, she would have vanished, but on that she was bound to hear him; and now the danger of her position commenced. While she had an active part to play, while she clung to him as a suppliant, it was easy enough for her to reject his proferred love, and cast from her his caressing words; but now – now that he had yielded, and was talking to her calmly and kindly as to her father's welfare, it was hard enough for her to do so. Then Mary Bold assisted her, but now she was quite on her brother's side. Mary said but little, but every word she did say gave some direct and deadly blow. The first thing she did was to make room for her brother between herself and Eleanor on the sofa: as the sofa was full large for three, Eleanor could not resent this, nor could she show suspicion by taking another seat; but she felt it to be a most unkind proceeding. And then Mary would talk as though they three were joined in some close peculiar bond together; as though they were in future always to wish together, contrive together, and act together; and Eleanor could not gainsay this; she could not make another speech, and say, 'Mr Bold and I are mere strangers, Mary, and are always to remain so!'

He explained to her that, though undoubtedly the proceeding against the hospital had commenced solely with himself, many others were now interested in the matter, some of whom were much more influential than himself: that it was to him alone, however, that the lawyers looked for instruction as to their doings, and, more important still, for the payment of their bills; and he promised that he would at once give them notice that it was his intention to abandon the cause. He thought, he said, that it was not probable that any active steps would be taken after he had seceded from the matter, though it was possible that some passing allusion might still be made to the hospital in the daily *Jupiter*. He promised, however, that he would use his best influence to prevent any further personal allusion being made to Mr Harding. He then suggested that he would on that afternoon ride over himself to Dr Grantly, and inform him of his altered intentions on the subject, and with this view, he postponed his immediate return to London.

This was all very pleasant, and Eleanor did enjoy a sort of triumph in the feeling that she had attained the object for which she had sought this interivew; but still the part of Iphigenia was to be played out. The gods had heard her prayer, granted her request, and were they not to have their promised sacrifice? Eleanor was not a girl to defraud them wilfully; so, as soon as she decently could, she got up for her bonnet.

'Are you going so soon?' said Bold, who half an hour since would have given a hundred pounds that he was in London, and she still at Barchester.

'Oh yes!' said she. 'I am so much obliged to you; papa will feel this to be so kind' (she did not quite appreciate all her father's feelings); 'of course I must tell him, and I will say that you will see the archdeacon.'

'But may I not say one word for myself?' said Bold.

'I'll fetch you your bonnet, Eleanor,' said Mary, in the act of leaving the room.

'Mary, Mary,' said she, getting up and catching her by her dress, 'don't go, I'll get my bonnet myself'; but Mary, the traitress, stood fast by the door, and permitted no such retreat. Poor Iphigenia!

And with a volley of impassioned love, John Bold poured forth the feelings of his heart, swearing, as men do, some truths and many falsehoods; and Eleanor repeated with every shade of vehemence the 'No, no, no' which had had a short time since so much effect; but now, alas! its strength was gone. Let her be never so vehement, her vehemence was not respected; all her 'No, no, noes' were met with counter asseverations, and at last were over-powered. The ground was cut from under her on every side: she was pressed to say whether her father would object; whether she herself had any aversion (aversion! God help her, poor girl! the word nearly made her jump into his arms); any other preference (this she loudly disclaimed); whether it was impossible that she should love him (Eleanor could not say that it was impossible): and so at last, all her defences demolished, all her maiden barriers swept away, she capitulated, or rather marched out with the honours of war, vanquished evidently, palpably vanquished, but still not reduced to the necessity of confessing it.

And so the altar on the shore of the modern Aulis reeked with no sacrifice.

CHAPTER 12

Mr Bold's Visit to Plumstead

WHETHER or no the ill-natured prediction made by certain ladies in the beginning of the last chapter, was or was not carried out to the letter, I am not in a position to state; Eleanor, however, certainly did feel herself to have been baffled, as she returned home with all her news to her father. Certainly she had been victorious, certainly she had achieved her object, certainly she was not unhappy, and yet she did not feel herself triumphant. Everything would run smooth now. Eleanor was not at all addicted to the Lydian school of romance;[1] she by no means objected to her lover because he came in at the door under the name of Absolute, instead of pulling her out of a window under the name of Beverley; and yet she felt that she had been imposed upon, and could hardly think of Mary Bold with sisterly charity. 'I did think I could have trusted Mary,' she said to herself over and over again. 'Oh that she should have dared to keep me in the room when I tried to get out!' Eleanor, however, felt that the game was up, and that she had now nothing further to do but to add to the budget of news which was prepared for her father, that John Bold was her accepted lover.

We will, however, now leave her on her way, and go with John Bold to Plumstead Episcopi, merely premising that Eleanor on reaching home will not find things so smooth as she fondly expected; two messengers had come, one to her father, and the other to the archdeacon, and each of them much opposed to her quiet mode of solving all their difficulties; the one in the shape of a number of the *Jupiter*; and the other in that of a further opinion from Sir Abraham Haphazard.

John Bold got on his horse and rode off to Plumstead Episcopi; not briskly and with eager spur, as men do ride when self-satisfied with their own intentions, but slowly, modestly, thoughtfully, and somewhat in dread of the coming interview. Now and again he would recur to the scene which was just over, support himself by the remembrance of the silence that gives consent, and exult as a happy lover; but even this feeling was not without a shade of remorse. Had he not shown himself childishly weak thus to yield up the resolve of many hours of thought to the tears of a pretty girl? How was he to meet his lawyer? How was he to back out of a matter in which his name was already so publicly concerned? What, oh what! was he to say to Tom Towers? While meditating these painful things he reached the lodge leading up to the arch-deacon's glebe,[2] and for the first time in his life found himself within the sacred precincts.

All the doctor's children were together on the slope of the lawn close to the road, as Bold rode up to the hall door. They were there holding high debate on matters evidently of deep interest at Plum-stead Episcopi, and the voices of the boys had been heard before the lodge gate was closed.

Florinda and Grizzel, frightened at the sight of so well-known an enemy to the family, fled on the first appearance of the horse-man, and ran in terror to their mother's arms; not for them was it, tender branches, to resent injuries, or as members of a church militant to put on armour against its enemies: but the boys stood their ground like heroes, and boldly demanded the business of the intruder.

'Do you want to see anybody here, sir?' said Henry, with a defiant eye and a hostile tone, which plainly said that at any rate no one there wanted to see the person so addressed; and as he spoke he brandished aloft his garden water-pot, holding it by the spout, ready for the braining of anyone.

'Henry,' said Charles James slowly, and with a certain dignity of diction, 'Mr Bold of course would not have come without wanting to see someone; if Mr Bold has a proper ground for wanting to see some person here, of course he has a right to come.'

But Samuel stepped lightly up to the horse's head, and offered his services. 'Oh, Mr Bold,' said he, 'papa, I'm sure, will be glad to see you; I suppose you want to see papa. Shall I hold your horse for you? Oh, what a very pretty horse!' and he turned his head and winked funnily at his brothers; 'papa has heard such good news about the old hospital today. We know you'll be glad to hear it, because you're such a friend of grandpapa Harding, and so much in love with aunt Nelly!'

'How d'ye do, lads?' said Bold, dismounting; 'I want to see your father if he's at home.'

'Lads!' said Henry, turning on his heel and addressing himself to his brother, but loud enough to be heard by Bold; 'lads, indeed! if we're lads, what does he call himself?'

Charles James condescended to say nothing further, but cocked his hat with much precision, and left the visitor to the care of his youngest brother.

Samuel stayed till the servant came, chatting and patting the horse; but as soon as Bold had disappeared through the front door, he stuck a switch under the animal's tail to make him kick, if possible.

The church reformer soon found himself *tête à tête* with the archdeacon in that same room, in that sanctum sanctorum³ of the rectory, to which we have already been introduced. As he entered he heard the click of a certain patent lock, but it struck him with no surprise: the worthy clergyman was no doubt hiding from eyes profane his last much-studied sermon, for the archdeacon, though he preached but seldom, was famous for his sermons. No room, Bold thought, could have been more becoming for a dignitary of the church; each wall was loaded with theology; over each separate bookcase was printed in small gold letters the names of those great divines whose works were ranged beneath: beginning from the early fathers in due chronological order, there were to be found the precious labours of the chosen servants of the church down to the last pamphlet written in opposition to the consecration of Dr Hampden;⁴ and raised above this were to be seen the busts of the greatest among the great: Chrysostom, St Augustine, Thomas à Becket, Cardinal Wolsey, Archbishop Laud, and Dr Philpotts.⁵

Every appliance that could make study pleasant and give ease to the over-toiled brain was there: chairs made to relieve each limb and muscle; reading-desks and writing-desks to suit every attitude; lamps and candles mechanically contrived to throw their light on any favoured spot, as the student might desire; a shoal of newspapers to amuse the few leisure moments which might be stolen from the labours of the day; and then from the window a view right through a bosky vista along which ran a broad green path from the rectory to the church, at the end of which the tawny-tinted fine old tower was seen with all its variegated pinnacles and parapets. Few parish churches in England are in better repair, or better worth keeping so, than that at Plumstead Episcopi; and yet it is built in a faulty style: the body of the church is low – so low that the nearly flat leaden roof would be visible from the churchyard, were it not for the carved parapet with which it is surrounded. It is cruciform, though the transepts are irregular, one being larger than the other; and the tower is much too high in proportion to the church: but the colour of the building is perfect; it is that rich yellow grey which one finds nowhere but in the south and west of England, and which is so strong a characteristic of most of our old houses of Tudor architecture. The stonework also is beautiful; the mullions of the windows and the thick tracery of the Gothic workmanship is as rich as fancy can desire; and though in gazing on such a structure, one knows by rule that the old priests who built it, built it wrong, one cannot bring oneself to wish that they should have made it other than it is.

When Bold was ushered into the book-room, he found its owner standing with his back to the empty fireplace ready to receive him, and he could not but perceive that that expansive brow was elated with triumph, and that those full heavy lips bore more prominently than usual an appearance of arrogant success.

'Well, Mr Bold,' said he – 'well, what can I do for you? Very happy, I can assure you, to do anything for such a friend of my father-in-law.'

'I hope you'll excuse my calling, Dr Grantly.'

'Certainly, certainly,' said the archdeacon; 'I can assure you, no apology is necessary from Mr Bold; only let me know what I can do for him.'

Dr Grantly was standing himself, and he did not ask Bold to sit, and therefore he had to tell his tale standing, leaning on the table, with his hat in his hand. He did, however, manage to tell it; and as the archdeacon never once interrupted him, or even encouraged him by a single word, he was not long in coming to the end of it.

'And so, Mr Bold, I'm to understand, I believe, that you are desirous of abandoning this attack upon Mr Harding.'

'Oh, Dr Grantly, there has been no attack, I can assure you –'

'Well, well, we won't quarrel about words; I should call it an attack – most men would so call an endeavour to take away from a man every shilling of income that he has to live upon; but it shan't be an attack, if you don't like it; you wish to abandon this – this little game of backgammon you've begun to play.'

'I intend to put an end to the legal proceedings which I have commenced.'

'I understand,' said the archdeacon. 'You've already had enough of it; well, I can't say that I am surprised; carrying on a losing lawsuit where one has nothing to gain, but everything to pay, is not pleasant.'

Bold turned very red in the face. 'You misinterpret my motives,' said he; 'but, however, that is of little consequence. I did not come to trouble you with my motives, but to tell you a matter of fact. Good morning, Dr Grantly.'

'One moment – one moment,' said the other. 'I don't exactly appreciate the taste which induced you to make any personal communication to me on the subject; but I dare say I'm wrong, I dare say your judgement is the better of the two; but as you have done me the honour – as you have, as it were, forced me into a certain amount of conversation on a subject which had better, perhaps, have been left to our lawyers, you will excuse me if I ask you to hear my reply to your communication.'

'I am in no hurry, Dr Grantly.'

'Well, I am, Mr Bold; my time is not exactly leisure time, and, therefore, if you please, we'll go to the point at once – you're going to abandon this lawsuit?' – and he paused for a reply.

'Yes, Dr Grantly, I am.'

'Having exposed a gentleman who was one of your father's warmest friends to all the ignominy and insolence which the press could heap upon his name; having somewhat ostentatiously declared that it was your duty as a man of high public virtue to protect those poor old fools whom you have humbugged there at the hospital, you now find that the game costs more than it's worth, and so you make up your mind to have done with it. A prudent resolution, Mr Bold; but it is a pity you should have been so long coming to it. Has it struck you that we may not now choose to give over? that we may find it necessary to punish the injury you have done to us? Are you aware, sir, that we have gone to enormous expense to resist this iniquitous attempt of yours?'

Bold's face was now furiously red, and he nearly crushed his hat between his hands; but he said nothing.

'We have found it necessary to employ the best advice that money could procure. Are you aware, sir, what may be the probable cost of securing the services of the attorney-general?'

'Not in the least, Dr Grantly.'

'I dare say not, sir. When you recklessly put this affair into the hands of your friend Mr Finney, whose six and eightpences and thirteen and fourpences may, probably, not amount to a large sum, you were indifferent as to the cost and suffering which such a proceeding might entail on others; but are you aware, sir, that these crushing costs must now come out of your own pocket?'

'Any demand of such a nature which Mr Harding's lawyer may have to make, will doubtless be made to my lawyer.'

'"Mr Harding's lawyer and my lawyer"! Did you come here merely to refer me to the lawyers? Upon my word I think the honour of your visit might have been spared! And now, sir, I'll tell you what my opinion is – my opinion is, that we shall not allow you to withdraw this matter from the courts.'

'You can do as you please, Dr Grantly; good morning.'

'Hear me out, sir,' said the archdeacon; 'I have here in my hands the last opinion given in this matter by Sir Abraham Haphazard. I dare say you have already heard of this – I dare say it has had something to do with your visit here today.'

'I know nothing whatever of Sir Abraham Haphazard or his opinion.'

'Be that as it may, here it is; he declares most explicitly that under no phasis⁶ of the affair whatever have you a leg to stand upon; that Mr Harding is as safe in his hospital as I am here in my rectory; that a more futile attempt to destroy a man was never made, than this which you have made to ruin Mr Harding. Here,' and he slapped the paper on the table, 'I have this opinion from the very first lawyer in the land; and under these circumstances you expect me to make you a low bow for your kind offer to release Mr Harding from the toils of your net! Sir, your net is not strong enough to hold him; sir, your net has fallen to pieces, and you knew that well enough before I told you – and now, sir, I'll wish you good morning, for I'm busy.'

Bold was now choking with passion; he had let the archdeacon run on, because he knew not with what words to interrupt him; but now that he had been so defied and insulted, he could not leave the room without some reply.

'Dr Grantly,' he commenced.

'I have nothing further to say or to hear,' said the archdeacon; 'I'll do myself the honour to order your horse:' and he rang the bell.

'I came here, Dr Grantly, with the warmest, kindest feelings –'

'Oh, of course you did; nobody doubts it.'

'With the kindest feelings – and they have been most grossly outraged by your treatment.'

'Of course they have – I have not chosen to see my father-in-law ruined; what an outrage that has been to your feelings!'

'The time will come, Dr Grantly, when you will understand why I called upon you today.'

'No doubt, no doubt. Is Mr Bold's horse there? That's right, open the front door – good morning, Mr Bold'; and the doctor stalked into his own drawing-room, closing the door behind him, and making it quite impossible that John Bold should speak another word.

As he got on his horse, which he was fain to do feeling like a dog turned out of a kitchen, he was again greeted by little Sammy.

'Good-bye, Mr Bold; I hope we may have the pleasure of seeing you again before long; I am sure papa will always be glad to see you.'

That was certainly the bitterest moment in John Bold's life; not even the remembrance of his successful love could comfort him; nay, when he thought of Eleanor, he felt that it was that very love which had brought him to such a pass. That he should have been so insulted, and be unable to reply! That he should have given up so much to the request of a girl, and then have had his motives so misunderstood! That he should have made so gross a mistake as this visit of his to the archdeacon's! He bit the top of his whip, till he penetrated the horn of which it was made: he struck the poor animal in his anger, and then was doubly angry with himself at his futile passion. He had been so completely checkmated, so palpably overcome! and what was he to do? He could not continue his action after pledging himself to abandon it; nor was there any revenge in that – it was the very step to which his enemy had endeavoured to goad him!

He threw the reins to the servant who came to take his horse, and rushed upstairs into his drawing-room, where his sister Mary was sitting.

'If there be a devil,' said he, 'a real devil here on earth, it is Dr Grantly.' He vouchsafed her no further intelligence, but again seizing his hat, he rushed out, and took his departure for London without another word to anyone.

CHAPTER 13

The Warden's Decision

THE meeting between Eleanor and her father was not so stormy as that described in the last chapter, but it was hardly more successful. On her return from Bold's house, she found her father in a strange state. He was not sorrowful and silent as he had been on that memorable day when his son-in-law lectured him as to all that he owed to his order; nor was he in his usual quiet mood. When Eleanor reached the hospital, he was walking quickly to and fro upon the lawn, and she soon saw that he was much excited.

'I am going to London, my dear,' he said as soon as he saw her.

'London, papa!'

'Yes, my dear, to London; I will have this matter settled some way: there are some things, Eleanor, which I cannot bear.'

'Oh, papa, what is it?' said she, leading him by the arm into the house – 'I had such good news for you, and now you make me fear I am too late'; and then, before he could let her know what had caused this sudden resolve, or could point to the fatal paper which lay on the table, she told him that the lawsuit was over, that Bold had commissioned her to assure her father in his name that it would be abandoned, that there was no further cause for misery, that the whole matter might be looked on as though it had never been discussed. She did not tell him with what determined vehemence she had obtained this concession in his favour, nor did she mention the price she was to pay for it.

The warden did not express himself peculiarly gratified at this intelligence, and Eleanor, though she had not worked for thanks, and was by no means disposed to magnify her own good offices, felt hurt at the manner in which her news was received.

'Mr Bold can act as he thinks proper, my love,' said he: 'if Mr Bold thinks that he has been wrong, of course he will discontinue what he is doing; but that cannot change my purpose.'

'Oh, papa!' she exclaimed, all but crying with vexation – 'I thought you would have been so happy – I thought all would have been right now.'

'Mr Bold,' continued he, 'has set great people to work; so great that I doubt they are now beyond his control. Read that, my dear': and the warden, doubling up a number of the *Jupiter*, pointed to the peculiar article which she was to read. It was to the last of the three leaders, which are generally furnished daily for the support of the nation, that Mr Harding directed her attention. It dealt some heavy blows on various clerical delinquents; on families who had received their tens of thousands yearly for doing nothing; on men who, as the article stated, rolled in wealth which they had neither earned nor inherited, and which was in fact stolen from the poorer clergy. It named some sons of bishops, and grandsons of arch-bishops; men great in their way, who had redeemed their disgrace in the eyes of many by the enormity of their plunder; and then having disposed of these leviathans, it descended to Mr Harding.

We alluded some few weeks since to an instance of similar injustice, though in a more humble scale, in which the warden of an almshouse at Barchester has become possessed of the income of the greater part of the whole institution. Why an almshouse should have a warden we cannot pretend to explain, nor can we say what special need twelve old men can have for the services of a separate clergyman, seeing that they have twelve reserved seats for themselves in Barchester Cathedral. But be this as it may, let the gentleman call himself warden or precentor, or what he will, let him be never so scrupulous in exacting religious duties from his twelve dependants, or never so negligent as regards the services of the cathedral, it appears palpably clear that he can be entitled to no portion of the revenue of the hospital, excepting that which the founder set apart for him; and it is equally clear that the founder did not intend that three fifths of his charity should be so consumed.

The case is certainly a paltry one after the tens of thousands with which we have been dealing, for the warden's income is after all but a poor eight hundred a year: eight hundred a year is not magnificent preferment of itself, and the warden may, for anything we know, be worth much more to the church; but if so, let the church pay him out of funds justly at its own disposal.

We allude to the question of the Barchester almshouse at the present moment, because we understand that a plea has been set up which will be peculiarly revolting to the minds of English churchmen. An action has

been taken against Mr Warden Harding, on behalf of the almsmen, by a
gentleman acting solely on public grounds, and it is to be argued that Mr
Harding takes nothing but what he receives as a servant of the hospital,
and that he is not himself responsible for the amount of stipend given to
him for his work. Such a plea would doubtless be fair, if anyone questioned
the daily wages of a bricklayer employed on the building, or the fee of the
charwoman who cleans it; but we cannot envy the feeling of a clergyman
of the Church of England who could allow such an argument to be put
into his mouth.

If this plea be put forward, we trust Mr Harding will be forced as a
witness to state the nature of his employment; the amount of work that
he does; the income which he receives, and the source from whence he
obtained his appointment. We do not think he will receive much public
sympathy to atone for the annoyance of such an examination.

As Eleanor read the article her face flushed with indignation,
and when she had finished it, she almost feared to look up at her
father.

'Well, my dear,' said he, 'what do you think of that – is it worth
while to be a warden at that price?'

'Oh, papa – dear papa.'

'Mr Bold can't unwrite that my dear – Mr Bold can't say that
that shan't be read by every clergyman at Oxford; nay, by every
gentleman in the land'; and then he walked up and down the
room, while Eleanor in mute despair followed him with her eyes
– 'and I'll tell you what, my dear,' he continued, speaking now
very calmly, and in a forced manner very unlike himself. 'Mr Bold
can't dispute the truth of every word in that article you have just
read – nor can I.' Eleanor stared at him, as though she scarcely
understood the words he was speaking. 'Nor can I, Eleanor: that's
the worst of all, or would be so if there were no remedy; I have
thought much of all this since we were together last night'; and
he came and sat beside her, and put his arm round her waist as
he had done then. 'I have thought much of what the archdeacon
has said, and of what this paper says; and I do believe I have no
right to be here.'

'No right to be warden of the hospital, papa?'

'No right to be warden with eight hundred a year; no right to
be warden with such a house as this; no right to spend in luxury

money that was intended for charity. Mr Bold may do as he pleases about his suit, but I hope he will not abandon it for my sake.'

Poor Eleanor! this was hard upon her. Was it for this she had made her great resolve! For this that she had laid aside her quiet demeanour, and taken upon her the rants of a tragedy heroine! One may work and not for thanks, but yet feel hurt at not receiving them; and so it was with Eleanor: one may be disinterested in one's good actions, and yet feel discontented that they are not recognized. Charity may be given with the left hand so privily that the right hand does not know it, and yet the left hand may regret to feel that it has no immediate reward. Eleanor had had no wish to burden her father with a weight of obligation, and yet she had looked forward to much delight from the knowledge that she had freed him from his sorrows: now such hopes were entirely over; all that she had done was of no avail; she had humbled herself to Bold in vain; the evil was utterly beyond her power to cure!

She had thought also how gently she would whisper to her father all that her lover had said to her about herself, and how impossible she had found it to reject him: and then she had anticipated her father's kindly kiss and close embrace as he gave his sanction to her love. Alas, she could say nothing of this now. In speaking of Mr Bold, her father put him aside as one whose thoughts and sayings and acts could be of no moment. Gentle reader, did you ever feel yourself snubbed? Did you ever, when thinking much of your own importance, find yourself suddenly reduced to a nonentity? Such was Eleanor's feeling now.

'They shall not put forward this plea on my behalf,' continued the warden. 'Whatever may be the truth of the matter, that at any rate is not true; and the man who wrote that article is right in saying that such a plea is revolting to an honest mind. I will go up to London, my dear, and see these lawyers myself, and if no better excuse can be made for me than that, I and the hospital will part.'

'But the archdeacon, papa?'

'I can't help it, my dear; there are some things which a man cannot bear – I cannot bear that' – and he put his hand upon the newspaper.

'But will the archdeacon go with you?'

To tell the truth Mr Harding had made up his mind to steal a march upon the archdeacon. He was aware that he could take no steps without informing his dread son-in-law, but he had resolved that he would send out a note to Plumstead Episcopi detailing his plans, but that the messenger should not leave Barchester till he himself had started for London; so that he might be a day before the doctor, who, he had no doubt, would follow him. In that day, if he had luck, he might arrange it all; he might explain to Sir Abraham that he, as warden, would have nothing further to do with the defence about to be set up; he might send in his official resignation to his friend the bishop, and so make public the whole transaction that even the doctor would not be able to undo what he had done. He knew too well the doctor's strength and his own weakness to suppose he could do this, if they both reached London together; indeed, he would never be able to get to London if the doctor knew of his intended journey in time to prevent it.

'No, I think not,' said he; 'I think I shall start before the archdeacon could be ready – I shall go early tomorrow morning.'

'That will be best, papa,' said Eleanor, showing that her father's ruse was appreciated.

'Why, yes, my love: the fact is, I wish to do all this before the archdeacon can – can interfere. There is a great deal of truth in all he says – he argues very well, and I can't always answer him; but there is an old saying, Nelly, "Everyone knows where his own shoe pinches!" He'll say that I want moral courage, and strength of character, and power of endurance, and it's all true; but I'm sure I ought not to remain here, if I have nothing better to put forward than a quibble: so, Nelly, we shall have to leave this pretty place.'

Eleanor's face brightened up, as she assured her father how cordially she agreed with him.

'True, my love,' said he, now again quite happy and at ease in his manner. 'What good to us is this place or all the money, if we are to be ill-spoken of?'

'Oh, papa, I am so glad.'

'My darling child. It did cost me a pang at first, Nelly, to think that you should lose your pretty drawing-room, and your ponies, and your garden: the garden will be the worst of all – but there is a garden at Crabtree, a very pretty garden.'

Crabtree Parva was the name of the small living which Mr

Harding had held as a minor canon, and which still belonged to
him. It was only worth some eighty pounds a year, and a small
house and glebe, all of which were now handed over to Mr
Harding's curate; but it was to Crabtree glebe that Mr Harding
thought of retiring. This parish must not be mistaken for that
other living, Crabtree Canonicorum as it is called. Crabtree
Canonicorum is a very nice thing; there are only two hundred
parishioners; there are four hundred acres of glebe; and the great
and small tithes,[1] which both go to the rector, are worth four
hundred pounds a year more. Crabtree Canonicorum is in the gift
of the dean and chapter, and is at this time possessed by the
Honourable and Reverend Dr Vesey Stanhope, who also fills the
prebendal stall[2] of Goosegorge in Barchester Chapter, and holds the
united rectory of Eiderdown and Stogpingum, or Stoke Pinquium
as it should be written. This is the same Dr Vesey Stanhope whose
hospitable villa on the Lake of Como is well known to the *élite* of
English travellers, and whose collection of Lombard butterflies is
supposed to be unique.

'Yes,' said the warden musing, 'there is a very pretty garden at
Crabtree, but I shall be sorry to disturb poor Smith.' Smith was the
curate of Crabtree, a gentleman who was maintaining a wife and
half a dozen children on the income arising from his profession.

Eleanor assured her father that as far as she was concerned, she
could leave her house and her ponies without a single regret: she
was only so happy that he was going – going where he would
escape all this dreadful turmoil.

'But we will take the music, my dear.'

And so they went on planning their future happiness, and
plotting how they would arrange it all without the interposition
of the archdeacon, and at last they again became confidential, and
then the warden did thank her for what she had done, and
Eleanor, lying on her father's shoulder, did find an opportunity to
tell her secret: and the father gave his blessing to his child, and
said that the man whom she loved was honest, good, and kind-
hearted, and right-thinking in the main – one who wanted only
a good wife to put him quite upright – 'a man, my love,' he ended
by saying, 'to whom I firmly believe that I can trust my treasure
with safety.'

'But what will Dr Grantly say?'

'Well, my dear, it can't be helped – we shall be out at Crabtree then.'

And Eleanor ran upstairs to prepare her father's clothes for his journey; and the warden returned to his garden to make his last adieus to every tree, and shrub, and shady nook that he knew so well.

CHAPTER 14

Mount Olympus

WRETCHED in spirit, groaning under the feeling of insult, self-condemning, and ill-satisfied in every way, Bold returned to his London lodgings. Ill as he had fared in his interview with the archdeacon, he was not less under the necessity of carrying out his pledge to Eleanor; and he went about his ungracious task with a heavy heart.

The attorneys whom he had employed in London received his instructions with surprise and evident misgiving: however, they could only obey, and mutter something of their sorrow that such heavy costs should only fall upon their own employer – especially as nothing was wanting but perseverance to throw them on the opposite party. Bold left the office which he had latterly so much frequented, shaking the dust from off his feet; and before he was down the stairs, an edict had already gone forth for the preparation of the bill.

He next thought of the newspapers. The case had been taken up by more than one; and he was well aware that the keynote had been sounded by the *Jupiter*. He had been very intimate with Tom Towers, and had often discussed with him the affairs of the hospital. Bold could not say that the articles in that paper had been written at his own instigation; he did not even know as a fact that they had been written by his friend. Tom Towers had never said that such a view of the case, or such a side in the dispute, would be taken by the paper with which he was connected. Very discreet in such matters was Tom Towers, and altogether indisposed to talk loosely of the concerns of that mighty engine of which it was his high privilege to move in secret some portion. Nevertheless, Bold believed that to him were owing those dreadful words which had caused him such panic at Barchester – and he conceived himself bound to prevent their repetition. With this view he betook himself from the attorneys' to that laboratory where, with amazing chemistry, Tom Towers compounded thunderbolts for the destruction of all that is evil, and for the furtherance of all that is good, in this and other hemispheres.

Who has not heard of Mount Olympus[1] – that high abode of all the powers of type, that favoured seat of the great goddess Pica,[2] that wondrous habitation of gods and devils, from whence, with cease-less hum of steam and never-ending flow of Castalian ink,[3] issue forth fifty thousand nightly edicts for the governance of a subject nation?

Velvet and gilding do not make a throne, nor gold and jewels a sceptre. It is a throne because the most exalted one sits there – and a sceptre because the most mighty one wields it. So it is with Mount Olympus. Should a stranger make his way thither at dull noonday, or during the sleepy hours of the silent afternoon, he would find no acknowledged temple of power and beauty, no fitting fane for the great Thunderer, no proud façades and pillared roofs to support the dignity of this greatest of earthly potentates. To the outward and uninitiated eye, Mount Olympus is a somewhat humble spot – un-distinguished, unadorned – nay, almost mean. It stands alone, as it were, in a mighty city, close to the densest throng of men, but par-taking neither of the noise nor the crowd; a small, secluded, dreary spot, tenanted, one would say, by quite unambitious people at the easiest rents. 'Is this Mount Olympus?' asks the unbelieving stranger. 'Is it from these small, dark, dingy buildings that those infallible laws proceed which cabinets are called upon to obey; by which bishops are to be guided, lords and commons controlled – judges instructed in law, generals in strategy, admirals in naval tactics, and orange-women in the management of their barrows?' 'Yes, my friend – from these walls. From here issue the only known infallible bulls[4] for the guidance of British souls and bodies. This little court is the Vatican of England. Here reigns a pope, self-nominated, self-consecrated – ay, and much stranger too – self-believing! – a pope whom, if you cannot believe him, I would advise you to disobey as silently as possible; a pope hitherto afraid of no Luther; a pope who manages his own inquisition, who punishes unbelievers as no most skilful inquisitor of Spain ever dreamt of doing – one who can ex-communicate thoroughly, fearfully, radically; put you beyond the pale of men's charity; make you odious to your dearest friends, and turn you into a monster to be pointed at by the finger!'

Oh heavens! and this is Mount Olympus!

It is a fact amazing to ordinary mortals that the *Jupiter* is never wrong. With what endless care, with what unsparing labour, do we not strive to get together for our great national council the men most fitting to compose it. And how we fail! Parliament is always wrong: look at the *Jupiter*, and see how futile are their meetings, how vain their council, how needless all their trouble! With what pride do we regard our chief ministers, the great servants of state, the oligarchs of the nation on whose wisdom we lean, to whom we look for guidance in our difficulties! But what are they to the writers of the *Jupiter*? They hold council together and with anxious thought painfully elaborate their country's good; but when all is done, the *Jupiter* declares that all is nought. Why should we look to Lord John Russell – why should we regard Palmerston and Gladstone,[5] when Tom Towers without a struggle can put us right? Look at our generals, what faults they make; at our admirals, how inactive they are. What money, honesty, and science can do, is done; and yet how badly are our troops brought together, fed, conveyed, clothed, armed, and managed. The most excellent of our good men do their best to man our ships, with the assistance of all possible external appliances, but in vain. All, all is wrong – alas! alas! Tom Towers, and he alone, knows all about it. Why, oh why, ye earthly ministers, why have ye not followed more closely this heaven-sent messenger that is among us?

Were it not well for us in our ignorance that we confided all things to the *Jupiter*? Would it not be wise in us to abandon useless talking, idle thinking, and profitless labour? Away with majorities in the House of Commons, with verdicts from judicial bench given after much delay, with doubtful laws, and the fallible attempts of humanity! Does not the *Jupiter*, coming forth daily with fifty thousand impressions[6] full of unerring decision on every mortal subject, set all matters sufficiently at rest? Is not Tom Towers here, able to guide us and willing?

Yes indeed – able and willing to guide all men in all things, so long as he is obeyed as autocrat should be obeyed – with undoubting submission: only let not ungrateful ministers seek other colleagues than those whom Tom Towers may approve; let church and state, law and physic, commerce and agriculture – the arts of war, and the arts of peace – all listen and obey, and all will be made perfect. Has not Tom Towers an all-seeing eye? From the diggings of Australia to those of California, right round the habitable globe, does he not know, watch, and chronicle the doings of everyone? From a bishopric in New Zealand to an unfortunate director of a north-west passage, is he not the only fit judge of capability? From the sewers of London to the Central Railway of India – from the palaces of St Petersburg to the cabins of Connaught, nothing can escape him. Britons have but to read, to obey, and be blessed. None but the fools doubt the wisdom of the *Jupiter*; none but the mad dispute its facts.

No established religion has ever been without its unbelievers, even in the country where it is the most firmly fixed; no creed has been without scoffers; no church has so prospered as to free itself entirely from dissent. There are those who doubt the *Jupiter*! They live and breathe the upper air walking here unscathed, though scorned – men, born of British mothers and nursed on English milk, who scruple not to say that Mount Olympus has its price, that Tom Towers can be bought for gold!

Such is Mount Olympus, the mouthpiece of all the wisdom of this great country. It may probably be said that no place in this nineteenth century is more worthy of notice. No treasury mandate armed with the signatures of all the government has half the power of one of those broadsheets, which fly forth from hence so abundantly, armed with no signature at all.

Some great man, some mighty peer – we'll say a noble duke – retires to rest feared and honoured by all his countrymen – fearless himself; if not a good man, at any rate a mighty man – too mighty to care much what men may say about his want of virtue. He rises in the morning degraded, mean, and miserable; an object of men's scorn, anxious only to retire as quickly as may be to some German obscurity, some unseen Italian privacy, or, indeed, anywhere out of sight. What has made this awful change? what has so afflicted him? An article has appeared in the *Jupiter*; some fifty lines of a narrow column have destroyed all his grace's equanimity, and banished him for ever from the world. No man knows who wrote the bitter words; the clubs talk confusedly of the matter, whispering to each other this and that name; while Tom Towers walks quietly along Pall Mall, with his coat buttoned close against the east wind, as though he were a mortal man, and not a god dispensing thunderbolts from Mount Olympus.

It was not to Mount Olympus that our friend Bold betook himself. He had before now wandered round that lonely spot, thinking how grand a thing it was to write articles for the *Jupiter*; considering within himself whether by any stretch of the powers within him he could ever come to such distinction; wondering how Tom Towers would take any little humble offering of his talents; calculating that Tom Towers himself must have once had a beginning, have once doubted as to his own success. Towers could not have been born a writer in the *Jupiter*. With such ideas, half ambitious and half awe-struck, had Bold regarded the silent-looking workshop of the gods; but he had never yet by word or sign attempted to influence the slightest word of his unerring friend. On such a course was he now intent; and not without much inward palpitation did he betake himself to the quiet abode of wisdom, where Tom Towers was to be found o' mornings inhaling ambrosia and sipping nectar in the shape of toast and tea.[7]

Not far removed from Mount Olympus, but somewhat nearer to the blessed regions of the West, is the most favoured abode of Themis.[8] Washed by the rich tide which now passes from the towers of Caesar to Barry's halls of eloquence;[9] and again back, with new offerings of a city's tribute, from the palaces of peers to the mart of merchants, stand those quiet walls which Law has delighted to honour by its presence. What a world within a world is the Temple! how quiet are its 'entangled walks', as someone lately has called them, and yet how close to the densest concourse of humanity! how gravely respectable its sober alleys, though removed but by a single step from the profanity of the Strand and the low iniquity of Fleet Street! Old St Dunstan, with its bell-smiting bludgeoners,[10] has been removed; the ancient shops with their faces full of pleasant history are passing away one by one; the bar itself is to go[11] – its doom has been pronounced by the *Jupiter*; rumour tells us of some huge building that is to appear in these latitudes dedicated to law,[12] subversive of the courts of Westminster, and antagonistic to the Rolls and Lincoln's Inn; but nothing yet threatens the silent beauty of the Temple: it is the medieval court of the metropolis.

Here, on the choicest spot of this choice ground, stands a lofty row of chambers, looking obliquely upon the sullied Thames; before the windows, the lawn of the Temple Gardens stretches with that dim yet delicious verdure so refreshing to the eyes of Londoners. If doomed to live within the thickest of London smoke, you would surely say that that would be your chosen spot. Yes, you, you whom I now address, my dear, middle-aged bachelor friend, can nowhere be so well domiciled as here. No one here will ask whether you are out or at home; alone or with friends: here no Sabbatarian will investigate your Sundays, no censorious land-lady will scrutinize your empty bottle, no valetudinarian neigh-bour will complain of late hours. If you love books, to what place are books so suitable? The whole spot is redolent of typography. Would you worship the Paphian goddess,[13] the groves of Cyprus are not more taciturn than those of the Temple. Wit and wine are always here, and always together; the revels of the Temple are as those of polished Greece, where the wildest worshipper of Bacchus[14] never forgot the dignity of the god whom he adored. Where can retirement be so complete as here? where can you be so sure of all the pleasures of society?

It was here that Tom Towers lived, and cultivated with eminent success the tenth Muse who now governs the periodical press.[15] But let it not be supposed that his chambers were such, or so comfort-less, as are frequently the gaunt abodes of legal aspirants. Four chairs, a half-filled deal bookcase with hangings of dingy green baize, an old office table covered with dusty papers, which are not moved once in six months, and an older Pembroke brother with rickety legs, for all daily uses[16] – a despatcher for the preparation of lobsters and coffee, and an apparatus for the cooking of toast and mutton chops; such utensils and luxuries as these did not suffice for the well-being of Tom Towers. He indulged in four rooms on the first floor, each of which was furnished, if not with the splendour, with probably more than the comfort of Stafford House.[17] Every addition that science and art have lately made to the luxuries of modern life was to be found there. The room in which he usually sat was surrounded by bookshelves carefully filled; nor was there a volume there which was not entitled to its place in such a collection, both by its intrinsic worth and exterior splen-dour: a pretty portable set of steps in one corner of the room showed that those even on the higher shelves were intended for use. The chamber contained but two works of art – the one, an admirable bust of Sir Robert Peel, by Power,[18] declared the individual politics of our friend; and the other, a singularly long figure of a female devotee, by Millais,[19] told equally plainly the school of art to which he was addicted. This picture was not hung, as pictures usually are, against the wall; there was no inch of wall vacant for such a purpose: it had a stand or desk erected for its own accomodation; and there on her pedestal, framed and glazed, stood the devotional lady looking intently at a lily as no lady ever looked before.[20]

Our modern artists, whom we style Pre-Raphaelites, have delighted to go back, not only to the finish and peculiar manner, but also to the subjects of the early painters. It is impossible to give them too much praise for the elaborate perseverance with which they have equalled the minute perfections of the masters from whom they take their inspiration: nothing probably can exceed the painting of some of these latterday pictures. It is, however, singular into what faults they fall as regards their subjects: they are not quite content to take the old stock groups – a Sebastian with his arrows, a Lucia with her eyes in a dish, a Lorenzo with a gridiron, or the virgin with two children. But they are anything but happy in their change. As a rule, no figure should be drawn in a position which it is impossible to suppose any figure should maintain. The patient endurance of St Sebastian, the wild ecstasy of St John in the Wilderness, the maternal love of the virgin, are feelings naturally portrayed by a fixed posture; but the lady with the stiff back and bent neck, who looks at her flower, and is still looking from hour to hour, gives us an idea of pain without grace, and abstraction without a cause.

It was easy, from his rooms, to see that Tom Towers was a Sybarite,[21] though by no means an idle one. He was lingering over his last cup of tea, surrounded by an ocean of newspapers, through which he had been swimming, when John Bold's card was brought in by his tiger.[22] This tiger never knew that his master was at home, though he often knew that he was not, and thus Tom Towers was never invaded but by his own consent. On this occasion, after twisting the card twice in his fingers, he signified to his attendant imp that he was visible; and the inner door was unbolted, and our friend announced.

I have before said that he of the *Jupiter* and John Bold were intimate. There was no very great difference in their ages, for Towers was still considerably under forty; and when Bold had been attending the London hospitals, Towers, who was not then the great man that he had since become, had been much with him. Then they had often discussed together the objects of their ambition and future prospects; then Tom Towers was struggling hard to maintain himself, as a briefless barrister, by shorthand reporting for any of the papers that would engage him; then he had not dared to dream of writing leaders for the *Jupiter*, or canvassing the conduct of cabinet ministers. Things had altered since that time: the briefless barrister was still briefless, but he now despised briefs: could he have been sure of a judge's seat, he would hardly have left his present career. It is true he wore no ermine, bore no outward marks of a world's respect; but with what a load of inward importance was he charged! It is true his name appeared in no large capitals; on no wall was chalked up TOM TOWERS FOR EVER — FREEDOM OF THE PRESS AND TOM TOWERS: but what member of Parliament had half his power? It is true that in far-off provinces men did not talk daily of Tom Towers, but they read the *Jupiter*, and acknowledged that without the *Jupiter* life was not worth having. This kind of hidden but still conscious glory suited the nature of the man. He loved to sit silent in a corner of his club and listen to the loud chattering of politicians, and to think how they all were in his power — how he could smite the loudest of them, were it worth his while to raise his pen for such a purpose. He loved to watch the great men of whom he daily wrote, and flatter himself that he was greater than any of them. Each of them was responsible to his country, each of them must answer if inquired into, each of them must endure abuse with good humour, and insolence without anger. But to whom was he, Tom Towers, responsible? No one could insult him; no one could inquire into him. He could speak out withering words, and no one could answer him: ministers courted him, though perhaps they knew not his name; bishops feared him; judges doubted their own verdicts unless he confirmed them; and generals, in their councils of war, did not consider more deeply what the enemy would do, than what the *Jupiter* would say. Tom Towers never boasted of the

Jupiter; he scarcely ever named the paper even to the most intimate of his friends; he did not even wish to be spoken of as connected with it; but he did not the less value his privileges, or think the less of his own importance. It is probable that Tom Towers considered himself the most powerful man in Europe; and so he walked on from day to day, studiously striving to look a man, but knowing within his breast that he was a god.

CHAPTER 15

Tom Towers, Dr Anticant, and Mr Sentiment

'AH, Bold! how are you? You haven't breakfasted?'

'Oh yes, hours ago. And how are you?'

When one Esquimau meets another, do the two, as an invariable rule, ask after each other's health? is it inherent in all human nature to make this obliging inquiry? Did any reader of this tale ever meet any friend or acquaintance without asking some such question, and did anyone ever listen to the reply? Sometimes a studiously courteous questioner will show so much thought in the matter as to answer it himself, by declaring that had he looked at you he needn't have asked; meaning thereby to signify that you are an absolute personification of health: but such persons are only those who premeditate small effects.

'I suppose you're busy?' inquired Bold.

'Why, yes, rather; or I should say rather not: if I have a leisure hour in the day, this is it.'

'I want to ask you if you can oblige me in a certain matter.'

Towers understood in a moment, from the tone of his friend's voice, that the certain matter referred to the newspaper. He smiled, and nodded his head, but made no promise.

'You know this lawsuit that I've been engaged in?' said Bold.

Tom Towers intimated that he was aware of the action which was pending about the hospital.

'Well, I've abandoned it.'

Tom Towers merely raised his eyebrows, thrust his hands into his trousers' pockets, and waited for his friend to proceed.

'Yes, I've given it up. I needn't trouble you with all the history; but the fact is that the conduct of Mr Harding – Mr Harding is the –'

'Oh yes, the master of the place; the man who takes all the money and does nothing,' said Tom Towers, interrupting him.

'Well, I don't know about that; but his conduct in the matter has been so excellent, so little selfish, so open, that I cannot

proceed in the matter to his detriment.' Bold's heart misgave him
as to Eleanor as he said this; and yet he felt that what he said was
not untrue. 'I think nothing should now be done till the wardenship be vacant.'

'And be again filled,' said Towers, 'as it certainly would, before
anyone heard of the vacancy; and the same objection would again
exist. It's an old story that of the vested rights of the incumbent;
but suppose the incumbent has only a vested wrong, and that the
poor of the town have a vested right, if they only knew how to get
at it: is not that something the case here?'

Bold couldn't deny it, but thought it was one of those cases
which required a good deal of management before any real good
could be done. It was a pity that he had not considered this before
he crept into the lion's mouth, in the shape of an attorney's office.

'It will cost you a good deal, I fear,' said Towers.

'A few hundreds,' said Bold – 'perhaps three hundred; I can't
help that, and am prepared for it.'

'That's philosophical; it's quite refreshing to hear a man talking
of his hundreds in so purely indifferent a manner. But I'm sorry
you are giving the matter up; it injures a man to commence a
thing of this kind, and not carry it through. Have you seen that?'
and he threw a small pamphlet across the table, which was all but
damp from the press.

Bold had not seen it nor heard of it; but he was well acquainted
with the author of it – a gentleman whose pamphlets, condem-
natory of all things in these modern days, had been a good deal
talked about of late.

Dr Pessimist Anticant was a Scotchman,[1] who had passed a
great portion of his early days in Germany; he had studied there
with much effect, and had learnt to look with German subtlety
into the root of things, and to examine for himself their intrinsic
worth and worthlessness. No man ever resolved more bravely
than he to accept as good nothing that was evil; to banish from
him as evil nothing that was good. 'Tis a pity that he should not
have recognized the fact that in this world no good is unalloyed,
and that there is but little evil that has not in it some seed of what
is goodly.

Returning from Germany, he had astonished the reading public by the vigour of his thoughts, put forth in the quaintest language. He cannot write English, said the critics. No matter, said the public; we can read what he does write, and that without yawning. And so Dr Pessimist Anticant became popular. Popularity spoilt him for all further real use, as it has done many another. While, with some diffidence, he confined his objurgations to the occasional follies or shortcomings of mankind; while he ridiculed the energy of the squire devoted to the slaughter of partridges, or the mistake of some noble patron who turned a poet into a gauger of beer-barrels, it was all well; we were glad to be told our faults and to look forward to the coming millennium, when all men, having sufficiently studied the works of Dr Anticant, would become truthful and energetic. But the doctor mistook the signs of the times and the minds of men, instituted himself censor of things in general, and began the great task of reprobating everything and everybody, without further promise of any millennium at all. This was not so well: and, to tell the truth, our author did not succeed in his undertaking. His theories were all beautiful, and the code of morals that he taught us certainly an improvement on the practices of the age. We all of us could, and many of us did, learn much from the doctor while he chose to remain vague, mysterious, and cloudy; but when he became practical, the charm was gone.

His allusion to the poet and the partridges was received very well.[2]

Oh, my poor brother (said he) slaughtered partridges a score of brace to each gun, and poets gauging ale-barrels, with sixty pounds a year, at Dumfries, are not the signs of a great era! perhaps of the smallest possible era yet written of. Whatever economies we pursue, political or other, let us see at once that this is the maddest of the uneconomic: partridges killed by our land magnates at, shall we say, a guinea a head, to be retailed in Leadenhall at one shilling and ninepence, with one poacher in limbo for every fifty birds! our poet, maker, creator, gauging ale, and that badly, with no leisure for making or creating, only a little leisure for drinking, and suchlike beer-barrel avocations! Truly, a cutting of blocks with fine razors while we scrape our chins so uncomfortably with rusty knives! Oh, my political economist, master of supply and demand, division of labour and high pressure – oh, my loud-speaking friend, tell me, if so much be in you, what is the demand for poets in these kingdoms of Queen Victoria, and what the vouchsafed supply?

This was all very well; this gave us some hope. We might do better with our next poet, when we got one; and though the partridges might not be abandoned, something could perhaps be done as to the poachers. We were unwilling, however, to take lessons in politics from so misty a professor; and when he came to tell us that the heroes of Westminster were naught, we began to think that he had written enough. His attack upon despatch boxes was not thought to have much in it; but as it is short, the doctor shall again be allowed to speak his sentiments:[3]

Could utmost ingenuity in the management of red tape avail anything to men lying gasping – we may say, all but dead; could despatch boxes with never-so-much velvet lining and Chubb's patent,[4] be of comfort to a people *in extremis*, I also, with so many others, would, with parched tongue, call on the name of Lord John Russell; or, my brother, at your advice, on Lord Aberdeen; or, my cousin, on Lord Derby,[5] at yours; being, with my parched tongue, indifferent in such matters. 'Tis all one. Oh, Derby! Oh, Gladstone! Oh, Palmerston! Oh, Lord John! Each comes running with serene face and despatch box. Vain physicians! though there were hosts of such, no despatch box will cure this disorder! What! are there other doctors' new names, disciples who have not burdened their souls with tape? Well, let us call again. Oh, Disraeli,[6] great oppositionist, man of the bitter brow! or, Oh, Molesworth,[7] great reformer, thou who promisest Utopia. They come; each with that serene face, and each – alas, me! alas, my country! – each with a despatch box!

Oh, the serenity of Downing Street!

My brothers, when hope was over on the battlefield, when no dimmest chance of victory remained, the ancient Roman could hide his face within his toga, and die gracefully. Can you and I do so now? If so, 'twere best for us; if not, oh my brothers, we must die disgracefully, for hope of life and victory I see none left to us in this world below. I for one cannot trust much to serene face and despatch box!

There might be truth in this, there might be depth of reasoning; but Englishmen did not see enough in the argument to induce them to withdraw their confidence from the present arrangements of the government, and Dr Anticant's monthly pamphlet on the decay of the world did not receive so much attention as his earlier works. He did not confine himself to politics in these publications,

but roamed at large over all matters of public interest, and found
everything bad. According to him nobody was true, and not only
nobody, but nothing; a man could not take off his hat to a lady
without telling a lie – the lady would lie again in smiling. The
ruffles of the gentleman's shirt would be fraught with deceit, and
the ladies' flounces full of falsehood. Was ever anything more
severe than that attack of his on chip-bonnets, or the anathemas
with which he endeavoured to dust the powder out of the bishops'
wigs?

The pamphlet which Tom Towers now pushed across the table
was entitled 'Modern Charity', and was written with the view of
proving how much in the way of charity was done by our pre-
decessors – how little by the present age; and it ended by a
comparison between ancient and modern times, very little to the
credit of the latter.[8]

'Look at this,' said Towers, getting up and turning over the
pages of the pamphlet, and pointing to a passage near the end;
'your friend the warden, who is so little selfish, won't like that, I
fear.' Bold read as follows:

Heavens, what a sight! Let us with eyes wide open see the godly man
of four centuries since, the man of the dark ages: let us see how he does
his god-like work, and, again, how the godly man of these latter days does
his.

Shall we say that the former is one walking painfully through the world,
regarding, as a prudent man, his worldly work, prospering in it as a
diligent man will prosper, but always with an eye to that better treasure
to which thieves do not creep in?[9] Is there not much nobility in that old
man, as, leaning on his oaken staff, he walks down the high street of his
native town, and receives from all courteous salutation and acknowledge-
ment of his worth? A noble old man, my august inhabitants of Belgrave
Square and suchlike vicinity[10] – a very noble old man, though employed no
better than in the wholesale carding of wool.

This carding of wool, however, did in those days bring with it much
profit, so that our ancient friend, when dying, was declared, in whatever
slang then prevailed, to cut up exceeding well. For sons and daughters
there was ample sustenance, with assistance of due industry; for friends
and relatives some relief for grief at this great loss; for aged dependants
comfort in declining years. This was much for one old man to get done
in that dark fifteenth century. But this was not all: coming generations of

poor wool-carders should bless the name of this rich one; and a hospital should be founded and endowed with his wealth for the feeding of such of the trade as could not, by diligent carding, any longer duly feed themselves.

'Twas thus that an old man in the fifteenth century did his god-like work to the best of his power, and not ignobly, as appears to me.

We will now take our godly man of latter days. He shall no longer be a wool-carder, for such are not now men of mark. We will suppose him to be one of the best of the good – one who has lacked no opportunities. Our old friend, was, after all, but illiterate; our modern friend shall be a man educated in all seemly knowledge; he shall, in short, be that blessed being – a clergyman of the Church of England!

And now, in what perfectest manner does he in this lower world get his god-like work done and put out of hand? Heavens! in the strangest of manners. Oh, my brother! in a manner not at all to be believed but by the most minute testimony of eyesight. He does it by the magnitude of his appetite – by the power of his gorge; his only occupation is to swallow the bread prepared with so much anxious care for these impoverished carders of wool – that, and to sing indifferently through his nose once in the week some psalm more or less long – the shorter the better, we should be inclined to say.

Oh, my civilized friends! – great Britons that never will be slaves, men advanced to infinite state of freedom and knowledge of good and evil – tell me, will you, what becoming monument you will erect to an highly educated clergyman of the Church of England?

Bold certainly thought that his friend would not like that: he could not conceive anything that he would like less than this. To what a world of toil and trouble had he, Bold, given rise by his indiscreet attack upon the hospital!

'You see,' said Towers, 'that this affair has been much talked of, and the public are with you. I am sorry you should give the matter up. Have you seen the first number of *The Almshouse*?'[11]

No; Bold had not seen *The Almshouse*. He had seen advertisements of Mr Popular Sentiment's new novel of that name, but had in no way connected it with Barchester Hospital, and had never thought a moment on the subject.

'It's a direct attack on the whole system,' said Towers. 'It'll go a long way to put down Rochester, and Barchester, and Dulwich,[12] and St Cross, and all such hotbeds of peculation. It's very clear that

Sentiment has been down to Barchester, and got up the whole story there; indeed, I thought he must have had it all from you. It's very well done, as you'll see: his first numbers always are.'

Bold declared that Mr Sentiment had got nothing from him, and that he was deeply grieved to find that the case had become so notorious.

'The fire has gone too far to be quenched,' said Towers; 'the building must go now; and as the timbers are all rotten, why, I should be inclined to say, the sooner the better. I expected to see you get some *éclat* in the matter.'[13]

This was all wormwood to Bold. He had done enough to make his friend the warden miserable for life, and had then backed out just when the success of his project was sufficient to make the question one of real interest. How weakly he had managed his business! He had already done the harm, and then stayed his hand when the good which he had in view was to be commenced. How delightful would it have been to have employed all his energy in such a cause – to have been backed by the *Jupiter*, and written up to by two of the most popular authors of the day! The idea opened a view into the very world in which he wished to live. To what might it not have given rise? what delightful intimacies – what public praise – to what Athenian banquets and rich flavour of Attic salt?[14]

This, however, was now past hope. He had pledged himself to abandon the cause; and could he have forgotten the pledge, he had gone too far to retreat. He was now, this moment, sitting in Tom Towers's room with the object of deprecating any further articles in the *Jupiter*, and, greatly as he disliked the job, his petition to that effect must be made.

'I couldn't continue it,' said he, 'because I found I was in the wrong.'

Tom Towers shrugged his shoulders. How could a successful man be in the wrong! 'In that case,' said he, 'of course you must abandon it.'

'And I called this morning to ask you also to abandon it,' said Bold.

'To ask me,' said Tom Towers with the most placid of smiles, and a consummate look of gentle surprise, as though Tom Towers was well aware that he of all men was the last to meddle in such matters.

'Yes,' said Bold, almost trembling with hesitation. 'The *Jupiter*, you know, has taken the matter up very strongly. Mr Harding has felt what it has said deeply; and I thought that if I could explain to you that he personally has not been to blame, these articles might be discontinued.'

How calmly impassive was Tom Towers's face, as this innocent little proposition was made! Had Bold addressed himself to the doorposts in Mount Olympus, they would have shown as much outward sign of assent or dissent. His quiescence was quite admirable; his discretion certainly more than human.

'My dear fellow,' said he, when Bold had quite done speaking, 'I really cannot answer for the *Jupiter*.'

'But if you saw that these articles were unjust, I think you would endeavour to put a stop to them: of course nobody doubts that you could, if you chose.'

'Nobody and everybody are always very kind, but unfortunately are generally very wrong.'

'Come, come, Towers,' said Bold, plucking up his courage, and remembering that for Eleanor's sake he was bound to make his best exertion; 'I have no doubt in my own mind but that you wrote the articles yourself; and very well written they were: it will be a great favour if you will in future abstain from any personal allusion to poor Harding.'

'My dear Bold,' said Tom Towers, 'I have a sincere regard for you. I have known you for many years, and value your friendship; I hope you will let me explain to you, without offence, that none who are connected with the public press can with propriety listen to interference.'

'Interference!' said Bold, 'I don't want to interfere.'

'Ah, but my dear fellow, you do; what else is it? You think that I am able to keep certain remarks out of a newspaper. Your information is probably incorrect, as most public gossip on such subjects is; but, at any rate, you think I have such power, and you ask me to use it: now that is interference.'

'Well, if you choose to call it so.'

'And now suppose for a moment that I had this power, and used

it as you wish: isn't it clear that it would be a great abuse? Certain
men are employed in writing for the public press; and if they are
induced either to write or to abstain from writing by private
motives, surely the public press would soon be of little value. Look
at the recognized worth of different newspapers, and see if it does
not mainly depend on the assurance which the public feel that
such a paper is, or is not, independent. You alluded to the *Jupiter*:
surely you cannot but see that the weight of the *Jupiter* is too great
to be moved by any private request, even though it should be made
to a much more influential person than myself: you've only to
think of this, and you'll see that I am right.'

The discretion of Tom Towers was boundless: there was no
contradicting what he said, no arguing against such propositions.
He took such high ground that there was no getting on it. 'The
public is defrauded,' said he, 'whenever private considerations are
allowed to have weight.' Quite true, thou greatest oracle of the
middle of the nineteenth century, thou sententious proclaimer of
the purity of the press – the public is defrauded when it is purposely
misled. Poor public! how often is it misled! against what a world
of fraud has it to contend!

Bold took his leave and got out of the room as quickly as he
could, inwardly denouncing his friend Tom Towers as a prig and
a humbug. 'I know he wrote those articles,' said Bold to himself;
'I know he got his information from me. He was ready enough to
take my word for gospel when it suited his own views, and to set
Mr Harding up before the public as an impostor on no other
testimony than my chance conversation; but when I offer him real
evidence opposed to his own views, he tells me that private
motives are detrimental to public justice! Confound his arrogance!
What is any public question but a conglomeration of private
interests? What is any newspaper article but an expression of the
views taken by one side? Truth! it takes an age to ascertain the
truth of any question! The idea of Tom Towers talking of public
motives and purity of purpose! Why, it wouldn't give him a
moment's uneasiness to change his politics tomorrow, if the paper
required it.'

Such were John Bold's inward exclamations as he made his way
out of the quiet labyrinth of the Temple; and yet there was no

position of wordly power so coveted in Bold's ambition as that held by the man of whom he was thinking. It was the impregnability of the place which made Bold so angry with the possessor of it, and it was the same quality which made it appear so desirable.

Passing into the Strand, he saw in a bookseller's window an announcement of the first number of *The Almshouse*; so he purchased a copy, and hurrying back to his lodgings, proceeded to ascertain what Mr Popular Sentiment had to say to the public on the subject which had lately occupied so much of his own attention.

In former times great objects were attained by great work. When evils were to be reformed, reformers set about their heavy task with grave decorum and laborious argument. An age was occupied in proving a grievance, and philosophical researches were printed in folio pages, which it took a life to write, and an eternity to read. We get on now with a lighter step, and quicker: ridicule is found to be more convincing than argument, imaginary agonies touch more than true sorrows, and monthly novels convince, when learned quartos fail to do so. If the world is to be set right, the work will be done by shilling numbers.[15]

Of all such reformers Mr Sentiment is the most powerful. It is incredible the number of evil practices he has put down: it is to be feared he will soon lack subjects, and that when he has made the working classes comfortable, and got bitter beer put into proper-sized pint bottles, there will be nothing further for him left to do. Mr Sentiment is certainly a very powerful man, and perhaps not the less so that his good poor people are so very good; his hard rich people so very hard; and the genuinely honest so very honest. Namby-pamby in these days is not thrown away if it be introduced in the proper quarters. Divine peeresses are no longer interesting, though possessed of every virtue; but a pattern peasant or an immaculate manufacturing hero may talk as much twaddle as one of Mrs Radcliffe's heroines,[16] and still be listened to. Perhaps, however, Mr Sentiment's great attraction is in his second-rate characters. If his heroes and heroines walk upon stilts, as heroes and heroines, I fear, ever must, their attendant satellites are as natural as though one met them in the street: they walk and talk like men and women, and live among our friends a rattling, lively life; yes, live, and will live till the names of their callings shall be forgotten in their own, and Bucket and Mrs Gamp will be the only words left to us to signify a detective police officer or a monthly nurse.[17]

The Almshouse opened with a scene in a clergyman's house. Every luxury to be purchased by wealth was described as being there: all the appearances of household indulgence generally found among the most self-indulgent of the rich were crowded into this abode. Here the reader was introduced to the demon of the book, the Mephistopheles[18] of the drama. What story was ever written without a demon? what novel, what history, what work of any sort, what world, would be perfect without existing principles both of good and evil? The demon of *The Almshouse* was the clerical owner of this comfortable abode. He was a man well stricken in years, but still strong to do evil: he was one who looked cruelly out of a hot, passionate, bloodshot eye; who had a huge red nose with a carbuncle, thick lips, and a great double, flabby chin, which swelled out into solid substance, like a turkey-cock's comb, when sudden anger inspired him: he had a hot, furrowed, low brow, from which a few grizzled hairs were not yet rubbed off by the friction of his handkerchief: he wore a loose unstarched white handkerchief, black loose ill-made clothes, and huge loose shoes, adapted to many corns and various bunions: his husky voice told tales of much daily port wine, and his language was not so decorous as became a clergyman. Such was the master of Mr Sentiment's *Almshouse*. He was a widower, but at present accompanied by two daughters, and a thin and somewhat insipid curate. One of the young ladies was devoted to her father and the fashionable world, and she of course was the favourite; the other was equally addicted to Puseyism and the curate.[19]

The second chapter of course introduced the reader to the more especial inmates of the hospital. Here were discovered eight old men; and it was given to be understood that four vacancies remained unfilled, through the perverse ill-nature of the clerical gentleman with the double chin. The state of these eight paupers was touchingly dreadful: sixpence-farthing a day had been sufficient for their diet when the almshouse was founded; and on sixpence-farthing a day were they still doomed to starve, though food was four times as dear, and money four times as plentiful. It was shocking to find how the conversation of these eight starved old men in their dormitory shamed that of the clergyman's family in his rich drawing-room. The absolute words they uttered were not perhaps spoken in the purest English, and it might be difficult to distinguish from their dialect to what part of the country they belonged; the beauty of the sentiment, however, amply atoned for the imperfection of the language; and it was really a pity that these eight old men could not be sent through the country as moral missionaries, instead of being immured and starved in that wretched almshouse.

Bold finished the number; and as he threw it aside, he thought that that at least had no direct appliance to Mr Harding, and that the absurdly strong colouring of the picture would disenable the work from doing either good or harm. He was wrong. The artist who paints for the million must use glaring colours, as no one knew better than Mr Sentiment when he described the inhabitants of his almshouse; and the radical reform which has now swept over such establishments has owed more to the twenty numbers of Mr Sentiment's novel, than to all the true complaints which have escaped from the public for the last half-century.

CHAPTER 16

A Long Day in London

THE warden had to make use of all his very moderate powers of intrigue to give his son-in-law the slip, and get out of Barchester without being stopped on his road. No schoolboy ever ran away from school with more precaution and more dread of detection; no convict, slipping down from a prison wall, ever feared to see the gaoler more entirely than Mr Harding did to see his son-in-law, as he drove up in the pony-carriage to the railway station on the morning of his escape to London.

The evening before he went, he wrote a note to the archdeacon, explaining that he should start on the morrow on his journey; that it was his intention to see the attorney-general if possible, and to decide on his future plans in accordance with what he heard from that gentleman; he excused himself for giving Dr Grantly no earlier notice by stating that his resolve was very sudden; and having entrusted this note to Eleanor, with the perfect, though not expressed, understanding that it was to be sent over to Plumstead Episcopi without haste, he took his departure.

He also prepared and carried with him a note for Sir Abraham Haphazard, in which he stated his name, explaining that he was the defendant in the case of 'The Queen on behalf of the Wool-carders of Barchester v. Trustees under the will of the late John Hiram', for so was the suit denominated, and begged the illustrious and learned gentleman to vouchsafe to him ten minutes' audience at any hour on the next day. Mr Harding calculated that for that one day he was safe; his son-in-law, he had no doubt, would arrive in town by an early train, but not early enough to reach the truant till he should have escaped from his hotel after breakfast; and could he thus manage to see the lawyer on that very day, the deed might be done before the archdeacon could interfere.

On his arrival in town the warden drove, as was his wont, to the Chapter Hotel and Coffee House, near St Paul's. His visits to London of late had not been frequent; but in those happy days when *Harding's Church Music* was going through the press, he had been often there; and as the publisher's house was in Paternoster Row, and the printer's press in Fleet Street, the Chapter Hotel and Coffee House had been convenient. It was a quiet, sombre, clerical house, beseeming such a man as the warden, and thus he afterwards frequented it. Had he dared, he would on this occasion have gone elsewhere to throw the archdeacon further off the scent; but he did not know what violent steps his son-in-law might take for his recovery if he were not found at his usual haunt, and he deemed it not prudent to make himself the object of a hunt through London.

Arrived at his inn, he ordered dinner, and went forth to the attorney-general's chambers. There he learnt that Sir Abraham was in Court, and would not probably return that day. He would go direct from Court to the House; all appointments were, as a rule, made at the chambers; the clerk could by no means promise an interview for the next day; was able, on the other hand, to say that such interview was, he thought, impossible; but that Sir Abraham would certainly be at the House in the course of the night, when an answer from himself might possibly be elicited.

To the House Mr Harding went, and left his note, not finding Sir Abraham there. He added a most piteous entreaty that he might be favoured with an answer that evening, for which he would return. He then journeyed back sadly to the Chapter Coffee House, digesting his great thoughts, as best he might, in a clattering omnibus, wedged in between a wet old lady and a journeyman glazier, returning from his work with his tools in his lap. In melancholy solitude he discussed his mutton chop and pint of port. What is there in this world more melancholy than such a dinner? A dinner, though alone, in a country hotel may be worthy of some energy; the waiter, if you are known, will make much of you; the landlord will make you a bow, and perhaps put the fish on the table; if you ring you are attended to, and there is some life about it. A dinner at a London eating-house is also lively enough, if it have no other attraction. There is plenty of noise and stir about it, and the rapid whirl of voices and rattle of dishes disperses sadness. But a solitary dinner in an old, respectable, sombre, solid London inn, where nothing makes any noise but the old waiter's creaking shoes; where one plate slowly goes and another slowly comes without a sound; where the two or three guests would as soon think of knocking each other down as of speaking; where the servants whisper, and the whole household is disturbed if an order be given above the voice – what can be more melancholy than a mutton chop and a pint of port in such a place?

Having gone through this, Mr Harding got into another omnibus, and again returned to the House. Yes, Sir Abraham was there, and was that moment on his legs, fighting eagerly for the hundred and seventh clause of the Convent Custody Bill.[1] Mr Harding's note had been delivered to him; and if Mr Harding would wait some two or three hours, Sir Abraham could be asked whether there was any answer. The House was not full, and perhaps Mr Harding might get admittance into the Strangers' Gallery, which admission, with the help of five shillings, Mr Harding was able to effect.

This bill of Sir Abraham's had been read a second time and passed into committee. A hundred and six clauses had already been discussed, and had occupied only four mornings and five evening sittings: nine of the hundred and six clauses were passed, fifty-five were withdrawn by consent, fourteen had been altered so as to mean the reverse of the original proposition, eleven had been postponed for further consideration, and seventeen had been directly negatived. The hundred and seventh ordered the bodily searching of nuns for Jesuitical symbols by aged clergymen, and was considered to be the real mainstay of the whole bill. No intention had ever existed to pass such a law as that proposed, but the government did not intend to abandon it till their object was fully attained by the discussion of this clause. It was known that it would be insisted on with terrible vehemence by Protestant Irish members, and as vehemently denounced by the Roman Catholic; and it was justly considered that no further union between the parties would be possible after such a battle. The innocent Irish fell into the trap as they always do, and whiskey and poplins became a drug in the market.

A florid-faced gentleman with a nice head of hair, from the south of Ireland, had succeeded in catching the speaker's eye by the time that Mr Harding had got into the gallery, and was denouncing the proposed sacrilege, his whole face glowing with a fine theatrical frenzy.

'And is this a Christian country?' said he. (Loud cheers; counter cheers from the ministerial benches. 'Some doubt as to that,' from a voice below in the gangway.) 'No, it can be no Christian country, in which the head of the bar, the lagal adviser (loud laughter and cheers) – yes, I say the lagal adviser of the crown (great cheers and laughter) – can stand up in his seat in this House (prolonged cheers and laughter), and attempt to lagalize indacent assaults on the bodies of religious ladies.' (Deafening cheers and laughter, which were prolonged till the honourable member resumed his seat.)

When Mr Harding had listened to this and much more of the same kind for about three hours, he returned to the door of the House, and received back from the messenger his own note, with the following words scrawled in pencil on the back of it: 'Tomorrow, 10 p.m. – my chambers. A.H.'

He was so far successful – but 10 p.m.: what an hour Sir Abraham had named for a legal interview! Mr Harding felt perfectly sure that long before that Dr Grantly would be in London. Dr Grantly could not, however, know that this interview had been arranged, nor could he learn it unless he managed to get hold of Sir Abraham before that hour; and as this was very improbable, Mr Harding determined to start from his hotel early, merely leaving word that he should dine out, and unless luck were much against him, he might still escape the archdeacon till his return from the attorney-general's chambers.

He was at breakfast at nine, and for the twentieth time consulted his *Bradshaw*[2] to see at what earliest hour Dr Grantly could arrive from Barchester. As he examined the columns, he was nearly petrified by the reflection that perhaps the archdeacon might come up by the night mail-train! His heart sank within him at the horrid idea, and for a moment he felt himself dragged back to Barchester without accomplishing any portion of his object. Then he remembered that had Dr Grantly done so, he would have been in the hotel, looking for him long since.

'Waiter,' said he, timidly.

The waiter approached, creaking in his shoes, but voiceless.

'Did any gentleman – a clergyman, arrive here by the night mail-train?'

'No, sir, not one,' whispered the waiter, putting his mouth nearly close to the warden's ear.

Mr Harding was reassured.

'Waiter,' said he again, and the waiter again creaked up; 'if anyone calls for me, I am going to dine out, and shall return about eleven o'clock.'

The waiter nodded, but did not this time vouchsafe any reply; and Mr Harding, taking up his hat, proceeded out to pass a long day in the best way he could, somewhere out of sight of the archdeacon.

Bradshaw had told him twenty times that Dr Grantly could not be at Paddington station till 2 p.m., and our poor friend might therefore have trusted to the shelter of the hotel for some hours longer with perfect safety; but he was nervous. There was no knowing what steps the archdeacon might take for his apprehension: a message by electric telegraph might desire the landlord of the hotel to set a watch upon him; some letter might come which he might find himself unable to disobey; at any rate, he could not feel himself secure in any place at which the archdeacon could expect to find him; and at 10 a.m. he started forth to spend twelve hours in London.

Mr Harding had friends in town, had he chosen to seek them; but he felt that he was in no humour for ordinary calls, and he did not now wish to consult with anyone as to the great step which he had determined to take. As he had said to his daughter, no one knows where the shoe pinches but the wearer. There are some points on which no man can be contented to follow the advice of another – some subjects on which a man can consult his own conscience only. Our warden had made up his mind that it was good for him at any cost to get rid of this grievance; his daughter was the only person whose concurrence appeared necessary to him, and she did concur with him most heartily. Under such circumstances he would not, if he could help it, consult anyone further, till advice would be useless. Should the archdeacon catch him, indeed, there would be much advice, and much consultation of a kind not to be avoided; but he hoped better things; and as he felt that he could not now converse on indifferent subjects, he resolved to see no one till after his interview with the attorney-general.

He determined to take sanctuary in Westminster Abbey, so he again went thither in an omnibus, and finding that the doors were not open for morning service, he paid his twopence, and went in as a sightseer. It occurred to him that he had no definite place of rest for the day, and that he should be absolutely worn out before his interview if he attempted to walk about from 10 a.m. to 10 p.m., so he sat himself down on a stone step, and gazed up at the figure of William Pitt,[3] who looks as though he had just entered the church for the first time in his life, and was anything but pleased at finding himself there.

He had been sitting unmolested about twenty minutes, when the verger asked him whether he wouldn't like to walk round. Mr Harding didn't want to walk anywhere, and declined, merely observing that he was waiting for the morning service. The verger, seeing that he was a clergyman, told him that the doors of the choir were now open, and showed him into a seat. This was a great point gained; the archdeacon would certainly not come to morning service at Westminster Abbey, even though he were in London; and here the warden could rest quietly, and, when the time came, duly say his prayers.

He longed to get up from his seat, and examine the music-books of the choristers, and the copy of the litany from which the service was chanted, to see how far the little details at Westminster corresponded with those at Barchester, and whether he thought his own voice would fill the church well from the Westminster precentor's seat. There would, however, be impropriety in such meddling, and he sat perfectly still, looking up at the noble roof, and guarding against the coming fatigues of the day.

By degrees two or three people entered: the very same damp old woman who had nearly obliterated him in the omnibus, or some other just like her; a couple of young ladies, with their veils down, and gilt crosses conspicuous on their prayer-books; an old man on crutches; a party who were seeing the abbey, and thought they might as well hear the service for their twopence, as opportunity served; and a young woman with her prayer-book done up in her handkerchief, who rushed in late, and, in her hurried entry, tumbled over one of the forms, and made such a noise that everyone, even the officiating minor canon, was startled, and she herself was so frightened by the echo of her own catastrophe, that she was nearly thrown into fits by the panic.

Mr Harding was not much edified by the manner of the service. The minor canon in question hurried in, somewhat late, in a surplice not in the neatest order, and was followed by a dozen choristers, who were also not as trim as they might have been: they all jostled into their places with a quick hurried step, and the service was soon commenced. Soon commenced, and soon over, for there was no music, and time was not unnecessarily lost in the chanting. On the whole, Mr Harding was of opinion that things were managed better at Barchester, though even there he knew that there was room for improvement.

It appears to us a question whether any clergyman can go through our church service with decorum, morning after morning, in an immense building, surrounded by not more than a dozen listeners. The best actors cannot act well before empty benches, and though there is, of course, a higher motive in one case than the other, still even the best of clergymen cannot but be influenced by their audience; and to expect that a duty should be well done under such circumstances, would be to require from human nature more than human power.

When the two ladies with the gilt crosses, the old man with his crutch, and the still palpitating housemaid were going, Mr Harding found himself obliged to go too. The verger stood in his way, and looked at him and looked at the door, and so he went. But he returned again in a few minutes, and re-entered with another twopence. There was no other sanctuary so good for him.

As he walked slowly down the nave, and then up one aisle, and then again down the nave and up the other aisle, he tried to think gravely of the step he was about to take. He was going to give up eight hundred a year voluntarily; and doom himself to live for the rest of his life on about a hundred and fifty. He knew that he had hitherto failed to realize this fact as he ought to do. Could he maintain his own independence and support his daughter on a hundred and fifty pounds a year without being a burden on anyone? His son-in-law was rich, but nothing could induce him to lean on his son-in-law after acting, as he intended to do, in most direct opposition to his counsel. The bishop was rich, but he was about to throw away the bishop's best gift, and that in a manner to injure materially the patronage of the giver: he could neither expect nor accept anything further from the bishop. There would be not only no merit, but positive disgrace, in giving up his wardenship, if he were not prepared to meet the world without it. Yes, he must from this time forward bound all his human wishes for himself and his daughter to the poor extent of so limited an income. He knew he had not thought sufficiently of this, that he had been carried away by enthusiasm, and had hitherto not brought home to himself the full reality of his position.

He thought most about his daughter, naturally. It was true that she was engaged, and he knew enough of his proposed son-in-law to be sure that his own altered circumstances would make no obstacle to such a marriage; nay, he was sure that the very fact of his poverty would induce Bold more anxiously to press the matter; but he disliked counting on Bold in this emergency, brought on, as it had been, by his doing. He did not like saying to himself, Bold has turned me out of my house and income, and, therefore, he must relieve me of my daughter; he preferred reckoning on Eleanor as the companion of his poverty and exile – as the sharer of his small income.

Some modest provision for his daughter had been long since made. His life was insured for three thousand pounds, and this sum was to go to Eleanor. The archdeacon, for some years past, had paid the premium, and had secured himself by the immediate possession of a small property which was to have gone to Mrs Grantly after her father's death. This matter, therefore, had been out of the warden's hands long since, as, indeed, had all the business transactions of his family, and his anxiety was, therefore, confined to his own life income.

Yes. A hundred and fifty per annum was very small, but still it might suffice; but how was he to chant the litany at the cathedral on Sunday mornings, and get the service done at Crabtree Parva? True, Crabtree Church was not quite a mile and a half from the cathedral; but he could not be in two places at once! Crabtree was a small village, and afternoon service might suffice, but still this went against his conscience; it was not right that his parishioners should be robbed of any of their privileges on account of his poverty. He might, to be sure, make some arrangement for doing weekday service at the cathedral, but he had chanted the litany at Barchester so long, and had a conscious feeling that he did it so well, that he was unwilling to give up the duty.

Thinking of such things, turning over in his own mind together small desires and grave duties, but never hesitating for a moment as to the necessity of leaving the hospital, Mr Harding walked up and down the abbey, or sat still meditating on the same stone step, hour after hour. One verger went and another came, but they did not disturb him; every now and then they crept up and looked at him, but they did so with a reverential stare, and, on the whole, Mr Harding found his retreat well chosen. About four o'clock his comfort was disturbed by an enemy in the shape of hunger; it was necessary that he should dine, and it was clear that he could not dine in the abbey; so he left his sanctuary not willingly, and betook himself to the neighbourhood of the Strand to look for food.

His eyes had become so accustomed to the gloom of the church, that they were dazed when he got out into the full light of day, and he felt confused and ashamed of himself, as though people were staring at him. He hurried along, still in dread of the arch-deacon, till he came to Charing Cross, and then remembered that in one of his passages through the Strand he had seen the words CHOPS AND STEAKS on a placard in a shop window. He remembered the shop distinctly; it was next door to a trunk-seller's, and there was a cigar shop on the other side. He couldn't go to his hotel for dinner, which to him hitherto was the only known mode of dining in London at his own expense; and, therefore, he would get a steak at the shop in the Strand. Archdeacon Grantly would certainly not come to such a place for his dinner.

He found the house easily – just as he had observed it, between the trunks and the cigars. He was rather daunted by the huge quantity of fish which he saw in the window. There were barrels of oysters, hecatombs of lobsters, a few tremendous-looking crabs, and a tub full of pickled salmon; not, however, being aware of any connection between shellfish and iniquity, he entered, and modestly asked a slatternly woman, who was picking oysters out of a great watery reservoir, whether he could have a mutton chop and a potato.

The woman looked somewhat surprised, but answered in the affirmative, and a slipshod girl ushered him into a long back room, filled with boxes for the accommodation of parties, in one of which he took his seat. In a more miserably forlorn place he could not have found himself: the room smelt of fish, and sawdust, and stale tobacco smoke, with a slight taint of escaped gas; everything was rough, and dirty, and disreputable; the cloth which they put before him was abominable; the knives and forks were bruised, and hacked, and filthy; and everything was impregnated with fish. He had one comfort, however: he was quite alone; there was no one there to look on his dismay; nor was it probable that anyone would come to do so. It was a London supper-house.[4] About one o'clock at night the place would be lively enough, but at the present time his seclusion was as deep as it had been in the abbey.

In about half an hour the untidy girl, not yet dressed for her evening labours, brought him his chop and potatoes, and Mr Harding begged for a pint of sherry. He was impressed with an idea, which was generally prevalent a few years since, and is not yet wholly removed from the minds of men, that to order a dinner at any kind of inn, without also ordering a pint of wine for the benefit of the landlord, was a kind of fraud; not punishable, indeed, by law, but not the less abominable on that account. Mr Harding remembered his coming poverty, and would willingly have saved his half-crown, but he thought he had no alternative; and he was soon put in possession of some horrid mixture procured from the neighbouring public house.

His chop and potatoes, however, were eatable, and having got over as best he might the disgust created by the knives and forks, he contrived to swallow his dinner. He was not much disturbed: one young man, with pale face and watery fish-like eyes, wearing his hat ominously on one side, did come in and stare at him, and ask the girl, audibly enough, 'Who that old cock was'; but the annoyance went no further, and the warden was left seated on his wooden bench in peace, endeavouring to distinguish the different scents arising from lobsters, oysters, and salmon.

Unknowing as Mr Harding was in the ways of London, he felt that he had somehow selected an ineligible dining-house, and that he had better leave it. It was hardly five o'clock – how was he to pass the time till ten? Five miserable hours! He was already tired, and it was impossible that he should continue walking so long. He thought of getting into an omnibus, and going out to Fulham for the sake of coming back in another: this, however, would be weary work, and as he paid his bill to the woman in the shop, he asked her if there were any place near where he could get a cup of coffee. Though she did keep a shellfish supper-house, she was very civil, and directed him to the cigar divan[5] on the other side of the street.

Mr Harding had not a much correcter notion of a cigar divan than he had of a London dinner-house, but he was desperately in want of rest, and went as he was directed. He thought he must have made some mistake when he found himself in a cigar shop, but the man behind the counter saw immediately that he was a stranger, and understood what he wanted. 'One shilling, sir – thank ye, sir – cigar, sir? – ticket for coffee, sir – you'll only have to call the waiter. Up those stairs, if you please, sir. Better take the cigar, sir – you can always give it to a friend you know. Well, sir, thank ye, sir – as you are so good, I'll smoke it myself.' And so Mr Harding ascended to the divan, with his ticket for coffee, but minus the cigar.

The place seemed much more suitable to his requirements than the room in which he had dined: there was, to be sure, a strong smell of tobacco, to which he was not accustomed; but after the shellfish, the tobacco did not seem disagreeable. There were quantities of books, and long rows of sofas. What on earth could be more luxurious than a sofa, a book, and a cup of coffee? An old waiter came up to him, with a couple of magazines and an evening paper. Was ever anything so civil? Would he have a cup of coffee, or would he prefer sherbet? Sherbet![6] Was he absolutely in an Eastern divan, with the slight addition of all the London periodicals? He had, however, an idea that sherbet should be drunk sitting cross-legged, and as he was not quite up to this, he ordered the coffee.

The coffee came, and was unexceptionable. Why, this divan was a paradise! The civil old waiter suggested to him a game of chess: though a chess-player he was not equal to this, so he declined, and, putting up his weary legs on the sofa, leisurely sipped his coffee, and turned over the pages of his *Blackwood*.⁷ He might have been so engaged for about an hour, for the old waiter enticed him to a second cup of coffee, when a musical clock began to play. Mr Harding then closed his magazine, keeping his place with his finger, and lay, listening with closed eyes to the clock. Soon the clock seemed to turn into a violoncello, with piano accompaniments, and Mr Harding began to fancy the old waiter was the Bishop of Barchester; he was inexpressibly shocked that the bishop should have brought him his coffee with his own hands; then Dr Grantly came in, with a basket full of lobsters, which he would not be induced to leave downstairs in the kitchen; and then the warden couldn't quite understand why so many people would smoke in the bishop's drawing-room; and so he fell fast asleep, and his dreams wandered away to his accustomed stall in Barchester Cathedral, and the twelve old men he was so soon about to leave for ever.

He was fatigued, and slept soundly for some time. Some sudden stop in the musical clock woke him at length, and he jumped up with a start, surprised to find the room quite full; it had been nearly empty when his nap began. With nervous anxiety he pulled out his watch, and found that it was half-past nine. He seized his hat, and, hurrying downstairs, started at a rapid pace for Lincoln's Inn.

It still wanted twenty minutes to ten when the warden found himself at the bottom of Sir Abraham's stairs, so he walked leisurely up and down the quiet inn to cool himself. It was a beautiful evening at the end of August. He had recovered from his fatigue; his sleep and the coffee had refreshed him, and he was surprised to find that he was absolutely enjoying himself, when the inn clock struck ten. The sound was hardly over before he knocked at Sir Abraham's door, and was informed by the clerk who received him that the great man would be with him immediately.

CHAPTER 17

Sir Abraham Haphazard

MR HARDING was shown into a comfortable inner sitting-room, looking more like a gentleman's bookroom than a lawyer's chambers, and there waited for Sir Abraham. Nor was he kept waiting long: in ten or fifteen minutes he heard a clatter of voices speaking quickly in the passage, and then the attorney-general entered.

'Very sorry to keep you waiting, Mr Warden,' said Sir Abraham, shaking hands with him; 'and sorry, too, to name so disagreeable an hour; but your notice was short, and as you said today, I named the very earliest hour that was not disposed of.'

Mr Harding assured him that he was aware that it was he that should apologize.

Sir Abraham was a tall thin man, with hair prematurely grey, but bearing no other sign of age; he had a slight stoop, in his neck rather than his back, acquired by his constant habit of leaning forward as he addressed his various audiences. He might be fifty years old, and would have looked young for his age, had not constant work hardened his features, and given him the appearance of a machine with a mind. His face was full of intellect, but devoid of natural expression. You would say he was a man to use, and then have done with; a man to be sought for on great emergencies, but ill adapted for ordinary services; a man whom you would ask to defend your property, but to whom you would be sorry to confide your love. He was bright as a diamond, and as cutting, and also as unimpressionable. He knew everyone whom to know was an honour, but he was without a friend; he wanted none, however, and knew not the meaning of the word in other than its parliamentary sense. A friend! Had he not always been sufficient to himself, and now, at fifty, was it likely that he should trust another? He was married, indeed, and had children, but what time had he for the soft idleness of conjugal felicity? His working days or term-times were occupied from his time of rising to the late hour at which he went to rest, and even his vacations were more full of labour than the busiest days of other men. He never quarrelled with his wife, but he never talked to her – he never had time to talk, he was so taken up with speaking. She, poor lady, was not unhappy; she had all that money could give her, she would probably live to be a peeress, and she really thought Sir Abraham the best of husbands.

Sir Abraham was a man of wit, and sparkled among the brightest at the dinner-tables of political grandees; indeed, he always sparkled; whether in society, in the House of Commons, or the courts of law, coruscations flew from him; glittering sparkles, as from hot steel, but no heat; no cold heart was ever cheered by warmth from him, no unhappy soul ever dropped a portion of its burden at his door.

With him success alone was praiseworthy, and he knew none so successful as himself. No one had thrust him forward; no powerful friends had pushed him along on his road to power. No, he was attorney-general, and would, in all human probability, be Lord Chancellor[1] by sheer dint of his own industry and his own talent. Who else in all the world rose so high with so little help? A premier, indeed! Who had ever been premier without mighty friends? An archbishop! Yes, the son or grandson of a great noble, or else, probably, his tutor. But he, Sir Abraham, had had no mighty lord at his back; his father had been a country apothecary, his mother a farmer's daughter. Why should he respect any but himself? And so he glitters along through the world, the brightest among the bright; and when his glitter is gone, and he is gathered to his fathers, no eye will be dim with a tear, no heart will mourn for its lost friend.

'And so, Mr Warden,' said Sir Abraham, 'all our trouble about this lawsuit is at an end.'

Mr Harding said he hoped so, but he didn't at all understand what Sir Abraham meant. Sir Abraham, with all his sharpness, could not have looked into his heart and read his intentions.

'All over. You need trouble yourself no further about it; of course they must pay the costs, and the absolute expense to you and Dr Grantly will be trifling – that is, compared with what it might have been if it had been continued.'

'I fear I don't quite understand you, Sir Abraham.'

'Don't you know that their attorneys have noticed us that they have withdrawn the suit?'

Mr Harding explained to the lawyer that he knew nothing of this, although he had heard in a roundabout way that such an intention had been talked of; and he also at length succeeded in making Sir Abraham understand that even this did not satisfy him. The attorney-general stood up, put his hands into his breeches' pockets, and raised his eyebrows, as Mr Harding proceeded to detail the grievance from which he now wished to rid himself.

'I know I have no right to trouble you personally with this matter, but as it is of most vital importance to me, as all my happiness is concerned in it, I thought I might venture to seek your own advice.'

Sir Abraham bowed, and declared his clients were entitled to the best advice he could give them; particularly a client so respectable in every way as the Warden of Barchester Hospital.

'A spoken word, Sir Abraham, is often of more value than volumes of written advice. The truth is, I am ill satisfied with this matter as it stands at present. I do see – I cannot help seeing, that the affairs of the hospital are not arranged according to the will of the founder.'

'None of such institutions are, Mr Harding, nor can they be; the altered circumstances in which we live do not admit of it.'

'Quite true – that is quite true; but I can't see that those altered circumstances give me a right to eight hundred a year. I don't know whether I ever read John Hiram's will, but were I to read it now I could not understand it. What I want you, Sir Abraham, to tell me, is this – am I, as warden, legally and distinctly entitled to the proceeds of the property, after the due maintenance of the twelve bedesmen?'

Sir Abraham declared that he couldn't exactly say in so many words that Mr Harding was legally entitled to, etc., etc., etc., and ended in expressing a strong opinion that it would be madness to raise any further question on the matter, as the suit was to be – nay, was, abandoned.

Mr Harding, seated in his chair, began to play a slow tune on an imaginary violoncello.

'Nay, my dear sir,' continued the attorney-general, 'there is no further ground for any question; I don't see that you have the power of raising it.'

'I can resign,' said Mr Harding, slowly playing away with his right hand, as though the bow were beneath the chair in which he was sitting.

'What! throw it up altogether?' said the attorney-general, gazing with utter astonishment at his client.

'Did you see those articles in the *Jupiter?*' said Mr Harding, piteously, appealing to the sympathy of the lawyer.

Sir Abraham said he had seen them. This poor little clergyman, cowed into such an act of extreme weakness by a newspaper article, was to Sir Abraham so contemptible an object, that he hardly knew how to talk to him as to a rational being.

'Hadn't you better wait,' said he, 'till Dr Grantly is in town with you? Wouldn't it be better to postpone any serious step till you can consult with him?'

Mr Harding declared vehemently that he could not wait, and Sir Abraham began seriously to doubt his sanity.

'Of course,' said the latter, 'if you have private means sufficient for your wants, and if this –'

'I haven't a sixpence, Sir Abraham,' said the warden.

'God bless me! Why, Mr Harding, how do you mean to live?'

Mr Harding proceeded to explain to the man of law that he meant to keep his precentorship – that was eighty pounds a year; and, also, that he meant to fall back upon his own little living of Crabtree, which was another eighty pounds. That, to be sure, the duties of the two were hardly compatible; but perhaps he might effect an exchange. And then, recollecting that the attorney-general would hardly care to hear how the service of a cathedral church is divided among the minor canons, stopped short in his explanations.

Sir Abraham listened in pitying wonder. 'I really think, Mr Harding, you had better wait for the archdeacon. This is a most serious step: one for which, in my opinion, there is not the slightest necessity; and, as you have done me the honour of asking my advice, I must implore you to do nothing without the approval of your friends. A man is never the best judge of his own position.'

'A man is the best judge of what he feels himself. I'd sooner beg my bread till my death than read such another article as those two that have appeared, and feel, as I do, that the writer has truth on his side.'

'Have you not a daughter, Mr Harding – an unmarried daughter?'

'I have,' said he, now standing also, but still playing away on his fiddle with his hand behind his back. 'I have, Sir Abraham; and she and I are completely agreed on this subject.'

'Pray excuse me, Mr Harding, if what I say seems impertinent: but surely it is you that should be prudent on her behalf. She is young, and does not know the meaning of living on an income of a hundred and fifty pounds a year. On her account give up this idea. Believe me, it is sheer Quixotism.'[2]

The warden walked away to the window, and then back to his chair; and then, irresolute what to say, took another turn to the window. The attorney-general was really extremely patient, but he was beginning to think that the interview had been long enough.

'But if this income be not justly mine, what if she and I have both to beg?' said the warden at last, sharply, and in a voice so different from that he had hitherto used, that Sir Abraham was startled. 'If so, it would be better to beg.'

'My dear sir, nobody now questions its justness.'

'Yes, Sir Abraham, one does question it – the most important of all witnesses against me – I question it myself. My God knows whether or no I love my daughter; but I would sooner that she and I should both beg, than that she should live in comfort on money which is truly the property of the poor. It may seem strange to you, Sir Abraham, it is strange to myself, that I should have been ten years in that happy home, and not have thought of these things, till they were so roughly dinned into my ears. I cannot boast of my conscience, when it required the violence of a public newspaper to awaken it; but, now that it is awake, I must obey it. When I came here I did not know that the suit was withdrawn by Mr Bold, and my object was to beg you to abandon my defence. As there is no action, there can be no defence; but it is, at any rate, as well that you should know that, from tomorrow, I shall cease to be the warden of the hospital. My friends and I differ on this subject, Sir Abraham, and that adds much to my sorrow: but it cannot be helped.' And, as he finished what he had to say, he played up such a tune as never before had graced the chambers of any attorney-general. He was standing up, gallantly fronting Sir Abraham, and his right arm passed with bold and rapid sweeps before him, as though he were embracing some huge instrument, which allowed him to stand thus erect; and with the fingers of his left hand he stopped, with preternatural velocity, a multitude of strings, which ranged from the top of his collar to the bottom of the lappet of his coat. Sir Abraham listened and looked in wonder. As he had never before seen Mr Harding, the meaning of these wild gesticulations was lost upon him; but he perceived that the gentleman who had a few minutes since been so subdued as to be unable to speak without hesitation, was now impassioned – nay, almost violent.

'You'll sleep on this, Mr Harding, and tomorrow –'

'I have done more than sleep on it,' said the warden; 'I have laid awake upon it, and that night after night. I found I could not sleep upon it; now I hope to do so.'

The attorney-general had no answer to make to this; so he expressed a quiet hope that whatever settlement was finally made would be satisfactory; and Mr Harding withdrew, thanking the great man for his kind attention.

Mr Harding was sufficiently satisfied with the interview to feel a glow of comfort as he descended into the small old square of Lincoln's Inn. It was a calm, bright, beautiful night, and by the light of the moon, even the chapel of Lincoln's Inn, and the sombre row of chambers, which surround the quadrangle, looked well. He stood still a moment to collect his thoughts; and reflect on what he had done, and was about to do. He knew that the attorney-general regarded him as little better than a fool, but that he did not mind; he and the attorney-general had not much in common between them; he knew also that others, whom he did care about, would think so too; but Eleanor, he was sure, would exult in what he had done, and the bishop, he trusted, would sympathize with him.

In the meantime he had to meet the archdeacon, and so he

walked slowly down Chancery Lane and along Fleet Street, feeling
sure that his work for the night was not yet over. When he reached
the hotel he rang the bell quietly, and with a palpitating heart; he
almost longed to escape round the corner, and delay the coming
storm by a further walk round St Paul's Churchyard, but he heard
the slow creaking shoes of the old waiter approaching, and he
stood his ground manfully.

CHAPTER 18

The Warden is Very Obstinate

'DR GRANTLY is here, sir,' greeted his ears before the door was well open, 'and Mrs Grantly; they have a sitting-room above, and are waiting up for you.'

There was something in the tone of the man's voice which seemed to indicate that even he looked upon the warden as a runaway schoolboy, just recaptured by his guardian, and that he pitied the culprit, though he could not but be horrified at the crime.

The warden endeavoured to appear unconcerned, as he said, 'Oh, indeed! I'll go upstairs at once'; but he failed signally: there was, perhaps, a ray of comfort in the presence of his married daughter; that is to say, of comparative comfort, seeing that his son-in-law was there: but how much would he have preferred that they should both have been safe at Plumstead Episcopi! However, upstairs he went, the waiter slowly preceding him; and on the door being opened the archdeacon was discovered standing in the middle of the room, erect, indeed, as usual, but oh! how sorrowful! and on a dingy sofa behind him reclined his patient wife.

'Papa, I thought you were never coming back,' said the lady; 'it's twelve o'clock.'

'Yes, my dear,' said the warden. 'The attorney-general named ten for my meeting; to be sure ten is late, but what could I do, you know? Great men will have their own way.'

And he gave his daughter a kiss, and shook hands with the doctor, and again tried to look unconcerned.

'And you have absolutely been with the attorney-general?' asked the archdeacon.

Mr Harding signified that he had.

'Good heavens, how unfortunate!' And the archdeacon raised his huge hands in the manner in which his friends are so accustomed to see him express disapprobation and astonishment. 'What will Sir Abraham think of it? Did you not know that it is not customary for clients to go direct to their counsel?'

'Isn't it!' asked the warden, innocently. 'Well, at any rate, I've done it now. Sir Abraham didn't seem to think it so very strange.'

The archdeacon gave a sigh that would have moved a man-of-war.

'But, papa, what did you say to Sir Abraham?' asked the lady.

'I asked him, my dear, to explain John Hiram's will to me. He couldn't explain it in the only way which would have satisfied me, and so I resigned the wardenship.'

'Resigned it!' said the archdeacon, in a solemn voice, sad and low, but yet sufficiently audible; a sort of whisper that Macready[1] would have envied, and the galleries have applauded with a couple of rounds. 'Resigned it! Good heavens!' and the dignitary of the Church sank back horrified into a horse-hair armchair.

'At least I told Sir Abraham that I would resign; and of course I must now do so.'

'Not at all,' said the archdeacon, catching a ray of hope. 'Nothing that you say in such a way to your own counsel can be in any way binding on you; of course you were there to ask his advice. I'm sure, Sir Abraham did not advise any such step.'

Mr Harding could not say that he had.

'I am sure he disadvised you from it,' continued the reverend cross-examiner.

Mr Harding could not deny this.

'I'm sure Sir Abraham must have advised you to consult your friends.'

To this proposition also Mr Harding was obliged to assent.

'Then your threat of resignation amounts to nothing, and we are just where we were before.'

Mr Harding was now standing on the rug, moving uneasily from one foot to the other. He made no distinct answer to the archdeacon's last proposition, for his mind was chiefly engaged on thinking how he could escape to bed. That his resignation was a thing finally fixed on, a fact all but completed, was not in his mind a matter of any doubt; he knew his own weakness; he knew how prone he was to be led; but he was not weak enough to give way now, to go back from the position to which his conscience had driven him, after having purposely come to London to declare his determination: he did not in the least doubt his resolution, but he greatly doubted his power of defending it against his son-in-law.

'You must be very tired, Susan,' said he: 'wouldn't you like to go to bed?'

But Susan didn't want to go till her husband went – she had an idea that her papa might be bullied if she were away: she wasn't tired at all, or at least she said so.

The archdeacon was pacing the room, expressing, by certain noddles of his head, his opinion of the utter fatuity of his father-in-law.

'Why,' at last he said – and angels might have blushed at the rebuke expressed in his tone and emphasis – 'why did you go off from Barchester so suddenly? Why did you take such a step without giving us notice, after what had passed at the palace?'

The warden hung his head, and made no reply: he could not condescend to say that he had not intended to give his son-in-law the slip; and as he had not the courage to avow it, he said nothing.

'Papa has been too much for you,' said the lady.

The archdeacon took another turn, and again ejaculated, 'Good heavens!' this time in a very low whisper, but still audible.

'I think I'll go to bed,' said the warden, taking up a side candle.

'At any rate you'll promise me to take no further step without consultation,' said the archdeacon. Mr Harding made no answer, but slowly proceeded to light his candle. 'Of course,' continued the other, 'such a declaration as that you made to Sir Abraham means nothing. Come, warden, promise me this. The whole affair, you see, is already settled, and that with very little trouble or expense. Bold has been compelled to abandon his action, and all you have to do is to remain quiet at the hospital.' Mr Harding still made no reply, but looked meekly into his son-in-law's face. The archdeacon thought he knew his father-in-law, but he was mistaken; he thought that he had already talked over a vacillating man to resign his promise. 'Come,' said he, 'promise Susan to give up this idea of resigning the wardenship.'

The warden looked at his daughter, thinking probably at the moment that if Eleanor were contented with him, he need not so much regard his other child, and said, 'I am sure Susan will not ask me to break my word, or to do what I know to be wrong.'

'Papa,' said she, 'it would be madness in you to throw up your preferment. What are you to live on?'

'God, that feeds the young ravens,² will take care of me also,' said Mr Harding, with a smile, as though afraid of giving offence by making his reference to scripture too solemn.

'Pish!' said the archdeacon, turning away rapidly; 'if the ravens persisted in refusing the food prepared for them, they wouldn't be fed.' A clergyman generally dislikes to be met in argument by any scriptural quotation; he feels as affronted as a doctor does, when recommended by an old woman to take some favourite dose, or as a lawyer when an unprofessional man attempts to put him down by a quibble.

'I shall have the living of Crabtree,' modestly suggested the warden.

'Eighty pounds a year!' sneered the archdeacon.

'And the precentorship,' said the father-in-law.

'It goes with the wardenship,' said the son-in-law. Mr Harding was prepared to argue this point, and began to do so, but Dr Grantly stopped him. 'My dear warden,' said he, 'this is all nonsense. Eighty pounds or a hundred and sixty makes very little difference. You can't live on it – you can't ruin Eleanor's prospects for ever. In point of fact, you can't resign; the bishop wouldn't accept it; the whole thing is settled. What I now want to do is to prevent any inconvenient tittle-tattle – any more newspaper articles.'

'That's what I want, too,' said the warden.

'And to prevent that,' continued the other, 'we mustn't let any talk of resignation get abroad.'

'But I shall resign,' said the warden, very, very meekly.

'Good heavens! Susan, my dear, what can I say to him?'

'But, papa,' said Mrs Grantly, getting up, and putting her arm through that of her father, 'what is Eleanor to do if you throw away your income?'

A hot tear stood in each of the warden's eyes as he looked round upon his married daughter. Why should one sister who was so rich predict poverty for another? some such idea as this was on his mind, but he gave no utterance to it. Then he thought of the pelican feeding its young with blood from its own breast, but he gave no utterance to that either; and then of Eleanor waiting for him at home, waiting to congratulate him on the end of all his trouble.

'Think of Eleanor, papa,' said Mrs Grantly.

'I do think of her,' said her father.

'And you will not do this rash thing!' The lady was really moved beyond her usual calm composure.

'It can never be rash to do right,' said he. 'I shall certainly resign this wardenship.'

'Then, Mr Harding, there is nothing before you but ruin,' said the archdeacon, now moved beyond all endurance. 'Ruin both for you and Eleanor. How do you mean to pay the monstrous expenses of this action?'

Mrs Grantly suggested that, as the action was abandoned, the costs would not be heavy.

'Indeed they will, my dear,' continued he. 'One cannot have the attorney-general up at twelve o'clock at night for nothing – but of course your father has not thought of this.'

'I will sell my furniture,' said the warden.

'Furniture!' ejaculated the other, with a most powerful sneer.

'Come, archdeacon,' said the lady, 'we needn't mind that at present. You know you never expected papa to pay the costs.'

'Such absurdity is enough to provoke Job,'³ said the archdeacon, marching quickly up and down the room. 'Your father is like a child. Eight hundred pounds a year! – eight hundred and eighty with the house – with nothing to do. The very place for him. And to throw that up because some scoundrel writes an article in a newspaper! Well – I have done my duty. If he chooses to ruin his child I cannot help it'; and he stood still at the fireplace, and looked at himself in a dingy mirror which stood on the chimneypiece.

There was a pause for about a minute, and then the warden, finding that nothing else was coming, lighted his candle, and quietly said, 'Good night.'

'Good night, papa,' said the lady.

And so the warden retired; but, as he closed the door behind him, he heard the well-known ejaculation – slower, lower, more solemn, more ponderous than ever – 'Good heavens!'

CHAPTER 19

The Warden Resigns

THE party met the next morning at breakfast; and a very sombre affair it was – very unlike the breakfasts at Plumstead Episcopi.

There were three thin, small, dry bits of bacon, each an inch long, served up under a huge old plated cover; there were four three-cornered bits of dry toast, and four square bits of buttered toast; there was a loaf of bread, and some oily-looking butter; and on the sideboard there were the remains of a cold shoulder of mutton. The archdeacon, however, had not come up from his rectory to St Paul's Churchyard to enjoy himself, and therefore nothing was said of the scanty fare.

The guests were as sorry as the viands – hardly anything was said over the breakfast-table. The archdeacon munched his toast in ominous silence, turning over bitter thoughts in his deep mind. The warden tried to talk to his daughter, and she tried to answer him; but they both failed. There were no feelings at present in common between them. The warden was thinking only of getting back to Barchester, and calculating whether the archdeacon would expect him to wait for him; and Mrs Grantly was preparing herself for a grand attack which she was to make on her father, as agreed upon between herself and her husband during their curtain confabulation of that morning.

When the waiter had creaked out of the room with the last of the teacups, the archdeacon got up and went to the window, as though to admire the view. The room looked out on a narrow passage which runs from St Paul's Churchyard to Paternoster Row; and Dr Grantly patiently perused the names of the three shopkeepers whose doors were in view. The warden still kept his seat at the table, and examined the pattern of the tablecloth; and Mrs Grantly, seating herself on the sofa, began to knit.

After a while the warden pulled his *Bradshaw* out of his pocket, and began laboriously to consult it. There was a train for Barchester at 10 a.m. That was out of the question, for it was nearly ten already. Another at 3 p.m.; another, the night mail-train, at 9 p.m. The three o'clock train would take him home to tea, and would suit very well.

'My dear,' said he, 'I think I shall go back home at three o'clock today. I shall get home at half-past-eight. I don't think there's anything to keep me in London.'

'The archdeacon and I return by the early train tomorrow, papa; won't you wait and go back with us?'

'Why, Eleanor will expect me tonight; and I've so much to do; and —'

'Much to do!' said the archdeacon *sotto voce*;[1] but the warden heard him.

'You'd better wait for us, papa.'

'Thank ye, my dear! I think I'll go this afternoon.' The tamest animal will turn when driven too hard, and even Mr Harding was beginning to fight for his own way.

'I suppose you won't be back before three?' said the lady, addressing her husband.

'I must leave this at two,' said the warden.

'Quite out of the question,' said the archdeacon, answering his wife, and still reading the shopkeepers' names; 'I don't suppose I shall be back till five.'

There was another long pause, during which Mr Harding continued to study his *Bradshaw*.

'I must go to Cox and Cummins,' said the archdeacon at last.

'Oh, to Cox and Cummins,' said the warden. It was quite a matter of indifference to him where his son-in-law went. The names of Cox and Cummins had now no interest in his ears. What had he to do with Cox and Cummins further, having already had his suit finally adjudicated upon in a court of conscience, a judgement without power of appeal fully registered, and the matter settled so that all the lawyers in London could not disturb it. The archdeacon could go to Cox and Cummins, could remain there all day in anxious discussion; but what might be said there was no longer matter of interest to him, who was so soon to lay aside the name of Warden of Barchester Hospital.

The archdeacon took up his shining new clerical hat, and put on his black new clerical gloves, and looked heavy, respectable, decorous, and opulent, a decided clergyman of the Church of England, every inch of him. 'I suppose I shall see you at Barchester the day after tomorrow,' said he.

The warden supposed he would.

'I must once more beseech you to take no further steps till you see my father; if you owe me nothing,' and the archdeacon looked as though he thought a great deal were due to him, 'at least you owe so much to my father'; and, without waiting for a reply, Dr Grantly wended his way to Cox and Cummins.

Mrs Grantly waited till the last fall of her husband's foot was heard, as he turned out of the court into St Paul's Churchyard, and then commenced her task of talking her father over.

'Papa,' she began, 'this is a most serious business.'

'Indeed it is,' said the warden, ringing the bell.

'I greatly feel the distress of mind you must have endured.'

'I am sure you do, my dear'; and he ordered the waiter to bring him pen, ink, and paper.

'Are you going to write, papa?'

'Yes, my dear – I am going to write my resignation to the bishop.'

'Pray, pray, papa, put it off till our return – pray put it off till you have seen the bishop – dear papa! for my sake, for Eleanor's! –'

'It is for your sake and Eleanor's that I do this. I hope, at least, that my children may never have to be ashamed of their father.'

'How can you talk about shame, papa?' and she stopped while the waiter creaked in with the paper, and then slowly creaked out again; 'how can you talk about shame? you know what all your friends think about this question.'

The warden spread his paper on the table, placing it on the meagre blotting-book which the hotel afforded, and sat himself down to write.

'You won't refuse me one request, papa?' continued his daughter; 'you won't refuse to delay your letter for two short days? – two days can make no possible difference.'

'My dear,' said he naïvely, 'if I waited till I got to Barchester, I might, perhaps, be prevented.'

'But surely you would not wish to offend the bishop?' said she.

'God forbid! The bishop is not apt to take offence, and knows me too well to take in bad part anything that I may be called on to do.'

'But, papa –'

'Susan,' said he, 'my mind on this subject is made up; it is not without much repugnance that I act in opposition to the advice of such men as Sir Abraham Haphazard and the archdeacon; but in this matter I can take no advice, I cannot alter the resolution to which I have come.'

'But two days, papa –'

'No – nor can I delay it. You may add to my present unhappiness by pressing me, but you cannot change my purpose; it will be a comfort to me if you will let the matter rest'; and, dipping his pen into the inkstand, he fixed his eyes intently on the paper.

There was something in his manner which taught his daughter to perceive that he was in earnest; she had at one time ruled supreme in her father's house, but she knew that there were moments when, mild and meek as he was, he would have his way, and the present was an occasion of the sort. She returned, therefore, to her knitting, and very shortly after left the room.

The warden was now at liberty to compose his letter, and, as it was characteristic of the man, it shall be given at full length. The official letter, which, when written, seemed to him to be too formally cold to be sent alone to so dear a friend, was accompanied by a private note: and both are here inserted.

The letter of resignation ran as follows:

Chapter Hotel, St Paul's
London, August, 18—

MY LORD BISHOP,

It is with the greatest pain that I feel myself constrained to resign into your Lordship's hands the wardenship of the hospital at Barchester which you so kindly conferred upon me, now nearly twelve years since.

I need not explain the circumstances which have made this step appear necessary to me. You are aware that a question has arisen as to the right of the warden to the income which has been allotted to the wardenship; it has seemed to me that this right is not well made out, and I hesitate to incur the risk of taking an income to which my legal claim appears doubtful.

The office of precentor of the cathedral is, as your Lordship is aware, joined to that of the warden; that is to say, the precentor has for many years been the warden of the hospital; there is, however, nothing to make the junction of the two offices necessary, and, unless you or the dean and chapter object to such an arrangement, I would wish to keep the precentorship. The income of this office will now be necessary to me; indeed, I do not know why I should be ashamed to say that I should have difficulty in supporting myself without it.

Your Lordship, and such others as you may please to consult on the matter, will at once see that my resignation of the wardenship need offer not the slightest bar to its occupation by another person. I am thought in the wrong by all those whom I have consulted in the matter; I have very little but an inward and an unguided conviction of my own to bring me to this step, and I shall, indeed, be hurt to find that any slur is thrown on the preferment which your kindness bestowed on me, by my resignation of it. I, at any rate for one, shall look on any successor whom you may appoint as enjoying a clerical situation of the highest respectability, and one to which your Lordship's nomination gives an indefeasible right.

I cannot finish this official letter without again thanking your Lordship for all your great kindness, and I beg to subscribe myself

Your Lordship's most obedient servant,
SEPTIMUS HARDING,
Warden of Barchester Hospital,
and Precentor of the cathedral.

He then wrote the following private note:

MY DEAR BISHOP,

I cannot send you the accompanying official letter without a warmer expression of thanks for all your kindness than would befit a document which may to a certain degree be made public. You, I know, will understand the feeling, and, perhaps, pity the weakness which makes me resign the hospital. I am not made of calibre strong enough to withstand public attack. Were I convinced that I stood on ground perfectly firm, that I was certainly justified in taking eight hundred a year under Hiram's will, I should feel bound by duty to retain the position, however unendurable might be the nature of the assault; but, as I do not feel this conviction, I cannot believe that you will think me wrong in what I am doing.

I had at one time an idea of keeping only some moderate portion of the income; perhaps three hundred a year, and of remitting the remainder to the trustees; but it occurred to me, and I think with reason, that by so doing I should place my successors in an invidious position, and greatly damage your patronage.

My dear friend, let me have a line from you to say that you do not blame me for what I am doing, and that the officiating vicar of Crabtree Parva will be the same to you as the warden of the hospital.

I am very anxious about the precentorship; the archdeacon thinks it must go with the wardenship; I think not, and that, having it, I cannot be ousted. I will, however, be guided by you and the dean. No other duty will suit me so well, or come so much within my power of adequate performance.

I thank you from my heart for the preferment which I am now giving up, and for all your kindness, and am, dear bishop, now as always,

Yours most sincerely,

SEPTIMUS HARDING

London, August, 18—

Having written these letters and made a copy of the former one for the benefit of the archdeacon, Mr Harding, whom we must now cease to call the warden, he having designated himself so for the last time, found that it was nearly two o'clock, and that he must prepare for his journey. Yes, from this time he never again admitted the name by which he had been so familiarly known, and in which, to tell the truth, he had rejoiced. The love of titles is common to all men, and a vicar or fellow is as pleased at becoming Mr Archdeacon or Mr Provost, as a lieutenant at getting his captaincy, or a city tallow-chandler in becoming Sir John on the occasion of a Queen's visit to a new bridge. But warden he was no longer, and the name of precentor, though the office was to him so dear, confers in itself no sufficient distinction; our friend, therefore, again became Mr Harding.

Mrs Grantly had gone out; he had, therefore, no one to delay him by further entreaties to postpone his journey; he had soon arranged his bag, and paid his bill, and, leaving a note for his daughter, in which he put the copy of his official letter, he got into a cab and drove away to the station with something of triumph in his heart.

Had he not cause for triumph? Had he not been supremely successful? Had he not for the first time in his life held his own purpose against that of his son-in-law, and manfully combated against great odds – against the archdeacon's wife as well as the archdeacon? Had he not gained a great victory, and was it not fit that he should step into his cab with triumph?

He had not told Eleanor when he would return, but she was on the look out for him by every train by which he could arrive, and the pony-carriage was at the Barchester station when the train drew up at the platform.

'My dear,' said he, sitting beside her, as she steered her little vessel to one side of the road to make room for the clattering omnibus as they passed from the station into the town; 'I hope you'll be able to feel a proper degree of respect for the vicar of Crabtree.'

'Dear papa,' said she, 'I am so glad.'

There was great comfort in returning home to that pleasant house, though he was to leave it so soon, and in discussing with his daughter all that he had done, and all that he had to do. It must take some time to get out of one house into another; the curate at Crabtree could not be abolished under six months, that is, unless other provision could be made for him; and then the furniture – the most of that must be sold to pay Sir Abraham Haphazard for sitting up till twelve at night. Mr Harding was strangely ignorant as to lawyers' bills; he had no idea, from twenty pounds to two thousand, as to the sum in which he was indebted for legal assistance. True, he had called in no lawyer himself; true, he had been no consenting party to the employment of either Cox and Cummins, or Sir Abraham; he had never been consulted on such matters – the archdeacon had managed all this himself, never for a moment suspecting that Mr Harding would take upon him to end the matter in a way of his own. Had the lawyers' bills been ten thousand pounds, Mr Harding could not have helped it; but he was not on that account disposed to dispute his own liability. The question never occurred to him; but it did occur to him that he had very little money at his banker's, that he could receive nothing further from the hospital, and that the sale of the furniture was his only resource.

'Not all, papa,' said Eleanor, pleadingly.

'Not quite all, my dear,' said he; 'that is, if we can help it. We must have a little at Crabtree – but it can only be a little; we must put a bold front on it, Nelly; it isn't easy to come down from affluence to poverty.'

And so they planned their future mode of life; the father taking comfort from the reflection that his daughter would soon be freed from it, and she resolving that her father would soon have in her own house a ready means of escape from the solitude of the Crabtree vicarage.

When the archdeacon left his wife and father-in-law at the Chapter Coffee House to go to Messrs Cox and Cummins, he had no very defined idea of what he had to do when he got there. Gentlemen when at law, or in any way engaged in matters requiring legal assistance, are very apt to go to their lawyers without much absolute necessity – gentlemen when doing so, are apt to describe such attendance as quite compulsory, and very disagreeable. The lawyers, on the other hand, do not at all see the necessity, though they quite agree as to the disagreeable nature of the visit – gentlemen when so engaged are usually somewhat gravelled[2] at finding nothing to say to their learned friends; they generally talk a little politics, a little weather, ask some few foolish questions about their suit, and then withdraw, having passed half an hour in a small, dingy waiting-room, in company with some junior assistant-clerk, and ten minutes with the members of the firm; the business is then over for which the gentleman has come up to London, probably a distance of a hundred and fifty miles. To be sure he goes to the play, and dines at his friend's club, and has a bachelor's liberty and bachelor's recreation for three or four days; and he could not probably plead the desire of such gratifications as a reason to his wife for a trip to London.

Married ladies, when your husbands find they are positively obliged to attend their legal advisers, the nature of the duty to be performed is generally of this description.

The archdeacon would not have dreamt of leaving London without going to Cox and Cummins; and yet he had nothing to say to them. The game was up; he plainly saw that Mr Harding in this matter was not to be moved; his only remaining business on this head was to pay the bill and have done with it: and I think it may be taken for granted, that whatever the cause may be that takes a gentleman to a lawyer's chambers, he never goes there to pay his bill.

Dr Grantly, however, in the eyes of Messrs Cox and Cummins represented the spiritualities of the diocese of Barchester, as Mr Chadwick did the temporalities, and was, therefore, too great a man to undergo the half-hour in the clerk's room. It will not be necessary that we should listen to the notes of sorrow in which the archdeacon bewailed to Mr Cox the weakness of his father-in-law, and the end of all their hopes of triumph; nor need we repeat the various exclamations of surprise with which the mournful intelligence was received. No tragedy occurred, though Mr Cox, a short and somewhat bull-necked man, was very near a fit of apoplexy when he first attempted to ejaculate that fatal word – resign!

Over and over again did Mr Cox attempt to enforce on the archdeacon the propriety of urging on Mr Warden the madness of the deed he was about to do.

'Eight hundred a year!' said Mr Cox.

'And nothing whatever to do!' said Mr Cummins, who had joined the conference.

'No private fortune, I believe,' said Mr Cox.

'Not a shilling,' said Mr Cummins, in a very low voice, shaking his head.

'I never heard of such a case in all my experience,' said Mr Cox.

'Eight hundred a year, and as nice a house as any gentleman could wish to hang up his hat in,' said Mr Cummins.

'And an unmarried daughter, I believe,' said Mr Cox, with much moral seriousness in his tone. The archdeacon only sighed as each separate wail was uttered, and shook his head, signifying that the fatuity of some people was past belief.

'I'll tell you what he might do,' said Mr Cummins, brightening up. 'I'll tell you how you might save it – let him exchange.'

'Exchange where?' said the archdeacon.

'Exchange for a living. There's Quiverful,[3] of Puddingdale; he has twelve children, and would be delighted to get the hospital. To be sure Puddingdale is only four hundred, but that would be saving something out of the fire: Mr Harding would have a curate, and still keep three hundred or three hundred and fifty.'

The archdeacon opened his ears and listened; he really thought the scheme might do.

'The newspapers,' continued Mr Cummins, 'might hammer away at Quiverful every day for the next six months without his minding them.'

The archdeacon took up his hat, and returned to his hotel, thinking the matter over deeply: at any rate he would sound Quiverful; a man with twelve children would do much to double his income.

CHAPTER 20

Farewell

On the morning after Mr Harding's return home, he received a note from the bishop full of affection, condolence, and praise. 'Pray come to me at once,' wrote the bishop, 'that we may see what had better be done; as to the hospital, I will not say a word to dissuade you; but I don't like your going to Crabtree: at any rate, come to me at once.'

Mr Harding did go to him at once; and long and confidential was the consultation between the two old friends. There they sat together the whole long day plotting to get the better of the archdeacon, and to carry out little schemes of their own, which they knew would be opposed by the whole weight of his authority.

The bishop's first idea was that Mr Harding, if left to himself, would certainly starve – not in the figurative sense in which so many of our ladies and gentlemen do starve on incomes from one to five hundred a year; not that he would be starved as regarded dress-coats, port wine, and pocket-money; but that he would positively perish of inanition for want of bread.

'How is a man to live, when he gives up all his income?' said the bishop to himself. And then the good-natured little man began to consider how his friend might be best rescued from a death so horrid and painful.

His first proposition to Mr Harding was that they should live together at the palace. He, the bishop, positively assured Mr Harding that he wanted another resident chaplain: not a young, working chaplain, but a steady, middle-aged chaplain; one who would dine and drink a glass of wine with him, talk about the archdeacon, and poke the fire. The bishop did not positively name all these duties, but he gave Mr Harding to understand that such would be the nature of the service required.

It was not without much difficulty that Mr Harding made his friend see that this would not suit him; that he could not throw up the bishop's preferment, and then come and hang on at the bishop's table; that he could not allow people to say of him that it was an easy matter to abandon his own income, as he was able to sponge on that of another person. He succeeded, however, in explaining that the plan would not do, and then the bishop brought forward another which he had in his sleeve. He, the bishop, had in his will left certain moneys to Mr Harding's two daughters, imagining that Mr Harding would himself want no such assistance during his own lifetime. This legacy amounted to three thousand pounds each, duty free; and he now pressed it as a gift on his friend.

'The girls, you know,' said he, 'will have it just the same when you're gone – and they won't want it sooner – and as for the interest during my lifetime, it isn't worth talking about. I have more than enough.'

With much difficulty and heartfelt sorrow, Mr Harding refused also this offer. No; his wish was to support himself, however poorly – not to be supported on the charity of anyone. It was hard to make the bishop understand this; it was hard to make him comprehend that the only real favour he could confer was the continuation of his independent friendship; but at last even this was done. At any rate, thought the bishop, he will come and dine with me from time to time, and if he be absolutely starving I shall see it.

Touching the precentorship, the bishop was clearly of opinion that it could be held without the other situation – an opinion from which no one differed; and it was therefore soon settled among all the parties concerned, that Mr Harding should still be the precentor of the cathedral.

On the day following Mr Harding's return, the archdeacon reached Plumstead full of Mr Cummins's scheme regarding Puddingdale and Mr Quiverful. On the very next morning he drove over to Puddingdale, and obtained the full consent of the wretched clerical Priam who was endeavouring to feed his poor Hecuba and a dozen of Hectors[1] on the small proceeds of his ecclesiastical kingdom. Mr Quiverful had no doubts as to the legal rights of the warden; his conscience would be quite clear as to accepting the income; and as to the *Jupiter*, he begged to assure the archdeacon that he was quite indifferent to any emanations from the profane portion of the periodical press.

Having so far succeeded, he next sounded the bishop; but here he was astonished by most unexpected resistance. The bishop did not think it would do. 'Not do, why not?' and seeing that his father was not shaken, he repeated the question in a severer form: 'Why not do, my lord?'

His lordship looked very unhappy, and shuffled about in his chair, but still didn't give way; he thought Puddingdale wouldn't do for Mr Harding; it was too far from Barchester.

'Oh! of course he'll have a curate.'

The bishop also thought that Mr Quiverful wouldn't do for the hospital; such an exchange wouldn't look well at such a time; and, when pressed harder, he declared he didn't think Mr Harding would accept of Puddingdale under any circumstances.

'How is he to live?' demanded the archdeacon.

The bishop, with tears in his eyes, declared that he had not the slightest conception how life was to be sustained within him at all.

The archdeacon then left his father, and went down to the hospital; but Mr Harding wouldn't listen at all to the Puddingdale scheme. To his eyes it had no attraction; it savoured of simony,[2] and was likely to bring down upon him harder and more deserved strictures than any he had yet received: he positively declined to become vicar of Puddingdale under any circumstances.

The archdeacon waxed wroth, talked big, and looked bigger; he said something about dependence and beggary, spoke of the duty every man was under to earn his bread, made passing allusions to the follies of youth and waywardness of age, as though Mr Harding were afflicted by both, and ended by declaring that he had done. He felt that he had left no stone unturned to arrange matters on the best and easiest footing; that he had, in fact, so arranged them, that he had so managed that there was no further need of any anxiety in the matter. And how had he been paid? His advice had been systematically rejected; he had been not only slighted, but distrusted and avoided; he and his measures had been utterly thrown over, as had been Sir Abraham, who, he had reason to know, was much pained at what had occurred. He now found it was useless to interfere any further, and he should retire. If any further assistance were required from him, he would probably be called on, and should be again happy to come forward. And so he left the hospital, and has not since entered it from that day to this.

And here we must take leave of Archdeacon Grantly. We fear that he is represented in these pages as being worse than he is; but we have had to do with his foibles, and not with his virtues. We have seen only the weak side of the man, and have lacked the opportunity of bringing him forward on his strong ground. That he is a man somewhat too fond of his own way, and not sufficiently scrupulous in his manner of achieving it, his best friends cannot deny. That he is bigoted in favour, not so much of his doctrines as of his cloth, is also true: and it is true that the possession of a large income is a desire that sits near his heart. Nevertheless, the archdeacon is a gentleman and a man of conscience; he spends his money liberally, and does the work he has to do with the best of his ability; he improves the tone of society of those among whom he lives. His aspirations are of a healthy, if not of the highest, kind. Though never an austere man, he upholds propriety of conduct both by example and precept. He is generous to the poor, and hospitable to the rich; in matters of religion he is sincere, and yet no Pharisee;[3] he is in earnest, and yet no fanatic. On the whole, the Archdeacon of Barchester is a man doing more good than harm – a man to be furthered and supported, though perhaps also to be controlled; and it is matter of regret to us that the course of our narrative has required that we should see more of his weakness than his strength.

Mr Harding allowed himself no rest till everything was prepared for his departure from the hospital. It may be as well to mention that he was not driven to the stern necessity of selling all his furniture: he had been quite in earnest in his intention to do so, but it was soon made known to him that the claims of Messrs Cox and Cummins made no such step obligatory. The archdeacon had thought it wise to make use of the threat of the lawyer's bill, to frighten his father-in-law into compliance; but he had no intention to saddle Mr Harding with costs, which had been incurred by no means exclusively for his benefit. The amount of the bill was added to the diocesan account, and was, in fact, paid out of the bishop's pocket, without any consciousness on the part of his lordship. A great part of his furniture he did resolve to sell, having no other means to dispose of it; and the ponies and carriage were transferred, by private contract, to the use of an old maiden lady in the city.

For his present use Mr Harding took a lodging in Barchester, and thither were conveyed such articles as he wanted for daily use – his music, books, and instruments, his own armchair, and Eleanor's pet sofa; her teapoy and his cellaret,[4] and also the slender but still sufficient contents of his wine-cellar. Mrs Grantly had much wished that her sister would reside at Plumstead, till her father's house at Crabtree should be ready for her; but Eleanor herself strongly resisted this proposal. It was in vain urged upon her that a lady in lodgings costs more than a gentleman; and that, under her father's present circumstances, such an expense should be avoided. Eleanor had not pressed her father to give up the hospital, in order that she might live at Plumstead Rectory, and he alone in his Barchester lodgings; nor did Eleanor think that she would be treating a certain gentleman very fairly, if she betook herself to the house which he would be the least desirous of entering of any in the county. So she got a little bedroom for herself behind the sitting-room, and just over the little back parlour of the chemist, with whom they were to lodge. There was somewhat of a savour of senna softened by peppermint about the place; but, on the whole, the lodgings were clean and comfortable.

The day had been fixed for the migration of the ex-warden, and all Barchester were in a state of excitement on the subject. Opinion was much divided as to the propriety of Mr Harding's conduct. The mercantile part of the community, the mayor and corporation, and council, also most of the ladies, were loud in his praise. Nothing could be more noble, nothing more generous, nothing more upright. But the gentry were of a different way of thinking – especially the lawyers and the clergymen. They said such conduct was very weak and undignified; that Mr Harding evinced a lamentable want of *esprit de corps*,[5] as well as courage; and that such an abdication must do much harm, and could do but little good.

On the evening before he left, he summoned all the bedesmen into his parlour to wish them good-bye. With Bunce he had been in frequent communication since his return from London, and had been at much pains to explain to the old man the cause of his resignation, without in any way prejudicing the position of his successor. The others, also, he had seen more or less frequently; and had heard from most of them separately some expression of regret at his departure; but he had postponed his farewell till the last evening.

He now bade the maid put wine and glasses on the table; and had the chairs arranged around the room; and sent Bunce to each of the men to request they would come and say farewell to their late warden. Soon the noise of aged scuffling feet was heard upon the gravel and in the little hall, and the eleven men who were enabled to leave their rooms were assembled.

'Come in, my friends, come in,' said the warden – he was still warden then. 'Come in, and sit down'; and he took the hand of Abel Handy, who was the nearest to him, and led the limping grumbler to a chair. The others followed slowly and bashfully: the infirm, the lame, and the blind; poor wretches! who had been so happy, had they but known it! Now their aged faces were covered with shame, and every kind word from their master was a coal of fire burning on their heads.

When first the news had reached them that Mr Harding was going to leave the hospital, it had been received with a kind of triumph – his departure was, as it were, a prelude to success. He had admitted his want of right to the money about which they were disputing; and as it did not belong to him, of course it did to them. The one hundred a year to each of them was actually becoming a reality; and Abel Handy was a hero, and Bunce a faint-hearted sycophant, worthy neither honour nor fellowship. But other tidings soon made their way into the old men's rooms. It was first notified to them that the income abandoned by Mr Harding would not come to them; and these accounts were confirmed by attorney Finney. They were then informed that Mr Harding's place would be at once filled by another. That the new warden could not be a kinder man they all knew; that he would be a less friendly one most suspected; and then came the bitter information that, from the moment of Mr Harding's departure, the twopence a day, his own peculiar gift, must of necessity be with-drawn.

And this was to be the end of all their mighty struggle – of their fight for their rights – of their petition, and their debates, and their hopes! They were to change the best of masters for a possible bad one, and to lose twopence a day each man! No; unfortunate as this was, it was not the worst, or nearly the worst, as will just now be seen.

'Sit down, sit down, my friends,' said the warden. 'I want to say a word to you, and to drink your healths, before I leave you. Come up here, Moody, here is a chair for you; come, Jonathan Crumple –' and by degrees he got the men to be seated. It was not surprising that they should hang back with faint hearts, having returned so much kindness with such deep ingratitude. Last of all of them came Bunce, and with sorrowful mien and slow step got into his accustomed seat near the fireplace.

When they were all in their places, Mr Harding rose to address them; and then finding himself not quite at home on his legs, he sat down again. 'My dear old friends,' said he, 'you all know that I am going to leave you.'

There was a sort of murmur ran round the room, intended, perhaps, to express regret at his departure; but it was but a murmur, and might have meant that or anything else.

'There has been lately some misunderstanding between us. You have thought, I believe, that you did not get all that you were entitled to, and that the funds of the hospital have not been properly disposed of. As for me, I cannot say what should be the disposition of these moneys, or how they should be managed, and I have therefore thought it best to go.'

'We never wanted to drive your reverence out of it,' said Handy.

'No, indeed, your reverence,' said Skulpit. 'We never thought it would come to this. When I signed the petition – that is, I didn't sign it, because –'

'Let his reverence speak, can't you?' said Moody.

'No,' continued Mr Harding; 'I am sure you did not wish to turn me out; but I thought it best to leave you. I am not a very good hand at a lawsuit, as you may all guess; and when it seemed necessary that our ordinary quiet mode of living should be disturbed, I thought it better to go. I am neither angry nor offended with any man in the hospital.'

Here Bunce uttered a kind of groan, very clearly expressive of disagreement.

'I am neither angry nor displeased with any man in the hospital,' repeated Mr Harding emphatically. 'If any man has been wrong – and I don't say any man has – he has erred through wrong advice. In this country all are entitled to look for their own rights, and you have done no more. As long as your interests and my interests were at variance, I could give you no counsel on this subject; but the connection between us has ceased; my income can no longer depend on your doings, and therefore, as I leave you, I venture to offer to you my advice.'

The men all declared that they would from henceforth be entirely guided by Mr Harding's opinion in their affairs.

'Some gentleman will probably take my place here very soon, and I strongly advise you to be prepared to receive him in a kindly spirit, and to raise no further question among yourselves as to the amount of his income. Were you to succeed in lessening what he has to receive, you would not increase your own allowance. The surplus would not go to you; your wants are adequately provided for, and your position could hardly be improved.'

'God bless your reverence, we knows it,' said Spriggs.

'It's all true, your reverence,' said Skulpit; 'we sees it all now.'

'Yes, Mr Harding,' said Bunce, opening his mouth for the first time; 'I believe they do understand it now, now that they've driven from under the same roof with them such a master as not one of them will ever know again – now that they're like to be in sore want of a friend.'

'Come, come, Bunce,' said Mr Harding, blowing his nose, and manoeuvring to wipe his eyes at the same time.

'Oh, as to that,' said Handy, 'we none of us never wanted to do Mr Harding no harm; if he's going now, it's not along of us; and I don't see for what Mr Bunce speaks up agen us that way.'

'You've ruined yourselves, and you've ruined me too, and that's why,' said Bunce.

'Nonsense, Bunce,' said Mr Harding; 'there's nobody ruined at all. I hope you'll let me leave you all friends, I hope you'll all drink a glass of wine in friendly feeling with me and with one another. You'll have a good friend, I don't doubt, in your new warden; and if ever you want any other, why after all I'm not going so far off but that I shall sometimes see you'; and then, having finished his speech, Mr Harding filled all the glasses, and himself handed each a glass to the men round him, and raising his own, said –

'God bless you all! you have my heartfelt wishes for your welfare. I hope you may live contented, and die trusting in the Lord Jesus Christ, and thankful to Almighty God for the good things he has given you. God bless you, my friends!' and Mr Harding drank his wine.

Another murmur, somewhat more articulate than the first, passed round the circle, and this time it was intended to imply a blessing on Mr Harding. It had, however, but little cordiality in it. Poor old men! how could they be cordial with their sore consciences and shamed faces? how could they bid God bless him with hearty voices and a true benison, knowing, as they did, that their vile cabal had driven him from his happy home. and sent him in his old age to seek shelter under a strange roof-tree? They did their best, however; they drank their wine, and withdrew.

As they left the hall door, Mr Harding shook hands with each of the men, and spoke a kind word to them about their individual cases and ailments; and so they departed, answering his questions in the fewest words, and retreated to their dens, a sorrowful repentant crew.

All but Bunce, who still remained to make his own farewell. 'There's poor old Bell,' said Mr Harding, 'I mustn't go without saying a word to him; come through with me, Bunce, and bring the wine with you'; and so they went through to the men's cottages, and found the old man propped up as usual in his bed.

'I've come to say good-bye to you, Bell,' said Mr Harding, speaking loud, for the old man was deaf.

'And are you going away, then, really?' asked Bell.

'Indeed I am, and I've brought you a glass of wine; so that we may part friends, as we lived, you know.'

The old man took the proffered glass in his shaking hands, and drank it eagerly. 'God bless you, Bell!' said Mr Harding; 'good-bye, my old friend.'

'And so you're really going?' the man again asked.

'Indeed I am, Bell.'

The poor old bedridden creature still kept Mr Harding's hand in his own, and the warden thought that he had met with something like warmth of feeling in the one of all his subjects from whom it was the least likely to be expected, for poor old Bell had nearly outlived all human feelings. 'And your reverence,' said he, and then he paused, while his old palsied head shook horribly, and his shrivelled cheeks sank lower within his jaws, and his glazy eye gleamed with a momentary light; 'and, your reverence, shall we get the hundred a year then?'

How gently did Mr Harding try to extinguish the false hope of money which had been so wretchedly raised to disturb the quiet of the dying man! One other week and his mortal coil would be shuffled off;⁶ in one short week would God resume his soul, and set it apart for its irrevocable doom; seven more tedious days and nights of senseless inactivity, and all would be over for poor Bell in this world; and yet, with his last audible words, he was demanding his moneyed rights, and asserting himself to be the proper heir of John Hiram's bounty! Not on him, poor sinner as he was, be the load of such sin!

Mr Harding returned to his parlour, meditating with a sick heart on what he had seen, and Bunce with him. We will not describe the parting of these two good men, for good men they were. It was in vain that the late warden endeavoured to comfort the heart of the old bedesman; poor old Bunce felt that his days of comfort were gone. The hospital had to him been a happy home, but it could be so no longer. He had had honour there, and friendship; he had recognized his master, and been recognized; all his wants, both of soul and body, had been supplied, and he had been a happy man. He wept grievously as he parted from his friend, and the tears of an old man are bitter. 'It is all over for me in this world,' said he, as he gave the last squeeze to Mr Harding's hand; 'I have now to forgive those who have injured me – and to die.'

And so the old man went out, and then Mr Harding gave way to his grief, and he too wept aloud.

CHAPTER 21

Conclusion

OUR tale is now done, and it only remains to us to collect the scattered threads of our little story, and to tie them into a seemly knot. This will not be a work of labour, either to the author or to his readers; we have not to deal with many personages, or with stirring events, and were it not for the custom of the thing, we might leave it to the imagination of all concerned to conceive how affairs at Barchester arranged themselves.

On the morning after the day last alluded to, Mr Harding, at an early hour, walked out of the hospital, with his daughter under his arm, and sat down quietly to breakfast at his lodgings over the chemist's shop. There was no parade about his departure; no one, not even Bunce, was there to witness it: had he walked to the apothecary's thus early to get a piece of court plaster,[1] or a box of lozenges, he could not have done it with less appearance of an important movement. There was a tear in Eleanor's eye as she passed through the big gateway and over the bridge; but Mr Harding walked with an elastic step, and entered his new abode with a pleasant face.

'Now, my dear,' said he, 'you have everything ready, and you can make tea here just as nicely as in the parlour at the hospital.' So Eleanor took off her bonnet and made the tea. After this manner did the late Warden of Barchester Hospital accomplish his flitting, and change his residence.

It was not long before the archdeacon brought his father to discuss the subject of a new warden. Of course he looked upon the nomination as his own, and he had in his eye three or four fitting candidates, seeing that Mr Cummins's plan as to the living of Puddingdale could not be brought to bear. How can I describe the astonishment which confounded him, when his father declared that he would appoint no successor to Mr Harding? 'If we can get the matter set to rights, Mr Harding will return.' said the bishop;

'and if we cannot, it will be wrong to put any other gentleman into so cruel a position.'

It was in vain that the archdeacon argued and lectured, and even threatened; in vain he my-lorded his poor father in his sternest manner; in vain his 'good heavens!' were ejaculated in a tone that might have moved a whole synod, let alone one weak and aged bishop. Nothing would induce his father to fill up the vacancy caused by Mr Harding's retirement.

Even John Bold would have pitied the feelings with which the archdeacon returned to Plumstead: the Church was falling, nay, already in ruins; its dignitaries were yielding without a struggle before the blows of its antagonists; and one of its most respected bishops, his own father – the man considered by all the world as being in such matters under his, Dr Grantly's control – had positively resolved to capitulate, and own himself vanquished!

And how fared the hospital under this resolve of its visitor? Badly indeed. It is now some years since Mr Harding left it, and the warden's house is still tenantless. Old Bell has died, and Billy Gazy; the one-eyed Spriggs has drunk himself to death, and three others of the twelve have been gathered into the churchyard mould. Six have gone, and the six vacancies remain unfilled! Yes, six have died, with no kind friend to solace their last moments, with no wealthy neighbour to administer comforts and ease the stings of death. Mr Harding, indeed, did not desert them; from him they had such consolation as a dying man may receive from his Christian pastor; but it was the occasional kindness of a stranger which ministered to them, and not the constant presence of a master, a neighbour, and a friend.

Nor were those who remained better off than those who died. Dissensions rose among them, and contests for pre-eminence; and then they began to understand that soon one among them would be the last – some one wretched being would be alone there in that now comfortless hospital – the miserable relic of what had once been so good and comfortable.

The building of the hospital itself has not been allowed to go to ruins. Mr Chadwick, who still holds his stewardship, and pays the accruing rents into an account opened at a bank for the purpose, sees to that; but the whole place has become disordered and ugly.

The warden's garden is a wretched wilderness, the drive and paths are covered with weeds, the flowerbeds are bare, and the unshorn lawn is now a mass of long damp grass and unwholesome moss. The beauty of the place is gone; its attractions have withered. Alas! a very few years since it was the prettiest spot in Barchester, and now it is a disgrace to the city.

Mr Harding did not go out to Crabtree Parva. An arrangement was made which respected the homestead of Mr Smith and his happy family, and put Mr Harding into possession of a small living within the walls of the city. It is the smallest possible parish, containing a part of the Cathedral Close and a few old houses adjoining. The church is a singular little Gothic building, perched over a gateway, through which the Close is entered, and is approached by a flight of stone steps which leads down under the archway of the gate. It is no bigger than an ordinary room – perhaps twenty-seven feet long by eighteen wide – but still it is a perfect church.[2] It contains an old carved pulpit and reading-desk, a tiny altar under a window filled with dark old-coloured glass, a font, some half-dozen pews, and perhaps a dozen seats for the poor, and also a vestry. The roof is high-pitched, and of black old oak, and the three large beams which support it run down to the side walls, and terminate in grotesquely carved faces – two devils and an angel on one side, two angels and a devil on the other. Such is the church of St Cuthbert at Barchester, of which Mr Harding became rector, with a clear income of seventy-five pounds a year.

Here he performs afternoon service every Sunday, and administers the Sacrament once in every three months. His audience is not large; and, had they been so, he could not have accommodated them: but enough come to fill his six pews, and on the front seat of those devoted to the poor is always to be seen our old friend Mr Bunce, decently arrayed in his bedesman's gown.

Mr Harding is still precentor of Barchester; and it is very rarely the case that those who attend the Sunday morning service miss the gratification of hearing him chant the litany, as no other man in England can do it. He is neither a discontented nor an unhappy man; he still inhabits the lodgings to which he went on leaving the hospital, but he now has them to himself. Three months after that time Eleanor became Mrs Bold, and of course removed to her husband's house.

There were some difficulties to be got over on the occasion of her marriage. The archdeacon, who could not so soon overcome his grief, would not be persuaded to grace the ceremony with his presence, but he allowed his wife and children to be there. The marriage took place at the palace, and the bishop himself officiated. It was the last occasion on which he ever did so; and, though he still lives, it is not probable that he will ever do so again.

Not long after the marriage, perhaps six months, when Eleanor's bridal-honours were fading, and persons were beginning to call her Mrs Bold without twittering, the archdeacon consented to meet John Bold at a dinner-party, and since that time they have become almost friends. The archdeacon firmly believes that his brother-in-law was, as a bachelor, an infidel, an unbeliever in the great truths of our religion; but that matrimony has opened his eyes, as it has those of others. And Bold is equally inclined to think that time has softened the asperities of the archdeacon's character. Friends though they are, they do not often revert to the feud of the hospital.

Mr Harding, we say, is not an unhappy man; he keeps his lodgings, but they are of little use to him, except as being the one spot on earth which he calls his own. His time is spent chiefly at his daughter's or at the palace; he is never left alone, even should he wish to be so; and within a twelvemonth of Eleanor's marriage his determination to live at his own lodging had been so far broken through and abandoned, that he consented to have his violoncello permanently removed to his daughter's house.

Every other day a message is brought to him from the bishop. 'The bishop's compliments, and his lordship is not very well today, and he hopes Mr Harding will dine with him.' This bulletin as to the old man's health is a myth; for though he is over eighty he is never ill, and will probably die some day, as a spark goes out, gradually and without a struggle. Mr Harding does dine with him very often, which means going to the palace at three and remaining till ten; and whenever he does not the bishop whines, and says that the port wine is corked, and complains that nobody attends to him, and frets himself off to bed an hour before his time.

It was long before the people of Barchester forgot to call Mr Harding by his long well-known name of Warden. It had become so customary to say Mr Warden, that it was not easily dropped. 'No, no,' he always says when so addressed, 'not warden now, only precentor.'

THE END

BOOK 2

Barchester Towers

BARCHESTER TOWERS

CHAPTER I

WHO WILL BE THE NEW BISHOP ?

In the latter days of July in the year 185—, a most important question was for ten days hourly asked in the cathedral city of Barchester, and answered every hour in various ways—Who was to be the new Bishop ?

The death of old Dr. Grantly, who had for many years filled that chair with meek authority, took place exactly as the ministry of Lord —— was going to give place to that of Lord ——. The illness of the good old man was long and lingering, and it became at last a matter of intense interest to those concerned whether the new appointment should be made by a conservative or liberal government.

It was pretty well understood that the out-going premier had made his selection, and that if the question rested with him, the mitre would descend on the head of Archdeacon Grantly, the old bishop's son. The archdeacon had long managed the affairs of the diocese ; and for some months previous to the demise of his father, rumour had confidently assigned to him the reversion of his father's honours.

Bishop Grantly died as he had lived, peaceably, slowly, without pain and without excitement. The breath ebbed from him almost imperceptibly, and for a month before his death, it was a question whether he were alive or dead.

A trying time was this for the archdeacon, for whom was designed the reversion of his father's see by those who then had the giving away of episcopal thrones. I would not be understood to say that the prime minister had in so many words promised the bishopric to Dr. Grantly. He was too discreet a man for that. There is a proverb with reference to the killing of cats, and those who know anything either of high or low government places, will

be well aware that a promise may be made without positive
words, and that an expectant may be put into the highest
state of encouragement, though the great man on whose
breath he hangs may have done no more than whisper
that ' Mr. So-and-so is certainly a rising man.'

Such a whisper had been made, and was known by those
who heard it to signify that the cures of the diocese of
Barchester should not be taken out of the hands of the
archdeacon. The then prime minister was all in all at
Oxford, and had lately passed a night at the house of the
master of Lazarus. Now the master of Lazarus—which
is, by the bye, in many respects the most comfortable,
as well as the richest college at Oxford,—was the archdeacon's most intimate friend and most trusted counsellor.
On the occasion of the prime minister's visit, Dr. Grantly
was of course present, and the meeting was very gracious.
On the following morning Dr. Gwynne, the master, told
the archdeacon that in his opinion the thing was settled.

At this time the bishop was quite on his last legs ; but
the ministry also were tottering. Dr. Grantly returned
from Oxford happy and elated, to resume his place in the
palace, and to continue to perform for the father the last
duties of a son ; which, to give him his due, he performed
with more tender care than was to be expected from his
usual somewhat worldly manners.

A month since the physicians had named four weeks as
the outside period during which breath could be supported
within the body of the dying man. At the end of the
month the physicians wondered, and named another
fortnight. The old man lived on wine alone, but at the
end of the fortnight he still lived ; and the tidings of the
fall of the ministry became more frequent. Sir Lamda
Mewnew and Sir Omicron Pie, the two great London
doctors, now came down for the fifth time, and declared,
shaking their learned heads, that another week of life
was impossible ; and as they sat down to lunch in the
episcopal dining-room, whispered to the archdeacon their
own private knowledge that the ministry must fall within
five days. The son returned to his father's room, and
after administering with his own hands the sustaining
modicum of madeira, sat down by the bedside to calculate
his chances.

The ministry were to be out within five days : his father was to be dead within—No, he rejected that view of the subject. The ministry were to be out, and the diocese might probably be vacant at the same period. There was much doubt as to the names of the men who were to succeed to power, and a week must elapse before a Cabinet was formed. Would not vacancies be filled by the out-going men during this week ? Dr. Grantly had a kind of idea that such would be the case, but did not know ; and then he wondered at his own ignorance on such a question.

He tried to keep his mind away from the subject, but he could not. The race was so very close, and the stakes were so very high. He then looked at the dying man's impassive, placid face. There was no sign there of death or disease ; it was something thinner than of yore, some-what grayer, and the deep lines of age more marked ; but, as far as he could judge, life might yet hang there for weeks to come. Sir Lamda Mewnew and Sir Omicron Pie had thrice been wrong, and might yet be wrong thrice again. The old bishop slept during twenty of the twenty-four hours, but during the short periods of his waking moments, he knew both his son and his dear old friend, Mr. Harding, the archdeacon's father-in-law, and would thank them tenderly for their care and love. Now he lay sleeping like a baby, resting easily on his back, his mouth just open, and his few gray hairs straggling from beneath his cap ; his breath was perfectly noiseless, and his thin, wan hand, which lay above the coverlid, never moved. Nothing could be easier than the old man's passage from this world to the next.

But by no means easy were the emotions of him who sat there watching. He knew it must be now or never. He was already over fifty, and there was little chance that his friends who were now leaving office would soon return to it. No probable British prime minister but he who was now in, he who was so soon to be out, would think of making a bishop of Dr. Grantly. Thus he thought long and sadly, in deep silence, and then gazed at that still living face, and then at last dared to ask himself whether he really longed for his father's death.

The effort was a salutary one, and the question was answered in a moment. The proud, wishful, worldly man,

sank on his knees by the bedside, and taking the bishop's
hand within his own, prayed eagerly that his sins might
be forgiven him.

His face was still buried in the clothes when the door
of the bed-room opened noiselessly, and Mr. Harding
entered with a velvet step. Mr. Harding's attendance
at that bedside had been nearly as constant as that of
the archdeacon, and his ingress and egress was as much
a matter of course as that of his son-in-law. He was
standing close beside the archdeacon before he was perceived, and would also have knelt in prayer had he not
feared that his doing so might have caused some sudden
start, and have disturbed the dying man. Dr. Grantly,
however, instantly perceived him, and rose from his knees.
As he did so Mr. Harding took both his hands, and pressed
them warmly. There was more fellowship between them
at that moment than there had ever been before, and it
so happened that after circumstances greatly preserved
the feeling. As they stood there pressing each other's
hands, the tears rolled freely down their cheeks.

' God bless you, my dears,'—said the bishop with
feeble voice as he woke—' God bless you—may God bless
you both, my dear children : ' and so he died.

There was no loud rattle in the throat, no dreadful
struggle, no palpable sign of death ; but the lower jaw
fell a little from its place, and the eyes, which had been
so constantly closed in sleep, now remained fixed and open.
Neither Mr. Harding nor Dr. Grantly knew that life was
gone, though both suspected it.

' I believe it 's all over,' said Mr. Harding, still pressing
the other's hands. ' I think—nay, I hope it is.'

' I will ring the bell,' said the other, speaking all but in
a whisper. ' Mrs. Phillips should be here.'

Mrs Phillips, the nurse, was soon in the room, and
immediately, with practised hand, closed those staring
eyes.

' It 's all over, Mrs. Phillips ? ' asked Mr. Harding.

' My lord 's no more,' said Mrs. Phillips, turning round
and curtseying low with solemn face ; ' his lordship 's gone
more like a sleeping babby than any that I ever saw.'

' It 's a great relief, archdeacon,' said Mr. Harding,
' a great relief—dear, good, excellent old man. Oh that

our last moments may be as innocent and as peaceful as his ! '

' Surely,' said Mrs. Phillips. ' The Lord be praised for all his mercies ; but, for a meek, mild, gentle-spoken Christian, his lordship was——' and Mrs. Phillips, with unaffected but easy grief, put up her white apron to her flowing eyes.

' You cannot but rejoice that it is over,' said Mr. Harding, still consoling his friend. The archdeacon's mind, however, had already travelled from the death chamber to the closet of the prime minister. He had brought himself to pray for his father's life, but now that that life was done, minutes were too precious to be lost. It was now useless to dally with the fact of the bishop's death—useless to lose perhaps everything for the pretence of a foolish sentiment.

But how was he to act while his father-in-law stood there holding his hand ? how, without appearing unfeeling, was he to forget his father in the bishop—to overlook what he had lost, and think only of what he might possibly gain ?

' No ; I suppose not,' said he, at last, in answer to Mr. Harding. ' We have all expected it so long.'

Mr. Harding took him by the arm and led him from the room. ' We will see him again to-morrow morning,' said he ; ' we had better leave the room now to the women.' And so they went down stairs.

It was already evening and nearly dark. It was most important that the prime minister should know that night that the diocese was vacant. Everything might depend on it ; and so, in answer to Mr. Harding's further consolation, the archdeacon suggested that a telegraph message should be immediately sent off to London. Mr. Harding who had really been somewhat surprised to find Dr. Grantly, as he thought, so much affected, was rather taken aback ; but he made no objection. He knew that the archdeacon had some hope of succeeding to his father's place, though he by no means knew how highly raised that hope had been.

' Yes,' said Dr. Grantly, collecting himself and shaking off his weakness, ' we must send a message at once ; we don't know what might be the consequence of delay. Will you do it ? '

' I ! oh yes ; certainly : I'll do anything, only I don't know exactly what it is you want.'

Dr. Grantly sat down before a writing table, and taking pen and ink, wrote on a slip of paper as follows :—

' By Electric Telegraph.
' For the Earl of ——, Downing Street, or elsewhere.
' " The Bishop of Barchester is dead."
' Message sent by the Rev. Septimus Harding.'

' There,' said he, ' just take that to the telegraph office at the railway station, and give it in as it is ; they'll probably make you copy it on to one of their own slips ; that 's all you'll have to do : then you'll have to pay them half-a-crown ; ' and the archdeacon put his hand in his pocket and pulled out the necessary sum.

Mr. Harding felt very much like an errand-boy, and also felt that he was called on to perform his duties as such at rather an unseemly time ; but he said nothing, and took the slip of paper and the proffered coin.

' But you've put my name into it, archdeacon.'

' Yes,' said the other, ' there should be the name of some clergyman you know, and what name so proper as that of so old a friend as yourself ? The Earl won't look at the name, you may be sure of that ; but my dear Mr. Harding, pray don't lose any time.'

Mr. Harding got as far as the library door on his way to the station, when he suddenly remembered the news with which he was fraught when he entered the poor bishop's bed-room. He had found the moment so inopportune for any mundane tidings, that he had repressed the words which were on his tongue, and immediately afterwards all recollection of the circumstance was for the time banished by the scene which had occurred.

' But, archdeacon,' said he, turning back, ' I forgot to tell you—The ministry are out.'

' Out ! ' ejaculated the archdeacon, in a tone which too plainly showed his anxiety and dismay, although under the circumstances of the moment he endeavoured to control himself : ' Out ! who told you so ? '

Mr. Harding explained that news to this effect had come down by electric telegraph, and that the tidings had been left at the palace door by Mr. Chadwick.

The archdeacon sat silent for awhile meditating, and Mr. Harding stood looking at him. 'Never mind,' said the archdeacon at last; 'send the message all the same. The news must be sent to some one, and there is at present no one else in a position to receive it. Do it at once, my dear friend; you know I would not trouble you, were I in a state to do it myself. A few minutes' time is of the greatest importance.'

Mr. Harding went out and sent the message, and it may be as well that we should follow it to its destination. Within thirty minutes of its leaving Barchester it reached the Earl of —— in his inner library. What elaborate letters, what eloquent appeals, what indignant remonstrances, he might there have to frame, at such a moment, may be conceived, but not described! How he was preparing his thunder for successful rivals, standing like a British peer with his back to the sea-coal fire, and his hands in his breeches pockets,—how his fine eye was lit up with anger, and his forehead gleamed with patriotism,—how he stamped his foot as he thought of his heavy associates,—how he all but swore as he remembered how much too clever one of them had been,—my creative readers may imagine. But was he so engaged? No: history and truth compel me to deny it. He was sitting easily in a lounging chair, conning over a Newmarket list, and by his elbow on the table was lying open an uncut French novel on which he was engaged.

He opened the cover in which the message was enclosed, and having read it, he took his pen and wrote on the back of it—

> 'For the Earl of ——,
>   'With the Earl of ——'s compliments,'

and sent it off again on its journey.

Thus terminated our unfortunate friend's chance of possessing the glories of a bishopric.

The names of many divines were given in the papers as that of the bishop elect. 'The British Grandmother' declared that Dr. Gwynne was to be the man, in compliment to the late ministry. This was a heavy blow to Dr. Grantly, but he was not doomed to see himself superseded by his friend. 'The Anglican Devotee' put forward

confidently the claims of a great London preacher of
austere doctrines; and 'The Eastern Hemisphere,' an
evening paper supposed to possess much official knowledge,
declared in favour of an eminent naturalist, a gentleman
most completely versed in the knowledge of rocks and
minerals, but supposed by many to hold on religious
subjects no special doctrines whatever. 'The Jupiter,'
that daily paper, which, as we all know, is the only true
source of infallibly correct information on all subjects,
for a while was silent, but at last spoke out. The merits
of all these candidates were discussed and somewhat
irreverently disposed of, and then 'The Jupiter' declared
that Dr. Proudie was to be the man.

Dr. Proudie was the man. Just a month after the
demise of the late bishop, Dr. Proudie kissed the Queen's
hand as his successor elect.

We must beg to be allowed to draw a curtain over the
sorrows of the archdeacon as he sat, sombre and sad at
heart, in the study of his parsonage at Plumstead Episcopi.
On the day subsequent to the despatch of the message he
heard that the Earl of —— had consented to undertake
the formation of a ministry, and from that moment he
knew that his chance was over. Many will think that
he was wicked to grieve for the loss of episcopal power,
wicked to have coveted it, nay, wicked even to have
thought about it, in the way and at the moments he had
done so.

With such censures I cannot profess that I completely
agree. The *nolo episcopari*, though still in use, is so
directly at variance with the tendency of all human
wishes, that it cannot be thought to express the true
aspirations of rising priests in the Church of England.
A lawyer does not sin in seeking to be a judge, or in com-
passing his wishes by all honest means. A young diplomate
entertains a fair ambition when he looks forward to be the
lord of a first-rate embassy; and a poor novelist when
he attempts to rival Dickens or rise above Fitzjeames,
commits no fault, though he may be foolish. Sydney
Smith truly said that in these recreant days we cannot
expect to find the majesty of St. Paul beneath the cassock
of a curate. If we look to our clergymen to be more than
men, we shall probably teach ourselves to think that they

are less, and can hardly hope to raise the character of the pastor by denying to him the right to entertain the aspirations of a man.

Our archdeacon was worldly—who among us is not so ? He was ambitious—who among us is ashamed to own that ' last infirmity of noble minds ! ' He was avaricious, my readers will say. No—it was for no love of lucre that he wished to be bishop of Barchester. He was his father's only child, and his father had left him great wealth. His preferment brought him in nearly three thousand a year. The bishopric, as cut down by the Ecclesiastical Commission, was only five. He would be a richer man as archdeacon than he could be as bishop. But he certainly did desire to play first fiddle ; he did desire to sit in full lawn sleeves among the peers of the realm ; and he did desire, if the truth must out, to be called ' My Lord ' by his reverend brethren.

His hopes, however, were they innocent or sinful, were not fated to be realised ; and Dr. Proudie was consecrated Bishop of Barchester.

CHAPTER II

HIRAM'S HOSPITAL ACCORDING TO ACT OF PARLIAMENT

It is hardly necessary that I should here give to the public any lengthened biography of Mr. Harding, up to the period of the commencement of this tale. The public cannot have forgotten how ill that sensitive gentleman bore the attack that was made on him in the columns of the Jupiter, with reference to the income which he received as warden of Hiram's Hospital, in the city of Barchester. Nor can it yet be forgotten that a law-suit was instituted against him on the matter of that charity by Mr. John Bold, who afterwards married his, Mr. Harding's, younger and then only unmarried daughter. Under pressure of these attacks, Mr. Harding had resigned his wardenship, though strongly recommended to abstain from doing so, both by his friends and by his lawyers. He did, however, resign it, and betook himself manfully to the duties of the small parish of St. Cuthbert's, in the city, of which he was vicar, continuing also to perform

those of precentor of the cathedral, a situation of small
emolument which had hitherto been supposed to be joined,
as a matter of course, to the wardenship of the Hospital
above spoken of.

When he left the hospital from which he had been so
ruthlessly driven, and settled himself down in his own
modest manner in the High Street of Barchester, he had
not expected that others would make more fuss about
it than he was inclined to do himself ; and the extent
of his hope was, that the movement might have been made
in time to prevent any further paragraphs in the Jupiter.
His affairs, however, were not allowed to subside thus
quietly, and people were quite as much inclined to talk
about the disinterested sacrifice he had made, as they had
before been to upbraid him for his cupidity.

The most remarkable thing that occurred, was the
receipt of an autograph letter from the Archbishop of
Canterbury, in which the primate very warmly praised
his conduct, and begged to know what his intentions were
for the future. Mr. Harding replied that he intended
to be rector of St. Cuthbert's, in Barchester : and so that
matter dropped. Then the newspapers took up his case,
the Jupiter among the rest, and wafted his name in
eulogistic strains through every reading-room in the nation.
It was discovered also, that he was the author of that great
musical work, Harding's Church music,—and a new
edition was spoken of, though, I believe, never printed.
It is, however, certain that the work was introduced into
the Royal Chapel at St. James's, and that a long criticism
appeared in the Musical Scrutator, declaring that in no
previous work of the kind had so much research been
joined with such exalted musical ability, and asserting
that the name of Harding would henceforward be known
wherever the Arts were cultivated, or Religion valued.

This was high praise, and I will not deny that Mr.
Harding was gratified by such flattery ; for if Mr. Harding
was vain on any subject, it was on that of music. But here
the matter rested. The second edition, if printed, was
never purchased ; the copies which had been introduced
into the Royal Chapel disappeared again, and were laid
by in peace, with a load of similar literature. Mr. Towers,
of the Jupiter, and his brethren, occupied themselves

with other names, and the undying fame promised to our
friend was clearly intended to be posthumous.

Mr. Harding had spent much of his time with his friend
the bishop, much with his daughter Mrs. Bold, now, alas,
a widow ; and had almost daily visited the wretched
remnant of his former subjects, the few surviving bedesmen
now left at Hiram's Hospital. Six of them were still
living. The number, according to old Hiram's will, should
always have been twelve. But after the abdication of their
warden, the bishop had appointed no successor to him,
no new occupants of the charity had been nominated,
and it appeared as though the hospital at Barchester
would fall into abeyance, unless the powers that be should
take some steps towards putting it once more into working
order.

During the past five years, the powers that be had not
overlooked Barchester Hospital, and sundry political
doctors had taken the matter in hand. Shortly after
Mr. Harding's resignation, the Jupiter had very clearly
shown what ought to be done. In about half a column
it had distributed the income, rebuilt the building, put
an end to all bickerings, regenerated kindly feeling, provided for Mr. Harding, and placed the whole thing on
a footing which could not but be satisfactory to the city
and Bishop of Barchester, and to the nation at large.
The wisdom of this scheme was testified by the number
of letters which ' Common Sense,' ' Veritas,' and ' One
that loves fair play ' sent to the Jupiter, all expressing
admiration, and amplifying on the details given. It is
singular enough that no adverse letter appeared at all,
and, therefore, none of course was written.

But Cassandra was not believed, and even the wisdom
of the Jupiter sometimes falls on deaf ears. Though other
plans did not put themselves forward in the columns
of the Jupiter, reformers of church charities were not
slack to make known in various places their different
nostrums for setting Hiram's Hospital on its feet again.
A learned bishop took occasion, in the Upper House,
to allude to the matter, intimating that he had communicated on the subject with his right reverend brother
of Barchester. The radical member for Staleybridge
had suggested that the funds should be alienated for the

education of the agricultural poor of the country, and he
amused the house by some anecdotes touching the supersti-
tion and habits of the agriculturists in question. A
political pamphleteer had produced a few dozen pages,
which he called ' Who are John Hiram's heirs ? ' intending
to give an infallible rule for the governance of all such
establishments ; and, at last, a member of the government
promised that in the next session a short bill should be
introduced for regulating the affairs of Barchester, and
other kindred concerns.

The next session came, and, contrary to custom, the
bill came also. Men's minds were then intent on other
things. The first threatenings of a huge war hung heavily
over the nation, and the question as to Hiram's heirs did
not appear to interest very many people either in or out
of the house. The bill, however, was read and re-read,
and in some undistinguished manner passed through its
eleven stages without appeal or dissent. What would John
Hiram have said in the matter, could he have predicted
that some forty-five gentlemen would take on themselves
to make a law altering the whole purport of his will,
without in the least knowing at the moment of their
making it, what it was that they were doing ? It is however to be hoped that the under-secretary for the Home
Office knew, for to him had the matter been confided.

The bill, however, did pass, and at the time at which
this history is supposed to commence, it had been ordained
that there should be, as heretofore, twelve old men in
Barchester Hospital, each with 1s. 4d. a day ; that there
should also be twelve old women to be located in a house
to be built, each with 1s. 2d. a day ; that there should be
a matron, with a house and 70l. a year ; a steward with
150l. a year ; and latterly, a warden with 450l. a year,
who should have the spiritual guidance of both establishments, and the temporal guidance of that appertaining
to the male sex. The bishop, dean, and warden were,
as formerly, to appoint in turn the recipients of the charity,
and the bishop was to appoint the officers. There was
nothing said as to the wardenship being held by the
precentor of the cathedral, nor a word as to Mr. Harding's
right to the situation.

It was not, however, till some months after the death

of the old bishop, and almost immediately consequent on the installation of his successor, that notice was given that the reform was about to be carried out. The new law and the new bishop were among the earliest works of a new ministry, or rather of a ministry who, having for a while given place to their opponents, had then returned to power ; and the death of Dr. Grantly occurred, as we have seen, exactly at the period of the change.

Poor Eleanor Bold ! How well does that widow's cap become her, and the solemn gravity with which she devotes herself to her new duties. Poor Eleanor !

Poor Eleanor ! I cannot say that with me John Bold was ever a favourite. I never thought him worthy of the wife he had won. But in her estimation he was most worthy. Hers was one of those feminine hearts which cling to a husband, not with idolatry, for worship can admit of no defect in its idol, but with the perfect tenacity of ivy. As the parasite plant will follow even the defects of the trunk which it embraces, so did Eleanor cling to and love the very faults of her husband. She had once declared that whatever her father did should in her eyes be right. She then transferred her allegiance, and became ever ready to defend the worst failings of her lord and master.

And John Bold was a man to be loved by a woman ; he was himself affectionate, he was confiding and manly ; and that arrogance of thought, unsustained by first-rate abilities, that attempt at being better than his neighbours which jarred so painfully on the feelings of his acquaintance, did not injure him in the estimation of his wife.

Could she even have admitted that he had a fault, his early death would have blotted out the memory of it. She wept as for the loss of the most perfect treasure with which mortal woman had ever been endowed ; for weeks after he was gone the idea of future happiness in this world was hateful to her ; consolation, as it is called, was insupportable, and tears and sleep were her only relief.

But God tempers the wind to the shorn lamb. She knew that she had within her the living source of other cares. She knew that there was to be created for her another subject of weal or woe, of unutterable joy or despairing sorrow, as God in his mercy might vouchsafe to her. At first this did but augment her grief ! To be the mother

of a poor infant, orphaned before it was born, brought
forth to the sorrows of an ever desolate hearth, nurtured
amidst tears and wailing, and then turned adrift into
the world without the aid of a father's care! There was
at first no joy in this.

By degrees, however, her heart became anxious for
another object, and, before its birth, the stranger was
expected with all the eagerness of a longing mother. Just
eight months after the father's death a second John Bold
was born, and if the worship of one creature can be innocent
in another, let us hope that the adoration offered over the
cradle of the fatherless infant may not be imputed as a sin.

It will not be worth our while to define the character of
the child, or to point out in how far the faults of the father
were redeemed within that little breast by the virtues of
the mother. The baby, as a baby, was all that was delightful, and I cannot foresee that it will be necessary for us
to inquire into the facts of his after life. Our present
business at Barchester will not occupy us above a year
or two at the furthest, and I will leave it to some other
pen to produce, if necessary, the biography of John Bold
the Younger.

But, as a baby, this baby was all that could be desired.
This fact no one attempted to deny. 'Is he not delightful?'
she would say to her father, looking up into his face from
her knees, her lustrous eyes overflowing with soft tears,
her young face encircled by her close widow's cap and her
hands on each side of the cradle in which her treasure
was sleeping. The grandfather would gladly admit that
the treasure was delightful, and the uncle archdeacon
himself would agree, and Mrs. Grantly, Eleanor's sister,
would re-echo the word with true sisterly energy; and
Mary Bold —— but Mary Bold was a second worshipper
at the same shrine.

The baby was really delightful; he took his food with
a will, struck out his toes merrily whenever his legs were
uncovered, and did not have fits. These are supposed to
be the strongest points of baby perfection, and in all these
our baby excelled.

And thus the widow's deep grief was softened, and
a sweet balm was poured into the wound which she had
thought nothing but death could heal. How much kinder

is God to us than we are willing to be to ourselves! At the loss of every dear face, at the last going of every well beloved one, we all doom ourselves to an eternity of sorrow, and look to waste ourselves away in an ever-running fountain of tears. How seldom does such grief endure! how blessed is the goodness which forbids it to do so! 'Let me ever remember my living friends, but forget them as soon as dead,' was the prayer of a wise man who understood the mercy of God. Few perhaps would have the courage to express such a wish, and yet to do so would only be to ask for that release from sorrow, which a kind Creator almost always extends to us.

I would not, however, have it imagined that Mrs. Bold forgot her husband. She daily thought of him with all conjugal love, and enshrined his memory in the innermost centre of her heart. But yet she was happy in her baby. It was so sweet to press the living toy to her breast, and feel that a human being existed who did owe, and was to owe everything to her; whose daily food was drawn from herself; whose little wants could all be satisfied by her; whose little heart would first love her and her only; whose infant tongue would make its first effort in calling her by the sweetest name a woman can hear. And so Eleanor's bosom became tranquil, and she set about her new duties eagerly and gratefully.

As regards the concerns of the world, John Bold had left his widow in prosperous circumstances. He had bequeathed to her all that he possessed, and that comprised an income much exceeding what she or her friends thought necessary for her. It amounted to nearly a thousand a year; and when she reflected on its extent, her dearest hope was to hand it over, not only unimpaired but increased, to her husband's son, to her own darling, to the little man who now lay sleeping on her knee, happily ignorant of the cares which were to be accumulated in his behalf.

When John Bold died she earnestly implored her father to come and live with her, but this Mr. Harding declined, though for some weeks he remained with her as a visitor. He could not be prevailed upon to forego the possession of some small home of his own, and so remained in the lodgings he had first selected over a chemist's shop in the High Street of Barchester.

CHAPTER III

DR. AND MRS. PROUDIE

THIS narrative is supposed to commence immediately after the installation of Dr. Proudie. I will not describe the ceremony, as I do not precisely understand its nature. I am ignorant whether a bishop be chaired like a member of parliament, or carried in a gilt coach like a lord mayor, or sworn in like a justice of peace, or introduced like a peer to the upper house, or led between two brethren like a knight of the garter; but I do know that every thing was properly done, and that nothing fit or becoming to a young bishop was omitted on the occasion.

Dr. Proudie was not the man to allow anything to be omitted that might be becoming to his new dignity. He understood well the value of forms, and knew that the due observance of rank could not be maintained unless the exterior trappings belonging to it were held in proper esteem. He was a man born to move in high circles; at least so he thought himself, and circumstances had certainly sustained him in this view. He was the nephew of an Irish baron by his mother's side, and his wife was the niece of a Scotch earl. He had for years held some clerical office appertaining to courtly matters, which had enabled him to live in London, and to entrust his parish to his curate. He had been preacher to the royal beefeaters, curator of theological manuscripts in the Ecclesiastical Courts, chaplain to the Queen's yeomanry guard, and almoner to his Royal Highness the Prince of Rappe-Blankenburg.

His residence in the metropolis, rendered necessary by the duties thus entrusted to him, his high connections, and the peculiar talents and nature of the man, recommended him to persons in power; and Dr. Proudie became known as a useful and rising clergyman.

Some few years since, even within the memory of many who are not yet willing to call themselves old, a liberal clergyman was a person not frequently to be met. Sydney Smith was such, and was looked on as little better than an infidel; a few others also might be named, but they

were 'raræ aves,' and were regarded with doubt and
distrust by their brethren. No man was so surely a tory
as a country rector—nowhere were the powers that be so
cherished as at Oxford.

When, however, Dr. Whately was made an archbishop,
and Dr. Hampden some years afterwards regius professor,
many wise divines saw that a change was taking place in
men's minds, and that more liberal ideas would henceforward be suitable to the priests as well as to the laity.
Clergymen began to be heard of who had ceased to
anathematise papists on the one hand, or vilify dissenters
on the other. It appeared clear that high church principles,
as they are called, were no longer to be surest claims to
promotion with at any rate one section of statesmen,
and Dr. Proudie was one among those who early in life
adapted himself to the views held by the whigs on most
theological and religious subjects. He bore with the
idolatry of Rome, tolerated even the infidelity of Socinian-
ism, and was hand and glove with the Presbyterian
Synods of Scotland and Ulster.

Such a man at such a time was found to be useful, and
Dr. Proudie's name began to appear in the newspapers.
He was made one of a commission who went over to Ireland
to arrange matters preparative to the working of the
national board ; he became honorary secretary to another
commission nominated to inquire into the revenues of
cathedral chapters ; and had had something to do with
both the regium donum and the Maynooth grant.

It must not on this account be taken as proved that
Dr. Proudie was a man of great mental powers, or even
of much capacity for business, for such qualities had not
been required in him. In the arrangement of those church
reforms with which he was connected, the ideas and
original conception of the work to be done were generally
furnished by the liberal statesmen of the day, and the
labour of the details was borne by officials of a lower rank.
It was, however, thought expedient that the name of
some clergyman should appear in such matters, and as
Dr. Proudie had become known as a tolerating divine,
great use of this sort was made of his name. If he did
not do much active good, he never did any harm ; he
was amenable to those who were really in authority, and

at the sittings of the various boards to which he belonged
maintained a kind of dignity which had its value.

He was certainly possessed of sufficient tact to answer
the purpose for which he was required without making
himself troublesome ; but it must not therefore be surmised that he doubted his own power, or failed to believe
that he could himself take a high part in high affairs when
his own turn came. He was biding his time, and patiently
looking forward to the days when he himself would sit
authoritative at some board, and talk and direct, and
rule the roast, while lesser stars sat round and obeyed,
as he had so well accustomed himself to do.

His reward and his time had now come. He was selected
for the vacant bishopric, and on the next vacancy which
might occur in any diocese would take his place in the
House of Lords, prepared to give not a silent vote in all
matters concerning the weal of the church establishment.
Toleration was to be the basis on which he was to fight
his battles, and in the honest courage of his heart he
thought no evil would come to him in encountering even
such foes as his brethren of Exeter and Oxford.

Dr. Proudie was an ambitious man, and before he was
well consecrated Bishop of Barchester, he had begun to
look up to archiepiscopal splendour, and the glories of
Lambeth, or at any rate of Bishopsthorpe. He was
comparatively young, and had, as he fondly flattered
himself, been selected as possessing such gifts, natural
and acquired, as must be sure to recommend him to a
yet higher notice, now that a higher sphere was opened
to him. Dr. Proudie was, therefore, quite prepared to
take a conspicuous part in all theological affairs appertaining to these realms ; and having such views, by no means
intended to bury himself at Barchester as his predecessor
had done. No : London should still be his ground : a
comfortable mansion in a provincial city might be well
enough for the dead months of the year. Indeed Dr.
Proudie had always felt it necessary to his position to
retire from London when other great and fashionable
people did so ; but London should still be his fixed residence, and it was in London that he resolved to exercise
that hospitality so peculiarly recommended to all bishops
by St. Paul. How otherwise could he keep himself before

the world ? how else give to the government, in matters
theological, the full benefit of his weight and talents ?

This resolution was no doubt a salutary one as regarded
the world at large, but was not likely to make him popular
either with the clergy or people of Barchester. Dr. Grantly
had always lived there ; and in truth it was hard for a
bishop to be popular after Dr. Grantly. His income had
averaged 9000*l.* a year ; his successor was to be rigidly
limited to 5000*l.* He had but one child on whom to spend
his money ; Dr. Proudie had seven or eight. He had been
a man of few personal expenses, and they had been confined to the tastes of a moderate gentleman ; but Dr.
Proudie had to maintain a position in fashionable society,
and had that to do with comparatively small means.
Dr. Grantly had certainly kept his carriage, as became
a bishop ; but his carriage, horses, and coachman, though
they did very well for Barchester, would have been almost
ridiculous at Westminster. Mrs. Proudie determined
that her husband's equipage should not shame her, and
things on which Mrs. Proudie resolved, were generally
accomplished.

From all this it was likely to result that Dr. Proudie
would not spend much money at Barchester ; whereas
his predecessor had dealt with the tradesmen of the city
in a manner very much to their satisfaction. The Grantlys,
father and son, had spent their money like gentlemen ;
but it soon became whispered in Barchester that Dr.
Proudie was not unacquainted with those prudent devices
by which the utmost show of wealth is produced from
limited means.

In person Dr. Proudie is a good-looking man ; spruce
and dapper, and very tidy. He is somewhat below middle
height, being about five feet four ; but he makes up for
the inches which he wants by the dignity with which he
carries those which he has. It is no fault of his own
if he has not a commanding eye, for he studies hard to
assume it. His features are well formed, though perhaps the
sharpness of his nose may give to his face in the eyes of
some people an air of insignificance. If so, it is greatly
redeemed by his mouth and chin, of which he is justly proud.

Dr. Proudie may well be said to have been a fortunate
man, for he was not born to wealth, and he is now bishop

of Barchester; but nevertheless he has his cares. He has a large family, of whom the three eldest are daughters, now all grown up and fit for fashionable life; and he has a wife. It is not my intention to breathe a word against the character of Mrs. Proudie, but still I cannot think that with all her virtues she adds much to her husband's happiness. The truth is that in matters domestic she rules supreme over her titular lord, and rules with a rod of iron. Nor is this all. Things domestic Dr. Proudie might have abandoned to her, if not voluntarily, yet willingly. But Mrs. Proudie is not satisfied with such home dominion, and stretches her power over all his movements, and will not even abstain from things spiritual. In fact, the bishop is henpecked.

The archdeacon's wife, in her happy home at Plumstead, knows how to assume the full privileges of her rank, and express her own mind in becoming tone and place. But Mrs. Grantly's sway, if sway she has, is easy and beneficent. She never shames her husband; before the world she is a pattern of obedience; her voice is never loud, nor her looks sharp: doubtless she values power, and has not unsuccessfully striven to acquire it; but she knows what should be the limits of a woman's rule.

Not so Mrs. Proudie. This lady is habitually authoritative to all, but to her poor husband she is despotic. Successful as has been his career in the eyes of the world, it would seem that in the eyes of his wife he is never right. All hope of defending himself has long passed from him; indeed he rarely even attempts self-justification; and is aware that submission produces the nearest approach to peace which his own house can ever attain.

Mrs. Proudie has not been able to sit at the boards and committees to which her husband has been called by the state; nor, as he often reflects, can she make her voice heard in the House of Lords. It may be that she will refuse to him permission to attend to this branch of a bishop's duties; it may be that she will insist on his close attendance to his own closet. He has never whispered a word on the subject to living ears, but he has already made his fixed resolve. Should such an attempt be made he will rebel. Dogs have turned against their masters, and even Neapolitans against their rulers, when oppression has been too severe. And Dr. Proudie feels within himself that if the cord be drawn too tight, he also can muster courage and resist.

The state of vassalage in which our bishop has been kept by his wife has not tended to exalt his character in the eyes of his daughters, who assume in addressing their father too much of that authority which is not properly belonging, at any rate, to them. They are, on the whole, fine engaging young ladies. They are tall and robust like their mother, whose high cheek-bones, and——, we may say auburn hair, they all inherit. They think somewhat too much of their grand uncles, who have not hitherto returned the compliment by thinking much of them. But now that their father is a bishop, it is probable that family ties will be drawn closer. Considering their connection with the church, they entertain but few prejudices against the pleasures of the world ; and have certainly not distressed their parents, as too many English girls have lately done, by any enthusiastic wish to devote themselves to the seclusion of a protestant nunnery. Dr. Proudie's sons are still at school.

One other marked peculiarity in the character of the bishop's wife must be mentioned. Though not averse to the society and manners of the world, she is in her own way a religious woman ; and the form in which this tendency shows itself in her is by a strict observance of Sabbatarian rule. Dissipation and low dresses during the week are, under her control, atoned for by three services, an evening sermon read by herself, and a perfect abstinence from any cheering employment on the Sunday. Unfortunately for those under her roof to whom the dissipation and low dresses are not extended, her servants namely and her husband, the compensating strictness of the Sabbath includes all. Woe betide the recreant housemaid who is found to have been listening to the honey of a sweetheart in the Regent's park, instead of the soul-stirring evening discourse of Mr. Slope. Not only is she sent adrift, but she is so sent with a character which leaves her little hope of a decent place. Woe betide the six-foot hero who escorts Mrs. Proudie to her pew in red plush breeches, if he slips away to the neighbouring beer-shop, instead of falling into the back seat appropriated

to his use. Mrs. Proudie has the eyes of Argus for such
offenders. Occasional drunkenness in the week may be
overlooked, for six feet on low wages are hardly to be
procured if the morals are always kept at a high pitch;
but not even for grandeur or economy will Mrs. Proudie
forgive a desecration of the Sabbath.

In such matters Mrs. Proudie allows herself to be often
guided by that eloquent preacher, the Rev. Mr. Slope,
and as Dr. Proudie is guided by his wife, it necessarily
follows that the eminent man we have named has obtained
a good deal of control over Dr. Proudie in matters concerning religion. Mr. Slope's only preferment has hitherto
been that of reader and preacher in a London district
church: and on the consecration of his friend the new
bishop, he readily gave this up to undertake the onerous
but congenial duties of domestic chaplain to his lordship.

Mr. Slope, however, on his first introduction must not
be brought before the public at the tail of a chapter.

CHAPTER IV

THE BISHOP'S CHAPLAIN

OF the Rev. Mr. Slope's parentage I am not able to
say much. I have heard it asserted that he is lineally
descended from that eminent physician who assisted at
the birth of Mr. T. Shandy, and that in early years he
added an ' e ' to his name, for the sake of euphony, as
other great men have done before him. If this be so,
I presume he was christened Obadiah, for that is his name,
in commemoration of the conflict in which his ancestor
so distinguished himself. All my researches on the subject
have, however, failed in enabling me to fix the date on
which the family changed its religion.

He had been a sizar at Cambridge, and had there conducted himself at any rate successfully, for in due process
of time he was an M.A., having university pupils under
his care. From thence he was transferred to London,
and became preacher at a new district church built on
the confines of Baker Street. He was in this position
when congenial ideas on religious subjects recommended

him to Mrs. Proudie, and the intercourse had become close and confidential.

Having been thus familiarly thrown among the Misses Proudie, it was no more than natural that some softer feeling than friendship should be engendered. There have been some passages of love between him and the eldest hope, Olivia; but they have hitherto resulted in no favourable arrangement. In truth, Mr. Slope having made a declaration of affection, afterwards withdrew it on finding that the doctor had no immediate worldly funds with which to endow his child; and it may easily be conceived that Miss Proudie, after such an announcement on his part, was not readily disposed to receive any further show of affection. On the appointment of Dr. Proudie to the bishopric of Barchester, Mr. Slope's views were in truth somewhat altered. Bishops, even though they be poor, can provide for clerical children, and Mr. Slope began to regret that he had not been more disinterested. He no sooner heard the tidings of the doctor's elevation, than he recommenced his siege, not violently, indeed, but respectfully, and at a distance. Olivia Proudie, however, was a girl of spirit: she had the blood of two peers in her veins, and, better still, she had another lover on her books; so Mr. Slope sighed in vain; and the pair soon found it convenient to establish a mutual bond of inveterate hatred.

It may be thought singular that Mrs. Proudie's friendship for the young clergyman should remain firm after such an affair; but, to tell the truth, she had known nothing of it. Though very fond of Mr. Slope herself, she had never conceived the idea that either of her daughters would become so, and remembering their high birth and social advantages, expected for them matches of a different sort. Neither the gentleman nor the lady found it necessary to enlighten her. Olivia's two sisters had each known of the affair, so had all the servants, so had all the people living in the adjoining houses on either side; but Mrs. Proudie had been kept in the dark.

Mr. Slope soon comforted himself with the reflection, that as he had been selected as chaplain to the bishop, it would probably be in his power to get the good things in the bishop's gift, without troubling himself with the bishop's daughter; and he found himself able to endure the pangs of rejected love. As he sat himself down in the railway carriage, confronting the bishop and Mrs. Proudie, as they started on their first journey to Barchester, he began to form in his own mind a plan of his future life. He knew well his patron's strong points, but he knew the weak ones as well. He understood correctly enough to what attempts the new bishop's high spirit would soar, and he rightly guessed that public life would better suit the great man's taste, than the small details of diocesan duty.

He, therefore, he, Mr. Slope, would in effect be bishop of Barchester. Such was his resolve; and to give Mr. Slope his due, he had both courage and spirit to bear him out in his resolution. He knew that he should have a hard battle to fight, for the power and patronage of the see would be equally coveted by another great mind—Mrs. Proudie would also choose to be bishop of Barchester. Mr. Slope, however, flattered himself that he could out-manœuvre the lady. She must live much in London, while he would always be on the spot. She would necessarily remain ignorant of much, while he would know everything belonging to the diocese. At first, doubtless, he must flatter and cajole, perhaps yield, in some things; but he did not doubt of ultimate triumph. If all other means failed, he could join the bishop against his wife, inspire courage into the unhappy man, lay an axe to the root of the woman's power, and emancipate the husband.

Such were his thoughts as he sat looking at the sleeping pair in the railway carriage, and Mr. Slope is not the man to trouble himself with such thoughts for nothing. He is possessed of more than average abilities, and is of good courage. Though he can stoop to fawn, and stoop low indeed, if need be, he has still within him the power to assume the tyrant; and with the power he has certainly the wish. His acquirements are not of the highest order, but such as they are they are completely under control, and he knows the use of them. He is gifted with a certain kind of pulpit eloquence, not likely indeed to be persuasive with men, but powerful with the softer sex. In his sermons he deals greatly in denunciations, excites the minds of his weaker hearers with a not unpleasant terror, and leaves an impression on their minds that all mankind are in a perilous state, and all womankind too, except those who attend regularly to the evening lectures in Baker Street. His looks and tones are extremely severe, so much so that one cannot but fancy that he regards the greater part of the world as being infinitely too bad for his care. As he walks through the streets, his very face denotes his horror of the world's wickedness; and there is always an anathema lurking in the corner of his eye.

In doctrine, he, like his patron, is tolerant of dissent, if so strict a mind can be called tolerant of anything. With Wesleyan-Methodists he has something in common, but his soul trembles in agony at the iniquities of the Puseyites. His aversion is carried to things outward as well as inward. His gall rises at a new church with a high pitched roof; a full-breasted black silk waistcoat is with him a symbol of Satan; and a profane jest-book would not, in his view, more foully desecrate the church seat of a Christian, than a book of prayer printed with red letters, and ornamented with a cross on the back. Most active clergymen have their hobby, and Sunday observances are his. Sunday, however, is a word which never pollutes his mouth—it is always ' the Sabbath.' The ' desecration of the Sabbath,' as he delights to call it, is to him meat and drink :—he thrives upon that as policemen do on the general evil habits of the community. It is the loved subject of all his evening discourses, the source of all his eloquence, the secret of all his power over the female heart. To him the revelation of God appears only in that one law given for Jewish observance. To him the mercies of our Saviour speak in vain, to him in vain has been preached that sermon which fell from divine lips on the mountain—' Blessed are the meek, for they shall inherit the earth '—' Blessed are the merciful, for they shall obtain mercy.' To him the New Testament is comparatively of little moment, for from it can he draw no fresh authority for that dominion which he loves to exercise over at least a seventh part of man's allotted time here below.

Mr. Slope is tall, and not ill made. His feet and hands are large, as has ever been the case with all his family, but he has a broad chest and wide shoulders to carry off these excrescences, and on the whole his figure is good. His countenance, however, is not specially prepossessing. His hair is lank, and of a dull pale reddish hue. It is always formed into three straight lumpy masses, each brushed with admirable precision, and cemented with much grease ; two of them adhere closely to the sides of his face, and the other lies at right angles above them. He wears no whiskers, and is always punctiliously shaven. His face is nearly of the same colour as his hair, though perhaps a little redder : it is not unlike beef,—beef, however, one would say, of a bad quality. His forehead is capacious and high, but square and heavy, and un-pleasantly shining. His mouth is large, though his lips are thin and bloodless ; and his big, prominent, pale brown eyes inspire anything but confidence. His nose, however, is his redeeming feature : it is pronounced straight and well-formed ; though I myself should have liked it better did it not possess a somewhat spongy, porous appearance, as though it had been cleverly formed out of a red coloured cork.

I never could endure to shake hands with Mr. Slope. A cold, clammy perspiration always exudes from him, the small drops are ever to be seen standing on his brow, and his friendly grasp is unpleasant.

Such is Mr. Slope—such is the man who has suddenly fallen into the midst of Barchester Close, and is destined there to assume the station which has heretofore been filled by the son of the late bishop. Think, oh, my medita-tive reader, what an associate we have here for those comfortable prebendaries, those gentlemanlike clerical doctors, those happy well-used well-fed minor canons, who have grown into existence at Barchester under the kindly wings of Bishop Grantly !

But not as a mere associate for these does Mr. Slope travel down to Barchester with the bishop and his wife. He intends to be, if not their master, at least the chief among them. He intends to lead, and to have followers ; he intends to hold the purse strings of the diocese, and draw round him an obedient herd of his poor and hungry brethren.

And here we can hardly fail to draw a comparison between the archdeacon and our new private chaplain ;

and despite the manifold faults of the former, one can hardly fail to make it much to his advantage.

Both men are eager, much too eager, to support and increase the power of their order. Both are anxious that the world should be priest-governed, though they have probably never confessed so much, even to themselves. Both begrudge any other kind of dominion held by man over man. Dr. Grantly, if he admits the Queen's supremacy in things spiritual, only admits it as being due to the *quasi* priesthood conveyed in the consecrating qualities of her coronation; and he regards things temporal as being by their nature subject to those which are spiritual. Mr. Slope's ideas of sacerdotal rule are of quite a different class. He cares nothing, one way or the other, for the Queen's supremacy; these to his ears are empty words, meaning nothing. Forms he regards but little, and such titular expressions as supremacy, consecration, ordination, and the like, convey of themselves no significance to him. Let him be supreme who can. The temporal king, judge, or gaoler, can work but on the body. The spiritual master, if he have the necessary gifts, and can duly use them, has a wider field of empire. He works upon the soul. If he can make himself be believed, he can be all powerful over those who listen. If he be careful to meddle with none who are too strong in intellect, or too weak in flesh, he may indeed be supreme. And such was the ambition of Mr. Slope.

Dr. Grantly interfered very little with the worldly doings of those who were in any way subject to him. I do not mean to say that he omitted to notice misconduct among his clergy, immorality in his parish, or omissions in his family; but he was not anxious to do so where the necessity could be avoided. He was not troubled with a propensity to be curious, and as long as those around him were tainted with no heretical leaning towards dissent, as long as they fully and freely admitted the efficacy of Mother Church, he was willing that that mother should be merciful and affectionate, prone to indulgence, and unwilling to chastise. He himself enjoyed the good things of this world, and liked to let it be known that he did so. He cordially despised any brother rector who thought harm of dinner-parties, or dreaded the dangers of a moderate claret-jug; consequently dinner-parties and claret-jugs were common in the diocese. He liked to give laws and to be obeyed in them implicity, but he endeavoured that his ordinances should be within the compass of the man, and not unpalatable to the gentle-man. He had ruled among his clerical neighbours now for sundry years, and as he had maintained his power without becoming unpopular, it may be presumed that he had exercised some wisdom.

Of Mr. Slope's conduct much cannot be said, as his grand career is yet to commence; but it may be premised that his tastes will be very different from those of the archdeacon. He conceives it to be his duty to know all the private doings and desires of the flock entrusted to his care. From the poorer classes he exacts an uncon-ditional obedience to set rules of conduct, and if disobeyed he has recourse, like his great ancestor, to the fulmina-tions of an Ernulfus: ' Thou shalt be damned in thy going in and in thy coming out—in thy eating and thy drinking,' &c. &c. &c. With the rich, experience has already taught him that a different line of action is necessary. Men in the upper walks of life do not mind being cursed, and the women, presuming that it be done in delicate phrase, rather like it. But he has not, therefore, given up so important a portion of believing Christians. With the men, indeed, he is generally at variance; they are hardened sinners, on whom the voice of the priestly charmer too often falls in vain; but with the ladies, old and young, firm and frail, devout and dissipated, he is, as he conceives, all powerful. He can reprove faults with so much flattery, and utter censure in so caressing a manner, that the female heart, if it glow with a spark of low church susceptibility, cannot withstand him. In many houses he is thus an admired guest: the husbands, for their wives' sake, are fain to admit him; and when once admitted it is not easy to shake him off. He has, however, a pawing, greasy way with him, which does not endear him to those who do not value him for their souls' sake, and he is not a man to make himself at once popular in a large circle such as is now likely to surround him at Barchester.

CHAPTER V

A MORNING VISIT

It was known that Dr. Proudie would immediately have to reappoint to the wardenship of the hospital under the act of Parliament to which allusion has been made; but no one imagined that any choice was left to him—no one for a moment thought that he could appoint any other than Mr. Harding. Mr. Harding himself, when he heard how the matter had been settled, without troubling himself much on the subject, considered it as certain that he would go back to his pleasant house and garden. And though there would be much that was melancholy, nay, almost heartrending, in such a return, he still was glad that it was to be so. His daughter might probably be persuaded to return there with him. She had, indeed, all but promised to do so, though she still entertained an idea that that greatest of mortals, that important atom of humanity, that little god upon earth, Johnny Bold her baby, ought to have a house of his own over his head.

Such being the state of Mr. Harding's mind in the matter, he did not feel any peculiar personal interest in the appointment of Dr. Proudie to the bishopric. He, as well as others at Barchester, regretted that a man should be sent among them who, they were aware, was not of their way of thinking; but Mr. Harding himself was not a bigoted man on points of church doctrine, and he was quite prepared to welcome Dr. Proudie to Barchester in a graceful and becoming manner. He had nothing to seek and nothing to fear; he felt that it behoved him to be on good terms with his bishop, and he did not anticipate any obstacle that would prevent it.

In such a frame of mind he proceeded to pay his respects at the palace the second day after the arrival of the bishop and his chaplain. But he did not go alone. Dr. Grantly proposed to accompany him, and Mr. Harding was not sorry to have a companion, who would remove from his shoulders the burden of the conversation in such an interview. In the affair of the consecration Dr. Grantly

had been introduced to the bishop, and Mr. Harding
had also been there. He had, however, kept himself in
the background, and he was now to be presented to the
great man for the first time.

The archdeacon's feelings were of a much stronger
nature. He was not exactly the man to overlook his own
slighted claims, or to forgive the preference shown to
another. Dr. Proudie was playing Venus to his Juno,
and he was prepared to wage an internecine war against
the owner of the wished-for apple, and all his satellites,
private chaplains, and others.

Nevertheless, it behoved him also to conduct himself
towards the intruder as an old archdeacon should conduct
himself to an incoming bishop; and though he was well
aware of all Dr. Proudie's abominable opinions as regarded
dissenters, church reform, the hebdomadal council, and
such like; though he disliked the man, and hated the
doctrines, still he was prepared to show respect to the
station of the bishop. So he and Mr. Harding called
together at the palace.

His lordship was at home, and the two visitors were
shown through the accustomed hall into the well-known
room, where the good old bishop used to sit. The furniture
had been bought at a valuation, and every chair and table,
every bookshelf against the wall, and every square in the
carpet, was as well known to each of them as their own
bedrooms. Nevertheless they at once felt that they were
strangers there. The furniture was for the most part
the same, yet the place had been metamorphosed. A
new sofa had been introduced, a horrid chintz affair,
most unprelatical and almost irreligious: such a sofa
as never yet stood in the study of any decent high church
clergyman of the Church of England. The old curtains
had also given away. They had, to be sure, become
dingy, and that which had been originally a rich and
goodly ruby had degenerated into a reddish brown. Mr.
Harding, however, thought the old reddish brown much
preferable to the gaudy buff-coloured trumpery moreen
which Mrs. Proudie had deemed good enough for her
husband's own room in the provincial city of Barchester.

Our friends found Dr. Proudie sitting on the old bishop's
chair, looking very nice in his new apron; they found, too,

Mr. Slope standing on the hearthrug, persuasive and eager, just as the archdeacon used to stand; but on the sofa they also found Mrs. Proudie, an innovation for which a precedent might in vain be sought in all the annals of the Barchester bishopric!

There she was, however, and they could only make the best of her. The introductions were gone through in much form. The archdeacon shook hands with the bishop, and named Mr. Harding, who received such an amount of greeting as was due from a bishop to a precentor. His lordship then presented them to his lady wife; the archdeacon first, with archidiaconal honours, and then the precentor with diminished parade. After this Mr. Slope presented himself. The bishop, it is true, did mention his name, and so did Mrs. Proudie too, in a louder tone; but Mr. Slope took upon himself the chief burden of his own introduction. He had great pleasure in making himself acquainted with Dr. Grantly; he had heard much of the archdeacon's good works in that part of the diocese in which his duties as archdeacon had been exercised (thus purposely ignoring the archdeacon's hitherto unlimited dominion over the diocese at large). He was aware that his lordship depended greatly on the assistance which Dr. Grantly would be able to give him in that portion of his diocese. He then thrust out his hand, and grasping that of his new foe, bedewed it unmercifully. Dr. Grantly in return bowed, looked stiff, contracted his eyebrows, and wiped his hand with his pocket-handkerchief. Nothing abashed, Mr. Slope then noticed the precentor, and descended to the grade of the lower clergy. He gave him a squeeze of the hand, damp indeed, but affectionate, and was very glad to make the acquaintance of Mr. ——; oh yes, Mr. Harding; he had not exactly caught the name—'Precentor in the cathedral,' surmised Mr. Slope. Mr. Harding confessed that such was the humble sphere of his work. 'Some parish duty as well,' suggested Mr. Slope. Mr. Harding acknowledged the diminutive incumbency of St. Cuthbert's. Mr. Slope then left him alone, having condescended sufficiently, and joined the conversation among the higher powers.

There were four persons there, each of whom considered

himself the most important personage in the diocese;
himself, indeed, or herself, as Mrs. Proudie was one of
them; and with such a difference of opinion it was not
probable that they would get on pleasantly together.
The bishop himself actually wore the visible apron, and
trusted mainly to that—to that and his title, both being
facts which could not be overlooked. The archdeacon
knew his subject, and really understood the business of
bishoping, which the others did not; and this was his
strong ground. Mrs. Proudie had her sex to back her,
and her habit of command, and was nothing daunted
by the high tone of Dr. Grantly's face and figure. Mr.
Slope had only himself and his own courage and tact to
depend on, but he nevertheless was perfectly self-assured,
and did not doubt but that he should soon get the better
of weak men who trusted so much to externals, as both
bishop and archdeacon appeared to do.

' Do you reside in Barchester, Dr. Grantly ? ' asked
the lady with her sweetest smile.

Dr. Grantly explained that he lived in his own parish
of Plumstead Episcopi, a few miles out of the city. Whereupon the lady hoped that the distance was not too great
for country visiting, as she would be so glad to make the
acquaintance of Mrs. Grantly. She would take the earliest
opportunity, after the arrival of her horses at Barchester;
their horses were at present in London; their horses were
not immediately coming down, as the bishop would be
obliged, in a few days, to return to town. Dr. Grantly
was no doubt aware that the bishop was at present much
called upon by the ' University Improvement Committee : '
indeed, the Committee could not well proceed without
him, as their final report had now to be drawn up. The
bishop had also to prepare a scheme for the ' Manufacturing Towns Morning and Evening Sunday School Society,'
of which he was a patron, or president, or director, and
therefore the horses would not come down to Barchester
at present; but whenever the horses did come down,
she would take the earliest opportunity of calling at
Plumstead Episcopi, providing the distance was not too
great for country visiting.

The archdeacon made his fifth bow : he had made one
at each mention of the horses; and promised that Mrs.

Grantly would do herself the honour of calling at the palace on an early day. Mrs. Proudie declared that she would be delighted : she hadn't liked to ask, not being quite sure whether Mrs. Grantly had horses ; besides, the distance might have been, &c. &c.

Dr. Grantly again bowed, but said nothing. He could have bought every individual possession of the whole family of the Proudies, and have restored them as a gift, without much feeling the loss ; and had kept a separate pair of horses for the exclusive use of his wife since the day of his marriage ; whereas Mrs. Proudie had been hitherto jobbed about the streets of London at so much a month during the season ; and at other times had managed to walk, or hire a smart fly from the livery stables.

' Are the arrangements with reference to the Sabbath-day schools generally pretty good in your archdeaconry ? ' asked Mr. Slope.

' Sabbath-day schools ! ' repeated the archdeacon with an affectation of surprise. ' Upon my word, I can't tell ; it depends mainly on the parson's wife and daughters. There is none at Plumstead.'

This was almost a fib on the part of the Archdeacon, for Mrs. Grantly has a very nice school. To be sure it is not a Sunday school exclusively, and is not so designated ; but that exemplary lady always attends there an hour before church, and hears the children say their catechism, and sees that they are clean and tidy for church, with their hands washed, and their shoes tied ; and Grisel and Florinda, her daughters, carry thither a basket of large buns, baked on the Saturday afternoon, and distribute them to all the children not especially under disgrace, which buns are carried home after church with considerable content, and eaten hot at tea, being then split and toasted. The children of Plumstead would indeed open their eyes if they heard their venerated pastor declare that there was no Sunday school in his parish.

Mr. Slope merely opened his eyes wider, and slightly shrugged his shoulders. He was not, however, prepared to give up his darling project.

' I fear there is a great deal of Sabbath travelling here,' said he. ' On looking at the '' Bradshaw,'' I see that there

are three trains in and three out every Sabbath. Could
nothing be done to induce the company to withdraw
them ? Don't you think, Dr. Grantly, that a little energy
might diminish the evil ? '

' Not being a director, I really can't say. But if you
can withdraw the passengers, the company, I dare say,
will withdraw the trains,' said the doctor. ' It's merely
a question of dividends.'

' But surely, Dr. Grantly,' said the lady, ' surely we
should look at it differently. You and I, for instance, in
our position : surely we should do all that we can to control
so grievous a sin. Don't you think so, Mr. Harding ? ' and
she turned to the precentor, who was sitting mute and
unhappy.

Mr. Harding thought that all porters and stokers,
guards, breaksmen, and pointsmen ought to have an
opportunity of going to church, and he hoped that they
all had.

' But surely, surely,' continued Mrs. Proudie, ' surely
that is not enough. Surely that will not secure such an
observance of the Sabbath as we are taught to conceive
is not only expedient but indispensable ; surely——'

Come what come might, Dr. Grantly was not to be
forced into a dissertation on a point of doctrine with
Mrs. Proudie, nor yet with Mr. Slope ; so without much
ceremony he turned his back upon the sofa, and began
to hope that Dr. Proudie had found that the palace repairs
had been such as to meet his wishes.

' Yes, yes,' said his lordship ; upon the whole he thought
so—upon the whole, he didn't know that there was much
ground for complaint ; the architect, perhaps, might have
——but his double, Mr. Slope, who had sidled over to
the bishop's chair, would not allow his lordship to finish
his ambiguous speech.

' There is one point I would like to mention, Mr. Archdeacon. His lordship asked me to step through the
premises, and I see that the stalls in the second stable
are not perfect.'

' Why—there's standing there for a dozen horses,'
said the archdeacon.

' Perhaps so,' said the other ; ' indeed, I've no doubt
of it ; but visitors, you know, often require so much

accommodation. There are so many of the bishop's
relatives who always bring their own horses.'

Dr. Grantly promised that due provision for the relatives'
horses should be made, as far at least as the extent of
the original stable building would allow. He would himself
communicate with the architect.

'And the coach-house, Dr. Grantly,' continued Mr.
Slope; 'there is really hardly room for a second carriage
in the large coach-house, and the smaller one, of course,
holds only one.'

'And the gas,' chimed in the lady; 'there is no gas
through the house, none whatever, but in the kitchen and
passages. Surely the palace should have been fitted
through with pipes for gas, and hot water too. There
is no hot water laid on anywhere above the ground-floor;
surely there should be the means of getting hot water
in the bed-rooms without having it brought in jugs from
the kitchen.'

The bishop had a decided opinion that there should be
pipes for hot water. Hot water was very essential for
the comfort of the palace. It was, indeed, a requisite in
any decent gentleman's house.

Mr. Slope had remarked that the coping on the garden
wall was in many places imperfect.

Mrs. Proudie had discovered a large hole, evidently
the work of rats, in the servants' hall.

The bishop expressed an utter detestation of rats. There
was nothing, he believed, in this world, that he so much
hated as a rat.

Mr. Slope had, moreover, observed that the locks of
the out-houses were very imperfect: he might specify
the coal-cellar, and the wood-house.

Mrs. Proudie had also seen that those on the doors of
the servants' bedrooms were in an equally bad condition;
indeed the locks all through the house were old-fashioned
and unserviceable.

The bishop thought that a great deal depended on a
good lock, and quite as much on the key. He had observed
that the fault very often lay with the key, especially if
the wards were in any way twisted.

Mr. Slope was going on with his catalogue of grievances,
when he was somewhat loudly interrupted by the arch-

deacon, who succeeded in explaining that the diocesan architect, or rather his foreman, was the person to be addressed on such subjects; and that he, Dr. Grantly, had inquired as to the comfort of the palace, merely as a point of compliment. He was sorry, however, that so many things had been found amiss: and then he rose from his chair to escape.

Mrs. Proudie, though she had contrived to lend her assistance in recapitulating the palatial dilapidations, had not on that account given up her hold of Mr. Harding, nor ceased from her cross-examinations as to the iniquity of Sabbatical amusements. Over and over again had she thrown out her ' Surely, surely,' at Mr. Harding's devoted head, and ill had that gentleman been able to parry the attack.

He had never before found himself subjected to such a nuisance. Ladies hitherto, when they had consulted him on religious subjects, had listened to what he might choose to say with some deference, and had differed, if they differed, in silence. But Mrs. Proudie interrogated him, and then lectured. ' Neither thou, nor thy son, nor thy daughter, nor thy man servant, nor thy maid servant,' said she, impressively, and more than once, as though Mr. Harding had forgotten the words. She shook her finger at him as she quoted the favourite law, as though menacing him with punishment; and then called upon him categorically to state whether he did not think that travelling on the Sabbath was an abomination and a desecration.

Mr. Harding had never been so hard pressed in his life. He felt that he ought to rebuke the lady for presuming so to talk to a gentleman and a clergyman many years her senior; but he recoiled from the idea of scolding the bishop's wife, in the bishop's presence, on his first visit to the palace; moreover, to tell the truth, he was somewhat afraid of her. She, seeing him sit silent and absorbed, by no means refrained from the attack.

' I hope, Mr. Harding,' said she, shaking her head slowly and solemnly, ' I hope you will not leave me to think that you approve of Sabbath travelling,' and she looked a look of unutterable meaning into his eyes.

There was no standing this, for Mr. Slope was now

looking at him, and so was the bishop, and so was the
archdeacon, who had completed his adieux on that side
of the room. Mr. Harding therefore got up also, and
putting out his hand to Mrs. Proudie said : ' If you will
come to St. Cuthbert's some Sunday, I will preach you
a sermon on that subject.'

And so the archdeacon and the precentor took their
departure, bowing low to the lady, shaking hands with
the lord, and escaping from Mr. Slope in the best manner
each could. Mr. Harding was again maltreated ; but
Dr. Grantly swore deeply in the bottom of his heart,
that no earthly consideration should ever again induce
him to touch the paw of that impure and filthy animal.

And now, had I the pen of a mighty poet, would I sing
in epic verse the noble wrath of the archdeacon. The
palace steps descend to a broad gravel sweep, from whence
a small gate opens out into the street, very near the
covered gateway leading into the close. The road from
the palace door turns to the left, through the spacious
gardens, and terminates on the London-road, half a mile
from the cathedral.

Till they had both passed this small gate and entered
the close, neither of them spoke a word ; but the precentor
clearly saw from his companion's face that a tornado
was to be expected, nor was he himself inclined to stop
it. Though by nature far less irritable than the archdeacon, even he was angry : he even—that mild and
courteous man—was inclined to express himself in anything but courteous terms.

CHAPTER VI

WAR

' GOOD heavens ! " exclaimed the archdeacon, as he
placed his foot on the gravel walk of the close, and raising
his hat with one hand, passed the other somewhat violently
over his now grizzled locks ; smoke issued forth from
the uplifted beaver as it were a cloud of wrath, and the
safety-valve of his anger opened, and emitted a visible
steam, preventing positive explosion and probable
apoplexy. ' Good heavens ! '—and the archdeacon

looked up to the gray pinnacles of the cathedral tower, making a mute appeal to that still living witness which had looked down on the doings of so many bishops of Barchester.

'I don't think I shall ever like that Mr. Slope,' said Mr. Harding.

'Like him!' roared the archdeacon, standing still for a moment to give more force to his voice; 'like him!' All the ravens of the close cawed their assent. The old bells of the tower, in chiming the hour, echoed the words; and the swallows flying out from their nests mutely expressed a similar opinion. Like Mr. Slope! Why no, it was not very probable that any Barchester-bred living thing should like Mr. Slope!

'Nor Mrs. Proudie either,' said Mr. Harding.

The archdeacon hereupon forgot himself. I will not follow his example, nor shock my readers by transcribing the term in which he expressed his feeling as to the lady who had been named. The ravens and the last lingering notes of the clock bells were less scrupulous, and repeated in corresponding echoes the very improper exclamation. The archdeacon again raised his hat, and another salutary escape of steam was effected.

There was a pause, during which the precentor tried to realise the fact that the wife of a bishop of Barchester had been thus designated, in the close of the cathedral, by the lips of its own archdeacon: but he could not do it.

'The bishop seems to be a quiet man enough,' suggested Mr. Harding, having acknowledged to himself his own failure.

'Idiot!' exclaimed the doctor, who for the nonce was not capable of more than such spasmodic attempts at utterance.

'Well, he did not seem very bright,' said Mr. Harding, 'and yet he has always had the reputation of a clever man. I suppose he's cautious and not inclined to express himself very freely.'

The new bishop of Barchester was already so contemptible a creature in Dr. Grantly's eyes, that he could not condescend to discuss his character. He was a puppet to be played by others; a mere wax doll, done up in an apron and a shovel hat, to be stuck on a throne or elsewhere,

and pulled about by wires as others chose. Dr. Grantly
did not choose to let himself down low enough to talk
about Dr. Proudie; but he saw that he would have to
talk about the other members of his household, the
coadjutor bishops, who had brought his lordship down,
as it were, in a box, and were about to handle the wires
as they willed. This in itself was a terrible vexation to
the archdeacon. Could he have ignored the chaplain,
and have fought the bishop, there would have been, at
any rate, nothing degrading in such a contest. Let the
Queen make whom she would bishop of Barchester;
a man, or even an ape, when once a bishop, would be a
respectable adversary, if he would but fight, himself.
But what was such a person as Dr. Grantly to do, when
such another person as Mr. Slope was put forward as his
antagonist?

If he, our archdeacon, refused the combat, Mr. Slope
would walk triumphant over the field, and have the
diocese of Barchester under his heel.

If, on the other hand, the archdeacon accepted as his
enemy the man whom the new puppet bishop put before
him as such, he would have to talk about Mr. Slope, and
write about Mr. Slope, and in all matters treat with Mr.
Slope, as a being standing, in some degree, on ground
similar to his own. He would have to meet Mr. Slope;
to——Bah! the idea was sickening. He could not bring
himself to have to do with Mr. Slope.

'He is the most thoroughly bestial creature that ever
I set my eyes upon,' said the archdeacon.

'Who—the bishop?' asked the other, innocently.

'Bishop! no—I'm not talking about the bishop. How
on earth such a creature got ordained!—they'll ordain
anybody now, I know; but he's been in the church these
ten years; and they used to be a little careful ten years ago.'

'Oh! you mean Mr. Slope.'

'Did you ever see any animal less like a gentleman?'
asked Dr. Grantly.

'I can't say I felt myself much disposed to like him.'

'Like him!' again shouted the doctor, and the assenting
ravens again cawed an echo; 'of course, you don't like
him: it's not a question of liking. But what are we to
do with him?'

' Do with him ? ' asked Mr. Harding.

' Yes—what are we to do with him ? How are we to treat him ? There he is, and there he'll stay. He has put his foot in that palace, and he will never take it out again till he's driven. How are we to get rid of him ? '

' I don't suppose he can do us much harm.'

' Not do harm !—Well, I think you'll find yourself of a different opinion before a month is gone. What would you say now, if he got himself put into the hospital ? Would that be harm ? '

Mr. Harding mused awhile, and then said he didn't think the new bishop would put Mr. Slope into the hospital.

' If he doesn't put him there, he'll put him somewhere else where he'll be as bad. I tell you that that man, to all intents and purposes, will be Bishop of Barchester ; ' and again Dr. Grantly raised his hat, and rubbed his hand thoughtfully and sadly over his head.

' Impudent scoundrel ! ' he continued after a while. ' To dare to cross-examine me about the Sunday schools in the diocese, and Sunday travelling too : I never in my life met his equal for sheer impudence. Why, he must have thought we were two candidates for ordination ! '

' I declare I thought Mrs. Proudie was the worst of the two,' said Mr. Harding.

' When a woman is impertinent, one must only put up with it, and keep out of her way in future ; but I am not inclined to put up with Mr. Slope. " Sabbath travelling ! " ' and the doctor attempted to imitate the peculiar drawl of the man he so much disliked : ' " Sabbath travelling ! " Those are the sort of men who will ruin the Church of England, and make the profession of a clergyman disreputable. It is not the dissenters or the papists that we should fear, but the set of canting, low-bred hypocrites who are wriggling their way in among us : men who have no fixed principle, no standard ideas of religion or doctrine, but who take up some popular cry, as this fellow has done about " Sabbath travelling." '

Dr. Grantly did not again repeat the question aloud, but he did so constantly to himself, ' What were they to do with Mr. Slope ? ' How was he openly, before the world, to show that he utterly disapproved of and abhorred such a man ?

Hitherto Barchester had escaped the taint of any extreme rigour of church doctrine. The clergymen of the city and neighbourhood, though very well inclined to promote high-church principles, privileges, and preroga- tives, had never committed themselves to tendencies, which are somewhat too loosely called Puseyite practices. They all preached in their black gowns, as their fathers had done before them ; they wore ordinary black cloth waistcoats ; they had no candles on their altars, either lighted or unlighted ; they made no private genuflexions, and were contented to confine themselves to such cere- monial observances as had been in vogue for the last hundred years. The services were decently and demurely read in their parish churches, chanting was confined to the cathedral, and the science of intoning was unknown. One young man who had come direct from Oxford as a curate to Plumstead had, after the lapse of two or three Sundays, made a faint attempt, much to the bewilderment of the poorer part of the congregation. Dr. Grantly had not been present on the occasion ; but Mrs. Grantly, who had her own opinion on the subject, immediately after the service expressed a hope that the young gentleman had not been taken ill, and offered to send him all kinds of condiments supposed to be good for a sore throat. After that there had been no more intoning at Plumstead Episcopi.

But now the archdeacon began to meditate on some strong measures of absolute opposition. Dr. Proudie and his crew were of the lowest possible order of Church of England clergymen, and therefore it behoved him, Dr. Grantly, to be of the very highest. Dr. Proudie would abolish all forms and ceremonies, and therefore Dr. Grantly felt the sudden necessity of multiplying them. Dr. Proudie would consent to deprive the church of all collective authority and rule, and therefore Dr. Grantly would stand up for the full power of convocation, and the renewal of all its ancient privileges.

It was true that he could not himself intone the service, but he could procure the co-operation of any number of gentlemanlike curates well trained in the mystery of doing so. He would not willingly alter his own fashion of dress, but he could people Barchester with young

clergymen dressed in the longest frocks, and in the highest-
breasted silk waistcoats. He certainly was not prepared
to cross himself, or to advocate the real presence ; but,
without going this length, there were various observances,
by adopting which he could plainly show his antipathy
to such men as Dr. Proudie and Mr. Slope.

All these things passed through his mind as he paced
up and down the close with Mr. Harding. War, war,
internecine war was in his heart. He felt that, as regarded
himself and Mr. Slope, one of the two must be annihilated
as far as the city of Barchester was concerned ; and he
did not intend to give way until there was not left to him
an inch of ground on which he could stand. He still
flattered himself that he could make Barchester too hot
to hold Mr. Slope, and he had no weakness of spirit to
prevent his bringing about such a consummation if it
were in his power.

' I suppose Susan must call at the palace,' said Mr.
Harding.

' Yes, she shall call there ; but it shall be once and once
only. I dare say " the horses " won't find it convenient
to come out to Plumstead very soon, and when that once
is done the matter may drop.'

' I don't suppose Eleanor need call. I don't think
Eleanor would get on at all well with Mrs. Proudie.'

' Not the least necessity in life,' replied the archdeacon,
not without the reflection that a ceremony which was
necessary for his wife, might not be at all binding on the
widow of John Bold. ' Not the slightest reason on earth
why she should do so, if she doesn't like it. For myself,
I don't think that any decent young woman should be
subjected to the nuisance of being in the same room with
that man.'

And so the two clergymen parted, Mr. Harding going
to his daughter's house, and the archdeacon seeking the
seclusion of his brougham.

The new inhabitants of the palace did not express any
higher opinion of their visitors than their visitors had
expressed of them. Though they did not use quite such
strong language as Dr. Grantly had done, they felt as
much personal aversion, and were quite as well aware
as he was that there would be a battle to be fought, and

that there was hardly room for Proudieism in Barchester as long as Grantlyism was predominant.

Indeed, it may be doubted whether Mr. Slope had not already within his breast a better prepared system of strategy, a more accurately-defined line of hostile conduct than the archdeacon. Dr. Grantly was going to fight because he found that he hated the man. Mr. Slope had predetermined to hate the man, because he foresaw the necessity of fighting him. When he had first reviewed the *carte du pays*, previous to his entry into Barchester, the idea had occurred to him of conciliating the archdeacon, of cajoling and flattering him into submission, and of obtaining the upper hand by cunning instead of courage. A little inquiry, however, sufficed to convince him that all his cunning would fail to win over such a man as Dr. Grantly to such a mode of action as that to be adopted by Mr. Slope; and then he determined to fall back upon his courage. He at once saw that open battle against Dr. Grantly and all Dr. Grantly's adherents was a necessity of his position, and he deliberately planned the most expedient methods of giving offence.

Soon after his arrival the bishop had intimated to the dean that, with the permission of the canon then in residence, his chaplain would preach in the cathedral on the next Sunday. The canon in residence happened to be the Hon. and Rev. Dr. Vesey Stanhope, who at this time was very busy on the shores of the Lake of Como, adding to that unique collection of butterflies for which he is so famous. Or, rather, he would have been in residence but for the butterflies and other such summer-day considerations; and the vicar-choral, who was to take his place in the pulpit, by no means objected to having his work done for him by Mr. Slope.

Mr. Slope accordingly preached, and if a preacher can have satisfaction in being listened to, Mr. Slope ought to have been gratified. I have reason to think that he was gratified, and that he left the pulpit with the conviction that he had done what he intended to do when he entered it.

On this occasion the new bishop took his seat for the first time in the throne allotted to him. New scarlet cushions and drapery had been prepared, with new gilt binding and new fringe. The old carved oak-wood of

the throne, ascending with its numerous grotesque
pinnacles half-way up to the roof of the choir, had been
washed, and dusted, and rubbed, and it all looked very
smart. Ah ! how often sitting there, in happy early days,
on those lowly benches in front of the altar, have I whiled
away the tedium of a sermon in considering how best
I might thread my way up amidst those wooden towers,
and climb safely to the topmost pinnacle !

All Barchester went to hear Mr. Slope ; either for that
or to gaze at the new bishop. All the best bonnets of
the city were there, and moreover all the best glossy
clerical hats. Not a stall but had its fitting occupant ;
for though some of the prebendaries might be away in
Italy or elsewhere, their places were filled by brethren,
who flocked into Barchester on the occasion. The dean
was there, a heavy old man, now too old, indeed, to attend
frequently in his place ; and so was the archdeacon. So
also were the chancellor, the treasurer, the precentor,
sundry canons and minor canons, and every lay member
of the choir, prepared to sing the new bishop in with due
melody and harmonious expression of sacred welcome.

The service was certainly very well performed. Such
was always the case at Barchester, as the musical education of the choir had been good, and the voices had been
carefully selected. The psalms were beautifully chanted ;
the Te Deum was magnificently sung ; and the litany
was given in a manner, which is still to be found at
Barchester, but, if my taste be correct, is to be found
nowhere else. The litany in Barchester cathedral has
long been the special task to which Mr. Harding's skill
and voice have been devoted. Crowded audiences
generally make good performers, and though Mr. Harding
was not aware of any extraordinary exertion on his part,
yet probably he rather exceeded his usual mark. Others
were doing their best, and it was natural that he should
emulate his brethren. So the service went on, and at
last Mr. Slope got into the pulpit.

He chose for his text a verse from the precepts addressed
by St. Paul to Timothy, as to the conduct necessary in
a spiritual pastor and guide, and it was immediately
evident that the good clergy of Barchester were to have
a lesson.

' Study to show thyself approved unto God, a workman that needeth not to be ashamed, rightly dividing the word of truth.' These were the words of his text, and with such a subject in such a place, it may be supposed that such a preacher would be listened to by such an audience. He was listened to with breathless attention, and not without considerable surprise. Whatever opinion of Mr. Slope might have been held in Barchester before he commenced his discourse, none of his hearers, when it was over, could mistake him either for a fool or a coward.

It would not be becoming were I to travestie a sermon, or even to repeat the language of it in the pages of a novel. In endeavouring to depict the characters of the persons of whom I write, I am to a certain extent forced to speak of sacred things. I trust, however, that I shall not be thought to scoff at the pulpit, though some may imagine that I do not feel all the reverence that is due to the cloth. I may question the infallibility of the teachers, but I hope that I shall not therefore be accused of doubt as to the thing to be taught.

Mr. Slope, in commencing his sermon, showed no slight tact in his ambiguous manner of hinting that, humble as he was himself, he stood there as the mouthpiece of the illustrious divine who sat opposite to him ; and having premised so much, he gave forth a very accurate definition of the conduct which that prelate would rejoice to see in the clergymen now brought under his jurisdiction. It is only necessary to say, that the peculiar points insisted upon were exactly those which were most distasteful to the clergy of the diocese, and most averse to their practice and opinions ; and that all those peculiar habits and privileges which have always been dear to high-church priests, to that party which is now scandalously called the high-and-dry church, were ridiculed, abused, and anathematised. Now, the clergymen of the diocese of Barchester are all of the high-and-dry church.

Having thus, according to his own opinion, explained how a clergyman should show himself approved unto God, as a workman that needeth not to be ashamed, he went on to explain how the word of truth should be divided ; and here he took a rather narrow view of the question, and fetched his arguments from afar. His

object was to express his abomination of all ceremonious
modes of utterance, to cry down any religious feeling
which might he excited, not by the sense, but by the
sound of words, and in fact to insult cathedral practices.
Had St. Paul spoken of rightly pronouncing instead of
rightly dividing the word of truth, this part of his sermon
would have been more to the purpose ; but the preacher's
immediate object was to preach Mr. Slope's doctrine,
and not St. Paul's, and he contrived to give the necessary
twist to the text with some skill.

He could not exactly say, preaching from a cathedral
pulpit, that chanting should be abandoned in cathedral
services. By such an assertion, he would have overshot
his mark and rendered himself absurd, to the delight of
his hearers. He could, however, and did, allude with
heavy denunciations to the practice of intoning in parish
churches, although the practice was all but unknown in
the diocese ; and from thence he came round to the undue
preponderance, which he asserted, music had over meaning
in the beautiful service which they had just heard. He
was aware, he said, that the practices of our ancestors
could not be abandoned at a moment's notice ; the feelings
of the aged would be outraged, and the minds of respectable men would be shocked. There were many, he was
aware, of not sufficient calibre of thought to perceive,
of not sufficient education to know, that a mode of service,
which was effective when outward ceremonies were of
more moment than inward feelings, had become all but
barbarous at a time when inward conviction was everything, when each word of the minister's lips should fall
intelligibly into the listener's heart. Formerly the
religion of the multitude had been an affair of the imagination : now, in these latter days, it had become necessary
that a Christian should have a reason for his faith—should
not only believe, but digest—not only hear, but understand. The words of our morning service, how beautiful,
how apposite, how intelligible they were, when read with
simple and distinct decorum ! but how much of the
meaning of the words was lost when they were produced
with all the meretricious charms of melody ! &c. &c.

Here was a sermon to be preached before Mr. Archdeacon Grantly, Mr. Precentor Harding, and the rest of

them! before a whole dean and chapter assembled in their own cathedral! before men who had grown old in the exercise of their peculiar services, with a full conviction of their excellence for all intended purposes! This too from such a man, a clerical *parvenu*, a man without a cure, a mere chaplain, an intruder among them; a fellow raked up, so said Dr. Grantly, from the gutters of Marylebone! They had to sit through it! None of them, not even Dr. Grantly, could close his ears, nor leave the house of God during the hours of service. They were under an obligation of listening, and that too, without any immediate power of reply.

There is, perhaps, no greater hardship at present inflicted on mankind in civilised and free countries, than the necessity of listening to sermons. No one but a preaching clergyman has, in these realms, the power of compelling an audience to sit silent, and be tormented. No one but a preaching clergyman can revel in platitudes, truisms, and untruisms, and yet receive, as his undisputed privilege, the same respectful demeanour as though words of impassioned eloquence, or persuasive logic, fell from his lips. Let a professor of law or physic find his place in a lecture-room, and there pour forth jejune words and useless empty phrases, and he will pour them forth to empty benches. Let a barrister attempt to talk without talking well, and he will talk but seldom. A judge's charge need be listened to per force by none but the jury, prisoner, and gaoler. A member of Parliament can be coughed down or counted out. Town-councillors can be tabooed. But no one can rid himself of the preaching clergyman. He is the bore of the age, the old man whom we Sindbads cannot shake off, the nightmare that disturbs our Sunday's rest, the incubus that overloads our religion and makes God's service distasteful. We are not forced into church! No: but we desire more than that. We desire not to be forced to stay away. We desire, nay, we are resolute, to enjoy the comfort of public worship; but we desire also that we may do so without an amount of tedium which ordinary human nature cannot endure with patience; that we may be able to leave the house of God, without that anxious longing for escape, which is the common consequence of common sermons.

With what complacency will a young parson deduce
false conclusions from misunderstood texts, and then
threaten us with all the penalties of Hades if we neglect
to comply with the injunctions he has given us! Yes,
my too self-confident juvenile friend, I do believe in those
mysteries, which are so common in your mouth; I do
believe in the unadulterated word which you hold there
in your hand; but you must pardon me if, in some things,
I doubt your interpretation. The bible is good, the
prayer-book is good, nay, you yourself would be acceptable,
if you would read to me some portion of those time-
honoured discourses which our great divines have
elaborated in the full maturity of their powers. But you
must excuse me, my insufficient young lecturer, if I yawn
over your imperfect sentences, your repeated phrases,
your false pathos, your drawlings and denouncings, your
humming and hawing, your oh-ing and ah-ing, your
black gloves and your white handkerchief. To me, it
all means nothing; and hours are too precious to be so
wasted——if one could only avoid it.

And here I must make a protest against the pretence,
so often put forward by the working clergy, that they are
overburdened by the multitude of sermons to be preached.
We are all too fond of our own voices, and a preacher is
encouraged in the vanity of making his heard by the
privilege of a compelled audience. His sermon is the
pleasant morsel of his life, his delicious moment of self-
exaltation. 'I have preached nine sermons this week,'
said a young friend to me the other day, with hand
languidly raised to his brow, the picture of an overburdened martyr. 'Nine this week, seven last week,
four the week before. I have preached twenty-three
sermons this month. It is really too much.' 'Too much,
indeed,' said I, shuddering; 'too much for the strength
of any one.' 'Yes,' he answered meekly, 'indeed it is;
I am beginning to feel it painfully.' 'Would,' said I,
'you could feel it—would that you could be made to
feel it.' But he never guessed that my heart was wrung
for the poor listeners.

There was, at any rate, no tedium felt in listening to
Mr. Slope on the occasion in question. His subject came
too home to his audience to be dull; and, to tell the truth,

Mr. Slope had the gift of using words forcibly. He was heard through his thirty minutes of eloquence with mute attention and open ears; but with angry eyes, which glared round from one enraged parson to another, with wide-spread nostrils from which already burst forth fumes of indignation, and with many shufflings of the feet and uneasy motions of the body, which betokened minds disturbed, and hearts not at peace with all the world.

At last the bishop, who, of all the congregation, had been most surprised, and whose hair almost stood on end with terror, gave the blessing in a manner not at all equal to that in which he had long been practising it in his own study, and the congregation was free to go their way.

CHAPTER VII

THE DEAN AND CHAPTER TAKE COUNSEL

ALL Barchester was in a tumult. Dr. Grantly could hardly get himself out of the cathedral porch before he exploded in his wrath. The old dean betook himself silently to his deanery, afraid to speak; and there sat, half stupefied, pondering many things in vain. Mr. Harding crept forth solitary and unhappy; and, slowly passing beneath the elms of the close, could scarcely bring himself to believe that the words which he had heard had proceeded from the pulpit of Barchester cathedral. Was he again to be disturbed? was his whole life to be shown up as a useless sham a second time? would he have to abdicate his precentorship, as he had his wardenship, and to give up chanting, as he had given up his twelve old bedesmen? And what if he did! Some other Jupiter, some other Mr. Slope, would come and turn him out of St. Cuthbert's. Surely he could not have been wrong all his life in chanting the litany as he had done! He began, however, to have his doubts. Doubting himself was Mr. Harding's weakness. It is not, however, the usual fault of his order.

Yes! all Barchester was in a tumult. It was not only the clergy who were affected. The laity also had listened to Mr. Slope's new doctrine, all with surprise, some with indignation, and some with a mixed feeling, in which dislike of the preacher was not so strongly blended. The old bishop and his chaplains, the dean and his canons and minor canons, the old choir, and especially Mr. Harding who was at the head of it, had all been popular in Barchester. They had spent their money and done good ; the poor had not been ground down ; the clergy in society had neither been overbearing nor austere ; and the whole repute of the city was due to its ecclesiastical importance. Yet there were those who had heard Mr. Slope with satisfaction.

It is so pleasant to receive a fillip of excitement when suffering from the dull routine of every-day life ! The anthems and Te Deums were in themselves delightful, but they had been heard so often ! Mr. Slope was certainly not delightful, but he was new, and, moreover, clever. They had long thought it slow, so said now many of the Barchesterians, to go on as they had done in their old humdrum way, giving ear to none of the religious changes which were moving the world without. People in advance of the age now had new ideas, and it was quite time that Barchester should go in advance. Mr. Slope might be right. Sunday certainly had not been strictly kept in Barchester, except as regarded the cathedral services. Indeed the two hours between services had long been appropriated to morning calls and hot luncheons. Then Sunday schools ! really more ought to have been done as to Sunday schools ; Sabbath-day schools Mr. Slope had called them. The late bishop had really not thought of Sunday schools as he should have done. (These people probably did not reflect that catechisms and collects are quite as hard work to the young mind as book-keeping is to the elderly ; and that quite as little feeling of worship enters into the one task as the other.) And then, as regarded that great question of musical services, there might be much to be said on Mr. Slope's side of the question. It certainly was the fact, that people went to the cathedral to hear the music, &c. &c.

And so a party absolutely formed itself in Barchester on Mr. Slope's side of the question ! This consisted, among the upper classes, chiefly of ladies. No man— that is, no gentleman—could possibly be attracted by

Mr. Slope, or consent to sit at the feet of so abhorrent a Gamaliel. Ladies are sometimes less nice in their appreciation of physical disqualification ; and, provided that a man speak to them well, they will listen, though he speak from a mouth never so deformed and hideous. Wilkes was most fortunate as a lover ; and the damp, sandy-haired, saucer-eyed, red-fisted Mr. Slope was powerful only over the female breast.

There were, however, one or two of the neighbouring clergy who thought it not quite safe to neglect the baskets in which for the nonce were stored the loaves and fishes of the diocese of Barchester. They, and they only, came to call on Mr. Slope after his performance in the cathedral pulpit. Among these Mr. Quiverful, the rector of Pudding-dale, whose wife still continued to present him from year to year with fresh pledges of her love, and so to increase his cares and, it is to be hoped, his happiness equally. Who can wonder that a gentleman, with fourteen living children and a bare income of 400*l.* a year, should look after the loaves and fishes, even when they are under the thumb of a Mr. Slope ?

Very soon after the Sunday on which the sermon was preached, the leading clergy of the neighbourhood held high debate together as to how Mr. Slope should be put down. In the first place he should never again preach from the pulpit of Barchester cathedral. This was Dr. Grantly's earliest dictum ; and they all agreed, providing only that they had the power to exclude him. Dr. Grantly declared that the power rested with the dean and chapter, observing that no clergyman out of the chapter had a claim to preach there, saving only the bishop himself. To this the dean assented, but alleged that contests on such a subject would be unseemly ; to which rejoined a meagre little doctor, one of the cathedral prebendaries, that the contest must be all on the side of Mr. Slope if every prebendary were always there ready to take his own place in the pulpit. Cunning little meagre doctor, whom it suits well to live in his own cosy house within Barchester close, and who is well content to have his little fling at Dr. Vesey Stanhope and other absentees, whose Italian villas, or enticing London homes, are more tempting than cathedral stalls and residences !

To this answered the burly chancellor, a man rather silent indeed, but very sensible, that absent prebendaries had their vicars, and that in such case the vicar's right to the pulpit was the same as that of the higher order. To which the dean assented, groaning deeply at these truths. Thereupon, however, the meagre doctor remarked that they would be in the hands of their minor canons, one of whom might at any hour betray his trust. Whereon was heard from the burly chancellor an ejaculation sounding somewhat like 'Pooh, pooh, pooh!' but it might be that the worthy man was but blowing out the heavy breath from his windpipe. Why silence him at all? suggested Mr. Harding. Let them not be ashamed to hear what any man might have to preach to them, unless he preached false doctrine; in which case, let the bishop silence him. So spoke our friend; vainly; for human ends must be attained by human means. But the dean saw a ray of hope out of those purblind old eyes of his. Yes, let them tell the bishop how distasteful to them was this Mr. Slope: a new bishop just come to his seat could not wish to insult his clergy while the gloss was yet fresh on his first apron.

Then up rose Dr. Grantly; and, having thus collected the scattered wisdom of his associates, spoke forth with words of deep authority. When I say up rose the arch-deacon, I speak of the inner man, which then sprang up to more immediate action, for the doctor had, bodily, been standing all along with his back to the dean's empty fire-grate, and the tails of his frock coat supported over his two arms. His hands were in his breeches pockets.

'It is quite clear that this man must not be allowed to preach again in this cathedral. We all see that, except our dear friend here, the milk of whose nature runs so softly, that he would not have the heart to refuse the Pope the loan of his pulpit, if the Pope would come and ask it. We must not, however, allow the man to preach again here. It is not because his opinion on church matters may be different from ours—with that one would not quarrel. It is because he has purposely insulted us. When he went up into the pulpit last Sunday, his studied object was to give offence to men who had grown old in reverence of those things of which he dared to speak so slightingly. What! to come here a stranger, a young, unknown, and unfriended stranger, and tell us, in the name of the bishop his master, that we are ignorant of our duties, old-fashioned, and useless! I don't know whether most to admire his courage or his impudence! And one thing I will tell you : that sermon originated solely with the man himself. The bishop was no more a party to it than was the dean here. You all know how grieved I am to see a bishop in this diocese holding the latitudinarian ideas by which Dr. Proudie has made himself conspicuous. You all know how greatly I should distrust the opinion of such a man. But in this matter I hold him to be blameless. I believe Dr. Proudie has lived too long among gentlemen to be guilty, or to instigate another to be guilty, of so gross an outrage. No! that man uttered what was untrue when he hinted that he was speaking as the mouthpiece of the bishop. It suited his ambitious views at once to throw down the gauntlet to us—at once to defy us here in the quiet of our own religious duties—here within the walls of our own loved cathedral —here where we have for so many years exercised our ministry without schism and with good repute. Such an attack upon us, coming from such a quarter, is abominable.'

'Abominable,' groaned the dean. 'Abominable,' muttered the meagre doctor. 'Abominable,' re-echoed the chancellor, uttering the sound from the bottom of his deep chest. 'I really think it was,' said Mr. Harding.

'Most abominable and most unjustifiable,' continued the archdeacon. 'But, Mr. Dean, thank God, that pulpit is still our own : your own, I should say. That pulpit belongs solely to the dean and chapter of Barchester Cathedral, and, as yet, Mr. Slope is no part of that chapter. You, Mr. Dean, have suggested that we should appeal to the bishop to abstain from forcing this man on us ; but what if the bishop allow himself to be ruled by his chaplain? In my opinion, the matter is in our own hands. Mr. Slope cannot preach there without permission asked and obtained, and let that permission be invariably refused. Let all participation in the ministry of the cathedral service be refused to him. Then, if the bishop choose to interfere, we shall know what answer to make to the bishop My

friend here has suggested that this man may again find
his way into the pulpit by undertaking the duty of some
of your minor canons; but I am sure that we may fully
trust to these gentlemen to support us, when it is known
that the dean objects to any such transfer.'

'Of course you may,' said the chancellor.

There was much more discussion among the learned
conclave, all of which, of course, ended in obedience to
the archdeacon's commands. They had too long been
accustomed to his rule to shake it off so soon; and in
this particular case they had none of them a wish to abet
the man whom he was so anxious to put down.

Such a meeting as that we have just recorded is not
held in such a city as Barchester unknown and untold
of. Not only was the fact of the meeting talked of in
every respectable house, including the palace, but the
very speeches of the dean, the archdeacon, and chancellor
were repeated; not without many additions and imaginary circumstances, according to the tastes and opinions
of the relaters.

All, however, agreed in saying that Mr. Slope was to
be debarred from opening his mouth in the cathedral of
Barchester; many believed that the vergers were to be
ordered to refuse him even the accommodation of a seat;
and some of the most far-going advocates for strong
measures, declared that his sermon was looked upon as
an indictable offence, and that proceedings were to be
taken against him for brawling.

The party who were inclined to defend him—the
enthusiastically religious young ladies, and the middle-
aged spinsters desirous of a move—of course took up his
defence the more warmly on account of this attack. If
they could not hear Mr. Slope in the cathedral, they would
hear him elsewhere; they would leave the dull dean, the
dull old prebendaries, and the scarcely less dull young
minor canons, to preach to each other; they would work
slippers and cushions, and hem bands for Mr. Slope, make
him a happy martyr, and stick him up in some new Sion
or Bethesda, and put the cathedral quite out of fashion.

Dr. and Mrs. Proudie at once returned to London.
They thought it expedient not to have to encounter any
personal application from the dean and chapter respecting

the sermon, till the violence of the storm had expended
itself; but they left Mr. Slope behind them nothing
daunted, and he went about his work zealously, flattering
such as would listen to his flattery, whispering religious
twaddle into the ears of foolish women, ingratiating
himself with the few clergy who would receive him,
visiting the houses of the poor, inquiring into all people,
prying into everything, and searching with his minutest
eye into all palatial dilapidations. He did not, however,
make any immediate attempt to preach again in the
cathedral.

And so all Barchester was by the ears.

CHAPTER VIII

THE EX-WARDEN REJOICES IN HIS PROBABLE RETURN TO THE HOSPITAL

AMONG the ladies in Barchester who have hitherto
acknowledged Mr. Slope as their spiritual director, must
not be reckoned either the widow Bold, or her sister-in-law.
On the first outbreak of the wrath of the denizens of the
close, none had been more animated against the intruder
than these two ladies. And this was natural. Who could
be so proud of the musical distinction of their own cathedral
as the favourite daughter of the precentor ? Who would
be so likely to resent an insult offered to the old choir ?
And in such matters Miss Bold and her sister-in-law had
but one opinion.

This wrath, however, has in some degree been mitigated,
and I regret to say that these ladies allowed Mr. Slope
to be his own apologist. About a fortnight after the
sermon had been preached, they were both of them not
a little surprised by hearing Mr. Slope announced, as the
page in buttons opened Mrs. Bold's drawing-room door.
Indeed, what living man could, by a mere morning visit,
have surprised them more ? Here was the great enemy
of all that was good in Barchester coming into their own
drawing-room, and they had no strong arm, no ready
tongue, near at hand for their protection. The widow
snatched her baby out of its cradle into her lap, and Mary

Bold stood up ready to die manfully in that baby's behalf, should, under any circumstances, such a sacrifice become necessary.

In this manner was Mr. Slope received. But when he left, he was allowed by each lady to take her hand, and to make his adieux as gentlemen do who have been graciously entertained! Yes; he shook hands with them, and was curtseyed out courteously, the buttoned page opening the door, as he would have done for the best canon of them all. He had touched the baby's little hand and blessed him with a fervid blessing; he had spoken to the widow of her early sorrows, and Eleanor's silent tears had not rebuked him; he had told Mary Bold that her devotion would be rewarded, and Mary Bold had heard the praise without disgust. And how had he done all this? how had he so quickly turned aversion into, at any rate, acquaintance? how had he overcome the enmity with which these ladies had been ready to receive him, and made his peace with them so easily?

My readers will guess from what I have written that I myself do not like Mr. Slope; but I am constrained to admit that he is a man of parts. He knows how to say a soft word in the proper place; he knows how to adapt his flattery to the ears of his hearers; he knows the wiles of the serpent, and he uses them. Could Mr. Slope have adapted his manners to men as well as to women, could he ever have learnt the ways of a gentleman, he might have risen to great things.

He commenced his acquaintance with Eleanor by praising her father. He had, he said, become aware that he had unfortunately offended the feelings of a man of whom he could not speak too highly; he would not now allude to a subject which was probably too serious for drawing-room conversation, but he would say, that it had been very far from him to utter a word in disparagement of a man, of whom all the world, at least the clerical world, spoke so highly as it did of Mr. Harding. And so he went on, unsaying a great deal of his sermon, expressing his highest admiration for the precentor's musical talents, eulogising the father and the daughter and the sister-in-law, speaking in that low silky whisper which he always had specially prepared for feminine ears, and, ultimately,

gaining his object. When he left, he expressed a hope
that he might again be allowed to call; and though
Eleanor gave no verbal assent to this, she did not express
dissent: and so Mr. Slope's right to visit at the widow's
house was established.

The day after this visit Eleanor told her father of it,
and expressed an opinion that Mr. Slope was not quite
so black as he had been painted. Mr. Harding opened
his eyes rather wider than usual when he heard what had
occurred, but he said little; he could not agree in any
praise of Mr. Slope,. and it was not his practice to say
much evil of any one. He did not, however, like the visit,
and simple-minded as he was, he felt sure that Mr. Slope
had some deeper motive than the mere pleasure of making
soft speeches to two ladies.

Mr. Harding, however, had come to see his daughter
with other purpose than that of speaking either good or
evil of Mr. Slope. He had come to tell her that the place
of warden in Hiram's hospital was again to be filled up,
and that in all probability he would once more return
to his old home and his twelve bedesmen.

'But,' said, he, laughing, 'I shall be greatly shorn of
my ancient glory.'

'Why so, papa?'

'This new act of parliament, that is to put us all on
our feet again,' continued he, 'settles my income at four
hundred and fifty pounds per annum.'

'Four hundred and fifty,' said she, 'instead of eight
hundred! Well; that is rather shabby. But still, papa,
you'll have the dear old house and the garden?'

'My dear,' said he, 'it's worth twice the money;'
and as he spoke he showed a jaunty kind of satisfaction
in his tone and manner, and in the quick, pleasant way
in which he paced Eleanor's drawing-room. 'It's worth
twice the money. I shall have the house and the garden,
and a larger income than I can possibly want.'

'At any rate, you'll have no extravagant daughter to
provide for;' and as she spoke, the young widow put
her arm within his, and made him sit on the sofa beside
her; 'at any rate you'll not have that expense.'

'No, my dear; and I shall be rather lonely without her;
but we won't think of that now. As regards income I shall

have plenty for all I want. I shall have my old house; and I don't mind owning now that I have felt sometimes the inconvenience of living in a lodging. Lodgings are very nice for young men, but at my time of life there is a want of——I hardly know what to call it, perhaps not respectability——'

'Oh, papa! I'm sure there's been nothing like that. Nobody has thought it; nobody in all Barchester has been more respected than you have been since you took those rooms in High Street. Nobody! Not the dean in his deanery, or the archdeacon out at Plumstead.'

'The archdeacon would not be much obliged to you if he heard you,' said he, smiling somewhat at the exclusive manner in which his daughter confined her illustration to the church dignitaries of the chapter of Barchester; 'but at any rate I shall be glad to get back to the old house. Since I heard that it was all settled, I have begun to fancy that I can't be comfortable without my two sitting-rooms.'

'Come and stay with me, papa, till it is settled—there's a dear papa.'

'Thank ye, Nelly. But no; I won't do that. It would make two movings. I shall be very glad to get back to my old men again. Alas! alas! There have six of them gone in these few last years. Six out of twelve! And the others I fear have had but a sorry life of it there. Poor Bunce, poor old Bunce!'

Bunce was one of the surviving recipients of Hiram's charity; an old man, now over ninety, who had long been a favourite of Mr. Harding's.

'How happy old Bunce will be,' said Mrs. Bold, clapping her soft hands softly. 'How happy they all will be to have you back again. You may be sure there will soon be friendship among them again when you are there.'

'But,' said he, half laughing, ' I am to have new troubles, which will be terrible to me. There are to be twelve old women, and a matron. How shall I manage twelve women and a matron!'

'The matron will manage the women of course.'

'And who'll manage the matron?' said he.

'She won't want to be managed. She'll be a great lady herself, I suppose. But, papa, where will the matron live ? She is not to live in the warden's house with you, is she ? '

' Well, I hope not, my dear.'

' Oh, papa, I tell you fairly, I won't have a matron for a new step-mother.'

' You shan't, my dear ; that is, if I can help it. But they are going to build another house for the matron and the women ; and I believe they haven't even fixed yet on the site of the building.'

' And have they appointed the matron ? ' said Eleanor.

' They haven't appointed the warden yet,' replied he.

' But there's no doubt about that, I suppose,' said his daughter.

Mr. Harding explained that he thought there was no doubt ; that the archdeacon had declared as much, saying that the bishop and his chaplain between them had not the power to appoint any one else, even if they had the will to do so, and sufficient impudence to carry out such a will. The archdeacon was of opinion, that though Mr. Harding had resigned his wardenship, and had done so unconditionally, he had done so under circumstances which left the bishop no choice as to his re-appointment, now that the affair of the hospital had been settled on a new basis by act of parliament. Such was the archdeacon's opinion, and his father-in-law received it without a shadow of doubt.

Dr. Grantly had always been strongly opposed to Mr. Harding's resignation of the place. He had done all in his power to dissuade him from it. He had considered that Mr. Harding was bound to withstand the popular clamour with which he was attacked for receiving so large an income as eight hundred a year from such a charity, and was not even yet satisfied that his father-in-law's conduct had not been pusillanimous and undignified. He looked also on this reduction of the warden's income as a shabby, paltry scheme on the part of government for escaping from a difficulty into which it had been brought by the public press. Dr. Grantly observed that the government had no more right to dispose of a sum of four hundred and fifty pounds a year out of the income of Hiram's legacy, than of nine hundred ; whereas, as he said, the bishop, dean, and chapter clearly had a right

to settle what sum should be paid. He also declared that
the government had no more right to saddle the charity
with twelve old women than with twelve hundred; and
he was, therefore, very indignant on the matter. He
probably forgot when so talking that government had
done nothing of the kind, and had never assumed any such
might or any such right. He made the common mistake
of attributing to the government, which in such matters
is powerless, the doings of parliament, which in such
matters is omnipotent.

But though he felt that the glory and honour of the
situation of warden of Barchester hospital were indeed
curtailed by the new arrangement; that the whole establishment had to a certain degree been made vile by the
touch of Whig commissioners; that the place with its
lessened income, its old women, and other innovations,
was very different from the hospital of former days;
still the archdeacon was too practical a man of the world
to wish that his father-in-law, who had at present little
more than 200l. per annum for all his wants, should refuse
the situation, defiled, undignified, and commission-ridden
as it was.

Mr. Harding had, accordingly, made up his mind that
he would return to his old home at the hospital, and to
tell the truth, had experienced almost a childish pleasure
in the idea of doing so. The diminished income was to
him not even the source of momentary regret. The matron
and the old women did rather go against the grain; but
he was able to console himself with the reflection, that,
after all, such an arrangement might be of real service
to the poor of the city. The thought that he must receive
his re-appointment as the gift of the new bishop, and
probably through the hands of Mr. Slope, annoyed him
a little; but his mind was set at rest by the assurance
of the archdeacon that there would be no favour in such
a presentation. The re-appointment of the old warden
would be regarded by all the world as a matter of course.
Mr. Harding, therefore, felt no hesitation in telling his
daughter that they might look upon his return to his old
quarters as a settled matter.

'And you won't have to ask for it, papa.'

'Certainly not, my dear. There is no ground on which

I could ask for any favour from the bishop, whom, indeed, I hardly know. Nor would I ask a favour, the granting of which might possibly be made a question to be settled by Mr. Slope. No,' said he, moved for a moment by a spirit very unlike his own, ' I certainly shall be very glad to go back to the hospital; but I should never go there, if it were necessary that my doing so should be the subject of a request to Mr. Slope.'

This little outbreak of her father's anger jarred on the present tone of Eleanor's mind. She had not learnt to like Mr. Slope, but she had learnt to think that he had much respect for her father; and she would, therefore, willingly use her efforts to induce something like good feeling between them.

' Papa,' said she, ' I think you somewhat mistake Mr. Slope's character.'

' Do I ? ' said he, placidly.

' I think you do, papa. I think he intended no personal disrespect to you when he preached the sermon which made the archdeacon and the dean so angry ! '

' I never supposed he did, my dear. I hope I never inquired within myself whether he did or no. Such a matter would be unworthy of any inquiry, and very unworthy of the consideration of the chapter. But I fear he intended disrespect to the ministration of God's services, as conducted in conformity with the rules of the Church of England.'

' But might it not be that he thought it his duty to express his dissent from that which you, and the dean, and all of us here so much approve ? '

' It can hardly be the duty of a young man rudely to assail the religious convictions of his elders in the church. Courtesy should have kept him silent, even if neither charity nor modesty could do so.'

' But Mr. Slope would say that on such a subject the commands of his heavenly Master do not admit of his being silent.'

' Nor of his being courteous, Eleanor ? '

' He did not say that, papa.'

' Believe me, my child, that Christian ministers are never called on by God's word to insult the convictions, or even the prejudices of their brethren ; and that religion is at any rate not less susceptible of urbane and courteous conduct among men, than any other study which men may take up. I am sorry to say that I cannot defend Mr. Slope's sermon in the cathedral. But come, my dear, put on your bonnet, and let us walk round the dear old gardens at the hospital. I have never yet had the heart to go beyond the court-yard since we left the place. Now I think I can venture to enter.'

Eleanor rang the bell, and gave a variety of imperative charges as to the welfare of the precious baby, whom, all but unwillingly, she was about to leave for an hour or so, and then sauntered forth with her father to revisit the old hospital. It had been forbidden ground to her as well as to him since the day on which they had walked forth together from its walls.

CHAPTER IX

THE STANHOPE FAMILY

It is now three months since Dr. Proudie began his reign, and changes have already been effected in the diocese which show at least the energy of an active mind. Among other things absentee clergymen have been favoured with hints much too strong to be overlooked. Poor dear old Bishop Grantly had on this matter been too lenient, and the archdeacon had never been inclined to be severe with those who were absent on reputable pretences, and who provided for their duties in a liberal way.

Among the greatest of the diocesan sinners in this respect was Dr. Vesey Stanhope. Years had now passed since he had done a day's duty; and yet there was no reason against his doing duty except a want of inclination on his own part. He held a prebendal stall in the diocese; one of the best residences in the close; and the two large rectories of Crabtree Canonicorum, and Stogpingum. Indeed, he had the cure of three parishes, for that of Eiderdown was joined to Stogpingum. He had resided in Italy for twelve years. His first going there had been attributed to a sore throat; and that sore throat, though never repeated in any violent manner, had stood him in such stead, that it had enabled him to live in easy idleness ever since.

He had now been summoned home—not, indeed, with rough violence, or by any peremptory command, but by a mandate which he found himself unable to disregard. Mr. Slope had written to him by the bishop's desire. In the first place, the bishop much wanted the valuable co-operation of Dr. Vesey Stanhope in the diocese; in the next, the bishop thought it his imperative duty to become personally acquainted with the most conspicuous of his diocesan clergy; then the bishop thought it essentially necessary for Dr. Stanhope's own interests, that Dr. Stanhope should, at any rate for a time, return to Barchester; and lastly, it was said that so strong a feeling was at the present moment evinced by the hierarchs of the church with reference to the absence of its clerical members, that it behoved Dr. Vesey Stanhope not to allow his name to stand among those which would probably in a few months be submitted to the councils of the nation.

There was something so ambiguously frightful in this last threat that Dr. Stanhope determined to spend two or three summer months at his residence in Barchester. His rectories were inhabited by his curates, and he felt himself from disuse to be unfit for parochial duty; but his prebendal home was kept empty for him, and he thought it probable that he might be able now and again to preach a prebendal sermon. He arrived, therefore, with all his family at Barchester, and he and they must be introduced to my readers.

The great family characteristic of the Stanhopes might probably be said to be heartlessness; but this want of feeling was, in most of them, accompanied by so great an amount of good nature as to make itself but little noticeable to the world. They were so prone to oblige their neighbours that their neighbours failed to perceive how indifferent to them was the happiness and well-being of those around them. The Stanhopes would visit you in your sickness (provided it were not contagious), would bring you oranges, French novels, and the last new bit of scandal, and then hear of your death or your recovery

with an equally indifferent composure. Their conduct
to each other was the same as to the world; they bore
and forebore: and there was sometimes, as will be seen,
much necessity for forbearing: but their love among
themselves rarely reached above this. It is astonishing
how much each of the family was able to do, and how
much each did, to prevent the well-being of the other
four.

For there were five in all; the doctor, namely, and
Mrs. Stanhope, two daughters, and one son. The doctor,
perhaps, was the least singular and most estimable of
them all, and yet such good qualities as he possessed
were all negative. He was a good looking rather plethoric
gentleman of about sixty years of age. His hair was
snow white, very plentiful, and somewhat like wool of
the finest description. His whiskers were very large and
very white, and gave to his face the appearance of a
benevolent sleepy old lion. His dress was always unexceptionable. Although he had lived so many years in Italy
it was invariably of a decent clerical hue, but it never
was hyperclerical. He was a man not given to much
talking, but what little he did say was generally well
said. His reading seldom went beyond romances and
poetry of the lightest and not always most moral description. He was thoroughly a *bon vivant;* an accomplished
judge of wine, though he never drank to excess; and
a most inexorable critic in all affairs touching the kitchen.
He had had much to forgive in his own family, since a
family had grown up around him, and had forgiven
everything—except inattention to his dinner. His weakness in that respect was now fully understood, and his
temper but seldom tried. As Dr. Stanhope was a clergyman, it may be supposed that his religious convictions
made up a considerable part of his character; but this
was not so. That he had religious convictions must be
believed; but he rarely obtruded them, even on his
children. This abstinence on his part was not systematic,
but very characteristic of the man. It was not that he
had predetermined never to influence their thoughts;
but he was so habitually idle that his time for doing so
had never come till the opportunity for doing so was gone
for ever. Whatever conviction the father may have had,

the children were at any rate but indifferent members
of the church from which he drew his income.

Such was Dr. Stanhope. The features of Mrs. Stanhope's
character were even less plainly marked than those of
her lord. The *far niente* of her Italian life had entered
into her very soul, and brought her to regard a state of
inactivity as the only earthly good. In manner and
appearance she was exceedingly prepossessing. She had
been a beauty, and even now, at fifty-five, she was a
handsome woman. Her dress was always perfect: she
never dressed but once in the day, and never appeared
till between three and four; but when she did appear,
she appeared at her best. Whether the toil rested partly
with her, or wholly with her handmaid, it is not for such
a one as the author even to imagine. The structure of
her attire was always elaborate, and yet never over
laboured. She was rich in apparel, but not bedizened
with finery; her ornaments were costly, rare, and such
as could not fail to attract notice, but they did not look
as though worn with that purpose. She well knew the
great architectural secret of decorating her constructions,
and never descended to construct a decoration. But
when we have said that Mrs. Stanhope knew how to dress,
and used her knowledge daily, we have said all. Other
purpose in life she had none. It was something, indeed,
that she did not interfere with the purposes of others.
In early life she had undergone great trials with reference
to the doctor's dinners; but for the last ten or twelve
years her eldest daughter Charlotte had taken that labour
off her hands, and she had had little to trouble her;—
little, that is, till the edict for this terrible English journey
had gone forth: since, then, indeed, her life had been
laborious enough. For such a one, the toil of being
carried from the shores of Como to the city of Barchester
is more than labour enough, let the care of the carriers
be ever so vigilant. Mrs. Stanhope had been obliged
to have every one of her dresses taken in from the effects
of the journey.

Charlotte Stanhope was at this time about thirty-five
years old; and, whatever may have been her faults, she
had none of those which belong particularly to old young
ladies. She neither dressed young, nor talked young,

nor indeed looked young. She appeared to be perfectly
content with her time of life, and in no way affected the
graces of youth. She was a fine young woman; and
had she been a man, would have been a very fine young
man. All that was done in the house, and that was not
done by servants, was done by her. She gave the orders,
paid the bills, hired and dismissed the domestics, made
the tea, carved the meat, and managed everything in
the Stanhope household. She, and she alone, could ever
induce her father to look into the state of his worldly
concerns. She, and she alone, could in any degree control
the absurdities of her sister. She, and she alone, prevented
the whole family from falling into utter disrepute and
beggary. It was by her advice that they now found themselves very unpleasantly situated in Barchester.

So far, the character of Charlotte Stanhope is not
unprepossessing. But it remains to be said, that the
influence which she had in her family, though it had been
used to a certain extent for their worldly well-being, had
not been used to their real benefit, as it might have been.
She had aided her father in his indifference to his professional duties, counselling him that his livings were as
much his individual property as the estates of his elder
brother were the property of that worthy peer. She had
for years past stifled every little rising wish for a return
to England which the doctor had from time to time
expressed. She had encouraged her mother in her idleness
in order that she herself might be mistress and manager
of the Stanhope household. She had encouraged and
fostered the follies of her sister, though she was always
willing, and often able, to protect her from their probable
result. She had done her best, and had thoroughly
succeeded in spoiling her brother, and turning him loose
upon the world an idle man without a profession, and
without a shilling that he could call his own.

Miss Stanhope was a clever woman, able to talk on
most subjects, and quite indifferent as to what the subject
was. She prided herself on her freedom from English
prejudice, and she might have added, from feminine
delicacy. On religion she was a pure freethinker, and
with much want of true affection, delighted to throw
out her own views before the troubled mind of her father.

To have shaken what remained of his Church of England faith would have gratified her much ; but the idea of his abandoning his preferment in the church had never once presented itself to her mind. How could he indeed, when he had no income from any other source ?

But the two most prominent members of the family still remain to be described. The second child had been christened Madeline, and had been a great beauty. We need not say had been, for she was never more beautiful than at the time of which we write, though her person for many years had been disfigured by an accident. It is unnecessary that we should give in detail the early history of Madeline Stanhope. She had gone to Italy when about seventeen years of age, and had been allowed to make the most of her surpassing beauty in the saloons of Milan, and among the crowded villas along the shores of the Lake of Como. She had become famous for adventures in which her character was just not lost, and had destroyed the hearts of a dozen cavaliers without once being touched in her own. Blood had flowed in quarrels about her charms, and she heard of these encounters with pleasurable excitement. It had been told of her that on one occasion she had stood by in the disguise of a page, and had seen her lover fall.

As is so often the case, she had married the very worst of those who sought her hand. Why she had chosen Paulo Neroni, a man of no birth and no property, a mere captain in the pope's guard, one who had come up to Milan either simply as an adventurer or else as a spy, a man of harsh temper and oily manners, mean in figure, swarthy in face, and so false in words as to be hourly detected, need not now be told. When the moment for doing so came, she had probably no alternative, He, at any rate, had become her husband ; and after a prolonged honeymoon among the lakes, they had gone together to Rome, the papal captain having vainly endeavoured to induce his wife to remain behind him.

Six months afterwards she arrived at her father's house a cripple, and a mother. She had arrived without even notice, with hardly clothes to cover her, and without one of those many ornaments which had graced her bridal *trousseau*. Her baby was in the arms of a poor girl from

Milan, whom she had taken in exchange for the Roman maid who had accompanied her thus far, and who had then, as her mistress said, become homesick and had returned. It was clear that the lady had determined that there should be no witness to tell stories of her life in Rome.

She had fallen, she said, in ascending a ruin, and had fatally injured the sinews of her knee; so fatally, that when she stood she lost eight inches of her accustomed height; so fatally, that when she essayed to move, she could only drag herself painfully along, with protruded hip and extended foot in a manner less graceful than that of a hunchback. She had consequently made up her mind, once and for ever, that she would never stand, and never attempt to move herself.

Stories were not slow to follow her, averring that she had been cruelly ill used by Neroni, and that to his violence had she owed her accident. Be that as it may, little had been said about her husband, but that little had made it clearly intelligible to the family that Signor Neroni was to be seen and heard of no more. There was no question as to re-admitting the poor ill used beauty to her old family rights, no question as to adopting her infant daughter beneath the Stanhope roof tree. Though heartless, the Stanhopes were not selfish. The two were taken in, petted, made much of, for a time all but adored, and then felt by the two parents to be great nuisances in the house. But in the house the lady was, and there she remained, having her own way, though that way was not very conformable with the customary usages of an English clergyman.

Madame Neroni, though forced to give up all motion in the world, had no intention whatever of giving up the world itself. The beauty of her face was uninjured, and that beauty was of a peculiar kind. Her copious rich brown hair was worn in Grecian *bandeaux* round her head, displaying as much as possible of her forehead and cheeks. Her forehead, though rather low, was very beautiful from its perfect contour and pearly whiteness. Her eyes were long and large, and marvellously bright; might I venture to say, bright as Lucifer's, I should perhaps best express the depth of their brilliancy. They were dreadful eyes to look at, such as would absolutely deter any man of quiet mind and easy spirit from attempting a passage of arms with such foes. There was talent in them, and the fire of passion and the play of wit, but there was no love. Cruelty was there instead, and courage, a desire of masterhood, cunning, and a wish for mischief. And yet, as eyes, they were very beautiful. The eyelashes were long and perfect, and the long steady unabashed gaze, with which she would look into the face of her admirer, fascinated while it frightened him. She was a basilisk from whom an ardent lover of beauty could make no escape. Her nose and mouth and teeth and chin and neck and bust were perfect, much more so at twenty-eight than they had been at eighteen. What wonder that with such charms still glowing in her face, and with such deformity destroying her figure, she should resolve to be seen, but only to be seen reclining on a sofa.

Her resolve had not been carried out without difficulty. She had still frequented the opera at Milan; she had still been seen occasionally in the saloons of the *noblesse*; she had caused herself to be carried in and out from her carriage, and that in such a manner as in no wise to disturb her charms, disarrange her dress, or expose her deformities. Her sister always accompanied her and a maid, a man-servant also, and on state occasions, two. It was impossible that her purpose could have been achieved with less: and yet, poor as she was, she had achieved her purpose. And then again the more dissolute Italian youths of Milan frequented the Stanhope villa and surrounded her couch, not greatly to her father's satisfaction. Sometimes his spirit would rise, a dark spot would show itself on his cheek, and he would rebel; but Charlotte would assuage him with some peculiar triumph of her culinary art, and all again would be smooth for a while.

Madeline affected all manner of rich and quaint devices in the garniture of her room, her person, and her feminine belongings. In nothing was this more apparent than in the visiting card which she had prepared for her use. For such an article one would say that she, in her present state, could have but small need, seeing how improbable it was that she should make a morning call: but not such was her own opinion. Her card was surrounded by

a deep border of gilding; on this she had imprinted, in
three lines,—

> 'La Signora Madeline
> 'Vesey Neroni.
> —Nata Stanhope.'

And over the name she had a bright gilt coronet, which
certainly looked very magnificent. How she had come
to concoct such a name for herself it would be difficult
to explain. Her father had been christened Vesey, as
another man is christened Thomas; and she had no more
right to assume it than would have the daughter of a
Mr. Josiah Jones to call herself Mrs. Josiah Smith, on
marrying a man of the latter name. The gold coronet
was equally out of place, and perhaps inserted with even
less excuse. Paulo Neroni had had not the faintest title
to call himself a scion of even Italian nobility. Had the
pair met in England Neroni would probably have been
a count; but they had met in Italy, and any such pretence
on his part would have been simply ridiculous. A coronet,
however, was a pretty ornament, and if it could solace
a poor cripple to have such on her card, who would
begrudge it to her?

Of her husband, or of his individual family, she never
spoke; but with her admirers she would often allude in
a mysterious way to her married life and isolated state,
and, pointing to her daughter, would call her the last of
the blood of the emperors, thus referring Neroni's extrac-
tion to the old Roman family from which the worst of
the Cæsars sprang.

The 'Signora' was not without talent, and not without
a certain sort of industry; she was an indomitable letter
writer, and her letters were worth the postage: they
were full of wit, mischief, satire, love, latitudinarian
philosophy, free religion, and, sometimes, alas! loose
ribaldry. The subject, however, depended entirely on
the recipient, and she was prepared to correspond with
any one but moral young ladies or stiff old women. She
wrote also a kind of poetry, generally in Italian, and short
romances, generally in French. She read much of a
desultory sort of literature, and as a modern linguist had
really made great proficiency. Such was the lady who
had now come to wound the hearts of the men of Barchester.

Ethelbert Stanhope was in some respects like his younger sister, but he was less inestimable as a man than she as a woman. His great fault was an entire absence of that principle which should have induced him, as the son of a man without fortune, to earn his own bread. Many attempts had been made to get him to do so, but these had all been frustrated, not so much by idleness on his part, as by a disinclination to exert himself in any way not to his taste. He had been educated at Eton, and had been intended for the Church, but had left Cambridge in disgust after a single term, and notified to his father his intention to study for the bar. Preparatory to that, he thought it well that he should attend a German university, and consequently went to Leipsic. There he remained two years, and brought away a knowledge of German and a taste for the fine arts. He still, however, intended himself for the bar, took chambers, engaged himself to sit at the feet of a learned pundit, and spent a season in London. He there found that all his aptitudes inclined him to the life of an artist, and he determined to live by painting. With this object he returned to Milan, and had himself rigged out for Rome. As a painter he might have earned his bread, for he wanted only diligence to excel; but when at Rome his mind was carried away by other things: he soon wrote home for money, saying that he had been converted to the Mother Church, that he was already an acolyte of the Jesuits, and that he was about to start with others to Palestine on a mission for converting Jews. He did go to Judèa, but being unable to convert the Jews, was converted by them. He again wrote home, to say that Moses was the only giver of perfect laws to the world, that the coming of the true Messiah was at hand, that great things were doing in Palestine, and that he had met one of the family of Sidonia, a most remarkable man, who was now on his way to Western Europe, and whom he had induced to deviate from his route with the object of calling at the Stanhope villa. Ethelbert then expressed his hope that his mother and sisters would listen to this wonderful prophet. His father he knew could not do so from pecuniary considerations. This Sidonia, however, did not take so strong a fancy to him as another of that

family once did to a young English nobleman. At least
he provided him with no heaps of gold as large as lions;
so that the Judaised Ethelbert was again obliged to draw
on the revenues of the Christian Church.

It is needless to tell how the father swore that he would
send no more money and receive no Jew; nor how
Charlotte declared that Ethelbert could not be left penni-
less in Jerusalem, and how ' La Signora Neroni' resolved
to have Sidonia at her feet. The money was sent, and
the Jew did come. The Jew did come, but he was not
at all to the taste of ' La Signora.' He was a dirty little
old man, and though he had provided no golden lions,
he had, it seems, relieved young Stanhope's necessities.
He positively refused to leave the villa till he had got
a bill from the doctor on his London bankers.

Ethelbert did not long remain a Jew. He soon reappeared at the villa without prejudices on the subject
of his religion, and with a firm resolve to achieve fame
and fortune as a sculptor. He brought with him some
models which he had originated at Rome, and which
really gave such fair promise that his father was induced
to go to further expense in furthering these views. Ethelbert opened an establishment, or rather took lodgings
and a workshop, at Carrara, and there spoilt much marble,
and made some few pretty images. Since that period,
now four years ago, he had alternated between Carrara
and the villa, but his sojourns at the workshop became
shorter and shorter, and those at the villa longer and
longer. 'Twas no wonder; for Carrara is not a spot in
which an Englishman would like to dwell.

When the family started for England he had resolved
not to be left behind, and with the assistance of his elder
sister had carried his point against his father's wishes.
It was necessary, he said, that he should come to England
for orders. How otherwise was he to bring his profession
to account?

In personal appearance Ethelbert Stanhope was the
most singular of beings. He was certainly very handsome.
He had his sister Madeline's eyes without their stare,
and without their hard cunning cruel firmness. They
were also very much lighter, and of so light and clear
a blue as to make his face remarkable, if nothing else did

so. On entering a room with him, Ethelbert's blue eyes would be the first thing you would see, and on leaving it almost the last you would forget. His light hair was very long and silky, coming down over his coat. His beard had been prepared in holy land, and was patriarchal. He never shaved, and rarely trimmed it. It was glossy, soft, clean, and altogether not unprepossessing. It was such, that ladies might desire to reel it off and work it into their patterns in lieu of floss silk. His complexion was fair and almost pink, he was small in height, and slender in limb, but well-made, and his voice was of peculiar sweetness.

In manner and dress he was equally remarkable. He had none of the *mauvaise honte* of an Englishman. He required no introduction to make himself agreeable to any person. He habitually addressed strangers, ladies as well as men, without any such formality, and in doing so never seemed to meet with rebuke. His costume cannot be described, because it was so various; but it was always totally opposed in every principle of colour and construction to the dress of those with whom he for the time consorted.

He was habitually addicted to making love to ladies, and did so without any scruple of conscience, or any idea that such a practice was amiss. He had no heart to touch himself, and was literally unaware that humanity was subject to such an infliction. He had not thought much about it; but, had he been asked, would have said, that ill-treating a lady's heart meant injuring her promotion in the world. His principles therefore forbade him to pay attention to a girl, if he thought any man was present whom it might suit her to marry. In this manner, his good nature frequently interfered with his amusement; but he had no other motive in abstaining from the fullest declarations of love to every girl that pleased his eye.

Bertie Stanhope, as he was generally called, was, however, popular with both sexes; and with Italians as well as English. His circle of acquaintance was very large, and embraced people of all sorts. He had no respect for rank, and no aversion to those below him. He had lived on familiar terms with English peers, German shopkeepers, and Roman priests. All people were nearly alike to him. He was above, or rather below, all prejudices. No virtue could charm him, no vice shock him. He had about him a natural good manner, which seemed to qualify him for the highest circles, and yet he was never out of place in the lowest. He had no principle, no regard for others, no self-respect, no desire to be other than a drone in the hive, if only he could, as a drone, get what honey was sufficient for him. Of honey, in his latter days, it may probably be presaged, that he will have but short allowance.

Such was the family of the Stanhopes, who, at this period, suddenly joined themselves to the ecclesiastical circle of Barchester close. Any stranger union, it would be impossible perhaps to conceive. And it was not as though they all fell down into the cathedral precincts hitherto unknown and untalked of. In such case no amalgamation would have been at all probable between the new comers and either the Proudie set or the Grantly set. But such was far from being the case. The Stanhopes were all known by name in Barchester, and Barchester was prepared to receive them with open arms. The doctor was one of her prebendaries, one of her rectors, one of her pillars of strength; and was, moreover, counted on, as a sure ally, both by Proudies and Grantlys.

He himself was the brother of one peer, and his wife was the sister of another—and both these peers were lords of whiggish tendency, with whom the new bishop had some sort of alliance. This was sufficient to give to Mr. Slope high hope that he might enlist Dr. Stanhope on his side, before his enemies could out-manœuvre him. On the other hand, the old dean had many many years ago, in the days of the doctor's clerical energies, been instrumental in assisting him in his views as to preferment; and many many years ago also, the two doctors, Stanhope and Grantly, had, as young parsons, been joyous together in the common rooms of Oxford. Dr. Grantly, consequently, did not doubt but that the new comer would range himself under his banners.

Little did any of them dream of what ingredients the Stanhope family was now composed.

CHAPTER X

MRS. PROUDIE'S RECEPTION—COMMENCED

THE bishop and his wife had only spent three or four days in Barchester on the occasion of their first visit. His lordship had, as we have seen, taken his seat on his throne; but his demeanour there, into which it had been his intention to infuse much hierarchal dignity, had been a good deal disarranged by the audacity of his chaplain's sermon. He had hardly dared to look his clergy in the face, and to declare by the severity of his countenance that in truth he meant all that his factotum was saying on his behalf; nor yet did he dare to throw Mr. Slope over, and show to those around him that he was no party to the sermon, and would resent it.

He had accordingly blessed his people in a shambling manner, not at all to his own satisfaction, and had walked back to his palace with his mind very doubtful as to what he would say to his chaplain on the subject. He did not remain long in doubt. He had hardly doffed his lawn when the partner of all his toils entered his study, and exclaimed even before she had seated herself—

'Bishop, did you ever hear a more sublime, more spirit-moving, more appropriate discourse than that?'

'Well, my love; ha—hum—he!' The bishop did not know what to say.

'I hope, my lord, you don't mean to say you disapprove?'

There was a look about the lady's eye which did not admit of my lord's disapproving at that moment. He felt that if he intended to disapprove, it must be now or never; but he also felt that it could not be now. It was not in him to say to the wife of his bosom that Mr. Slope's sermon was ill-timed, impertinent and vexatious.

'No, no,' replied the bishop. 'No, I can't say I disapprove—a very clever sermon and very well intended, and I dare say will do a great deal of good.' This last praise was added, seeing that what he had already said by no means satisfied Mrs. Proudie.

'I hope it will,' said she. 'I am sure it was well deserved.

Did you ever in your life, bishop, hear anything so like play-acting as the way in which Mr. Harding sings the litany ? I shall beg Mr. Slope to continue a course of sermons on the subject till all that is altered. We will have at any rate, in our cathedral, a decent, godly, modest morning service. There must be no more play-acting here now ; ' and so the lady rang for lunch.

The bishop knew more about cathedrals and deans, and precentors and church services than his wife did, and also more of a bishop's powers. But he thought it better at present to let the subject drop.

' My dear,' said he, ' I think we must go back to London on Tuesday. I find my staying here will be very inconvenient to the Government.'

The bishop knew that to this proposal his wife would not object ; and he also felt that by thus retreating from the ground of battle, the heat of the fight might be got over in his absence.

' Mr. Slope will remain here, of course ? ' said the lady.

' Oh, of course,' said the bishop.

Thus, after less than a week's sojourn in his palace, did the bishop fly from Barchester ; nor did he return to it for two months, the London season being then over. During that time Mr. Slope was not idle, but he did not again essay to preach in the cathedral. In answer to Mrs. Proudie's letters, advising a course of sermons, he had pleaded that he would at any rate wish to put off such an undertaking till she was there to hear them.

He had employed his time in consolidating a Proudie and Slope party—or rather a Slope and Proudie party, and he had not employed his time in vain. He did not meddle with the dean and chapter, except by giving them little teasing intimations of the bishop's wishes about this and the bishop's feelings about that, in a manner which was to them sufficiently annoying, but which they could not resent. He preached once or twice in a distant church in the suburbs of the city, but made no allusion to the cathedral service. He commenced the establishment of two ' Bishop's Barchester Sabbath-day Schools,' gave notice of a proposed ' Bishop's Barchester Young Men's Sabbath Evening Lecture Room,'—and wrote three or four letters to the manager of the Barchester branch railway, informing him how anxious the bishop was that the Sunday trains should be discontinued.

At the end of two months, however, the bishop and the lady reappeared; and as a happy harbinger of their return, heralded their advent by the promise of an evening party on the largest scale. The tickets of invitation were sent out from London—they were dated from Bruton Street, and were despatched by the odious Sabbath breaking railway, in a huge brown paper parcel to Mr. Slope. Everybody calling himself a gentleman, or herself a lady, within the city of Barchester, and a circle of two miles round it, was included. Tickets were sent to all the diocesan clergy, and also to many other persons of priestly note, of whose absence the bishop, or at least the bishop's wife, felt tolerably confident. It was intended, however, to be a thronged and noticeable affair, and preparations were made for receiving some hundreds.

And now there arose considerable agitation among the Grantlyites whether or no they would attend the episcopal bidding. The first feeling with them all was to send the briefest excuses both for themselves and their wives and daughters. But by degrees policy prevailed over passion. The archdeacon perceived that he would be making a false step if he allowed the cathedral clergy to give the bishop just ground of umbrage. They all met in conclave and agreed to go. They would show that they were willing to respect the office, much as they might dislike the man. They agreed to go. The old dean would crawl in, if it were but for half an hour. The chancellor, treasurer, archdeacon, prebendaries, and minor canons would all go, and would all take their wives. Mr. Harding was especially bidden to do so, resolving in his heart to keep himself far removed from Mrs. Proudie. And Mrs. Bold was determined to go, though assured by her father that there was no necessity for such a sacrifice on her part. When all Barchester was to be there, neither Eleanor nor Mary Bold understood why they should stay away. Had they not been invited separately ? and had not a separate little note from the chaplain, couched in the most respectful language, been enclosed with the huge episcopal card ?

And the Stanhopes would be there, one and all. Even

the lethargic mother would so far bestir herself on such
an occasion. They had only just arrived. The card was
at the residence waiting for them. No one in Barchester
had seen them ; and what better opportunity could they
have of showing themselves to the Barchester world ?
Some few old friends, such as the archdeacon and his
wife, had called, and had found the doctor and his eldest
daughter ; but the *élite* of the family were not yet known.

The doctor indeed wished in his heart to prevent the
signora from accepting the bishop's invitation ; but she
herself had fully determined that she would accept it.
If her father was ashamed of having his daughter carried
into a bishop's palace, she had no such feeling.

' Indeed, I shall,' she had said to her sister who had
gently endeavoured to dissuade her, by saying that the
company would consist wholly of parsons and parsons'
wives. ' Parsons, I suppose, are much the same as other
men, if you strip them of their black coats ; and as to
their wives, I dare say they won't trouble me. You may
tell papa I don't at all mean to be left at home.'

Papa was told, and felt that he could do nothing but
yield. He also felt that it was useless for him now to be
ashamed of his children. Such as they were, they had
become such under his auspices ; as he had made his bed,
so he must lie upon it ; as he had sown his seed, so must
he reap his corn. He did not indeed utter such reflections
in such language, but such was the gist of his thoughts.
It was not because Madeline was a cripple that he shrank
from seeing her make one of the bishop's guests ; but
because he knew that she would practise her accustomed
lures, and behave herself in a way that could not fail
of being distasteful to the propriety of Englishwomen.
These things had annoyed but not shocked him in Italy.
There they had shocked no one ; but here in Barchester,
here among his fellow parsons, he was ashamed that they
should be seen. Such had been his feelings, but he repressed them. What if his brother clergymen were
shocked ! They could not take from him his preferment
because the manners of his married daughter were too free.

La Signora Neroni had, at any rate, no fear that she
would shock anybody. Her ambition was to create a
sensation, to have parsons at her feet, seeing that the

manhood of Barchester consisted mainly of parsons,
and to send, if possible, every parson's wife home with
a green fit of jealousy. None could be too old for her,
and hardly any too young. None too sanctified, and
none too worldly. She was quite prepared to entrap the
bishop himself, and then to turn up her nose at the bishop's
wife. She did not doubt of success, for she had always
succeeded; but one thing was absolutely necessary, she
must secure the entire use of a sofa.

The card sent to Dr. and Mrs. Stanhope and family,
had been so sent in an envelope, having on the cover
Mr. Slope's name. The signora soon learnt that Mrs.
Proudie was not yet at the palace, and that the chaplain
was managing everything. It was much more in her line
to apply to him than to the lady, and she accordingly
wrote him the prettiest little billet in the world. In five
lines she explained everything, declared how impossible
it was for her not to be desirous to make the acquaintance
of such persons as the Bishop of Barchester and his wife,
and she might add also of Mr. Slope, depicted her own
grievous state, and concluded by being assured that Mrs.
Proudie would forgive her extreme hardihood in petition-
ing to be allowed to be carried to a sofa. She then enclosed
one of her beautiful cards. In return she received as
polite an answer from Mr. Slope—a sofa should be kept
in the large drawing-room, immediately at the top of the
grand stairs, especially for her use.

And now the day of the party had arrived. The bishop
and his wife came down from town, only on the morning
of the eventful day, as behoved such great people to do;
but Mr. Slope had toiled day and night to see that everything should be in right order. There had been much to
do. No company had been seen in the palace since heaven
knows when. New furniture had been required, new pots
and pans, new cups and saucers, new dishes and plates.
Mrs. Proudie had at first declared that she would condescend to nothing so vulgar as eating and drinking;
but Mr. Slope had talked, or rather written her out of
economy! Bishops should be given to hospitality, and
hospitality meant eating and drinking. So the supper
was conceded; the guests, however, were to stand as they
consumed it.

There were four rooms opening into each other on the
first floor of the house, which were denominated the
drawing-rooms, the reception-room, and Mrs. Proudie's
boudoir. In olden days one of these had been Bishop
Grantly's bed-room, and another his common sitting-
room and study. The present bishop, however, had been
moved down into a back parlour, and had been given to
understand, that he could very well receive his clergy in the
dining-room, should they arrive in too large a flock to
be admitted into his small sanctum. He had been unwilling to yield, but after a short debate had yielded.

Mrs. Proudie's heart beat high as she inspected her
suite of rooms. They were really very magnificent, or
at least would be so by candlelight; and they had nevertheless been got up with commendable economy. Large
rooms when full of people and full of light look well,
because they are large, and are full, and are light. Small
rooms are those which require costly fittings and rich
furniture. Mrs. Proudie knew this, and made the most
of it; she had therefore a huge gas lamp with a dozen
burners hanging from each of the ceilings.

People were to arrive at ten, supper was to last from
twelve till one, and at half-past one everybody was to
be gone. Carriages were to come in at the gate in the
town and depart at the gate outside. They were desired
to take up at a quarter before one. It was managed
excellently, and Mr. Slope was invaluable.

At half-past nine the bishop and his wife and their
three daughters entered the great reception-room, and
very grand and very solemn they were. Mr. Slope was
down-stairs giving the last orders about the wine. He
well understood that curates and country vicars with
their belongings did not require so generous an article
as the dignitaries of the close. There is a useful gradation
in such things, and Marsala at 20s. a dozen did very well
for the exterior supplementary tables in the corner.

'Bishop,' said the lady, as his lordship sat himself
down, 'don't sit on that sofa, if you please; it is to be
kept separate for a lady.'

The bishop jumped up and seated himself on a cane-
bottomed chair. 'A lady?' he inquired meekly; 'do
you mean one particular lady, my dear?'

'Yes, Bishop, one particular lady,' said his wife, disdaining to explain.

'She has got no legs, papa,' said the youngest daughter, tittering.

'No legs!' said the bishop, opening his eyes.

'Nonsense, Netta, what stuff you talk,' said Olivia. 'She has got legs, but she can't use them. She has always to be kept lying down, and three or four men carry her about everywhere.'

'Laws, how odd!' said Augusta. 'Always carried about by four men! I'm sure I shouldn't like it. Am I right behind, mamma? I feel as if I was open;' and she turned her back to her anxious parent.

'Open! to be sure you are,' said she, 'and a yard of petticoat strings hanging out. I don't know why I pay such high wages to Mrs. Richards, if she can't take the trouble to see whether or no you are fit to be looked at,' and Mrs. Proudie poked the strings here, and twitched the dress there, and gave her daughter a shove and a shake, and then pronounced it all right.

'But,' rejoined the bishop, who was dying with curiosity about the mysterious lady and her legs, 'who is it that is to have the sofa? What's her name, Netta?'

A thundering rap at the front door interrupted the conversation. Mrs. Proudie stood up and shook herself gently, and touched her cap on each side as she looked in the mirror. Each of the girls stood on tiptoe, and re-arranged the bows on their bosoms; and Mr. Slope rushed up stairs three steps at a time.

'But who is it, Netta?' whispered the bishop to his youngest daughter.

'La Signora Madeline Vesey Neroni,' whispered back the daughter; 'and mind you don't let any one sit upon the sofa.'

'La Signora Madeline Vicinironi!' muttered, to himself, the bewildered prelate. Had he been told that the Begum of Oude was to be there, or Queen Pomara of the Western Isles, he could not have been more astonished. La Signora Madeline Vicinironi, who, having no legs to stand on, had bespoken a sofa in his drawing-room!—who could she be? He however could now make no further inquiry, as Dr. and Mrs. Stanhope were announced. They

had been sent on out of the way a little before the time,
in order that the signora might have plenty of time to
get herself conveniently packed into the carriage.

The bishop was all smiles for the prebendary's wife,
and the bishop's wife was all smiles for the prebendary.
Mr. Slope was presented, and was delighted to make the
acquaintance of one of whom he had heard so much.
The doctor bowed very low, and then looked as though
he could not return the compliment as regarded Mr.
Slope, of whom, indeed, he had heard nothing. The
doctor, in spite of his long absence, knew an English
gentleman when he saw him.

And then the guests came in shoals: Mr. and Mrs.
Quiverful and their three grown daughters. Mr. and
Mrs. Chadwick and their three daughters. The burly
chancellor and his wife and clerical son from Oxford.
The meagre little doctor without incumbrance. Mr.
Harding with Eleanor and Miss Bold. The dean leaning
on a gaunt spinster, his only child now living with him,
a lady very learned in stones, ferns, plants, and vermin,
and who had written a book about petals. A wonderful
woman in her way was Miss Trefoil. Mr. Finnie, the
attorney, with his wife, was to be seen, much to the dismay
of many who had never met him in a drawing-room before.
The five Barchester doctors were all there, and old Scalpen,
the retired apothecary and toothdrawer, who was first
taught to consider himself as belonging to the higher
orders by the receipt of the bishop's card. Then came
the archdeacon and his wife, with their elder daughter
Griselda, a slim pale retiring girl of seventeen, who kept
close to her mother, and looked out on the world with
quiet watchful eyes, one who gave promise of much beauty
when time should have ripened it.

And so the rooms became full, and knots were formed,
and every new comer paid his respects to my lord and
passed on, not presuming to occupy too much of the great
man's attention. The archdeacon shook hands very
heartily with Doctor Stanhope, and Mrs. Grantly seated
herself by the doctor's wife. And Mrs. Proudie moved
about with well regulated grace, measuring out the
quantity of her favours to the quality of her guests, just
as Mr. Slope had been doing with the wine. But the sofa

was still empty, and five-and-twenty ladies and five
gentlemen had been courteously warned off it by the
mindful chaplain.

'Why doesn't she come?' said the bishop to himself.
His mind was so preoccupied with the signora, that he
hardly remembered how to behave himself *en bishop*.

At last a carriage dashed up to the hall steps with a
very different manner of approach from that of any other
vehicle that had been there that evening. A perfect
commotion took place. The doctor, who heard it as he
was standing in the drawing-room, knew that his daughter
was coming, and retired into the furthest corner, where
he might not see her entrance. Mrs. Proudie perked
herself up, feeling that some important piece of business
was in hand. The bishop was instinctively aware that
La Signora Vicinironi was come at last, and Mr. Slope
hurried into the hall to give his assistance.

He was, however, nearly knocked down and trampled
on by the cortège that he encountered on the hall steps.
He got himself picked up as well as he could, and followed
the cortège up stairs. The signora was carried head
foremost, her head being the care of her brother and an
Italian man-servant who was accustomed to the work;
her feet were in the care of the lady's maid and the lady's
Italian page; and Charlotte Stanhope followed to see
that all was done with due grace and decorum. In this
manner they climbed easily into the drawing-room, and
a broad way through the crowd having been opened, the
signora rested safely on her couch. She had sent a servant
beforehand to learn whether it was a right or a left hand
sofa, for it required that she should dress accordingly,
particularly as regarded her bracelets.

And very becoming her dress was. It was white velvet,
without any other garniture than rich white lace worked
with pearls across her bosom, and the same round the
armlets of her dress. Across her brow she wore a band
of red velvet, on the centre of which shone a magnificent
Cupid in mosaic, the tints of whose wings were of the most
lovely azure, and the colour of his chubby cheeks the
clearest pink. On the one arm which her position required
her to expose she wore three magnificent bracelets, each
of different stones. Beneath her on the sofa, and over the

cushion and head of it, was spread a crimson silk mantle or shawl, which went under her whole body and concealed her feet. Dressed as she was and looking as she did, so beautiful and yet so motionless, with the pure brilliancy of her white dress brought out and strengthened by the colour beneath it, with that lovely head, and those large bold bright staring eyes, it was impossible that either man or woman should do other than look at her.

Neither man nor woman for some minutes did do other.

Her bearers too were worthy of note. The three servants were Italian, and though perhaps not peculiar in their own country, were very much so in the palace at Barchester. The man especially attracted notice, and created a doubt in the mind of some whether he were a friend or a domestic. The same doubt was felt as to Ethelbert. The man was attired in a loose-fitting common black cloth morning coat. He had a jaunty fat well-pleased clean face, on which no atom of beard appeared, and he wore round his neck a loose black silk neckhandkerchief. The bishop essayed to make him a bow, but the man, who was well-trained, took no notice of him, and walked out of the room quite at his ease, followed by the woman and the boy.

Ethelbert Stanhope was dressed in light blue from head to foot. He had on the loosest possible blue coat, cut square like a shooting coat, and very short. It was lined with silk of azure blue. He had on a blue satin waistcoat, a blue neckhandkerchief which was fastened beneath his throat with a coral ring, and very loose blue trowsers which almost concealed his feet. His soft glossy beard was softer and more glossy than ever.

The bishop, who had made one mistake, thought that he also was a servant, and therefore tried to make way for him to pass. But Ethelbert soon corrected the error.

CHAPTER XI

MRS. PROUDIE'S RECEPTION—CONCLUDED

'BISHOP OF BARCHESTER, I presume?' said Bertie Stanhope, putting out his hand, frankly; 'I am delighted to make your acquaintance. We are in rather close quarters here, a'nt we?'

In truth they were. They had been crowded up behind the head of the sofa: the bishop in waiting to receive his guest, and the other in carrying her; and they now had hardly room to move themselves.

The bishop gave his hand quickly, and made his little studied bow, and was delighted to make——. He couldn't go on, for he did not know whether his friend was a signor, or a count, or a prince.

'My sister really puts you all to great trouble,' said Bertie.

'Not at all!' The bishop was delighted to have the opportunity of welcoming the Signora Vicinironi—so at least he said—and attempted to force his way round to the front of the sofa. He had, at any rate, learnt that his strange guests were brother and sister. The man, he presumed, must be Signor Vicinironi—or count, or prince, as it might be. It was wonderful what good English he spoke. There was just a twang of foreign accent, and no more.

'Do you like Barchester on the whole?' asked Bertie.

The bishop, looking dignified, said that he did like Barchester.

'You've not been here very long, I believe,' said Bertie.

'No—not long,' said the bishop, and tried again to make his way between the back of the sofa and a heavy rector, who was staring over it at the grimaces of the signora.

'You weren't a bishop before, were you?'

Dr. Proudie explained that this was the first diocese he had held.

'Ah—I thought so,' said Bertie; 'but you are changed about sometimes, a'nt you?'

'Translations are occasionally made,' said Dr. Proudie; 'but not so frequently as in former days.'

' They've cut them all down to pretty nearly the same figure, haven't they ? ' said Bertie.

To this the bishop could not bring himself to make any answer, but again attempted to move the rector.

' But the work, I suppose, is different ? ' continued Bertie. ' Is there much to do here, at Barchester ? ' This was said exactly in the tone that a young Admiralty clerk might use in asking the same question of a brother acolyte at the Treasury.

' The work of a bishop of the Church of England,' said Dr. Proudie, with considerable dignity, ' is not easy. The responsibility which he has to bear is very great indeed.'

' Is it ? ' said Bertie, opening wide his wonderful blue eyes. ' Well ; I never was afraid of responsibility. I once had thoughts of being a bishop, myself.'

' Had thoughts of being a bishop ! ' said Dr. Proudie, much amazed.

' That is, a parson—a parson first, you know, and a bishop afterwards. If I had once begun, I'd have stuck to it. But, on the whole, I like the Church of Rome the best.'

The bishop could not discuss the point, so he remained silent.

' Now, there's my father,' continued Bertie ; ' he hasn't stuck to it. I fancy he didn't like saying the same thing over so often. By the bye, Bishop, have you seen my father ? '

The bishop was more amazed than ever. Had he seen his father ? ' No,' he replied ; ' he had not yet had the pleasure : he hoped he might ; ' and, as he said so, he resolved to bear heavy on that fat, immovable rector, if ever he had the power of doing so.

' He's in the room somewhere,' said Bertie, ' and he'll turn up soon. By the bye, do you know much about the Jews ? '

At last the bishop saw a way out. ' I beg your pardon,' said he ; ' but I'm forced to go round the room.'

' Well—I believe I'll follow in your wake,' said Bertie. ' Terribly hot—isn't it ? ' This he addressed to the fat rector with whom he had brought himself into the closest contact. ' They've got this sofa into the worst possible part of the room; suppose we move it. Take care, Madeline.'

The sofa had certainly been so placed that those who were behind it found great difficulty in getting out;—there was but a narrow gangway, which one person could stop. This was a bad arrangement, and one which Bertie thought it might be well to improve.

'Take care, Madeline,' said he; and turning to the fat rector, added, ' Just help me with a slight push.'

The rector's weight was resting on the sofa, and unwittingly lent all its impetus to accelerate and increase the motion which Bertie intentionally originated. The sofa rushed from its moorings, and ran half-way into the middle of the room. Mrs. Proudie was standing with Mr. Slope in front of the signora, and had been trying to be condescending and sociable; but she was not in the very best of tempers; for she found that, whenever she spoke to the lady, the lady replied by speaking to Mr. Slope. Mr. Slope was a favourite, no doubt; but Mrs. Proudie had no idea of being less thought of than the chaplain. She was beginning to be stately, stiff, and offended, when unfortunately the castor of the sofa caught itself in her lace train, and carried away there is no saying how much of her garniture. Gathers were heard to go, stitches to crack, plaits to fly open, flounces were seen to fall, and breadths to expose themselves;—a long ruin of rent lace disfigured the carpet, and still clung to the vile wheel on which the sofa moved.

So, when a granite battery is raised, excellent to the eyes of warfaring men, is its strength and symmetry admired. It is the work of years. Its neat embrasures, its finished parapets, its casemated stories, show all the skill of modern science. But, anon, a small spark is applied to the treacherous fusee—a cloud of dust arises to the heavens—and then nothing is to be seen but dirt and dust and ugly fragments.

We know what was the wrath of Juno when her beauty was despised. We know too what storms of passion even celestial minds can yield. As Juno may have looked at Paris on Mount Ida, so did Mrs. Proudie look on Ethelbert Stanhope when he pushed the leg of the sofa into her lace train.

'Oh, you idiot, Bertie!' said the signora, seeing what
had been done, and what were to be the consequences.

'Idiot!' re-echoed Mrs. Proudie, as though the word
were not half strong enough to express the required
meaning; 'I'll let him know——;' and then looking
round to learn, at a glance, the worst, she saw that at
present it behoved her to collect the scattered *débris* of
her dress.

Bertie, when he saw what he had done, rushed over the
sofa, and threw himself on one knee before the offended
lady. His object, doubtless, was to liberate the torn
lace from the castor; but he looked as though he were
imploring pardon from a goddess.

'Unhand it, sir!' said Mrs. Proudie. From what
scrap of dramatic poetry she had extracted the word
cannot be said; but it must have rested on her memory,
and now seemed opportunely dignified for the occasion.

'I'll fly to the looms of the fairies to repair the damage,
if you'll only forgive me,' said Ethelbert, still on his
knees.

'Unhand it, sir!' said Mrs. Proudie, with redoubled
emphasis, and all but furious wrath. This allusion to
the fairies was a direct mockery, and intended to turn
her into ridicule. So at least it seemed to her. 'Unhand
it, sir!' she almost screamed.

'It's not me; it's the cursed sofa,' said Bertie, looking
imploringly in her face, and holding up both his hands
to show that he was not touching her belongings, but
still remaining on his knees.

Hereupon the signora laughed; not loud, indeed, but
yet audibly. And as the tigress bereft of her young will
turn with equal anger on any within reach, so did Mrs.
Proudie turn upon her female guest.

'Madam!' she said—and it is beyond the power of
prose to tell of the fire which flashed from her eyes.

The signora stared her full in the face for a moment,
and then turning to her brother said, playfully, 'Bertie,
you idiot, get up.'

By this time the bishop, and Mr. Slope, and her three
daughters were around her, and had collected together
the wide ruins of her magnificence. The girls fell into
circular rank behind their mother, and thus following

her and carrying out the fragments, they left the reception-rooms in a manner not altogether devoid of dignity. Mrs. Proudie had to retire and re-array herself.

As soon as the constellation had swept by, Ethelbert rose from his knees, and turning with mock anger to the fat rector, said : ' After all it was your doing, sir—not mine. But perhaps you are waiting for preferment, and so I bore it.'

Whereupon there was a laugh against the fat rector, in which both the bishop and the chaplain joined ; and thus things got themselves again into order.

' Oh ! my lord, I am so sorry for this accident,' said the signora, putting out her hand so as to force the bishop to take it. ' My brother is so thoughtless. Pray sit down, and let me have the pleasure of making your acquaintance. Though I am so poor a creature as to want a sofa, I am not so selfish as to require it all.' Madeline could always dispose herself so as to make room for a gentleman, though, as she declared, the crinoline of her lady friends was much too bulky to be so accommodated.

' It was solely for the pleasure of meeting you that I have had myself dragged here,' she continued. ' Of course, with your occupation, one cannot even hope that you should have time to come to us, that is, in the way of calling. And at your English dinner-parties all is so dull and so stately. Do you know, my lord, that in coming to England my only consolation has been the thought that I should know you ; ' and she looked at him with the look of a she-devil.

The bishop, however, thought that she looked very like an angel, and accepting the proffered seat, sat down beside her. He uttered some platitude as to his deep obligation for the trouble she had taken, and wondered more and more who she was.

' Of course you know my sad story ? ' she continued.

The bishop didn't know a word of it. He knew, however, or thought he knew, that she couldn't walk into a room like other people, and so made the most of that. He put on a look of ineffable distress, and said that he was aware how God had afflicted her.

The signora just touched the corner of her eyes with the most lovely of pocket-handkerchiefs. Yes, she said—

she had been sorely tried—tried, she thought, beyond
the common endurance of humanity; but while her child
was left to her, everything was left. ' Oh! my lord,'
she exclaimed, ' you must see that infant—the last bud
of a wondrous tree: you must let a mother hope that
you will lay your holy hands on her innocent head, and
consecrate her for female virtues. May I hope it ?' said
she, looking into the bishop's eye, and touching the
bishop's arm with her hand.

The bishop was but a man, and said she might. After
all, what was it but a request that he would confirm her
daughter ?—a request, indeed, very unnecessary to make,
as he should do so as a matter of course, if the young lady
came forward in the usual way.

' The blood of Tiberius,' said the signora, in all but
a whisper; ' the blood of Tiberius flows in her veins.
She is the last of the Neros!'

The bishop had heard of the last of the Visigoths, and
had floating in his brain some indistinct idea of the last
of the Mohicans, but to have the last of the Neros thus
brought before him for a blessing was very staggering.
Still he liked the lady: she had a proper way of thinking,
and talked with more propriety than her brother. But
who were they ? It was now quite clear that that blue
madman with the silky beard was not a Prince Vicinironi.
The lady was married, and was of course one of the
Vicinironis by right of the husband. So the bishop went
on learning.

' When will you see her ?' said the signora with a start.

' See whom ?' said the bishop.

' My child,' said the mother.

' What is the young lady's age ?' asked the bishop.

' She is just seven,' said the signora.

' Oh,' said the bishop, shaking his head; ' she is much
too young—very much too young.'

' But in sunny Italy you know, we do not count by
years,' and the signora gave the bishop one of her very
sweetest smiles.

' But indeed, she is a great deal too young,' persisted
the bishop; ' we never confirm before——'

' But you might speak to her; you might let her hear
from your consecrated lips, that she is not a castaway

because she is a Roman; that she may be a Nero and yet a Christian; that she may owe her black locks and dark cheeks to the blood of the pagan Cæsars, and yet herself be a child of grace; you will tell her this, won't you, my friend?'

The friend said he would, and asked if the child could say her catechism.

'No,' said the signora, 'I would not allow her to learn lessons such as those in a land ridden over by priests, and polluted by the idolatry of Rome. It is here, here in Barchester, that she must first be taught to lisp those holy words. Oh, that you could be her instructor!'

Now, Dr. Proudie certainly liked the lady, but, seeing that he was a bishop, it was not probable that he was going to instruct a little girl in the first rudiments of her catechism; so he said he'd send a teacher.

'But you'll see her, yourself, my lord?'

The bishop said he would, but where should he call.

'At papa's house,' said the signora, with an air of some little surprise at the question.

The bishop actually wanted the courage to ask her who was her papa; so he was forced at last to leave her without fathoming the mystery. Mrs. Proudie, in her second best, had now returned to the rooms, and her husband thought it as well that he should not remain in too close conversation with the lady whom his wife appeared to hold in such slight esteem. Presently he came across. his youngest daughter.

'Netta,' said he, 'do you know who is the father of that Signora Vicinironi?'

'It isn't Vicinironi, papa,' said Netta; 'but Vesey Neroni, and she's Doctor Stanhope's daughter. But I must go and do the civil to Griselda Grantly; I declare nobody has spoken a word to the poor girl this evening.'

Dr. Stanhope! Dr. Vesey Stanhope! Dr. Vesey Stanhope's daughter, of whose marriage with a dissolute Italian scamp he now remembered to have heard something! And that impertinent blue cub who had examined him as to his episcopal bearings was old Stanhope's son, and the lady who had entreated him to come and teach her child the catechism was old Stanhope's daughter! the daughter of one of his own prebendaries! As these things

flashed across his mind, he was nearly as angry as his
wife had been. Nevertheless, he could not but own that
the mother of the last of the Neros was an agreeable
woman.

Dr. Proudie tripped out into the adjoining room, in
which were congregated a crowd of Grantlyite clergymen,
among whom the archdeacon was standing pre-eminent,
while the old dean was sitting nearly buried in a huge
arm-chair by the fire-place. The bishop was very anxious
to be gracious, and, if possible, to diminish the bitterness
which his chaplain had occasioned. Let Mr. Slope do
the *fortiter in re*, he himself would pour in the *suaviter
in modo*.

'Pray don't stir, Mr. Dean, pray don't stir,' he said,
as the old man essayed to get up; 'I take it as a great
kindness, your coming to such an *omnium gatherum* as
this. But we have hardly got settled yet, and Mrs. Proudie
has not been able to see her friends as she would wish
to do. Well, Mr. Archdeacon, after all, we have not been
so hard upon you at Oxford.'

'No,' said the archdeacon; 'you've only drawn our
teeth and cut out our tongues; you've allowed us still
to breathe and swallow.'

'Ha, ha, ha!' laughed the bishop; 'it's not quite so
easy to cut out the tongue of an Oxford magnate,—and
as for teeth,—ha, ha, ha! Why, in the way we've left
the matter, it's very odd if the heads of colleges don't
have their own way quite as fully as when the hebdomadal
board was in all its glory; what do you say, Mr. Dean?'

'An old man, my lord, never likes changes,' said the
dean.

'You must have been sad bunglers if it is so,' said the
archdeacon; 'and indeed, to tell the truth, I think you
have bungled it. At any rate, you must own this; you
have not done the half what you boasted you would do.'

'Now, as regards your system of professors——' began
the chancellor slowly. He was never destined to get
beyond such beginning.

'Talking of professors,' said a soft clear voice, close
behind the chancellor's elbow; 'how much you Englishmen might learn from Germany; only you are all too
proud.'

The bishop looking round, perceived that that abominable young Stanhope had pursued him. The dean stared at him, as though he were some unearthly apparition; so also did two or three prebendaries and minor canons. The archdeacon laughed.

'The German professors are men of learning,' said Mr. Harding, 'but——'

'German professors!' groaned out the chancellor, as though his nervous system had received a shock which nothing but a week of Oxford air could cure.

'Yes,' continued Ethelbert; not at all understanding why a German professor should be contemptible in the eyes of an Oxford don. 'Not but what the name is best earned at Oxford. In Germany the professors do teach; at Oxford, I believe they only profess to do so, and sometimes not even that. You'll have those universities of yours about your ears soon, if you don't consent to take a lesson from Germany.'

There was no answering this. Dignified clergymen of sixty years of age could not condescend to discuss such a matter with a young man with such clothes and such a beard.

'Have you got good water out at Plumstead, Mr. Archdeacon?' said the bishop by way of changing the conversation.

'Pretty good,' said Dr. Grantly.

'But by no means so good as his wine, my lord,' said a witty minor canon.

'Nor so generally used,' said another; 'that is for inward application.'

'Ha, ha, ha!' laughed the bishop, 'a good cellar of wine is a very comfortable thing in a house.'

'Your German professors, sir, prefer beer, I believe,' said the sarcastic little meagre prebendary.

'They don't think much of either,' said Ethelbert; 'and that perhaps accounts for their superiority. Now the Jewish professor——'

The insult was becoming too deep for the spirit of Oxford to endure, so the archdeacon walked off one way and the chancellor another, followed by their disciples, and the bishop and the young reformer were left together on the hearth-rug.

' I was a Jew once myself,' began Bertie.

The bishop was determined not to stand another examination, or be led on any terms into Palestine; so he again remembered that he had to do something very particular, and left young Stanhope with the dean. The dean did not get the worst of it, for Ethelbert gave him a true account of his remarkable doings in the Holy Land.

' Oh, Mr. Harding,' said the bishop, overtaking the ci-devant warden; ' I wanted to say one word about the hospital. You know, of course, that it is to be filled up.'

Mr. Harding's heart beat a little, and he said that he had heard so.

' Of course,' continued the bishop; ' there can be only one man whom I could wish to see in that situation. I don't know what your own views may be, Mr. Harding——'

' They are very simply told, my lord,' said the other; ' to take the place if it be offered me, and to put up with the want of it should another man get it.'

The bishop professed himself delighted to hear it; Mr. Harding might be quite sure that no other man would get it. There were some few circumstances which would in a slight degree change the nature of the duties. Mr. Harding was probably aware of this, and would, perhaps, not object to discuss the matter with Mr. Slope. It was a subject to which Mr. Slope had given a good deal of attention.

Mr. Harding felt, he knew not why, oppressed and annoyed. What could Mr. Slope do to him? He knew that there were to be changes. The nature of them must be communicated to the warden through somebody, and through whom so naturally as the bishop's chaplain. 'Twas thus he tried to argue himself back to an easy mind, but in vain.

Mr. Slope in the mean time had taken the seat which the bishop had vacated on the signora's sofa, and remained with that lady till it was time to marshal the folk to supper. Not with contented eyes had Mrs. Proudie seen this. Had not this woman laughed at her distress, and had not Mr. Slope heard it? Was she not an intriguing Italian woman, half wife and half not, full of affectation, airs, and impudence? Was she not horribly bedizened with velvet and pearls, with velvet and pearls, too, which had not been torn off her back ? Above all, did she not pretend to be more beautiful than her neighbours ? To say that Mrs. Proudie was jealous would give a wrong idea of her feelings. She had not the slightest desire that Mr. Slope should be in love with herself. But she desired the incense of Mr. Slope's spiritual and temporal services, and did not choose that they should be turned out of their course to such an object as Signora Neroni. She considered also that Mr. Slope ought in duty to hate the signora ; and it appeared from his manner that he was very far from hating her.

'Come, Mr. Slope,' she said, sweeping by, and looking all that she felt ; ' can't you make yourself useful ? Do pray take Mrs. Grantly down to supper.'

Mrs. Grantly heard and escaped. The words were hardly out of Mrs. Proudie's mouth, before the intended victim had stuck her hand through the arm of one of her husband's curates, and saved herself. What would the archdeacon have said had he seen her walking down stairs with Mr. Slope ?

Mr. Slope heard also, but was by no means so obedient as was expected. Indeed, the period of Mr. Slope's obedience to Mrs. Proudie was drawing to a close. He did not wish yet to break with her, nor to break with her at all, if it could be avoided. But he intended to be master in that palace, and as she had made the same resolution it was not improbable that they might come to blows.

Before leaving the signora he arranged a little table before her, and begged to know what he should bring her. She was quite indifferent, she said—nothing—anything. It was now she felt the misery of her position, now that she must be left alone. Well, a little chicken, some ham, and a glass of champagne.

Mr. Slope had to explain, not without blushing for his patron, that there was no champagne.

Sherry would do just as well. And then Mr. Slope descended with the learned Miss Trefoil on his arm. Could she tell him, he asked, whether the ferns of Barsetshire were equal to those of Cumberland ? His strongest worldly passion was for ferns — and before she could answer him he left her wedged between the door and the sideboard. It was fifty minutes before she escaped, and even then unfed.

'You are not leaving us, Mr. Slope,' said the watchful lady of the house, seeing her slave escaping towards the door, with stores of provisions held high above the heads of the guests.

Mr. Slope explained that the Signora Neroni was in want of her supper.

'Pray, Mr. Slope, let her brother take it to her,' said Mrs. Proudie, quite out loud. 'It is out of the question that you should be so employed. Pray, Mr. Slope, oblige me ; I am sure Mr. Stanhope will wait upon his sister.'

Ethelbert was most agreeably occupied in the furthest corner of the room, making himself both useful and agreeable to Mrs. Proudie's youngest daughter.

'I couldn't get out, madam, if Madeline were starving for her supper,' said he ; 'I'm physically fixed, unless I could fly.'

The lady's anger was increased by seeing that her daughter also had gone over to the enemy ; and when she saw, that in spite of her remonstrances, in the teeth of her positive orders, Mr. Slope went off to the drawing-room, the cup of her indignation ran over, and she could not restrain herself. 'Such manners I never saw,' she said, muttering. 'I cannot, and will not permit it ;' and then, after fussing and fuming for a few minutes, she pushed her way through the crowd, and followed Mr. Slope.

When she reached the room above, she found it absolutely deserted, except by the guilty pair. The signora was sitting very comfortably up to her supper, and Mr. Slope was leaning over her and administering to her wants. They had been discussing the merits of Sabbath-day schools, and the lady had suggested that as she could not possibly go to the children, she might be indulged in the wish of her heart by having the children brought to her.

'And when shall it be, Mr. Slope ?' said she.

Mr. Slope was saved the necessity of committing himself to a promise by the entry of Mrs. Proudie. She swept close up to the sofa so as to confront the guilty pair, stared full at them for a moment, and then said as she

passed on to the next room, 'Mr. Slope, his lordship is
especially desirous of your attendance below; you will
greatly oblige me if you will join him.' And so she
stalked on.

Mr. Slope muttered something in reply, and prepared
to go down stairs. As for the bishop's wanting him, he
knew his lady patroness well enough to take that assertion
at what it was worth; but he did not wish to make
himself the hero of a scene, or to become conspicuous
for more gallantry than the occasion required.

'Is she always like this?' said the signora.

'Yes—always—madam,' said Mrs. Proudie, returning;
'always the same—always equally adverse to impropriety
of conduct of every description;' and she stalked back
through the room again, following Mr. Slope out of the door.

The signora couldn't follow her, or she certainly would
have done so. But she laughed loud, and sent the sound
of it ringing through the lobby and down the stairs after
Mrs. Proudie's feet. Had she been as active as Grimaldi,
she could probably have taken no better revenge.

'Mr. Slope,' said Mrs. Proudie, catching the delinquent
at the door, 'I am surprised that you should leave my
company to attend on such a painted Jezebel as that.'

'But she's lame, Mrs. Proudie, and cannot move.
Somebody must have waited upon her.'

'Lame,' said Mrs. Proudie; 'I'd lame her if she
belonged to me. What business had she here at all?—
such impertinence—such affectation.'

In the hall and adjacent rooms all manner of cloaking
and shawling was going on, and the Barchester folk were
getting themselves gone. Mrs. Proudie did her best to
smirk at each and every one, as they made their adieux,
but she was hardly successful. Her temper had been
tried fearfully. By slow degrees, the guests went.

'Send back the carriage quick,' said Ethelbert, as
Dr. and Mrs. Stanhope took their departure.

The younger Stanhopes were left to the very last, and
an uncomfortable party they made with the bishop's
family. They all went into the dining room, and then the
bishop observing that 'the lady' was alone in the
drawing-room, they followed him up. Mrs. Proudie kept
Mr. Slope and her daughters in close conversation, resolving

that he should not be indulged, nor they polluted. The bishop, in mortal dread of Bertie and the Jews, tried to converse with Charlotte Stanhope about the climate of Italy. Bertie and the signora had no resource but in each other.

' Did you get your supper, at last, Madeline ? ' said the impudent or else mischievous young man.

' Oh, yes,' said Madeline ; ' Mr. Slope was so very kind as to bring it me. I fear, however, he put himself to more inconvenience than I wished.'

Mrs. Proudie looked at her, but said nothing. The meaning of her look might have been thus translated : ' If ever you find yourself within these walls again, I'll give you leave to be as impudent and affected, and as mischievous as you please.'

At last the carriage returned with the three Italian servants, and La Signora Madeline Vesey Neroni was carried out, as she had been carried in.

The lady of the palace retired to her chamber by no means contented with the result of her first grand party at Barchester.

CHAPTER XII

SLOPE VERSUS HARDING

Two or three days after the party, Mr. Harding received a note, begging him to call on Mr. Slope, at the palace, at an early hour the following morning. There was nothing uncivil in the communication, and yet the tone of it was thoroughly displeasing. It was as follows :

' My dear Mr. Harding,—Will you favour me by calling on me at the palace to-morrow morning at 9.30 A.M. The bishop wishes me to speak to you touching the hospital. I hope you will excuse my naming so early an hour. I do so as my time is greatly occupied. If, however, it is positively inconvenient to you, I will change it to 10. You will, perhaps, be kind enough to let me have a note in reply.

' Believe me to be,
' My dear Mr. Harding,
' Your assured friend,
' OBH. SLOPE.

' The Palace, Monday morning,
' 20th August, 185—.'

Mr. Harding neither could nor would believe anything of the sort; and he thought, moreover, that Mr. Slope was rather impertinent to call himself by such a name. His assured friend, indeed! How many assured friends generally fall to the lot of a man in this world? And by what process are they made? and how much of such process had taken place as yet between Mr. Harding and Mr. Slope? Mr. Harding could not help asking himself these questions as he read and re-read the note before him. He answered it, however, as follows:

' Dear Sir,—I will call at the palace to-morrow at 9.30 A.M. as you desire.

' Truly yours,
' S. Harding.

' High Street, Barchester, Monday.'

And on the following morning, punctually at half-past nine, he knocked at the palace door, and asked for Mr. Slope.

The bishop had one small room allotted to him on the ground-floor, and Mr. Slope had another. Into this latter Mr. Harding was shown, and asked to sit down. Mr. Slope was not yet there. The ex-warden stood up at the window looking into the garden, and could not help thinking how very short a time had passed since the whole of that house had been open to him, as though he had been a child of the family, born and bred in it. He remembered how the old servants used to smile as they opened the door to him; how the familiar butler would say, when he had been absent a few hours longer than usual, ' A sight of you, Mr. Harding, is good for sore eyes; ' how the fussy housekeeper would swear that he couldn't have dined, or couldn't have breakfasted, or couldn't have lunched. And then, above all, he remembered the pleasant gleam of inward satisfaction which always spread itself over the old bishop's face, whenever his friend entered his room.

A tear came into each eye as he reflected that all this was gone. What use would the hospital be to him now? He was alone in the world, and getting old; he would soon, very soon have to go, and leave it all, as his dear old friend had gone;—go, and leave the hospital, and his accustomed place in the cathedral, and his haunts and pleasures, to younger and perhaps wiser men. That chanting of his!—perhaps, in truth, the time for it had gone by. He felt as though the world were sinking from his feet; as though this, this was the time for him to turn with confidence to those hopes which he had preached with confidence to others. 'What,' said he to himself, ' can a man's religion be worth, if it does not support him against the natural melancholy of declining years?' And, as he looked out through his dimmed eyes into the bright parterres of the bishop's garden, he felt that he had the support which he wanted.

Nevertheless, he did not like to be thus kept waiting. If Mr. Slope did not really wish to see him at half-past nine o'clock, why force him to come away from his lodgings with his breakfast in his throat? To tell the truth, it was policy on the part of Mr. Slope. Mr. Slope had made up his mind that Mr. Harding should either accept the hospital with abject submission, or else refuse it altogether; and had calculated that he would probably be more quick to do the latter, if he could be got to enter upon the subject in an ill-humour. Perhaps Mr. Slope was not altogether wrong in his calculation.

It was nearly ten when Mr. Slope hurried into the room, and, muttering something about the bishop and diocesan duties, shook Mr. Harding's hand ruthlessly, and begged him to be seated.

Now the air of superiority which this man assumed, did go against the grain of Mr. Harding; and yet he did not know how to resent it. The whole tendency of his mind and disposition was opposed to any contra-assumption of grandeur on his own part, and he hadn't the worldly spirit or quickness necessary to put down insolent pretensions by downright and open rebuke, as the archdeacon would have done. There was nothing for Mr. Harding but to submit, and he accordingly did so.

' About the hospital, Mr. Harding?' began Mr. Slope, speaking of it as the head of a college at Cambridge might speak of some sizarship which had to be disposed of.

Mr. Harding crossed one leg over another, and then one hand over the other on the top of them, and looked Mr. Slope in the face; but he said nothing.

' It 's to be filled up again,' said Mr. Slope. Mr. Harding
said that he had understood so.

' Of course, you know, the income will be very much
reduced,' continued Mr. Slope. ' The bishop wished to
be liberal, and he therefore told the government that he
thought it ought to be put at not less than £450. I think
on the whole the bishop was right ; for though the services
required will not be of a very onerous nature, they will
be more so than they were before. And it is, perhaps, well
that the clergy immediately attached to the cathedral
town should be made as comfortable as the extent of the
ecclesiastical means at our disposal will allow. Those
are the bishop's ideas, and I must say mine also.'

Mr. Harding sat rubbing one hand on the other, but
said not a word.

' So much for the income, Mr. Harding. The house
will, of course, remain to the warden, as before. It should,
however, I think, be stipulated that he should paint
inside every seven years, and outside every three years,
and be subject to dilapidations, in the event of vacating,
either by death or otherwise. But this is a matter on
which the bishop must yet be consulted.'

Mr. Harding still rubbed his hands, and still sat silent,
gazing up into Mr. Slope's unprepossessing face.

' Then, as to the duties,' continued he, ' I believe, if
I am rightly informed, there can hardly be said to have
been any duties hitherto,' and he gave a sort of half laugh,
as though to pass off the accusation in the guise of a
pleasantry.

Mr. Harding thought of the happy, easy years he had
passed in his old home ; of the worn-out, aged men whom
he had succoured ; of his good intentions ; and of his
work, which had certainly been of the lightest. He thought
of these things, doubting for a moment whether he did
or did not deserve the sarcasm. He gave his enemy the
benefit of the doubt, and did not rebuke him. He merely
observed, very tranquilly, and perhaps with too much
humility, that the duties of the situation, such as they
were, had, he believed, been done to the satisfaction of
the late bishop.

Mr. Slope again smiled, and this time the smile was
intended to operate against the memory of the late bishop,

rather than against the energy of the ex-warden; and so it was understood by Mr. Harding. The colour rose to his cheeks, and he began to feel very angry.

'You must be aware, Mr. Harding, that things are a good deal changed in Barchester,' said Mr. Slope.

Mr. Harding said that he was aware of it. 'And not only in Barchester, Mr. Harding, but in the world at large. It is not only in Barchester that a new man is carrying out new measures and casting away the useless rubbish of past centuries. The same thing is going on throughout the country. Work is now required from every man who receives wages; and they who have to superintend the doing of work, and the paying of wages, are bound to see that this rule is carried out. New men, Mr. Harding, are now needed, and are now forthcoming in the church, as well as in other professions.'

All this was wormwood to our old friend. He had never rated very high his own abilities or activity; but all the feelings of his heart were with the old clergy, and any antipathies of which his heart was susceptible, were directed against those new, busy, uncharitable, self-lauding men, of whom Mr. Slope was so good an example.

'Perhaps,' said he, 'the bishop will prefer a new man at the hospital?'

'By no means,' said Mr. Slope. 'The bishop is very anxious that you should accept the appointment; but he wishes you should understand beforehand what will be the required duties. In the first place, a Sabbath-day school will be attached to the hospital.'

'What! for the old men?' asked Mr. Harding.

'No, Mr. Harding, not for the old men, but for the benefit of the children of such of the poor of Barchester as it may suit. The bishop will expect that you shall attend this school, and the teachers shall be under your inspection and care.'

Mr. Harding slipped his topmost hand off the other, and began to rub the calf of the leg which was supported.

'As to the old men,' continued Mr. Slope, 'and the old women who are to form a part of the hospital, the bishop is desirous that you shall have morning and evening service on the premises every Sabbath, and one week-day service; that you shall preach to them once at least on

Sundays; and that the whole hospital be always collected
for morning and evening prayer. The bishop thinks that
this will render it unnecessary that any separate seats in
the cathedral should be reserved for the hospital inmates.'

Mr. Slope paused, but Mr. Harding still said nothing.

' Indeed, it would be difficult to find seats for the
women; and, on the whole, Mr. Harding, I may as well
say at once, that for people of that class the cathedral
service does not appear to me the most useful,—even
if it be so for any class of people.'

' We will not discuss that, if you please,' said Mr.
Harding.

' I am not desirous of doing so; at least, not at the
present moment. I hope, however, you fully understand
the bishop's wishes about the new establishment of the
hospital; and if, as I do not doubt, I shall receive from
you an assurance that you accord with his lordship's
views, it will give me very great pleasure to be the bearer
from his lordship to you of the presentation to the appointment.'

' But if I disagree with his lordship's views ? ' asked
Mr. Harding.

' But I hope you do not,' said Mr. Slope.

' But if I do ? ' again asked the other.

' If such unfortunately should be the case, which I can
hardly conceive, I presume your own feelings will dictate
to you the propriety of declining the appointment.'

' But if I accept the appointment, and yet disagree with
the bishop, what then ? '

This question rather bothered Mr. Slope. It was true
that he had talked the matter over with the bishop, and
had received a sort of authority for suggesting to Mr.
Harding the propriety of a Sunday school, and certain
hospital services; but he had no authority for saying
that these propositions were to be made peremptory
conditions attached to the appointment. The bishop's
idea had been that Mr. Harding would of course consent,
and that the school would become, like the rest of those
new establishments in the city, under the control of his
wife and his chaplain. Mr. Slope's idea had been more
correct. He intended that Mr. Harding should refuse
the situation, and that an ally of his own should get it;

but he had not conceived the possibility of Mr. Harding openly accepting the appointment, and as openly rejecting the conditions.

'It is not, I presume, probable,' said he, 'that you will accept from the hands of the bishop a piece of preferment, with a fixed predetermination to disacknowledge the duties attached to it.'

'If I become warden,' said Mr. Harding, 'and neglect my duty, the bishop has means by which he can remedy the grievance.'

'I hardly expected such an argument from you, or I may say the suggestion of such a line of conduct,' said Mr. Slope, with a great look of injured virtue.

'Nor did I expect such a proposition.'

'I shall be glad at any rate to know what answer I am to make to his lordship,' said Mr. Slope.

'I will take an early opportunity of seeing his lordship myself,' said Mr. Harding.

'Such an arrangement,' said Mr. Slope, 'will hardly give his lordship satisfaction. Indeed, it is impossible that the bishop should himself see every clergyman in the diocese on every subject of patronage that may arise. The bishop, I believe, did see you on the matter, and I really cannot see why he should be troubled to do so again.'

'Do you know, Mr. Slope, how long I have been officiating as a clergyman in this city?' Mr. Slope's wish was now nearly fulfilled. Mr. Harding had become angry, and it was probable that he might commit himself.

'I really do not see what that has to do with the question. You cannot think the bishop would be justified in allowing you to regard as a sinecure a situation that requires an active man, merely because you have been employed for many years in the cathedral.'

'But it might induce the bishop to see me, if I asked him to do so. I shall consult my friends in this matter, Mr. Slope; but I mean to be guilty of no subterfuge,—you may tell the bishop that as I altogether disagree with his views about the hospital, I shall decline the situation if I find that any such conditions are attached to it as those you have suggested;' and so saying, Mr. Harding took his hat and went his way.

Mr. Slope was contented. He considered himself at liberty to accept Mr. Harding's last speech as an absolute refusal of the appointment. At least, he so represented it to the bishop and to Mrs. Proudie.

' That is very surprising,' said the bishop.

' Not at all,' said Mrs. Proudie ; ' you little know how determined the whole set of them are to withstand your authority.'

' But Mr. Harding was so anxious for it,' said the bishop.

' Yes,' said Mr. Slope, ' if he can hold it without the slightest acknowledgment of your lordship's jurisdiction.'

' That is out of the question,' said the bishop.

' I should imagine it to be quite so,' said the chaplain.

' Indeed, I should think so,' said the lady.

' I really am sorry for it,' said the bishop.

' I don't know that there is much cause for sorrow,' said the lady. ' Mr. Quiverful is a much more deserving man, more in need of it, and one who will make himself much more useful in the close neighbourhood of the palace.'

' I suppose I had better see Quiverful ? ' said the chaplain.

' I suppose you had,' said the bishop.

CHAPTER XIII

THE RUBBISH CART

MR. HARDING was not a happy man as he walked down the palace pathway, and stepped out into the close. His preferment and pleasant house were a second time gone from him ; but that he could endure. He had been schooled and insulted by a man young enough to be his son ; but that he could put up with. He could even draw from the very injuries, which had been inflicted on him, some of that consolation, which we may believe martyrs always receive from the injustice of their own sufferings, and which is generally proportioned in its strength to the extent of cruelty with which martyrs are treated. He had admitted to his daughter that he wanted the comfort of his old home, and yet he could have returned to his lodgings in the High Street, if not with exultation, at least with satisfaction, had that been all. But the venom of the

chaplain's harangue had worked into his blood, and sapped
the life of his sweet contentment.

'New men are carrying out new measures, and are
carting away the useless rubbish of past centuries!'
What cruel words these had been; and how often are they
now used with all the heartless cruelty of a Slope! A man
is sufficiently condemned if it can only be shown that
either in politics or religion he does not belong to some new
school established within the last score of years. He may
then regard himself as rubbish and expect to be carted
away. A man is nothing now unless he has within him a
full appreciation of the new era; an era in which it would
seem that neither honesty nor truth is very desirable, but
in which success is the only touchstone of merit. We
must laugh at every thing that is established. Let the joke
be ever so bad, ever so untrue to the real principles of
joking; nevertheless we must laugh—or else beware the
cart. We must talk, think, and live up to the spirit of the
times, and write up to it too, if that cacoethes be upon us,
or else we are nought. New men and new measures, long
credit and few scruples, great success or wonderful ruin,
such are now the tastes of Englishmen who know how to
live. Alas, alas! under such circumstances Mr. Harding
could not but feel that he was an Englishman who did not
know how to live. This new doctrine of Mr. Slope and the
rubbish cart, new at least at Barchester, sadly disturbed
his equanimity.

'The same thing is going on throughout the whole
country!' 'Work is now required from every man who
receives wages!' And had he been living all his life
receiving wages, and doing no work? Had he in truth so
lived as to be now in his old age justly reckoned as rubbish
fit only to be hidden away in some huge dust hole? The
school of men to whom he professes to belong, the Grantlys,
the Gwynnes, and the old high set of Oxford divines, are
afflicted with no such self-accusations as these which
troubled Mr. Harding. They, as a rule, are as satisfied
with the wisdom and propriety of their own conduct as can
be any Mr. Slope, or any Dr. Proudie, with his own. But
unfortunately for himself Mr. Harding had little of this
self-reliance. When he heard himself designated as rubbish
by the Slopes of the world, he had no other resource than

to make inquiry within his own bosom as to the truth of the designation. Alas, alas! the evidence seemed generally to go against him.

He had professed to himself in the bishop's parlour that in these coming sources of the sorrow of age, in these fits of sad regret from which the latter years of few reflecting men can be free, religion would suffice to comfort him. Yes, religion could console him for the loss of any worldly good ; but was his religion of that active sort which would enable him so to repent of misspent years as to pass those that were left to him in a spirit of hope for the future ? And such repentance itself, is it not a work of agony and of tears ? It is very easy to talk of repentance ; but a man has to walk over hot ploughshares before he can complete it ; to be skinned alive as was St. Bartholomew ; to be stuck full of arrows as was St. Sebastian ; to lie broiling on a gridiron like St. Lorenzo! How if his past life required such repentance as this ? had he the energy to go through with it ?

Mr. Harding after leaving the palace, walked slowly for an hour or so beneath the shady elms of the close, and then betook himself to his daughter's house. He had at any rate made up his mind that he would go out to Plumstead to consult Dr. Grantly, and that he would in the first instance tell Eleanor what had occurred.

And now he was doomed to undergo another misery. Mr. Slope had forestalled him at the widow's house. He had called there on the preceding afternoon. He could not, he had said, deny himself the pleasure of telling Mrs. Bold that her father was about to return to the pretty house at Hiram's hospital. He had been instructed by the bishop to inform Mr. Harding that the appointment would now be made at once. The bishop was of course only too happy to be able to be the means of restoring to Mr. Harding the preferment which he had so long adorned. And then by degrees Mr. Slope had introduced the subject of the pretty school which he hoped before long to see attached to the hospital. He had quite fascinated Mrs. Bold by his description of this picturesque, useful, and charitable appendage, and she had gone so far as to say that she had no doubt her father would approve, and that she herself would gladly undertake a class.

Any one who had heard the entirely different tone, and seen the entirely different manner in which Mr. Slope had spoken of this projected institution to the daughter and to the father, could not have failed to own that Mr. Slope was a man of genius. He said nothing to Mrs. Bold about the hospital sermons and services, nothing about the exclusion of the old men from the cathedral, nothing about dilapidation and painting, nothing about carting away the rubbish. Eleanor had said to herself that certainly she did not like Mr. Slope personally, but that he was a very active, zealous clergyman, and would no doubt be useful in Barchester. All this paved the way for much additional misery to Mr. Harding.

Eleanor put on her happiest face as she heard her father on the stairs, for she thought she had only to congratulate him ; but directly she saw his face, she knew that there was but little matter for congratulation. She had seen him with the same weary look of sorrow on one or two occasions before, and remembered it well. She had seen him when he first read that attack upon himself in the Jupiter which had ultimately caused him to resign the hospital ; and she had seen him also when the archdeacon had persuaded him to remain there against his own sense of propriety and honour. She knew at a glance that his spirit was in deep trouble.

' Oh, papa, what is it ? ' said she, putting down her boy to crawl upon the floor.

' I came to tell you, my dear,' said he, ' that I am going out to Plumstead : you won't come with me, I suppose ? '

' To Plumstead, papa ? Shall you stay there ? '

' I suppose I shall, to night : I must consult the archdeacon about this weary hospital. Ah me ! I wish I had never thought of it again.'

' Why, papa, what is the matter ? '

' I've been with Mr. Slope, my dear, and he isn't the pleasantest companion in the world, at least not to me.' Eleanor gave a sort of half blush ; but she was wrong if she imagined that her father in any way alluded to her acquaintance with Mr. Slope.

' Well, papa.'

' He wants to turn the hospital into a Sunday school and a preaching house ; and I suppose he will have his way.

I do not feel myself adapted for such an establishment, and therefore, I suppose, I must refuse the appointment.'

' What would be the harm of the school, papa ? '

' The want of a proper schoolmaster, my dear.'

' But that would of course be supplied.'

' Mr. Slope wishes to supply it by making me his schoolmaster. But as I am hardly fit for such work, I intend to decline.'

' Oh, papa ! Mr. Slope doesn't intend that. He was here yesterday, and what he intends——'

' He was here yesterday, was he ? ' asked Mr. Harding.

' Yes, papa.'

' And talking about the hospital ? '

' He was saying how glad he would be, and the bishop too, to see you back there again. And then he spoke about the Sunday school ; and to tell the truth I agreed with him ; and I thought you would have done so too. Mr. Slope spoke of a school, not inside the hospital, but just connected with it, of which you would be the patron and visitor ; and I thought you would have liked such a school as that ; and I promised to look after it and to take a class —and it all seemed so very——. But, oh, papa ! I shall be so miserable if I find I have done wrong.'

' Nothing wrong at all, my dear,' said he, gently, very gently rejecting his daughter's caress. ' There can be nothing wrong in your wishing to make yourself useful ; indeed, you ought to do so by all means. Every one must now exert himself who would not choose to go to the wall.' Poor Mr. Harding thus attempted in his misery to preach the new doctrine to his child. ' Himself or herself, it 's all the same,' he continued ; ' you will be quite right, my dear, to do something of this sort ; but——'

' Well, papa.'

' I am not quite sure that if I were you I would select Mr. Slope for my guide.'

' But I never have done so, and never shall.'

' It would be very wicked of me to speak evil of him, for to tell the truth I know no evil of him ; but I am not quite sure that he is honest. That he is not gentleman-like in his manners, of that I am quite sure.'

' I never thought of taking him for my guide, papa.'

' As for myself, my dear,' continued he, ' we know the

old proverb—' It 's bad teaching an old dog tricks.' I must decline the Sunday school, and shall therefore probably decline the hospital also. But I will first see your brother-in-law.' So he took up his hat, kissed the baby, and withdrew, leaving Eleanor in as low spirits as himself.

All this was a great aggravation to his misery. He had so few with whom to sympathise, that he could not afford to be cut off from the one whose sympathy was of the most value to him. And yet it seemed probable that this would be the case. He did not own to himself that he wished his daughter to hate Mr. Slope; yet had she expressed such a feeling there would have been very little bitterness in the rebuke he would have given her for so uncharitable a state of mind. The fact, however, was that she was on friendly terms with Mr. Slope, that she coincided with his views, adhered at once to his plans, and listened with delight to his teaching. Mr. Harding hardly wished his daughter to hate the man, but he would have preferred that to her loving him.

He walked away to the inn to order a fly, went home to put up his carpet bag, and then started for Plumstead. There was, at any rate, no danger that the archdeacon would fraternise with Mr. Slope; but then he would recommend internecine war, public appeals, loud reproaches, and all the paraphernalia of open battle. Now that alternative was hardly more to Mr. Harding's taste than the other.

When Mr. Harding reached the parsonage he found that the archdeacon was out, and would not be home till dinner-time, so he began his complaint to his elder daughter. Mrs. Grantly entertained quite as strong an antagonism to Mr. Slope as did her husband; she was also quite as alive to the necessity of combating the Proudie faction, of supporting the old church interest of the close, of keeping in her own set such of the loaves and fishes as duly belonged to it; and was quite as well prepared as her lord to carry on the battle without giving or taking quarter. Not that she was a woman prone to quarrelling, or ill inclined to live at peace with her clerical neighbours; but she felt, as did the archdeacon, that the presence of Mr. Slope in Barchester was an insult to every one connected with the late bishop, and that his assumed dominion in the diocese was a

spiritual injury to her husband. Hitherto people had little
guessed how bitter Mrs. Grantly could be. She lived on
the best of terms with all the rectors' wives around her.
She had been popular with all the ladies connected with
the close. Though much the wealthiest of the ecclesiastical matrons of the county, she had so managed her affairs
that her carriage and horses had given umbrage to none.
She had never thrown herself among the county grandees
so as to excite the envy of other clergymen's wives. She
had never talked too loudly of earls and countesses, or
boasted that she gave her governess sixty pounds a year,
or her cook seventy. Mrs. Grantly had lived the life of a
wise, discreet, peace-making woman; and the people of
Barchester were surprised at the amount of military vigour
she displayed as general of the feminine Grantlyite forces.

Mrs. Grantly soon learnt that her sister Eleanor had
promised to assist Mr. Slope in the affairs of the hospital;
and it was on this point that her attention soon fixed itself.

' How can Eleanor endure him ? ' said she.

' He is a very crafty man,' said her father, ' and his craft
has been successful in making Eleanor think that he is a
meek, charitable, good clergyman. God forgive me, if I
wrong him, but such is not his true character in my opinion.'

' His true character, indeed ! ' said she, with something
approaching to scorn for her father's moderation. ' I only
hope he won't have craft enough to make Eleanor forget
herself and her position.'

' Do you mean marry him ? ' said he, startled out of his
usual demeanour by the abruptness and horror of so
dreadful a proposition.

' What is there so improbable in it ? Of course that
would be his own object if he thought he had any chance
of success. Eleanor has a thousand a year entirely at her
own disposal, and what better fortune could fall to Mr.
Slope's lot than the transferring of the disposal of such a
fortune to himself ? '

' But you can't think she likes him, Susan ? '

' Why not ? ' said Susan. ' Why shouldn't she like him ?
He 's just the sort of man to get on with a woman left as she
is, with no one to look after her.'

' Look after her ! ' said the unhappy father; ' don't we
look after her ? '

'Ah, papa, how innocent you are! Of course it was to
be expected that Eleanor should marry again. I should be
the last to advise her against it, if she would only wait the
proper time, and then marry at least a gentleman.'

'But you don't really mean to say that you suppose
Eleanor has ever thought of marrying Mr. Slope? Why,
Mr. Bold has only been dead a year.'

'Eighteen months,' said his daughter. 'But I don't
suppose Eleanor has ever thought about it. It is very
probable, though, that he has, and that he will try and
make her do so; and that he will succeed too, if we don't
take care what we are about.'

This was quite a new phase of the affair to poor Mr.
Harding. To have thrust upon him as his son-in-law, as
the husband of his favourite child, the only man in the
world whom he really positively disliked, would be a misfortune which he felt he would not know how to endure
patiently. But then, could there be any ground for so
dreadful a surmise? In all worldly matters he was apt to
look upon the opinion of his eldest daughter, as one
generally sound and trustworthy. In her appreciation of
character, of motives, and the probable conduct both of
men and women, she was usually not far wrong. She had
early foreseen the marriage of Eleanor and John Bold;
she had at a glance deciphered the character of the new
bishop and his chaplain; could it possibly be that her
present surmise should ever come forth as true?

'But you don't think that she likes him?' said Mr.
Harding again.

'Well, papa, I can't say that I think she dislikes him as
she ought to do. Why is he visiting there as a confidential
friend, when he never ought to have been admitted inside
the house? Why is it that she speaks to him about your
welfare and your position, as she clearly has done? At the
bishop's party the other night, I saw her talking to him for
half an hour at the stretch.'

'I thought Mr. Slope seemed to talk to nobody there but
that daughter of Stanhope's,' said Mr. Harding, wishing to
defend his child.

'Oh, Mr. Slope is a cleverer man than you think of, papa,
and keeps more than one iron in the fire.'

To give Eleanor her due, any suspicion as to the slightest

inclination on her part towards Mr. Slope was a wrong to her. She had no more idea of marrying Mr. Slope than she had of marrying the bishop ; and the idea that Mr. Slope would present himself as a suitor had never occurred to her. Indeed, to give her her due again, she had never thought about suitors since her husband's death. But nevertheless it was true that she had overcome all that repugnance to the man which was so strongly felt for him by the rest of the Grantly faction. She had forgiven him his sermon. She had forgiven him his low church tendencies, his Sabbath schools, and puritanical observances. She had forgiven his pharisaical arrogance, and even his greasy face and oily vulgar manners. Having agreed to overlook such offences as these, why should she not in time be taught to regard Mr. Slope as a suitor ?

And as to him, it must also be affirmed that he was hitherto equally innocent of the crime imputed to him. How it had come to pass that a man whose eyes were generally so widely open to everything around him had not perceived that this young widow was rich as well as beautiful, cannot probably now be explained. But such was the fact. Mr. Slope had ingratiated himself with Mrs. Bold, merely as he had done with other ladies, in order to strengthen his party in the city. He subsequently amended his error ; but it was not till after the interview between him and Mr. Harding.

CHAPTER XIV

THE NEW CHAMPION

THE archdeacon did not return to the parsonage till close upon the hour of dinner, and there was therefore no time to discuss matters before that important ceremony. He seemed to be in an especial good humour, and welcomed his father-in-law with a sort of jovial earnestness that was usual with him when things on which he was intent were going on as he would have them.

' It's all settled, my dear,' said he to his wife as he washed his hands in his dressing-room, while she, according to her wont, sat listening in the bedroom ; ' Arabin has agreed to accept the living. He'll be here next week.'

And the archdeacon scrubbed his hands and rubbed his
face with a violent alacrity, which showed that Arabin's
coming was a great point gained.

'Will he come here to Plumstead?' said the wife.

'He has promised to stay a month with us,' said the
archdeacon, 'so that he may see what his parish is like.
You'll like Arabin very much. He's a gentleman in every
respect, and full of humour.'

'He's very queer, isn't he?' asked the lady.

'Well—he is a little odd in some of his fancies; but
there's nothing about him you won't like. He is as staunch
a churchman as there is at Oxford. I really don't know
what we should do without Arabin. It's a great thing for
me to have him so near me; and if anything can put
Slope down, Arabin will do it.'

The Reverend Francis Arabin was a fellow of Lazarus,
the favoured disciple of the great Dr. Gwynne, a high
churchman at all points; so high, indeed, that at one
period of his career he had all but toppled over into the cess-
pool of Rome; a poet and also a polemical writer, a great
pet in the common rooms at Oxford, an eloquent clergyman, a droll, odd, humorous, energetic, conscientious man,
and, as the archdeacon had boasted of him, a thorough
gentleman. As he will hereafter be brought more closely
to our notice, it is now only necessary to add, that he had
just been presented to the vicarage of St. Ewold by Dr.
Grantly, in whose gift as archdeacon the living lay. St.
Ewold is a parish lying just without the city of Barchester.
The suburbs of the new town, indeed, are partly within its
precincts, and the pretty church and parsonage are not
much above a mile distant from the city gate.

St. Ewold is not a rich piece of preferment—it is worth
some three or four hundred a year at most, and has
generally been held by a clergyman attached to the
cathedral choir. The archdeacon, however, felt, when the
living on this occasion became vacant, that it imperatively
behoved him to aid the force of his party with some tower
of strength, if any such tower could be got to occupy St.
Ewold's. He had discussed the matter with his brethren
in Barchester; not in any weak spirit as the holder of
patronage to be used for his own or his family's benefit, but
as one to whom was committed a trust, on the due ad-

ministration of which much of the church's welfare might depend. He had submitted to them the name of Mr. Arabin, as though the choice had rested with them all in conclave, and they had unanimously admitted that, if Mr. Arabin would accept St. Ewold's no better choice could possibly be made.

If Mr. Arabin would accept St. Ewold's! There lay the difficulty. Mr. Arabin was a man standing somewhat prominently before the world, that is, before the Church of England world. He was not a rich man, it is true, for he held no preferment but his fellowship; but he was a man not over anxious for riches, not married of course, and one whose time was greatly taken up in discussing, both in print and on platforms, the privileges and practices of the church to which he belonged. As the archdeacon had done battle for its temporalities, so did Mr. Arabin do battle for its spiritualities; and both had done so conscientiously; that is, not so much each for his own benefit as for that of others.

Holding such a position as Mr. Arabin did, there was much reason to doubt whether he would consent to become the parson of St. Ewold's, and Dr. Grantly had taken the trouble to go himself to Oxford on the matter. Dr. Gwynne and Dr. Grantly together had succeeded in persuading this eminent divine that duty required him to go to Barchester. There were wheels within wheels in this affair. For some time past Mr. Arabin had been engaged in a tremendous controversy with no less a person than Mr. Slope, respecting the apostolic succession. These two gentlemen had never seen each other, but they had been extremely bitter in print. Mr. Slope had endeavoured to strengthen his cause by calling Mr. Arabin an owl, and Mr. Arabin had retaliated by hinting that Mr. Slope was an infidel. This battle had been commenced in the columns of the daily Jupiter, a powerful newspaper, the manager of which was very friendly to Mr. Slope's view of the case. The matter, however, had become too tedious for the readers of the Jupiter, and a little note had therefore been appended to one of Mr. Slope's most telling rejoinders, in which it had been stated that no further letters from the reverend gentleman could be inserted except as advertisements.

Other methods of publication were, however, found less

expensive than advertisements in the Jupiter; and the war went on merrily. Mr. Slope declared that the main part of the consecration of a clergyman was the self-devotion of the inner man to the duties of the ministry. Mr. Arabin contended that a man was not consecrated at all, had, indeed, no single attribute of a clergyman, unless he became so through the imposition of some bishop's hands, who had become a bishop through the imposition of other hands, and so on in a direct line to one of the apostles. Each had repeatedly hung the other on the horns of a dilemma; but neither seemed to be a whit the worse for the hanging; and so the war went on merrily.

Whether or no the near neighbourhood of the foe may have acted in any way as an inducement to Mr. Arabin to accept the living of St. Ewold, we will not pretend to say; but it had at any rate been settled in Dr. Gwynne's library, at Lazarus, that he would accept it, and that he would lend his assistance towards driving the enemy out of Barchester, or, at any rate, silencing him while he remained there. Mr. Arabin intended to keep his rooms at Oxford, and to have the assistance of a curate at St. Ewold; but he promised to give as much time as possible to the neighbourhood of Barchester, and from so great a man Dr. Grantly was quite satisfied with such a promise. It was no small part of the satisfaction derivable from such an arrangement that Bishop Proudie would be forced to institute into a living, immediately under his own nose, the enemy of his favourite chaplain.

All through dinner the archdeacon's good humour shone brightly in his face. He ate of the good things heartily, he drank wine with his wife and daughter, he talked pleasantly of his doings at Oxford, told his father-in-law that he ought to visit Dr. Gwynne at Lazarus, and launched out again in praise of Mr. Arabin.

' Is Mr. Arabin married, papa?' asked Griselda.

' No, my dear; the fellow of a college is never married.'

' Is he a young man, papa?'

' About forty, I believe,' said the archdeacon.

' Oh!' said Griselda. Had her father said eighty, Mr. Arabin would not have appeared to her to be very much older.

When the two gentlemen were left alone over their wine,

Mr. Harding told his tale of woe. But even this, sad as it was, did not much diminish the archdeacon's good humour, though it greatly added to his pugnacity.

' He can't do it,' said Dr. Grantly over and over again, as his father-in-law explained to him the terms on which the new warden of the hospital was to be appointed ; ' he can't do it. What he says is not worth the trouble of listening to. He can't alter the duties of the place.'

' Who can't ? ' asked the ex-warden.

' Neither the bishop nor the chaplain, nor yet the bishop's wife, who, I take it, has really more to say to such matters than either of the other two. The whole body corporate of the palace together have no power to turn the warden of the hospital into a Sunday schoolmaster.'

' But the bishop has the power to appoint whom he pleases, and——'

' I don't know that ; I rather think he'll find he has no such power. Let him try it, and see what the press will say. For once we shall have the popular cry on our side. But Proudie, ass as he is, knows the world too well to get such a hornet's nest about his ears.'

Mr. Harding winced at the idea of the press. He had had enough of that sort of publicity, and was unwilling to be shown up a second time either as a monster or as a martyr. He gently remarked that he hoped the newspapers would not get hold of his name again, and then suggested that perhaps it would be better that he should abandon his object. ' I am getting old,' said he ; ' and after all I doubt whether I am fit to undertake new duties.'

' New duties ! ' said the archdeacon : ' don't I tell you there shall be no new duties ? '

' Or, perhaps, old duties either,' said Mr. Harding ; ' I think I will remain content as I am.' The picture of Mr. Slope carting away the rubbish was still present to his mind.

The archdeacon drank off his glass of claret, and prepared himself to be energetic. ' I do hope,' said he, ' that you are not going to be so weak as to allow such·a man as Mr. Slope to deter you from doing what you know it is your duty to do. You know it is your duty to resume your place at the hospital now that parliament has so settled the stipend as to remove those difficulties which induced you

to resign it. You cannot deny this; and should your
timidity now prevent you from doing so, your conscience
will hereafter never forgive you;' and as he finished this
clause of his speech, he pushed over the bottle to his
companion.

'Your conscience will never forgive you,' he continued.
'You resigned the place from conscientious scruples,
scruples which I greatly respected, though I did not share
them. All your friends respected them, and you left your
old house as rich in reputation as you were ruined in
fortune. It is now expected that you will return. Dr.
Gwynne was saying only the other day——'

'Dr. Gwynne does not reflect how much older a man I
am now than when he last saw me.'

'Old—nonsense!' said the archdeacon; 'you never
thought yourself old till you listened to the impudent trash
of that coxcomb at the palace.'

'I shall be sixty-five if I live till November,' said Mr.
Harding.

'And seventy-five, if you live till November ten years,'
said the archdeacon. 'And you bid fair to be as efficient
then as you were ten years ago. But for heaven's sake let
us have no pretence in this matter. Your plea of old age
is only a pretence. But you're not drinking your wine.
It is only a pretence. The fact is, you are half afraid of
this Slope, and would rather subject yourself to comparative poverty and discomfort, than come to blows with a
man who will trample on you, if you let him.'

'I certainly don't like coming to blows, if I can help it.'

'Nor I neither—but sometimes we can't help it. This
man's object is to induce you to refuse the hospital, that
he may put some creature of his own into it; that he may
show his power, and insult us all by insulting you, whose
cause and character are so intimately bound up with that
of the chapter. You owe it to us all to resist him in this,
even if you have no solicitude for yourself. But surely, for
your own sake, you will not be so lily-livered as to fall into
this trap which he has baited for you, and let him take the
very bread out of your mouth without a struggle.'

Mr. Harding did not like being called lily-livered, and
was rather inclined to resent it. 'I doubt there is any true
courage,' said he, 'in squabbling for money.'

' If honest men did not squabble for money, in this
wicked world of ours, the dishonest men would get it all;
and I do not see that the cause of virtue would be much
improved. No,—we must use the means which we have.
If we were to carry your argument home, we might give
away every shilling of revenue which the church has; and
I presume you are not prepared to say that the church
would be strengthened by such a sacrifice.' The archdeacon filled his glass and then emptied it, drinking with
much reverence a silent toast to the well-being and
permanent security of those temporalities which were so
dear to his soul.

' I think all quarrels between a clergyman and his bishop
should be avoided,' said Mr. Harding.

' I think so too; but it is quite as much the duty of the
bishop to look to that as of his inferior. I tell you what,
my friend; I'll see the bishop in this matter, that is, if you
will allow me; and you may be sure I will not compromise
you. My opinion is, that all this trash about the Sunday-
schools and the sermons has originated wholly with Slope
and Mrs. Proudie, and that the bishop knows nothing
about it. The bishop can't very well refuse to see me, and
I'll come upon him when he has neither his wife nor his
chaplain by him. I think you'll find that it will end in his
sending you the appointment without any condition whatever. And as to the seats in the cathedral, we may safely
leave that to Mr. Dean. I believe the fool positively thinks
that the bishop could walk away with the cathedral if he
pleased.'

And so the matter was arranged between them. Mr.
Harding had come expressly for advice, and therefore felt
himself bound to take the advice given him. He had
known, moreover, beforehand, that the archdeacon would
not hear of his giving the matter up, and accordingly
though he had in perfect good faith put forward his own
views, he was prepared to yield.

They therefore went into the drawing-room in good
humour with each other, and the evening passed pleasantly
in prophetic discussions on the future wars of Arabin and
Slope. The frogs and the mice would be nothing to them,
nor the angers of Agamemnon and Achilles. How the
archdeacon rubbed his hands, and plumed himself on the

success of his last move. He could not himself descend into the arena with Slope, but Arabin would have no such scruples. Arabin was exactly the man for such work, and the only man whom he knew that was fit for it.

The archdeacon's good humour and high buoyancy continued till, when reclining on his pillow, Mrs. Grantly commenced to give him her view of the state of affairs at Barchester. And then certainly he was startled. The last words he said that night were as follows :—

' If she does, by heaven I'll never speak to her again. She dragged me into the mire once, but I'll not pollute myself with such filth as that——' And the archdeacon gave a shudder which shook the whole room, so violently was he convulsed with the thought which then agitated his mind.

Now in this matter, the widow Bold was scandalously ill-treated by her relatives. She had spoken to the man three or four times, and had expressed her willingness to teach in a Sunday-school. Such was the full extent of her sins in the matter of Mr. Slope. Poor Eleanor ! But time will show.

The next morning Mr. Harding returned to Barchester, no further word having been spoken in his hearing respecting Mr. Slope's acquaintance with his younger daughter. But he observed that the archdeacon at breakfast was less cordial than he had been on the preceding evening.

CHAPTER XV

THE WIDOW'S SUITORS

MR. SLOPE lost no time in availing himself of the bishop's permission to see Mr. Quiverful, and it was in his interview with this worthy pastor that he first learned that Mrs. Bold was worth the wooing. He rode out to Puddingdale to communicate to the embryo warden the good will of the bishop in his favour, and during the discussion on the matter it was not unnatural that the pecuniary resources of Mr. Harding and his family should become the subject of remark.

Mr. Quiverful, with his fourteen children and his four hundred a year, was a very poor man, and the prospect of

this new preferment, which was to be held together with
his living, was very grateful to him. To what clergyman
so circumstanced would not such a prospect be very
grateful ?   But Mr. Quiverful had long been acquainted
with Mr. Harding, and had received kindness at his hands,
so that his heart misgave him as he thought of supplanting
a friend at the hospital.   Nevertheless, he was extremely
civil, cringingly civil, to Mr. Slope ; treated him quite as
the great man ; entreated this great man to do him the
honour to drink a glass of sherry, at which, as it was very
poor Marsala, the now pampered Slope turned up his nose ;
and ended by declaring his extreme obligation to the
bishop and Mr. Slope, and his great desire to accept the
hospital, if—if it were certainly the case that Mr. Harding
had refused it.

What man, as needy as Mr. Quiverful, would have been
more disinterested ?

'Mr. Harding did positively refuse it,' said Mr. Slope,
with a certain air of offended dignity, 'when he heard of
the conditions to which the appointment is now subjected.
Of course, you understand, Mr. Quiverful, that the same
conditions will be imposed on yourself.'

Mr. Quiverful cared nothing for the conditions.   He
would have undertaken to preach any number of sermons
Mr. Slope might have chosen to dictate, and to pass every
remaining hour of his Sundays within the walls of a Sunday-
school.   What sacrifices, or, at any rate, what promises,
would have been too much to make for such an addition
to his income, and for such a house !   But his mind still
recurred to Mr. Harding.

'To be sure,' said he ; 'Mr. Harding's daughter is very
rich, and why should he trouble himself with the hospital ? '

'You mean Mrs. Grantly,' said Slope.

'I meant his widowed daughter,' said the other.   'Mrs.
Bold has twelve hundred a year of her own, and I suppose
Mr. Harding means to live with her.'

'Twelve hundred a year of her own ! ' said Slope, and
very shortly afterwards took his leave, avoiding, as far as
it was possible for him to do, any further allusion to the
hospital.   Twelve hundred a year, said he to himself, as he
rode slowly home.   If it were the fact that Mrs. Bold had
twelve hundred a year of her own, what a fool would he be

to oppose her father's return to his old place. The train of Mr. Slope's ideas will probably be plain to all my readers. Why should he not make the twelve hundred a year his own ? and if he did so, would it not be well for him to have a father-in-law comfortably provided with the good things of this world ? would it not, moreover, be much more easy for him to gain the daughter, if he did all in his power to forward the father's views ?

These questions presented themselves to him in a very forcible way, and yet there were many points of doubt. If he resolved to restore to Mr. Harding his former place, he must take the necessary steps for doing so at once ; he must immediately talk over the bishop, quarrel on the matter with Mrs. Proudie whom he knew he could not talk over, and let Mr. Quiverful know that he had been a little too precipitate as to Mr. Harding's positive refusal. That he could effect all this, he did not doubt ; but he did not wish to effect it for nothing. He did not wish to give way to Mr. Harding, and then be rejected by the daughter. He did not wish to lose one influential friend before he had gained another.

And thus he rode home, meditating many things in his mind. It occurred to him that Mrs. Bold was sister-in-law to the archdeacon ; and that not even for twelve hundred a year would he submit to that imperious man. A rich wife was a great desideratum to him, but success in his profession was still greater ; there were, moreover, other rich women who might be willing to become wives ; and after all, this twelve hundred a year might, when inquired into, melt away into some small sum utterly beneath his notice. Then also he remembered that Mrs. Bold had a son.

Another circumstance also much influenced him, though it was one which may almost be said to have influenced him against his will. The vision of the Signora Neroni was perpetually before his eyes. It would be too much to say that Mr. Slope was lost in love, but yet he thought, and kept continually thinking, that he had never seen so beautiful a woman. He was a man whose nature was open to such impulses, and the wiles of the Italianised charmer had been thoroughly successful in imposing upon his thoughts. We will not talk about his heart : not that he

had no heart, but because his heart had little to do with
his present feelings. His taste had been pleased, his eyes
charmed, and his vanity gratified. He had been dazzled
by a sort of loveliness which he had never before seen, and
had been caught by an easy, free, voluptuous manner
which was perfectly new to him. He had never been so
tempted before, and the temptation was now irresistible.
He had not owned to himself that he cared for this woman
more than for others around him ; but yet he thought
often of the time when he might see her next, and made,
almost unconsciously, little cunning plans for seeing her
frequently.

He had called at Dr. Stanhope's house the day after the
bishop's party, and then the warmth of his admiration had
been fed with fresh fuel. If the signora had been kind in
her manner and flattering in her speech when lying upon
the bishop's sofa, with the eyes of so many on her, she had
been much more so in her mother's drawing-room, with no
one present but her sister to repress either her nature or
her art. Mr. Slope had thus left her quite bewildered, and
could not willingly admit into his brain any scheme, a part
of which would be the necessity of his abandoning all
further special friendship with this lady.

And so he slowly rode along very meditative.

And here the author must beg it to be remembered that
Mr. Slope was not in all things a bad man. His motives,
like those of most men, were mixed ; and though his
conduct was generally very different from that which we
would wish to praise, it was actuated perhaps as often as
that of the majority of the world by a desire to do his duty.
He believed in the religion which he taught, harsh, unpalatable, uncharitable as that religion was. He believed
those whom he wished to get under his hoof, the Grantlys
and Gwynnes of the church, to be the enemies of that
religion. He believed himself to be a pillar of strength,
destined to do great things ; and with that subtle, selfish,
ambiguous sophistry to which the minds of all men are so
subject, he had taught himself to think that in doing much
for the promotion of his own interests he was doing much
also for the promotion of religion. But Mr. Slope had
never been an immoral man. Indeed, he had resisted
temptations to immorality with a strength of purpose that

was creditable to him. He had early in life devoted himself to works which were not compatible with the ordinary pleasures of youth, and he had abandoned such pleasures not without a struggle. It must therefore be conceived that he did not admit to himself that he warmly admired the beauty of a married woman without heartfelt stings of conscience; and to pacify that conscience, he had to teach himself that the nature of his admiration was innocent.

And thus he rode along meditative and ill at ease. His conscience had not a word to say against his choosing the widow and her fortune. That he looked upon as a godly work rather than otherwise; as a deed which, if carried through, would redound to his credit as a Christian. On that side lay no future remorse, no conduct which he might probably have to forget, no inward stings. If it should turn out to be really the fact that Mrs. Bold had twelve hundred a year at her own disposal, Mr. Slope would rather look upon it as a duty which he owed his religion to make himself the master of the wife and the money; as a duty too, in which some amount of self-sacrifice would be necessary. He would have to give up his friendship with the signora, his resistance to Mr. Harding, his antipathy—no, he found on mature self-examination, that he could not bring himself to give up his antipathy to Dr. Grantly. He would marry the lady as the enemy of her brother-in-law if such an arrangement suited her; if not, she must look elsewhere for a husband.

It was with such resolve as this that he reached Barchester. He would at once ascertain what the truth might be as to the lady's wealth, and having done this, he would be ruled by circumstances in his conduct respecting the hospital. If he found that he could turn round and secure the place for Mr. Harding without much self-sacrifice, he would do so; but if not, he would woo the daughter in opposition to the father. But in no case would he succumb to the archdeacon.

He saw his horse taken round to the stable, and immediately went forth to commence his inquiries. To give Mr. Slope his due, he was not a man who ever let much grass grow under his feet.

Poor Eleanor! She was doomed to be the intended victim of more schemes than one.

About the time that Mr. Slope was visiting the vicar of Puddingdale, a discussion took place respecting her charms and wealth at Dr. Stanhope's house in the close. There had been morning callers there, and people had told some truth and also some falsehood respecting the property which John Bold had left behind him. By degrees the visitors went, and as the doctor went with them, and as the doctor's wife had not made her appearance, Charlotte Stanhope and her brother were left together. He was sitting idly at the table, scrawling caricatures of Barchester notables, then yawning, then turning over a book or two, and evidently at a loss how to kill his time without much labour.

'You haven't done much, Bertie, about getting any orders,' said his sister.

'Orders !' said he ; ' who on earth is there at Barchester to give one orders ? Who among the people here could possibly think it worth his while to have his head done into marble ? '

' Then you mean to give up your profession,' said she.

' No, I don't,' said he, going on with some absurd portrait of the bishop. 'Look at that, Lotte ; isn't it the little man all over, apron and all ? I'd go on with my profession at once, as you call it, if the governor would set me up with a studio in London ; but as to sculpture at Barchester—I suppose half the people here don't know what a torso means.'

' The governor will not give you a shilling to start you in London,' said Lotte. 'Indeed, he can't give you what would be sufficient, for he has not got it. But you might start yourself very well, if you pleased.'

' How the deuce am I to do it ? ' said he.

' To tell you the truth, Bertie, you'll never make a penny by any profession.'

' That's what I often think myself,' said he, not in the least offended. ' Some men have a great gift of making money, but they can't spend it. Others can't put two shillings together, but they have a great talent for all sorts of outlay. I begin to think that my genius is wholly in the latter line.'

' How do you mean to live then ? ' asked the sister.

' I suppose I must regard myself as a young raven, and

look for heavenly manna ; besides, we have all got something when the governor goes.'

' Yes—you'll have enough to supply yourself with gloves
and boots ; that is, if the Jews have not got the possession
of it all. I believe they have the most of it already. I
wonder, Bertie, at your indifference ; that you, with your
talents and personal advantages, should never try to settle
yourself in life. I look forward with dread to the time
when the governor must go. Mother, and Madeline, and
I,—we shall be poor enough, but you will have absolutely
nothing.'

' Sufficient for the day is the evil thereof,' said Bertie.

' Will you take my advice ? ' said his sister.

' *Cela dépend*,' said the brother.

' Will you marry a wife with money ? '

' At any rate,' said he, ' I won't marry one without :
wives with money a'nt so easy to get now-a-days ; the
parsons pick them all up.'

' And a parson will pick up the wife I mean for you, if
you do not look quickly about it ; the wife I mean is
Mrs. Bold.'

' Whew-w-w-w ! ' whistled Bertie, ' a widow ! '

' She is very beautiful,' said Charlotte.

' With a son and heir all ready to my hand,' said Bertie.

' A baby that will very likely die,' said Charlotte.

' I don't see that,' said Bertie. ' But however, he may
live for me—I don't wish to kill him ; only, it must be
owned that a ready-made family is a drawback.'

' There is only one after all,' pleaded Charlotte.

' And that a very little one, as the maid-servant said,'
rejoined Bertie.

' Beggars mustn't be choosers, Bertie ; you can't have
everything.'

' God knows I am not unreasonable,' said he, ' nor yet
opinionated ; and if you'll arrange it all for me, Lotte, I'll
marry the lady. Only mark this ; the money must be sure,
and the income at my own disposal, at any rate for the
lady's life.'

Charlotte was explaining to her brother that he must
make love for himself if he meant to carry on the matter,
and was encouraging him to do so, by warm eulogiums on
Eleanor's beauty, when the signora was brought into the

drawing-room. When at home, and subject to the gaze of none but her own family, she allowed herself to be dragged about by two persons, and her two bearers now deposited her on her sofa. She was not quite so grand in her apparel as she had been at the bishop's party, but yet she was dressed with much care, and though there was a look of care and pain about her eyes, she was, even by daylight, extremely beautiful.

' Well, Madeline ; so I'm going to be married,' Bertie began, as soon as the servants had withdrawn.

' There's no other foolish thing left, that you haven't done,' said Madeline, ' and therefore you are quite right to try that.'

' Oh, you think it's a foolish thing, do you ? ' said he. ' There's Lotte advising me to marry by all means. But on such a subject your opinion ought to be the best ; you have experience to guide you.'

' Yes, I have,' said Madeline, with a sort of harsh sadness in her tone, which seemed to say—What is it to you if I am sad ? I have never asked your sympathy.

Bertie was sorry when he saw that she was hurt by what he said, and he came and squatted on the floor close before her face to make his peace with her.

' Come, Mad, I was only joking ; you know that. But in sober earnest, Lotte is advising me to marry. She wants me to marry this Mrs. Bold. She's a widow with lots of tin, a fine baby, a beautiful complexion, and the *George and Dragon* hotel up in the High Street. By Jove, Lotte, if I marry her, I'll keep the public house myself— it's just the life to suit me.'

' What ? ' said Madeline, ' that vapid swarthy creature in the widow's cap, who looked as though her clothes had been stuck on her back with a pitchfork ! ' The signora never allowed any woman to be beautiful.

' Instead of being vapid,' said Lotte, ' I call her a very lovely woman. She was by far the loveliest woman in the rooms the other night ; that is, excepting you, Madeline.'

Even the compliment did not soften the asperity of the maimed beauty. ' Every woman is charming according to Lotte,' she said ; ' I never knew an eye with so little true appreciation. In the first place, what woman on earth

could look well in such a thing as that she had on her
head ? '

' Of course she wears a widow's cap ; but she'll put that
off when Bertie marries her.'

' I don't see any of course in it,' said Madeline.   ' The
death of twenty husbands should not make me undergo
such a penance.   It is as much a relic of paganism as the
sacrifice of a Hindoo woman at the burning of her husband's
body.   If not so bloody, it is quite as barbarous, and quite
as useless.'

' But you don't blame her for that,' said Bertie. ' She
does it because it's the custom of the country. People
would think ill of her if she didn't do it.'

' Exactly,' said Madeline.   ' She is just one of those
English nonentities who would tie her head up in a bag for
three months every summer, if her mother and her grandmother had tied up their heads before her. It would never
occur to her, to think whether there was any use in sub-
mitting to such a nuisance.'

' It's very hard, in a country like England, for a young
woman to set herself in opposition to prejudices of that
sort,' said the prudent Charlotte.

' What you mean is, that it's very hard for a fool not to
be a fool,' said Madeline.

Bertie Stanhope had been so much knocked about the
world from his earliest years, that he had not retained
much respect for the gravity of English customs ; but even
to his mind an idea presented itself, that, perhaps in a wife,
true British prejudice would not in the long run be less
agreeable than Anglo-Italian freedom from restraint. He
did not exactly say so, but he expressed the idea in another
way.

' I fancy,' said he, ' that if I were to die, and then walk,
I should think that my widow looked better in one of those
caps than any other kind of head-dress.'

' Yes—and you'd fancy also that she could do nothing
better than shut herself up and cry for you, or else burn
herself. But she would think differently. She'd probably
wear one of those horrid she-helmets, because she'd want
the courage not to do so ; but she'd wear it with a heart
longing for the time when she might be allowed to throw it
off. I hate such shallow false pretences. For my part, I

would let the world say what it pleased, and show no grief if I felt none;—and perhaps not, if I did.'

'But wearing a widow's cap won't lessen her fortune,' said Charlotte.

'Or increase it,' said Madeline. 'Then why on earth does she do it?'

'But Lotte's object is to make her put it off,' said Bertie.

'If it be true that she has got twelve hundred a year quite at her own disposal, and she be not utterly vulgar in her manners, I would advise you to marry her. I dare say she is to be had for the asking: and as you are not going to marry her for love, it doesn't much matter whether she is good-looking or not. As to your really marrying a woman for love, I don't believe *you* are fool enough for that.'

'Oh, Madeline!' exclaimed her sister.

'And oh, Charlotte!' said the other.

'You don't mean to say that no man can love a woman unless he be a fool?'

'I mean very much the same thing,—that any man who is willing to sacrifice his interest to get possession of a pretty face is a fool. Pretty faces are to be had cheaper than that. I hate your mawkish sentimentality, Lotte. You know as well as I do in what way husbands and wives generally live together; you know how far the warmth of conjugal affection can withstand the trial of a bad dinner, of a rainy day, or of the least privation which poverty brings with it; you know what freedom a man claims for himself, what slavery he would exact from his wife if he could! And you know also how wives generally obey. Marriage means tyranny on one side and deceit on the other. I say that a man is a fool to sacrifice his interests for such a bargain. A woman, too generally, has no other way of living.'

'But Bertie has no other way of living,' said Charlotte.

'Then, in God's name, let him marry Mrs. Bold,' said Madeline. And so it was settled between them.

But let the gentle-hearted reader be under no apprehension whatsoever. It is not destined that Eleanor shall marry Mr. Slope or Bertie Stanhope. And here, perhaps, it may be allowed to the novelist to explain his views on a very important point in the art of telling tales. He

ventures to reprobate that system which goes so far to
violate all proper confidence between the author and his
readers, by maintaining nearly to the end of the third
volume a mystery as to the fate of their favourite personage. Nay, more, and worse than this, is too frequently
done. Have not often the profoundest efforts of genius
been used to baffle the aspirations of the reader, to raise
false hopes and false fears, and to give rise to expectations
which are never to be realised ? Are not promises all but
made of delightful horrors, in lieu of which the writer
produces nothing but most commonplace realities in his
final chapter ? And is there not a species of deceit in this
to which the honesty of the present age should lend no
countenance ?

And what can be the worth of that solicitude which a
peep into the third volume can utterly dissipate ? What
the value of those literary charms which are absolutely
destroyed by their enjoyment ? When we have once
learnt what was that picture before which was hung Mrs.
Radcliffe's solemn curtain, we feel no further interest about
either the frame or the veil. They are to us, merely a
receptacle for old bones, an inappropriate coffin, which we
would wish to have decently buried out of our sight.

And then, how grievous a thing it is to have the pleasure
of your novel destroyed by the ill-considered triumph of
a previous reader. ' Oh, you needn't be alarmed for
Augusta, of course she accepts Gustavus in the end.'
' How very ill-natured you are, Susan,' says Kitty, with
tears in her eyes ; ' I don't care a bit about it now.' Dear
Kitty, if you will read my book, you may defy the ill-
nature of your sister. There shall be no secret that she can
tell you. Nay, take the last chapter if you please—learn
from its pages all the results of our troubled story, and the
story shall have lost none of its interest, if indeed there be
any interest in it to lose.

Our doctrine is, that the author and the reader should
move along together in full confidence with each other.
Let the personages of the drama undergo ever so complete a
comedy of errors among themselves, but let the spectator
never mistake the Syracusan for the Ephesian ; otherwise
he is one of the dupes, and the part of a dupe is never
dignified.

I would not for the value of this chapter have it believed by a single reader that my Eleanor could bring herself to marry Mr. Slope, or that she should be sacrificed to a Bertie Stanhope. But among the good folk of Barchester many believed both the one and the other.

CHAPTER XVI

BABY WORSHIP

' DIDDLE, diddle, diddle, diddle, dum, dum, dum,' said or sung Eleanor Bold.

' Diddle, diddle, diddle, diddle, dum, dum, dum,' continued Mary Bold, taking up the second part in this concerted piece.

The only audience at the concert was the baby, who however gave such vociferous applause, that the performers presuming it to amount to an encore, commenced again.

' Diddle, diddle, diddle, diddle, dum, dum, dum : hasn't he got lovely legs ? ' said the rapturous mother.

' H'm 'm 'm 'm 'm,' simmered Mary, burying her lips in the little fellow's fat neck, by way of kissing him.

' H'm 'm 'm 'm 'm,' simmered the mamma, burying her lips also in his fat round short legs. ' He's a dawty little bold darling, so he is ; and he has the nicest little pink legs in all the world, so he has ; ' and the simmering and the kissing went on over again, and as though the ladies were very hungry, and determined to eat him.

' Well, then, he's his own mother's own darling : well, he shall—oh, oh—Mary, Mary—did you ever see ? What am I to do ? My naughty, naughty, naughty, naughty little Johnny.' All these energetic exclamations were elicited by the delight of the mother in finding that her son was strong enough, and mischievous enough, to pull all her hair out from under her cap. ' He's been and pulled down all mamma's hair, and he's the naughtiest, naughtiest, naughtiest little man that ever, ever, ever, ever, ever——'

A regular service of baby worship was going on. Mary Bold was sitting on a low easy chair, with the boy in her lap, and Eleanor was kneeling before the object of her idolatry. As she tried to cover up the little fellow's face

with her long, glossy, dark brown locks, and permitted him
to pull them hither and thither, as he would, she looked
very beautiful in spite of the widow's cap which she still
wore. There was a quiet, enduring, grateful sweetness
about her face, which grew so strongly upon those who
knew her, as to make the great praise of her beauty which
came from her old friends, appear marvellously exaggerated to those who were only slightly acquainted with
her. Her loveliness was like that of many landscapes,
which require to be often seen to be fully enjoyed. There
was a depth of dark clear brightness in her eyes which was
lost upon a quick observer, a character about her mouth
which only showed itself to those with whom she familiarly
conversed, a glorious form of head the perfect symmetry
of which required the eye of an artist for its appreciation.
She had none of that dazzling brilliancy, of that voluptuous
Rubens beauty, of that pearly whiteness, and those
vermilion tints, which immediately entranced with the
power of a basilisk men who came within reach of Madeline
Neroni. It was all but impossible to resist the signora, but
no one was called upon for any resistance towards Eleanor.
You might begin to talk to her as though she were your
sister, and it would not be till your head was on your pillow,
that the truth and intensity of her beauty would flash upon
you; that the sweetness of her voice would come upon
your ear. A sudden half-hour with the Neroni, was like
falling into a pit; an evening spent with Eleanor like an
unexpected ramble in some quiet fields of asphodel.

' We'll cover him up till there sha'n't be a morsel of his
little 'ittle 'ittle 'ittle nose to be seen,' said the mother,
stretching her streaming locks over the infant's face. The
child screamed with delight, and kicked till Mary Bold was
hardly able to hold him.

At this moment the door opened, and Mr. Slope was
announced. Up jumped Eleanor, and with a sudden quick
motion of her hands pushed back her hair over her shoulders. It would have been perhaps better for her that she
had not, for she thus showed more of her confusion than
she would have done had she remained as she was. Mr.
Slope, however, immediately recognised her loveliness, and
thought to himself, that irrespective of her fortune, she
would be an inmate that a man might well desire for his

house, a partner for his bosom's care very well qualified
to make care lie easy. Eleanor hurried out of the room to
re-adjust her cap, muttering some unnecessary apology
about her baby. And while she is gone, we will briefly go
back and state what had been hitherto the results of Mr.
Slope's meditations on his scheme of matrimony.

His inquiries as to the widow's income had at any rate
been so far successful as to induce him to determine to go
on with the speculation. As regarded Mr. Harding, he had
also resolved to do what he could without injury to himself.
To Mrs. Proudie he determined not to speak on the matter,
at least not at present. His object was to instigate a little
rebellion on the part of the bishop. He thought that such
a state of things would be advisable not only in respect to
Messrs. Harding and Quiverful, but also in the affairs of the
diocese generally. Mr. Slope was by no means of opinion
that Dr. Proudie was fit to rule, but he conscientiously
thought it wrong that his brother clergy should be subjected
to petticoat government. He therefore made up his mind
to infuse a little of his spirit into the bishop, sufficient to
induce him to oppose his wife, though not enough to make
him altogether insubordinate.

He had therefore taken an opportunity of again speaking
to his lordship about the hospital, and had endeavoured to
make it appear that after all it would be unwise to exclude
Mr. Harding from the appointment. Mr. Slope, however,
had a harder task than he had imagined. Mrs. Proudie,
anxious to assume to herself as much as possible of the
merit of patronage, had written to Mrs. Quiverful, request-
ing her to call at the palace ; and had then explained to
that matron, with much mystery, condescension, and
dignity, the good that was in store for her and her progeny.
Indeed Mrs. Proudie had been so engaged at the very time
that Mr. Slope had been doing the same with the husband
at Puddingdale Vicarage, and had thus in a measure
committed herself. The thanks, the humility, the gratitude, the surprise of Mrs. Quiverful had been very overpowering ; she had all but embraced the knees of her
patroness, and had promised that the prayers of fourteen
unprovided babes (so Mrs. Quiverful had described her
own family, the eldest of which was a stout young woman
of three-and-twenty) should be put up to heaven morning

and evening for the munificent friend whom God had sent
to them. Such incense as this was not unpleasing to Mrs.
Proudie, and she made the most of it. She offered her
general assistance to the fourteen unprovided babes, if,
as she had no doubt, she should find them worthy;
expressed a hope that the eldest of them would be fit to
undertake tuition in her Sabbath schools, and altogether
made herself a very great lady in the estimation of Mrs.
Quiverful.

Having done this, she thought it prudent to drop a few
words before the bishop, letting him know that she had
acquainted the Puddingdale family with their good
fortune; so that he might perceive that he stood committed to the appointment. The husband well understood
the *ruse* of his wife, but he did not resent it. He knew that
she was taking the patronage out of his hands; he was
resolved to put an end to her interference, and re-assume
his powers. But then he thought this was not the best
time to do it. He put off the evil hour, as many a man in
similar circumstances has done before him.

Such having been the case, Mr. Slope naturally encountered a difficulty in talking over the bishop, a difficulty
indeed which he found could not be overcome except at
the cost of a general outbreak at the palace. A general
outbreak at the present moment might be good policy, but
it also might not. It was at any rate not a step to be lightly
taken. He began by whispering to the bishop that he
feared that public opinion would be against him if Mr.
Harding did not reappear at the hospital. The bishop
answered with some warmth that Mr. Quiverful had been
promised the appointment on Mr. Slope's advice. ' Not
promised!' said Mr. Slope. ' Yes, promised,' replied the
bishop, ' and Mrs. Proudie has seen Mrs. Quiverful on the
subject.' This was quite unexpected on the part of Mr.
Slope, but his presence of mind did not fail him, and he
turned the statement to his own account.

' Ah, my lord,' said he, ' we shall all be in scrapes if the
ladies interfere.'

This was too much in unison with my lord's feelings
to be altogether unpalatable, and yet such an allusion to
interference demanded a rebuke. My lord was somewhat
astounded also, though not altogether made miserable, by

finding that there was a point of difference between his
wife and his chaplain.

' I don't know what you mean by interference,' said the
bishop mildly. ' When Mrs. Proudie heard that Mr.
Quiverful was to be appointed, it was not unnatural that
she should wish to see Mrs. Quiverful about the schools.
I really cannot say that I see any interference.'

' I only speak, my lord, for your own comfort,' said
Slope ; ' for your own comfort and dignity in the diocese.
I can have no other motive. As far as personal feelings go,
Mrs. Proudie is the best friend I have. I must always
remember that. But still, in my present position, my first
duty is to your lordship.'

' I'm sure of that, Mr. Slope, I am quite sure of that ; '
said the bishop mollified : ' and you really think that Mr.
Harding should have the hospital ? '

' Upon my word, I'm inclined to think so. I am quite
prepared to take upon myself the blame of first suggesting
Mr. Quiverful's name. But since doing so, I have found
that there is so strong a feeling in the diocese in favour of
Mr. Harding, that I think your lordship should give way.
I hear also that Mr. Harding has modified the objections
he first felt to your lordship's propositions. And as to
what has passed between Mrs. Proudie and Mrs. Quiverful,
the circumstance may be a little inconvenient, but I really
do not think that that should weigh in a matter of so much
moment.'

And thus the poor bishop was left in a dreadfully un-
decided state as to what he should do. His mind, however,
slightly inclined itself to the appointment of Mr. Harding,
seeing that by such a step, he should have the assistance
of Mr. Slope in opposing Mrs. Proudie.

Such was the state of affairs at the palace, when Mr.
Slope called at Mrs. Bold's house, and found her playing
with her baby. When she ran out of the room, Mr. Slope
began praising the weather to Mary Bold, then he praised
the baby and kissed him, and then he praised the mother,
and then he praised Miss Bold herself. Mrs. Bold, however,
was not long before she came back.

' I have to apologise for calling at so very early an hour,'
began Mr. Slope, ' but I was really so anxious to speak to
you that I hope you and Miss Bold will excuse me.'

Eleanor muttered something in which the words
'certainly,' and 'of course,' and 'not early at all,' were
just audible, and then apologised for her own appearance,
declaring with a smile, that her baby was becoming such
a big boy that he was quite unmanageable.

'He's a great big naughty boy,' said she to the child;
'and we must send him away to a great big rough romping
school, where they have great big rods, and do terrible
things to naughty boys who don't do what their own
mammas tell them;' and she then commenced another
course of kissing, being actuated thereto by the terrible
idea of sending her child away which her own imagination
had depicted.

'And where the masters don't have such beautiful long
hair to be dishevelled,' said Mr. Slope, taking up the joke
and paying a compliment at the same time.

Eleanor thought he might as well have left the compliment alone; but she said nothing and looked nothing,
being occupied as she was with the baby.

'Let me take him,' said Mary. 'His clothes are nearly
off his back with his romping,' and so saying she left the
room with the child. Miss Bold had heard Mr. Slope say
he had something pressing to say to Eleanor, and thinking
that she might be *de trop*, took this opportunity of getting
herself out of the room.

'Don't be long, Mary,' said Eleanor, as Miss Bold shut
the door.

'I am glad, Mrs. Bold, to have the opportunity of having
ten minutes' conversation with you alone,' began Mr.
Slope. 'Will you let me openly ask you a plain question?'

'Certainly,' said she.

'And I am sure you will give me a plain and open
answer.'

'Either that or none at all,' said she, laughing.

'My question is this, Mrs. Bold; is your father really
anxious to go back to the hospital?'

'Why do you ask me?' said she. 'Why don't you ask
himself?'

'My dear Mrs. Bold, I'll tell you why. There are
wheels within wheels, all of which I would explain to you,
only I fear that there is not time. It is essentially necessary that I should have an answer to this question, other-

wise I cannot know how to advance your father's wishes ; and it is quite impossible that I should ask himself. No one can esteem your father more than I do, but I doubt if this feeling is reciprocal.' It certainly was not. 'I must be candid with you as the only means of avoiding ultimate consequences, which may be most injurious to Mr. Harding. I fear there is a feeling, I will not even call it a prejudice, with regard to myself in Barchester, which is not in my favour. You remember that sermon——'

'Oh ! Mr. Slope, we need not go back to that,' said Eleanor.

'For one moment, Mrs. Bold. It is not that I may talk of myself, but because it is so essential that you should understand how matters stand. That sermon may have been ill-judged,—it was certainly misunderstood ; but I will say nothing about that now ; only this, that it did give rise to a feeling against myself which your father shares with others. It may be that he has proper cause, but the result is that he is not inclined to meet me on friendly terms. I put it to yourself whether you do not know this to be the case.'

Eleanor made no answer, and Mr. Slope, in the eagerness of his address, edged his chair a little nearer to the widow's seat, unperceived by her.

'Such being so,' continued Mr. Slope, 'I cannot ask him this question as I can ask it of you. In spite of my delin-quencies since I came to Barchester you have allowed me to regard you as a friend.' Eleanor made a little motion with her head which was hardly confirmatory, but Mr. Slope if he noticed it, did not appear to do so. 'To you I can speak openly, and explain the feelings of my heart. This your father would not allow. Unfortunately the bishop has thought it right that this matter of the hospital should pass through my hands. There have been some details to get up with which he would not trouble himself, and thus it has come to pass that I was forced to have an interview with your father on the matter.'

'I am aware of that,' said Eleanor.

'Of course,' said he. 'In that interview Mr. Harding left the impression on my mind that he did not wish to return to the hospital.'

'How could that be ?' said Eleanor, at last stirred up to

forget the cold propriety of demeanour which she had determined to maintain.

' My dear Mrs. Bold, I give you my word that such was the case,' said he, again getting a little nearer to her. ' And what is more than that, before my interview with Mr. Harding, certain persons at the palace, I do not mean the bishop, had told me that such was the fact. I own, I hardly believed it ; I own, I thought that your father would wish on every account, for conscience' sake, for the sake of those old men, for old association, and the memory of dear days long gone by, on every account I thought that he would wish to resume his duties. But I was told that such was not his wish ; and he certainly left me with the impression that I had been told the truth.'

' Well ! ' said Eleanor, now sufficiently roused on the matter.

' I hear Miss Bold's step,' said Mr. Slope ; ' would it be asking too great a favour to beg you to——I know you can manage anything with Miss Bold.'

Eleanor did not like the word manage, but still she went out, and asked Mary to leave them alone for another quarter of an hour.

' Thank you, Mrs. Bold,—I am so very grateful for this confidence. Well, I left your father with this impression. Indeed, I may say that he made me understand that he declined the appointment.'

' Not the appointment,' said Eleanor. ' I am sure he did not decline the appointment. But he said that he would not agree,—that is, that he did not like the scheme about the schools and the services, and all that. I am quite sure he never said that he wished to refuse the place.'

' Oh, Mrs. Bold ! ' said Mr. Slope, in a manner almost impassioned. ' I would not, for the world, say to so good a daughter a word against so good a father. But you must, for his sake, let me show you exactly how the matter stands at present. Mr. Harding was a little flurried when I told him of the bishop's wishes about the school. I did so, perhaps, with the less caution because you yourself had so perfectly agreed with me on the same subject. He was a little put out and spoke warmly. ' Tell the bishop,' said he, ' that I quite disagree with him,—and shall not return to the hospital as such conditions are attached to it.' What

he said was to that effect; indeed, his words were, if
anything, stronger than those. I had no alternative but to
repeat them to his lordship, who said that he could look on
them in no other light than a refusal. He also had heard
the report that your father did not wish for the appointment, and putting all these things together, he thought he
had no choice but to look for some one else. He has
consequently offered the place to Mr. Quiverful.'

' Offered the place to Mr. Quiverful ! ' repeated Eleanor,
her eyes suffused with tears. ' Then, Mr. Slope, there is an
end of it.'

' No, my friend—not so,' said he. ' It is to prevent such
being the end of it that I am now here. I may at any rate
presume that I have got an answer to my question, and
that Mr. Harding is desirous of returning.'

' Desirous of returning—of course he is,' said Eleanor ;
' of course he wishes to have back his house and his income,
and his place in the world ; to have back what he gave up
with such self-denying honesty, if he can have them without restraints on his conduct to which at his age it would
be impossible that he should submit. How can the bishop
ask a man of his age to turn schoolmaster to a pack of
children ? '

' Out of the question,' said Mr. Slope, laughing slightly ;
' of course no such demand shall be made on your father.
I can at any rate promise you that I will not be the medium
of any so absurd a requisition. We wished your father to
preach in the hospital, as the inmates may naturally be
too old to leave it ; but even that shall not be insisted on.
We wished also to attach a Sabbath-day school to the
hospital, thinking that such an establishment could not
but be useful under the surveillance of so good a clergyman
as Mr. Harding, and also under your own. But, dear Mrs.
Bold ; we won't talk of these things now. One thing is
clear ; we must do what we can to annul this rash offer the
bishop has made to Mr. Quiverful. Your father wouldn't
see Quiverful, would he ? Quiverful is an honourable man,
and would not, for a moment, stand in your father's way.'

' What ? ' said Eleanor ; ' ask a man with fourteen
children to give up his preferment ! I am quite sure he
will do no such thing.'

' I suppose not,' said Slope ; and he again drew near to

Mrs. Bold, so that now they were very close to each other.
Eleanor did not think much about it, but instinctively
moved away a little. How greatly would she have increased the distance could she have guessed what had been
said about her at Plumstead! 'I suppose not. But it is
out of the question that Quiverful should supersede your
father,—quite out of the question. The bishop has been
too rash. An idea occurs to me, which may, perhaps.
with God's blessing, put us right. My dear Mrs. Bold,
would you object to seeing the bishop yourself?'
    'Why should not my father see him?' said Eleanor.
She had once before in her life interfered in her father's
affairs, and then not to much advantage. She was older
now, and felt that she should take no step in a matter so
vital to him without his consent.
    'Why, to tell the truth,' said Mr. Slope, with a look of
sorrow, as though he greatly bewailed the want of charity
in his patron, ' the bishop fancies that he has cause of
anger against your father. I fear an interview would lead
to further ill will.'
    'Why,' said Eleanor, ' my father is the mildest, the
gentlest man living.'
    'I only know,' said Slope, ' that he has the best of
daughters. So you would not see the bishop? As to
getting an interview, I could manage that for you without
the slightest annoyance to yourself.'
    'I could do nothing, Mr. Slope, without consulting my
father.'
    'Ah!' said he, ' that would be useless; you would then
only be your father's messenger. Does anything occur to
yourself? Something must be done. Your father shall
not be ruined by so ridiculous a misunderstanding.'
    Eleanor said that nothing occurred to her, but that it
was very hard; and the tears came to her eyes and rolled
down her cheeks. Mr. Slope would have given much to
have had the privilege of drying them; but he had tact
enough to know that he had still a great deal to do before
he could even hope for any privilege with Mrs. Bold.
    'It cuts me to the heart to see you so grieved,' said he.
' But pray let me assure you that your father's interests
shall not be sacrificed if it be possible for me to protect
them. I will tell the bishop openly what are the facts.

I will explain to him that he has hardly the right to appoint any other than your father, and will show him that if he does so he will be guilty of great injustice,—and you, Mrs. Bold, you will have the charity at any rate to believe this of me, that I am truly anxious for your father's welfare,— for his and for your own.'

The widow hardly knew what answer to make. She was quite aware that her father would not be at all thankful to Mr. Slope; she had a strong wish to share her father's feelings; and yet she could not but acknowledge that Mr. Slope was very kind. Her father, who was generally so charitable to all men, who seldom spoke ill of any one, had warned her against Mr. Slope, and yet she did not know how to abstain from thanking him. What interest could he have in the matter but that which he professed? Nevertheless there was that in his manner which even she distrusted. She felt, she did not know why, that there was something about him which ought to put her on her guard.

Mr. Slope read all this in her hesitating manner just as plainly as though she had opened her heart to him. It was the talent of the man that he could so read the inward feelings of women with whom he conversed. He knew that Eleanor was doubting him, and that if she thanked him she would only do so because she could not help it; but yet this did not make him angry or even annoy him. Rome was not built in a day.

' I did not come for thanks,' continued he, seeing her hesitation; ' and do not want them—at any rate before they are merited. But this I do want, Mrs. Bold, that I may make to myself friends in this fold to which it has pleased God to call me as one of the humblest of his shepherds. If I cannot do so, my task here must indeed be a sad one. I will at any rate endeavour to deserve them.'

' I'm sure,' said she, ' you will soon make plenty of friends.' She felt herself obliged to say something.

' That will be nothing unless they are such as will sympathise with my feelings; unless they are such as I can reverence and admire—and love. If the best and purest turn away from me, I cannot bring myself to be satisfied with the friendship of the less estimable. In such case I must live alone.'

'Oh! I'm sure you will not do that, Mr. Slope.'
Eleanor meant nothing, but it suited him to appear to
think some special allusion had been intended.

'Indeed, Mrs. Bold, I shall live alone, quite alone as far
as the heart is concerned, if those with whom I yearn to
ally myself turn away from me. But enough of this; I
have called you my friend, and I hope you will not contradict me. I trust the time may come when I may also
call your father so. May God bless you, Mrs. Bold, you
and your darling boy. And tell your father from me that
what can be done for his interest shall be done.'

And so he took his leave, pressing the widow's hand
rather more closely than usual. Circumstances, however,
seemed just then to make this intelligible, and the lady did
not feel called on to resent it.

'I cannot understand him,' said Eleanor to Mary Bold,
a few minutes afterwards. 'I do not know whether he is
a good man or a bad man—whether he is true or false.'

'Then give him the benefit of the doubt,' said Mary,
'and believe the best.'

'On the whole, I think I do,' said Eleanor. 'I think I do
believe that he means well—and if so, it is a shame that we
should revile him, and make him miserable while he is
among us. But, oh, Mary, I fear papa will be disappointed
in the hospital.'

CHAPTER XVII

WHO SHALL BE COCK OF THE WALK ?

ALL this time things were going on somewhat uneasily
at the palace. The hint or two which Mr. Slope had given
was by no means thrown away upon the bishop. He had
a feeling that if he ever meant to oppose the now almost
unendurable despotism of his wife, he must lose no further
time in doing so; that if he ever meant to be himself
master in his own diocese, let alone his own house, he
should begin at once. It would have been easier to have
done so from the day of his consecration than now, but
easier now than when Mrs. Proudie should have succeeded
in thoroughly mastering the diocesan details. Then the
proffered assistance of Mr. Slope was a great thing for him,

a most unexpected and invaluable aid. Hitherto he had
looked on the two as allied forces ; and had considered
that as allies they were impregnable. He had begun to
believe that his only chance of escape would be by the
advancement of Mr. Slope to some distant and rich preferment. But now it seemed that one of his enemies, certainly
the least potent of them, but nevertheless one very important, was willing to desert his own camp. Assisted by
Mr. Slope what might he not do ? He walked up and
down his little study, almost thinking that the time might
come when he would be able to appropriate to his own use
the big room up stairs, in which his predecessor had
always sat.

As he revolved these things in his mind a note was
brought to him from Archdeacon Grantly, in which that
divine begged his lordship to do him the honour of seeing
him on the morrow—would his lordship have the kindness
to name an hour ? Dr. Grantly's proposed visit would
have reference to the reappointment of Mr. Harding to the
wardenship of Barchester hospital. The bishop having
read his note was informed that the archdeacon's servant
was waiting for an answer.

Here at once a great opportunity offered itself to the
bishop of acting on his own responsibility. He bethought
himself however of his new ally, and rang the bell for Mr.
Slope. It turned out that Mr. Slope was not in the house ;
and then, greatly daring, the bishop with his own unassisted
spirit wrote a note to the archdeacon saying that he would
see him, and naming an hour for doing so. Having
watched from his study-window that the messenger got
safely off from the premises with this despatch, he began
to turn over in his mind what step he should next take.

To-morrow he would have to declare to the archdeacon
either that Mr. Harding should have the appointment, or
that he should not have it. The bishop felt that he could
not honestly throw over the Quiverfuls without informing
Mrs. Proudie, and he resolved at last to brave the lioness
in her den and tell her that circumstances were such that
it behoved him to reappoint Mr. Harding. He did not feel
that he should at all derogate from his new courage by
promising Mrs. Proudie that the very first piece of available preferment at his disposal should be given to Quiverful

to atone for the injury done to him. If he could mollify
the lioness with such a sop, how happy would he think his
first efforts to have been !

Not without many misgivings did he find himself in
Mrs. Proudie's boudoir. He had at first thought of sending
for her. But it was not at all impossible that she might
chose to take such a message amiss, and then also it might
be some protection to him to have his daughters present
at the interview. He found her sitting with her account
books before her nibbling the end of her pencil evidently
mersed in pecuniary difficulties, and harassed in mind by
the multiplicity of palatial expenses, and the heavy cost
of episcopal grandeur. Her daughters were around her.
Olivia was reading a novel, Augusta was crossing a note
to her bosom friend in Baker Street, and Netta was
working diminutive coach wheels for the bottom of a
petticoat. If the bishop could get the better of his wife in
her present mood, he would be a man indeed. He might
then consider the victory his own for ever. After all, in
such cases the matter between husband and wife stands
much the same as it does between two boys at the same
school, two cocks in the same yard, or two armies on the
same continent. The conqueror once is generally the
conqueror for ever after. The prestige of victory is every
thing.

' Ahem—my dear,' began the bishop, ' if you are dis-
engaged, I wished to speak to you.' Mrs. Proudie put her
pencil down carefully at the point to which she had dotted
her figures, marked down in her memory the sum she had
arrived at, and then looked up, sourly enough, into her
helpmate's face. ' If you are busy, another time will do
as well,' continued the bishop, whose courage like Bob
Acres' had oozed out, now that he found himself on the
ground of battle.

' What is it about, Bishop ? ' asked the lady.

' Well—it was about those Quiverfuls—but I see you
are engaged. Another time will do just as well for me.'

' What about the Quiverfuls ? It is quite understood
I believe, that they are to come to the hospital. There is
to be no doubt about that, is there ? ' and as she spoke she
kept her pencil sternly and vigorously fixed on the column
of figures before her.

' Why, my dear, there is a difficulty,' said the bishop.

' A difficulty!' said Mrs. Proudie, ' what difficulty? The place has been promised to Mr. Quiverful, and of course he must have it. He has made all his arrangements. He has written for a curate for Puddingdale, he has spoken to the auctioneer about selling his farm, horses, and cows, and in all respects considers the place as his own. Of course he must have it.'

Now, bishop, look well to thyself, and call up all the manhood that is in thee. Think how much is at stake. If now thou art not true to thy guns, no Slope can hereafter aid thee. How can he who deserts his own colours at the first smell of gunpowder expect faith in any ally. Thou thyself hast sought the battle-field; fight out the battle manfully now thou art there. Courage, bishop, courage! Frowns cannot kill, nor can sharp words break any bones. After all the apron is thine own. She can appoint no wardens, give away no benefices, nominate no chaplains, an' thou art but true to thyself. Up, man, and at her with a constant heart.

Some little monitor within the bishop's breast so addressed him. But then there was another monitor there which advised him differently, and as follows. Remember, bishop, she is a woman, and such a woman too as thou well knowest: a battle of words with such a woman is the very mischief. Were it not better for thee to carry on this war, if it must be waged, from behind thine own table in thine own study? Does not every cock fight best on his own dunghill? Thy daughters also are here, the pledges of thy love, the fruits of thy loins; is it well that they should see thee in the hour of thy victory over their mother? nay, is it well that they should see thee in the possible hour of thy defeat? Besides, hast thou not chosen thy opportunity with wonderful little skill, indeed with no touch of that sagacity for which thou art famous? Will it not turn out that thou art wrong in this matter, and thine enemy right; that thou hast actually pledged thyself in this matter of the hospital, and that now thou wouldest turn upon thy wife because she requires from thee but the fulfilment of thy promise? Art thou not a Christian bishop, and is not thy word to be held sacred whatever be the result? Return, bishop, to thy sanctum

on the lower floor, and postpone thy combative propensities for some occasion in which at least thou mayest fight
the battle against odds less tremendously against thee.

All this passed within the bishop's bosom while Mrs.
Proudie still sat with her fixed pencil, and the figures
of her sum still enduring on the tablets of her memory.
'£4 17s. 7d.' she said to herself. ' Of course Mr. Quiverful
must have the hospital,' she said out loud to her lord.

' Well, my dear, I merely wanted to suggest to you that
Mr. Slope seems to think that if Mr. Harding be not
appointed, public feeling in the matter would be against
us, and that the press might perhaps take it up.'

' Mr. Slope seems to think ! ' said Mrs. Proudie, in a tone
of voice which plainly showed the bishop that he was right
in looking for a breach in that quarter. ' And what has
Mr. Slope to do with it ? I hope, my lord, you are not
going to allow yourself to be governed by a chaplain.' And
now in her eagerness the lady lost her place in her account.

' Certainly not, my dear. Nothing I can assure you is
less probable. But still Mr. Slope may be useful in finding
how the wind blows, and I really thought that if we could
give something else as good to the Quiverfuls——'

' Nonsense,' said Mrs. Proudie ; ' it would be years
before you could give them anything else that could suit
them half as well, and as for the press and the public, and
all that, remember there are two ways of telling a story.
If Mr. Harding is fool enough to tell his tale, we can also
tell ours. The place was offered to him, and he refused it.
It has now been given to some one else, and there's an end
of it. At least, I should think so.'

' Well, my dear, I rather believe you are right ; ' said the
bishop, and sneaking out of the room, he went down stairs,
troubled in his mind as to how he should receive the archdeacon on the morrow. He felt himself not very well just
at present ; and began to consider that he might, not
improbably, be detained in his room the next morning by
an attack of bile. He was, unfortunately, very subject to
bilious annoyances.

' Mr. Slope, indeed ! I'll Slope him,' said the indignant
matron to her listening progeny. ' I don't know what has
come to Mr. Slope. I believe he thinks he is to be Bishop
of Barchester himself, because I've taken him by the

hand, and got your father to make him his domestic chaplain.'

'He was always full of impudence,' said Olivia; 'I told you so once before, mamma.' Olivia, however, had not thought him too impudent when once before he had proposed to make her Mrs. Slope.

'Well, Olivia, I always thought you liked him,' said Augusta, who at that moment had some grudge against her sister. 'I always disliked the man, because I think him thoroughly vulgar.'

'There you're wrong,' said Mrs. Proudie; 'he's not vulgar at all; and what is more, he is a soul-stirring, eloquent preacher; but he must be taught to know his place if he is to remain in this house.'

'He has the horridest eyes I ever saw in a man's head,' said Netta; 'and I tell you what, he's terribly greedy; did you see all the currant pie he ate yesterday ? '

When Mr. Slope got home he soon learnt from the bishop, as much from his manner as his words, that Mrs. Proudie's behests in the matter of the hospital were to be obeyed. Dr. Proudie let fall something as to ' this occasion only,' and ' keeping all affairs about patronage exclusively in his own hands.' But he was quite decided about Mr. Harding; and as Mr. Slope did not wish to have both the prelate and the prelatess against him, he did not at present see that he could do anything but yield.

He merely remarked that he would of course carry out the bishop's views, and that he was quite sure that if the bishop trusted to his own judgment things in the diocese would certainly be well ordered. Mr. Slope knew that if you hit a nail on the head often enough, it will penetrate at last.

He was sitting alone in his room on the same evening when a light knock was made on his door, and before he could answer it the door was opened, and his patroness appeared. He was all smiles in a moment, but so was not she also. She took, however, the chair that was offered to her, and thus began her expostulation :—

'Mr. Slope, I did not at all approve your conduct the other night with that Italian woman. Any one would have thought that you were her lover.'

'Good gracious, my dear madam,' said Mr. Slope, with a look of horror. 'Why, she is a married woman.'

' That's more than I know,' said Mrs. Proudie ; ' however she chooses to pass for such. But married or not married, such attention as you paid to her was improper. I cannot believe that you would wish to give offence in my drawing-room, Mr. Slope ; but I owe it to myself and my daughters to tell you that I disapprove your conduct.'

Mr. Slope opened wide his huge protruding eyes, and stared out of them with a look of well-feigned surprise. ' Why, Mrs. Proudie,' said he, ' I did but fetch her something to eat when she said she was hungry.'

' And you have called on her since,' continued she, looking at the culprit with the stern look of a detective policeman in the act of declaring himself.

Mr. Slope turned over in his mind whether it would be well for him to tell this termagant at once that he should call on whom he liked, and do what he liked ; but he remembered that his footing in Barchester was not yet sufficiently firm, and that it would be better for him to pacify her.

' I certainly called since at Dr. Stanhope's house, and certainly saw Madame Neroni.'

' Yes, and you saw her alone,' said the episcopal Argus.

' Undoubtedly, I did,' said Mr. Slope, ' but that was because nobody else happened to be in the room. Surely it was no fault of mine if the rest of the family were out.'

' Perhaps not ; but I assure you, Mr. Slope, you will fall greatly in my estimation if I find that you allow yourself to be caught by the lures of that woman. I know women better than you do, Mr. Slope, and you may believe me that that signora, as she calls herself, is not a fitting companion for a strict evangelical, unmarried young clergyman.'

How Mr. Slope would have liked to laugh at her, had he dared ! But he did not dare. So he merely said, ' I can assure you, Mrs. Proudie, the lady in question is nothing to me.'

' Well, I hope not, Mr. Slope. But I have considered it my duty to give you this caution ; and now there is another thing I feel myself called on to speak about ; it is your conduct to the bishop, Mr. Slope.'

' My conduct to the bishop,' said he, now truly surprised and ignorant what the lady alluded to.

' Yes, Mr. Slope ; your conduct to the bishop. It is by no means what I would wish to see it.'

' Has the bishop said anything, Mrs. Proudie ? '

' No, the bishop has said nothing. He probably thinks that any remarks on the matter will come better from me, who first introduced you to his lordship's notice. The fact is, Mr. Slope, you are a little inclined to take too much upon yourself.'

An angry spot showed itself on Mr. Slope's cheeks, and it was with difficulty that he controlled himself. But he did do so, and sat quite silent while the lady went on.

' It is the fault of many young men in your position, and therefore the bishop is not inclined at present to resent it. You will, no doubt, soon learn what is required from you, and what is not. If you will take my advice, however, you will be careful not to obtrude advice upon the bishop in any matter touching patronage. If his lordship wants advice, he knows where to look for it.' And then having added to her counsel a string of platitudes as to what was desirable and what not desirable in the conduct of a strictly evangelical, unmarried young clergyman, Mrs. Proudie retreated, leaving the chaplain to his thoughts.

The upshot of his thoughts was this, that there certainly was not room in the diocese for the energies of both himself and Mrs. Proudie, and that it behoved him quickly to ascertain whether his energies or hers were to prevail.

CHAPTER XVIII

THE WIDOW'S PERSECUTION

EARLY on the following morning Mr. Slope was summoned to the bishop's dressing-room, and went there fully expecting that he should find his lordship very indignant, and spirited up by his wife to repeat the rebuke which she had administered on the previous day. Mr. Slope had resolved that at any rate from him he would not stand it, and entered the dressing-room in rather a combative disposition ; but he found the bishop in the most placid and gentlest of humours. His lordship complained of being rather unwell, had a slight headache, and

was not quite the thing in his stomach; but there was
nothing the matter with his temper.

'Oh, Slope,' said he, taking the chaplain's proffered
hand, 'Archdeacon Grantly is to call on me this morning,
and I really am not fit to see him. I fear I must trouble
you, to see him for me;' and then Dr. Proudie proceeded to
explain what it was that must be said to Dr. Grantly. He
was to be told in fact in the civilest words in which the
tidings could be conveyed, that Mr. Harding having refused
the wardenship, the appointment had been offered to Mr.
Quiverful and accepted by him.

Mr. Slope again pointed out to his patron that he
thought he was perhaps not quite wise in his decision, and
this he did *sotto voce*. But even with this precaution it was
not safe to say much, and during the little that he did say,
the bishop made a very slight, but still a very ominous
gesture with his thumb towards the door which opened
from his dressing-room to some inner sanctuary. Mr.
Slope at once took the hint, and said no more; but he
perceived that there was to be confidence between him and
his patron, that the league desired by him was to be made,
and that this appointment of Mr. Quiverful was to be the
last sacrifice offered on the altar of conjugal obedience.
All this Mr. Slope read in the slight motion of the bishop's
thumb, and he read it correctly. There was no need of
parchments and seals, of attestations, explanations, and
professions. The bargain was understood between them,
and Mr. Slope gave the bishop his hand upon it. The
bishop understood the little extra squeeze, and an intelligible gleam of assent twinkled in his eye.

'Pray be civil to the archdeacon, Mr. Slope,' said he out
loud; 'but make him quite understand that in this
matter Mr. Harding has put it out of my power to oblige
him.'

It would be a calumny on Mrs. Proudie to suggest that
she was sitting in her bed-room with her ear at the keyhole
during this interview. She had within her a spirit of
decorum which prevented her from descending to such
baseness. To put her ear to a key-hole or to listen at a
chink, was a trick for a housemaid.

Mrs. Proudie knew this, and therefore she did not do it;
but she stationed herself as near to the door as she well

could, that she might, if possible, get the advantage which the housemaid would have had, without descending to the housemaid's artifice.

It was little, however, that she heard, and that little was only sufficient to deceive her. She saw nothing of that friendly pressure, perceived nothing of that concluded bargain; she did not even dream of the treacherous resolves which those two false men had made together to upset her in the pride of her station, to dash the cup from her lip before she had drank of it, to sweep away all her power before she had tasted its sweets! Traitors that they were; the husband of her bosom, and the outcast whom she had fostered and brought to the warmth of the world's brightest fireside! But neither of them had the magnanimity of this woman. Though two men have thus leagued themselves together against her, even yet the battle is not lost.

Mr. Slope felt pretty sure that Dr. Grantly would decline the honour of seeing him, and such turned out to be the case. The archdeacon, when the palace door was opened to him, was greeted by a note. Mr. Slope presented his compliments, &c. &c. The bishop was ill in his room, and very greatly regretted, &c. &c. Mr. Slope had been charged with the bishop's views, and if agreeable to the archdeacon, would do himself the honour, &c. &c. The archdeacon, however, was not agreeable, and having read his note in the hall, crumpled it up in his hand, and muttering something about sorrow for his lordship's illness, took his leave, without sending as much as a verbal message in answer to Mr. Slope's note.

' Ill! ' said the archdeacon to himself as he flung himself into his brougham. ' The man is absolutely a coward. He is afraid to see me. Ill, indeed! ' The archdeacon was never ill himself, and did not therefore understand that any one else could in truth be prevented by illness from keeping an appointment. He regarded all such excuses as subterfuges, and in the present instance he was not far wrong.

Dr. Grantly desired to be driven to his father-in-law's lodgings in the High Street, and hearing from the servant that Mr. Harding was at his daughter's, followed him to Mrs. Bold's house, and there found him. The archdeacon was fuming with rage when he got into the drawing-room, and had by this time nearly forgotten the pusillanimity of the bishop in the villany of the chaplain.

'Look at that,' said he, throwing Mr. Slope's crumpled note to Mr. Harding. 'I am to be told that if I choose I may have the honour of seeing Mr. Slope, and that too, after a positive engagement with the bishop.'

'But he says the bishop is ill,' said Mr. Harding.

'Pshaw! You don't mean to say that you are deceived by such an excuse as that. He was well enough yesterday. Now I tell you what, I will see the bishop; and I will tell him also very plainly what I think of his conduct. I will see him, or else Barchester will soon be too hot to hold him.'

Eleanor was sitting in the room, but Dr. Grantly had hardly noticed her in his anger. Eleanor now said to him, with the greatest innocence, 'I wish you had seen Mr. Slope, Dr. Grantly, because I think perhaps it might have done good.'

The archdeacon turned on her with almost brutal wrath. Had she at once owned that she had accepted Mr. Slope for her second husband, he could hardly have felt more convinced of her belonging body and soul to the Slope and Proudie party than he now did on hearing her express such a wish as this. Poor Eleanor!

'See him!' said the archdeacon glaring at her; 'and why am I to be called on to lower myself in the world's esteem and my own by coming in contact with such a man as that? I have hitherto lived among gentlemen, and do not mean to be dragged into other company by anybody.'

Poor Mr. Harding well knew what the archdeacon meant, but Eleanor was as innocent as her own baby. She could not understand how the archdeacon could consider himself to be dragged into bad company by condescending to speak to Mr. Slope for a few minutes when the interests of her father might be served by his doing so.

'I was talking for a full hour yesterday to Mr. Slope,' said she, with some little assumption of dignity, 'and I did not find myself lowered by it.'

'Perhaps not,' said he. 'But if you'll be good enough to allow me, I shall judge for myself in such matters. And I tell you what, Eleanor; it will be much better for you if you will allow yourself to be guided also by the advice of those who are your friends. If you do not you will be apt to find that you have no friends left who can advise you.'

Eleanor blushed up to the roots of her hair. But even now she had not the slightest idea of what was passing in the archdeacon's mind. No thought of love-making or love-receiving had yet found its way to her heart since the death of poor John Bold; and if it were possible that such a thought should spring there, the man must be far different from Mr. Slope that could give it birth.

Nevertheless Eleanor blushed deeply, for she felt she was charged with improper conduct, and she did so with the more inward pain because her father did not instantly rally to her side; that father for whose sake and love she had submitted to be the receptacle of Mr. Slope's confidence. She had given a detailed account of all that had passed to her father; and though he had not absolutely agreed with her about Mr. Slope's views touching the hospital, yet he had said nothing to make her think that she had been wrong in talking to him.

She was far too angry to humble herself before her brother-in-law. Indeed, she had never accustomed herself to be very abject before him, and they had never been confidential allies. 'I do not the least understand what you mean, Dr. Grantly,' said she. 'I do not know that I can accuse myself of doing anything that my friends should disapprove. Mr. Slope called here expressly to ask what papa's wishes were about the hospital; and as I believe he called with friendly intentions I told him.'

'Friendly intentions!' sneered the archdeacon.

'I believe you greatly wrong Mr. Slope,' continued Eleanor; 'but I have explained this to papa already; and as you do not seem to approve of what I say, Dr. Grantly, I will with your permission leave you and papa together,' and so saying she walked slowly out of the room.

All this made Mr. Harding very unhappy. It was quite clear that the archdeacon and his wife had made up their minds that Eleanor was going to marry Mr. Slope. Mr. Harding could not really bring himself to think that she would do so, but yet he could not deny that circumstances made it appear that the man's company was not disagreeable to her. She was now constantly seeing him, and yet she received visits from no other unmarried gentleman.

She always took his part when his conduct was canvassed, although she was aware how personally objectionable he was to her friends. Then, again, Mr. Harding felt that if she should choose to become Mrs. Slope, he had nothing that he could justly urge against her doing so. She had full right to please herself, and he, as a father, could not say that she would disgrace herself by marrying a clergyman who stood so well before the world as Mr. Slope did. As for quarrelling with his daughter on account of such a marriage, and separating himself from her as the arch-deacon had threatened to do, that, with Mr. Harding, would be out of the question. If she should determine to marry this man, he must get over his aversion as best he could. His Eleanor, his own old companion in their old happy home, must still be the friend of his bosom, the child of his heart. Let who would cast her off, he would not. If it were fated that he should have to sit in his old age at the same table with that man whom of all men he disliked the most, he would meet his fate as best he might. Anything to him would be preferable to the loss of his daughter.

Such being his feelings, he hardly knew how to take part with Eleanor against the archdeacon, or with the arch-deacon against Eleanor. It will be said that he should never have suspected her.—Alas! he never should have done so. But Mr. Harding was by no means a perfect character. In his indecision, his weakness, his proneness to be led by others, his want of self-confidence, he was very far from being perfect. And then it must be remembered that such a marriage as that which the archdeacon contem-plated with disgust, which we who know Mr. Slope so well would regard with equal disgust, did not appear so monstrous to Mr. Harding, because in his charity he did not hate the chaplain as the archdeacon did, and as we do.

He was, however, very unhappy when his daughter left the room, and he had recourse to an old trick of his that was customary to him in his times of sadness. He began playing some slow tune upon an imaginary violoncello, drawing one hand slowly backwards and forwards as though he held a bow in it, and modulating the unreal cords with the other.

'She'll marry that man as sure as two and two make four,' said the practical archdeacon.

' I hope not, I hope not,' said the father. ' But if she does, what can I say to her ? I have no right to object to him.'

' No right ! ' exclaimed Dr. Grantly.

' No right as her father. He is in my own profession, and for aught we know a good man.'

To this the archdeacon would by no means assent. It was not well, however, to argue the case against Eleanor in her own drawing-room, and so they both walked forth and discussed the matter in all its bearings under the elm trees of the close. Mr. Harding also explained to his son-in-law what had been the purport, at any rate the alleged purport, of Mr. Slope's last visit to the widow. He, however, stated that he could not bring himself to believe that Mr. Slope had any real anxiety such as that he had pretended. ' I cannot forget his demeanour to myself,' said Mr. Harding, ' and it is not possible that his ideas should have changed so soon.'

' I see it all,' said the archdeacon. ' The sly *tartufe !* He thinks to buy the daughter by providing for the father. He means to show how powerful he is, how good he is, and how much he is willing to do for her *beaux yeux ;* yes, I see it all now. But we'll be too many for him yet, Mr. Harding ; ' he said, turning to his companion with some gravity, and pressing his hand upon the other's arm. ' It would, perhaps, be better for you to lose the hospital than get it on such terms.'

' Lose it ! ' said Mr. Harding ; ' why I've lost it already. I don't want it. I've made up my mind to do without it. I'll withdraw altogether. I'll just go and write a line to the bishop and tell him that I withdraw my claim altogether.'

Nothing would have pleased him better than to be allowed to escape from the trouble and difficulty in such a manner. But he was now going too fast for the archdeacon.

' No—no—no ! we'll do no such thing,' said Dr. Grantly ; ' we'll still have the hospital. I hardly doubt but that we'll have it. But not by Mr. Slope's assistance. If that be necessary we'll lose it ; but we'll have it, spite of his teeth, if we can. Arabin will be at Plumstead to-morrow ; you must come over and talk to him.'

The two now turned into the cathedral library, which was used by the clergymen of the close as a sort of ecclesiastical club-room, for writing sermons and sometimes letters; also for reading theological works, and sometimes magazines and newspapers. The theological works were not disturbed, perhaps, quite as often as from the appearance of the building the outside public might have been led to expect. Here the two allies settled on their course of action. The archdeacon wrote a letter to the bishop, strongly worded, but still respectful, in which he put forward his father-in-law's claim to the appointment, and expressed his own regret that he had not been able to see his lordship when he called. Of Mr. Slope he made no mention whatsoever. It was then settled that Mr. Harding should go out to Plumstead on the following day; and after considerable discussion on the matter, the archdeacon proposed to ask Eleanor there also, so as to withdraw her, if possible, from Mr. Slope's attentions. 'A week or two,' said he, ' may teach her what he is, and while she is there she will be out of harm's way. Mr. Slope won't come there after her.'

Eleanor was not a little surprised when her brother-in-law came back and very civilly pressed her to go out to Plumstead with her father. She instantly perceived that her father had been fighting her battles for her behind her back. She felt thankful to him, and for his sake she would not show her resentment to the archdeacon by refusing his invitation. But she could not, she said, go on the morrow; she had an invitation to drink tea at the Stanhopes which she had promised to accept. She would, she added, go with her father on the next day, if he would wait; or she would follow him.

' The Stanhopes!' said Dr. Grantly; ' I did not know you were so intimate with them.'

' I did not know it myself,' said she, ' till Miss Stanhope called yesterday. However, I like her very much, and I have promised to go and play chess with some of them.'

' Have they a party there?' said the archdeacon, still fearful of Mr. Slope.

' Oh, no,' said Eleanor; ' Miss Stanhope said there was to be nobody at all. But she had heard that Mary had left me for a few weeks, and she had learnt from some one that

I play chess, and so she came over on purpose to ask me to go in.'

' Well, that's very friendly,' said the ex-warden. ' They certainly do look more like foreigners than English people, but I dare say they are none the worse for that.'

The archdeacon was inclined to look upon the Stanhopes with favourable eyes, and had nothing to object on the matter. It was therefore arranged that Mr. Harding should postpone his visit to Plumstead for one day, and then take with him Eleanor, the baby, and the nurse.

Mr. Slope is certainly becoming of some importance in Barchester.

CHAPTER XIX

BARCHESTER BY MOONLIGHT

THERE was much cause for grief and occasional perturbation of spirits in the Stanhope family, but yet they rarely seemed to be grieved or to be disturbed. It was the peculiar gift of each of them that each was able to bear his or her own burden without complaint, and perhaps without sympathy. They habitually looked on the sunny side of the wall, if there was a gleam on either side for them to look at ; and, if there was none, they endured the shade with an indifference which, if not stoical, answered the end at which the Stoics aimed. Old Stanhope could not but feel that he had ill-performed his duties as a father and a clergyman ; and could hardly look forward to his own death without grief at the position in which he would leave his family. His income for many years had been as high as 3000*l.* a year, and yet they had among them no other provision than their mother's fortune of 10,000*l.* He had not only spent his income, but was in debt. Yet with all this, he seldom showed much outward sign of trouble.

It was the same with the mother. If she added little to the pleasures of her children she detracted still less : she neither grumbled at her lot, nor spoke much of her past or future sufferings ; as long as she had a maid to adjust her dress, and had those dresses well made, nature with her was satisfied. It was the same with the children. Charlotte never rebuked her father with the prospect of their future

poverty, nor did it seem to grieve her that she was becoming an old maid so quickly; her temper was rarely
ruffled, and, if we might judge by her appearance, she was
always happy. The signora was not so sweet-tempered,
but she possessed much enduring courage; she seldom
complained—never, indeed, to her family. Though she
had a cause for affliction which would have utterly broken
down the heart of most women as beautiful as she and as
devoid of all religious support, yet, she bore her suffering
in silence, or alluded to it only to elicit the sympathy and
stimulate the admiration of the men with whom she flirted.
As to Bertie, one would have imagined from the sound of
his voice and the gleam of his eye that he had not a sorrow
nor a care in the world. Nor had he. He was incapable
of anticipating to-morrow's griefs. The prospect of future
want no more disturbed his appetite than does that of the
butcher's knife disturb the appetite of the sheep.

Such was the usual tenour of their way; but there
were rare exceptions. Occasionally the father would
allow an angry glance to fall from his eye, and the lion
would send forth a low dangerous roar as though he
meditated some deed of blood. Occasionally also Madame
Neroni would become bitter against mankind, more than
usually antagonistic to the world's decencies, and would
seem as though she was about to break from her moorings
and allow herself to be carried forth by the tide of her
feelings to utter ruin and shipwreck. She, however, like
the rest of them, had no real feelings, could feel no true
passion. In that was her security. Before she resolved on
any contemplated escapade she would make a small
calculation, and generally summed up that the Stanhope
villa or even Barchester close was better than the world
at large.

They were most irregular in their hours. The father was
generally the earliest in the breakfast-parlour, and
Charlotte would soon follow and give him his coffee; but
the others breakfasted anywhere, anyhow, and at any
time. On the morning after the archdeacon's futile visit
to the palace, Dr. Stanhope came down stairs with an
ominously dark look about his eyebrows; his white locks
were rougher than usual, and he breathed thickly and
loudly as he took his seat in his arm-chair. He had open

letters in his hand, and when Charlotte came into the
room he was still reading them. She went up and kissed
him as was her wont, but he hardly noticed her as she did
so, and she knew at once that something was the matter.

'What's the meaning of that ? ' said he, throwing over
the table a letter with a Milan post-mark. Charlotte was
a little frightened as she took it up, but her mind was
relieved when she saw that it was merely the bill of their
Italian milliner. The sum total was certainly large, but
not so large as to create an important row.

'It's for our clothes, papa, for six months before we
came here. The three of us can't dress for nothing you
know.'

'Nothing, indeed ! ' said he, looking at the figures,
which in Milanese denominations were certainly monstrous.

'The man should have sent it to me,' said Charlotte.

'I wish he had with all my heart—if you would have
paid it. I see enough in it, to know that three quarters of
it are for Madeline.'

'She has little else to amuse her, sir,' said Charlotte with
true good nature.

'And I suppose he has nothing else to amuse him,' said
the doctor, throwing over another letter to his daughter.
It was from some member of the family of Sidonia, and
politely requested the father to pay a small trifle of 700*l.*,
being the amount of a bill discounted in favour of Mr.
Ethelbert Stanhope, and now overdue for a period of nine
months.

Charlotte read the letter, slowly folded it up, and put it
under the edge of the tea-tray.

'I suppose he has nothing to amuse him but discounting
bills with Jews. Does he think I'll pay that ? '

'I am sure he thinks no such thing,' said she.

'And who does he think will pay it ? '

'As far as honesty goes I suppose it won't much matter
if it is never paid,' said she. 'I dare say he got very little
of it.'

'I suppose it won't much matter either,' said the father,
'if he goes to prison and rots there. It seems to me that
that's the other alternative.'

Dr. Stanhope spoke of the custom of his youth. But
his daughter, though she had lived so long abroad, was

much more completely versed in the ways of the English
world. ' If the man arrests him,' said she, ' he must go
through the court.'

It is thus, thou great family of Sidonia—it is thus that
we Gentiles treat thee, when, in our extremest need, thou
and thine have aided us with mountains of gold as big as
lions,—and occasionally with wine-warrants and orders
for dozens of dressing-cases.

' What, and become an insolvent ? ' said the doctor.

' He's that already,' said Charlotte, wishing always to
get over a difficulty.

' What a condition,' said the doctor, ' for the son of a
clergyman of the Church of England.'

' I don't see why clergymen's sons should pay their
debts more than other young men,' said Charlotte.

' He's had as much from me since he left school as is held
sufficient for the eldest son of many a nobleman,' said the
angry father.

' Well, sir,' said Charlotte, ' give him another chance.'

' What ! ' said the doctor, ' do you mean that I am to pay
that Jew ? '

' Oh no ! I wouldn't pay him, he must take his chance ;
and if the worst comes to the worst, Bertie must go abroad.
But I want you to be civil to Bertie, and let him remain
here as long as we stop. He has a plan in his head, that
may put him on his feet after all.'

' Has he any plan for following up his profession ? '

' Oh, he'll do that too ; but that must follow. He's
thinking of getting married.'

Just at that moment the door opened, and Bertie came
in whistling. The doctor immediately devoted himself to
his egg, and allowed Bertie to whistle himself round to his
sister's side without noticing him.

Charlotte gave a sign to him with her eye, first glancing
at her father, and then at the letter, the corner of which
peeped out from under the tea-tray. Bertie saw and understood, and with the quiet motion of a cat abstracted the
letter, and made himself acquainted with its contents.
The doctor, however, had seen him, deep as he appeared
to be mersed in his egg-shell, and said in his harshest voice,
' Well, sir, do you know that gentleman ? '

' Yes, sir,' said Bertie. ' I have a sort of acquaintance

with him, but none that can justify him in troubling you.
If you will allow me, sir, I will answer this.'

'At any rate I sha'n't,' said the father, and then he
added, after a pause, ' Is it true, sir, that you owe the
man 700*l*. ? '

' Well,' said Bertie, ' I think I should be inclined to
dispute the amount, if I were in a condition to pay him
such of it as I really do owe him.'

' Has he your bill for 700*l*. ? ' said the father, speaking
very loudly and very angrily.

' Well, I believe he has,' said Bertie ; ' but all the money
I ever got from him was 150*l*.'

' And what became of the 550*l*. ? '

' Why, sir ; the commission was 100*l*. or so, and I took
the remainder in paving-stones and rocking-horses.'

' Paving-stones and rocking-horses ! ' said the doctor,
' where are they ? '

' Oh, sir, I suppose they are in London somewhere—but
I'll inquire if you wish for them.'

' He's an idiot,' said the doctor, ' and it's sheer folly to
waste more money on him. Nothing can save him from
ruin,' and so saying, the unhappy father walked out of the
room.

' Would the governor like to have the paving-stones ? '
said Bertie to his sister.

' I'll tell you what,' said she. ' If you don't take care,
you will find yourself loose upon the world without even
a house over your head : you don't know him as well as I
do. He's very angry.'

Bertie stroked his big beard, sipped his tea, chatted over
his misfortunes in a half comic, half serious tone, and
ended by promising his sister that he would do his very
best to make himself agreeable to the widow Bold. Then
Charlotte followed her father to his own room and softened
down his wrath, and persuaded him to say nothing more
about the Jew bill discounter, at any rate for a few weeks.
He even went so far as to say he would pay the 700*l*., or at
any rate settle the bill, if he saw a certainty of his son's
securing for himself anything like a decent provision in
life. Nothing was said openly between them about poor
Eleanor : but the father and the daughter understood
each other.

They all met together in the drawing-room at nine o'clock, in perfect good humour with each other; and about that hour Mrs. Bold was announced. She had never been in the house before, though she had of course called; and now she felt it strange to find herself there in her usual evening dress, entering the drawing-room of these strangers in this friendly unceremonious way, as though she had known them all her life. But in three minutes they made her at home. Charlotte tripped down stairs and took her bonnet from her, and Bertie came to relieve her from her shawl, and the signora smiled on her as she could smile when she chose to be gracious, and the old doctor shook hands with her in a kind benedictory manner that went to her heart at once, and made her feel that he must be a good man.

She had not been seated for above five minutes when the door again opened, and Mr. Slope was announced. She felt rather surprised, because she was told that nobody was to be there, and it was very evident from the manner of some of them, that Mr. Slope was unexpected. But still there was not much in it. In such invitations a bachelor or two more or less are always spoken of as nobodies, and there was no reason why Mr. Slope should not drink tea at Dr. Stanhope's as well as Eleanor herself. He, however, was very much surprised and not very much gratified at finding that his own embryo spouse made one of the party. He had come there to gratify himself by gazing on Madame Neroni's beauty, and listening to and returning her flattery: and though he had not owned as much to himself, he still felt that if he spent the evening as he had intended to do, he might probably not thereby advance his suit with Mrs. Bold.

The signora, who had no idea of a rival, received Mr. Slope with her usual marks of distinction. As he took her hand, she made some confidential communication to him in a low voice, declaring that she had a plan to communicate to him after tea, and was evidently prepared to go on with her work of reducing the chaplain to a state of captivity. Poor Mr. Slope was rather beside himself. He thought that Eleanor could not but have learnt from his demeanour that he was an admirer of her own, and he had also flattered himself that the idea was not unacceptable

to her. What would she think of him if he now devoted
himself to a married woman !

But Eleanor was not inclined to be severe in her criticisms on him in this respect, and felt no annoyance of any
kind, when she found herself seated between Bertie and
Charlotte Stanhope. She had no suspicion of Mr. Slope's
intentions ; she had no suspicion even of the suspicion of
other people ; but still she felt well pleased not to have
Mr. Slope too near to her.

And she was not ill-pleased to have Bertie Stanhope
near her. It was rarely indeed that he failed to make an
agreeable impression on strangers. With a bishop indeed
who thought much of his own dignity it was possible that
he might fail, but hardly with a young and pretty woman·
He possessed the tact of becoming instantly intimate with
women without giving rise to any fear of impertinence.
He had about him somewhat of the propensities of a tame
cat. It seemed quite natural that he should be petted,
caressed, and treated with familiar good nature, and that
in return he should purr, and be sleek and graceful, and
above all never show his claws. Like other tame cats, however, he had his claws, and sometimes made them dangerous.

When tea was over Charlotte went to the open window
and declared loudly that the full harvest moon was much
too beautiful to be disregarded, and called them all to look
at it. To tell the truth, there was but one there who cared
much about the moon's beauty, and that one was not
Charlotte ; but she knew how valuable an aid to her
purpose the chaste goddess might become, and could easily
create a little enthusiasm for the purpose of the moment.
Eleanor and Bertie were soon with her. The doctor was
now quiet in his arm-chair, and Mrs. Stanhope in hers,
both prepared for slumber.

' Are you a Whewellite or a Brewsterite, or a t'other-
manite, Mrs. Bold ? ' said Charlotte, who knew a little
about everything, and had read about a third of each of
the books to which she alluded.

' Oh ! ' said Eleanor ; ' I have not read any of the books,
but I feel sure that there is one man in the moon at least,
if not more.'

' You don't believe in the pulpy gelatinous matter ? '
said Bertie.

' I heard about that,' said Eleanor ; ' and I really think it's almost wicked to talk in such a manner. How can we argue about God's power in the other stars from the laws which he has given for our rule in this one ? '

' How indeed ! ' said Bertie. ' Why shouldn't there be a race of salamanders in Venus ? and even if there be nothing but fish in Jupiter, why shouldn't the fish there be as wide awake as the men and women here ? '

' That would be saying very little for them,' said Charlotte. ' I am for Dr. Whewell myself ; for I do not think that men and women are worth being repeated in such countless worlds. There may be souls in other stars, but I doubt their having any bodies attached to them. But come, Mrs. Bold, let us put our bonnets on and walk round the close. If we are to discuss sidereal questions, we shall do so much better under the towers of the cathedral, than stuck in this narrow window.'

Mrs. Bold made no objection, and a party was made to walk out. Charlotte Stanhope well knew the rule as to three being no company, and she had therefore to induce her sister to allow Mr. Slope to accompany them.

' Come, Mr. Slope,' she said ; ' I'm sure you'll join us. We shall be in again in a quarter of an hour, Madeline.'

Madeline read in her eye all that she had to say, knew her object, and as she had to depend on her sister for so many of her amusements, she felt that she must yield. It was hard to be left alone while others of her own age walked out to feel the soft influence of the bright night, but it would be harder still to be without the sort of sanction which Charlotte gave to all her flirtations and intrigues. Charlotte's eye told her that she must give up just at present for the good of the family, and so Madeline obeyed.

But Charlotte's eyes said nothing of the sort to Mr. Slope. He had no objection at all to the *tête-à-tête* with the signora, which the departure of the other three would allow him, and gently whispered to her, ' I shall not leave you alone.'

' Oh, yes,' said she ; ' go—pray go, pray go, for my sake. Do not think that I am so selfish. It is understood that nobody is kept within for me. You will understand this too when you know me better. Pray join them, Mr. Slope, but when you come in speak to me for five minutes before you leave us.'

Mr. Slope understood that he was to go, and he therefore joined the party in the hall. He would have had no objection at all to this arrangement, if he could have secured Mrs. Bold's arm; but this of course was out of the question. Indeed, his fate was very soon settled, for no sooner had he reached the hall-door than Miss Stanhope put her hand within his arm, and Bertie walked off with Eleanor just as naturally as though she were already his own property.

And so they sauntered forth: first they walked round the close, according to their avowed intent; then they went under the old arched gateway below St. Cuthbert's little church, and then they turned behind the grounds of the bishop's palace, and so on till they came to the bridge just at the edge of the town, from which passers-by can look down into the gardens of Hiram's Hospital; and here Charlotte and Mr. Slope, who were in advance, stopped till the other two came up to them. Mr. Slope knew that the gable-ends and old brick chimneys which stood up so prettily in the moonlight, were those of Mr. Harding's late abode, and would not have stopped on such a spot, in such company, if he could have avoided it; but Miss Stanhope would not take the hint which he tried to give.

' This is a very pretty place, Mrs. Bold,' said Charlotte; ' by far the prettiest place near Barchester. I wonder your father gave it up.'

It was a very pretty place, and now by the deceitful light of the moon looked twice larger, twice prettier, twice more antiquely picturesque than it would have done in truth-telling daylight. Who does not know the air of complex multiplicity and the mysterious interesting grace which the moon always lends to old gabled buildings half surrounded, as was the hospital, by fine trees ! As seen from the bridge on the night of which we are speaking, Mr. Harding's late abode did look very lovely; and though Eleanor did not grieve at her father's having left it, she felt at the moment an intense wish that he might be allowed to return.

' He is going to return to it almost immediately, is he not ? ' asked Bertie.

Eleanor made no immediate reply. Many such a question

passes unanswered, without the notice of the questioner ;
but such was not now the case. They all remained silent
as though expecting her to reply, and after a moment or
two, Charlotte said, ' I believe it is settled that Mr. Harding
returns to the hospital, is it not ? '

' I don't think anything about it is settled yet,' said
Eleanor.

' But it must be a matter of course,' said Bertie ; ' that
is, if your father wishes it ; who else on earth could hold it
after what has occurred ? '

Eleanor quietly made her companion understand that
the matter was one which she could not discuss in the
present company ; and then they passed on ; Charlotte
said she would go a short way up the hill out of the town
so as to look back upon the towers of the cathedral, and as
Eleanor leant upon Bertie's arm for assistance in the walk,
she told him how the matter stood between her father and
the bishop.

' And, he,' said Bertie, pointing on to Mr. Slope, ' what
part does he take in it ? '

Eleanor explained how Mr. Slope had at first endeavoured to tyrannise over her father, but how he had
latterly come round, and done all he could to talk the
bishop over in Mr. Harding's favour. ' But my father,'
said she, ' is hardly inclined to trust him ; they all say he
is so arrogant to the old clergymen of the city.'

' Take my word for it,' said Bertie, ' your father is right.
If I am not very much mistaken, that man is both arrogant
and false.'

They strolled up to the top of the hill, and then returned
through the fields by a footpath which leads by a small
wooden bridge, or rather a plank with a rustic rail to it,
over the river to the other side of the cathedral from that
at which they had started. They had thus walked round
the bishop's grounds, through which the river runs, and
round the cathedral and adjacent fields, and it was past
eleven before they reached the doctor's door.

' It is very late,' said Eleanor, ' it will be a shame to
disturb your mother again at such an hour.'

' Oh,' said Charlotte, laughing, ' you won't disturb
mamma ; I dare say she is in bed by this time, and
Madeline would be furious if you did not come in and

see her. Come, Bertie, take Mrs. Bold's bonnet from her.'

They went up stairs, and found the signora alone, reading. She looked somewhat sad and melancholy, but not more so perhaps than was sufficient to excite additional interest in the bosom of Mr. Slope; and she was soon deep in whispered intercourse with that happy gentleman, who was allowed to find a resting-place on her sofa. The signora had a way of whispering that was peculiarly her own, and was exactly the reverse of that which prevails among great tragedians. The great tragedian hisses out a positive whisper, made with bated breath, and produced by inarticulated tongue-formed sounds, but yet he is audible through the whole house. The signora however used no hisses, and produced all her words in a clear silver tone, but they could only be heard by the ear into which they were poured.

Charlotte hurried and skurried about the room hither and thither, doing, or pretending to do many things; and then saying something about seeing her mother, ran up stairs. Eleanor was thus left alone with Bertie, and she hardly felt an hour fly by her. To give Bertie his due credit, he could not have played his cards better. He did not make love to her, nor sigh, nor look languishing; but he was amusing and familiar, yet respectful; and when he left Eleanor at her own door at one o'clock, which he did by the bye with the assistance of the now jealous Slope, she thought that he was one of the most agreeable men, and the Stanhopes decidedly the most agreeable family, that she had ever met.

CHAPTER XX

MR. ARABIN

THE Rev. Francis Arabin, fellow of Lazarus, late professor of poetry at Oxford, and present vicar of St. Ewold, in the diocese of Barchester, must now be introduced personally to the reader. And as he will fill a conspicuous place in the volume, it is desirable that he should be made to stand before the reader's eye by the aid of such portraiture as the author is able to produce.

It is to be regretted that no mental method of daguerreotype or photography has yet been discovered, by which the characters of men can be reduced to writing and put into grammatical language with an unerring precision of truthful description. How often does the novelist feel, ay, and the historian also and the biographer, that he has conceived within his mind and accurately depicted on the tablet of his brain the full character and personage of a man, and that nevertheless, when he flies to pen and ink to perpetuate the portrait, his words forsake, elude, disappoint, and play the deuce with him, till at the end of a dozen pages the man described has no more resemblance to the man conceived than the sign board at the corner of the street has to the Duke of Cambridge ?

And yet such mechanical descriptive skill would hardly give more satisfaction to the reader than the skill of the photographer does to the anxious mother desirous to possess an absolute duplicate of her beloved child. The likeness is indeed true ; but it is a dull, dead, unfeeling, inauspicious likeness. The face is indeed there, and those looking at it will know at once whose image it is ; but the owner of the face will not be proud of the resemblance.

There is no royal road to learning ; no short cut to the acquirement of any valuable art. Let photographers and daguerreotypers do what they will, and improve as they may with further skill on that which skill has already done, they will never achieve a portrait of the human face divine. Let biographers, novelists, and the rest of us groan as we may under the burdens which we so often feel too heavy for our shoulders ; we must either bear them up like men, or own ourselves too weak for the work we have undertaken. There is no way of writing well and also of writing easily.

Labor omnia vincit improbus. Such should be the chosen motto of every labourer, and it may be that labour, if adequately enduring, may suffice at last to produce even some not untrue resemblance of the Rev. Francis Arabin.

Of his doings in the world, and of the sort of fame which he has achieved, enough has been already said. It has also been said that he is forty years of age, and still un-

married. He was the younger son of a country gentleman
of small fortune in the north of England. At an early
age he went to Winchester, and was intended by his father
for New College ; but though studious as a boy, he was
not studious within the prescribed limits ; and at the
age of eighteen he left school with a character for talent,
but without a scholarship. All that he had obtained, over
and above the advantage of his character, was a gold
medal for English verse, and hence was derived a strong
presumption on the part of his friends that he was destined
to add another name to the imperishable list of English
poets.

From Winchester he went to Oxford, and was entered
as a commoner at Balliol. Here his special career very
soon commenced. He utterly eschewed the society of
fast men, gave no wine parties, kept no horses, rowed no
boats, joined no rows, and was the pride of his college
tutor. Such at least was his career till he had taken his
little go ; and then he commenced a course of action which,
though not less creditable to himself as a man, was hardly
so much to the taste of the tutor. He became a member
of a vigorous debating society, and rendered himself remarkable there for humorous energy. Though always in earnest, yet his earnestness was always droll. To be true in his
ideas, unanswerable in his syllogisms, and just in his
aspirations was not enough for him. He had failed, failed
in his own opinion as well as that of others when others
came to know him, if he could not reduce the arguments
of his opponents to an absurdity, and conquer both by
wit and reason. To say that his object was ever to raise
a laugh, would be most untrue. He hated such common
and unnecessary evidence of satisfaction on the part of
his hearers. A joke that required to be laughed at was,
with him, not worth uttering. He could appreciate by
a keener sense than that of his ears the success of his wit,
and would see in the eyes of his auditory whether or no
he was understood and appreciated.

He had been a religious lad before he left school. That
is, he had addicted himself to a party in religion, and
having done so had received that benefit which most men
do who become partisans in such a cause. We are much
too apt to look at schism in our church as an unmitigated

evil. Moderate schism, if there may be such a thing, at
any rate calls attention to the subject, draws in supporters
who would otherwise have been inattentive to the matter,
and teaches men to think upon religion. How great an
amount of good of this description has followed that
movement in the Church of England which commenced
with the publication of Froude's Remains !

As a boy young Arabin took up the cudgels on the side
of the Tractarians, and at Oxford he sat for a while at
the feet of the great Newman. To this cause he lent all
his faculties. For it he concocted verses, for it he made
speeches, for it he scintillated the brightest sparks of his
quiet wit. For it he ate and drank and dressed, and had
his being. In due process of time he took his degree, and
wrote himself B.A., but he did not do so with any remarkable amount of academical éclat. He had occupied
himself too much with high church matters, and the
polemics, politics, and outward demonstrations usually
concurrent with high churchmanship, to devote himself
with sufficient vigour to the acquisition of a double first.
He was not a double first, nor even a first class man ;
but he revenged himself on the university by putting
firsts and double firsts out of fashion for the year, and
laughing down a species of pedantry which at the age of
twenty-three leaves no room in a man's mind for graver
subjects than conic sections or Greek accents.

Greek accents, however, and conic sections were
esteemed necessaries at Balliol, and there was no admittance there for Mr. Arabin within the list of its fellows.
Lazarus, however, the richest and most comfortable
abode of Oxford dons, opened its bosom to the young
champion of a church militant. Mr. Arabin was ordained,
and became a fellow soon after taking his degree, and
shortly after that was chosen professor of poetry.

And now came the moment of his great danger. After
many mental struggles, and an agony of doubt which may
be well surmised, the great prophet of the Tractarians
confessed himself a Roman Catholic. Mr. Newman left
the Church of England, and with him carried many a
waverer. He did not carry off Mr. Arabin, but the escape
which that gentleman had was a very narrow one. He
left Oxford for a while that he might meditate in complete

peace on the step which appeared to him to be all but
unavoidable, and shut himself up in a little village on
the sea-shore of one of our remotest counties, that he
might learn by communing with his own soul whether
or no he could with a safe conscience remain within the
pale of his mother church.

Things would have gone badly with him there had he
been left entirely to himself. Every thing was against
him: all his worldly interests required him to remain
a Protestant; and he looked on his worldly interests as
a legion of foes, to get the better of whom was a point of
extremest honour. In his then state of ecstatic agony
such a conquest would have cost him little; he could
easily have thrown away all his livelihood; but it cost
him much to get over the idea that by choosing the Church
of England he should be open in his own mind to the
charge that he had been led to such a choice by unworthy
motives. Then his heart was against him: he loved
with a strong and eager love the man who had hitherto
been his guide, and yearned to follow his footsteps. His
tastes were against him: the ceremonies and pomps of
the Church of Rome, their august feasts and solemn fasts,
invited his imagination and pleased his eye. His flesh
was against him: how great an aid would it be to a poor,
weak, wavering man to be constrained to high moral
duties, self-denial, obedience, and chastity by laws which
were certain in their enactments, and not to be broken
without loud, palpable, unmistakable sin! Then his faith
was against him: he required to believe so much; panted
so eagerly to give signs of his belief; deemed it so insufficient to wash himself simply in the waters of Jordan;
that some great deed, such as that of forsaking everything
for a true church, had for him allurements almost past
withstanding.

Mr. Arabin was at this time a very young man, and
when he left Oxford for his far retreat was much too
confident in his powers of fence, and too apt to look down
on the ordinary sense of ordinary people, to expect aid
in the battle that he had to fight from any chance inhabitants of the spot which he had selected. But Providence
was good to him; and there, in that all but desolate place,
on the storm-beat shore of that distant sea, he met one

who gradually calmed his mind, quieted his imagination, and taught him something of a Christian's duty. When Mr. Arabin left Oxford, he was inclined to look upon the rural clergymen of most English parishes almost with contempt. It was his ambition, should he remain within the fold of their church, to do somewhat towards redeeming and rectifying their inferiority, and to assist in infusing energy and faith into the hearts of Christian ministers, who were, as he thought, too often satisfied to go through life without much show of either.

And yet it was from such a one that Mr. Arabin in his extremest need received that aid which he so much required. It was from the poor curate of a small Cornish parish that he first learnt to know that the highest laws for the governance of a Christian's duty must act from within and not from without; that no man can become a serviceable servant solely by obedience to written edicts; and that the safety which he was about to seek within the gates of Rome was no other than the selfish freedom from personal danger which the bad soldier attempts to gain who counterfeits illness on the eve of battle.

Mr. Arabin returned to Oxford a humbler but a better and a happier man; and from that time forth he put his shoulder to the wheel as a clergyman of the Church for which he had been educated. The intercourse of those among whom he familiarly lived kept him staunch to the principles of that system of the Church to which he had always belonged. Since his severance from Mr. Newman, no one had had so strong an influence over him as the head of his college. During the time of his expected apostacy, Dr. Gwynne had not felt much predisposition in favour of the young fellow. Though a High Churchman himself within moderate limits, Dr. Gwynne felt no sympathy with men who could not satisfy their faiths with the Thirty-nine Articles. He regarded the enthusiasm of such as Newman as a state of mind more nearly allied to madness than to religion; and when he saw it evinced by very young men, was inclined to attribute a good deal of it to vanity. Dr. Gwynne himself, though a religious man, was also a thoroughly practical man of the world, and he regarded with no favourable eye the tenets of any one who looked on the two things as incompatible. When he found that Mr. Arabin was a half Roman, he began to regret all he had done towards bestowing a fellowship on so unworthy a recipient; and when again he learnt that Mr. Arabin would probably complete his journey to Rome, he regarded with some satisfaction the fact that in such case the fellowship would be again vacant.

When, however, Mr. Arabin returned and professed himself a confirmed Protestant, the master of Lazarus again opened his arms to him, and gradually he became the pet of the college. For some little time he was saturnine, silent, and unwilling to take any prominent part in university broils; but gradually his mind recovered, or rather made its tone, and he became known as a man always ready at a moment's notice to take up the cudgels in opposition to anything that savoured of an evangelical bearing. He was great in sermons, great on platforms, great at after dinner conversations, and always pleasant as well as great. He took delight in elections, served on committees, opposed tooth and nail all projects of university reform, and talked jovially over his glass of port of the ruin to be anticipated by the Church, and of the sacrilege daily committed by the Whigs. The ordeal through which he had gone, in resisting the blandishments of the lady of Rome, had certainly done much towards the strengthening of his character. Although in small and outward matters he was self-confident enough, nevertheless in things affecting the inner man he aimed at a humility of spirit which would never have been attractive to him but for that visit to the coast of Cornwall. This visit he now repeated every year.

Such is an interior view of Mr. Arabin at the time when he accepted the living of St. Ewold. Exteriorly, he was not a remarkable person. He was above the middle height, well made, and very active. His hair which had been jet black, was now tinged with gray, but his face bore no sign of years. It would perhaps be wrong to say that he was handsome, but his face was, nevertheless, pleasant to look upon. The cheek bones were rather too high for beauty, and the formation of the forehead too massive and heavy: but the eyes, nose, and mouth were perfect. There was a continual play of lambent fire about his eyes, which gave promise of either pathos or humour whenever he essayed to speak, and that promise was rarely broken. There was a gentle play about his mouth which declared that his wit never descended to sarcasm, and that there was no ill-nature in his repartee.

Mr. Arabin was a popular man among women, but more so as a general than a special favourite. Living as a fellow at Oxford, marriage with him had been out of the question, and it may be doubted whether he had ever allowed his heart to be touched. Though belonging to a Church in which celibacy is not the required lot of its ministers, he had come to regard himself as one of those clergymen to whom to be a bachelor is almost a necessity. He had never looked for parochial duty, and his career at Oxford was utterly incompatible with such domestic joys as a wife and nursery. He looked on women, therefore, in the same light that one sees them regarded by many Romish priests. He liked to have near him that which was pretty and amusing, but women generally were little more to him than children. He talked to them without putting out all his powers, and listened to them without any idea that what he should hear from them could either actuate his conduct or influence his opinion.

Such was Mr. Arabin, the new vicar of St. Ewold, who is going to stay with the Grantlys, at Plumstead Episcopi.

Mr. Arabin reached Plumstead the day before Mr. Harding and Eleanor, and the Grantly family were thus enabled to make his acquaintance and discuss his qualifications before the arrival of the other guests. Griselda was surprised to find that he looked so young; but she told Florinda her younger sister, when they had retired for the night, that he did not talk at all like a young man: and she decided with the authority that seventeen has over sixteen, that he was not at all nice, although his eyes were lovely. As usual, sixteen implicitly acceded to the dictum of seventeen in such a matter, and said that he certainly was not nice. They then branched off on the relative merits of other clerical bachelors in the vicinity, and both determined without any feeling of jealousy between them that a certain Rev. Augustus Green was by many degrees the most estimable of the lot. The gentleman in question had certainly much in his favour, as, having a comfortable allowance from his father, he could devote the whole proceeds of his curacy to violet gloves and unexceptionable neck ties. Having thus fixedly resolved that the new comer had nothing about him to shake the pre-eminence of the exalted Green, the two girls went to sleep in each other's arms, contented with themselves and the world.

Mrs. Grantly at first sight came to much the same conclusion about her husband's favourite as her daughters had done, though, in seeking to measure his relative value, she did not compare him to Mr. Green; indeed, she made no comparison by name between him and any one else; but she remarked to her husband that one person's swans were very often another person's geese, thereby clearly showing that Mr. Arabin had not yet proved his qualifications in swanhood to her satisfaction.

'Well, Susan,' said he, rather offended at hearing his friend spoken of so disrespectfully, 'if you take Mr. Arabin for a goose, I cannot say that I think very highly of your discrimination.'

'A goose! No of course, he's not a goose. I've no doubt he's a very clever man. But you're so matter-of-fact, archdeacon, when it suits your purpose, that one can't trust oneself to any *façon de parler*. I've no doubt Mr. Arabin is a very valuable man—at Oxford, and that he'll be a good vicar at St. Ewold. All I mean is, that having passed one evening with him, I don't find him to be absolutely a paragon. In the first place, if I am not mistaken, he is a little inclined to be conceited.'

'Of all the men that I know intimately,' said the archdeacon, 'Arabin is, in my opinion, the most free from any taint of self-conceit. His fault is that he's too diffident.'

'Perhaps so,' said the lady; 'only I must own I did not find it out this evening.'

Nothing further was said about him. Dr. Grantly thought that his wife was abusing Mr. Arabin merely because he had praised him; and Mrs. Grantly knew that it was useless arguing for or against any person in favour of or in opposition to whom the archdeacon had already pronounced a strong opinion.

In truth they were both right. Mr. Arabin was a diffident man in social intercourse with those whom he did

not intimately know; when placed in situations which
it was his business to fill, and discussing matters with
which it was his duty to be conversant, Mr. Arabin was
from habit brazen-faced enough. When standing on a
platform in Exeter Hall, no man would be less mazed
than he by the eyes of the crowd before him; for such
was the work which his profession had called on him to
perform; but he shrank from a strong expression of
opinion in general society, and his doing so not uncom-
monly made it appear that he considered the company
not worth the trouble of his energy. He was averse to
dictate when the place did not seem to him to justify
dictation; and as those subjects on which people wished
to hear him speak were such as he was accustomed to
treat with decision, he generally shunned the traps there
were laid to allure him into discussion, and, by doing so,
not unfrequently subjected himself to such charges as
those brought against him by Mrs. Grantly.

Mr. Arabin, as he sat at his open window, enjoying the
delicious moonlight and gazing at the gray towers of the
church, which stood almost within the rectory grounds,
little dreamed that he was the subject of so many friendly
or unfriendly criticisms. Considering how much we are
all given to discuss the characters of others, and discuss
them often not in the strictest spirit of charity, it is singular
how little we are inclined to think that others can speak
ill-naturedly of us, and how angry and hurt we are when
proof reaches us that they have done so. It is hardly
too much to say that we all of us occasionally speak of our
dearest friends in a manner in which those dearest friends
would very little like to hear themselves mentioned;
and that we nevertheless expect that our dearest friends
shall invariably speak of us as though they were blind
to all our faults, but keenly alive to every shade of our
virtues.

It did not occur to Mr. Arabin that he was spoken of
at all. It seemed to him, when he compared himself with
his host, that he was a person of so little consequence
to any, that he was worth no one's words or thoughts.
He was utterly alone in the world as regarded domestic
ties and those inner familiar relations which are hardly
possible between others than husbands and wives, parents

and children, or brothers and sisters. He had often discussed with himself the necessity of such bonds for a man's happiness in this world, and had generally satisfied himself with the answer that happiness in this world is not a necessity. Herein he deceived himself, or rather tried to do so. He, like others, yearned for the enjoyment of whatever he saw enjoyable ; and though he attempted, with the modern stoicism of so many Christians, to make himself believe that joy and sorrow were matters which here should be held as perfectly indifferent, these things were not indifferent to him. He was tired of his Oxford rooms and his college life. He regarded the wife and children of his friend with something like envy ; he all but coveted the pleasant drawing-room, with its pretty windows opening on to lawns and flower-beds, the apparel of the comfortable house, and—above all—the air of home which encompassed it all.

It will be said that no time can have been so fitted for such desires on his part as this, when he had just possessed himself of a country parish, of a living among fields and gardens, of a house which a wife would grace. It is true there was a difference between the opulence of Plumstead and the modest economy of St. Ewold ; but surely Mr. Arabin was not a man to sigh after wealth ! Of all men, his friends would have unanimously declared he was the last to do so. But how little our friends know us ! In his period of stoical rejection of this world's happiness, he had cast from him as utter dross all anxiety as to fortune. He had, as it were, proclaimed himself to be indifferent to promotion, and those who chiefly admired his talents, and would mainly have exerted themselves to secure to them their deserved reward, had taken him at his word. And now, if the truth must out, he felt himself disappointed —disappointed not by them but by himself. The daydream of his youth was over, and at the age of forty he felt that he was not fit to work in the spirit of an apostle. He had mistaken himself, and learned his mistake when it was past remedy. He had professed himself indifferent to mitres and diaconal residences, to rich livings and pleasant glebes, and now he had to own to himself that he was sighing for the good things of other men, on whom in his pride he had ventured to look down.

Not for wealth, in its vulgar sense, had he ever sighed;
not for the enjoyment of rich things had he ever longed;
but for the allotted share of worldly bliss, which a wife,
and children, and happy home could give him, for that
usual amount of comfort which he had ventured to reject
as unnecessary for him, he did now feel that he would
have been wiser to have searched.

He knew that his talents, his position, and his friends
would have won for him promotion, had he put himself
in the way of winning it. Instead of doing so, he had
allowed himself to be persuaded to accept a living which
would give him an income of some 300*l.* a year, should he,
by marrying, throw up his fellowship. Such, at the age
of forty, was the worldly result of labour, which the world
had chosen to regard as successful. The world also thought
that Mr. Arabin was, in his own estimation, sufficiently
paid. Alas! alas! the world was mistaken; and Mr.
Arabin was beginning to ascertain that such was the case.

And here, may I beg the reader not to be hard in his
judgment upon this man. Is not the state at which he
has arrived, the natural result of efforts to reach that
which is not the condition of humanity? Is not modern
stoicism, built though it be on Christianity, as great an
outrage on human nature as was the stoicism of the
ancients? The philosophy of Zeno was built on true
laws, but on true laws misunderstood, and therefore mis-
applied. It is the same with our Stoics here, who would
teach us that wealth and worldly comfort and happiness
on earth are not worth the search. Alas, for a doctrine
which can find no believing pupils and no true teachers!

The case of Mr. Arabin was the more singular, as he
belonged to a branch of the Church of England well inclined
to regard its temporalities with avowed favour, and had
habitually lived with men who were accustomed to much
worldly comfort. But such was his idiosyncrasy, that
these very facts had produced within him, in early life,
a state of mind that was not natural to him. He was
content to be a High Churchman, if he could be so on
principles of his own, and could strike out a course showing
a marked difference from those with whom he consorted.
He was ready to be a partisan as long as he was allowed
to have a course of action and of thought unlike that of

his party. His party had indulged him, and he began to feel that his party was right and himself wrong, just when such a conviction was too late to be of service to him. He discovered, when such discovery was no longer serviceable, that it *would* have been worth his while to have worked for the usual pay assigned to work in this world, and have earned a wife and children, with a carriage for them to sit in; to have earned a pleasant dining-room, in which his friends could drink his wine, and the power of walking up the high street of his country town, with the knowledge that all its tradesmen would have gladly welcomed him within their doors. Other men arrived at those convictions in their start in life, and so worked up to them. To him they had come when they were too late to be of use.

It has been said that Mr. Arabin was a man of pleasantry and it may be thought that such a state of mind as that described, would be antagonistic to humour. But surely such is not the case. Wit is the outward mental casing of the man, and has no more to do with the inner mind of thoughts and feelings than have the rich brocaded garments of the priest at the altar with the asceticism of the anchorite below them, whose skin is tormented with sackcloth, and whose body is half flayed with rods. Nay, will not such a one often rejoice more than any other in the rich show of his outer apparel? Will it not be food for his pride to feel that he groans inwardly, while he shines outwardly? So it is with the mental efforts which men make. Those which they show forth daily to the world are often the opposites of the inner workings of the spirit.

In the archdeacon's drawing-room, Mr. Arabin had sparkled with his usual unaffected brilliancy, but when he retired to his bed-room, he sat there sad, at his open window, repining within himself that he also had no wife, no bairns, no soft sward of lawn duly mown for him to lie on, no herd of attendant curates, no bowings from the banker's clerks, no rich rectory. That apostleship that he had thought of had evaded his grasp, and he was now only vicar of St. Ewold's, with a taste for a mitre. Truly he had fallen between two stools.

CHAPTER XXI

ST. EWOLD'S PARSONAGE

WHEN Mr. Harding and Mrs. Bold reached the rectory on the following morning, the archdeacon and his friend were at St. Ewold's. They had gone over that the new vicar might inspect his church, and be introduced to the squire, and were not expected back before dinner. Mr. Harding rambled out by himself, and strolled, as was his wont at Plumstead, about the lawn and round the church ; and as he did so, the two sisters naturally fell into conversation about Barchester.

There was not much sisterly confidence between them. Mrs. Grantly was ten years older than Eleanor, and had been married while Eleanor was yet a child. They had never, therefore, poured into each other's ears their hopes and loves ; and now that one was a wife and the other a widow, it was not probable that they would begin to do so. They lived too much asunder to be able to fall into that kind of intercourse which makes confidence between sisters almost a necessity ; and, moreover, that which is so easy at eighteen is often very difficult at twenty-eight. Mrs. Grantly knew this, and did not, therefore, expect confidence from her sister ; and yet she longed to ask her whether in real truth Mr. Slope was agreeable to her.

It was by no means difficult to turn the conversation to Mr. Slope. That gentleman had become so famous at Barchester, had so much to do with all clergymen connected with the city, and was so specially concerned in the affairs of Mr. Harding, that it would have been odd if Mr. Harding's daughters had not talked about him. Mrs. Grantly was soon abusing him, which she did with her whole heart ; and Mrs. Bold was nearly as eager to defend him. She positively disliked the man, would have been delighted to learn that he had taken himself off so that she should never see him again, had indeed almost a fear of him, and yet she constantly found herself taking his part. The abuse of other people, and abuse of a nature that she felt to be unjust, imposed this necessity on her, and at last made Mr. Slope's defence an habitual course of argument with her.

From Mr. Slope the conversation turned to the Stan-hopes, and Mrs. Grantly was listening with some interest to Eleanor's account of the family, when it dropped out that Mr. Slope made one of the party.

' What ! ' said the lady of the rectory, ' was Mr. Slope there too ? '

Eleanor merely replied that such had been the case.

' Why, Eleanor, he must be very fond of you, I think; he seems to follow you everywhere.'

Even this did not open Eleanor's eyes. She merely laughed, and said that she imagined Mr. Slope found other attraction at Dr. Stanhope's. And so they parted. Mrs. Grantly felt quite convinced that the odious match would take place ; and Mrs. Bold as convinced that that unfortunate chaplain, disagreeable as he must be allowed to be, was more sinned against than sinning.

The archdeacon of course heard before dinner that Eleanor had remained the day before in Barchester with the view of meeting Mr. Slope, and that she had so met him. He remembered how she had positively stated that there were to be no guests at the Stanhopes, and he did not hesitate to accuse her of deceit. Moreover, the fact, or rather presumed fact, of her being deceitful on such a matter, spoke but too plainly in evidence against her as to her imputed crime of receiving Mr. Slope as a lover.

' I am afraid that anything we can do will be too late,' said the archdeacon. ' I own I am fairly surprised. I never liked your sister's taste with regard to men ; but still I did not give her credit for—ugh ! '

' And so soon, too,' said Mrs. Grantly, who thought more, perhaps, of her sister's indecorum in having a lover before she had put off her weeds, than her bad taste in having such a lover as Mr. Slope.

' Well, my dear, I shall be sorry to be harsh, or to do anything that can hurt your father ; but, positively, neither that man nor his wife shall come within my doors.'

Mrs. Grantly sighed, and then attempted to console herself and her lord by remarking that, after all, the thing was not accomplished yet. Now that Eleanor was at Plumstead, much might be done to wean her from her fatal passion. Poor Eleanor !

The evening passed off without anything to make it

remarkable. Mr. Arabin discussed the parish of St. Ewold
with the archdeacon, and Mrs. Grantly and Mr. Harding,
who knew the personages of the parish, joined in. Eleanor
also knew them, but she said little. Mr. Arabin did not
apparently take much notice of her, and she was not in
a humour to receive at that time with any special grace
any special favourite of her brother-in-law. Her first
idea on reaching her bed-room was that a much pleasanter
family party might be met at Dr. Stanhope's than at the
rectory. She began to think that she was getting tired
of clergymen and their respectable humdrum wearisome
mode of living, and that after all, people in the outer world,
who had lived in Italy, London, or elsewhere, need not
necessarily be regarded as atrocious and abominable.
The Stanhopes, she had thought, were a giddy, thoughtless,
extravagant set of people ; but she had seen nothing wrong
about them, and had, on the other hand, found that they
thoroughly knew how to make their house agreeable. It
was a thousand pities, she thought, that the archdeacon
should not have a little of the same *savoir vivre*. Mr.
Arabin, as we have said, did not apparently take much
notice of her ; but yet he did not go to bed without feeling
that he had been in company with a very pretty woman ;
and as is the case with most bachelors, and some married
men, regarded the prospect of his month's visit at Plumstead in a pleasanter light, when he learnt that a very
pretty woman was to share it with him.

Before they all retired it was settled that the whole
party should drive over on the following day to inspect
the parsonage at St. Ewold. The three clergymen were
to discuss dilapidations, and the two ladies were to lend
their assistance in suggesting such changes as might be
necessary for a bachelor's abode. Accordingly, soon after
breakfast, the carriage was at the door. There was only
room for four inside, and the archdeacon got upon the
box. Eleanor found herself opposite to Mr. Arabin, and
was, therefore, in a manner forced into conversation
with him. They were soon on comfortable terms together ;
and had she thought about it, she would have thought
that, in spite of his black cloth, Mr. Arabin would not
have been a bad addition to the Stanhope family party.

Now that the archdeacon was away, they could all

trifle. Mr. Harding began by telling them in the most innocent manner imaginable an old legend about Mr. Arabin's new parish. There was, he said, in days of yore, an illustrious priestess of St. Ewold, famed through the whole country for curing all manner of diseases. She had a well, as all priestesses have ever had, which well was extant to this day, and shared in the minds of many of the people the sanctity which belonged to the consecrated ground of the parish church. Mr. Arabin declared that he should look on such tenets on the part of his parishioners as anything but orthodox. And Mrs. Grantly replied that she so entirely disagreed with him as to think that no parish was in a proper state that had not its priestess as well as its priest. 'The duties are never well done,' said she, ' unless they are so divided.'

' I suppose, papa,' said Eleanor, ' that in the olden times the priestess bore all the sway herself. Mr. Arabin, perhaps, thinks that such might be too much the case now if a sacred lady were admitted within the parish.'

' I think, at any rate,' said he, ' that it is safer to run no such risk. No priestly pride has ever exceeded that of sacerdotal females. A very lowly curate I might, perhaps, essay to rule ; but a curatess would be sure to get the better of me.'

' There are certainly examples of such accidents happening,' said Mrs. Grantly. ' They do say that there is a priestess at Barchester who is very imperious in all things touching the altar. Perhaps the fear of such a fate as that is before your eyes.

When they were joined by the archdeacon on the gravel before the vicarage, they descended again to grave dulness. Not that Archdeacon Grantly was a dull man ; but his frolic humours were of a cumbrous kind ; and his wit, when he was witty, did not generally extend itself to his auditory. On the present occasion he was soon making speeches about wounded roofs and walls, which he declared to be in want of some surgeon's art. There was not a partition that he did not tap, nor a block of chimneys that he did not narrowly examine ; all water-pipes, flues, cisterns, and sewers underwent an investigation ; and he even descended, in the care of his friend, so far as to bore sundry boards in the floors with a bradawl.

Mr. Arabin accompanied him through the rooms, trying to look wise in such domestic matters, and the other three also followed. Mrs. Grantly showed that she had not herself been priestess of a parish twenty years for nothing, and examined the bells and window panes in a very knowing way.

'You will, at any rate, have a beautiful prospect out of your own window, if this is to be your private sanctum,' said Eleanor. She was standing at the lattice of a little room up stairs, from which the view certainly was very lovely. It was from the back of the vicarage, and there was nothing to interrupt the eye between the house and the glorious gray pile of the cathedral. The intermediate ground, however, was beautifully studded with timber. In the immediate foreground ran the little river which afterwards skirted the city; and, just to the right of the cathedral, the pointed gables and chimneys of Hiram's Hospital peeped out of the elms which encompass it.

'Yes,' said he, joining her. 'I shall have a beautifully complete view of my adversaries. I shall sit down before the hostile town, and fire away at them at a very pleasant distance. I shall just be able to lodge a shot in the hospital, should the enemy ever get possession of it; and as for the palace, I have it within full range.'

'I never saw anything like you clergymen,' said Eleanor; 'you are always thinking of fighting each other.'

'Either that,' said he, 'or else supporting each other. The pity is that we cannot do the one without the other. But are we not here to fight? Is not ours a church militant? What is all our work but fighting, and hard fighting, if it be well done?'

'But not with each other.'

'That's as it may be. The same complaint which you make of me for battling with another clergyman of our own church, the Mohammedan would make against me for battling with the error of a priest of Rome. Yet, surely, you would not be inclined to say that I should be wrong to do battle with such as him. A pagan, too, with his multiplicity of gods, would think it equally odd that the Christian and the Mohammedan should disagree.'

'Ah! but you wage your wars about trifles so bitterly.'

'Wars about trifles,' said he, 'are always bitter,

especially among neighbours. When the differences are
great, and the parties comparative strangers, men quarrel
with courtesy. What combatants are ever so eager as
two brothers ? '

'But do not such contentions bring scandal on the
church ? '

'More scandal would fall on the church if there were
no such contentions. We have but one way to avoid
them—that of acknowledging a common head of our
church, whose word on all points of doctrine shall be
authoritative. Such a termination of our difficulties
is alluring enough. It has charms which are irresistible
to many, and all but irresistible, I own, to me.'

'You speak now of the Church of Rome ? ' said Eleanor.

'No,' said he, 'not necessarily of the Church of Rome ;
but of a church with a head. Had it pleased God to
vouchsafe to us such a church our path would have been
easy. But easy paths have not been thought good for
us.' He paused and stood silent for a while, thinking of
the time when he had so nearly sacrificed all he had, his
powers of mind, his free agency, the fresh running waters
of his mind's fountain, his very inner self, for an easy
path in which no fighting would be needed ; and then
he continued :—'What you say is partly true ; our contentions do bring on us some scandal. The outer world,
though it constantly reviles us for our human infirmities,
and throws in our teeth the fact that being clergymen we
are still no more than men, demands of us that we should
do our work with godlike perfection. There is nothing
godlike about us : we differ from each other with the
acerbity common to man—we triumph over each other
with human frailty—we allow differences on subjects
of divine origin to produce among us antipathies and
enmities which are anything but divine. This is all true.
But what would you have in place of it ? There is no
infallible head for a church on earth. This dream of
believing man has been tried, and we see in Italy and in
Spain what has come of it. Grant that there are and have
been no bickerings within the pale of the Pope's Church.
Such an assumption would be utterly untrue ; but let
us grant it, and then let us say which church has incurred
the heavier scandals.'

There was a quiet earnestness about Mr. Arabin, as he half acknowledged and half defended himself from the charge brought against him, which surprised Eleanor. She had been used all her life to listen to clerical discussion; but the points at issue between the disputants had so seldom been of more than temporal significance as to have left on her mind no feeling of reverence for such subjects. There had always been a hard worldly leaven of the love either of income or of power in the strains she had heard; there had been no panting for the truth; no aspirations after religious purity. It had always been taken for granted by those around her that they were indubitably right, that there was no ground for doubt, that the hard uphill work of ascertaining what the duty of a clergyman should be had been already accomplished in full; and that what remained for an active militant parson to do, was to hold his own against all comers. Her father, it is true, was an exception to this; but then he was so essentially anti-militant in all things, that she classed him in her own mind apart from all others. She had never argued the matter within herself, or considered whether this common tone was or was not faulty; but she was sick of it without knowing that she was so. And now she found to her surprise and not without a certain pleasurable excitement, that this new comer among them spoke in a manner very different from that to which she was accustomed.

'It is so easy to condemn,' said he, continuing the thread of his thoughts. 'I know no life that must be so delicious as that of a writer for newspapers, or a leading member of the opposition—to thunder forth accusations against men in power; show up the worst side of everything that is produced; to pick holes in every coat; to be indignant, sarcastic, jocose, moral, or supercilious; to damn with faint praise, or crush with open calumny! What can be so easy as this when the critic has to be responsible for nothing? You condemn what I do; but put yourself in my position and do the reverse, and then see if I cannot condemn you.'

'Oh! Mr. Arabin, I do not condemn you.'

'Pardon me, you do, Mrs. Bold—you as one of the world; you are now the opposition member; you are now composing your leading article, and well and bitterly you do it. "Let dogs delight to bark and bite;" you fitly begin with an elegant quotation; "but if we are to have a church at all, in heaven's name let the pastors who preside over it keep their hands from each other's throats. Lawyers can live without befouling each other's names; doctors do not fight duels. Why is it that clergymen alone should indulge themselves in such unrestrained liberty of abuse against each other?" and so you go on reviling us for our ungodly quarrels, our sectarian propensities, and scandalous differences. It will, however, give you no trouble to write another article next week in which we, or some of us, shall be twitted with an unseemly apathy in matters of our vocation. It will not fall on you to reconcile the discrepancy; your readers will never ask you how the poor parson is to be urgent in season and out of season, and yet never come in contact with men who think widely differently from him. You, when you condemn this foreign treaty, or that official arrangement, will have to incur no blame for the graver faults of any different measure. It is so easy to condemn; and so pleasant too; for eulogy charms no listeners as detraction does.'

Eleanor only half followed him in his raillery, but she caught his meaning. 'I know I ought to apologise for presuming to criticise you,' she said; ' but I was thinking with sorrow of the ill-will that has lately come among us at Barchester, and I spoke more freely than I should have done.'

'Peace on earth and good-will among men, are, like heaven, promises for the future;' said he, following rather his own thoughts than hers. 'When that prophecy is accomplished, there will no longer be any need for clergymen.'

Here they were interrupted by the archdeacon, whose voice was heard from the cellar shouting to the vicar.

'Arabin, Arabin,'—and then turning to his wife, who was apparently at his elbow—'where has he gone to? This cellar is perfectly abominable. It would be murder to put a bottle of wine into it till it has been roofed, walled, and floored. How on earth old Goodenough ever got on with it, I cannot guess. But then Goodenough never had a glass of wine that any man could drink.'

'What is it, archdeacon?' said the vicar, running down stairs, and leaving Eleanor above to her meditations.

'This cellar must be roofed, walled, and floored,' repeated the archdeacon. 'Now mind what I say, and don't let the architect persuade you that it will do; half of these fellows know nothing about wine. This place as it is now would be damp and cold in winter, and hot and muggy in summer. I wouldn't give a straw for the best wine that ever was vinted, after it had lain here a couple of years.'

Mr. Arabin assented, and promised that the cellar should be reconstructed according to the archdeacon's receipt.

'And, Arabin, look here; was such an attempt at a kitchen grate ever seen?'

'The grate is really very bad,' said Mrs. Grantly; 'I am sure the priestess won't approve of it, when she is brought home to the scene of her future duties. Really, Mr. Arabin, no priestess accustomed to such an excellent well as that above could put up with such a grate as this.'

'If there must be a priestess at St. Ewold's at all, Mrs. Grantly, I think we will leave her to her well, and not call down her divine wrath on any of the imperfections rising from our human poverty. However, I own I am amenable to the attractions of a well-cooked dinner, and the grate shall certainly be changed.'

By this time the archdeacon had again ascended, and was now in the dining-room. 'Arabin,' said he, speaking in his usual loud clear voice, and with that tone of dictation which was so common to him; 'you must positively alter this dining-room, that is, remodel it altogether; look here, it is just sixteen feet by fifteen; did anybody ever hear of a dining-room of such proportions!' and the archdeacon stepped the room long-ways and cross-ways with ponderous steps, as though a certain amount of ecclesiastical dignity could be imparted even to such an occupation as that by the manner of doing it. 'Barely sixteen; you may call it a square.'

'It would do very well for a round table,' suggested the ex-warden.

Now there was something peculiarly unorthodox in the archdeacon's estimation in the idea of a round table.

He had always been accustomed to a goodly board of
decent length, comfortably elongating itself according
to the number of the guests, nearly black with perpetual
rubbing, and as bright as a mirror. Now round dinner
tables are generally of oak, or else of such new construction as not to have acquired the peculiar hue which was
so pleasing to him. He connected them with what he
called the nasty new fangled method of leaving a cloth
on the table, as though to warn people that they were
not to sit long. In his eyes there was something democratic
and parvenue in a round table. He imagined that dissenters and calico-printers chiefly used them, and perhaps
a few literary lions more conspicuous for their wit than
their gentility. He was a little flurried at the idea of
such an article being introduced into the diocese by a
protégé of his own, and at the instigation of his father-
in-law.

'A round dinner-table,' said he, with some heat, ' is
the most abominable article of furniture that ever was
invented. I hope that Arabin has more taste than to
allow such a thing in his house.'

Poor Mr. Harding felt himself completely snubbed, and
of course said nothing further; but Mr. Arabin, who had
yielded submissively in the small matters of the cellar
and kitchen grate, found himself obliged to oppose reforms
which might be of a nature too expensive for his pocket.

'But it seems to me, archdeacon, that I can't very well
lengthen the room without pulling down the wall, and
if I pull down the wall, I must build it up again; then
if I throw out a bow on this side, I must do the same on
the other, then if I do it for the ground floor, I must
carry it up to the floor above. That will be putting a new
front to the house, and will cost, I suppose, a couple of
hundred pounds. The ecclesiastical commissioners will
hardly assist me when they hear that my grievance consists
in having a dining-room only sixteen feet long.'

The archdeacon proceeded to explain that nothing
would be easier than adding six feet to the front of the
dining-room, without touching any other in the house.
Such irregularities of construction in small country houses
were, he said, rather graceful than otherwise, and he
offered to pay for the whole thing out of his own pocket.

if it cost more than forty pounds. Mr. Arabin, however, was firm, and, although the archdeacon fussed and fumed about it, would not give way.

Forty pounds, he said, was a matter of serious moment to him, and his friends, if under such circumstances they would be good-natured enough to come to him at all, must put up with the misery of a square room. He was willing to compromise matters by disclaiming any intention of having a round table.

' But,' said Mrs. Grantly, ' what if the priestess insists on having both the rooms enlarged ? '

' The priestess in that case must do it for herself, Mrs. Grantly.'

' I have no doubt she will be well able to do so,' replied the lady ; ' to do that and many more wonderful things. I am quite sure that the priestess of St. Ewold, when she does come, won't come empty-handed.'

Mr. Arabin, however, did not appear well inclined to enter into speculative expenses on such a chance as this, and therefore, any material alterations in the house, the cost of which could not fairly be made to lie at the door either of the ecclesiastical commissioners or of the estate of the late incumbent, were tabooed. With this essential exception, the archdeacon ordered, suggested, and carried all points before him in a manner very much to his own satisfaction. A close observer, had there been one there, might have seen that his wife had been quite as useful in the matter as himself. No one knew better than Mrs. Grantly the appurtenances necessary to a comfortable house. She did not, however, think it necessary to lay claim to any of the glory which her lord and master was so ready to appropriate as his own.

Having gone through their work effectually and systematically, the party returned to Plumstead well satisfied with their expedition.

CHAPTER XXII

THE THORNES OF ULLATHORNE

On the following Sunday Mr. Arabin was to read himself in at his new church. It was agreed at the rectory that the archdeacon should go over with him and assist at the reading-desk, and that Mr. Harding should take the archdeacon's duty at Plumstead Church. Mrs. Grantly had her school and her buns to attend to, and professed that she could not be spared; but Mrs. Bold was to accompany them. It was further agreed also, that they would lunch at the squire's house, and return home after the afternoon service.

Wilfred Thorne, Esq., of Ullathorne, was the squire of St. Ewold's; or rather the squire of Ullathorne; for the domain of the modern landlord was of wider notoriety than the fame of the ancient saint. He was a fair specimen of what that race has come to in our days, which a century ago was, as we are told, fairly represented by Squire Western. If that representation be a true one, few classes of men can have made faster strides in improvement. Mr. Thorne, however, was a man possessed of quite a sufficient number of foibles to lay him open to much ridicule. He was still a bachelor, being about fifty, and was not a little proud of his person. When living at home at Ullathorne there was not much room for such pride, and there therefore he always looked like a gentleman, and like that which he certainly was, the first man in his parish. But during the month or six weeks which he annually spent in London, he tried so hard to look like a great man there also, which he certainly was not, that he was put down as a fool by many at his club. He was a man of considerable literary attainment in a certain way and on certain subjects. His favourite authors were Montaigne and Burton, and he knew more perhaps than any other man in his own county, and the next to it, of the English essayists of the two last centuries. He possessed complete sets of the 'Idler,' the 'Spectator,' the 'Tatler,' the 'Guardian,' and the 'Rambler;' and would discourse by hours together on the superiority of such publications to anything which has since been produced in our Edinburghs and Quarterlies. He was a great proficient in all questions of genealogy, and knew enough of almost every gentleman's family in England to say of what blood and lineage were descended all those who had any claim to be considered as possessors of any such luxuries. For blood and lineage he himself had a most profound respect. He counted back his own ancestors to some period long antecedent to the Conquest; and could tell you, if you would listen to him, how it had come to pass that they, like Cedric the Saxon, had been permitted to hold their own among the Norman barons. It was not, according to his showing, on account of any weak complaisance on the part of his family towards their Norman neighbours. Some Ealfried of Ullathorne once fortified his own castle, and held out, not only that, but the then existing cathedral of Barchester also, against one Geoffrey De Burgh, in the time of King John; and Mr. Thorne possessed the whole history of the siege written on vellum, and illuminated in a most costly manner. It little signified that no one could read the writing, as, had that been possible, no one could have understood the language. Mr. Thorne could, however, give you all the particulars in good English, and had no objection to do so.

It would be unjust to say that he looked down on men whose families were of recent date. He did not do so. He frequently consorted with such, and had chosen many of his friends from among them. But he looked on them as great millionaires are apt to look on those who have small incomes; as men who have Sophocles at their fingers' ends regard those who know nothing of Greek. They might doubtless be good sort of people, entitled to much praise for virtue, very admirable for talent, highly respectable in every way; but they were without the one great good gift. Such was Mr. Thorne's way of thinking on this matter; nothing could atone for the loss of good blood; nothing could neutralise its good effects. Few indeed were now possessed of it, but the possession was on that account the more precious. It was very pleasant to hear Mr. Thorne descant on this matter. Were you in your ignorance to surmise that such a one was of a good family because the head of his family was a baronet

of an old date, he would open his eyes with a delightful
look of affected surprise, and modestly remind you that
baronetcies only dated from James I. He would gently
sigh if you spoke of the blood of the Fitzgeralds and De
Burghs ; would hardly allow the claims of the Howards
and Lowthers ; and has before now alluded to the Talbots
as a family who had hardly yet achieved the full honours
of a pedigree.

In speaking once of a wide spread race whose name
had received the honours of three coronets, scions from
which sat for various constituencies, some one of whose
members had been in almost every cabinet formed during
the present century, a brilliant race such as there are
few in England, Mr. Thorne had called them all ' dirt.' He
had not intended any disrespect to these men. He admired
them in many senses, and allowed them their privileges
without envy. He had merely meant to express his feeling
that the streams which ran through their veins were not
yet purified by time to that perfection, had not become
so genuine an ichor, as to be worthy of being called blood
in the genealogical sense.

When Mr. Arabin was first introduced to him, Mr.
Thorne had immediately suggested that he was one of the
Arabins of Uphill Stanton. Mr. Arabin replied that he
was a very distant relative of the family alluded to. To
this Mr. Thorne surmised that the relationship could not
be very distant. Mr. Arabin assured him that it was so
distant that the families knew nothing of each other.
Mr. Thorne laughed his gentle laugh at this, and told
Mr. Arabin that there was now existing no branch of his
family separated from the parent stock at an earlier date
than the reign of Elizabeth ; and that therefore Mr.
Arabin could not call himself distant. Mr. Arabin himself
was quite clearly an Arabin of Uphill Stanton.

' But,' said the vicar, ' Uphill Stanton has been sold
to the De Greys, and has been in their hands for the last
fifty years.'

' And when it has been there one hundred and firty,
if it unluckily remain there so long,' said Mr. Thorne,
' your descendants will not be a whit the less entitled
to describe themselves as being of the family of Uphill Stanton. Thank God, no De Grey can buy that

—and, thank God—no Arabin, and no Thorne, can sell it.'

In politics, Mr. Thorne was an unflinching conservative. He looked on those fifty-three Trojans, who, as Mr. Dod tells us, censured free trade in November, 1852, as the only patriots left among the public men of England. When that terrible crisis of free trade had arrived, when the repeal of the corn laws was carried by those very men whom Mr. Thorne had hitherto regarded as the only possible saviours of his country, he was for a time paralysed. His country was lost ; but that was comparatively a small thing. Other countries had flourished and fallen, and the human race still went on improving under God's providence. But now all trust in human faith must for ever be at an end. Not only must ruin come, but it must come through the apostasy of those who had been regarded as the truest of true believers. Politics in England, as a pursuit for gentlemen, must be at an end. Had Mr. Thorne been trodden under foot by a Whig, he could have borne it as a Tory and a martyr ; but to be so utterly thrown over and deceived by those he had so earnestly supported, so thoroughly trusted, was more than he could endure and live. He therefore ceased to live as a politician, and refused to hold any converse with the world at large on the state of the country.

Such were Mr. Thorne's impressions for the first two or three years after Sir Robert Peel's apostasy ; but by degrees his temper, as did that of others, cooled down. He began once more to move about, to frequent the bench and the market, and to be seen at dinners, shoulder to shoulder with some of those who had so cruelly betrayed him. It was a necessity for him to live, and that plan of his for avoiding the world did not answer. He, however, and others around him who still maintained the same staunch principles of protection—men like himself, who were too true to flinch at the cry of a mob—had their own way of consoling themselves. They were, and felt themselves to be, the only true depositaries left of certain Eleusinian mysteries, of certain deep and wondrous services of worship by which alone the gods could be rightly approached. To them and them only was it now given to know these things, and to perpetuate them, if that might still be done, by the careful and secret education of their children.

We have read how private and peculiar forms of worship have been carried on from age to age in families, which to the outer world have apparently adhered to the services of some ordinary church. And so by degrees it was with Mr. Thorne. He learnt at length to listen calmly while protection was talked of as a thing dead, although he knew within himself that it was still quick with a mystic life. Nor was he without a certain pleasure that such knowledge though given to him should be debarred from the multitude. He became accustomed to hear, even among country gentlemen, that free trade was after all not so bad, and to hear this without dispute, although conscious within himself that everything good in England had gone with his old palladium. He had within him something of the feeling of Cato, who gloried that he could kill himself because Romans were no longer worthy of their name. Mr. Thorne had no thought of killing himself, being a Christian, and still possessing his 4000*l.* a year; but the feeling was not on that account the less comfortable.

Mr. Thorne was a sportsman, and had been active though not outrageous in his sports. Previous to the great downfall of politics in his country, he had supported the hunt by every means in his power. He had preserved game till no goose or turkey could show a tail in the parish of St. Ewold's. He had planted gorse covers with more care than oaks and larches. He had been more anxious for the comfort of his foxes than of his ewes and lambs. No meet had been more popular than Ullathorne; no man's stables had been more liberally open to the horses of distant men than Mr. Thorne's; no man had said more, written more, or done more to keep the club up. The theory of protection could expand itself so thoroughly in the practices of a country hunt! But when the great ruin came; when the noble master of the Barsetshire hounds supported the recreant minister in the House of Lords, and basely surrendered his truth, his manhood, his friends, and his honour for the hope of a garter, then Mr. Thorne gave up the hunt. He did not cut his covers, for that would not have been the act of a gentleman. He did not kill his foxes, for that according to his light would have been murder. He did not say that his covers should not be drawn, or his earths stopped, for that would have been illegal according to the by-laws prevailing among country gentlemen. But he absented himself from home on the occasion of every meet at Ullathorne, left the covers to their fate, and could not be persuaded to take his pink coat out of the press, or his hunters out of his stable. This lasted for two years, and then by degrees he came round. He first appeared at a neighbouring meet on a pony, dressed in his shooting coat, as though he had trotted in by accident; then he walked up one morning on foot to see his favourite gorse drawn, and when his groom brought his mare out by chance, he did not refuse to mount her. He was next persuaded, by one of the immortal fifty-three, to bring his hunting materials over to the other side of the county, and take a fortnight with the hounds there; and so gradually he returned to his old life. But in hunting as in other things he was only supported by an inward feeling of mystic superiority to those with whom he shared the common breath of outer life.

Mr. Thorne did not live in solitude at Ullathorne. He had a sister, who was ten years older than himself, and who participated in his prejudices and feelings so strongly, that she was a living caricature of all his foibles. She would not open a modern quarterly, did not choose to see a magazine in her drawing-room, and would not have polluted her fingers with a shred of the 'Times' for any consideration. She spoke of Addison, Swift, and Steele, as though they were still living, regarded De Foe as the best known novelist of his country, and thought of Fielding as a young but meritorious novice in the fields of romance. In poetry, she was familiar with names as late as Dryden, and had once been seduced into reading the 'Rape of the Lock;' but she regarded Spenser as the purest type of her country's literature in this line. Genealogy was her favourite insanity. Those things which are the pride of most genealogists were to her contemptible. Arms and mottoes set her beside herself. Ealfried of Ullathorne had wanted no motto to assist him in cleaving to the brisket Geoffrey De Burgh; and

Ealfried's great grandfather, the gigantic Ullafrid, had required no other arms than those which nature gave him to hurl from the top of his own castle a cousin of the base invading Norman. To her all modern English names were equally insignificant : Hengist, Horsa, and such like, had for her ears the only true savour of nobility. She was not contented unless she could go beyond the Saxons ; and would certainly have christened her children, had she had children, by the names of the ancient Britons. In some respects she was not unlike Scott's Ulrica, and had she been given to cursing, she would certainly have done so in the names of Mista, Skogula, and Zernebock. Not having submitted to the embraces of any polluting Norman, as poor Ulrica had done, and having assisted no parricide, the milk of human kindness was not curdled in her bosom. She never cursed, therefore, but blessed rather. This, however, she did in a strange uncouth Saxon manner that would have been unintelligible to any peasants but her own.

As a politician, Miss Thorne had been so thoroughly disgusted with public life by base deeds long antecedent to the Corn Law question, that that had but little moved her. In her estimation her brother had been a fast young man, hurried away by a too ardent temperament into democratic tendencies. Now happily he was brought to sounder views by seeing the iniquity of the world. She had not yet reconciled herself to the Reform Bill, and still groaned in spirit over the defalcations of the Duke as touching the Catholic Emancipation. If asked whom she thought the Queen should take as her counsellor, she would probably have named Lord Eldon ; and when reminded that that venerable man was no longer present in the flesh to assist us, she would probably have answered with a sigh that none now could help us but the dead.

In religion, Miss Thorne was a pure Druidess. We would not have it understood by that, that she did actually in these latter days assist at any human sacrifices, or that she was in fact hostile to the Church of Christ. She had adopted the Christian religion as a milder form of the worship of her ancestors, and always appealed to her doing so as evidence that she had no prejudices against reform, when it could be shown that reform was salutary.

This reform was the most modern of any to which she had
as yet acceded, it being presumed that British ladies
had given up their paint and taken to some sort of petticoats before the days of St. Augustine.   That further
feminine step in advance which combines paint and
petticoats together, had not found a votary in Miss Thorne.

But she was a Druidess in this, that she regretted she
knew not what in the usages and practices of her Church.
She sometimes talked and constantly thought of good
things gone by, though she had but the faintest idea of
what those good things had been.   She imagined that
a purity had existed which was now gone; that a piety
had adorned our pastors and a simple docility our people,
for which it may be feared history gave her but little true
warrant.   She was accustomed to speak of Cranmer as
though he had been the firmest and most simple-minded
of martyrs, and of Elizabeth as though the pure Protestant
faith of her people had been the one anxiety of her life.
It would have been cruel to undeceive her, had it been
possible; but it would have been impossible to make her
believe that the one was a time-serving priest, willing
to go any length to keep his place, and that the other was
in heart a papist, with this sole proviso, that she should
be her own pope.

And so Miss Thorne went on sighing and regretting,
looking back to the divine right of kings as the ruling
axiom of a golden age, and cherishing, low down in the
bottom of her heart of hearts, a dear unmentioned wish
for the restoration of some exiled Stuart.   Who would
deny her the luxury of her sighs, or the sweetness of her
soft regrets!

In her person and her dress she was perfect, and well
she knew her own perfection.   She was a small elegantly
made old woman, with a face from which the glow of her
youth had not departed without leaving some streaks of
a roseate hue.   She was proud of her colour, proud of her
grey hair which she wore in short crisp curls peering out
all around her face from the dainty white lace cap.   To
think of all the money that she spent in lace used to break
the heart of poor Mrs. Quiverful with her seven daughters.
She was proud of her teeth, which were still white and
numerous, proud of her bright cheery eye, proud of her

short jaunty step, and very proud of the neat, precise, small feet with which those steps were taken. She was proud also, ay, very proud, of the rich brocaded silk in which it was her custom to ruffle through her drawing-room.

We know what was the custom of the lady of Branksome—

> Nine-and-twenty knights of fame
> Hung their shields in Branksome Hall.

The lady of Ullathorne was not so martial in her habits, but hardly less costly. She might have boasted that nine-and-twenty silken skirts might have been produced in her chamber, each fit to stand alone. The nine-and-twenty shields of the Scottish heroes were less independent, and hardly more potent to withstand any attack that might be made on them. Miss Thorne when fully dressed might be said to have been armed cap-a-pie, and she was always fully dressed, as far as was ever known to mortal man.

For all this rich attire Miss Thorne was not indebted to the generosity of her brother. She had a very comfortable independence of her own, which she divided among juvenile relatives, the milliners, and the poor, giving much the largest share to the latter. It may be imagined, therefore, that with all her little follies she was not unpopular. All her follies have, we believe, been told. Her virtues were too numerous to describe, and not sufficiently interesting to deserve description.

While we are on the subject of the Thornes, one word must be said of the house they lived in. It was not a large house, nor a fine house, nor perhaps to modern ideas a very commodious house; but by those who love the peculiar colour and peculiar ornaments of genuine Tudor architecture it was considered a perfect gem. We beg to own ourselves among the number, and therefore take this opportunity to express our surprise that so little is known by English men and women of the beauties of English architecture. The ruins of the Colosseum, the Campanile at Florence, St. Mark's, Cologne, the Bourse and Notre Dame, are with our tourists as familiar as household words; but they know nothing of the glories

of Wiltshire, Dorsetshire, and Somersetshire. Nay, we
much question whether many noted travellers, men who
have pitched their tents perhaps under Mount Sinai,
are not still ignorant that there are glories in Wiltshire,
Dorsetshire, and Somersetshire. We beg that they will
go and see.

Mr. Thorne's house was called Ullathorne Court, and
was properly so called ; for the house itself formed two
sides of a quadrangle, which was completed on the other
two sides by a wall about twenty feet high. This wall
was built of cut stone, rudely cut indeed, and now much
worn, but of a beautiful rich tawny yellow colour, the
effect of that stonecrop of minute growth, which it had
taken three centuries to produce. The top of this wall
was ornamented by huge round stone balls of the same
colour as the wall itself. Entrance into the court was
had through a pair of iron gates, so massive that no one
could comfortably open or close them, consequently they
were rarely disturbed. From the gateway two paths led
obliquely across the court ; that to the left reaching the
hall-door, which was in the corner made by the angle of
the house, and that to the right leading to the back
entrance, which was at the further end of the longer
portion of the building.

With those who are now adepts in contriving house
accommodation, it will militate much against Ullathorne
Court, that no carriage could be brought to the hall-door.
If you enter Ullathorne at all, you must do so, fair reader,
on foot, or at least in a bath-chair. No vehicle drawn
by horses ever comes within that iron gate. But this
is nothing to the next horror that will encounter you.
On entering the front door, which you do by no very
grand portal, you find yourself immediately in the dining-
room. What,—no hall ? exclaims my luxurious friend,
accustomed to all the comfortable appurtenances of
modern life. Yes, kind sir ; a noble hall, if you will but
observe it ; a true old English hall of excellent dimensions
for a country gentleman's family ; but, if you please,
no dining-parlour.

Both Mr. and Miss Thorne were proud of this peculiarity
of their dwelling, though the brother was once all but
tempted by his friends to alter it. They delighted in

the knowledge that they, like Cedric, positively dined
in their true hall, even though they so dined tête-à-tête.
But though they had never owned, they had felt and
endeavoured to remedy the discomfort of such an arrangement.   A huge screen partitioned off the front door and
a portion of the hall, and from the angle so screened off
a second door led into a passage, which ran along the
larger side of the house next to the courtyard.   Either
my reader or I must be a bad hand at topography, if it
be not clear that the great hall forms the ground-floor of
the smaller portion of the mansion, that which was to
your left as you entered the iron gate, and that it occupies
the whole of this wing of the building.   It must be equally
clear that it looks out on a trim mown lawn, through
three quadrangular windows with stone mullions, each
window divided into a larger portion at the bottom, and
a smaller portion at the top, and each portion again divided
into five by perpendicular stone supporters.   There may
be windows which give a better light than such as these,
and it may be, as my utilitarian friend observes, that the
giving of light is the desired object of a window.   I will
not argue the point with him.   Indeed I cannot.   But I
shall not the less die in the assured conviction that no
sort of description of window is capable of imparting half
so much happiness to mankind as that which had been
adopted at Ullathorne Court.   What—not an oriel ?
says Miss Diana de Midellage.   No, Miss Diana ; not even
an oriel, beautiful as is an oriel window.   It has not about
it so perfect a feeling of quiet English homely comfort.
Let oriel windows grace a college, or the half public
mansion of a potent peer ; but for the sitting room of
quiet country ladies, of ordinary homely folk, nothing
can equal the square mullioned windows of the Tudor
architects.

   The hall was hung round with family female insipidities
by Lely, and unprepossessing male Thornes in red coats
by Kneller ; each Thorne having been let into a panel
in the wainscoting, in the proper manner.   At the further
end of the room was a huge fire-place, which afforded
much ground of difference between the brother and sister.
An antiquated grate that would hold about a hundred
weight of coal, had been stuck on to the hearth, by Mr.

Thorne's father. This hearth had of course been intended
for the consumption of wood fagots, and the iron dogs
for the purpose were still standing, though half buried
in the masonry of the grate. Miss Thorne was very
anxious to revert to the dogs. The dear good old creature
was always glad to revert to anything, and had she been
systematically indulged, would doubtless in time have
reflected that fingers were made before forks, and have
reverted accordingly. But in the affairs of the fire-place,
Mr. Thorne would not revert. Country gentlemen around
him, all had comfortable grates in their dining-rooms.
He was not exactly the man to have suggested a modern
usage; but he was not so far prejudiced as to banish
those which his father had prepared for his use. Mr.
Thorne had, indeed, once suggested that with very little
contrivance the front door might have been so altered,
as to open at least into the passage; but on hearing this,
his sister Monica, such was Miss Thorne's name, had been
taken ill, and had remained so for a week. Before she
came down stairs she received a pledge from her brother
that the entrance should never be changed in her lifetime.

At the end of the hall opposite to the fire-place a door
led into the drawing-room, which was of equal size, and
lighted with precisely similar windows. But yet the
aspect of the room was very different. It was papered,
and the ceiling, which in the hall showed the old rafters,
was whitened and finished with a modern cornice. Miss
Thorne's drawing-room, or, as she always called it, withdrawing-room, was a beautiful apartment. The windows
opened on to the full extent of the lovely trim garden;
immediately before the windows were plots of flowers
in stiff, stately, stubborn little beds, each bed surrounded
by a stone coping of its own; beyond, there was a low
parapet wall, on which stood urns and images, fawns,
nymphs, satyrs, and a whole tribe of Pan's followers;
and then again, beyond that, a beautiful lawn sloped
away to a sunk fence which divided the garden from the
park. Mr. Thorne's study was at the end of the drawing
room, and beyond that were the kitchen and the offices.
Doors opened into both Miss Thorne's withdrawing-room
and Mr. Thorne's sanctum from the passage above alluded
to; which, as it came to the latter room, widened itself

so as to make space for the huge black oak stairs, which led to the upper regions.

Such was the interior of Ullathorne Court. But having thus described it, perhaps somewhat too tediously, we beg to say that it is not the interior to which we wish to call the English tourist's attention, though we advise him to lose no legitimate opportunity of becoming acquainted with it in a friendly manner. It is the outside of Ullathorne that is so lovely. Let the tourist get admission at least into the garden, and fling himself on that soft sward just opposite to the exterior angle of the house. He will there get the double frontage, and enjoy that which is so lovely—the expanse of architectural beauty without the formal dulness of one long line.

It is the colour of Ullathorne that is so remarkable. It is all of that delicious tawny hue which no stone can give, unless it has on it the vegetable richness of centuries. Strike the wall with your hand, and you will think that the stone has on it no covering, but rub it carefully, and you will find that the colour comes off upon your finger. No colourist that ever yet worked from a palette has been able to come up to this rich colouring of years crowding themselves on years.

Ullathorne is a high building for a country house, for it possesses three stories; and in each story, the windows are of the same sort as that described, though varying in size, and varying also in their lines athwart the house. Those of the ground floor are all uniform in size and position. But those above are irregular both in size and place, and this irregularity gives a bizarre and not unpicturesque appearance to the building. Along the top, on every side, runs a low parapet, which nearly hides the roof, and at the corners are more figures of fawns and satyrs.

Such is Ullathorne House. But we must say one word of the approach to it, which shall include all the description which we mean to give of the church also. The picturesque old church of St. Ewold's stands immediately opposite to the iron gates which open into the court, and is all but surrounded by the branches of the lime trees, which form the avenue leading up to the house from both sides. This avenue is magnificent, but it would lose much of its value

in the eyes of many proprietors, by the fact that the road
through it is not private property.   It is a public lane
between hedge rows, with a broad grass margin on each
side of the road, from which the lime trees spring.   Ullathorne Court, therefore, does not stand absolutely surrounded by its own grounds, though Mr. Thorne is owner
of all the adjacent land.   This, however, is the source of
very little annoyance to him.   Men, when they are
acquiring property, think much of such things, but they
who live where their ancestors have lived for years, do
not feel the misfortune.   It never occurred either to Mr.
or Miss Thorne that they were not sufficiently private,
because the world at large might, if it so wished, walk
or drive by their iron gates.   That part of the world which
availed itself of the privilege was however very small.

Such a year or two since were the Thornes of Ullathorne.
Such, we believe, are the inhabitants of many an English
country home.   May it be long before their number
diminishes.

CHAPTER XXIII

MR. ARABIN READS HIMSELF IN AT ST. EWOLD'S

ON the Sunday morning the archdeacon with his sister-
in-law and Mr. Arabin drove over to Ullathorne, as had
been arranged.   On their way thither the new vicar
declared himself to be considerably disturbed in his mind
at the idea of thus facing his parishioners for the first time.
He had, he said, been always subject to *mauvaise honte* and
an annoying degree of bashfulness, which often unfitted
him for any work of a novel description ; and now he felt
this so strongly that he feared he should acquit himself
badly in St. Ewold's reading-desk.   He knew, he said, that
those sharp little eyes of Miss Thorne would be on him, and
that they would not approve.   All this the archdeacon
greatly ridiculed.   He himself knew not, and had never
known, what it was to be shy.   He could not conceive that
Miss Thorne, surrounded as she would be by the peasants
of Ullathorne, and a few of the poorer inhabitants of the
suburbs of Barchester, could in any way affect the composure of a man well accustomed to address the learned

congregation of St. Mary's at Oxford, and he laughed accordingly at the idea of Mr. Arabin's modesty.

Thereupon Mr. Arabin commenced to subtilise. The change, he said, from St. Mary's to St. Ewold's was quite as powerful on the spirits as would be that from St. Ewold's to St. Mary's. Would not a peer who, by chance of fortune, might suddenly be driven to herd among navvies be as afraid of the jeers of his companions, as would any navvy suddenly exalted to a seat among the peers ? Whereupon the archdeacon declared with a loud laugh that he would tell Miss Thorne that her new minister had likened her to a navvy. Eleanor, however, pronounced such a conclusion to be unfair ; a comparison might be very just in its proportions which did not at all assimilate the things compared. But Mr. Arabin went on subtilising, regarding neither the archdeacon's raillery nor Eleanor's defence. A young lady, he said, would execute with most perfect self-possession a difficult piece of music in a room crowded with strangers, who would not be able to express herself in intelligible language, even on any ordinary subject and among her most intimate friends, if she were required to do so standing on a box somewhat elevated among them. It was all an affair of education, and he at forty found it difficult to educate himself anew.

Eleanor dissented on the matter of the box ; and averred she could speak very well about dresses, or babies, or legs of mutton from any box, provided it were big enough for her to stand upon without fear, even though all her friends were listening to her. The archdeacon was sure she would not be able to say a word ; but this proved nothing in favour of Mr. Arabin. Mr. Arabin said that he would try the question out with Mrs. Bold, and get her on a box some day when the rectory might be full of visitors. To this Eleanor assented, making condition that the visitors should be of their own set, and the archdeacon cogitated in his mind, whether by such a condition it was intended that Mr. Slope should be included, resolving also that, if so, the trial would certainly never take place in the rectory drawing-room at Plumstead.

And so arguing, they drove up to the iron gates of Ullathorne Court.

Mr. and Miss Thorne were standing ready dressed for

church in the hall, and greeted their clerical visitors with cordiality. The archdeacon was an old favourite. He was a clergyman of the old school, and this recommended him to the lady. He had always been an opponent of free trade as long as free trade was an open question ; and now that it was no longer so, he, being a clergyman, had not been obliged, like most of his lay Tory companions, to read his recantation. He could therefore be regarded as a supporter of the immaculate fifty-three, and was on this account a favourite with Mr. Thorne. The little bell was tinkling, and the rural population of the parish were standing about the lane, leaning on the church stile, and against the walls of the old court, anxious to get a look at their new minister as he passed from the house to the rectory. The arch- deacon's servant had already preceded them thither with the vestments.

They all went forth together ; and when the ladies passed into the church the three gentlemen tarried a moment in the lane, that Mr. Thorne might name to the vicar with some kind of one-sided introduction, the most leading among his parishioners.

' Here are our churchwardens, Mr. Arabin ; Farmer Greenacre and Mr. Stiles. Mr. Stiles has the mill as you go into Barchester ; and very good churchwardens they are.'

' Not very severe, I hope,' said Mr. Arabin : the two ecclesiastical officers touched their hats, and each made a leg in the approved rural fashion, assuring the vicar that they were very glad to have the honour of seeing him, and adding that the weather was very good for the harvest. Mr. Stiles being a man somewhat versed in town life, had an impression of his own dignity, and did not quite like leaving his pastor under the erroneous idea that he being a church- warden kept the children in order during church time. 'Twas thus he understood Mr. Arabin's allusion to his severity, and hastened to put matters right by observing that ' Sexton Clodheve looked to the younguns, and perhaps sometimes there may be a thought too much stick going on during sermon.' Mr. Arabin's bright eye twinkled as he caught that of the archdeacon ; and he smiled to himself as he observed how ignorant his officers were of the nature of their authority, and of the surveillance which it was their duty to keep even over himself.

Mr. Arabin read the lessons and preached. It was enough to put a man a little out, let him have been ever so used to pulpit reading, to see the knowing way in which the farmers cocked their ears, and set about a mental criticism as to whether their new minister did or did not fall short of the excellence of him who had lately departed from them. A mental and silent criticism it was for the existing moment, but soon to be made public among the elders of St. Ewold's over the green graves of their children and forefathers. The excellence, however, of poor old Mr. Goodenough had not been wonderful, and there were few there who did not deem that Mr. Arabin did his work sufficiently well, in spite of the slightly nervous affection which at first impeded him, and which nearly drove the archdeacon beside himself.

But the sermon was the thing to try the man. It often surprises us that very young men can muster courage to preach for the first time to a strange congregation. Men who are as yet but little more than boys, who have but just left, what indeed we may not call a school, but a seminary intended for their tuition as scholars, whose thoughts have been mostly of boating, cricketing, and wine parties, ascend a rostrum high above the heads of the submissive crowd, not that they may read God's word to those below, but that they may preach their own word for the edification of their hearers. It seems strange to us that they are not stricken dumb by the new and awful solemnity of their position. How am I, just turned twenty-three, who have never yet passed ten thoughtful days since the power of thought first came to me, how am I to instruct these greybeards, who with the weary thinking of so many years have approached so near the grave ? Can I teach them their duty ? Can I explain to them that which I so imperfectly understand, that which years of study may have made so plain to them ? Has my newly acquired privilege, as one of God's ministers, imparted to me as yet any fitness for the wonderful work of a preacher ?

It must be supposed that such ideas do occur to young clergymen, and yet they overcome, apparently with ease, this difficulty which to us appears to be all but insurmountable. We have never been subjected in the way of ordination to the power of a bishop's hands. It may be that there is in them something that sustains the spirit and banishes the natural modesty of youth. But for ourselves we must own that the deep affection which Dominie Sampson felt for his young pupils has not more endeared him to us than the bashful spirit which sent him mute and inglorious from the pulpit when he rose there with the futile attempt to preach God's gospel.

There is a rule in our church which forbids the younger order of our clergymen to perform a certain portion of the service. The absolution must be read by a minister in priest's orders. If there be no such minister present, the congregation can have the benefit of no absolution but that which each may succeed in administering to himself. The rule may be a good one, though the necessity for it hardly comes home to the general understanding. But this forbearance on the part of youth would be much more appreciated if it were extended likewise to sermons. The only danger would be that congregations would be too anxious to prevent their young clergymen from advancing themselves in the ranks of the ministry. Clergymen who could not preach would be such blessings that they would be bribed to adhere to their incompetence.

Mr. Arabin, however, had not the modesty of youth to impede him, and he succeeded with his sermon even better than with the lessons. He took for his text two verses out of the second epistle of St. John, ' Whosoever transgresseth, and abideth not in the doctrine of Christ, hath not God. He that abideth in the doctrine of Christ he hath both the Father and Son. If there come any unto you and bring not this doctrine, receive him not into your house, neither bid him God speed.' He told them that the house of theirs to which he alluded was this their church in which he now addressed them for the first time ; that their most welcome and proper manner of bidding him God speed would be their patient obedience to his teaching of the gospel ; but that he could put forward no claim to such conduct on their part unless he taught them the great Christian doctrine of works and faith combined. On this he enlarged, but not very amply, and after twenty minutes succeeded in sending his new friends home to their baked mutton and pudding well pleased with their new minister.

Then came the lunch at Ullathorne. As soon as they

were in the hall Miss Thorne took Mr. Arabin's hand, and
assured him that she received him into her house, into
the temple, she said, in which she worshipped, and bade
him God speed with all her heart. Mr. Arabin was touched,
and squeezed the spinster's hand without uttering a
word in reply. Then Mr. Thorne expressed a hope
that Mr. Arabin found the church easy to fill, and
Mr. Arabin having replied that he had no doubt he
should do so as soon as he had learnt to pitch his voice
to the building, they all sat down to the good things before
them.

Miss Thorne took special care of Mrs. Bold. Eleanor
still wore her widow's weeds, and therefore had about
her that air of grave and sad maternity which is the lot
of recent widows. This opened the soft heart of Miss
Thorne, and made her look on her young guest as though
too much could not be done for her. She heaped chicken
and ham upon her plate, and poured out for her a full
bumper of port wine. When Eleanor, who was not sorry
to get it, had drunk a little of it, Miss Thorne at once
essayed to fill it again. To this Eleanor objected, but in
vain. Miss Thorne winked and nodded and whispered,
saying that it was the proper thing and must be done,
and that she knew all about it; and so she desired Mrs.
Bold to drink it up, and not mind any body.

' It is your duty, you know, to support yourself,' she
said into the ear of the young mother; ' there's more
than yourself depending on it;' and thus she coshered
up Eleanor with cold fowl and port wine. How it is that
poor men's wives, who have no cold fowl and port wine
on which to be coshered up, nurse their children without
difficulty, whereas the wives of rich men, who eat and
drink everything that is good, cannot do so, we will for
the present leave to the doctors and the mothers to settle
between them.

And then Miss Thorne was great about teeth. Little
Johnny Bold had been troubled for the last few days with
his first incipient masticator, and with that freemasonry
which exists among ladies, Miss Thorne became aware
of the fact before Eleanor had half finished her wing.
The old lady prescribed at once a receipt which had been
much in vogue in the young days of her grandmother,

and warned Eleanor with solemn voice against the fallacies of modern medicine.

'Take his coral, my dear,' said she, 'and rub it well with carrot-juice; rub it till the juice dries on it, and then give it him to play with——'

'But he hasn't got a coral,' said Eleanor.

'Not got a coral!' said Miss Thorne, with almost angry vehemence. 'Not got a coral—how can you expect that he should cut his teeth? Have you got Daffy's Elixir?'

Eleanor explained that she had not. It had not been ordered by Mr. Rerechild, the Barchester doctor whom she employed; and then the young mother mentioned some shockingly modern succedaneum, which Mr. Rerechild's new lights had taught him to recommend.

Miss Thorne looked awfully severe. 'Take care, my dear,' said she, 'that the man knows what he's about; take care he doesn't destroy your little boy. But'—and she softened into sorrow as she said it, and spoke more in pity than in anger—'but I don't know who there is in Barchester now that you can trust. Poor dear old Doctor Bumpwell, indeed——'

'Why, Miss Thorne, he died when I was a little girl.'

'Yes, my dear, he did, and an unfortunate day it was for Barchester. As to those young men that have come up since' (Mr. Rerechild, by the bye, was quite as old as Miss Thorne herself), 'one doesn't know where they came from or who they are, or whether they know anything about their business or not.'

'I think there are very clever men in Barchester,' said Eleanor.

'Perhaps there may be; only I don't know them; and it's admitted on all sides that medical men arn't now what they used to be. They used to be talented, observing, educated men. But now any whipper-snapper out of an apothecary's shop can call himself a doctor. I believe no kind of education is now thought necessary.'

Eleanor was herself the widow of a medical man, and felt a little inclined to resent all these hard sayings. But Miss Thorne was so essentially good-natured that it was impossible to resent anything she said. She therefore sipped her wine and finished her chicken.

'At any rate, my dear, don't forget the carrot-juice, and by all means get him a coral at once. My grandmother Thorne had the best teeth in the county, and carried them to the grave with her at eighty. I have heard her say it was all the carrot-juice. She couldn't bear the Barchester doctors. Even poor old Dr. Bumpwell didn't please her.' It clearly never occurred to Miss Thorne that some fifty years ago Dr. Bumpwell was only a rising man, and therefore as much in need of character in the eyes of the then ladies of Ullathorne, as the present doctors were in her own.

The archdeacon made a very good lunch, and talked to his host about turnip-drillers and new machines for reaping; while the host, thinking it only polite to attend to a stranger, and fearing that perhaps he might not care about turnip crops on a Sunday, mooted all manner of ecclesiastical subjects.

'I never saw a heavier lot of wheat, Thorne, than you've got there in that field beyond the copse. I suppose that's guano,' said the archdeacon.

'Yes, guano. I get it from Bristol myself. You'll find you often have a tolerable congregation of Barchester people out here, Mr. Arabin. They are very fond of St. Ewold's, particularly of an afternoon, when the weather is not too hot for the walk.'

'I am under an obligation to them for staying away to-day, at any rate,' said the vicar. 'The congregation can never be too small for a maiden sermon.'

'I got a ton and a half at Bradley's in High Street,' said the archdeacon, 'and it was a complete take in. I don't believe there was five hundred-weight of guano in it.'

'That Bradley never has anything good,' said Miss Thorne, who had just caught the name during her whisperings with Eleanor. 'And such a nice shop as there used to be in that very house before he came. Wilfred, don't you remember what good things old Ambleoff used to have?'

'There have been three men since Ambleoff's time,' said the archdeacon, 'and each as bad as the other. But who gets it for you at Bristol, Thorne?'

'I ran up myself this year and bought it out of the

ship. I am afraid as the evenings get shorter, Mr. Arabin,
you'll find the reading desk too dark. I must send a
fellow with an axe and make him lop off some of those
branches.'

Mr. Arabin declared that the morning light at any rate
was perfect, and deprecated any interference with the
lime trees. And then they took a stroll out among the
trim parterres, and Mr. Arabin explained to Mrs. Bold
the difference between a naiad and a dryad, and dilated
on vases and the shapes of urns. Miss Thorne busied
herself among her pansies ; and her brother, finding it
quite impracticable to give anything of a peculiarly
Sunday tone to the conversation, abandoned the attempt,
and had it out with the archdeacon about the Bristol
guano.

At three o'clock they again went into church ; and now
Mr. Arabin read the service and the archdeacon preached.
Nearly the same congregation was present, with some
adventurous pedestrians from the city, who had not
thought the heat of the mid-day August sun too great to
deter them. The archdeacon took his text from the
Epistle of Philemon. ' I beseech thee for my son Onesimus,
whom I have begotten in my bonds.' From such a text
it may be imagined the kind of sermon which Dr. Grantly
preached, and on the whole it was neither dull, nor bad,
nor out of place.

He told them that it had become his duty to look about
for a pastor for them, to supply the place of one who had
been long among them ; and that in this manner he
regarded as a son him whom he had selected, as St. Paul
had regarded the young disciple whom he sent forth. Then
he took a little merit to himself for having studiously
provided the best man he could without reference to
patronage or favour ; but he did not say that the best
man according to his views was he who was best able to
subdue Mr. Slope, and make that gentleman's situation
in Barchester too hot to be comfortable. As to the bonds,
they had consisted in the exceeding struggle which he had
made to get a good clergyman for them. He deprecated
any comparison between himself and St. Paul, but said
that he was entitled to beseech them for their good will
towards Mr. Arabin, in the same manner that the apostle

had besought Philemon and his household with regard
to Onesimus.

The archdeacon's sermon, text, blessing and all, was
concluded within the half hour. Then they shook hands
with their Ullathorne friends, and returned to Plumstead.
'Twas thus that Mr. Arabin read himself in at St. Ewold's.

CHAPTER XXIV

MR. SLOPE MANAGES MATTERS VERY CLEVERLY AT PUDDINGDALE

THE next two weeks passed pleasantly enough at
Plumstead. The whole party there assembled seemed
to get on well together. Eleanor made the house agreeable,
and the archdeacon and Mrs. Grantly seemed to have
forgotten her iniquity as regarded Mr. Slope. Mr. Harding
had his violoncello, and played to them while his daughters
accompanied him. Johnny Bold, by the help either of
Mr. Rerechild or else by that of his coral and carrot-juice,
got through his teething troubles. There had been
gaieties too of all sorts. They had dined at Ullathorne,
and the Thornes had dined at the Rectory. Eleanor had
been duly put to stand on her box, and in that position
had found herself quite unable to express her opinion on
the merits of flounces, such having been the subject given
to try her elocution. Mr. Arabin had of course been much
in his own parish, looking to the doings at his vicarage,
calling on his parishioners, and taking· on himself the
duties of his new calling. But still he had been every
evening at Plumstead, and Mrs. Grantly was partly willing
to agree with her husband that he was a pleasant inmate
in a house.

They had also been at a dinner party at Dr. Stanhope's,
of which Mr. Arabin had made one. He also, moth-like,
burnt his wings in the flames of the signora's candle. Mrs.
Bold, too, had been there, and had felt somewhat displeased with the taste, want of taste she called it, shown
by Mr. Arabin in paying so much attention to Madame
Neroni. It was as infallible that Madeline should displease
and irritate the women, as that she should charm and

captivate the men. The one result followed naturally
on the other. It was quite true that Mr. Arabin had been
charmed. He thought her a very clever and a very
handsome woman; he thought also that her peculiar
affliction entitled her to the sympathy of all. He had
never, he said, met so much suffering joined to such
perfect beauty and so clear a mind. 'Twas thus he spoke
of the signora coming home in the archdeacon's carriage;
and Eleanor by no means liked to hear the praise. It was,
however, exceedingly unjust of her to be angry with
Mr. Arabin, as she had herself spent a very pleasant
evening with Bertie Stanhope, who had taken her down
to dinner, and had not left her side for one moment after
the gentlemen came out of the dining-room. It was unfair
that she should amuse herself with Bertie and yet begrudge
her new friend his license of amusing himself with Bertie's
sister. And yet she did so. She was half angry with him
in the carriage, and said something about meretricious
manners. Mr. Arabin did not understand the ways of
women very well, or else he might have flattered himself
that Eleanor was in love with him.

But Eleanor was not in love with him. How many
shades there are between love and indifference, and how
little the graduated scale is understood! She had now
been nearly three weeks in the same house with Mr. Arabin,
and had received much of his attention, and listened daily
to his conversation. He had usually devoted at least
some portion of his evening to her exclusively. At Dr.
Stanhope's he had devoted himself exclusively to another.
It does not require that a woman should be in love to be
irritated at this; it does not require that she should even
acknowledge to herself that it is unpleasant to her.
Eleanor had no such self-knowledge. She thought in her
own heart that it was only on Mr. Arabin's account that
she regretted that he could condescend to be amused by
the signora. 'I thought he had more mind,' she said to
herself, as she sat watching her baby's cradle on her return
from the party. 'After all, I believe Mr. Stanhope is the
pleasanter man of the two.' Alas for the memory of poor
John Bold! Eleanor was not in love with Bertie Stanhope,
nor was she in love with Mr. Arabin. But her devotion
to her late husband was fast fading, when she could revolve

in her mind, over the cradle of his infant, the faults and failings of other aspirants to her favour.

Will any one blame my heroine for this ? Let him or her rather thank God for all His goodness,—for His mercy endureth for ever.

Eleanor, in truth, was not in love ; neither was Mr. Arabin. Neither indeed was Bertie Stanhope, though he had already found occasion to say nearly as much as that he was. The widow's cap had prevented him from making a positive declaration, when otherwise he would have considered himself entitled to do so on a third or fourth interview. It was, after all, but a small cap now, and had but little of the weeping-willow left in its construction. It is singular how these emblems of grief fade away by unseen gradations. Each pretends to be the counterpart of the forerunner, and yet the last little bit of crimped white crape that sits so jauntily on the back of the head, is as dissimilar to the first huge mountain of woe which disfigured the face of the weeper, as the state of the Hindoo is to the jointure of the English dowager.

But let it be clearly understood that Eleanor was in love with no one, and that no one was in love with Eleanor. Under these circumstances her anger against Mr. Arabin did not last long, and before two days were over they were both as good friends as ever. She could not but like him, for every hour spent in his company was spent pleasantly. And yet she could not quite like him, for there was always apparent in his conversation a certain feeling on his part that he hardly thought it worth his while to be in earnest. It was almost as though he were playing with a child. She knew well enough that he was in truth a sober thoughtful man, who in some matters and on some occasions could endure an agony of earnestness. And yet to her he was always gently playful. Could she have seen his brow once clouded she might have learnt to love him.

So things went on at Plumstead, and on the whole not unpleasantly, till a huge storm darkened the horizon, and came down upon the inhabitants of the rectory with all the fury of a water-spout. It was astonishing how in a few minutes the whole face of the heavens was changed. The party broke up from breakfast in perfect harmony ; but fierce passions had arisen before the evening, which did not admit of their sitting at the same board for dinner. To explain this, it will be necessary to go back a little.

It will be remembered that the bishop expressed to Mr. Slope in his dressing-room, his determination that Mr. Quiverful should be confirmed in his appointment to the hospital, and that his lordship requested Mr. Slope to communicate this decision to the archdeacon. It will also be remembered that the archdeacon had indignantly declined seeing Mr. Slope, and had, instead, written a strong letter to the bishop, in which he all but demanded the situation of warden for Mr. Harding. To this letter the archdeacon received an immediate formal reply from Mr. Slope, in which it was stated, that the bishop had received and would give his best consideration to the archdeacon's letter.

The archdeacon felt himself somewhat checkmated by this reply. What could he do with a man who would neither see him, nor argue with him by letter, and who had undoubtedly the power of appointing any clergyman he pleased ? He had consulted with Mr. Arabin, who had suggested the propriety of calling in the aid of the master of Lazarus. ' If,' said he, ' you and Dr. Gwynne formally declare your intention of waiting upon the bishop, the bishop will not dare to refuse to see you ; and if two such men as you are see him together, you will probably not leave him without carrying your point.'

The archdeacon did not quite like admitting the necessity of his being backed by the master of Lazarus before he could obtain admission into the episcopal palace of Barchester ; but still he felt that the advice was good, and he resolved to take it. He wrote again to the bishop, expressing a hope that nothing further would be done in the matter of the hospital, till the consideration promised by his lordship had been given, and then sent off a warm appeal to his friend the master, imploring him to come to Plumstead and assist in driving the bishop into compliance. The master had rejoined, raising some difficulty, but not declining ; and the archdeacon had again pressed his point, insisting on the necessity for immediate action. Dr. Gwynne unfortunately had the gout, and could therefore name no immediate day, but still agreed to come,

if it should be finally found necessary. So the matter
stood, as regarded the party at Plumstead.

But Mr. Harding had another friend fighting his battle
for him, quite as powerful as the master of Lazarus, and
this was Mr. Slope. Though the bishop had so pertina-
ciously insisted on giving way to his wife in the matter of
the hospital, Mr. Slope did not think it necessary to
abandon his object. He had, he thought, daily more and
more reason to imagine that the widow would receive
his overtures favourably, and he could not but feel that
Mr. Harding at the hospital, and placed there by his
means, would be more likely to receive him as a son-in-law,
than Mr. Harding growling in opposition and disappointment under the archdeacon's wing at Plumstead. Moreover, to give Mr. Slope due credit, he was actuated by
greater motives even than these. He wanted a wife, and
he wanted money, but he wanted power more than either.
He had fully realised the fact that he must come to blows
with Mrs. Proudie. He had no desire to remain in
Barchester as her chaplain. Sooner than do so, he would
risk the loss of his whole connection with the diocese.
What ! was he to feel within him the possession of no
ordinary talents ; was he to know himself to be courageous,
firm, and, in matters where his conscience did not interfere,
unscrupulous ; and yet be contented to be the working
factotum of a woman-prelate ? Mr. Slope had higher
ideas of his own destiny. Either he or Mrs. Proudie must
go to the wall ; and now had come the time when he would
try which it should be.

The bishop had declared that Mr. Quiverful should
be the new warden. As Mr. Slope went down stairs
prepared to see the archdeacon if necessary, but fully
satisfied that no such necessity would arise, he declared
to himself that Mr. Harding should be warden. With
the object of carrying this point, he rode over to Puddingdale, and had a further interview with the worthy expectant of clerical good things. Mr. Quiverful was on
the whole a worthy man. The impossible task of bringing
up as ladies and gentlemen fourteen children on an income
which was insufficient to give them with decency the
common necessaries of life, had had an effect upon him
not beneficial either to his spirit, or his keen sense of

honour. Who can boast that he would have supported such a burden with a different result ? Mr. Quiverful was an honest, pains-taking, drudging man ; anxious, indeed, for bread and meat, anxious for means to quiet his butcher and cover with returning smiles the now sour countenance of the baker's wife, but anxious also to be right with his own conscience. He was not careful, as another might be who sat on an easier worldly seat, to stand well with those around him, to shun a breath which might sully his name, or a rumour which might affect his honour. He could not afford such niceties of conduct, such moral luxuries. It must suffice for him to be ordinarily honest according to the ordinary honesty of the world's ways, and to let men's tongues wag as they would.

He had felt that his brother clergymen, men whom he had known for the last twenty years, looked coldly on him from the first moment that he had shown himself willing to sit at the feet of Mr. Slope ; he had seen that their looks grew colder still, when it became bruited about that he was to be the bishop's new warden at Hiram's hospital. This was painful enough ; but it was the cross which he was doomed to bear. He thought of his wife, whose last new silk dress was six years in wear. He thought of all his young flock, whom he could hardly take to church with him on Sundays, for there were not decent shoes and stockings for them all to wear. He thought of the well-worn sleeves of his own black coat, and of the stern face of the draper from whom he would fain ask for cloth to make another, did he not know that the credit would be refused him. Then he thought of the comfortable house in Barchester, of the comfortable income, of his boys sent to school, of his girls with books in their hands instead of darning needles, of his wife's face again covered with smiles, and of his daily board again covered with plenty. He thought of these things ; and do thou also, reader, think of them, and then wonder, if thou canst, that Mr. Slope had appeared to him to possess all those good gifts which could grace a bishop's chaplain. 'How beautiful upon the mountains are the feet of him that bringeth good tidings.'

Why, moreover, should the Barchester clergy have

looked coldly on Mr. Quiverful ? Had they not all shown
that they regarded with complacency the loaves and
fishes of their mother church ? Had they not all, by some
hook or crook, done better for themselves than he had
done ? They were not burdened as he was burdened.
Dr. Grantly had five children, and nearly as many thousands a year on which to feed them. It was very well for
him to turn up his nose at a new bishop who could do
nothing for him, and a chaplain who was beneath his
notice ; but it was cruel in a man so circumstanced to
set the world against the father of fourteen children
because he was anxious to obtain for them an honourable
support ! He, Mr. Quiverful, had not asked for the
wardenship ; he had not even accepted it till he had
been assured that Mr. Harding had refused it. How hard
then that he should be blamed for doing that which not to
have done would have argued a most insane imprudence ?

Thus in this matter of the hospital poor Mr. Quiverful
had his trials ; and he had also his consolations. On the
whole the consolations were the more vivid of the two.
The stern draper heard of the coming promotion, and
the wealth of his warehouse was at Mr. Quiverful's disposal.
Coming events cast their shadows before, and the coming
event of Mr. Quiverful's transference to Barchester produced a delicious shadow in the shape of a new outfit for
Mrs. Quiverful and her three elder daughters. Such consolations come home to the heart of a man, and quite
home to the heart of a woman. Whatever the husband
might feel, the wife cared nothing for frowns of dean,
archdeacon, or prebendary. To her the outsides and
insides of her husband and fourteen children were everything. In her bosom every other ambition had been
swallowed up in that maternal ambition of seeing them
and him and herself duly clad and properly fed. It had
come to that with her that life had now no other purpose.
She recked nothing of the imaginary rights of others.
She had no patience with her husband when he declared
to her that he could not accept the hospital unless he
knew that Mr. Harding had refused it. Her husband had
no right to be Quixotic at the expense of fourteen children.
The narrow escape of throwing away his good fortune
which her lord had had, almost paralysed her. Now,

indeed, they had received the full promise not only from
Mr. Slope, but also from Mrs. Proudie. Now, indeed,
they might reckon with safety on their good fortune.
But what if all had been lost ? What if her fourteen
bairns had been resteeped to the hips in poverty by the
morbid sentimentality of their father ? Mrs. Quiverful
was just at present a happy woman, but yet it nearly
took her breath away when she thought of the risk they
had run.

' I don't know what your father means when he talks
so much of what is due to Mr. Harding,' she said to her
eldest daughter. ' Does he think that Mr. Harding would
give him 450*l.* a year out of fine feeling ? And what
signifies it whom he offends, as long as he gets the place ?
He does not expect anything better. It passes me to
think how your father can be so soft, while everybody
around him is so griping.'

Thus, while the outer world was accusing Mr. Quiverful
of rapacity for promotion and of disregard to his honour,
the inner world of his own household was falling foul of
him, with equal vehemence, for his willingness to sacrifice
their interest to a false feeling of sentimental pride. It
is astonishing how much difference the point of view
makes in the aspect of all that we look at !

Such were the feelings of the different members of the
family at Puddingdale on the occasion of Mr. Slope's
second visit. Mrs. Quiverful, as soon as she saw his horse
coming up the avenue from the vicarage gate, hastily
packed up her huge basket of needlework, and hurried
herself and her daughter out of the room in which she
was sitting with her husband. ' It's Mr. Slope,' she said.
' He's come to settle with you about the hospital. I do
hope we shall now be able to move at once.' And she
hastened to bid the maid of all work go to the door, so
that the welcome great man might not be kept waiting.

Mr. Slope thus found Mr. Quiverful alone. Mrs. Quiverful went off to her kitchen and back settlements with
anxious beating heart, almost dreading that there might
be some slip between the cup of her happiness and the
lip of her fruition, but yet comforting herself with the
reflection that after what had taken place, any such slip
could hardly be possible.

Mr. Slope was all smiles as he shook his brother clergyman's hand, and said that he had ridden over because he
thought it right at once to put Mr. Quiverful in possession
of the facts of the matter regarding the wardenship of the
hospital. As he spoke, the poor expectant husband and
father saw at a glance that his brilliant hopes were to
be dashed to the ground, and that his visitor was now
there for the purpose of unsaying what on his former visit
he had said. There was something in the tone of the
voice, something in the glance of the eye, which told the
tale. Mr. Quiverful knew it all at once. He maintained
his self-possession, however, smiled with a slight unmean-
ing smile, and merely said that he was obliged to Mr. Slope
for the trouble he was taking.

' It has been a troublesome matter from first to last,'
said Mr. Slope ; ' and the bishop has hardly known how
to act. Between ourselves—but mind this of course must
go no further, Mr. Quiverful.'

Mr. Quiverful said that of course it should not. ' The
truth is, that poor Mr. Harding has hardly known his
own mind. You remember our last conversation, no
doubt.'

Mr. Quiverful assured him that he remembered it very
well indeed.

' You will remember that I told you that Mr. Harding
had refused to return to the hospital.'

Mr. Quiverful declared that nothing could be more
distinct on his memory.

' And acting on this refusal, I suggested that you should
take the hospital,' continued Mr. Slope.

' I understood you to say that the bishop had authorised
you to offer it to me.'

' Did I ? did I go so far as that ? Well, perhaps it may
be, that in my anxiety in your behalf I did commit myself
further than I should have done. So far as my own
memory serves me, I don't think I did go quite so far as
that. But I own I was very anxious that you should get
it ; and I may have said more than was quite prudent.'

' But,' said Mr. Quiverful, in his deep anxiety to prove
his case, ' my wife received as distinct a promise from
Mrs. Proudie as one human being could give to another.'

Mr. Slope smiled, and gently shook his head. He meant

that smile for a pleasant smile, but it was diabolical in
the eyes of the man he was speaking to. ' Mrs. Proudie ! '
he said. ' If we are to go to what passes between the
ladies in these matters, we shall really be in a nest of
troubles from which we shall never extricate ourselves.
Mrs. Proudie is a most excellent lady, kind-hearted,
charitable, pious, and in every way estimable. But,
my dear Mr. Quiverful, the patronage of the diocese is
not in her hands.'

Mr. Quiverful for a moment sat panic-stricken and
silent. ' Am I to understand, then, that I have received
no promise ? ' he said, as soon as he had sufficiently
collected his thoughts.

' If you will allow me, I will tell you exactly how the
matter rests. You certainly did receive a promise con-
ditional on Mr. Harding's refusal. I am sure you will do
me the justice to remember that you yourself declared
that you could accept the appointment on no other
condition than the knowledge that Mr. Harding had
declined it.'

' Yes,' said Mr. Quiverful ; ' I did say that, certainly.'

' Well ; it now appears that he did not refuse it.'

' But surely you told me, and repeated it more than
once, that he had done so in your own hearing.'

' So I understood him. But it seems I was in error.
But don't for a moment, Mr. Quiverful, suppose that
I mean to throw you over. No. Having held out my
hand to a man in your position, with your large family
and pressing claims, I am not now going to draw it back
again. I only want you to act with me fairly and honestly.'

' Whatever I do, I shall endeavour at any rate to act
fairly,' said the poor man, feeling that he had to fall back
for support on the spirit of martyrdom within him.

' I am sure you will,' said the other. ' I am sure you
have no wish to obtain possession of an income which
belongs by all right to another. No man knows better
than you do Mr. Harding's history, or can better appreciate
his character. Mr. Harding is very desirous of returning
to his old position, and the bishop feels that he is at the
present moment somewhat hampered, though of course
he is not bound, by the conversation which took place
on the matter between you and me.'

'Well,' said Mr. Quiverful, dreadfully doubtful as to what his conduct under such circumstances should be, and fruitlessly striving to harden his nerves with some of that instinct of self-preservation which made his wife so bold.

'The wardenship of this little hospital is not the only thing in the bishop's gift, Mr. Quiverful, nor is it by many degrees the best. And his lordship is not the man to forget any one whom he has once marked with approval. If you would allow me to advise you as a friend——'

'Indeed I shall be most grateful to you,' said the poor vicar of Puddingdale——

'I should advise you to withdraw from any opposition to Mr. Harding's claims. If you persist in your demand, I do not think you will ultimately succeed. Mr. Harding has all but a positive right to the place. But if you will allow me to inform the bishop that you decline to stand in Mr. Harding's way, I think I may promise you—though, by the bye, it must not be taken as a formal promise—that the bishop will not allow you to be a poorer man than you would have been had you become warden.'

Mr. Quiverful sat in his arm chair silent, gazing at vacancy. What was he to say? All this that came from Mr. Slope was so true. Mr. Harding had a right to the hospital. The bishop had a great many good things to give away. Both the bishop and Mr. Slope would be excellent friends and terrible enemies to a man in his position. And then he had no proof of any promise; he could not force the bishop to appoint him.

'Well, Mr. Quiverful, what do you say about it?'

'Oh, of course, whatever you think fit, Mr. Slope. It's a great disappointment, a very great disappointment. I won't deny that I am a very poor man, Mr. Slope.'

'In the end, Mr. Quiverful, you will find that it will have been better for you.'

The interview ended in Mr. Slope receiving a full renunciation from Mr. Quiverful of any claim he might have to the appointment in question. It was only given verbally and without witnesses; but then the original promise was made in the same way.

Mr. Slope again assured him that he should not be forgotten, and then rode back to Barchester, satisfied that he would now be able to mould the bishop to his wishes.

CHAPTER XXV

FOURTEEN ARGUMENTS IN FAVOUR OF MR. QUIVERFUL'S CLAIMS

WE have most of us heard of the terrible anger of a lioness when, surrounded by her cubs, she guards her prey. Few of us wish to disturb the mother of a litter of puppies when mouthing a bone in the midst of her young family. Medea and her children are familiar to us, and so is the grief of Constance. Mrs. Quiverful, when she first heard from her husband the news which he had to impart, felt within her bosom all the rage of a lioness, the rapacity of the hound, the fury of the tragic queen, and the deep despair of the bereaved mother.

Doubting, but yet hardly fearing, what might have been the tenor of Mr. Slope's discourse, she rushed back to her husband as soon as the front door was closed behind the visitor. It was well for Mr. Slope that he so escaped,— the anger of such a woman, at such a moment, would have cowed even him. As a general rule, it is highly desirable that ladies should keep their temper; a woman when she storms always makes herself ugly, and usually ridiculous also. There is nothing so odious to man as a virago. Though Theseus loved an Amazon, he showed his love but roughly; and from the time of Theseus downward, no man ever wished to have his wife remarkable rather for forward prowess than retiring gentleness. A low voice ' is an excellent thing in woman.'

Such may be laid down as a very general rule; and few women should allow themselves to deviate from it, and then only on rare occasions. But if there be a time when a woman may let her hair to the winds, when she may loose her arms, and scream out trumpet-tongued to the ears of men, it is when nature calls out within her not for her own wants, but for the wants of those whom her womb has borne, whom her breasts have suckled, for those who look to her for their daily bread as naturally as man looks to his Creator.

There was nothing poetic in the nature of Mrs. Quiverful. She was neither a Medea nor a Constance. When angry, she spoke out her anger in plain words, and in a tone which might have been modulated with advantage; but she did so, at any rate, without affectation. Now, without knowing it, she rose to a tragic vein.

'Well, my dear; we are not to have it.' Such were the words with which her ears were greeted when she entered the parlour, still hot from the kitchen fire. And the face of her husband spoke even more plainly than his words:—

> E'en such a man, so faint, so spiritless,
> So dull, so dead in look, so woe-begone,
> Drew Priam's curtain in the dead of night.

'What!' said she,—and Mrs. Siddons could not have put more passion into a single syllable,—'What! not have it? who says so?' And she sat opposite to her husband, with her elbows on the table, her hands clasped together, and her coarse, solid, but once handsome face stretched over it towards him.

She sat as silent as death while he told his story, and very dreadful to him her silence was. He told it very lamely and badly, but still in such a manner that she soon understood the whole of it.

'And so you have resigned it?' said she.

'I have had no opportunity of accepting it,' he replied. 'I had no witnesses to Mr. Slope's offer, even if that offer would bind the bishop. It was better for me, on the whole, to keep on good terms with such men than to fight for what I should never get!'

'Witnesses!' she screamed, rising quickly to her feet, and walking up and down the room. 'Do clergymen require witnesses to their words? He made the promise in the bishop's name, and if it is to be broken I'll know the reason why. Did he not positively say that the bishop had sent him to offer you the place?'

'He did, my dear. But that is now nothing to the purpose.'

'It is everything to the purpose, Mr. Quiverful. Witnesses indeed! and then to talk of *your* honour being questioned, because you wish to provide for fourteen children. It is everything to the purpose; and so they shall know, if I scream it into their ears from the town cross of Barchester.'

' You rorget, Letitia, that the bishop has so many things
in his gift. We must wait a little longer. That is all.'

' Wait! Shall we feed the children by waiting? Will
waiting put George, and Tom, and Sam, out into the
world? Will it enable my poor girls to give up some of
their drudgery? Will waiting make Bessy and Jane fit
even to be governesses? Will waiting pay for the things
we got in Barchester last week?'

' It is all we can do, my dear. The disappointment
is as much to me as to you; and yet, God knows, I feel
it more for your sake than my own.'

Mrs. Quiverful was looking full into her husband's
face, and saw a small hot tear appear on each of those
furrowed cheeks. This was too much for her woman's
heart. He also had risen, and was standing with his back
to the empty grate. She rushed towards him, and, seizing
him in her arms, sobbed aloud upon his bosom.

' You are too good, too soft, too yielding,' she said
at last. ' These men, when they want you, they use you
like a cat's-paw; and when they want you no longer,
they throw you aside like an old shoe. This is twice they
have treated you so.'

' In one way this will be all for the better,' argued he.
' It will make the bishop feel that he is bound to do something for me.'

' At any rate, he shall hear of it,' said the lady, again
reverting to her more angry mood. ' At any rate he shall
hear of it, and that loudly; and so shall she. She little
knows Letitia Quiverful, if she thinks I will sit down
quietly with the loss after all that passed between us at
the palace. If there's any feeling within her, I'll make
her ashamed of herself,'—and she paced the room again,
stamping the floor as she went with her fat heavy foot.
' Good heavens! what a heart she must have within her
to treat in such a way as this the father of fourteen
unprovided children!'

Mr. Quiverful proceeded to explain that he didn't think
that Mrs. Proudie had had anything to do with it.

' Don't tell me,' said Mrs. Quiverful; ' I know more
about it than that. Doesn't all the world know that
Mrs. Proudie is bishop of Barchester, and that Mr. Slope
is merely her creature? Wasn't it she that made me the

promise, just as though the thing was in her own particular
gift ? I tell you, it was that woman who sent him over
here to-day, because, for some reason of her own, she
wants to go back from her word.'

' My dear, you're wrong—'

' Now, Q., don't be so soft,' she continued. ' Take my
word for it, the bishop knows no more about it than
Jemima does.' Jemima was the two-year-old. ' And if
you'll take my advice, you'll lose no time in going over
and seeing him yourself.'

Soft, however, as Mr. Quiverful might be, he would
not allow himself to be talked out of his opinion on this
occasion ; and proceeded with much minuteness to
explain to his wife the tone in which Mr. Slope had spoken
of Mrs. Proudie's interference in diocesan matters. As
he did so, a new idea gradually instilled itself into the
matron's head, and a new course of conduct presented
itself to her judgment. What if, after all, Mrs. Proudie
knew nothing of this visit of Mr. Slope's ? In that case,
might it not be possible that that lady would still be
staunch to her in this matter, still stand her friend, and,
perhaps, possibly carry her through in opposition to Mr.
Slope ? Mrs. Quiverful said nothing as this vague hope
occurred to her, but listened with more than ordinary
patience to what her husband had to say. While he was
still explaining that in all probability the world was
wrong in its estimation of Mrs. Proudie's power and
authority, she had fully made up her mind as to her course
of action. She did not, however, proclaim her intention.
She shook her head ominously as he continued his narra-
tion ; and when he had completed she rose to go, merely
observing that it was cruel, cruel treatment. She then
asked him if he would mind waiting for a late dinner
instead of dining at their usual hour of three, and, having
received from him a concession on this point, she proceeded to carry her purpose into execution.

She determined that she would at once go to the palace ;
that she would do so, if possible, before Mrs. Proudie
could have had an interview with Mr. Slope ; and that
she would be either submissive piteous and pathetic, or
else indignant violent and exacting, according to the
manner in which she was received.

She was quite confident in her own power. Strengthened
as she was by the pressing wants of fourteen children,
she felt that she could make her way through legions of
episcopal servants, and force herself, if need be, into the
presence of the lady who had so wronged her. She had
no shame about it, no *mauvaise honte*, no dread of archdeacons. She would, as she declared to her husband,
make her wail heard in the market-place if she did not
get redress and justice. It might be very well for an
unmarried young curate to be shamefaced in such matters ;
it might be all right that a snug rector, really in want of
nothing, but still looking for better preferment, should
carry on his affairs decently under the rose. But Mrs.
Quiverful, with fourteen children, had given over being
shamefaced, and, in some things, had given over being
decent. If it were intended that she should be ill used in
the manner proposed by Mr. Slope, it should not be done
under the rose. All the world should know of it.

In her present mood, Mrs. Quiverful was not over
careful about her attire. She tied her bonnet under her
chin, threw her shawl over her shoulders, armed herself
with the old family cotton umbrella, and started for
Barchester. A journey to the palace was not quite so
easy a thing for Mrs. Quiverful as for our friend at Plumstead. Plumstead is nine miles from Barchester, and
Puddingdale is but four. But the archdeacon could
order round his brougham, and his high-trotting fast bay
gelding would take him into the city within the hour.
There was no brougham in the coach-house of Puddingdale
Vicarage, no bay horse in the stables. There was no
method of locomotion for its inhabitants but that which
nature has assigned to man.

Mrs. Quiverful was a broad heavy woman, not young,
nor given to walking. In her kitchen, and in the family
dormitories, she was active enough ; but her pace and
gait were not adapted for the road. A walk into Barchester
and back in the middle of an August day would be to
her a terrible task, if not altogether impracticable. There
was living in the parish, about half a mile from the
vicarage on the road to the city, a decent, kindly farmer,
well to do as regards this world, and so far mindful of the
next that he attended his parish church with decent

regularity. To him Mrs. Quiverful had before now appealed in some of her more pressing family troubles, and had not appealed in vain. At his door she now presented herself, and, having explained to his wife that most urgent business required her to go at once to Barchester, begged that Farmer Subsoil would take her thither in his tax-cart. The farmer did not reject her plan ; and, as soon as Prince could be got into his collar, they started on their journey.

Mrs. Quiverful did not mention the purpose of her business, nor did the farmer alloy his kindness by any unseemly questions. She merely begged to be put down at the bridge going into the city, and to be taken up again at the same place in the course of two hours. The farmer promised to be punctual to his appointment, and the lady, supported by her umbrella, took the short cut to the close, and in a few minutes was at the bishop's door.

Hitherto she had felt no dread with regard to the coming interview. She had felt nothing but an indignant longing to pour forth her claims, and declare her wrongs, if those claims were not fully admitted. But now the difficulty of her situation touched her a little. She had been at the palace once before, but then she went to give grateful thanks. Those who have thanks to return for favours received find easy admittance to the halls of the great. Such is not always the case with men, or even with women, who have favours to beg. Still less easy is access for those who demand the fulfilment of promises already made.

Mrs. Quiverful had not been slow to learn the ways of the world. She knew all this, and she knew also that her cotton umbrella and all but ragged shawl would not command respect in the eyes of the palatial servants. If she were too humble, she knew well that she would never succeed. To overcome by imperious overbearing with such a shawl as hers upon her shoulders, and such a bonnet on her head, would have required a personal bearing very superior to that with which nature had endowed her. Of this also Mrs. Quiverful was aware. She must make it known that she was the wife of a gentleman and a clergyman, and must yet condescend to conciliate.

The poor lady knew but one way to overcome these difficulties at the very threshold of her enterprise, and to

this she resorted. Low as were the domestic funds at
Puddingdale, she still retained possession of half-a-crown,
and this she sacrificed to the avarice of Mrs. Proudie's
metropolitan sesquipedalian serving-man. She was, she
said, Mrs. Quiverful of Puddingdale, the wife of the Rev.
Mr. Quiverful. She wished to see Mrs. Proudie. It was
indeed quite indispensable that she should see Mrs.
Proudie. James Fitzplush looked worse than dubious,
did not know whether his lady were out, or engaged, or in
her bed-room; thought it most probable she was subject
to one of these or to some other cause that would make
her invisible; but Mrs. Quiverful could sit down in the
waiting-room while inquiry was being made of Mrs.
Proudie's maid.

'Look here, my man,' said Mrs. Quiverful; 'I must
see her;' and she put her card and half-a-crown—think
of it, my reader, think of it; her last half-crown—into
the man's hand, and sat herself down on a chair in the
waiting-room.

Whether the bribe carried the day, or whether the
bishop's wife really chose to see the vicar's wife, it boots
not now to inquire. The man returned, and begging
Mrs. Quiverful to follow him, ushered her into the presence
of the mistress of the diocese.

Mrs. Quiverful at once saw that her patroness was in
a smiling humour. Triumph sat throned upon her brow,
and all the joys of dominion hovered about her curls.
Her lord had that morning contested with her a great
point. He had received an invitation to spend a couple
of days with the archbishop. His soul longed for the
gratification. Not a word, however, in his grace's note
alluded to the fact of his being a married man; and, if
he went at all, he must go alone. This necessity would
have presented no insurmountable bar to the visit, or
have militated much against the pleasure, had he been
able to go without any reference to Mrs. Proudie. But
this he could not do. He could not order his portmanteau
to be packed, and start with his own man, merely telling
the lady of his heart that he would probably be back on
Saturday. There are men—may we not rather say
monsters?—who do such things; and there are wives—
may we not rather say slaves?—who put up with such

usage. But Doctor and Mrs. Proudie were not among the number.

The bishop, with some beating about the bush, made the lady understand that he very much wished to go. The lady, without any beating about the bush, made the bishop understand that she wouldn't hear of it. It would be useless here to repeat the arguments that were used on each side, and needless to record the result. Those who are married will understand very well how the battle was lost and won ; and those who are single will never understand it till they learn the lesson which experience alone can give. When Mrs. Quiverful was shown into Mrs. Proudie's room, that lady had only returned a few minutes from her lord. But before she left him she had seen the answer to the archbishop's note written and sealed. No wonder that her face was wreathed with smiles as she received Mrs. Quiverful.

She instantly spoke of the subject which was so near the heart of her visitor. ' Well, Mrs. Quiverful,' said she, ' is it decided yet when you are to move into Barchester ? '

' That woman,' as she had an hour or two since been called, became instantly re-endowed with all the graces that can adorn a bishop's wife. Mrs. Quiverful immediately saw that her business was to be piteous, and that nothing was to be gained by indignation ; nothing, indeed, unless she could be indignant in company with her patroness.

' Oh, Mrs. Proudie,' she began, ' I fear we are not to move to Barchester at all.'

' Why not ? ' said that lady sharply, dropping at a moment's notice her smiles and condescension, and turning with her sharp quick way to business which she saw at a glance was important.

And then Mrs. Quiverful told her tale. As she progressed in the history of her wrongs she perceived that the heavier she leant upon Mr. Slope the blacker became Mrs. Proudie's brow, but that such blackness was not injurious to her own cause. When Mr. Slope was at Puddingdale vicarage that morning she had regarded him as the creature of the lady-bishop ; now she perceived that they were enemies. She admitted her mistake to herself without any pain or humiliation. She had but one feeling, and that was confined to her family. She cared little how she twisted and turned among these new comers at the bishop's palace so long as she could twist her husband into the warden's house. She cared not which was her friend or which was her enemy, if only she could get this preferment which she so sorely wanted.

She told her tale, and Mrs. Proudie listened to it almost in silence. She told how Mr. Slope had cozened her husband into resigning his claim, and had declared that it was the bishop's will that none but Mr. Harding should be warden. Mrs. Proudie's brow became blacker and blacker. At last she started from her chair, and begging Mrs. Quiverful to sit and wait for her return, marched out of the room.

'Oh, Mrs. Proudie, it's for fourteen children—for fourteen children.' Such was the burden that fell on her ear as she closed the door behind her.

CHAPTER XXVI

MRS. PROUDIE WRESTLES AND GETS A FALL

It was hardly an hour since Mrs. Proudie had left her husband's apartment victorious, and yet so indomitable was her courage that she now returned thither panting for another combat. She was greatly angry with what she thought was his duplicity. He had so clearly given her a promise on this matter of the hospital. He had been already so absolutely vanquished on that point. Mrs. Proudie began to feel that if every affair was to be thus discussed and battled about twice and even thrice, the work of the diocese would be too much even for her.

Without knocking at the door she walked quickly into her husband's room, and found him seated at his office table, with Mr. Slope opposite to him. Between his fingers was the very note which he had written to the archbishop in her presence——and it was open! Yes, he had absolutely violated the seal which had been made sacred by her approval. They were sitting in deep conclave, and it was too clear that the purport of the archbishop's invitation had been absolutely canvassed again, after it had been already debated and decided on in obedience to her behests ! Mr. Slope rose from his chair, and bowed slightly. The two opposing spirits looked each other fully in the face, and they knew that they were looking each at an enemy.

' What is this, bishop, about Mr. Quiverful ? ' said she, coming to the end of the table and standing there.

Mr. Slope did not allow the bishop to answer, but replied himself. ' I have been out to Puddingdale this morning, ma'am, and have seen Mr. Quiverful. Mr. Quiverful has abandoned his claim to the hospital, because he is now aware that Mr. Harding is desirous to fill his old place. Under these circumstances I have strongly advised his lordship to nominate Mr. Harding.'

' Mr. Quiverful has not abandoned anything,' said the lady, with a very imperious voice. ' His lordship's word has been pledged to him, and it must be respected.'.

The bishop still remained silent. He was anxiously desirous of making his old enemy bite the dust beneath his feet. His new ally had told him that nothing was more easy for him than to do so. The ally was there now at his elbow to help him, and yet his courage failed him. It is so hard to conquer when the prestige of former victories is all against one. It is so hard for the cock who has once been beaten out of his yard to resume his courage and again take a proud place upon a dunghill.

' Perhaps I ought not to interfere,' said Mr. Slope, ' but yet——'

' Certainly you ought not,' said the infuriated dame.

' But yet,' continued Mr. Slope, not regarding the interruption, ' I have thought it my imperative duty to recommend the bishop not to slight Mr. Harding's claims.'

' Mr. Harding should have known his own mind,' said the lady.

' If Mr. Harding be not replaced at the hospital, his lordship will have to encounter much ill will, not only in the diocese, but in the world at large. Besides, taking a higher ground, his lordship, as I understood, feels it to be his duty to gratify, in this matter, so very worthy a man and so good a clergyman as Mr. Harding.'

' And what is to become of the Sabbath-day school, and of the Sunday services in the hospital ? ' said Mrs. Proudie,

with something very nearly approaching to a sneer on
her face.

'I understand that Mr. Harding makes no objection
to the Sabbath-day school,' said Mr. Slope. 'And as to
the hospital services, that matter will be best discussed
after his appointment. If he has any permanent objection,
then, I fear, the matter must rest.'

'You have a very easy conscience in such matters,
Mr. Slope,' said she.

'I should not have an easy conscience,' he rejoined,
'but a conscience very far from being easy, if anything
said or done by me should lead the bishop to act un-
advisedly in this matter. It is clear that in the interview
I had with Mr. Harding, I misunderstood him——'

'And it is equally clear that you have misunderstood
Mr. Quiverful,' said she, now at the top of her wrath.
'What business have you at all with these interviews?
Who desired you to go to Mr. Quiverful this morning?
Who commissioned you to manage this affair? Will you
answer me, sir?—who sent you to Mr. Quiverful this
morning?'

There was a dead pause in the room. Mr. Slope had
risen from his chair, and was standing with his hand on
the back of it, looking at first very solemn and now very
black. Mrs. Proudie was standing as she had at first
placed herself, at the end of the table, and as she interrogated her foe she struck her hand upon it with almost
more than feminine vigour. The bishop was sitting in
his easy chair twiddling his thumbs, turning his eyes now
to his wife, and now to his chaplain, as each took up the
cudgels. How comfortable it would be if they could
fight it out between them without the necessity of any
interference on his part; fight it out so that one should
kill the other utterly, as far as diocesan life was concerned,
so that he, the bishop, might know clearly by whom it
behoved him to be led. There would be the comfort of
quiet in either case; but if the bishop had a wish as to
which might prove the victor, that wish was certainly
not antagonistic to Mr. Slope.

'Better the d—— you know than the d—— you don't
know,' is an old saying, and perhaps a true one; but the
bishop had not yet realised the truth of it.

' Will you answer me, sir ? ' she repeated. ' Who instructed you to call on Mr. Quiverful this morning ? ' There was another pause. ' Do you intend to answer me, sir ? '

' I think, Mrs. Proudie, that under all the circumstances it will be better for me not to answer such a question,' said Mr. Slope. Mr. Slope had many tones in his voice, all duly under his command ; among them was a sanctified low tone, and a sanctified loud tone ; and he now used the former.

' Did any one send you, sir ? '

' Mrs. Proudie,' said Mr. Slope, ' I am quite aware how much I owe to your kindness. I am aware also what is due by courtesy from a gentleman to a lady. But there are higher considerations than either of those, and I hope I shall be forgiven if I now allow myself to be actuated solely by them. My duty in this matter is to his lordship, and I can admit of no questioning but from him. He has approved of what I have done, and you must excuse me if I say, that having that approval and my own, I want none other.'

What horrid words were these which greeted the ear of Mrs. Proudie ? The matter was indeed too clear. There was premeditated mutiny in the camp. Not only had ill-conditioned minds become insubordinate by the fruition of a little power, but sedition had been overtly taught and preached. The bishop had not yet been twelve months in his chair, and rebellion had already reared her hideous head within the palace. Anarchy and misrule would quickly follow, unless she took immediate and strong measures to put down the conspiracy which she had detected.

' Mr. Slope,' she said, with slow and dignified voice, differing much from that which she had hitherto used, ' Mr. Slope, I will trouble you, if you please, to leave the apartment. I wish to speak to my lord alone.'

Mr. Slope also felt that everything depended on the present interview. Should the bishop now be repetticoated, his thraldom would be complete and for ever. The present moment was peculiarly propitious for rebellion. The bishop had clearly committed himself by breaking the seal of the answer to the archbishop ; he had therefore

fear to influence him. Mr. Slope had told him that no
consideration ought to induce him to refuse the archbishop's invitation; he had therefore hope to influence
him. He had accepted Mr. Quiverful's resignation, and
therefore dreaded having to renew that matter with his
wife. He had been screwed up to the pitch of asserting
a will of his own, and might possibly be carried on till
by an absolute success he should have been taught how
possible it was to succeed. Now was the moment for
victory or rout. It was now that Mr. Slope must make
himself master of the diocese, or else resign his place and
begin his search for fortune again. He saw all this plainly.
After what had taken place any compromise between
him and the lady was impossible. Let him once leave the
room at her bidding, and leave the bishop in her hands, and
he might at once pack up his portmanteau and bid adieu
to episcopal honours, Mrs. Bold, and the Signora Neroni.

And yet it was not so easy to keep his ground when he
was bidden by a lady to go; or to continue to make a
third in a party between a husband and wife when the
wife expressed a wish for a *tête-à-tête* with her husband.

'Mr. Slope,' she repeated, 'I wish to be alone with
my lord.'

'His lordship has summoned me on most important
diocesan business,' said Mr. Slope, glancing with uneasy
eye at Dr. Proudie. He felt that he must trust something
to the bishop, and yet that trust was so woefully ill-placed.
'My leaving him at the present moment is, I fear, impossible.'

'Do you bandy words with me, you ungrateful man?'
said she. 'My lord, will you do me the favour to beg
Mr. Slope to leave the room?'

My lord scratched his head, but for the moment said
nothing. This was as much as Mr. Slope expected from
him, and was on the whole, for him, an active exercise
of marital rights.

'My lord,' said the lady, 'is Mr. Slope to leave this
room, or am I?'

Here Mrs. Proudie made a false step. She should not
have alluded to the possibility of retreat on her part.
She should not have expressed the idea that her order
for Mr. Slope's expulsion could be treated otherwise than

by immediate obedience. In answer to such a question the bishop naturally said in his own mind, that as it was necessary that one should leave the room, perhaps it might be as well that Mrs. Proudie did so. He did say so in his own mind, but externally he again scratched his head and again twiddled his thumbs.

Mrs. Proudie was boiling over with wrath. Alas, alas! could she but have kept her temper as her enemy did, she would have conquered as she had ever conquered. But divine anger got the better of her, as it has done of other heroines, and she fell.

'My lord,' said she, 'am I to be vouchsafed an answer or am I not?'

At last he broke his deep silence and proclaimed himself a Slopeite. 'Why, my dear,' said he, 'Mr. Slope and I are very busy.'

That was all. There was nothing more necessary. He had gone to the battle-field, stood the dust and heat of the day, encountered the fury of the foe, and won the victory. How easy is success to those who will only be true to themselves!

Mr. Slope saw at once the full amount of his gain, and turned on the vanquished lady a look of triumph which she never forgot and never forgave. Here he was wrong. He should have looked humbly at her, and with meek entreating eye have deprecated her anger. He should have said by his glance that he asked pardon for his success, and that he hoped forgiveness for the stand which he had been forced to make in the cause of duty. So might he perchance have somewhat mollified that imperious bosom, and prepared the way for future terms. But Mr. Slope meant to rule without terms. Ah, forgetful, inexperienced man! Can you cause that little trembling victim to be divorced from the woman that possesses him? Can you provide that they shall be separated at bed and board? Is he not flesh of her flesh and bone of her bone, and must he not so continue? It is very well now for you to stand your ground, and triumph as she is driven ignominiously from the room; but can you be present when those curtains are drawn, when that awful helmet of proof has been tied beneath the chin, when the small remnants of the bishop's prowess shall be cowed

by the tassel above his head ? Can you then intrude
yourself when the wife wishes ' to speak to my lord alone ' ?

But for the moment Mr. Slope's triumph was complete ;
for Mrs. Proudie without further parley left the room,
and did not forget to shut the door after her. Then
followed a close conference between the new allies, in
which was said much which it astonished Mr. Slope to
say and the bishop to hear. And yet the one said it and
the other heard it without ill will. There was no mincing
of matters now. The chaplain plainly told the bishop
that the world gave him credit for being under the governance of his wife ; that his credit and character in the
diocese were suffering ; that he would surely get himself
into hot water if he allowed Mrs. Proudie to interfere in
matters which were not suitable for a woman's powers ;
and in fact that he would become contemptible if he did
not throw off the yoke under which he groaned. The
bishop at first hummed and hawed, and affected to deny
the truth of what was said. But his denial was not stout
and quickly broke down. He soon admitted by silence
his state of vassalage, and pledged himself, with Mr. Slope's
assistance, to change his courses. Mr. Slope also did not
make out a bad case for himself. He explained how it
grieved him to run counter to a lady who had always been
his patroness, who had befriended him in so many ways,
who had, in fact, recommended him to the bishop's
notice ; but, as he stated, his duty was now imperative ;
he held a situation of peculiar confidence, and was immediately and especially attached to the bishop's person.
In such a situation his conscience required that he should
regard solely the bishop's interests, and therefore he had
ventured to speak out.

The bishop took this for what it was worth, and Mr.
Slope only intended that he should do so. It gilded the
pill which Mr. Slope had to administer, and which the
bishop thought would be less bitter than that other pill
which he had so long been taking.

' My lord,' had his immediate reward, like a good child.
He was instructed to write and at once did write another
note to the archbishop accepting his grace's invitation.
This note Mr. Slope, more prudent than the lady, himself
took away and posted with his own hands. Thus he made

sure that this act of self-jurisdiction should be as nearly
as possible a *fait accompli.* He begged, and coaxed, and
threatened the bishop with a view of making him also
write at once to Mr. Harding ; but the bishop, though
temporarily emancipated from his wife, was not yet
enthralled to Mr. Slope. He said, and probably said truly,
that such an offer must be made in some official form ;
that he was not yet prepared to sign the form ; and that
he should prefer seeing Mr. Harding before he did so.
Mr. Slope might, however, beg Mr. Harding to call upon
him. Not disappointed with his achievement Mr. Slope
went his way. He first posted the precious note which
he had in his pocket, and then pursued other enterprises
in which we must follow him in other chapters.

Mrs. Proudie, having received such satisfaction as was
to be derived from slamming her husband's door, did not
at once betake herself to Mrs. Quiverful. Indeed for the
first few moments after her repulse she felt that she could
not again see that lady. She would have to own that she
had been beaten, to confess that the diadem had passed
from her brow, and the sceptre from her hand ! No, she
would send a message to her with the promise of a letter
on the next day or the day after. Thus resolving, she
betook herself to her bed-room ; but here she again
changed her mind. The air of that sacred enclosure
somewhat restored her courage, and gave her more heart.
As Achilles warmed at the sight of his armour, as Don
Quixote's heart grew strong when he grasped his lance,
so did Mrs. Proudie look forward to fresh laurels, as her
eye fell on her husband's pillow. She would not despair.
Having so resolved, she descended with dignified mien
and refreshed countenance to Mrs. Quiverful.

This scene in the bishop's study took longer m the
acting than in the telling. We have not, perhaps, had the
whole of the conversation. At any rate Mrs. Quiverful
was beginning to be very impatient, and was thinking
that farmer Subsoil would be tired of waiting for her,
when Mrs. Proudie returned. Oh ! who can tell the
palpitations of that maternal heart, as the suppliant
looked into the face of the great lady to see written there
either a promise of house, income, comfort and future
competence, or else the doom of continued and ever

increasing poverty. Poor mother! poor wife! there was
little there to comfort you!

'Mrs. Quiverful,' thus spoke the lady with considerable
austerity, and without sitting down herself, 'I find that
your husband has behaved in this matter in a very weak
and foolish manner.'

Mrs. Quiverful immediately rose upon her feet, thinking
it disrespectful to remain sitting while the wife of the
bishop stood. But she was desired to sit down again,
and made to do so, so that Mrs. Proudie might stand
and preach over her. It is generally considered an offensive
thing for a gentleman to keep his seat while another is
kept standing before him, and we presume the same law
holds with regard to ladies. It often is so felt; but we
are inclined to say that it never produces half the discomfort or half the feeling of implied inferiority that is
shown by a great man who desires his visitor to be seated
while he himself speaks from his legs. Such a solecism
in good breeding, when construed into English, means
this: 'The accepted rules of courtesy in the world require
that I should offer you a seat; if I did not do so, you
would bring a charge against me in the world of being
arrogant and ill-mannered; I will obey the world; but,
nevertheless, I will not put myself on an equality with
you. You may sit down, but I won't sit with you. Sit,
therefore, at my bidding, and I'll stand and talk at you!'

This was just what Mrs. Proudie meant to say; and
Mrs. Quiverful, though she was too anxious and too
flurried thus to translate the full meaning of the manœuvre,
did not fail to feel its effect. She was cowed and uncomfortable, and a second time essayed to rise from her chair.

'Pray be seated, Mrs. Quiverful, pray keep your seat.
Your husband, I say, has been most weak and most
foolish. It is impossible, Mrs. Quiverful, to help people
who will not help themselves. I much fear that I can
now do nothing for you in this matter.'

'Oh! Mrs. Proudie—don't say so,' said the poor woman
again jumping up.

'*Pray* be seated Mrs. Quiverful. I much fear that I
can do nothing further for you in this matter. Your
husband has, in a most unaccountable manner, taken upon
himself to resign that which I was empowered to offer

him. As a matter of course, the bishop expects that his
clergy shall know their own minds. What he may ultimately do—what we may finally decide on doing—I
cannot now say. Knowing the extent of your family—'
 ' Fourteen children, Mrs. Proudie, fourteen of them !
and barely bread,—barely, bread ! It's hard for the
children of a clergyman, it's hard for one who has always
done his duty respectably ! ' Not a word fell from her
about herself ; but the tears came streaming down her
big coarse cheeks, on which the dust of the August road
had left its traces.

Mrs. Proudie has not been portrayed in these pages as
an agreeable or an amiable lady. There has been no
intention to impress the reader much in her favour. It
is ordained that all novels should have a male and a female
angel, and a male and a female devil. If it be considered
that this rule is obeyed in these pages, the latter character
must be supposed to have fallen to the lot of Mrs. Proudie.
But she was not all devil. There was a heart inside that
stiff-ribbed bodice, though not, perhaps, of large dimensions, and certainly not easily accessible. Mrs. Quiverful,
however, did gain access, and Mrs. Proudie proved herself
a woman. Whether it was the fourteen children with
their probable bare bread and their possible bare backs,
or the respectability of the father's work, or the mingled
dust and tears on the mother's face, we will not pretend
to say. But Mrs. Proudie was touched.

She did not show it as other women might have done.
She did not give Mrs. Quiverful eau-de-Cologne, or order
her a glass of wine. She did not take her to her toilet
table, and offer her the use of brushes and combs, towels
and water. She did not say soft little speeches and coax
her kindly back to equanimity. Mrs. Quiverful, despite
her rough appearance, would have been as amenable to
such little tender cares as any lady in the land. But
none such were forthcoming. Instead of this, Mrs. Proudie
slapped one hand upon the other, and declared—not with
an oath ; for as a lady and a Sabbatarian and a she-bishop,
she could not swear,—but with an adjuration, that ' she
wouldn't have it done.'

The meaning of this was that she wouldn't have Mr.
Quiverful's promised appointment cozened away by the

treachery of Mr. Slope and the weakness of her husband.
This meaning she very soon explained to Mrs. Quiverful.

' Why was your husband such a fool,' said she, now
dismounted from her high horse and sitting confidentially
down close to her visitor, ' as to take the bait which that
man threw to him ? If he had not been so utterly foolish,
nothing could have prevented your going to the hospital.'

Poor Mrs. Quiverful was ready enough with her own
tongue in accusing her husband to his face of being soft,
and perhaps did not always speak of him to her children
quite so respectfully as she might have done. But she
did not at all like to hear him abused by others, and began
to vindicate him, and to explain that of course he had
taken Mr. Slope to be an emissary from Mrs. Proudie
herself ; that Mr. Slope was thought to be peculiarly her
friend ; and that, therefore, Mr. Quiverful would have
been failing in respect to her had he assumed to doubt
what Mr. Slope had said.

Thus mollified Mrs. Proudie again declared that ' she
would not have it done,' and at last sent Mrs. Quiverful
home with an assurance that, to the furthest stretch of
her power and influence in the palace, the appointment
of Mr. Quiverful should be insisted on. As she repeated
the word ' insisted,' she thought of the bishop in his
night-cap, and with compressed lips slightly shook her
head. Oh! my aspiring pastors, divines to whose ears
nolo episcopari are the sweetest of words, which of you
would be a bishop on such terms as these ?

Mrs. Quiverful got home in the farmer's cart, not indeed
with a light heart, but satisfied that she had done right
in making her visit.

CHAPTER XXVII

A LOVE SCENE

MR. SLOPE, as we have said, left the palace with a
feeling of considerable triumph. Not that he thought that
his difficulties were all over ; he did not so deceive himself ;
but he felt that he had played his first move well, as well
as the pieces on the board would allow ; and that he had
nothing with which to reproach himself. He first of all

posted the letter to the archbishop, and having made that
sure he proceeded to push the advantage which he had
gained. Had Mrs. Bold been at home, he would have
called on her; but he knew that she was at Plumstead,
so he wrote the following note. It was the beginning of
what, he trusted, might be a long and tender series of
epistles.

'My dear Mrs. Bold,—You will understand perfectly
that I cannot at present correspond with your father.
I heartily wish that I could, and hope the day may be
not long distant when mists shall have cleared away, and
we may know each other. But I cannot preclude myself
from the pleasure of sending you these few lines to say
that Mr. Q. has to-day, in my presence, resigned any
title that he ever had to the wardenship of the hospital,
and that the bishop has assured me that it is his intention
to offer it to your esteemed father.

'Will you, with my respectful compliments, ask him,
who I believe is now a fellow-visitor with you, to call on
the bishop either on Wednesday or Thursday, between
ten and one. *This is by the bishop's desire.* If you will
so far oblige me as to let me have a line naming either
day, and the hour which will suit Mr. Harding, I will
take care that the servants shall have orders to show him
in without delay. Perhaps I should say no more,—but
still I wish you could make your father understand that
no subject will be mooted between his lordship and him,
which will refer at all to the method in which he may
choose to perform his duty. I for one, am persuaded that
no clergyman could perform it more satisfactorily than he
did, or than he will do again.

'On a former occasion I was indiscreet and much too
impatient, considering your father's age and my own.
I hope he will not now refuse my apology. I still hope
also that with your aid and sweet pious labours, we may
live to attach such a Sabbath school to the old endowment,
as may, by God's grace and furtherance, be a blessing to
the poor of this city.

'You will see at once that this letter is confidential.
The subject, of course, makes it so. But, equally of
course, it is for your parent's eye as well as for your own,
should you think proper to show it to him.

' I hope my darling little friend Johnny is as strong as ever,—dear little fellow. Does he still continue his rude assaults on those beautiful long silken tresses ?

' I can assure you your friends miss you from Barchester sorely ; but it would be cruel to begrudge you your sojourn among flowers and fields during this truly sultry weather.

'Pray believe me, my dear Mrs. Bold,
'Yours most sincerely,
'OBADIAH SLOPE.

'Barchester, Friday.'

Now this letter, taken as a whole, and with the consideration that Mr. Slope wished to assume a great degree of intimacy with Eleanor, would not have been bad, but for the allusion to the tresses. Gentlemen do not write to ladies about their tresses, unless they are on very intimate terms indeed. But Mr. Slope could not be expected to be aware of this. He longed to put a little affection into his epistle, and yet he thought it injudicious, as the letter would, he knew, be shown to Mr. Harding. He would have insisted that the letter should be strictly private and seen by no eyes but Eleanor's own, had he not felt that such an injunction would have been disobeyed. He therefore restrained his passion, did not sign himself ' yours affectionately,' and contented himself instead with the compliment to the tresses.

Having finished his letter, he took it to Mrs. Bold's house, and learning there, from the servant, that things were to be sent out to Plumstead that afternoon, left it, with many injunctions, in her hands.

We will now follow Mr. Slope so as to complete the day with him, and then return to his letter and its momentous fate in the next chapter.

There is an old song which gives us some very good advice about courting :—

> It's gude to be off with the auld luve
> Before ye be on wi' the new.

Of the wisdom of this maxim Mr. Slope was ignorant, and accordingly, having written his letter to Mrs. Bold, he proceeded to call upon the Signora Neroni. Indeed it

was hard to say which was the old love and which the new,
Mr. Slope having been smitten with both so nearly at the
same time. Perhaps he thought it not amiss to have two
strings to his bow. But two strings to Cupid's bow are
always dangerous to him on whose behalf they are to be
used. A man should remember that between two stools
he may fall to the ground.

But in sooth Mr. Slope was pursuing Mrs. Bold in
obedience to his better instincts, and the signora in
obedience to his worser. Had he won the widow and worn
her, no one could have blamed him. You, O reader, and
I, and Eleanor's other friends would have received the
story of such a winning with much disgust and disappointment; but we should have been angry with Eleanor,
not with Mr. Slope. Bishop, male and female, dean and
chapter and diocesan clergy in full congress, could have
found nothing to disapprove of in such an alliance. Convocation itself, that mysterious and mighty synod, could
in no wise have fallen foul of it. The possession of 1000*l.*
a year and a beautiful wife would not at all have hurt
the voice of the pulpit charmer, or lessened the grace and
piety of the exemplary clergyman.

But not of such a nature were likely to be his dealings
with the Signora Neroni. In the first place he knew that
her husband was living, and therefore he could not woo
her honestly. Then again she had nothing to recommend
her to his honest wooing had such been possible. She was
not only portionless, but also from misfortune unfitted to be
chosen as the wife of any man who wanted a useful mate.
Mr. Slope was aware that she was a helpless hopeless
cripple.

But Mr. Slope could not help himself. He knew that
he was wrong in devoting his time to the back drawing-
room in Dr. Stanhope's house. He knew that what took
place there would if divulged utterly ruin him with Mrs.
Bold. He knew that scandal would soon come upon his
heels and spread abroad among the black coats of Barchester some tidings, exaggerated tidings, of the sighs
which he poured into the lady's ears. He knew that he
was acting against the recognised principles ·of his life,
against those laws of conduct by which he hoped to achieve
much higher success. But as we have said, he could not

help himself. Passion, for the first time in his life, passion
was too strong for him.

As for the signora, no such plea can be put forward
for her, for in truth she cared no more for Mr. Slope than
she did for twenty others who had been at her feet before
him. She willingly, nay greedily, accepted his homage.
He was the finest fly that Barchester had hitherto afforded
to her web; and the signora was a powerful spider that
made wondrous webs, and could in no way live without
catching flies. Her taste in this respect was abominable,
for she had no use for the victims when caught. She could
not eat them matrimonially, as young lady-flies do whose
webs are most frequently of their mothers' weaving. Nor
could she devour them by any escapade of a less legitimate
description. Her unfortunate affliction precluded her
from all hope of levanting with a lover. It would be
impossible to run away with a lady who required three
servants to move her from a sofa.

The signora was subdued by no passion. Her time for
love was gone. She had lived out her heart, such heart
as she had ever had, in her early years, at an age when
Mr. Slope was thinking of the second book of Euclid and
his unpaid bill at the buttery hatch. In age the lady was
younger than the gentleman; but in feelings, in knowledge
of the affairs of love, in intrigue, he was immeasurably
her junior. It was necessary to her to have some man at
her feet. It was the one customary excitement of her
life. She delighted in the exercise of power which this
gave her; it was now nearly the only food for her ambition; she would boast to her sister that she could make
a fool of any man, and the sister, as little imbued with
feminine delicacy as herself, good naturedly thought it
but fair that such amusement should be afforded to a poor
invalid who was debarred from the ordinary pleasures of life.

Mr. Slope was madly in love, but hardly knew it. The
signora spitted him, as a boy does a cockchafer on a cork,
that she might enjoy the energetic agony of his gyrations.
And she knew very well what she was doing.

Mr. Slope having added to his person all such adorn-
ments as are possible to a clergyman making a morning
visit, such as a clean neck tie, clean handkerchief, new
gloves, and a *soupçon* of not unnecessary scent called about

three o'clock at the doctor's door. At about this hour the signora was almost always alone in the back drawing-room. The mother had not come down. The doctor was out or in his own room. Bertie was out, and Charlotte at any rate left the room if any one called whose object was specially with her sister. Such was her idea of being charitable and sisterly.

Mr. Slope, as was his custom, asked for Mr. Stanhope, and was told, as was the servant's custom, that the signora was in the drawing-room. Upstairs he accordingly went. He found her, as he always did, lying on her sofa with a French volume before her, and a beautiful little inlaid writing case open on her table. At the moment of his entrance she was in the act of writing.

' Ah my friend,' said she, putting out her left hand to him across her desk, ' I did not expect you to-day and was this very instant writing to you——'

Mr. Slope, taking the soft fair delicate hand in his, and very soft and fair and delicate it was, bowed over it his huge red head and kissed it. It was a sight to see, a deed to record if the author could fitly do it, a picture to put on canvass. Mr. Slope was big, awkward, cumbrous, and having his heart in his pursuit was ill at ease. The lady was fair, as we have said, and delicate ; every thing about her was fine and refined ; her hand in his looked like a rose lying among carrots, and when he kissed it he looked as a cow might do on finding such a flower among her food. She was graceful as a couchant goddess, and, moreover, as self-possessed as Venus must have been when courting Adonis.

Oh, that such grace and such beauty should have condescended to waste itself on such a pursuit !

' I was in the act of writing to you,' said she, ' but now my scrawl may go into the basket ; ' and she raised the sheet of gilded note paper from off her desk as though to tear it.

' Indeed it shall not,' said he, laying the embargo of half a stone weight of human flesh and blood upon the devoted paper. ' Nothing that you write for my eyes, signora, shall be so desecrated,' and he took up the letter, put that also among the carrots and fed on it, and then proceeded to read it.

' Gracious me ! Mr. Slope,' said she, ' I hope you don't
mean to say that you keep all the trash I write to you.
Half my time I don't know what I write, and when I do,
I know it is only fit for the back of the fire. I hope you
have not that ugly trick of keeping letters.'

' At any rate, I don't throw them into a waste-paper
basket. If destruction is their doomed lot, they perish
worthily, and are burnt on a pyre, as Dido was of old.'

' With a steel pen stuck through them, of course,' said
she, ' to make the simile more complete. Of all the ladies
of my acquaintance I think Lady Dido was the most
absurd. Why did she not do as Cleopatra did ? Why did
she not take out her ships and insist on going with him ?
She could not bear to lose the land she had got by a
swindle ; and then she could not bear the loss of her
lover. So she fell between two stools. Mr. Slope, whatever
you do, never mingle love and business.'

Mr. Slope blushed up to his eyes, and over his mottled
forehead to the very roots of his hair. He felt sure that
the signora knew all about his intentions with reference
to Mrs. Bold. His conscience told him that he was detected.
His doom was to be spoken ; he was to be punished for
his duplicity, and rejected by the beautiful creature before
him. Poor man. He little dreamt that had all his intentions with reference to Mrs. Bold been known to the
signora, it would only have added zest to that lady's
amusement. It was all very well to have Mr. Slope at
her feet, to show her power by making an utter fool of
a clergyman, to gratify her own infidelity by thus proving
the little strength which religion had in controlling the
passions even of a religious man ; but it would be an
increased gratification if she could be made to understand
that she was at the same time alluring her victim away
from another, whose love if secured would be in every
way beneficent and salutary.

The signora had indeed discovered with the keen instinct
of such a woman, that Mr. Slope was bent on matrimony
with Mrs. Bold, but in alluding to Dido she had not thought
of it. She instantly perceived, however, from her lover's
blushes, what was on his mind, and was not slow in taking
advantage of it.

She looked him full in the face, not angrily, nor yet

with a smile, but with an intense and overpowering gaze ;
and then holding up her forefinger, and slightly shaking
her head she said :—

'Whatever you do, my friend, do not mingle love and
business. Either stick to your treasure and your city of
wealth, or else follow your love like a true man. But
never attempt both. If you do, you'll have to die with
a broken heart as did poor Dido. Which is it to be with
you, Mr. Slope, love or money ? '

Mr. Slope was not so ready with a pathetic answer as
he usually was with touching episodes in his extempore
sermons. He felt that he ought to say something pretty,
something also that should remove the impression on the
mind of his lady love. But he was rather put about how
to do it.

'Love,' said he, ' true overpowering love, must be the
strongest passion a man can feel ; it must control every
other wish, and put aside every other pursuit. But with
me love will never act in that way unless it be returned ; '
and he threw upon the signora a look of tenderness which
was intended to make up for all the deficiencies of his
speech.

'Take my advice,' said she. ' Never mind love. After
all, what is it ? The dream of a few weeks. That is all
its joy. The disappointment of a life is its Nemesis. Who
was ever successful in true love ? Success in love argues
that the love is false. True love is always despondent or
tragical. Juliet loved, Haidee loved, Dido loved, and
what came of it ? Troilus loved and ceased to be a man.'

'Troilus loved and was fooled,' said the more manly
chaplain. ' A man may love and yet not be a Troilus.
All women are not Cressids.'

'No ; all women are not Cressids. The falsehood is
not always on the woman's side. Imogen was true, but
how was she rewarded ? Her lord believed her to be the
paramour of the first he who came near her in his absence.
Desdemona was true and was smothered. Ophelia was
true and went mad. There is no happiness in love, except
at the end of an English novel. But in wealth, money,
houses, lands, goods and chattels, in the good things of
this world, yes, in them there is something tangible,
something that can be retained and enjoyed.'

' Oh, no,' said Mr. Slope, feeling himself bound to enter some protest against so very unorthodox a doctrine, ' this world's wealth will make no one happy.'

' And what will make you happy—you—you ? ' said she, raising herself up, and speaking to him with energy across the table. ' From what source do you look for happiness ? Do not say that you look for none ? I shall not believe you. It is a search in which every human being spends an existence.'

' And the search is always in vain,' said Mr. Slope. ' We look for happiness on earth, while we ought to be content to hope for it in heaven.'

' Pshaw ! you preach a doctrine which you know you don't believe. It is the way with you all. If you know that there is no earthly happiness, why do you long to be a bishop or a dean ? Why do you want lands and income ? '

' I have the natural ambition of a man,' said he.

' Of course you have, and the natural passions ; and therefore I say that you don't believe the doctrine you preach. St. Paul was an enthusiast. He believed so that his ambition and passions did not war against his creed. So does the Eastern fanatic who passes half his life erect upon a pillar. As for me, I will believe in no belief that does not make itself manifest by outward signs. I will think no preaching sincere that is not recommended by the practice of the preacher.'

Mr. Slope was startled and horrified, but he felt that he could not answer. How could he stand up and preach the lessons of his Master, being there as he was, on the devil's business ? He was a true believer, otherwise this would have been nothing to him. He had audacity for most things, but he had not audacity to make a play-thing of the Lord's word. All this the signora understood, and felt much interest as she saw her cockchafer whirl round upon her pin.

' Your wit delights in such arguments,' said he, ' but your heart and your reason do not go along with them.'

' My heart ! ' said she ; ' you quite mistake the principles of my composition if you imagine that there is such a thing about me.' After all, there was very little that was false in anything that the signora said. If Mr. Slope allowed himself to be deceived it was his own fault.

Nothing could have been more open than her declarations about herself.

The little writing table with her desk was still standing before her, a barrier, as it were, against the enemy. She was sitting as nearly upright as she ever did, and he had brought a chair close to the sofa, so that there was only the corner of the table between him and her. It so happened that as she spoke her hand lay upon the table, and as Mr. Slope answered her he put his hand upon hers.

'No heart!' said he. 'That is a heavy charge which you bring against yourself, and one of which I cannot find you guilty——'

She withdrew her hand, not quickly and angrily, as though insulted by his touch, but gently and slowly.

'You are in no condition to give a verdict on the matter,' said she, 'as you have not tried me. No; don't say that you intend doing so, for you know you have no intention of the kind; nor indeed have I either. As for you, you will take your vows where they will result in something more substantial than the pursuit of such a ghostlike, ghastly love as mine——'

'Your love should be sufficient to satisfy the dream of a monarch,' said Mr. Slope, not quite clear as to the meaning of his words.

'Say an archbishop, Mr. Slope,' said she. Poor fellow! she was very cruel to him. He went round again upon his cork on this allusion to his profession. He tried, however, to smile, and gently accused her of joking on a matter, which was, he said, to him of such vital moment.

'Why—what gulls do you men make of us,' she replied. 'How you fool us to the top of our bent; and of all men you clergymen are the most fluent of your honeyed caressing words. Now look me in the face, Mr. Slope, boldly and openly.'

Mr. Slope did look at her with a languishing loving eye, and as he did so, he again put forth his hand to get hold of hers.

'I told you to look at me boldly, Mr. Slope; but confine your boldness to your eyes.'

'Oh, Madeline!' he sighed.

'Well, my name is Madeline,' said she; 'but none except my own family usually call me so. Now look me

in the face, Mr. Slope. Am I to understand that you say
you love me ? '

Mr. Slope never had said so. If he had come there with
any formed plan at all, his intention was to make love to
the lady without uttering any such declaration. It was,
however, quite impossible that he should now deny his
love. He had, therefore, nothing for it, but to go down
on his knees distractedly against the sofa, and swear that
he did love her with a love passing the love of man.

The signora received the assurance with very little
palpitation or appearance of surprise. ' And now answer
me another question,' said she ; ' when are you to be
married to my dear friend Eleanor Bold ? '

Poor Mr. Slope went round and round in mortal agony.
In such a condition as his it was really very hard for him
to know what answer to give. And yet no answer would
be his surest condemnation. He might as well at once
plead guilty to the charge brought against him.

' And why do you accuse me of such dissimulation ? '
said he.

' Dissimulation ! I said nothing of dissimulation. I
made no charge against you, and make none. Pray don't
defend yourself to me. You swear that you are devoted
to my beauty, and yet you are on the eve of matrimony
with another. I feel this to be rather a compliment. It
is to Mrs. Bold that you must defend yourself. That you
may find difficult ; unless, indeed, you can keep her in
the dark. You clergymen are cleverer than other men.'

' Signora, I have told you that I loved you, and now
you rail at me ? '

' Rail at you. God bless the man ; what would he
have ? Come, answer me this at your leisure,—not without
thinking now, but leisurely and with consideration,—
Are you not going to be married to Mrs. Bold ? '

' I am not,' said he. And as he said it, he almost hated,
with an exquisite hatred, the woman whom he could not
help loving with an exquisite love.

' But surely you are a worshipper of hers ? '

' I am not,' said Mr. Slope, to whom the word worshipper
was peculiarly distasteful. The signora had conceived
that it would be so.

' I wonder at that,' said she. ' Do you not admire her ?

To my eye she is the perfection of English beauty. And then she is rich too. I should have thought she was just the person to attract you. Come, Mr. Slope, let me give you advice on this matter. Marry the charming widow! she will be a good mother to your children, and an excellent mistress of a clergyman's household.'

'Oh, signora, how can you be so cruel?'

'Cruel,' said she, changing the voice of banter which she had been using for one which was expressively earnest in its tone; 'is that cruelty?'

'How can I love another, while my heart is entirely your own?'

'If that were cruelty, Mr. Slope, what might you say of me if I were to declare that I returned your passion? What would you think if I bound you even by a lover's oath to do daily penance at this couch of mine? What can I give in return for a man's love? Ah, dear friend, you have not realised the conditions of my fate.'

Mr. Slope was not on his knees all this time. After his declaration of love he had risen from them as quickly as he thought consistent with the new position which he now filled, and as he stood was leaning on the back of his chair. This outburst of tenderness on the Signora's part quite overcame him, and made him feel for the moment that he could sacrifice everything to be assured of the love of the beautiful creature before him, maimed, lame, and already married as she was,

'And can I not sympathise with your lot?' said he, now seating himself on her sofa, and pushing away the table with his foot.

'Sympathy is so near to pity!' said she. 'If you pity me, cripple as I am, I shall spurn you from me.'

'Oh, Madeline, I will only love you,' and again he caught her hand and devoured it with kisses. Now she did not draw it from him, but sat there as he kissed it, looking at him with her great eyes, just as a great spider would look at a great fly that was quite securely caught.

'Suppose Signor Neroni were to come to Barchester,' said she, 'would you make his acquaintance?'

'Signor Neroni!' said he.

'Would you introduce him to the bishop, and Mrs. Proudie, and the young ladies?' said she, again having

recourse to that horrid quizzing voice which Mr. Slope
so particularly hated.

'Why do you ask such a question ? ' said he.

'Because it is necessary that you should know that
there is a Signor Neroni. I think you had forgotten it.'

'If I thought that you retained for that wretch one
particle of the love of which he was never worthy, I would
die before I would distract you by telling you what I feel.
No ! were your husband the master of your heart, I might
perhaps love you ; but you should never know it.'

'My heart again ! how you talk. And you consider
then, that if a husband be not master of his wife's heart,
he has no right to her fealty ; if a wife ceases to love,
she may cease to be true. Is that your doctrine on this
matter, as a minister of the Church of England ? '

Mr. Slope tried hard within himself to cast off the
pollution with which he felt that he was defiling his soul.
He strove to tear himself away from the noxious siren
that had bewitched him. But he could not do it. He
could not be again heart free. He had looked for rapturous
joy in loving this lovely creature, and he already found
that he met with little but disappointment and self-rebuke.
He had come across the fruit of the Dead Sea, so sweet
and delicious to the eye, so bitter and nauseous to the
taste. He had put the apple to his mouth, and it had
turned to ashes between his teeth. Yet he could not tear
himself away. He knew, he could not but know, that
she jeered at him, ridiculed his love, and insulted the
weakness of his religion. But she half permitted his
adoration, and that half permission added such fuel to
his fire that all the fountain of his piety could not quench
it. He began to feel savage, irritated, and revengeful.
He meditated some severity of speech, some taunt that
should cut her, as her taunts cut him. He reflected as
he stood there for a moment, silent before her, that if he
desired to quell her proud spirit, he should do so by being
prouder even than herself ; that if he wished to have her
at his feet suppliant for his love it behoved him to conquer
her by indifference. All this passed through his mind.
As far as dead knowledge went, he knew, or thought he
knew, how a woman should be tamed. But when he
essayed to bring his tactics to bear, he failed like a child.

What chance has dead knowledge with experience in any of the transactions between man and man? What possible chance between man and woman? Mr. Slope loved furiously, insanely, and truly; but he had never played the game of love. The signora did not love at all, but she was up to every move of the board. It was Philidor pitted against a school-boy.

And so she continued to insult him, and he continued to bear it.

'Sacrifice the world for love!' said she, in answer to some renewed vapid declaration of his passion, 'how often has the same thing been said, and how invariably with the same falsehood!'

'Falsehood,' said he. 'Do you say that I am false to you? do you say that my love is not real?'

'False? of course it is false, false as the father of false-hood—if indeed falsehoods need a sire and are not self-begotten since the world began. You are ready to sacrifice the world for love? Come let us see what you will sacrifice. I care nothing for nuptial vows. The wretch, I think you were kind enough to call him so, whom I swore to love and obey, is so base that he can only be thought of with repulsive disgust. In the council chamber of my heart I have divorced him. To me that is as good as though aged lords had gloated for months over the details of his licentious life. I care nothing for what the world can say. Will you be as frank? Will you take me to your home as your wife? Will you call me Mrs. Slope before bishop, dean, and prebendaries?' The poor tortured wretch stood silent, not knowing what to say. 'What! you won't do that. Tell me, then, what part of the world is it that you will sacrifice for my charms?'

'Were you free to marry, I would take you to my house to-morrow and wish no higher privilege.'

'I am free;' said she, almost starting up in her energy. For though there was no truth in her pretended regard for her clerical admirer, there was a mixture of real feeling in the scorn and satire with which she spoke of love and marriage generally. 'I am free; free as the winds. Come; will you take me as I am? Have your wish sacrifice the world, and prove yourself a true man.'

Mr. Slope should have taken her at her word. She

would have drawn back, and he would have had the full
advantage of the offer. But he did not. Instead of doing
so, he stood wrapt in astonishment, passing his fingers
through his lank red hair, and thinking as he stared upon
her animated countenance that her wondrous beauty
grew more and more wonderful as he gazed on it. ' Ha !
ha ! ha ! ' she laughed out loud. ' Come Mr. Slope ; don't
talk of sacrificing the world again. People beyond one-
and-twenty should never dream of such a thing. You
and I, if we have the dregs of any love left in us, if we have
the remnants of a passion remaining in our hearts, should
husband our resources better. We are not in our *première
jeunesse.* The world is a very nice place. Your world,
at any rate, is so. You have all manner of fat rectories
to get, and possible bishoprics to enjoy. Come, confess ;
on second thoughts you would not sacrifice such things
for the smiles of a lame lady ? '

It was impossible for him to answer this. In order to
be in any way dignified, he felt that he must be silent.

' Come,' said she—' don't boody with me : don't be
angry because I speak out some home truths. Alas, the
world, as I have found it, has taught me bitter truths.
Come, tell me that I am forgiven. Are we not to be
friends ? ' and she again put out her hand to him.

He sat himself down in the chair beside her, and took
her proffered hand and leant over her.

' There,' said she, with her sweetest softest smile—a
smile to withstand which a man should be cased in triple
steel, ' there ; seal your forgiveness on it,' and she raised
it towards his face. He kissed it again and again, and
stretched over her as though desirous of extending the
charity of his pardon beyond the hand that was offered
to him. She managed, however, to check his ardour.
For one so easily allured as this poor chaplain, her hand
was surely enough.

' Oh, Madeline ! ' said he, ' tell me that you love me—
do you—do you love me ? '

' Hush,' said she. ' There is my mother's step. Our
tête-à-tête has been of monstrous length. Now you had
better go. But we shall see you soon again, shall we not ? '

Mr. Slope promised that he would call again on the
following day.

' And, Mr. Slope,' she continued, ' pray answer my note.
You have it in your hand, though I declare during these
two hours you have not been gracious enough to read it.
It is about the Sabbath school and the children. You
know how anxious I am to have them here. I have been
learning the catechism myself, on purpose. You must
manage it for me next week. I will teach them, at any
rate, to submit themselves to their spiritual pastors and
masters.'

Mr. Slope said but little on the subject of Sabbath
schools, but he made his adieu, and betook himself home
with a sad heart, troubled mind, and uneasy conscience.

CHAPTER XXVIII

MRS. BOLD IS ENTERTAINED BY DR. AND MRS. GRANTLY AT PLUMSTEAD

IT will be remembered that Mr. Slope, when leaving his
billet doux at the house of Mrs. Bold, had been informed
that it would be sent out to her at Plumstead that afternoon. The archdeacon and Mr. Harding had in fact come
into town together in the brougham, and it had been
arranged that they should call for Eleanor's parcels as they
left on their way home. Accordingly they did so call, and
the maid, as she handed to the coachman a small basket
and large bundle carefully and neatly packed, gave in at
the carriage window Mr. Slope's epistle. The archdeacon,
who was sitting next to the window, took it, and immediately recognised the hand-writing of his enemy.

' Who left this ? ' said he.

' Mr. Slope called with it himself, your reverence,' said
the girl ; ' and was very anxious that missus should have
it to-day.'

So the brougham drove off, and the letter was left in the
archdeacon's hand. He looked at it as though he held a
basket of adders. He could not have thought worse of the
document had he read it and discovered it to be licentious
and atheistical. He did, moreover, what so many wise
people are accustomed to do in similar circumstances ; he
immediately condemned the person to whom the letter was
written, as though she were necessarily a *particeps criminis.*

Poor Mr. Harding, though by no means inclined to forward Mr. Slope's intimacy with his daughter, would have given anything to have kept the letter from his son-in-law. But that was now impossible. There it was in his hand ; and he looked as thoroughly disgusted as though he were quite sure that it contained all the rhapsodies of a favoured lover.

' It's very hard on me,' said he, after awhile, ' that this should go on under my roof.'

Now here the archdeacon was certainly most unreasonable. Having invited his sister-in-law to his house, it was a natural consequence that she should receive her letters there. And if Mr. Slope chose to write to her, his letter would, as a matter of course, be sent after her. Moreover, the very fact of an invitation to one's house implies confidence on the part of the inviter. He had shown that he thought Mrs. Bold to be a fit person to stay with him by his asking her to do so, and it was most cruel to her that he should complain of her violating the sanctity of his roof-tree, when the laches committed were none of her committing.

Mr. Harding felt this ; and felt also that when the archdeacon talked thus about his roof, what he said was most offensive to himself as Eleanor's father. If Eleanor did receive a letter from Mr. Slope, what was there in that to pollute the purity of Dr. Grantly's household ? He was indignant that his daughter should be so judged and so spoken of ; and he made up his mind that even as Mrs. Slope she must be dearer to him than any other creature on God's earth. He almost broke out, and said as much ; but for the moment he restrained himself.

' Here,' said the archdeacon, handing the offensive missile to his father-in-law ; ' I am not going to be the bearer of his love letters. You are her father, and may do as you think fit with it.'

By doing as he thought fit with it, the archdeacon certainly meant that Mr. Harding would be justified in opening and reading the letter, and taking any steps which might in consequence be necessary. To tell the truth, Dr. Grantly did feel rather a stronger curiosity than was justified by his outraged virtue, to see the contents of the letter. Of course he could not open it himself, but he

wished to make Mr. Harding understand that he, as
Eleanor's father, would be fully justified in doing so. The
idea of such a proceeding never occurred to Mr. Harding.
His authority over Eleanor ceased when she became the
wife of John Bold. He had not the slightest wish to pry
into her correspondence. He consequently put the letter
into his pocket, and only wished that he had been able to
do so without the archdeacon's knowledge. They both sat
silent during half the journey home, and then Dr. Grantly
said, ' Perhaps Susan had better give it to her. She can
explain to her sister, better than either you or I can do,
how deep is the disgrace of such an acquaintance.'

' I think you are very hard upon Eleanor,' replied Mr.
Harding. ' I will not allow that she has disgraced herself,
nor do I think it likely that she will do so. She has a right
to correspond with whom she pleases, and I shall not take
upon myself to blame her because she gets a letter from
Slope.'

' I suppose,' said Dr. Grantly, ' you don't wish her to
marry the man. I suppose you'll admit that she would
disgrace herself if she did do so.'

' I do not wish her to marry him,' said the perplexed
father ; ' I do not like him, and do not think he would
make a good husband. But if Eleanor chooses to do so, I
shall certainly not think that she disgraces herself.'

' Good heavens ! ' exclaimed Dr. Grantly, and threw
himself back into the corner of his brougham. Mr. Harding
said nothing more, but commenced playing a dirge, with
an imaginary fiddle bow upon an imaginary violoncello,
for which there did not appear to be quite room enough in
the carriage ; and he continued the tune, with sundry
variations, till he arrived at the rectory door.

The archdeacon had been meditating sad things in his
mind. Hitherto he had always looked on his father-in-law
as a true partisan, though he knew him to be a man devoid
of all the combative qualifications for that character. He
had felt no fear that Mr. Harding would go over to the
enemy, though he had never counted much on the ex-
warden's prowess in breaking the hostile ranks. Now,
however, it seemed that Eleanor, with her wiles, had
completely trepanned and bewildered her father, cheated
him out of his judgment, robbed him of the predilections

and tastes of his life, and caused him to be tolerant of a
man whose arrogance and vulgarity would, a few years
since, have been unendurable to him. That the whole
thing was as good as arranged between Eleanor and Mr.
Slope there was no longer any room to doubt. That
Mr. Harding knew that such was the case, even this could
hardly be doubted. It was too manifest that he at any
rate suspected it, and was prepared to sanction it.

And to tell the truth, such was the case. Mr. Harding
disliked Mr. Slope as much as it was in his nature to dislike
any man. Had his daughter wished to do her worst to
displease him by a second marriage, she could hardly have
succeeded better than by marrying Mr. Slope. But, as he
said to himself now very often, what right had he to
condemn her if she did nothing that was really wrong ?
If she liked Mr. Slope it was her affair. It was indeed
miraculous to him that a woman with such a mind, so
educated, so refined, so nice in her tastes, should like such
a man. Then he asked himself whether it was possible
that she did so ?

Ah, thou weak man ; most charitable, most Christian,
but weakest of men ! Why couldst thou not have asked
herself ? Was she not the daughter of thy loins, the child
of thy heart, the best beloved to thee of all humanity ?
Had she not proved to thee, by years of closest affection,
her truth and goodness and filial obedience ? And yet,
knowing and feeling all this, thou couldst endure to go
groping in darkness, hearing her named in strains which
wounded thy loving heart, and being unable to defend her
as thou shouldst have done !

Mr. Harding had not believed, did not believe, that his
daughter meant to marry this man ; but he feared to
commit himself to such an opinion. If she did do it there
would be then no means of retreat. The wishes of his heart
were—First, that there should be no truth in the archdeacon's surmises ; and in this wish he would have fain
trusted entirely, had he dared so to do ; Secondly, that the
match might be prevented, if unfortunately, it had been
contemplated by Eleanor ; Thirdly, that should she be so
infatuated as to marry this man, he might justify his conduct, and declare that no cause existed for his separating
himself from her.

He wanted to believe her incapable of such a marriage; he wanted to show that he so believed of her; but he wanted also to be able to say hereafter, that she had done nothing amiss, if she should unfortunately prove herself to be different from what he thought her to be.

Nothing but affection could justify such fickleness; but affection did justify it. There was but little of the Roman about Mr. Harding. He could not sacrifice his Lucretia even though she should be polluted by the accepted addresses of the clerical Tarquin at the palace. If Tarquin could be prevented, well and good; but if not, the father would still open his heart to his daughter, and accept her as she presented herself, Tarquin and all.

Dr. Grantly's mind was of a stronger calibre, and he was by no means deficient in heart. He loved with an honest genuine love his wife and children and friends. He loved his father-in-law; and was quite prepared to love Eleanor too, if she would be one of his party, if she would be on his side, if she would regard the Slopes and the Proudies as the enemies of mankind, and acknowledge and feel the comfortable merits of the Gwynnes and Arabins. He wished to be what he called ' safe ' with all those whom he had admitted to the penetralia of his house and heart. He could luxuriate in no society that was deficient in a certain feeling of faithful staunch high-churchism, which to him was tantamount to freemasonry. He was not strict in his lines of definition. He endured without impatience many different shades of Anglo-church conservatism; but with the Slopes and Proudies he could not go on all fours.

He was wanting in, moreover, or perhaps it would be more correct to say, he was not troubled by that womanly tenderness which was so peculiar to Mr. Harding. His feelings towards his friends were, that while they stuck to him he would stick to them; that he would work with them shoulder and shoulder; that he would be faithful to the faithful. He knew nothing of that beautiful love which can be true to a false friend.

And thus these two men, each miserable enough in his own way, returned to Plumstead.

It was getting late when they arrived there, and the ladies had already gone up to dress. Nothing more was said as the two parted in the hall. As Mr. Harding passed

to his own room he knocked at Eleanor's door and handed
in the letter. The archdeacon hurried to his own territory,
there to unburden his heart to his faithful partner.

What colloquy took place between the marital chamber
and the adjoining dressing-room shall not be detailed.
The reader, now intimate with the persons concerned, can
well imagine it. The whole tenor of it also might be read
in Mrs. Grantly's brow as she came down to dinner.

Eleanor, when she received the letter from her father's
hand, had no idea from whom it came. She had never seen
Mr. Slope's hand-writing, or if so had forgotten it; and
did not think of him as she twisted the letter as people do
twist letters when they do not immediately recognise their
correspondents either by the writing or the seal. She was
sitting at her glass brushing her hair, and rising every other
minute to play with her boy who was sprawling on the bed,
and who engaged pretty nearly the whole attention of the
maid as well as of his mother.

At last, sitting before her toilet table, she broke the seal,
and turning over the leaf saw Mr. Slope's name. She first
felt surprised, and then annoyed, and then anxious. As
she read it she became interested. She was so delighted to
find that all obstacles to her father's return to the hospital
were apparently removed that she did not observe the
fulsome language in which the tidings were conveyed.
She merely perceived that she was commissioned to tell her
father that such was the case, and she did not realise the
fact that such a communication should not have been
made, in the first instance, to her by an unmarried young
clergyman. She felt, on the whole, grateful to Mr. Slope,
and anxious to get on her dress that she might run with the
news to her father. Then she came to the allusion to her
own pious labours, and she said in her heart that Mr. Slope
was an affected ass. Then she went on again and was
offended by her boy being called Mr. Slope's darling—he
was nobody's darling but her own; or at any rate not the
darling of a disagreeable stranger like Mr. Slope. Lastly
she arrived at the tresses and felt a qualm of disgust. She
looked up in the glass, and there they were before her, long
and silken, certainly, and very beautiful. I will not say
but that she knew them to be so, but she felt angry with
them and brushed them roughly and carelessly. She

crumpled the letter up with angry violence, and resolved,
almost without thinking of it, that she would not show it
to her father. She would merely tell him the contents of it.
She then comforted herself again with her boy, had her
dress fastened, and went down to dinner.

As she tripped down the stairs she began to ascertain
that there was some difficulty in her situation. She could
not keep from her father the news about the hospital, nor
could she comfortably confess the letter from Mr. Slope
before the Grantlys. Her father had already gone down.
She had heard his step upon the lobby. She resolved
therefore to take him aside, and tell him her little bit of
news. Poor girl ! she had no idea how severely the unfortunate letter had already been discussed.

When she entered the drawing-room the whole party
were there, including Mr. Arabin, and the whole party
looked glum and sour. The two girls sat silent and apart
as though they were aware that something was wrong.
Even Mr. Arabin was solemn and silent. Eleanor had not
seen him since breakfast. He had been the whole day at
St. Ewold's, and such having been the case it was natural
that he should tell how matters were going on there. He
did nothing of the kind, however, but remained solemn and
silent. They were all solemn and silent. Eleanor knew in
her heart that they had been talking about her, and her
heart misgave her as she thought of Mr. Slope and his letter.
At any rate she felt it to be quite impossible to speak to her
father alone while matters were in this state.

Dinner was soon announced, and Dr. Grantly, as was his
wont, gave Eleanor his arm. But he did so as though the
doing it were an outrage on his feelings rendered necessary
by sternest necessity. With quick sympathy Eleanor felt
this, and hardly put her fingers on his coat sleeve. It may
be guessed in what way the dinner-hour was passed. Dr.
Grantly said a few words to Mr. Arabin, Mr. Arabin said a
few words to Mrs. Grantly, she said a few words to her
father, and he tried to say a few words to Eleanor. She
felt that she had been tried and found guilty of something,
though she knew not what. She longed to say out to them
all, ' Well, what is it that I have done ; out with it, and let
me know my crime ; for heaven's sake let me hear the
worst of it ; ' but she could not. She could say nothing,

but sat there silent, half feeling that she was guilty, and trying in vain to pretend even to eat her dinner.

At last the cloth was drawn, and the ladies were not long following it. When they were gone the gentlemen were somewhat more sociable but not much so. They could not of course talk over Eleanor's sins. The archdeacon had indeed so far betrayed his sister-in-law as to whisper into Mr. Arabin's ear in the study, as they met there before dinner, a hint of what he feared. He did so with the gravest and saddest of fears, and Mr. Arabin became grave and apparently sad enough as he heard it. He opened his eyes and his mouth and said in a sort of whisper ' Mr. Slope ! ' in the same way as he might have said ' The Cholera ! ' had his friend told him that that horrid disease was in his nursery. ' I fear so, I fear so,' said the arch- deacon, and then together they left the room.

We will not accurately analyse Mr. Arabin's feelings on receipt of such astounding tidings. It will suffice to say that he was surprised, vexed, sorrowful, and ill at ease. He had not perhaps thought very much about Eleanor, but he had appreciated her influence, and had felt that close intimacy with her in a country house was pleasant to him, and also beneficial. He had spoken highly of her intelli- gence to the archdeacon, and had walked about the shrubberies with her, carrying her boy on his back. When Mr. Arabin had called Johnny his darling, Eleanor was not angry.

Thus the three men sat over their wine, all thinking of the same subject, but unable to speak of it to each other. So we will leave them, and follow the ladies into the drawing-room.

Mrs. Grantly had received a commission from her husband, and had undertaken it with some unwillingness. He had desired her to speak gravely to Eleanor, and to tell her that, if she persisted in her adherence to Mr. Slope, she could no longer look-for the countenance of her present friends. Mrs. Grantly probably knew her sister better than the doctor did, and assured him that it would be in vain to talk to her. The only course likely to be of any service in her opinion was to keep Eleanor away from Barchester. Perhaps she might have added, for she had a very keen eye in such things, that there might also be ground for hope

in keeping Eleanor near Mr. Arabin. Of this, however, she
said nothing.   But the archdeacon would not be talked
over ; he spoke much of his conscience, and declared that
if Mrs. Grantly would not do it he would. So instigated,
the lady undertook the task, stating, however, her full
conviction that her interference would be worse than useless. And so it proved.

As soon as they were in the drawing-room Mrs. Grantly
found some excuse for sending her girls away, and then
began her task. She knew well that she could exercise but
very slight authority over her sister. Their various modes
of life, and the distance between their residences, had
prevented any very close confidence. They had hardly
lived together since Eleanor was a child. Eleanor had
moreover, especially in latter years, resented in a quiet
sort of way the dictatorial authority which the archdeacon
seemed to exercise over her father, and on this account had
been unwilling to allow the archdeacon's wife to exercise
authority over herself.

' You got a note just before dinner, I believe,' began the
eldest sister.

Eleanor acknowledged that she had done so, and felt
that she turned red as she acknowledged it. She would
have given anything to have kept her colour, but the more
she tried to do so the more signally she failed.

' Was it not from Mr. Slope ? '

Eleanor said that the letter was from Mr. Slope.

' Is he a regular correspondent of yours, Eleanor ? '

' Not exactly,' said she, already beginning to feel angry
at the cross-examination. She determined, and why it
would be difficult to say, that nothing should induce her to
tell her sister Susan what was the subject of the letter.
Mrs. Grantly, she knew, was instigated by the archdeacon,
and she would not plead to any arraignment made against
her by him.

' But, Eleanor dear, why do you get letters from Mr.
Slope at all, knowing, as you do, he is a person so distasteful
to papa, and to the archdeacon, and indeed to all your
friends ? '

' In the first place, Susan, I don't get letters from him ;
and in the next place, as Mr. Slope wrote the one letter
which I have got, and as I only received it, which I could

not very well help doing, as papa handed it to me, I think you had better ask Mr. Slope instead of me.'

' What was his letter about, Eleanor ? '

' I cannot tell you,' said she, ' because it was confidential. It was on business respecting a third person.'

' It was in no way personal to yourself, then ? '

' I won't exactly say that, Susan,' said she, getting more and more angry at her sister's questions.

' Well, I must say it's rather singular,' said Mrs. Grantly, affecting to laugh, ' that a young lady in your position should receive a letter from an unmarried gentleman of which she will not tell the contents, and which she is ashamed to show to her sister.'

' I am not ashamed,' said Eleanor blazing up ; ' I am not ashamed of anything in the matter ; only I do not choose to be cross-examined as to my letters by any one.'

' Well, dear,' said the other, ' I cannot but tell you that I do not think Mr. Slope a proper correspondent for you.'

' If he be ever so improper, how can I help his having written to me ? But you are all prejudiced against him to such an extent, that that which would be kind and generous in another man is odious and impudent in him. I hate a religion that teaches one to be so onesided in one's charity.'

' I am sorry, Eleanor, that you hate the religion you find here ; but surely you should remember that in such matters the archdeacon must know more of the world than you do. I don't ask you to respect or comply with me, although I am, unfortunately, so many years your senior ; but surely, in such a matter as this, you might consent to be guided by the archdeacon. He is most anxious to be your friend if you will let him.'

' In such a matter as what ? ' said Eleanor very testily. ' Upon my word I don't know what this is all about.'

' We all want you to drop Mr. Slope.'

' You all want me to be as illiberal as yourselves. That I shall never be. I see no harm in Mr. Slope's acquaintance, and I shall not insult the man by telling him that I do. He has thought it necessary to write to me, and I do not want the archdeacon's advice about the letter. If I did I would ask it.'

' Then, Eleanor, it is my duty to tell you,' and now she spoke with a tremendous gravity, ' that the archdeacon thinks that such a correspondence is disgraceful, and that he cannot allow it to go on in his house.'

Eleanor's eyes flashed fire as she answered her sister, jumping up from her seat as she did so. ' You may tell the archdeacon that wherever I am I shall receive what letters I please and from whom I please. And as for the word disgraceful, if Dr. Grantly has used it of me he has been unmanly and inhospitable,' and she walked off to the door. ' When papa comes from the dining-room I will thank you to ask him to step up to my bed-room. I will show him Mr. Slope's letter, but I will show it to no one else.' And so saying she retreated to her baby.

She had no conception of the crime with which she was charged. The idea that she could be thought by her friends to regard Mr. Slope as a lover, had never flashed upon her. She conceived that they were all prejudiced and illiberal in their persecution of him, and therefore she would not join in the persecution, even though she greatly disliked the man.

Eleanor was very angry as she seated herself in a low chair by her open window at the foot of her child's bed. ' To dare to say I have disgraced myself,' she repeated to herself more than once. ' How papa can put up with that man's arrogance ! I will certainly not sit down to dinner in his house again unless he begs my pardon for that word.' And then a thought struck her that Mr. Arabin might perchance hear of her ' disgraceful ' correspondence with Mr. Slope, and she turned crimson with pure vexation. Oh, if she had known the truth ? If she could have conceived that Mr. Arabin had been informed as a fact that she was going to marry Mr. Slope !

She had not been long in her room before her father joined her. As he left the drawing-room Mrs. Grantly took her husband into the recess of the window, and told him how signally she had failed.

' I will speak to her myself before I go to bed,' said the archdeacon.

' Pray do no such thing,' said she ; ' you can do no good and will only make an unseemly quarrel in the house. You have no idea how headstrong she can be.'

The archdeacon declared that as to that he was quite indifferent. He knew his duty and would do it. Mr. Harding was weak in the extreme in such matters. He would not have it hereafter on his conscience that he had not done all that in him lay to prevent so disgraceful an alliance. It was in vain that Mrs. Grantly assured him that speaking to Eleanor angrily would only hasten such a crisis, and render it certain if at present there were any doubt. He was angry, self-willed, and sore. The fact that a lady of his household had received a letter from Mr. Slope had wounded his pride in the sorest place, and nothing could control him.

Mr. Harding looked worn and woebegone as he entered his daughter's room. These sorrows worried him sadly. He felt that if they were continued he must go to the wall in the manner so kindly prophesied to him by the chaplain. He knocked gently at his daughter's door, waited till he was distinctly bade to enter, and then appeared as though he and not she were the suspected criminal.

Eleanor's arm was soon within his, and she had soon kissed his forehead and caressed him, not with joyous but with eager love. 'Oh, papa,' she said, 'I do so want to speak to you. They have been talking about me down stairs to-night; don't you know they have, papa ? '

Mr. Harding confessed with a sort of murmur that the archdeacon had been speaking of her.

' I shall hate Dr. Grantly soon—'

' Oh my dear ! '

' Well ; I shall. I cannot help it. He is so uncharitable, so unkind, so suspicious of every one that does not worship himself : and then he is so monstrously arrogant to other people who have a right to their opinions as well as he has to his own.'

' He is an earnest eager man, my dear : but he never means to be unkind.'

' He is unkind, papa, most unkind. There, I got that letter from Mr. Slope before dinner. It was you yourself who gave it to me. There ; pray read it. It is all for you. It should have been addressed to you. You know how they have been talking about it down stairs. You know how they behaved to me at dinner. And since dinner Susan has been preaching to me, till I could not remain in the room with her. Read it, papa ; and then say whether that is a letter that need make Dr. Grantly so outrageous.'

Mr. Harding took his arm from his daughter's waist, and slowly read the letter. She expected to see his countenance lit with joy as he learnt that his path back to the hospital was made so smooth ; but she was doomed to disappointment, as had once been the case before on a somewhat similar occasion. His first feeling was one of unmitigated disgust that Mr. Slope should have chosen to interfere in his behalf. He had been anxious to get back to the hospital, but he would have infinitely sooner resigned all pretensions to the place, than have owed it in any manner to Mr. Slope's influence in his favour. Then he thoroughly disliked the tone of Mr. Slope's letter ; it was unctuous, false, and unwholesome, like the man. He saw, which Eleanor had failed to see, that much more had been intended than was expressed. The appeal to Eleanor's pious labours as separate from his own grated sadly against his feelings as a father. And then when he came to the ' darling boy ' and the ' silken tresses,' he slowly closed and folded the letter in despair. It was impossible that Mr. Slope should so write unless he had been encouraged. It was impossible Eleanor should have received such a letter, and have received it without annoyance, unless she were willing to encourage him. So at least Mr. Harding argued to himself.

How hard it is to judge accurately of the feelings of others. Mr. Harding, as he came to the close of the letter, in his heart condemned his daughter for indelicacy, and it made him miserable to do so. She was not responsible for what Mr. Slope might write. True. But then she expressed no disgust at it. She had rather expressed approval of the letter as a whole. She had given it to him to read, as a vindication for herself and also for him. The father's spirits sank within him as he felt that he could not acquit her.

And yet it was the true feminine delicacy of Eleanor's mind which brought her on this condemnation. Listen to me, ladies, and I beseech you to acquit her. She thought of this man, this lover of whom she was so unconscious, exactly as her father did, exactly as the Grantlys did.

At least she esteemed him personally as they did. But
she believed him to be in the main an honest man, and one
truly inclined to assist her father. She felt herself bound,
after what had passed, to show this letter to Mr. Harding.
She thought it necessary that he should know what Mr.
Slope had to say. But she did not think it necessary to
apologise for, or condemn, or even allude to the vulgarity
of the man's tone, which arose, as does all vulgarity, from
ignorance. It was nauseous to her to have a man like
Mr. Slope commenting on her personal attractions ; and
she did not think it necessary to dilate with her father
upon what was nauseous. She never supposed they could
disagree on such a subject. It would have been painful
for her to point it out, painful for her to speak strongly
against a man of whom, on the whole, she was anxious to
think and speak well. In encountering such a man she had
encountered what was disagreeable, as she might do in
walking the streets. But in such encounters she never
thought it necessary to dwell on what disgusted her.

And he, foolish weak loving man, would not say one
word, though one word would have cleared up everything.
There would have been a deluge of tears, and in ten
minutes every one in the house would have understood
how matters really were. The father would have been
delighted. The sister would have kissed her sister and
begged a thousand pardons. The archdeacon would have
apologised and wondered, and raised his eyebrows, and
gone to bed a happy man. And Mr. Arabin—Mr. Arabin
would have dreamt of Eleanor, have awoke in the morning
with ideas of love, and retired to rest the next evening with
schemes of marriage. But, alas ! all this was not to be.

Mr. Harding slowly folded the letter, handed it back to
her, kissed her forehead and bade God bless her. He then
crept slowly away to his own room.

As soon as he had left the passage another knock was
given at Eleanor's door, and Mrs. Grantly's very demure
own maid, entering on tiptoe, wanted to know would Mrs.
Bold be so kind as to speak to the archdeacon for two
minutes, in the archdeacon's study, if not disagreeable.
The archdeacon's compliments, and he wouldn't detain
her two minutes.

Eleanor thought it was very disagreeable ; she was

tired and fagged and sick at heart; her present feelings
towards Dr. Grantly were anything but those of affection.
She was, however, no coward, and therefore promised to
be in the study in five minutes. So she arranged her
hair, tied on her cap, and went down with a palpitating
heart.

CHAPTER XXIX

A SERIOUS INTERVIEW

THERE are people who delight in serious interviews,
especially when to them appertains the part of offering
advice or administering rebuke, and perhaps the archdeacon was one of these. Yet on this occasion he did not
prepare himself for the coming conversation with much
anticipation of pleasure. Whatever might be his faults
he was not an inhospitable man, and he almost felt that
he was sinning against hospitality in upbraiding Eleanor
in his own house. Then, also he was not quite sure that
he would get the best of it. His wife had told him that he
decidedly would not, and he usually gave credit to what
his wife said. He was, however, so convinced of what he
considered to be the impropriety of Eleanor's conduct, and
so assured also of his own duty in trying to check it, that
his conscience would not allow him to take his wife's
advice and go to bed quietly.

Eleanor's face as she entered the room was not such as
to reassure him. As a rule she was always mild in manner
and gentle in conduct; but there was that in her eye
which made it not an easy task to scold her. In truth she
had been little used to scolding. No one since her child-
hood had tried it but the archdeacon, and he had generally
failed when he did try it. He had never done so since her
marriage; and now, when he saw her quiet easy step, as
she entered his room, he almost wished that he had taken
his wife's advice.

He began by apologising for the trouble he was giving
her. She begged him not to mention it, assured him that
walking down stairs was no trouble to her at all, and then
took a seat and waited patiently for him to begin his attack.

' My dear Eleanor,' he said, ' I hope you believe me
when I assure you that you have no sincerer friend than

I am.' To this Eleanor answered nothing, and therefore he proceeded. ' If you had a brother of your own I should not probably trouble you with what I am going to say. But as it is I cannot but think that it must be a comfort to you to know that you have near you one who is as anxious for your welfare as any brother of your own could be.'

' I never had a brother,' said she.

' I know you never had, and it is therefore that I speak to you.'

' I never had a brother,' she repeated; ' but I have hardly felt the want. Papa has been to me both father and brother.'

' Your father is the fondest and most affectionate of men. But—'

' He is—the fondest and most affectionate of men, and the best of counsellors. While he lives I can never want advice.'

This rather put the archdeacon out. He could not exactly contradict what his sister-in-law said about her father; and yet he did not at all agree with her. He wanted her to understand that he tendered his assistance because her father was a soft good-natured gentleman, not sufficiently knowing in the ways of the world; but he could not say this to her. So he had to rush into the subject-matter of his proffered counsel without any acknowledgment on her part that she could need it, or would be grateful for it.

' Susan tells me that you received a letter this evening from Mr. Slope.'

' Yes; papa brought it in the brougham. Did he not tell you?'

' And Susan says that you objected to let her know what it was about.'

' I don't think she asked me. But had she done so I should not have told her. I don't think it nice to be asked about one's letters. If one wishes to show them one does so without being asked.'

' True. Quite so. What you say is quite true. But is not the fact of your receiving letters from Mr. Slope, which you do not wish to show to your friends, a circumstance which must excite some—some surprise—some suspicion—'

'Suspicion!' said she, not speaking above her usual voice, speaking still in a soft womanly tone, but yet with indignation; 'suspicion! and who suspects me, and of what?' And then there was a pause, for the archdeacon was not quite ready to explain the ground of his suspicion. 'No, Dr. Grantly, I did not choose to show Mr. Slope's letter to Susan. I could not show it to any one till papa had seen it. If you have any wish to read it now, you can do so,' and she handed the letter to him over the table.

This was an amount of compliance which he had not at all expected, and which rather upset him in his tactics. However, he took the letter, perused it carefully, and then refolding it, kept it on the table under his hand. To him it appeared to be in almost every respect the letter of a declared lover; it seemed to corroborate his worst suspicions; and the fact of Eleanor's showing it to him was all but tantamount to a declaration on her part, that it was her pleasure to receive love-letters from Mr. Slope. He almost entirely overlooked the real subject-matter of the epistle; so intent was he on the forthcoming courtship and marriage.

'I'll thank you to give it me back, if you please, Dr. Grantly.'

He took it in his hand and held it up, but made no immediate overture to return it. 'And Mr. Harding has seen this?' said he.

'Of course he has,' said she; 'it was written that he might see it. It refers solely to his business—of course I showed it to him.'

'And, Eleanor, do you think that that is a proper letter for you—for a person in your condition—to receive from Mr. Slope?'

'Quite a proper letter,' said she, speaking, perhaps, a little out of obstinacy; probably forgetting at the moment the objectionable mention of her silken curls.

'Then, Eleanor, it is my duty to tell you that I wholly differ from you.'

'So I suppose,' said she, instigated now by sheer opposition and determination not to succumb. 'You think Mr. Slope is a messenger direct from Satan. I think he is an industrious, well meaning clergyman It's a pity that

we differ as we do. But, as we do differ, we had probably
better not talk about it.'

Here Eleanor undoubtedly put herself in the wrong.
She might probably have refused to talk to Dr. Grantly
on the matter in dispute without any impropriety ; but
having consented to listen to him, she had no business to
tell him that he regarded Mr. Slope as an emissary from the
evil one ; nor was she justified in praising Mr. Slope, seeing
that in her heart of hearts she did not think well of him.
She was, however, wounded in spirit, and angry and bitter.
She had been subjected to contumely and cross-questioning
and ill-usage through the whole evening. No one, not even
Mr. Arabin, not even her father, had been kind to her.
All this she attributed to the prejudice and conceit of the
archdeacon, and therefore she resolved to set no bounds
to her antagonism to him. She would neither give nor
take quarter. He had greatly presumed in daring to
question her about her correspondence, and she was
determined to show that she thought so.

'Eleanor, you are forgetting yourself,' said he, looking
very sternly at her. 'Otherwise you would never tell me
that I conceive any man to be a messenger from Satan.'

'But you do,' said she. 'Nothing is too bad for him.
Give me that letter, if you please ; ' and she stretched out
her hand and took it from him. 'He has been doing his
best to serve papa, doing more than any of papa's friends
could do ; and yet, because he is the chaplain of a bishop
whom you don't like, you speak of him as though he had
no right to the usage of a gentleman.'

'He has done nothing for your father.'

'I believe that he has done a great deal ; and, as far as
I am concerned, I am grateful to him. Nothing that you
can say can prevent my being so. I judge people by their
acts, and his, as far as I can see them, are good.' She then
paused for a moment. 'If you have nothing further to
say, I shall be obliged by being permitted to say good
night—I am very tired.'

Dr. Grantly had, as he thought, done his best to be
gracious to his sister-in-law. He had endeavoured not to
be harsh to her, and had striven to pluck the sting from his
rebuke. But he did not intend that she should leave him
without hearing him.

' I have something to say, Eleanor ; and I fear I must trouble you to hear it. You profess that it is quite proper that you should receive from Mr. Slope such letters as that you have in your hand. Susan and I think very differently. You are, of course, your own mistress, and much as we both must grieve should anything separate you from us, we have no power to prevent you from taking steps which may lead to such a separation. If you are so wilful as to reject the counsel of your friends, you must be allowed to cater for yourself. But Eleanor, I may at any rate ask you this. Is it worth your while to break away from all those you have loved—from all who love you—for the sake of Mr. Slope ? '

' I don't know what you mean, Dr. Grantly ; I don't know what you're talking about. I don't want to break away from anybody.'

' But you will do so if you connect yourself with Mr. Slope. Eleanor, I must speak out to you. You must choose between your sister and myself and our friends, and Mr. Slope and his friends. I say nothing of your father, as you may probably understand his feelings better than I do.'

' What do you mean, Dr. Grantly ? What am I to understand ? I never heard such wicked prejudice in my life.'

' It is no prejudice, Eleanor. I have known the world longer than you have done. Mr. Slope is altogether beneath you. You ought to know and feel that he is so. Pray—pray think of this before it is too late.'

' Too late ! '

' Or if you will not believe me, ask Susan ; you cannot think she is prejudiced against you. Or even consult your father, he is not prejudiced against you. Ask Mr. Arabin ——,'

' You haven't spoken to Mr. Arabin about this ! ' said she, jumping up and standing before him.

' Eleanor, all the world in and about Barchester will be speaking of it soon.'

' But have you spoken to Mr. Arabin about me and Mr. Slope ? '

' Certainly I have, and he quite agrees with me.'

' Agrees with what ? ' said she. ' I think you are trying to drive me mad.'

' He agrees with me and Susan that it is quite impossible you should be received at Plumstead as Mrs. Slope.'

Not being favourites with the tragic muse we do not dare to attempt any description of Eleanor's face when she first heard the name of Mrs. Slope pronounced as that which would or should or might at some time appertain to herself. The look, such as it was, Dr. Grantly did not soon forget. For a moment or two she could find no words to express her deep anger and deep disgust ; and, indeed, at this conjuncture, words did not come to her very freely.

' How dare you be so impertinent ? ' at last she said ; and then hurried out of the room, without giving the archdeacon the opportunity of uttering another word. It was with difficulty she contained herself till she reached her own room ; and then locking the door, she threw herself on her bed and sobbed as though her heart would break.

But even yet she had no conception of the truth. She had no idea that her father and her sister had for days past conceived in sober earnest the idea that she was going to marry this man. She did not even then believe that the archdeacon thought that she would do so. By some manœuvre of her brain, she attributed the origin of the accusation to Mr. Arabin, and as she did so her anger against him was excessive, and the vexation of her spirit almost unendurable. She could not bring herself to think that the charge was made seriously. It appeared to her most probable that the archdeacon and Mr. Arabin had talked over her objectionable acquaintance with Mr. Slope ; that Mr. Arabin, in his jeering, sarcastic way, had suggested the odious match as being the severest way of treating with contumely her acquaintance with his enemy ; and that the archdeacon, taking the idea from him, thought proper to punish her by the allusion. The whole night she lay awake thinking of what had been said, and this appeared to be the most probable solution.

But the reflection that Mr. Arabin should have in any way mentioned her name in connection with that of Mr. Slope was overpowering ; and the spiteful ill-nature of the archdeacon, in repeating the charge to her, made her wish to leave his house almost before the day had broken. One thing was certain : nothing should make her stay there beyond the following morning, and nothing should make

Men wanting both are mated with the best
And loftiest of God's feminine creation,
Whose love takes no distinction but of gender,
And ridicules the very name of choice.

And so he went on, troubled much in his mind.

He had but an uneasy ride of it that morning, and little good did he do at St. Ewold's.

The necessary alterations in his house were being fast completed, and he walked through the rooms, and went up and down the stairs and rambled through the garden ; but he could not wake himself to much interest about them. He stood still at every window to look out and think upon Mr. Slope. At almost every window he had before stood and chatted with Eleanor. She and Mrs. Grantly had been there continually, and while Mrs. Grantly had been giving orders, and seeing that orders had been complied with, he and Eleanor had conversed on all things appertaining to a clergyman's profession. He thought how often he had laid down the law to her, and how sweetly she had borne with his somewhat dictatorial decrees. He remembered her listening intelligence, her gentle but quick replies, her interest in all that concerned the church, in all that concerned him ; and then he struck his riding whip against the window sill, and declared to himself that it was impossible that Eleanor Bold should marry Mr. Slope.

And yet he did not really believe, as he should have done, that it was impossible. He should have known her well enough to feel that it was truly impossible. He should have been aware that Eleanor had that within her which would surely protect her from such degradation. But he, like so many others, was deficient in confidence in woman. He said to himself over and over again that it was impossible that Eleanor Bold should become Mrs. Slope, and yet he believed that she would do so. And so he rambled about, and could do and think of nothing. He was thoroughly uncomfortable, thoroughly ill at ease, cross with himself and every body else, and feeding in his heart on animosity towards Mr. Slope. This was not as it should be, as he knew and felt ; but he could not help himself. In truth Mr. Arabin was now in love with Mrs. Bold, though ignorant of the fact himself. He was in love, and, though forty years old. was in love without being aware of it. He her sit down to breakfast in company with Dr. Grantly. When she thought of the man whose name had been linked with her own, she cried from sheer disgust. It was only because she would be thus disgusted, thus pained and shocked and cut to the quick, that the archdeacon had spoken the horrid word. He wanted to make her quarrel with Mr. Slope, and therefore he had outraged her by his abominable vulgarity. She determined that at any rate he should know that she appreciated it.

Nor was the archdeacon a bit better satisfied with the result of his serious interview than was Eleanor. He gathered from it, as indeed he could hardly fail to do, that she was very angry with him; but he thought that she was thus angry, not because she was suspected of an intention to marry Mr. Slope, but because such an intention was imputed to her as a crime. Dr. Grantly regarded this supposed union with disgust; but it never occurred to him that Eleanor was outraged, because she looked at it exactly in the same light.

He returned to his wife vexed and somewhat disconsolate, but, nevertheless, confirmed in his wrath against his sister-in-law. 'Her whole behaviour,' said he, 'has been most objectionable. She handed me his love letter to read as though she were proud of it. And she is proud of it. She is proud of having this slavering, greedy man at her feet. She will throw herself and John Bold's money into his lap; she will ruin her boy, disgrace her father and you, and be a wretched miserable woman.'

His spouse who was sitting at her toilet table, continued her avocations, making no answer to all this. She had known that the archdeacon would gain nothing by interfering; but she was too charitable to provoke him by saying so while he was in such deep sorrow.

'This comes of a man making such a will as that of Bold's,' he continued. 'Eleanor is no more fitted to be trusted with such an amount of money in her own hands than is a charity-school girl.' Still Mrs. Grantly made no reply. 'But I have done my duty; I can do nothing further. I have told her plainly that she cannot be allowed to form a link of connection between me and that man. From henceforward it will not be in my power to make her welcome at Plumstead. I cannot have Mr. Slope's love letters coming here. Susan, I think you had better let her understand that as her mind on this subject seems to be irrevocably fixed, it will be better for all parties that she should return to Barchester.'

Now Mrs. Grantly was angry with Eleanor, nearly as angry as her husband; but she had no idea of turning her sister out of the house. She, therefore, at length spoke out, and explained to the archdeacon in her own mild seducing way, that he was fuming and fussing and fretting himself very unnecessarily. She declared that things, if left alone, would arrange themselves much better than he could arrange them; and at last succeeded in inducing him to go to bed in a somewhat less inhospitable state of mind.

On the following morning Eleanor's maid was commissioned to send word into the dining-room that her mistress was not well enough to attend prayers, and that she would breakfast in her own room. Here she was visited by her father and declared to him her intention of returning immediately to Barchester. He was hardly surprised by the announcement. All the household seemed to be aware that something had gone wrong. Every one walked about with subdued feet, and people's shoes seemed to creak more than usual. There was a look of conscious intelligence on the faces of the women: and the men attempted, but in vain, to converse as though nothing were the matter. All this had weighed heavily on the heart of Mr. Harding; and when Eleanor told him that her immediate return to Barchester was a necessity, he merely sighed piteously, and said that he would be ready to accompany her.

But here she objected strenuously. She had a great wish, she said, to go alone; a great desire that it might be seen that her father was not implicated in her quarrel with Dr. Grantly. To this at last he gave way; but not a word passed between them about Mr. Slope—not a word was said, not a question asked as to the serious interview on the preceding evening. There was, indeed, very little confidence between them, though neither of them knew why it should be so. Eleanor once asked him whether he would not call upon the bishop; but he answered rather tartly that he did not know—he did not think he should, but he could not say just at present. And so they parted.

Each was miserably anxious for some show of affection, for some return of confidence, for some sign of the feeling that usually bound them together. But none was given. The father could not bring himself to question his daughter about her supposed lover; and the daughter would not sully her mouth by repeating the odious word with which Dr. Grantly had roused her wrath. And so they parted.

There was some trouble in arranging the method of Eleanor's return. She begged her father to send for a postchaise; but when Mrs. Grantly heard of this, she objected strongly. If Eleanor would go away in dudgeon with the archdeacon, why should she let all the servants and all the neighbourhood know that she had done so? So at last Eleanor consented to make use of the Plumstead carriage; and as the archdeacon had gone out immediately after breakfast and was not to return till dinner-time, she also consented to postpone her journey till after lunch, and to join the family at that time. As to the subject of the quarrel not a word was said by any one. The affair of the carriage was arranged by Mr. Harding, who acted as Mercury between the two ladies; they, when they met, kissed each other very lovingly, and then sat down each to her crochet work as though nothing was amiss in all the world.

CHAPTER XXX

ANOTHER LOVE SCENE

But there was another visitor at the rectory whose feelings in this unfortunate matter must be somewhat strictly analysed. Mr. Arabin had heard from his friend of the probability of Eleanor's marriage with Mr. Slope with amazement, but not with incredulity. It has been said that he was not in love with Eleanor, and up to this period this certainly had been true. But as soon as he heard that she loved some one else, he began to be very fond of her himself. He did not make up his mind that he wished to have her for his wife; he had never thought of her, and did not now think of her, in connection with himself; but he experienced an inward indefinable feeling of deep regret, a gnawing sorrow, an unconquerable depression of spirits, and also a species of self-abasement that he—he Mr. Arabin—had not done something to prevent that other he, that vile he, whom he so thoroughly despised, from carrying off this sweet prize.

Whatever man may have reached the age of forty unmarried without knowing something of such feelings must have been very successful or else very cold hearted.

Mr. Arabin had never thought of trimming the sails of his bark so that he might sail as convoy to this rich argosy. He had seen that Mrs. Bold was beautiful, but he had not dreamt of making her beauty his own. He knew that Mrs. Bold was rich, but he had had no more idea of appropriating her wealth than that of Dr. Grantly. He had discovered that Mrs. Bold was intelligent, warm-hearted, agreeable, sensible, all, in fact, that a man could wish his wife to be ; but the higher were her attractions, the greater her claims to consideration, the less had he imagined that he might possibly become the possessor of them. Such had been his instinct rather than his thoughts, so humble and so diffident. Now his diffidence was to be rewarded by his seeing this woman, whose beauty was to his eyes perfect, whose wealth was such as to have deterred him from thinking of her, whose widowhood would have silenced him had he not been so deterred, by his seeing her become the prey of——Obadiah Slope !

On the morning of Mrs. Bold's departure he got on his horse to ride over to St. Ewold's. As he rode he kept muttering to himself a line from Van Artevelde,

> How little flattering is woman's love.

And then he strove to recall his mind and to think of other affairs, his parish, his college, his creed—but his thoughts would revert to Mr. Slope and the Flemish chieftain.——

> When we think upon it,
> How little flattering is woman's love,
> Given commonly to whosoe'er is nearest
> And propped with most advantage.

It was not that Mrs. Bold should marry any one but him ; he had not put himself forward as a suitor ; but that she should marry Mr. Slope—and so he repeated over again—

> Outward grace
> Nor inward light is needful—day by day